Kegan Paul, Trench and Co.

Ancient And Modern Britons

A Retrospect VOL. II

Kegan Paul, Trench and Co.

Ancient And Modern Britons
A Retrospect VOL. II

ISBN/EAN: 9783741196744

Manufactured in Europe, USA, Canada, Australia, Japa

Cover: Foto ©Andreas Hilbeck / pixelio.de

Manufactured and distributed by brebook publishing software
(www.brebook.com)

Kegan Paul, Trench and Co.

Ancient And Modern Britons

ANCIENT AND MODERN BRITONS.

ANCIENT

AND

MODERN BRITONS:

A RETROSPECT.

VOL. II.

LONDON:
KEGAN PAUL, TRENCH & CO., 1 PATERNOSTER SQUARE.
1884.

CONTENTS.

BOOK III.

CHAPTER I.

PAGE

Will Marshall and his Biographers—Our Seventeenth-Century Seamen—Seventeenth-Century Cavaliers—Marshall's "Position"—"Banished Dukes" and their Successors—The Typical Moss-Trooper—"Moors or Saracens"—Characteristics of the Borderers—Descriptive Titles—The Minstrels of Britain—Representatives of Archaic Scotland—"The Great Distinguishing Feature" of Gypsyism—Gypsy Lords and Lairds—Gentle Blood—Will Marshall again—His Exploits—Might *versus* Right—Last Years of the Tory Chief—His Death and Burial—His Characteristics—The Galloway Marshalls—The Old Order "Yielding Place to New"—1692 and 1792—Marshall's "Position" Defined . 3

CHAPTER II.

"The Ancient Nobility of the Country"—Northumbria in the, Ninth Century—Forgotten Kings—The Baillie Clan—Gypsy Cavaliers—"Friends at Court"—The Berwickshire Gordons—The Principal Tories in Scotland—The Baillies and the Faws—The Castes of Gypsydom—The Decay of Nomadism—A Daughter of the Tories—A Descent from Sir William Wallace—Baillies, Settled and Unsettled—The Dresses of the Cavaliers—Gypsy Complexions—White Gypsies 52

CHAPTER III.

The "Black Divisions" of North Britain—The Egyptian Kingdom of Carrick—The Enemies of Bruce—Fate of the Carrick Kingship—The Tory Kennedys—Tribal Feuds of the Eighteenth Century . . 87

CHAPTER IV.

PAGE

British Ethnology—The Faw Territory—Scoto-Pictish Scotland—Tory Passports—The Hieroglyphics of the Scots—The Egyptian Invaders of Britain—"The Sculptured Stones of Scotland"—Extinct British Animals—Egyptian Features in Gaelic—Egypt in the British Islands —The Era of the Scotch Hieroglyphs—The Religious Ceremonial of Asia and Europe—The Magians of the East and the West .   . 101

CHAPTER V.

The Beginnings of "Gypsydom" in Scotland—The Kingdoms of North Britain—"The Improvement of the Isles"—Rival Sovereignties— The Kingdom of Ettrick-Forest—Annexed by Scotia—Gypsy Colours —The Chief of the Ruthvens—A Scoto-Saracen Nation—The Border Country—Kings of the Border—Invasion of Liddesdale—British Indians: "Commonly Called Egyptians"—Gypsy Supremacy—A Reign of Terror—A Gypsy Gentlewoman—Plain Speaking and Tall Talk — Scott, Considered as an Antiquary — The Value of his Romances   128

CHAPTER VI.

Civilization and Barbarism—The People of Ettrickdale—Burghers *versus* "Savages"—Conquest of the Scots—Army of King David of Scotia —Colonists and Natives of "the Moors' Country"—Conquerors and Conquered—Early Scotland—Immigrations from the Continent—The Winning Side 168

CHAPTER VII.

The Tory Tribes of the Borders—A "Black Quarter" of Wigtownshire— Differing Complexions of Tories—The Dukes of Ancient Northumbria —"Country Keepers" 188

CHAPTER VIII.

Esther and David Blythe—Representative Border Tories—Some of Esther's Traits—Border "Thrift"—Old Border Customs—Tweed-dale Moss-Troopers Described—Inter-Tribal Feuds—The Two Populations of the Borders—The Moss-Troopers, of Fiction and of Fact .   .   . 199

CHAPTER IX.

Tory Provinces—Archaic Britain—Nationalism and Provincialism .   . 218

CHAPTER X.

PAGE

Mediæval Gentry—Yeomen and Nobles—Nomadic "Courtiers"—The "Courtier" and the "Villain": in the Fifteenth Century and in the Eighteenth—The Combative Castes of Britain—The Fifteenth Century—Gypsies of "The Upper Class"—The Decline of Gypsyism—Increase of "Peace-Lovers"—Clans of Sorners—"The Doones of Badgery"—Past Aristocracies—Cavalier Traits—The Tories of Modern Days—Habits of the Seventeenth-Century Royalists — Melanochroic Confederacies—The Tory Clans of England—"Something like Gypsies"—The Various Grades of Gypsydom—Blue-Blooded Romani Families—"Two Entirely Different and Even Hostile Races"—Cavaliers, as we Really Know Them—The Remains of Gypsyism   .   .   .   225

CHAPTER XI.

Egyptian Bishops—Fire-Worship, Astrology, &c.—"*Magi* and Enchanters and Soothsayers"—Marriage Ceremonies—"Marrying O'er the Sword"—Marital Rights—Sacred Circles—Black Monks—Priestly Emblems and Ceremonial—Sanctity of the Horse—Christians or Pagans?—Chanting and Incantation—The Ritual of the East—The Creed of Christianity—Heathen Aristocracies in Britain—Regimental Traditions—"Black Bandsmen"   275

CHAPTER XII.

The Tongues of Gypsydom—The Decline of "Rom" and "Romany"—Language of the Welsh Bards—"Romance" and "Romanes"—Troubadours, or Jugglers, or Gypsies—The Jugglers' Language—Edinburgh in the Fifteenth and Sixteenth Centuries—Gypsies, Nomadic and Stationary—"Egyptians," or "Moors," or "Moryans"—Buffoons and Actors—The Jugglers' "Contempt for Agriculturists"—French and British Romanes—Knight-Errantry—The Latest Phase of "Romance"—The Language of the Lists—The Sorners and Vagrants of History—The Ghost of an Ancient System.   .   .   .   310

CHAPTER XIII.

The Romani—The Romani of Annandale, Clydesdale, and Tweeddale—The Romani of Italy—The Romani of Egypt and Ethiopia—The Egyptians of Ancient Scotia—The Roman Language—The Language of the Romani—Roman customs   345

CHAPTER XIV.

Warfare by Legislation—The People Legislated Against—Nomads and their Enemies—"Glamour," "Witchcraft," and "Sorcery"—The Modern-British Nationality—"As Others See Us"   .   .   .   363

CHAPTER XV.

Orthoepic Changes—The Accent of the Elizabethans—"Tory" Meanings and Accentuation—Dental Sounds—Labial Sounds—Old-Fashioned British Castes 377

CHAPTER XVI.

The Component Parts of British Gypsydom—The Modernized British—The White Races—Our Ancestry—The Real Gypsies—Race Mixtures—The Black Tribes of Denmark—Tartar Lords—Tudors and Pagans—Numismatical Evidence—Asia in Europe—"The Turban'd Race of Termagaunt"—Advent of the Black Heathen—"Fire-Rain" and "Fire-Drakes"—Magical Arts—Persecution of the *Magi*—Star-Gazers—The *Magi* of Ireland—Galloway Cannon-Founders—Egyptian Arts and Sciences—Antagonistic Principles—The Sakas—British Huns—Painting and Scarifying—"Gypsy" and "Tory" 392

Appendix 443

BOOK III.

VOL. II.

ANCIENT

AND

MODERN BRITONS.

——◆◆——

CHAPTER I.

IF it is not yet too late in the day to look up the antecedents of the famous Galloway Pict, "Billy Marshall," the results obtained from such a research would almost certainly repay the trouble of obtaining them. He is introduced by several modern writers, though he was really of "the antique world." Not only because of his way of living, but literally so on account of his great age. For, although he lived on almost to the close of last century, his birth is placed as far back as the year 1671. This fact, therefore, gives him a great value; for if, like other true "gypsies," he clung tenaciously to all the customs of his forefathers—as far as the times would let him—then, in Billy Marshall, we have a representative of the Galloway Pict of the seventeenth century.

Without attempting anything that can be dignified by the name of "research," let us see what some of these modern writers say of him. Of these, none has a better right to the first word than Scott: and this is what he tells us* of the Galloway chief:—

"Meg Merrilies is in Galloway considered as having had her origin in the traditions concerning the celebrated Flora Marshal, one of the royal consorts of Willie Marshal, more commonly called the *Caird* [Tinker] of Barullion, King of the Gipsies of the Western ·Lowlands.

* In his "Additional Note" to "Guy Mannering."

That potentate was himself deserving of notice, from the following peculiarities. He was born in the parish of Kirkmichael, about the year
1671 ; and as he died at Kirkcudbright, 23rd November, 1792, he must
then have been in the one hundred and twentieth year of his age. It
cannot be said that this unusually long lease of existence was noted
by any peculiar excellence of conduct or habits of life. Willie had
been pressed or enlisted in the army seven times ; and had deserted as
often ; besides three times running away from the naval service. He
had been seventeen times lawfully married ; and besides such a reasonably large share of matrimonial comforts, was, after his hundredth year,
the avowed father of four children, by less legitimate affections. He
subsisted, in his extreme old age, by a pension from the present Earl of
Selkirk's grandfather. Will Marshal is buried in Kirkcudbright Church,
where his monument is still shown, decorated with a scutcheon suitably
blazoned with two tups' horns and two *cutty* spoons."

Beyond giving the details of one of his many robberies,
and stating that his consort, Flora, was finally " banished to
New England, whence she never returned,"—Scott does not
say more about Billy Marshall.

The compilers of the *New Annual Register* for 1792 thought
that his death was worthy of notice as one of the " Principal Occurrences " of that year. And this is the entry :—

"December 31. Lately died, at Kirkcudbright, in Scotland, aged 120,
Wm. Marshal, tinker. He was a native of the parish of Kirkmichael, in
the shire of Ayr. He retained his senses almost to the last hour of his
life ; and remembered distinctly to have seen King William's fleet,
when on their way to Ireland, riding at anchor in the Solway frith, close by
the Bay of Kirkcudbright, and the transports lying in the harbour. He
was present at the siege of Derry, where having lost his uncle, who
commanded a king's frigate, he returned home, enlisted into the Dutch
service, went to Holland, and soon after came back to his native country. He was buried in the Churchyard of Kirkcudbright. A great
concourse of people of all ranks attended his funeral, and paid due
respect to his astonishing age. The Countess of Selkirk, who, for a
course of years, had liberally contributed to his support, on this occasion,
discharged the expense of his funeral"

An extract has already been made from the sketch given
to us by the author of the *Gallovidian Encyclopedia, more
suo ;*—but it will be well to quote the whole account ; as it is
that of a Galloway-man.

"BILLY MARSHALL.—The famous Gallovidian gypsy, or *tinkler.* He
was of the family of the Marshalls, who have been tinklers in the south
of Scotland time out of mind. He was a short, thick-set little fellow, with
dark quick eyes ; and, being a good boxer, also famous at the *quarter-*

staff, he soon became eminent in his core ; and having done some won-derful trick by which he got clear off, he was advanced to be the chief of the most important tribe of vagabonds that ever marauded the country. The following was that trick :—He and his gang being in the neighbour-hood of Glasgow when there was a great fair to be held in it, himself and two or three more of his stamp, having painted their faces with *keel,* they went to the fair and enlisted, getting each so much cash. They then deserted to their crew in the wild mountain glen, leaving the sol-diers without a single cue [clue?] whereby to find them. For all, Billy once really took the *bounty,* joined the army, and went to the wars in Flanders ; but one day he accosted his commanding officer, who was a Galloway gentleman, this way : ' Sir, ha'e ye ony word to send to your friends in Scotland at present ?' ' What by that ?' returned the officer ' Is there any person going home?' ' Ay,' continued Billy, ' Keltonhill fair is just at hand. I ha'e never been absent frae it since my shanks could carry me to it, nor do I intend to let this year be the first.' The officer, knowing his nature, knew it would be vain to try to keep him in the ranks, so bade him tell his father and friends how he was ; he also gave him a note to take to his sweetheart. So Marshall departed, was at Keltonhill fair accordingly, and ever after that paid much respect to the family of Maculloch of Ardwell.

It is not my intention to give a lengthened portrait of this character, as one of the above family, who personally knew him, has done this for me, and much better, than I could, in *Blackwood's Magazine.* Suffice it to say, that the *Corse o' Slakes** was a favourite haunt of his. There did he frequently waylay the unwary, and sometimes deprived them of both life and purse. Billy's gang were seldom ever beat by any others. When they met at fairs, he generally drove all before him ; for the Irish took up with him from Down and Derry,—and who can overcome them at the handling of the *stick ?* To those country *Cock Lairds* who were kind to him, he would do them no injury, but all the good in his power ; whereas, those who were his foes,—Billy was upside with them.

He would not have cared to have *taken up lodging* [did not scruple to, &c.,]—he and his core—in one of these gentlemen's *kills,†*—to have purloined the greater part of the poultry, and roasted them with the wood of the roof of said *kill*—to have there staid a week, perhaps, in spite of everybody—gone away at his own time—and left a world of desolation behind him. It was in one of these scenes that he drank,

---

* "CORSE O' SLAKES.— . . . . In Galloway there was no roads so wild as the one which leads over the celebrated pass of the above name, between *Cairnsmoor* and *Cairnhattie ;* it is a perfect Alpine pass, and was a haunt of *Billy Marshall* and his gang in the days of yore ; even yet it is frequently selected as a suitable station for the ' bludgeon tribe.' " ("Gallov. Encyc.") This district lies on the eastern side of Wigtown Bay. On the western side, in a corner of the southward-jutting promontory known as The Maghers (*magh,* a marsh), is the Fell of Barullion or Barhullion, from which Marshall derived one of his titles. The map shows a ruined fort upon its summit.

† Outhouses.

May ne'er waur be amang us—a toast that can be construed in many shapes. Thus'did he flounder on through a long life. When he got old, his people though, in a great measure, forsook him.

It seems that he had both the good and bad qualities of man about him in a very large degree. He was kind, yet he was a murderer—an honest soul, yet a thief—at times a generous savage—at other times a wild Pagan. He knew both civil and uncivilized life—the dark and fair side of human nature. In short, he understood much of the world—had no fear—a happy constitution—was seldom sick—could sleep on a moor as soundly as in a feather-bed—took whisky to excess—died in Kirkcudbright at the age of 120 years—was buried there in state by the Hammermen, which body would not permit the Earl of Selkirk to lay his head in the grave, merely because his Lordship was not one of their incorporated tribe. Such was the end of Billy Marshall, a brother of Meg Merriless [*sic*]."

Mr. Simson's *History* only makes casual reference* to Marshall, repeating one or two of the facts already quoted ; and adding—on the authority of Sir Walter Scott—a little adventure of his with two Highland pipers, who had sought shelter in a certain cavern in Galloway, which had long been the retreat of Marshall and his band. The writer in *Blackwood*, referred to by McTaggart, is also cited—to this effect : " Who were his descendants I cannot tell ; I am sure he could not do it himself, if he were living. It is known that they were prodigiously numerous ; I dare say numberless." Which is quite in accordance with the statements made, in this respect, by the other writers quoted.

Although Mr. Leland's experience of "Gypsies" does not seem to take in those of Scotland, yet the fame of the celebrated Galloway chief has reached him also. Speaking of the surname, Marshall, he says (*Gypsies*, p. 306,) that it is "as much Scotch as English, especially in Dumfriesshire and Galloway, in which latter region, in Saint Cuthbert's churchyard, lies buried the 'old man' of the race, who died at the age of one hundred and seven."

Who *was* this man ? And what is one to make of all these statements, apparently so much at variance with each other ? Is there, in all history, a figure more difficult to *place*. In this "William Marshall, tinker," we have a real historical man ; and yet one who contradicts the received ideas of history, at every turn. The king of the Galloway "gypsies,"

---

* At pages 148-9 (note), 265 (note), and 388 (note).

lurking in some mountain defile with his gang of dark-skinned, crimson-visaged desperadoes, ready to rob and murder
at the first opportunity, differs very little from the leader of
any band of dark-skinned, crimson-visaged Wasaji braves,
ambuscading in some Western gulch. And yet this Scottish
"Indian" was the nephew of a naval officer in the service of
William of Orange.

If we reflect, however, the contrast is not so very violent
as it at first appears. Setting aside the figure of the *officer*,
let us recall the probable appearance of the ordinary British
tar of the seventeenth century. His head (like that of the
half-Indian, half-sailor Macleod, who rowed Dr. Johnson) was
uncovered, and his hair was probably plaited into a long
pigtail at the back. His nether garment was a short petticoat
or kilt like the Malay *sarong*. Of anything resembling
trousers, he was quite innocent. He may logically be
assumed to have tattooed himself more thoroughly—and
more seriously—than his representative of the nineteenth
century. And since Nelson's sailors went into action naked
to the waist,—it is not unlikely that those of King William's
fleet carried this notion still farther. That, in short, the
painted Gallowaymen that assailed King Robert Bruce were
not more naked than they.*

* The use of clothing seems to have been far from prevalent in the British
Islands, only a few generations ago. A last-century writer (of a very inferior
grade), known as *Dougal Graham*, makes one of his characters—a woman living
near Edinburgh—state that her grandparents wore little or no clothing. And
these people may be placed at about the middle of the seventeenth century.
Mr. Borrow, again ("Wild Wales," Vol. II. p. 305), describes a Welshman of
last century as "stripping himself stark naked" on the occasion of an encounter
with a rival. And Carleton, in his "Battle of the Factions," shows us one of
the combatants in a like condition; and, from his way of referring to this, it
would seem that—though not the rule—it was not an odd thing for one or more
of the participators in an Irish faction-fight, in the beginning of this century, to
be absolutely nude. Indeed, one of the descriptions in Mrs. Houstoun's
"Twenty Years in the Wild West" (of Ireland) leads one to assume that, even
at the present day, garments are not regarded as essentials by certain existing
natives of the United Kingdom. The glances that have previously been cast upon
Ireland have shown that that island has contained unclothed races for many centuries. Spenser's "naked rebels"; the "carrows" who used to gamble away
the mantle that was their only garment, after which they were content to "truss"
themselves with straw and leaves; those fourteenth-century kings of the neighbourhood of Dublin (*Dubhlinn*, "the black pool or water"); and the nobles of
that or a later period, who, on entering their wigwams, cast aside their sole

Suppose this to have been the case—and there is every reason to suppose it was so,—are we to imagine that the leaders of such warriors differed *entirely* from them in fashion? The "love-lock" of the seventeenth-century cavaliers may or may not have a racial meaning ;—but, at any rate, worn as it was "on the left side, depending from the ear, and decorated with a knot of riband ; " its effect, combined with a dark complexion, must have been very gypsy-like.* And there must have been many such "gypsies" among the cavaliers of the seventeenth-century: not the least notable of whom was Charles the Second, who was—if Marvell's picture is a true one—" of a tall stature, and of *sable hue* " (which shows how little of the Norman remained in his race by his time). Although his father had, very sensibly, snipped off *his* love-lock in the year 1646,† there is no evidence that the fashion was not continued by the Royalists for a considerable time afterwards. The seventeenth century was undoubtedly too near our own time to be an era in which a dynastic or political movement also denoted a struggle between *races ;* (although the historian must find it difficult to put down his finger on the exact date when racial feelings ceased to be an important factor in British politics).‡ And it would be impossible to show that the wearers of the "love-locks" were mostly men of swarthy complexion. But when such of them as resembled Charles II. in complexion, had played the not

garment as a matter of course : all these—whether they were of one race or diverse—regarded the wearing of clothes as scarcely necessary, or not at all. And the " Abram-men " of England were of the same opinion. There are other races now alive who hold similar views, and we are often inclined to stamp them as "savages," for this reason alone. But perhaps we are too much swayed by custom in deciding thus. The early Greeks and Romans do not seem to have worn overmuch clothing. And an incident in St. Peter's life shows that he did not always think it necessary to put on the " fisher's coat " that seems to have constituted his apparel ; while, in the same memorable epoch, there is mention of a "young man " who escaped his captors by leaving his only garment, a linen cloth, in their hands. Yet it can scarcely be argued that any of these last-mentioned people were "savages."

* See note to Dekker's "Gull's Hornbook," ed. 1812, p. 137. Compare with this fashion the long locks of the Hebridean women, "depending from the ear, and decorated with a knot of riband."

† *Ibid.*

‡ It will be seen, at a later page, that there are some grounds for believing that the seventeenth-century struggles really were, to some extent—perhaps, to a considerable extent—of a racial nature.

uncommon part of Roger Wildrake ; and having run through all their patrimony, found—as many of them did—that the only course left open to them was to " go and beg their food,"

> " Or with a base and boisterous sword enforce
> A thievish living on the common road,"—

it is difficult to see wherein such men differed from the " flash " gentlemen-gypsies described by Simson. Positively, there was *no* difference between them.

So that the incompatibility between Marshall, the gypsy, and Marshall (if he was a paternal uncle), the naval officer, becomes less and less as you regard the facts of the case. It is even possible that that latter worthy was not unacquainted with the war-paint of his forefathers. Thackeray describes the "Chevalier de Balibari" as painting *his* face, in accordance with the custom of his time. But as this practice may be nothing more than that species of *Pictism* which is now practised by a portion of the gentler sex ; and as its claim to be regarded as a "survival" may reasonably be disallowed; this point cannot be pressed. Against such a conjecture, it might also be objected that such portraits as we possess of seventeenth-century officers, do not give any hint of this *Pictish* proclivity. To which, on the other hand, it might be replied, that, as the custom of putting on war-paint was only practised when going into action, it would not make itself apparent on ordinary occasions. But it is most likely that the practice had been abandoned by the upper ranks—of whatever race—for many generations ; since statutes had been passed against tattooing many centuries previously. Still, such habits are tremendously tenacious, and we know that tattooing is not given up even yet ; and that painting the face was quite common among the most conservative section of our own population, so lately as the latter part of last century. As for the side-locks of the gypsy and the Cavalier, they seem to have been retained in the army till about the same period : since Washington Irving, in making his "General Harbottle" the representative of the British "soldier of the old school," pictures him "with powdered head, *side locks, and pigtail.*"

It is quite evident that " William Marshall, tinker ; " " king of the gipsies of the Western Lowlands ; " " the Caird of

Barullion ;" whose family had been "tinklers in the south of Scotland time out of mind," but whose uncle commanded a royal frigate ; private soldier, and deserter ; thief and murderer ; *sorner* and brigand—it is quite evident that he was not a nobody. The license allowed him by his commanding officer, during time of war, may not signify much ; though it is unlikely that, then or now, an ordinary private would be quietly permitted to desert, after giving due notice of his intention to do so. But, apart from this, and apart from the rank held by his uncle, which some might dispute as a myth of his own making, there yet remains the significant fact that, for many years, he was supported by an Earl and a Countess of Selkirk,—the latter of whom defrayed the expense of his funeral—no trivial matter in Scotland, in the year 1792, when "a great concourse of people" attended to pay "due respect," after the fashion of the country and the time. "His astonishing age" is by no means a satisfactory explanation of this final honour ; or of the fact that the Earl of Selkirk made an ineffectual effort to take the most important place in the last ceremony ; a place which the hammermen* of Galloway did not hold him entitled to occupy.

What had he to recommend him ? From our modern point of view he was simply a disreputable old scamp. He was more than that : he was a notorious murderer and thief. Viewed in this light alone, it is impossible to understand why he should have been the pensioner of a noble family ; or why an earl should have desired to act the part of "chief mourner" at his funeral. That he was utterly disreputable in the restricted sense which this word is sometimes understood to bear, is beyond question. Although Scott states that he had been "seventeen times lawfully married," it is not to be imagined that he had outlived sixteen consecutive "wives," before he wedded his seventeenth spouse. A glance at Mr. Simson's valuable chapter on the "gypsy" marriage and divorce ceremonies, will show how unnecessary it is to suppose this, even though Marshall had been a monogamist gypsy (a most unlikely combination). The ceremony of divorce consists (or did consist) of the performance of certain

---

* Who, by the way, get the credit of bearing the expense of the funeral, according to Mactaggart. These *Hammer-men* were evidently no other than the *Tinkers* of Galloway.

observances round the body of a horse, sacrificed for the occasion ; the time, noon ; the officiating priest, any gypsy who may be selected by lot, even the husband himself, if need be. Marshall himself may be the gypsy whose summary procedure, in this way, is related by Mr. Simson. "I have been informed (he says, at page 274,) of an instance of a gipsy falling out with his wife, and, in the heat of his passion, shooting his own horse* dead on the spot with his pistol, and forthwith performing the ceremony of divorce over the animal, without allowing himself a moment's time for reflection on the subject." As this event "took place many years ago, in a wild, sequestered spot between Galloway and Ayrshire," the gypsy in question was very likely one of Marshall's followers, if not that chief himself.

It is apparent, then, that the King of the Gypsies of the Western Lowlands might have been lawfully married, and as lawfully divorced from his seventeen wives, all within the space of one year. But the probability is that—like others of his race, in the Hebrides, on the Borders, or among the moors of the Ochils ; or, like his far back ancestors in the East—Marshall was an open and avowed polygamist. And that however his mode of life was opposed to modern ideas, there was nothing in it that was not sanctioned by the customs and the creed of his race. For in him, as in the other Scottish examples briefly indicated, we have a specimen of our *pagan* ancestors : one to whom Christianity was nothing, because he had never forsaken the religion of his forefathers : and in whose eyes the modern laws were no laws ; although those of his tribe (inherited from a remote antiquity) were inviolable.

This is the standing-point from which we shall most likely learn the true position in history of this celebrated "gypsy." Mactaggart's explanation of the circumstance that led to his appointment as King over the South-Western Picts is not a very satisfactory one ; although it is no doubt the relation of

---

* Both the horse and the fire-arms tend to confirm the statement that this "took place many years ago," when *gypsies* were still formidable marauders— mounted and armed—moss-troopers, bog-trotters, or "hobylers." Which period is remembered by their civilized descendants under the designation of "the riding days."

an episode in his life. It can scarcely be believed that a
successful trick of this sort would, of itself, entitle him to the
chiefship of a people so tenacious of old customs, and so
ready to recognize the rights of high descent. Much more
likely is it, that, by examining the pedigree of this particular
Marshall family (if that can yet be done) we shall find the
key to the triple mystery of his own station, of his uncle's
rank, and of the honour paid to him by a family of consideration. That he was the lineal representative of a family
of ancient standing, seems exceedingly probable. It may be
remembered that the *King of the Faws* (of the eastern
Anglo-Scottish border-country) who was buried at Jarrow,
on January 13, 1756,* bore the name of Francis Heron.
Though this name has had representatives in Kircudbright-
shire for several centuries, it seems to have been originally
Northumbrian ; and it is well-known in Border history. Scott
has introduced it into *Marmion*, as everybody knows : in the
persons of "Sir Hugh the Heron" and his frail spouse.
Scott adds, in a note, that "Hugh" is a fictitious personage ;
the original being William Heron of Ford. At any rate the
Herons were, at that date, a powerful border family. But
although,— like the Douglases—they have never ceased to be
represented, in some degree, by families of good position,
yet the fate of the main line of that race has apparently
been similar to that of the Douglases. We know that, since
1455, the genuine *Douglases* have been outlaws and wanderers :
what we call *gypsies*. So, although their decadence must
have been of later date, we find that the power of one branch
(presumably, not so much a *branch* as the main *stem*) of this
ancient clan had shrivelled into the shadowy sovereignty of
the *tories* of their race—and these alone—by the year 1756.
That Francis Heron, the acknowledged chief of the Northumbrian Picts (that is, of the *Irreconcilables* of this division
of the race), in the eighteenth century, was the purest representative of the chiefs of the Heron clan is most probable.
Any one who has paid the slightest attention to the pedigrees
of families or of clans, knows that—where that pedigree is
of any considerable length, the nominal wearer of the family
honours is, as likely as not, in a very slight degree the de-

* Halliwell's "Dictionary" ; under the word *Faw-gang.*

scendant of the founder—and often is of wholly alien blood.
The play of *New Men and Old Acres* is the oldest in the
world. Indeed, it is almost impossible that, in a country
which has been governed by a great variety of races—as this
has—any one family could remain in power through every
change. Although every successive chieftain had no more
principle in him than the Vicar of Bray, his family must lose
its power one day. Mr. Disraeli has some very true remarks
of this sort in *Sybil.* But the fact is too patent to require
argument. To take examples from this particular neighbourhood : not only did the purest-blooded *Douglases* cease to
belong to the successful and governmental party after the
fifteenth century, but so also was it with the *Graemes,*
wherever situated. Graeme of Claverhouse, for example,
may or may not have inherited a share of the blood of those
from whom he derived his surname. But the purest Stirlingshire *Graemes* of modern times were the swarthy marauders
of last century. And although more than one honourable
family lays claim to the blood of the Graemes of the
Debatable Land, we know that the greater portion of that
clan was exterminated, or expatriated, and that those of
them who were sent into Ireland (and whose descendants
probably bear other and various names to-day) or those who,
as the *gypsies* of the Debatable Lands, resented so strongly
the attempted partition of the territory of their forefathers,✷
must be regarded as, without doubt, the genuine " Graemes
of the Debatable Land." And as Francis Heron, King of
the South-Eastern Faws in 1756, was the possible, and
probable head of the mediæval clan of the Herons (by right
of blood), so William Marshall, King of the South-Western
Faws,† at the same period, was as likely the lineal descendant of a race of powerful border chiefs. The surname of
his ancestors might even have been Heron also. For
Marshall is not necessarily an old name. It does not indicate a particular family any more than Faa, or Fall does,

---

✷ Simson, pp. 149–50 : already referred to.

† It may not be strictly correct to use Faw, " of *various* colours," in connection
with those Picts who appear to have only made use of iron ore, or ruddle. But,
in the meantime, *Faw* and *Pict* may be used with some freedom.—The expressions
South-East and *South*-West are, of course, here used from the Scottish standing-
point.

though it eventually, like Faa, or Fall, attached itself to one particular line. (This, however, may be said of all surnames.) Like Stewart, Constable, and other names, it originally signified an office. For example, Sir George Bowes of Streatham, Durham (*inter alia*, father-in-law of Knox the Reformer), was Knight Marshall, or *Miles Marescallus*, of his province: and Sir William Keith, who was "great marischal of Scotland" in the fifteenth century, became Earl Marischal; the name of his descendant, the eighth earl, being written "Earl *Marshall*." So that if the Northumbrian Herons, who held various high offices, were at any time *Marischals* of the Borders, it is not at all unlikely that this dignity might cling to one branch of the family as a surname. It is of some importance to notice that although settled in Galloway for several centuries, the Scottish Herons trace their origin to the older Northumbrian stock. And it is a curious coincidence (if a coincidence) that the history of the *word* itself* shows that it has borne the meaning—not only of "a marshall of a kingdom or of a camp "—but also of "a blacksmith," "a farrier,"—that is, in Galloway, a *Tinkler.*

Therefore, if the Faw King represented an ancient and powerful—though decayed—race, it is easily understood how the Selkirk family, knowing this; and perhaps aware that, in point of descent, "William Marshall, tinker" was greatly their superior ;—possibly aware also that he was, genealogically regarded, the head of one of the families from which they traced their descent ;—would pay him a respect which was immeasurably above his merits. Looked at in this light —his robberies and murders were only the excusable ravages of an irreclaimable Border moss-trooping chief ; his numerous wives and mistresses were the lawful consorts of a man of his rank, race, and religion ; his custom of *sorning* on a country

---

* "MARSHAL, a master of the horse ; variously applied as a title of honour. . . . . The original sense is ' horse-servant,' a farrier or groom ; it rose to be a title of honour, like *constable.* . . . . Old French *mareschal* (mod. F. *maréchal*) 'a marshall of a kingdom or of a camp (an honourable place), also a blacksmith, farrier ; . . . . O.H.G. *marah*, a battle-horse, whence the fem. *merihd*, a mare . . . . and *schalh*, M.H.G. *shale*, a servant, whence G. *schalk*, a knave, a rogue," &c. (Professor Skeat's "Etymological Dictionary.") That *marshal* was used in Scotland during the fifteenth and sixteenth centuries, in the sense of *farrier*, is seen from various entries in the Treasurer's Accounts.

laird for days at a time, without leave asked or given, was only the inherited right of *coshering*, practised by the *Sorohen,* or nobles of his race, for countless generations ; the two ram's horns and horn-spoons, crossed, that were sculptured on his tombstone, were the armorial bearings of a chief whose people had never recognized the right of any Norman-Feudal herald to modify or alter these ; the tomb-stone itself ought rather to be regarded as the latest of the non-Christian " sculptered stones of Scotland," than as any ordinary Christian tablet,—the church itself being, for the moment, a druidical temple, such as those within whose precincts the earlier " Moors " used to bury their dead ;—and all such particulars ought to be held to prove the purity of the Faw chief's descent, as much as did the scarlet war-paint on his face, or the swarthy skin which it overlay.

As for his uncle, the sea-captain, we have seen that, at a time long after his, the " gypsy " fashion of side-locks* and pigtail still prevailed among the officers of the sister service ; while it is by no means certain that the use of war-paint had wholly died out in his day, among the higher classes. It was at least quite a recent thing among the Blue Donalds and Green Colins who led the Hebridean pirates : it, or its kindred practice of tattooing. Among the ordinary seamen of his ship, most of these peculiarities formed part and parcel of their life. And if Marshall, the elder, did not *adopt* any of these customs which our British sailors have inherited from the Frisians who once manned the South-British navy, he might easily have *inherited* them from those Frisians who settled in one portion of his native Galloway—Dumfries,† " the town of the Frisians." There is no mention of the outward appearance of this elder Marshall, but it may be assumed

---

* The word " fore-lock " is also somewhat suggestive. Though I am not aware of any proof of the fashion, the name seems certainly to hint at a long lock trained over the forehead, not very different from the North-American scalplock (and perhaps grown for the same purpose).

† Skene's " Celtic Scotland," Vol. III. p. 25. In speaking of the Frisian origin of the British navy—in a previous chapter—it was stated that, as a separate people, the Frisians of Britain had ceased to exist. This is likely ; though, as in the navy, many of their customs must have lingered long in the districts wherein they settled. It is possible, however, that one or other of the " gypsy " families of Dumfriesshire are of pure Frisian descent.

that he was not unlike his nephew—and, if so, not unlike
another celebrated Galloway "gypsy"—the notorious
adventurer, Paul Jones. This man's "forebears," in the preceding generation or so, do not display any peculiarly "gypsy"
proclivities : rather the reverse. But his own nature and outward appearance suggest a descent from such men as that
famous land-pirate, Billy Marshall ; who, indeed, may have
had reason to include Paul Jones among his numerous descendants.* Marshall, it may be remembered, is pictured to
us as "a short, thick-set little fellow, with dark quick eyes ; "
and the same writer says† of the formidable corsair, that " he
was a short thick little fellow, above five feet eight in height,
of a dark swarthy complexion." He, too, was a native of
Galloway. Although a man " above five feet eight " is only
"little" in the eyes of tall men, yet the general appearance
of Jones's figure—short and thick-set—is a token of what Mr.
Simson might call "a thorough gypsy ; " for he tells us‡ that,
" with gipsies of mixed blood, the individual, if he takes after
the Gipsy, is apt to be short and thick-set." And there is a
Scotch word,§ interchangeable with other Scotch terms for a
female "gypsy," which has also the radical meaning of short
and "stumpy." Therefore, although not described as a
"gypsy," and although born and brought up among people
of settled habits, Paul Jones—by his manner of life and his

---

* The surnames borne by this man's parents were Paul and McDuff, and his
mother's father is said to have been a local farmer. But as Paul Jones (or, more
correctly, John Paul) was born in 1747, and as the date of Marshall's birth is
usually fixed at about 1671, the latter might easily have been the grandfather, or
the great-grandfather, of the former.

† McTaggart, at pages 373 and 376 of his "Encyclopedia."

‡ "History of the Gipsies," p. 139, note.

§ *Cutty.* McTaggart enlarges this into *cutty-glies,* the complete etymology of
which he explains to his own satisfaction. Physically, he describes a "cutty" of
this sort as "a little squat-made female " ; and since he ascribes certain moral
(or immoral) characteristics to women of this description, it is quite evident that
he, unknowingly, refers to the women of a particular *race. Cutty*—along with
gypsy, quean, and *randy*—is used in ordinary Scotch phraseology, in an uncomplimentary sense. Mr. Simson believes the last of these words is the "gypsy"
rance, or *raunie,* "a queen." If so, all these four words are applicable to gypsy
women ; but when used *by* gypsies they are honourable—*dis*-honourable when
used by civilized people. And this is quite consistent with facts. For as the
half-tamed *raunie* is a "queen" to her people, but a "quean" to those of more
settled habits, so are *gypsies* synonymous with *thieves* and *blacks*—in the estimation
of the latter class.

physical characteristics—was nearly as much entitled to be styled a "gypsy" as was his renowned compatriot (and possible ancestor); and as much entitled to be so denominated as was Marshall's uncle, the naval officer.*

It would be tedious and difficult to ferret out other modern examples of the sea-faring "gypsy;" but such types must have been more and more numerous the farther one goes back in time. Allan Mac Ruari, the black-skinned Hebridean pirate of the fifteenth century, is one notable instance: and others of the same kind may be seen in those "Blue-skins"—Green and Blue Colins and Donalds—that infested the Hebridean creeks at about that period or later. *In Highland tradition, there are many "sea-tinkers"—such as "the black smith of Drontheim":—and in this Galloway district, specially, the legendary Blackamoor, Black Murray, or Black-Douglas, is remembered in one account as a sea-rover, and in another as one of a company of sea-faring "Moors or Saracens." And—as on the land, so on the sea —they assume quite *national* proportions, when one looks at them from a still greater distance; before their numbers had been diminished by conquest, or their individuality rendered indistinct by their blending with white-skinned races. When, in short, they were savage. sea-faring "black heathen;" known under various historical names; sacking churches and monasteries, killing and ravishing; and, at one time, actually conquering the greater portion of the British Islands.

Apparently, then, this patriarchal leader of the *tory* section of the Galloway Faws was a genuine descendant of the ancient Moors, or Picts. Of the conservative remnants of these races, other examples were seen in the *Graemes, Moors,* or *Gypsies* of the Debatable Land: who proved the purity of their ancestry—if in no other way—by the resistance they offered to the would-be claimants of their territory; in doing which they showed, instinctively, that they, and no other, were *the graemes* of that "debatable" district.

---

* More so. Because Paul Jones, though he eventually rose to positions of real eminence in foreign services, seems to have been a mere marauder at the first. Whereas, for anything we know to the contrary, this British naval officer of the seventeenth century had never occupied a more equivocal position than that in which he momentarily appears to view.

And they themselves are well aware of their history. Like
all other "gypsies," their traditions and songs are full
of reference to that history which is partly the history of
the general population of these islands, but which is
distinctly that of their forefathers. "As far as I can
judge (says Mr. Simson, p. 306), from the few and short
specimens which I have myself heard, and had reported to
me, the subjects of the songs of the Scottish gipsies, (I mean
those composed by themselves,) are chiefly their plunderings,
their robberies, and their sufferings. The numerous and
deadly conflicts which they had among themselves, also
afforded them themes for the exercise of their muse. My
father, in his youth, often heard them singing songs, wholly
in their own language. They appear to have been very fond
of our* ancient Border marauding songs, which celebrate the
daring exploits of the lawless freebooters on the frontiers
of Scotland and England. They were constantly singing
these compositions among themselves. The song composed
on Hughie Graeme, the horse-stealer, published in the second
volume of Sir Walter Scott's 'Border Mintrelsy,' was a great
favourite with the Tinklers." So many of these Border *Moors*
were distinguished by this title of *Graeme, Grim*, or *Black*, that
one cannot very easily discriminate ; but this "Hughie the
graeme," apparently the most ferocious of all those who bore
that name, seems to be the same as " Graeme, the Border
Outlaw," and " Graeme, the Outlaw of Galloway." Perhaps,
so, perhaps not. We saw that a redoubtable *Douglas*
(known historically under that equivalent of *Graeme, Moor,
Murray, Black*, &c.) was "Archibald the Grim," or black ;
and one or other of the three titles just given may apply to
a descendant of his. Like the Douglases proper, "Graeme
the Border Outlaw " was lord of a castle,—thereby a *Black
Castle*,—situated " at the head of the Vale of Fleet."† Again,
"Graeme, the Outlaw of Galloway," is only styled "a freebooter" and "a ruffian named Graeme ;" but his home is

---

* Really, *their* "ancient Border marauding songs," though the language is a
newer form of speech than theirs—out of which, to some extent, it has been
evolved. To some extent, also, those songs are the property of the civilized
mixed-bloods who apparently form the greatest part of the Border population.

† "Historical and Traditional Tales of the South of Scotland." John
Nicholson, Kirkcudbright, 1843, p. 304.

the Debatable Land. Of him, it is said, "many acts of bloody cruelty, too gross to be mentioned, are on record." The account of him from which these expressions are quoted,* gives the following sketch of the Debatable Land and its occupants, which, although partly a repetition of former statements, is worth extracting :—

"The people of the English borders, in common with those of Scotland, were in those days nothing less than clans of lawless banditti who were engaged in predatory excursions. The track which they occupied extended about fifty miles in length and six in breadth, and was called 'the debateable land,' both nations laying claim to it, though in fact it belonged to neither,† as their utmost efforts were ineffectual for the subjection of its inhabitants, whose dexterity in the art of thieving was such, that they could twist a cow's horn, or mark a horse, so that its owner could not know either again . . . . Since the union of Scotland and England, those scenes of contention and barbarism, which rendered existence and property equally precarious, have been gradually disappearing . . . .

"However, it was not with the English borderers alone that the Scotch clans were always at war. Deadly quarrels often arose among themselves which were not quelled during a lapse of centuries . . . . It was only on occasions of general warfare between the monarchs of the contending nations of England and Scotland, that these ancient feuds were laid aside,—when the chieftain of each opposing clan forgetting their former deadly enmity, joined the common cause against their hostile foe. But even at that period, and on the eve of battle, some fancied insult would again add fuel to the half-smothered flame, their former animosities would again break forth, and bloodshed and murder reigned triumphant.

The writer of this—since he distinguishes between "the freebooters of the forests," and "these opposing clans," and for other apparent reasons,—did not know that the moss-trooping thieves he described were popularly known as "Gypsies." But had he been writing an appendix to Mr. Simson's *History*, he could not have used more appropriate

* "Historical and Traditional Tales of the South of Scotland," pp. 31-34.
† This is a simple fact. So long as the laws of the British Government were successfully defied in this scrap of territory, or, as we have seen they were, in portions of the Hebrides, the larger of the British Islands was not really a "United Kingdom." Contemptible though the opposition was, it was, nevertheless, the latest assertion of a sovereignty which was not Modern-British, whether we call it, somewhat vaguely, "Pictish," or, more distinctly, "Black-Danish." The first term includes the second.

language. That book gives two examples (at pp. 142-3 and
148) of that "dexterity in the art of thieving" which so
characterized the Borderers,—only Mr. Simson calls his moss-
troopers, "Gypsies." But the two sets of men are, in every
respect, identical. The Border writer when he says of the
"lawless banditti" of the debatable lands, "engaged in
predatory excursions,"—"Deadly quarrels often arose among
themselves, which were not quelled during the lapse of centuries,"—might almost be accused of copying Mr. Simson's
very words—who tells us of "the numerous and deadly conflicts which they [the *gypsies*] had among themselves;" of
which he gives us many instances,—and the inveterate
character of which he dwells upon (pp. 236-7), with reference
to the never-ending feud between the Baillies and those *Faws*
to whom this descriptive epithet eventually clung as a surname. And when the Galloway writer adds that the outlawed *Graeme* stipulated for "a sum of money in the meantime, and a future annuity, by way of black-meal," he indicates a notorious practice of such *gypsies* as Henry [the] Faa,
who exacted a similar tribute from "men of considerable
fortune" on the southern Border, in the beginning of the
eighteenth century;—of such *gypsies* as the leader of that
tribe which a modern writer* tells us "for years levied black
mail over the county of Aberdeen," about the same period;
—or of those "black watches," generally, who, we saw in a
preceding chapter, used to traverse the Highlands (about
that era), and to whom there was yearly paid "in *black-mail*
or *watch-money*, openly and privately," the sum of five
thousand pounds: and, in all these cases, as in that of "the
tribute of the blacke armie," which a white-skinned nation of
Wales was forced to pay to the swarthy pirates whom history
knows as Danes, or Cimbri;—or as in that of the yearly sum
exacted from the Roman Empire in the fifth century, by the
probable kinsmen and ancestors of these Black Danes,—the
equally swarthy Huns;—in all these cases, the tax was most
fitly and naturally designated "*black*" mail, or tribute.

The distinction, then, between such *Graemes* as "Hughie
Graeme, the horse-stealer," and such *Graemes* as are mentioned by various "Gypsy" writers under the title of *Gypsies*,

* Dr. John Brown, in his sketch of "A Jacobite Family."

is only one of nomenclature. And even this distinction vanishes when one reflects that " *Graeme,*" strictly interpreted, is " *Moor,*" or " black man." Indeed (to dwell for a moment longer upon this particular branch of the race), the nicknames of those of the clan who were—in Scott's opinion —the probable associates of the celebrated " Hughie," might be those of any Gypsy gang. Such names as " Flaugh-tail," " Nimble Willie," " Mickle Willie," and " Muckle Willie Grame," accord well with " The Whistler " (*Black Duncan's* adopted son), " Muckle William Ruthven," " Little Wull " (Ruthven), " Gley'd Neckit Will " (supposed by Mr. Simson to have been " old Will Faa," a Yetholm chief), and suchlike. The use of nicknames seems indeed to have been regarded as a peculiarity of the black races, since a nickname is sometimes spoken of as a ". black."* It may be said that the use of descriptive names is not peculiar to any race ; but is merely a primitive custom. And this may be readily admitted without any damage to the argument. For it is only another way of saying that the *tories* of Scotland are nothing else than archaic Scotchmen.

And this is what everything goes to prove. In whatever part of Scotland we have looked at them, the *tories,* or robbers, or moss troopers, or " gypsies," have been seen to be *tories* in the modern sense of that word.† They are Scotch-

* "What a fool I was to give him a black," says Tom Brown, on the occasion of his fishing adventure, when he realizes that he hasn't improved his position by addressing the keeper as " Velveteens."

Prize-fighters, who have been identified with " gypsies " from the earliest records, are also known rather by their nick-names than by any other ; and bear such titles as " The Game Chicken," " The Tipton Slasher," or " The Putney Pet." Minstrels, or harpers, who also are " gypsies," follow the same custom. In Mr. Burnand's amusing " Little Holiday " (*Punch,* No. 2,148), we are told that the Bard whom he meets " has a title in his own language, which translated means ' The Soaring Eagle ' ;" and that " all the Bards have descriptive titles, such as The Roaring Lion, The Howling Deer, and so forth. It reminds me (adds the chronicler) of the names in Fenimore Cooper's novels about the Redskins," which is a very suitable observation. It is worth remarking that this Bard, when he makes his appearance, is black-haired, and generally so like a "foreigner" that his appearance gives rise to a most ludicrous situation. Of course, the adventure is half-mythical ; but this minstrel has precisely the appearance he ought to have—as a member of that brotherhood whose oldest living representative speaks the " gypsy " of Wales as his mother-tongue.

† That is to say, accepting *Toryism* as the equivalent of *Orientalism,* or the abhorrence of change and innovation : the caricature, so to speak, of that con-

men who have not progressed : "Scotchmen," that is, in the most comprehensive acceptation of the term,—whatever race-names they may have borne when they landed in North Britain.   Like their kinsmen, the swarthy minstrels and jugglers of the southern portion of the island,—during mediæval times,—the "Moorish" divisions of the Scotch nation have been the minstrels of the north.   And, conversely, the minstrels,—wherever they can be seen—are "Moors."   The songs that the people of the North-West used to "carol as they went along," were the ancient songs of that district : and the singers were "Gypsies:" members of that (then) "lowest rank of peasantry," whose females, in the speech of the local aristocracy were "black girls," and whose "vernacular" was "black speech."   Of these Highland gypsy minstrels the latest distinct example is, perhaps, the gypsy composer of "Macpherson's *Lament*;" though the well-known ballad of "Donald Caird," or "Gypsy Donald,"—which pictures a most typical gypsy,—shows that this characteristic of his people was once taken for granted.*

servative tendency which is one of the safeguards of civilization, and which is a very different thing from absolute *Toryism.* For the latter means simply the resistance of all progress ; and is, therefore, as great an impediment in the way of the advance of civilization and liberty as is its antithesis, Radicalism.   The word "Tory "—as used for the last century or two—is, of course, merely a nickname, and is inapplicable (in its strict sense) to the most extreme political Conservative of modern times.

    * Scott's version is called " *Donald* Caird's come again," but it is set to the air of an older ballad—"*Malcolm* Caird's come again." In either case *Caird* is evidently not used as a surname, but as signifying "gypsy." The line alluded to is the opening one, " Donald Caird can lilt and sing."

    That the gypsy of the Highlands is even yet a Minstrel, or Piper, is seen from the description given of these people in the sketch of "Two Little Tinkers " by the author of "John Halifax."   Mrs. Craik explains that Highland Tinkers "are not gipsies" ; but, as she speaks of the "brown skins " of the two in question, and as the father of one of them is "an ugly wee *black* man," one may be excusably allowed to think otherwise. We are here told that these Tinkers "live the roughest, wildest, most wandering of lives, ' tinkering ' pots and pans, and going about in bands, each band having attached to it one absolute idler, the ' piper,' who plays his bagpipes at feasts and weddings, and is usually the most confirmed drunkard of the whole."   This is *precisely* the character of the ancient Bard, Minstrel, or Jongleur, of mediæval and of earlier times : of those days when "to be a Bard freed a man."   And such Gypsy-Pipers are much truer representatives of that caste than are those specimens attached to modern mansions (and modern chiefs) in the Highlands of Scotland—often as artificially created as were Catherine of Russia's "happy peasants."

So also with the Minstrelsy of the Scottish Border. Where-ever we have looked for special examples of the Border Minstrels, we have found them among the kindred of those tawny people who sang so "bonnily" before the Earl of Cassilis' gate ; and wiled away the love of his Lady. When we ask for the singers of those ancient Border songs—of battle, and rapine, and love,—we are directed—not to the civil-ized, prosaic folk that constitute the general Border popula-tion ; and whose blood is either wholly that of the phleg-matic white-skinned peoples, or is largely dashed with it ;— but to the dusky dwellers among the camps, who are so attached to those " ancient Border marauding songs " that they are " constantly singing them among themselves." And who can so perfectly appreciate such minstrelsy,—impreg-nated as it is with a spirit of reckless daring and lawlessness, *utterly opposed to the ideas of modern civilization,—but quite in consonance with the creed of the gypsies,*—as those lingering representatives of that archaic life ? Everywhere have the Minstrels and the gypsies gone hand-in-hand. The man who laments the decay of " Minstrelsy," and he who mourns the approaching death of " Gypsydom,'" must read the self-same page of history, if they want to know when these flourished most.

As with their rhythmic traditions, so with their spoken legends. Just as the oldest living harper in Wales owns the speech of those " Gypsies " as his mother-tongue, so is the folk-lore of the Welsh Gypsy equally the property of the general population there. In giving us a " Gypsy " story, Mr. Leland tells us of British Merlin.* " Alike in Wales and Turkey," says the *Encyclopædia* writer, the " Gypsy " tales " may be identified with those of other Aryan races ; scarce one has yet been published but its counterpart may be found

---

* It is true that the gypsy narrator of the story states that—" A Welsher told me that story." ¿But, then, what *kind* of " Welsher "? If of the same race as the Welsh Minstrels, the preservers of tradition, he was a Welsh *gypsy*. This very form of " Welshman " is significant. For it has become identified with a certain class of men, unpleasantly prominent on race-courses, the members of which are —or were—described in Scotland as " blacks," and in England and elsewhere as " blacklegs " at the present day.

It is surely unnecessary to add that the connection between the Welsh *Minstrel* and the *Welsher* has been broken off long ago.

in Grimm's, Ralston's, or other collection of European folk-lore." And when Mr. Campbell collected his famous West Highland Tales, he gathered them, in great measure, from the lips of "Tinkers." A previous chapter has shown us that the inherited superstitions, of the existing "Scotch" people, and the obsolete customs of a portion of their ances-tors, are the superstitions and the customs of the Scottish "Gypsies."* We have seen that the "turf-built cots" of the "vagrant gypsies" on "Yeta's banks" were quite common last century in Inchegall, *The Isles of the Foreigners*, and commoner still throughout Scotland, at an earlier date. And

---

* Mr. Leland advances as plausible, if not capable of proof, that a common nursery rhyme (used for "counting out") is good sense in "gypsy," though nonsense in "English." The version he takes begins with "ekkeri. akkery, u-kery an"; that given by Dr. John Brown in "Pet Marjorie" goes thus—

"Wonery, twoery, tickery, seven;
Alibi, crackaby, ten, and eleven;"

and so on; and this is the version familiar to all Scotch children. In any case, Mr. Leland's theory as to the manner in which this rhyme became first known to non-gypsy children is—with all deference to him—very difficult to accept. But in view of the facts above stated, it is quite a superfluous theory. For the children of Scotland—not to regard others at present—have clearly obtained this rhyme, with many other customs, by *inheritance*. It has been previously pointed out that the Scotch game of *Jing-ga-ring* is almost certainly an archaic marriage ceremony; whether the etymology of its title (and burden) be connected with the word *Zingari* or not. Possibly it is the very ceremony indicated by McTaggart under the words "Owre Boggie," *i.e.*, "*too moor-ish*." "People (he says) are said to be married in an *owre boggie* manner" when they are married "contrary to the common laws" by men of the stamp of the Gretna Green blacksmith, who were popularly known as *auld bogyies*.

These are only two examples out of the mass. Men who have studied those nursery rhymes and games know how much sense lies hidden in what, at first sight, seems a heap of nonsense. It would be going too far to say that children never *invent* games and rhymes, or that all nonsense-verses were once sense; but it has become apparent within this century that our children are, in a measure, our *historians*. Children, it must be remembered, form a separate caste as much as does the Army, the Navy, or the Church; and, like any of these, their ways are deserving of the most precise analysis for the sake of the historical facts they teach. All of these, as distinct societies or castes, are to-day using certain words, and performing certain acts, that have been handed down to them, *as castes*, from remote ages. And although the members of these societies, in some cases, make use of words and actions which it would puzzle them to explain clearly, yet each of these was once full of meaning. So is it, as we have been lately taught, with the traditions of childhood. And it might be said that almost all—if not all —rhymes of the *one-ery, two-ery* order, and all burdens such as *lero, lero, lillibu-lero*, and of the *tol de-rol* kind generally, are quite intelligible and translateable. The former of these burdens, indeed, is stated to have been Irish-Gaelic.

that, so lately as 1547, the whole of the soldiery of the Scottish army at the Battle of Pinkie, were housed "in gypsy tents;"—at that time "the common building of the country,"—though now only used by the scattered Irreconcilables of the race. Is it a matter for surprise that the songs and legends of these yet un-tamed *Scots* are those which commemorate the deeds of those far-back days, when a large section of the people of Scotland were in customs, in blood, and in the fierceness of their disposition—" Gypsies " ?

From whatever side we regard them, we see that the so-called "gypsies" of Scotland are simply Scotchmen who have fallen behind in the march of progress. This is as evident in their old-fashioned customs, language, and ideas, as it is in the marked individuality of their physical natures,—the result of their aversion to mix their blood with that of other types. But as we see the remains of the ancestral stock in the *physique* of the general population of Scotland, so we find kindred evidence in the surnames common throughout the country. Of these, many have already been given—such as Black, Brown, Dunn, Grey, Duff, or Dow, Dougal, Glass, Douglas, and others,—all indicative of swarthy ancestors : while others show that at one time or another, nearer or more remote, the *bard* or *caird* of an obsolete polity has become the progenitor of modernized Bairds and Cairds.

But the general character of these Scottish "Gypsies" is what stamps them so clearly as archaic Scots. They are people who are still in the swaddling-clothes of civilization—who have never outgrown the ideas that were prevalent centuries ago, but are now as dead as the dodo. They still think that " a dexterous theft or robbery is one of the most meritorious actions they can perform," just as their savage ancestors thought—whether these were called Border moss-troopers or Highland banditti.* They have not yet realized that tribal life has been out of vogue for many generations, and that Scotland developed first a national existence, and then became

---

* Compare Simson's "History," pp. 96 and 164, or Dr. John Brown's story of Mary Yorston (quoted at second-hand in his review of " Biggar "), with Burt's Letter xxiii., or Scott's remarks upon the Borders, or with the statutes that were enacted from time to time against fire-raising, sorning, and plundering.

identified with a newer nation still, out of which has grown a great and world-wide empire. Those wretched "gypsies" still think that a Baillie is the born enemy of a "Faa;"— though the vast majority of their kindred recognized, ages ago, that a "Scotchman" had no rightful enemy north of the Borders,—later on, that a "Briton" (to use this makeshift of a word) had no legitimate foe but a Frenchman,—later still, that it was doubtful whether he ought to have any enemy at all.   And, while the general British population regards the whole world as the scene for its battles and aggrandisements, —if these must be,—these representatives of thirty generations back are incapable of looking further afield than their own parish or district ; or of imagining anything more heroic than the midnight plundering of farm-yards and stables, or the commission of some act of violence and murder.*

These characteristics—even more than the obvious links of custom (such as polygamy and painting, or tattooing) that join them to the past—distinctly mark them out as the little-altered descendants of the earlier Scottish races.   And, of them all, the practice of *sorning* is not the least emphatic. "The great distinguishing feature in the character of the gipsies (says Mr. Simson, at page 164,) is an incurable propensity for theft and robbery, and taking openly and forcibly (sorning) whatever answers their purpose.   A Gipsy of about twenty-one years of age, stated to me that his forefathers considered it quite lawful, among themselves, to take from others, not of their own fraternity, any article they stood in need of."   These are not the ways of a straggling and disunited caste of beggars, hypothetically assumed to have entered the country in comparatively recent times.   They are most visibly the evidences of bygone *power*, which did not require either to *beg* for lodging or gear ; but which followed out its own royal pleasure.   Not only does this custom of sorning show, by its inherent nature, that it is the right of a decayed aristocracy ; but we have seen that there is actual, historical proof that the men who first (so far as we can see) practised it, were

---

* Probably an acquaintanceship with modern "Scottish Gypsies" would convince one that these remarks do not apply to those of the present day.   They bear more exactly upon the period chiefly spoken of by the elder Simson—say, eighty years ago.

the nobles of the territory—Irish or Scotch—wherein it was law. And of this defunct sovereignty, one is forever feeling the touch, in whatever way one examines this " Gypsy " question.

Even quite lately, they were the actual rulers of the Debatable Land. Small though that territory was, it was under their sway. And men are yet living who can remember how this or that " moss," or moor-land was virtually possessed by the intractable "gypsies" that haunted it ;—unless, momentarily, if a military or constabulary force should happen to be present. Last century, we see them in several places, exacting tribute from all who would dwell peaceably within their territory ; much in the same way as (though certainly in a lesser degree than) the monarchs of this or that African district will protect European traders on somewhat similar terms.* And prior to last century—and farther and farther back—we see them as armed bands, desolating whole districts, over which —earlier still—they were the nominal as well as the virtual lords.

If we take individual cases, we see again this tendency. Much weight need not necessarily be attached to the fact that, instead of being mere vagrants, under the ban of the law, the " Gypsies" of Peeblesshire were, so lately as 1772, employed as " peace officers, constables, or country-keepers." And not only in Peeblesshire. " A gipsy chief, of the name of Pat Gillespie, was keeper for the county of Fife. He rode on horseback, armed with a sword and pistols, attended by four men on foot, carrying staves and batons. He appears to have been a sort of travelling justice of the peace. The practice seems to have been general. About the commencement of the late French war, a man of the name of Robert Scott (Rob the Laird,) was keeper for the counties of Peebles, Selkirk, and Roxburgh."† But, if not *very* significant, these

---

* Only in these African cases the representatives of modern civilization are numerically few ; whereas, at so recent a date as last century, the peaceably-disposed section of the community formed a distinct majority, and, had it been necessary, could have stamped out the " black-mail " banditti in a month. But partly from the disunited character of the general population, partly from sheer laziness, and partly for the sake of peace, the lairds, farmers, and others continued (as we have seen) to tacitly acknowledge—by the yearly payment of "black ' tribute—the right of "gypsy" chiefs to assert their sovereignty over various districts.

† Simson, pp. 218 and 343-4 ; also pp. 253-4.

statements are, at least, quite in accordance with the belief
that "gypsies," have not always been degraded outlaws. Nor
are they at variance, either, with other remarks of Mr. Simson's as to the social accomplishments formerly possessed by
" gypsies,"* who—in dress, in manners, and in education—
were distinctly entitled to be ranked as " gentlemen." Such
men, for example, as Alexander Brown, of the Lochgellie
band ; the Fifeshire gypsy, Charles Wilson ; and, pre-eminently, William Baillie,—of whom Mr. Simson's great-grandfather, " who knew him well, used to say that he was the
handsomest, the best dressed, the best looking, and the best
bred man he ever saw." This " Captain " Baillie appears to
have been quite an ideal " knight of the road : " " the stories
that are told of this splendid gypsy are numerous and interesting." Mr. Simson's conjectures as to his pedigree are very
conflicting. At one time, he tells us that he was " taken
notice of by the first in the land," *because* he gave himself
out to be a natural son of one of the Baillies of Lamington ;
at another, that he was " in all probability, a descendant of
Towla Bailyow," one of those who rebelled against John the
Pict, " Lord and Earl of Little Egypt," in the reign of James V.
of Scotland. If, therefore, his surname came to him from
his reputed father, this William Baillie, though a chief of the
very highest *gypsy* rank, was *not* " in all probability " a descendant of Towla Bailyow, or Baillie. But, as these Bailyows, or Baillies, as a clan, were once the most powerful of
their race, the likelihood is that this eighteenth-century
Baillie was the representative of this ancient stock. Had his
title to consideration been a bastard connection with a family
of merely local power, and of Modern, or Norman, or Feudal
descent (socially), he could not have been looked up to, on
that account, by the general population ;—and he certainly
could not have been, on that account, regarded—as he was—
by all the gypsies of Scotland as belonging to their very
highest caste.

These Baillies, or Bailyows, will be spoken of again. But
the point at present to be attended to is the former high
social position of Scottish " Gypsies." Although landless,
generally, it will be seen that, in many cases, they were dis-

* Simson, pp. 149-50, 157, 199, 202, 213-215.

tinguished by titles of respect. William Baillie was "Captain" and "Mr." Baillie: Robert Scott, the peace officer, was "Rob *the Laird ;*" while a third, Mr. Walker, of Thirkstane, Yetholm, was a veritable "laird." Earlier than these, "Johnny Faw," who ran away with the Countess of Cassilis, was, according to one account, "a gallant young knight, a Sir John Faa of Dunbar ;"* and that John Faw, or John the Pict, who is spoken of in an act of James V. as "Lord and Earl of Little Egypt," is also referred to in McLaurin's *Criminal Trials* as "this peer ;" and is stated to have been possessed of "divers sums of money, jewels, clothes and other goods, to the quantity of a great sum of money." Old William Faa, who died 1783-4, "persisted to the last that he himself was the male descendant, in a direct line, from the Earl of Little Egypt," and though he does not appear to have claimed that title, he was the acknowledged head of the Yetholm bands ; and, at his funeral, it is said that "his corpse was escorted betwixt Coldstream and Yetholm by above three hundred asses." Whether this "Little Egypt" was situated within the bounds of modern Scotland may be doubted—although there are two Egypts in that country at the present day. But, at any rate, this particular Faw—he of whom McLaurin speaks as "this peer"—was acknowledged in all seriousness as the bearer of that title, both by his suzerain, James V., King of Scots, and also, in 1553, in a writ of Mary, Queen of Scots :† having been quite plainly

* Anderson's "Scottish Nation," Vol. I. p. 606. The Earl of Cassilis is said to have overtaken his fugitive wife at "a ford over the Doon, still called ' the gypsies' steps,' a few miles from the Castle." (This name may be regarded as another form of "the Black Ford.") It is stated that the incident of her flight has been worked into a piece of tapestry, "which is said still to be preserved at Culzean Castle," in which she is represented "mounted behind her lover, gorgeously attired, on a superb white horse, and surrounded by a group of persons who bear no resemblance to a band of gipsies." The tapestry may or may not be a representation of this event ; but it would be curious to learn the ideas of the writer just quoted, regarding the outward appearance of the Scottish "gypsy" of two hundred and fifty years ago.

† The founder of this dynasty of Kings and Queens "of Scots" was himself a Norman, and it is likely that for several generations after the Norman Conquest of Britain the successful race still remained on the surface, little affected by the strata underneath (although by the time of Charles II., as we have noticed, they had reverted to a "gypsy" type, whether through his French mother, or by earlier alliances). But there is nothing inconsistent in a "King of Scots" regarding an

regarded as a man of rank by both these monarchs.
Another gypsy earldom, and a rather disagreeable one, is
that of " Earl of Hell."   It seems that it is quite " a favourite
title among the Tinklers,"—and that it is also to be met with
in modern Burmah.   This title is—or has lately been—borne
by a borderer of the name of Young ; and it was also
attached to a celebrated "gypsy," or "*dubh-glas*," of the
Lochmaben district, otherwise known as " Little Wull
Ruthven "—his tribe, the Ruthvens, being famous in "gypsy"
annals.   One of those " Earls of Hell " bore, according to
Mactaggart, the alternative title of " Laird o' Slagarie," and
his mansion was apparently at Auchenhoul, presumably in
Kirkcudbrightshire.   Although the Galloway writer states
that he was " one of the wildest wretches ever known in the
world," he does not call either him or his friends, *Black Jock*
and *Major Gaw*, by the title of "Gypsy" :* though it is
probable that all these would not have been mis-named, had
he done so.   Here again, we have, as in the case of Mr.
Walker of Thirkstane, a modern example of the " laird " who
is both "laird" and "gypsy,"—and it is likely that the
family-name of this proprietor of Slagarie and Auchenhoul
(for Mactaggart writes of these places as having an actual
geographical existence) is known to those acquainted with
the annals of Galloway.   Yet another " gypsy " who is
visibly a man of good birth—though of decayed fortune—
is the "caird" or tinker, described in Dr. John Brown's
sketch of a Jacobite Family.   Dr. Brown says of this man,
John Gunn, that he, " had come of gentle blood, the Gunns

"Egyptian" chief with a certain amount of favour ; for the Early Scots, it will
be remembered, were " Egyptians " in name, in colour, and in certain customs,
of which the use of hieroglyphics is one. We saw that, fully a century after
James V., a "Scot" was regarded (in Edinburgh) as synonymous with a
" mosser," or "thief," or "gypsy," and that (Simson, p. 113), in 1612, the
modernized and hybrid aristocracy of the clan Scott were obliged to " cut " that
section of their kindred that still adhered to the ancestral customs of thieving
and murdering, which customs had been voted vulgar by the ruling class of the
country.

* Probably for a reason indicated in the above note. " Gypsy " had long
been an opprobrious term, and the purest-blooded members of that race having
been long dispossessed of their lands, a " gypsy " was almost always a vagabond.
Therefore, the few that did retain something of their ancient power were not
likely to be identified with "gypsies."

of Ross-shire." He was Captain of a band of Cairds that "for years levied black mail over the county of Aberdeen;" and, although latterly he occupied the modest position of domestic servant in the " Jacobite family " written of, he continued to retain " his secret headship of the Cairds, ... using this often in Robin Hood fashion, generously, for his friends." Now, if " gentle " blood means—as it is conventionally held to mean—the blood of a ruling race, this John Gunn, being of the North-Scottish Gunns, had inherited " gentle " blood. For that tribe was at one time dominant in *Gallibh* (pronounced *Galliv*, a variety of *Galloway* and *Galway*); as Caithness used to be called, on account of its settlement by *Galls*, or foreigners. Those Gunns are believed by some to be descended from Olave the Black, who was the Prince, or Leod of Man and the South Hebrides in the thirteenth century, and who was evidently, by blood, a *dubh-gall.* The name of *Gunn*, or *Gun*, is said to be the same as the Welsh *Gwynn* and the Manx *Gawn.* If so, it is probably the same as the Scotch *Gawain* (pronounced *Gawn*), *Gavin*, *Gowan*, *Gove*, *Gow*, and, perhaps, *Cowan*—which names, Mr. Cosmo Innes has said, and with reason, are probably varieties of the Gaelic *Gobha*, or *Gobhainn*. If sprung from the black Leod of Man (who, by the way, would connect them with Hebridean Macleods and Welsh Lloyds) the Gunns of Gallibh might well have a descendant who was, by blood, well fitted to lead a band of eighteenth century "gypsies." And, that such was his ancestry, is very probable. For the racial characteristics are everywhere the same. Whether we look at John Gunn and his swarthy comrades levying blackmail throughout Aberdeenshire ; or at his savage ancestors exacting Dane-gelt, or " the tribute of the blacke armie," many centuries earlier ; we see the same fierce, piratical race. Or, if we examine the accounts regarding the *Gunn* sept of that race, during the intervening period, we learn that " the long, the many, the horrible encounters which happened between these two trybes,"—the Gunns and the *Sliochd-Iain-Abarach*, or the Seed of Abarach John,*—" with the blood-

---

* This *Abarach* John was the second son of Black Angus (*circa* 1400), chief of the race of Mackay, or Morgan. This tribe is assumed to have descended

shed and infinite spoils committed in every part of the diocy
of Catteynes by them and their associats, are of so disordered
and troublesome memorie," that the historian of the Earldom
of Sutherland waives the details of them.*   So that, in this
" inveterat deidlie feud " between those two savage races, we
have a northern counterpart of the immemorial warfare of the
more southern Baillies and Faas.   Thus John Gunn, in being
the Captain of an eighteenth-century league of "gypsies,"
proved himself to be a true representative of the Gunn
tribe,—just as the "gypsies" of the Debatable Land showed
themselves to be genuine Graemes,—or as the "Gypsies" of
Galloway are undoubtedly the purest *Douglases* of Galloway:
(though, in these, and in many other instances, such surnames
have come down to men who—as often as not—also inherit
the blood of the founder ; but whose ancestors have, in each
successive generation, laid themselves open to receive the culture of their time, and have not hesitated to ally themselves
with other races ;—by these means modifying and almost
wholly transforming the parent type.)   And, if John Gunn
as a typical *Gunn* was a typical *Gypsy*, he fully bore out—in
either aspect—the etymology of his name.   For, if the word
Gunn be really another spelling of Manx *Gawn*, and Scotch,
or English *Gawain*,—the meaning of which is found in
Gaelic dictionaries,—then "Gunn" is simply an equivalent of
"Caird."   Since *Gobhainn* (pronounced, variously, *Gawv'n*,

from the earlier races of Caithness, prior to the Black-Danish invasion, according
to one account : and the word *Morgan* is perhaps identical with *Moryan*, which
in sixteenth-century Britain signified a "Moor," and was applied to more than
one black-skinned Briton of that period.   Their name of *Siol Mhorgan*, or race of
Morgan seems also to point to a later Danish origin.   The Morgans of Wales (says
Mr. Wirt Sikes) believe their surname to be derived from a word signifying "the
sea," from which they themselves came.   This reminds one that all the words relating to the *Mauri, Moors, Morrows, Moravienses* or *Moray-men*, suggest the same
origin ; and that the words signifying *morass* or *marsh*, like the thing they denote,
seem to be the outcome of (Cornish and Armorican) *mor*, (Gaelic) *muir*, (Latin)
mare, the sea.   Which agrees with the fact that the early *Mauri* of Scotland were
Meatæ or marsh-dwellers.   Now, the radical meaning of *Abarach* is "marshy."
So that *Abarach* John is twice connected with the marsh-dwellers : both as
Abarach and as *Morgan*.   (It is immaterial whether his home was *Loch-abar* or
Strath-'n-abhair : either signifies a marshy situation.)   The Morgans of Wales and
of Caithness may, therefore, have sprung from any sea-faring or marsh-dwelling
people at or before the era of the Black Danes.

 * Anderson's "Scottish Nation," Vol. II. p. 385.

Govan, Gavin, and *Gawn)* and *Ceard* (pronounced *Caird*) are synonyms for " smith " or " tinker."*

Thus, these desultory glances at the pedigrees of individual " gypsies " disclose to us that the position of the Galloway chief, Billy Marshall, is in no way unique ; and they help to make us understand how—though stained with crimes that, if he had as many lives as a cat, would assuredly have hanged him at the present day—he was so respected for the vanished power of his race, that a nobleman strove for precedence at his grave, and the whole neighbourhood turned out to honour his memory. Whatever may have been the particular lineage of this Pictish chief, he was—as nearly as may be—an exact reproduction of those savage, swarthy, polygamous Picts of Galloway, whose existence as a national power may be said to have received its deathblow in the year 1455.

There is something so fascinating in the personality of this man—the latest visible specimen of the Galloway *Pict*—that one may be pardoned for reverting again to the consideration of his attributes ; and, indeed, it seems hardly excusable to content one's-self with a mere passing reference to what is probably the most detailed account of him, published in this century,—the article, namely, that was contributed to *Blackwood's Magazine* by one who was personally acquainted with

---

* Armstrong states that the Cornish *ceard* (sometimes spelled *keard*, though this does not alter the pronunciation) signifies "an artificer" generally. This accounts for the fact that a *tinker* is in Cornwall a *tinkeard*, "the original having been in all probability (says Mr. Robert Hunt) *staen* or *ystaen-cerdd*, a worker in tin." In Gaelic, *ceard* is so rarely used in the sense of "tradesman" or "artificer" generally, and so exclusively—almost—to denote an iron or tin worker ; that it is seldom found with a complementary word specifying the variety of *ceard*. But a Gaelic equivalent for the Cornish *staen-cerdd* does exist : in the shape of *ceard staoin*, a tinsmith. A Tinker proper, however, is a *Ceard* (pronounced *Caird*).

It is curious that the common Scotch equivalent for *Tinker*—namely, *Tinkler* —used as far back as the twelfth century, has apparently quite a different history from *Tinker*, though the two words approach each other so closely.

It may be noticed also that the name of the Scottish " Earl of Little Egypt," in whose favour James IV. of Scotland granted a letter of recommendation to the King of Denmark in the year 1506, was Anthony *Gavin* (referred to at pp. 99 and 100 of Mr. Simson's " History "). There really seems no good reason for believing that this " Little Egypt " was situated outside of North Britain. The surname of its lord, at any rate, is one of the oldest in these islands, and—as *Gawain*—is familiar to every reader of the Arthurian legends.

this " tory " king. The writer of that article was a mere youth when he made Marshall's acquaintance,—and the "gypsy" patriarch was then within a few years of his death. Therefore, the particulars he gives can only be regarded as *absolutely* trustworthy, in so far as they relate to the short interview which he describes : as far, also, as various statements which his position, as the descendant of a Galloway family of Marshall's acquaintance—entitled him to make. In his account, as in those previously quoted, there are certain discrepancies apparent : but it must be remembered that, if Marshall actually reached the great age with which he is credited (and on this point there is wonderfully little disagreement), the chief events of his life had taken place long before his oldest biographer was born. The following are some of the statements made in the *Blackwood* article ; contributed to the August number of the year 1817 :—

" . . . . . . I am one of an old family in the stewartry of Galloway, with whom Billy was intimate for nearly a whole century. He visited regularly, twice a year, my great-grandfather, grandfather, and father, and partook, I daresay, of their hospitality . . . . . . [The writer's great-grand-mother] died at the advanced age of one hundred and four ; her age was correctly known. She said that *Wull Marshal* was a man when she was a *bitt callant* (provincially, in Galloway, a very young girl). She had no doubt as to his being fifteen or sixteen years older than herself, and he survived her several years . . . . . . Billy Marshal's account of himself was this : he was born in or about the year 1666 ; but he might have been mistaken as to the exact year of his birth ;[*] however, the fact never was doubted, of his having been a private soldier in the army of King William, at the battle of the Boyne. It was also well known, that he was a private in some of the British regiments which served under the great Duke of Marlborough in Germany, about the year 1705. But at this period, Billy's military career in the service of his country ended : [and the story of his desertion from

---

[*] This version, it will be seen, places his birth five years earlier than the date usually given. But the above writer is probably not far wrong when he states that " his great age never was disputed to the extent of more than three or four years : the oldest people in the country allowed the account to be correct."

the army, in order to attend Keltonhill Fair, is given much
as Mactaggart gives it ;—with the addition that his commanding officer was one of the family of the McGuffogs of
Ruscoe] .... it was about this period, that, either elec-
tively, or by usurpation, he was placed at the head of that
*mighty** people in the south-west, whom he governed with
equal prudence and talent for the long space of eighty or
ninety years. Some of his admirers assert that he was of
royal ancestry, and that he succeeded by the laws of hereditary succession ; but no regular annals of *Billy's house* were
kept, and oral tradition and testimony weigh heavily against
this assertion. From any research I have been able to make,
I am strongly disposed to think that, in this crisis of his
life, Billy Marshal had been no better than Julius Cæsar,
Richard III., Oliver Cromwell, Hyder Ally, or Napoleon
Bonaparte : ...... it was shrewdly suspected that [he] ...
had stained his character and his hands with human blood.
His predecessor died very suddenly, it never was supposed
by his own hand, and he was buried as privately about
the foot of Cairnsmuir, Craig Nelder, or the Corse of
Slakes ......

"For a great period of his long life, he reigned with
sovereign sway over a numerous and powerful gang of gypsy
tinkers, who took their range over Carrick in Ayrshire, the
Carrick mountains, and over the stewartry and shire of Galloway ; and now and then ... they crossed at Donaghadee,
and visited the counties of Down and Derry. His long reign
was in the main fortunate for himself and his people. Only one
great calamity befel him and them, during that long space of
time in which he held the reins of government. It may
have been already suspected, that with Billy Marshal ambition was a ruling passion ; and this bane of human fortune
had stimulated in him a desire to extend his dominions, from
the Brigg end of Dumfries to the Newton of Ayr, at a time
when he well knew the Braes of Glen-Nap, and the Water
of Doon, to be his western precinct. He reached the Newton of Ayr, which I believe is in Kyle ; but there he was

---

* The underlinings in these extracts are repeated from the original. It is
necessary to do this in order to show that various words are used with mock
gravity, though, in several instances, the italics are rather superfluous.

opposed, and compelled to recross the river, by a powerful
body of tinkers from Argyle or Dumbarton. He said, in
his *bulletins*, that they were supported by strong bodies of
Irish sailors, and Kyle colliers. Billy had no artillery, but
his cavalry and infantry suffered very severely. He was
obliged to leave a great part of his baggage, provisions, and
camp equipage, behind him ; consisting of kettles, pots, pans,
blankets, crockery, horns, pigs, poultry, &c. A large proportion of shelties,* asses, and mules, were driven into the
water and drowned, which occasioned a heavy loss in creels,
panniers, hampers, tinkers' tools, and cooking utensils ; and
although he was as well appointed, as to a *medical staff*, as
such expeditions usually were, in addition to those who were
missing many died of their wounds. However, on reaching
Maybole with his broken and dispirited troops, he was joined
by a faithful ally from the county of Down ; who, unlike
other allies on such occasions, did not forsake him in his
adversity. This junction enabled our hero to rally, and pursue in his turn : a pitched battle was again fought, somewhere
about the Brigg of Doon or Alloway Kirk ; when both sides,
as is usual, claimed a victory ; but, however this may have
been, it is believed that this disaster, which happened
A.D. 1712, had slaked the thirst of Billy's ambition. He
was many years in recovering from the effects of this great
political error."

Before making a concluding extract from this account, it
may be well to notice another episode in Marshall's life ;
placed at about the year 1723. During the eighteenth century, the appropriation of common-lands by the adjacent
proprietors was going on all over Scotland. This—a fruitful
source of litigation between rival lairds—was a course of
action that was wholly unjustifiable: and, though now a
grievance of too old a date for fretting over, it was resented
very much at the time by those who assuredly possessed a
distinct right to the use of such "commonties," though not
themselves the owners, in fee, of any land whatever. We
have seen that the "tories" of the Debatable Land protested
most resolutely against the appropriation of their ancestral

---

* The small "Galloways" or "Irish hobbies" that gave to these moss-troopers
the designation of "hobbylers"—at a somewhat earlier period.

territory, supporting their protest by force of arms. A similar movement took place in Galloway, about the same period.
When the landed proprietors of South-Western Scotland—
seeing the manifest advantage (to themselves) of extending
their landmarks as widely as possible—began to build "march-
dykes," or boundary-walls, across stretches of land which did
not belong to them, the aggrieved parties (small farmers,
cottars, and "gypsies") combined to defeat the aggrandising
aims of their wealthier neighbours. Their plan of action
was first suggested at the annual Fair of Keltonhill, and the
prime mover in the proceedings was "the celebrated Gipsy-
chief, the redoubted William Marshall." The course which
he and his fellow "Levellers" followed, was simply to knock
down the offending "dykes"—thus earning their temporary
title of "Levellers." "Having divided themselves into companies of about fifty men, they appointed a person of suitable
age or influence to each, as commander, whom they styled
captain." (And, although this crowd was composed to a
large extent of peaceable agriculturists, this very title of
"captain," and the systematic way in which the thing was
gone about, indicates strongly the supervision of the "gypsy"
chief.) "The mode of their operations was this: they arranged themselves in companies along the ill-fated fence ;
and, their instruments of destruction* being applied to it, at
the word of command, it was overthrown with shouts of
exultation that might have been heard at the distance of
several miles." This kind of thing appears to have gone
on throughout various parts of Galloway, and so determined
was the attitude of the country people that it became necessary to despatch several troops of dragoons "from Dumfries,
Ayr, and even Edinburgh, to assist in terminating the disorder
and apprehending the delinquents." Without discussing
whether the term "delinquents" was not more applicable to
those who unwarrantably transformed communal land into
private freehold property,—it may be stated that after various
slight skirmishes, which would have ended most seriously had
it not been for the self-control and sagacity displayed by the

---

* "Each man was furnished with a strong *kent* (or piece of wood) from six to
eight feet in length, which he fixed into the dyke at the approved distance from
the foundation, and from his neighbour."

military, this movement was quelled ; and much trouble and bloodshed was saved—though undoubtedly at the expense of equity.

The book from which this information is obtained* gives some additional particulars regarding Marshall and his clan. "Two bands of gipsies (it is stated), at this time, and for some years afterwards, infested the district (of Galloway), and occasioned great loss to the inhabitants, by constantly committing all sortsof depredations. One of them, headed by Isaac Miller, acted as fortune-tellers, tinkers, and manufacturers of horn spoons ; but they lived chiefly by theft. The other, commanded by William Baillie,† represented themselves as horse dealers : but they were in reality horse stealers and robbers. William Marshall, commonly called Billy Marshall, belonged to the first-mentioned party ; but having killed his chief, at Maybole, who he considered was on terms of too much intimacy with his wife or mistress, Billy entered the army.‡ He afterwards returned, however, and followed his former calling." '

From the same source we learn that, in the year 1732, "Margaret and Isabell Marshall," with others of the same kind, were brought before the quarter sessions for the Stewartry of Kirkcudbright, "as being vagrant people of no certain residence, guilty of theft, pickery, and sorners and oppressors of the country, and so common nauseances, and therefore ought to be punished in terms of the acts of parliament made against sorners, vagrants, Egyptians, &c." The two male prisoners (one of whom was John Johnstone, the Annandale chief, who was afterwards hanged at Dumfries ; as Mr. Simson incidentally mentions), " acknowledge that they kept two durks or hangers that they had for defending of their

* Mackenzie's " History of Galloway," in which, at pages 401-3, 433-4, and ₄493 (note) of Vol. II., there are various statements made regarding Marshall or his kindred.

† As Mr. Simson states that the Baillies were the chiefs-paramount of all the Scottish " gypsies," this William Baillie could only have been present in Marshall's territory as a *sovereign*, not as a rival *chieftain*.

‡ The *Blackwood* writer places the murder of his predecessor *after* his desertion from the army. And this version is more likely to be correct than the one just quoted above, since the place of chief was rendered vacant by the deed. Apparently, then, this Isaac Miller was " King of the Galloway gypsies " in the beginning of the eighteenth century.

persons." All these prisoners were sentenced "to be burnt
on the cheeks severally, by the hand of the common hangman,
and thereafter to be severally whipped on their naked shoulders, from one end of the Bridge-end of Dumfries to the
other by the hangman," and after this punishment to be banished out of the Stewartry of Kirkcudbright "for ever."
That these Marshalls were related to the chief of their clan is
quite likely. There is no doubt, whatever, regarding Anne
Gibson, "daughter of William Marshall, the gipsy and robber
who had long harassed Galloway,"—who was transported to
"his Majesty's plantations," in the year 1750. Nor is there
doubt, either, as to the ancestry of "'Black Matthew Marshall,' grandson of the said chieftain," who is referred to in
Blackwood (Sept. 1817). But the "prodigiously numerous"
descendants of this celebrated "Galloway" scarcely merit
attention.

The first—and only—occasion on which the *Blackwood*
contributor saw his redoubtable fellow-countryman, is described in these words :—

"The writer of this, in the month of May, 1789, had
returned to Galloway after a long absence : he soon learned
that Billy Marshal, of whom he had heard so many tales in
his childhood, was still in existence. Upon one occasion he
went to Newton-Stewart, with the late Mr. McCulloch of
Barholm, and the late Mr. Hannay of Bargaly, to dine with
Mr. Samuel McCaul. Billy Marshal then lived at the hamlet
or clachan of Polnure, a spot beautifully situated on the burn
or stream of that name ; we called on our old hero, he was
at home, he never *denied* himself, and soon appeared ; he
walked slowly, but firmly towards the carriage, and asked
Mr. Hannay, who was a warm friend of his,* how he was ?
Mr. Hannay asked if he knew who was in the carriage ? He
answered, that his eyes 'had failed him a *gude dale ;*' but
added, that he saw his friend Barholm, and that he could see
a youth sitting betwixt them, whom he did not know. I was
introduced and had a gracious shake of his hand. He told

---

* This friendship had an odd beginning ; for one of the stories told (by Sir
Walter Scott) of Billy Marshall relates to a highway robbery committed by him
on "the Laird of Bargally," who, no doubt, was either this Mr. Hannay or his
predecessor.

me I was setting out in life, and admonished me to '*tak care o' my han', and do naething to dishonor the gude stock o' folk that I was come o'* ; he added, that I was the fourth generation of us he had been ' acquaint wi'.' Each of us paid a small pecuniary tribute of respect,—I attempted to add to mine, but Barholm told me he had fully as much as would be put to a good use. We were returning the same way, betwixt ten and eleven at night, ... the moon shone clear, and all nature was quiet, excepting Polnure burn, and the dwelling of Billy Marshall,—the postillion stopt . . . . and turning round with a voice which indicated terror, he said, ' Gude guide us, *there's folk singing psalms in the wud !* ' My companions awoke and listened,—Barholm said, ' psalms, sure enough ; ' but Bargaly said ' the deil a bit o' them are psalms.' We went on, and stopt again at the door of the old king : we then heard Billy go through a great many stanzas of a song, in such a way that convinced us that his memory and voice had, at any rate, not failed him ; he was joined by a numerous and powerful chorus. It is quite needless to be so minute as to give any account of the song which Billy sung ; it will be enough to say, that my friend Barholm was completely wrong, in supposing it to be a psalm ; it resembled in no particular, psalm, paraphrase, or hymn. We called him out again,—he appeared much brisker than he was in the morning : we advised him to go to bed ; but he replied, that ' he *didna think* he wad *be muckle in his bed that night*, they had *to tak the* country in the morning ' (meaning, that they were to begin a ramble over the country), and that they ' were just *takin a wee drap drink* to the health of our honours, wi' the lock siller we had gi'en them.' I shook hands with him for the last time,—he then called himself above one hundred and twenty years of age ! "

How long he continued to live in this retreat does not appear, but he is said to have died in the town of Kirkcudbright (which lies about twenty miles to the south-east of Polnure), three years and a half after the meeting recorded above, on the 28th of November, 1792. The circumstances of his burial have already been related ; but a slightly different version must be referred to here. This version not only states that " he subsisted in his extreme old age by a

pension from Dunbar, Earl of Selkirk," but it adds that
"Lord Daer attended his funeral as chief mourner, to the
churchyard of Kirkcudbright, and laid his head in the
grave."* Instead of the Earl of Selkirk himself, we have
here his second son, the "noble youthful Daer" who entertained Burns. And this statement is a flat contradiction of
Mactaggart's account; whether we take Lord Daer or his
father as having been "chief mourner." Mactaggart, it will
be remembered, affirms that the gypsy king "was buried in
state by the Hammer-men, *which boay would not permit the
Earl of Selkirk to lay his head in the grave*, merely because
his Lordship was not one of their incorporated tribe." One
would think that, even at this date, it would be no very difficult matter to ascertain which is the correct version.

Scott states that the grave of this savage chief was within
the *church* of Kirkcudbright: others say, the church-*yard*.
As the present building is of modern date, and built on a
new site, it is possible that Marshall's grave was situated
within the precincts of the old church. But if the "armorial
bearings" upon his tombstone were sculptured shortly after
his burial, it seems plain that that stone did not form a
portion of the flagged pavement of the church. For these
emblems are cut upon the reverse side of the stone, which is
now standing erect. This is only worth referring to for the
reason that to be buried *within* the walls of a church was
apparently a special honour paid only to the memory of men
of consideration, in former times; the rank and file being
relegated to the churchyard itself. Be this as it may, the
tombstone of this "Tinkler" chief is still to be seen in the
churchyard of Kirkcudbright, remounted on a modern base
(evidently by the hands of those of his kindred, whose
remains, after lives of less famous but of more honourable

---

* Mackenzie's "History of Galloway," Vol. II. p. 403 (note). One of the
facts given in this book—namely, that Marshall killed his chief at Maybole in
Ayrshire—is taken from the "Life of James Allan." Another reference to
Marshall, in this "History of Galloway," is the following extract from Chalmers's
"Caledonia":—"William Marshall, a tinker, died in Kirkcudbright on the
28th of November, 1792, in the 120th year of his age." And the only additional
reference I have encountered is the announcement of his death in the *Scots
Magazine* of December, 1792—"[Nov.] 28, at Kirkcudbright, aged 120, William
Marshall, tinker. He was a native of the parish of Kirkmichael, Ayrshire."

description, are lying beside his). The inscription on his gravestone is simply this :

THE REMAINS OF
WILLIAM MARSHALL,
TINKER, WHO DIED
28th Nov! 1792,
At the advanced age of
120 YEARS.

And on the back, rudely carved, are the two ram's-horns and " cutty-spoons " crossed, of which Scott and others speak.

The *Blackwood* writer sums up the character of his hero in words that echo the sentiments expressed by Mactaggart and by Scott:—"It is usual for writers to give the character along with the death of their prince or hero : I would like to be excused from the performance of any such task as drawing the character of Billy Marshal ; but it may be done in a few words, by saying that he had from nature a strong mind, with a vigorous and active person ; and that, either naturally or by acquirement, he possessed every *mental* and *personal* quality which was requisite for one who was placed in his *high station*, and who held sovereign power over his *fellow creatures* for so great a length of time: I would be glad if I could, with impartiality, close my account here ; but it becomes my duty to add, that (from expediency, it is believed, not from choice,) with the exception of intemperate drinking, treachery, and ingratitude, he practised every crime which is incident to human nature, those of the deepest dye, I am afraid, cannot with truth be included in the exception ; in short, his people met with an irreparable loss in the death of their king and leader ; but it never was alleged, that the moral world sustained any loss by the death of the man."

The poetical effusions with which Mactaggart concludes his references to the gypsy king do not throw much additional light upon the subject.   In these, various allusions are made to certain of Marshall's most notable points—those, at least, which latterly distinguished him and his kind from their more " respectable " neighbours ; to his many drinking-bouts, to his cudgel-fights, to his amorous nature, and to the annual gathering of all the Galloway gypsies, with their " wallets and cuddies" [asses], at the great fair of Keltonhill, beside the old town of Carlingwark, now known under its modern name of Castle-Douglas. And, like the writer quoted above, Mactaggart recognizes in Marshall the last real leader of the gypsies of Galloway :—

> "The duddy deils, in mountain glen,
> Lamenteth ane and a' man ;
> For sic a king they'll never ken,
> In bonny Gallowa man."

The author of the *Gallovidian Encyclopedia* is the only one who tells us that Marshall was of an old Galloway stock, for the *Blackwood* contributor throws doubt upon his claims to an ancestral right to the chiefship ; although it may be noted that he proves " Wull Marshall" to have been a *somebody* during his earliest manhood. This *Blackwood* writer —himself, presumably, of good descent—states that this distinguished gypsy "visited regularly, twice a year" his own ancestors as far back as the time of his great-grandfather, at which date Marshall cannot have been older than thirty or thereabouts ; and the same writer mentions that his great-grandmother knew him when she was "a very young girl," Marshall being her senior by fifteen or sixteen years ;—that is to say, he was a well-known personage at that period. The fact that he was in a position to *sorn* upon a country gentleman twice a year, "partaking of his hospitality," (and in return respecting the belongings of his host) speaks for itself. But the other statements of this writer are sufficient to prove his early celebrity. Since they place the date of his "accession" at the very beginning of the eighteenth century, and record his famous battle near the Water of Doon as having taken place in the year 1712. These facts, however, do no more than show that he reached his height at an early date. Mactaggart speaks much more distinctly as to his antecedents. He tells us that "he was of the family of the Marshalls, *who have been tinklers in the south of Scotland time out of mind.*" This, a local tradition, given to us by a local man,—is worthy of some consideration. If it be true that his people were known by the name of Marshall for

very many generations (and this is pretty clearly what Mactaggart means to convey), then any one attempting to trace
his pedigree would not require to regard him as the descendant of men bearing such surnames as Heron or Douglas,
along with the *office* of Marshall, as was suggested. His
own surname is enough of itself.

There were really Marshalls in Galloway at an early date :
one finds them on the surface. Among those Scotchmen
who swore fealty to Edward I. in the year 1296, there was
a certain lord of Toskerton, in Galloway, *dictus marescallus,
miles,* "at other times called John le Mareschal de Toskerton,
who held the land of Toskerton, in that shire . . . and who
was forfeited by Robert I." ("Bruce"). This was most likely
the "John Mareschal" and "John le Mareschal, knight,"
who appears as the recipient of wages due to him by
Edward III. of England, for services rendered to that
monarch, during the first half of the fourteenth century.*
From which it becomes probable that this John Marshall
was one of those very "Galloways" who sought to check
the career of Bruce, during his struggle for the monarchy.
The forfeiture of his lands by Bruce, and the fact that he
(for we may reasonably assume that it was he) was in the
pay of the English king afterwards ; this English king being
the sworn foe of the Brucean dynasty—argues strongly in
support of this belief. If he was himself a "Galloway" by
blood, he was then a *Pict,* or *dubhglass,* or *Moor,* or *gypsy.* The
languages used in designating him give no clue whatever to
his race. But when we hear it said that the Marshalls of
Galloway, represented last century by the "little dark-grey
man," of whom we have been speaking, had been "Tinklers"
in that neighbourhood "time out of mind," and when we
remember that the "Tinklers of Galloway" (to use the commonest Scotch equivalent of "gypsy," or "Moor," or "Pict,")
were the relentless foes of Bruce ; and that this fourteenth-
century Galwegian leader, John Marshall, was throughout,
one of Bruce's most consistent enemies—aiding the English
king after his own lands had been forfeited as the penalty of
his opposition ; then the probability that the Marshall of

* Mackenzie's "History of Galloway," Vol. I. pp. 198 and 294. At either
page the facts are taken from Chalmers's "Caledonia."

the fourteenth century, like him of the eighteenth, was a
Pict, Moor, or *Gypsy* of Galloway, becomes very great.   And
it is quite likely that William Marshall, born 1671, was a
lineal descendant of this John Marshall, born in the thirteenth
century.   There would be less reason for believing this if it
were not for the fact that, although used to denote an *office,*
then and subsequently—the word "Marshall" appears to
have adhered *as a surname* to this particular lord of Toskerton.   Although previously styled "John *le* Mareschal," on
more than one occasion, the last reference made to him
(1346–7) speaks of "John Mareschal;" not "John *the* Marshall" nor "John of Toskerton," but simply "John Marshall."
Wherefore, one may fairly assume that his male descendants
continued to bear that designation, as a surname.

It is curious to reflect upon the fact, already noticed, that
the word "marshall," is etymologically considered, almost a
synonym for "gypsy."   We have seen that "gypsies" are
or were most notable horse-dealers and farriers: and that
a "marshall" has been a "farrier," in France and Britain.
Sometimes the word was amplified into "horse-marshall."
The exact meaning must have been unknown to those who
used this expression: since a "marshall" was a *marah-chal,*
or "horse-fellow."*   (Of which compound word, the first
portion survives in our English *mare,* and the word *chal* is
still used to denote "a man," among our "tory" classes.)
This word "marshall," in more than one of its meanings,
would thus be a very appropriate designation of those
"travelling justices of the peace," referred to by Mr. Simson,
who supervised certain districts of Scotland, so recently as
last century, who were mounted men, and "gypsies."   A
specimen of these was seen in the Fifeshire "gypsy" chief,
Gillespie, who "rode on horseback, armed with a sword and
pistols attended by four men on foot, carrying staves and
batons."   Such men were styled "peace-officers," "constables," and "country-keepers."   One of these names,

---

* "The 'Ingliss hors Marschael' often occurs in the [Scottish] Treasurer's
Accounts: 1498, April 22, 'Item, giffin be the Kingis command to the Ingliss
hors Merchael, to hele the broun geldin, 18s.'" (Note to Kennedy's "Flyting";
Patterson's edition of Dunbar's poems.)   See also Skeat's "Etymological
Dictionary."

" constable," is compared by Mr. Skeat to " marshal," in the fluctuations it has experienced. Both have been used to denote men of the highest rank : both are now used (in America and in the British Islands) to denote the less exalted office of "policeman," though in France "marshal" is still held in great esteem. In the Scotland of last century, such a "constable" as this Fifeshire chief assuredly held a position much above that of a "constable" of to-day. There is, in fact, no modern British official who can be regarded as his equivalent. And it may be that the "gypsy" Gillespie represents a still higher function, in remoter times. If such hypothetical officials were those known to history as the "marshals" of this or that district, and if they were of the same race as those eighteenth-century "travelling justices of the peace," then such officials, *marshals* and *constables*, were selected from the "gypsy" races. If the central government of Scotland desired to keep the mosstrooping gypsies in check, it is certain that no better peace-officers could be found than those mosstroopers who were loyal to the crown.

There is less of speculation in the consideration of the word "Tinkler." For we know that the twelfth-century "Tinklers" were recognized by William the Lion as forming a distinct portion of the population of North Britain. Like *marshal* and *constable*, *tinkler* has deteriorated during the lapse of time. Whether it is still the common Scotch term for a "gypsy," or whether that word, and "tinker," are now more generally used ; it is pretty evident that no one wishing to do honour to the memory of a famous leader would put "Tinker" on his tombstone,—as was done at Kirkcudbright in 1792. It is a difficult thing for men of this generation to realise that Scotch "tinkers" were feared by the farming and labouring classes, and entertained by landed gentry of the highest rank (sometimes unwillingly), only a hundred and fifty years ago. And that these "nobles and gentlemen" paid a yearly tribute to such people ; either in the form of money, or by giving them and their followers house-room and food whenever they chose to demand it.

The real explanation can be nothing but this. That these nomadic *sorners* were decayed *Sorohen*, or nobles ; that they represented a system that ante-dated the polity under which these modern squires and nobles had gradually grown into power: that that ancient system—founded upon force—had not yet, a hundred and fifty years ago, subsided into what we should now call its proper level: and that the newer system, "the reign of law," was not yet powerful enough to assert itself completely, in the face of force. That is what "black mail" signified: that must be the true position of those to whom that tribute was paid.

Even in William Marshall's brief existence (for the longest life seems short when one tries to measure the life of societies), we can see the indications of this tendency—the setting of the one star and the growing splendour of the other. When he was living in his little cottage at Polnure, content to accept as a favour the gifts that he would once have forcibly taken as a right, addressing as "your honour" men of a class which he once counted beneath his own, all his following compressible into the narrow limits of his cottage-walls, his greatest exploit the robbery of a farm-yard or a hen-roost, Billy Marshall was hardly one remove above the common "blackguard" of to-day. But eighty years earlier? When he was at the head of a powerful confederacy that terrorized all the peaceable agriculturists and townsfolk of Galloway; when he exercised an absolute sway over such outlaws "from the Briggend of Dumfries to the Braes of Glen-Nap and the Water of Doon;" when he could quarter himself and his own immediate followers, wives, mistresses, and kinsmen, upon any of the "nobility and gentry" of that territory, without fear of opposition; when, although known to be guilty of innumerable robberies and murders, no man presumed to have him brought to justice; when, backed by a powerful force of painted savages, mounted, armed, and equipped as completely as any Tartar tribe on the war-path, he encountered an opposing force on the banks of the Doon, and fought a battle as important (if we count by bloodshed) as many that we now think worth chronicling in our newspapers—what was this "Tinker Chief" then? He was something—or, at least, he *represented* something—that was vastly greater than the largest lordship in Galloway. He was either landless, or he was the greatest land-lord in that

territory. If his own forefathers had ever possessed a parch-
ment-right to any estate there, that estate had passed away
from them in the days of Bruce. The Marshall-Picts had
become "gypsies" a century and a half before the Douglas-
Picts. What his position *by descent* was, is uncertain : but
there is no doubt as to what it was in effect. If you look at
a map of Scotland, you will see what the boundaries, beyond
which, "he well knew," he ought not to pass, really signifies.
"From the Briggend of Dumfries" means from the present
town of Maxwellton, the western bank of the river Nith.
"To the Braes of Glen-Nap and the Water of Doon" defines
his limits on the West—the ocean, and on the North-west
the northern extremity of the district of Carrick. And the
country so bounded is the province of *Galloway*, as it existed
after the twelfth century*—say, after the Norman conquest
of Scotland. Outside of this province, the Picts of Galloway
knew they had no right to go : that, if they tried to enlarge
their boundaries, they were invading a foreign country and
must fight their way. That they did try to do this, under
Marshall's leadership, we have seen, and with what result.

If "Billy Marshall," when he came of age, in the year 1692,
had taken to civilized courses, and had become "a respectable member of society," it is probable that his descendants
would now occupy a position of eminence, with all their
alliances duly entered in the stud-books, and the family-
pedigree so clearly printed that no one could question its
authenticity. But he did not do so. He preferred to live
the wild marauding life of his forefathers, at that time still
followed by many thousand British people. Instead of going
with the tide, as he ought to have done, he stood still. He
was a *tory*, as that word was then understood. And, as his
natural powers were almost incredibly strong, he lived through
a period of changes that affected him and his kind to a
tremendous extent. He lived to see the practices that, in

* Galloway-after-the-twelfth-century is commonly defined as consisting of the
modern counties of Kirkcudbright and Wigtown. But Marshall's province takes
in also the district of Carrick—the southern portion of Ayrshire. And, on the
strength of this fact, though it savours of "begging the question," I am inclined
to think that Carrick ought to be counted a part of Modern Galloway, and that
it has only been omitted through a loose fashion of expressing Galloway by
modern *counties*.

his boyhood, had been condoned and even practised by men of rank, placed in the catalogue of *crimes.* To kill a man, or to steal a horse, was a small matter in seventeenth-century Galloway; at the close of the eighteenth century the man who did either of these things was a *criminal.* When *young* Marshall "took the country" at the head of a powerful body of mosstroopers, he was simply a Border Chief of a type that was then becoming old-fashioned; when Marshall the patri-arch—never altering, to the very end of his life—started off with his meagre band on such an expedition, after a night of drinking and unholy songs, he and his comrades were nothing better than a gang of outcasts and thieves. And it is because his biographers have persisted in regarding him in the light of modern times, never thinking how Marshall would have fitted into the social life of 1692, that these writers—and others like them—have seen nothing but what was ludicrous in the "gypsy's" claims to rank, and that of the highest kind. Such men—no doubt without intending it—take up precisely the position of the British snob who regards all the natives of India as so many "damned niggers;" although it was only by dint of being very polite to such "niggers" that we gained a footing in Hindostan. Because the Red Indian of America is merely a "gypsy" in certain States of the Union, is one to deny the historical fact that a century ago he was the ruler of these districts, in whose eyes the wander-ing white trader was the "gypsy"? Philip, the Pokanoket chief—to take an example more near the time we are speak-ing of—was a real power in the New England of 1676, and a terror to half the colony; but if he had lived, on the scene of his old exploits, to witness the Declaration of Independ-ence, what "power" would there have been remaining to him? If he had *then* been rash enough to take the life of a colonist, he would simply have been treated as a male-factor. In his day-to-day existence, he would have found it necessary to work, or steal, or beg; and any assertion on his part of vanished greatness would have been received with an incredulous smile by men of newer growth and unacquainted with the history of him and his tribe. To judge Marshall by what he was in 1792, is to form a very imperfect idea of what he must have been a century earlier.

Setting aside his claims to high descent—which seem to have been disputed—it is enough to gauge Will Marshall by the rank he actually held for eighty or ninety years, by whatever token his right to that position had been admitted by his fellow-countrymen. And his position, as understood by himself and his followers, was this: he had no equal in the whole of Galloway. Farmers and farm-labourers and shop-keepers were nobodies in the estimation of the Galloway "gypsies;" and the "landed gentry" were so many vassals whose duty it was to furnish them with food and lodging when required, on peril of incessant trouble by robbery and murder. To men who lived after the old fashion, these "aristocrats," though no doubt of their own stock (in many cases) were only half-gentlemen. The Border "gypsy" regarded farmers with unbounded contempt; and farmer-lords were only a degree higher. All these people—sedentary people, *civilized* people as we now recognize them—were only there to be plundered and "sorned" upon. The deeds by which these landowners held their estates were worthless in the eyes of the Galloway Pict, whose only title was the strong arm. Until they began to encroach too much upon the uncultivated country, and to build walls across common-lands, these peaceable agriculturists and traders might live according to their own fashion, and transfer, or *pretend* to transfer, the land from one to another. But let no one attempt to enter Galloway by force! Parchments and other legal procedures were harmless enough; but forcible invasion of their territory by outside "gypsies" was an affair of another order. That large communities of men could continue to live an archaic life, quite blind to the march of progress as seen in other communities within the same territory, seems wonderful nowadays. But "gypsydom" can never be rightly understood until this possibility is admitted as an actual fact.

So that "Billy Marshall"—a landless vagabond, according to modern ideas—was really the greatest landowner in Galloway—in his own estimation and in that of his followers. While this or that nobleman possessed an estate of such and such an extent, the Gypsy Chief reigned over a territory whose limits were the limits of *Galloway.* And, however much he and his like had suffered by the spread of modern civilization ; and although the terms of "gypsy" and "tinker" have now become expressive of the lowest classes in our social scale ; yet these Galloway marauders of last century represent the latest phase of a very ancient and powerful system.   The plain little tombstone, with its simple inscription and grotesque emblems, that has been raised over the remains of "William Marshall, Tinker," in the old churchyard overlooking Kirkcudbright town, records the existence of an incorrigible old heathen, possessed, up to the last, of all the faults and all the virtues of the savage chief.   Such people as he have quite fallen into disrepute throughout the British Islands.   And yet no one of his contemporaries filled a position that was more intensely interesting.   For this man was really nothing less than the latest representative of the Pictish lords of Galloway.

CHAPTER II.

GENERALLY, this remembrance of ancient rank forms one of
the most striking features of "gypsydom." "With British
gipsies (says the writer in the "Encyclopædia Britannica,")
one is bewildered by the host of *soi-disant* kings and queens,
from King John Buelle, laid side by side with Athelstan in
Malmesbury Abbey in 1657, down to the gipsy queen of the
United States, Matilda Stanley, royally buried at Dayton,
Ohio, in 1878." The two cases cited are not the most appropriate in a consideration of the Scottish divisions of the
race, but the remark itself applies with equal force to Scotland. Mr. Simson refers again and again to the high "pretensions" of certain castes of North British gypsies.

That so many families claiming royal lineage should be
found among our lowest classes is not astonishing. History
tells us of change after change in the ruling dynasties of
these islands, and of the advent of races the most varied in
time and origin. During the last two thousand years enough
kings and nobles have sunk from power to furnish a royal
pedigree to half the population of the country. It is true
that the present Royal Family, and the present aristocracy,
inherit, to some extent, the blood of extinct dynasties. But
only to some extent. The Prince of Wales has lawfully
succeeded to various dignities ; but these are of such opposite
origin that they cannot possibly be typified in the person of
one man. He cannot be, at the same time, a typical Prince
of Wales and a typical Prince of Scotland ; a genuine Duke
of Cornwall and as genuine a Duke of Rothesay ; a perfect
specimen of the Lords of the Isles and an equally perfect
Earl of Chester ; he cannot be a thoroughbred Plantagenet,
Stewart, Tudor, and Guelph—though a certain proportion of
the blood of each may run in his veins. The circumstances
that developed such titles have been matters of history for

many generations; the titles themselves are now merely so many graceful honours, attaching by right of birth to the Heir Apparent.

When, in a struggle between two factions, the one went under, the chiefs of that faction were the very last that were likely to appear in the ranks of the new aristocracy. They were either killed or outlawed. The Douglases that obtained lands and power in the latter part of the fifteenth century were not the *chiefs* of their race. These were hunted down and killed ; or, when they managed to survive, it was only as marauding banditti, or "gypsies." So, during the civil wars that divided England at the same period, we are told that "eighty princes of the blood, and the larger proportion of the ancient nobility of the country" were slain ; and that " many noble families were either extirpated on the field and the scaffold, or completely ruined." But when a family is " completely ruined," it does not cease to exist. Being landless and penniless it disappears from the sight of all " respectable" people, and the heralds very soon omit to chronicle the births and alliances of its members. But they do get born and married, nevertheless. And at what point does such a family cease to forget its ancestry ? Do the "banished Duke" and his courtiers think themselves churls because their places have been usurped ; or do they cease to address each other by their titles because they have to camp like gypsies in leafy Arden ? And if their lost power is never regained, do they not still continue to be kings and nobles, in their own eyes ? Was the posterity of the Douglas leaders likely to forget its headship of the Picts of Galloway, although the Douglas lands and honours had been given to a younger and half-breed branch, and to strangers ? Were they not still, by virtue of their blood, Kings of the Faws, or *dubh-glasses*, of the South-West of Scotland ?

It has just been said that such " banished Dukes " camped *like* gypsies among the woods and fastnesses. But there was more than *likeness ;* there was *identity*. When such dispossessed nobles had to live from day to day, without either revenue or beeves of their own, after what fashion did they live ? Fate had decreed that the deer in the forest, and the cattle in the fields were no longer theirs, *legally ;* but it is

not to be supposed that, therefore, they starved. The idyllic
life of Shakespeare's courtly outlaws may have been theirs
occasionally, but they did not live from year's end to year's
end singing catches "under the greenwood tree." If they
were dispossessed Scottish nobles of the fifteenth century
(as the black Douglases were), they would shelter themselves
from the rain and snow under the covering of the turf-built,
conical wigwams, or the low, half-open tents of skin, or of
canvas, which were then "the common building of their
country," though we now call them the habitations of
"gypsies." And if these outlawed nobles were the descendants of any of the earlier *Mauri*, or "blackamoors" of
Scotland, or of the later "black foreigners," as were the
Galloway earls just referred to, and as were innumerable
other clans of the race of "Dubh of the three black divisions," then these coteries of marauding "kings" and
"dukes" were, *in every detail*, the people whom writers generally speak of as "gypsies." And, however ridiculous seemed
their high-sounding titles to people who were ignorant of
their history, these landless lords had once a legal right to
the titles they so uselessly clung to in their degradation.
The "gypsy" *rya* had been once the *ri* of Scottish history.*

The "king" of early British history, in general, was much
more *regulus* than *rex ;* more *riah* than *king*. With regard to
North Britain more particularly, this is pointed out by Mr.
Skene in various places (*e.g.,* "Celtic Scotland," Vol. I.
p. 343). And Northumbria, during the ninth century, was
partitioned into various districts, whose rulers were certainly
nothing more than *reguli.* "There is no doubt that not long
before the accession of Kenneth Mac Alpin to the Pictish
throne the kingdom of Northumbria seems to have fallen into
a state of complete disintegration, and we find a number of

---

* This word *rya* is usually placed side by side with the Hindu *rawah*, with
which it is almost identical. But it is almost, or altogether, the same (also) as
the *ri* or *righ* of Gaelic. (The shorter spelling appears to be the earlier.) No
doubt the pronunciation of this word, in Gaelic, is usually *ree*, but it is also *ry ;*
as in Dal-*ry* (the king's dale), of which one spelling- -*Dal-a-raidhe* (Dalriada)—
gives, according to Gaelic pronunciation, exactly the sound of Dal-a-*rayah*. In
Gaelic also, as in "gypsy," *ri* or *rya* is rather "a kinglet," "a chief," " a
gentleman," than a modern king. The many "kings" of Mr. Campbell's
"West Highland Tales" could not, it is clear, have been what we understand by
"king." But they were exactly like the *rya*, or chief of the "gypsies."

independent chiefs. or 'duces' as they are termed, appearing
in different parts of the country and engaging in conflict with
the kings and with each other, slaying and being slain, conspiring against the king and being conspired against in their
turn, expelling him and each other, and being expelled. Out
of this confusion, however, one family emerges who appear
as lords of Bamborough and for a time govern Bernicia."
("Celtic Scotland," Vol. I. p. 373.) And we are told that
"these dukes, or lords of Bamborough, seem to have had
some connection with Galloway." Northumbria—a country
vastly greater than modern *Northumberland*, since it took in
South-Eastern Scotland up to the Forth—was thus, a thousand years ago, altogether given over to marauding "kings"
and "dukes," who—according to Mr. Skene—were, in a great
measure, *Picts*, that is, *Faws*. Therefore, the chief difference
(and it is a vital one) between the Northumbria of the ninth
century, as pictured by a historian of unsurpassed ability,
and the Northumbria of the eighteenth century, as described
by the chief historian of the Scottish gypsies, is this—that, in
the ninth century, these painted tribes constituted the ruling,
if not the only power within that territory, whereas in the
eighteenth century the system that we call civilization had
almost wholly asserted its supremacy over barbarism. It
matters little, at the present moment, whether that civilization was matured by a gradually-refining aristocracy of bar-
barians, or by the influx of people of a newer and higher
race, or by a combination of two such elements. It is
enough that it was so. It is quite clear that Mr. Simson's
Northumbrian "gypsydom" was virtually the wreck of Mr.
Skene's Northumbrian Picticism. Or, if this is not quite
clear at this juncture, it is more likely to become so as the
question is more closely examined. Thus the whole of the
South of Scotland (for Skene's Galloway of the ninth century is not very different from his Northumbria of the same
period) was, a thousand years ago, the scene of many
rival conflicts between warring tribes of Picts, or Faws. And
this includes the North of England also, since Northumbria
included, at least, the modern county of Northumberland, as
well as a large division of Southern Scotland.

These Northumbrian chieftains were called "dukes" by

the monkish chroniclers who wrote about them.   It is as well
to speak of them as "dukes."   We call them *duces* (in the
singular, *dux*), but no one can say that they were not spoken of
as *dukes*. If there is one thing more uncertain than another, in
questions of an archæological nature, it is this question of
accent.   No one can say how the word *duces* was enunciated
in the ninth century.   It is not unlikely (since we are told
that *veni, vidi, vici* was pronounced *waynie, weedie, weekie,*)
that these *duces* were spoken of as *dukes*.   Or, perhaps, in the
now obsolete accent (though it is quite a recent one, among
men of good education), as *dooks*.   At any rate, ninth-century
Northumbria was distracted by the rivalries of innumerable
Faw dukes, very much as eighteenth century Northumbria
was, except that the latter was little more than the shadow
of the former (so far as concerns the doings of this particular
race).

Ninth-century Northumbria—or Galloway of the same
period—is, of course, a great distance beyond the epoch of
the Wars of the Roses.   But the principle involved is the
same.   At whatever period one chooses to glance, one seen
innumerable jealousies between rival tribes, or kingdoms;
and, out of this turmoil of rivalry, one dynasty emerges
triumphant.   It may be "the lords of Bamborough" in the
tenth century, or it may be the Tudors in the fifteenth,—but,
at whatever time, one particular chiefship gains the ascendency over the others, and these others, whether the scene
be Northumbria or England, disappear from history.   But
the leaders of these varying factions counted themselves
"kings" quite as much as did those who eventually triumphed.
History—that arch time-server—may have ignored them
from the date of their final defeat, but "kings" these leaders
would still hold themselves to be.   And, at the remote period
to which we are just now referring,—the ninth and tenth centuries, namely,—these "kings" and "dukes," of Galloway
and Northumbria, were largely *Picts*, or *Faws*—that is,
Gypsies.

Our popular nursery tales are full of references to such
reguli; who prove, by their ways and the extent of their
dominion, that their power and importance is very limited.
The West Highland Tales are full, also, of such "kings":

and Mr. Campbell received a great number of those traditions from the narrations of "Tinklers." He names several. There is the *King of Sorcha,* and the *King of Laidheann ;* and we have already referred to the *King of Rualay.* Many of such kingdoms are nameless now. Others are still well-known in Europe ; and these may, or may not (as recorded in legend) point to a great antiquity. Such are the *King of France,* the *King of Spain,* the *King of Greece.* A title may easily be borne by a "king," long after he has left the country. that gave him his right to it. Whatever their origin, there were several ' kings' and 'nobles' of this sort in fifteenth-century Scotland ; as the books of the Lord High Treasurer shew. " In a ' King of Rowmais' . . . 'the Erle of Greece' . . . 'King Cristal' . . . and the 'King of Cipre,'" says the *Encyclopædia* writer, quoting from these records, " one dimly recognizes four Gipsy chiefs." And the "Lord and Earl of Little Egypt" was formally acknowledged as a "peer" in sixteenth-century Scotland.

Nothing but patience, and the critical examinations of scholars, can ever tell us who such people really were. Until the last generation or so, everything has been hearsay— or mostly so. History of the Tales-of-a-Grandfather sort has been quite content to accept everything printed as *truth.* Writers of that kind slump the earlier nations of Britain under such a comprehensive and vague description as "the Picts and Scots." Others tell us a little more by character-izing them as so many "black herds ;" and relate how they crossed the fenny waters of the Forth basin ("the Scythian Vale,") in their skin canoes, and ravaged Wales and Southern Britain. But they tell us nothing of the titles of their chiefs. They were only the leaders of these "black herds of *painted people* and *vagabonds,*"—*Picts* and *Scots.* Such leaders,— black of skin, savage in nature, and yet possessed of the evi-dences of a certain civilization (having jewels, gold ornaments, chessmen of gold, of ivory, or of bone),—are confusedly remem-bered in the popular traditions of Wales, of the Western High-lands, and probably of other portions of the United King-dom. And these legendary tales, in many cases, reveal those savage chieftains as the kings, or *reguli,* or dukes of various neighbourhoods ; in the centre of which is their stronghold. As, for example, the castle of the black "giant" Gwrnach, in the Welsh *Mabinogion ;* or that of the Black Oppressor, or of the Black Knight of Lancashire ; or, more historically, that of the Black Dubh-glass of Galloway—whose memory is still execrated in that territory.

Without any more remarks of a general nature, let us turn again to the consideration of the *tory* classes of Scotland, as these have figured in modern times, and regarding them under their popular designation of *gypsies* or *tinklers.* By scrutinising the person of a famous Galloway *gypsy*, we saw that, in place of his bearing out—in the history of his family and in his own characteristics—the accepted theory that such people have straggled into Britain within the last few centries, " Billy Marshall " displayed most strongly the attributes that were the property of one or more of the earliest known inhabitants of his fatherland. Let us see if any evidence of a parallel kind can be gleaned by the consideration of any other Scottish *gypsy* of comparatively recent date.

It may be remembered that, although Marshall was the King of all the Tories in Galloway, there was some reference made to another leader, of the same kind of people and in the same territory, who was his contemporary. This man was named William Baillie, and the writer who spoke of him in this connection stated that he and his followers " represented themselves as horse dealers, but they were in reality horse stealers and robbers."

The recognition of *two* separate bands of these people, living in the same territory but acknowledging a different head, would at first sight seem antagonistic to the belief that Marshall reigned supreme over *tory* Galloway. And it really was not strictly accurate to say that that leader had no " equal " in that province. This slip may be amended by saying that he was the supreme chief of the Galloway gypsies, *when William Baillie was outside of the bounds of Galloway.* The reason for making this amendment will become apparent when we look into the statements that are made by Mr. Simson and others with regard to the Baillie sept of the Scottish "gypsies." If William Marshall, like other gypsies of equal rank, was a kinglet, or rye ; William

Baillie was very much more. For he was a king, a *baurie rye*, a very great gentleman indeed.

Of all the modern titular nobles, described by Mr. Simson as Scottish *gypsies*, the head of the Baillie clan was *facile princeps*. There was, it is true, a perpetual rivalry between the Baillies and the Faws for the right to the "gypsy crown :" but until we can learn the pedigree of the family that was specially distinguished by this latter name (once, as we have seen, applied collectively to the Clarkes, the Winters, the Herons, and other Border tribes ; and plainly signifying *Pict*) —it is needless to speculate upon their possible right to the supremacy. But with the Baillies it is otherwise.

So lately as the latter part of the last century, the leaders of this formidable clan were men who arrogated to themselves the rank of gentlemen, and bore themselves as such. Not "gentlemen" of the stamp that the heroine of the Wife of Bath's Tale holds up for example (and which, of course, is the highest kind), but "gentlemen" of the Roger Wildrake order ; "swashbucklers ;" "cavaliers."* This is seen in a story told by Mr. Simson (at page 196). "About the year 1770," he tells us, "the mother of the Baillies received some personal injury, or rather insult, at a fair at Biggar, from a gardener of the name of John Cree. The insult was instantly resented by the gipsies ; but Cree was luckily protected by his friends. In contempt and defiance of the whole multitude in the market, four of the Baillies—Matthew, James, William, and John—all brothers, appeared on horseback, dressed in scarlet, and armed with broadswords, and, parading through the crowd, threatened to be avenged of the gardener, and those who had assisted him. Burning with revenge, they threw off their coats, rolled up the sleeves of their shirts to

---

* The word "cavalier" has only an offensive meaning nowadays when used as an adjective—the sense it then bears being "arrogant," "overbearing," "rude." It is with this shade of its meaning in view that it is used substantively above. And it is not out of place to remark that the word "rogue," which was ultimately applied to vagabonds and "gypsies," signified originally a man of a "cavalier" disposition. Mr. Skeat, in his "Etymological Dictionary," shows us that—as French *rogue*, and Breton *rog*—this word is an equivalent of "arrogant, proud, haughty, presumptuous, brusque." Therefore, "cavalier" and "rogue" can be used with equal fitness, in speaking of those *sorners, masterful beggars, and such like runners about*, who retarded so much the progress of civilization.

the shoulder, like butchers when at work, and, with their
naked and brawny arms, and glittering swords in their
clenched hands, furiously rode up and down the fair, threatening death to all who should oppose them. Their bare arms,
naked weapons, and resolute looks, showed that they were
prepared to slaughter their enemies without mercy. No one
dared to interfere with them, till the minister of the parish
appeased their rage, and persuaded them to deliver up their
swords. It was found absolutely necessary, however, to keep
a watch upon the gardener's house, for six months after the
occurrence, to protect him and his family from the vengeance
of the vindictive gipsies."

William Baillie, the grandfather of these four "gypsies,"
has already been spoken of. He was "well known, over the
greater part of Scotland, as chief of his tribe within the
kingdom." A contemporary of his has described him as
"the handsomest, the best dressed, the best looking, and the
best bred man he ever saw." And another writer sketches
him thus :—"Before any considerable fair, if the gang were
at a distance from the place where it was to be held, whoever
of them were appointed to go, went singly, or, at most, never
above two travelled together. A day or so after, Mr. Baillie
himself followed, mounted like a nobleman—[Mr. Simson's
ancestor, previously quoted, states that "he generally rode
one of the best horses the kingdom could produce ; himself
attired in the finest scarlet, with his greyhounds following
him, as if he had been a man of the first rank : "]—and, as
journeys, in those days, were almost all performed on horseback, he sometimes rode, for many miles, with gentlemen of
the first respectability in the country. And, as he could discourse readily and fluently on almost any topic, he was often
taken to be some country gentleman of property, as his dress
and manners seemed to indicate."

We shall find a parallel case to this of the Baillies (though
there are many others), by looking southward to Exmoor,
where, in the persons of the notorious Doones of "Badgery,"
precisely the same characteristics are seen. It may be convenient to refer to that clan more particularly,—but every
reader of *Lorna Doone* is aware that they also were the dread
of their district, being guilty of endless acts of murder and

rapine ; that they—like other "gypsies"—were never busier than at local fairs ; that they—like the Baillies—were men of proud bearing and good education; to which qualities they —like the Baillies—added the claim of high descent. And it is beyond question that such men, if found among the Royalists of the preceding century, would not have differed —in any degree—from many of their fellow-cavaliers. However dark in complexion a Baillie was, he was not likely to be swarthier than Charles II.: if he wore a gypsy love-lock, tied with a gaudy ribbon, so did his brother cavaliers: if he swaggered, and bullied, and rode through a crowd of pea-sants with threatening looks and a brandished sword, so would every alternate one of his comrades have done, had they fancied themselves similarly insulted : and if, by a politi-cal revolution, or by personal extravagance, such a family as the Scottish Baillies had found themselves wholly bereft of land and treasure ; and, finding themselves thus, had resorted to means of violence, "enforcing a living on the common road ;" they would only have acted as scores of ruined seven-teenth and eighteenth-century " gentlemen " actually did. In every way, such men were *tories*. Their fault lay in not recognizing the changed sentiment of the times. What at one time was a common practice of the ruling classes (even of the blood-royal, if Shakespeare's *Prince Henry* may be taken as a true picture)—became regarded, in course of time, as criminal and disreputable. The swagger, the gay dresses, the long hair, and the life of dissipation and crime, that were inseparable concomitants of "Gypsy" life,—though latterly regarded with disfavour by men of good station, were pre-cisely the characteristics of the nobility of an earlier age. Later on—such qualities, and the language of the classes who displayed them, received the same contemptuous name,— *flash*. At the present day, no one with pretensions to good-breeding would imitate the "loud" manners, and ostentatious style of dressing of the cavaliers. Nor is it nowadays counted more honourable for a reduced gentleman to live by *sorning* and robbery, than to follow an honest calling, however humble. So much higher is the nineteenth-century standard of gentil-ity than that of the days of the Charleses.

Although convicted of the deliberate murder of his wife,

James Baillie—one of the four brothers that distinguished themselves at Biggar Fair—succeeded in obtaining a royal pardon, "on condition that he transported himself beyond seas within a limited time, otherwise the pardon was to have no effect." Not only did he quite ignore this condition, but, on regaining his liberty, he resumed his former brigand existence ; and, three years later, he was again sentenced to be hanged. Again he was pardoned, on the same condition ; and again he scouted its terms. How often, afterwards, he was imprisoned, and how often he attained his liberty, in one way or another, is not particularly stated. But the fact that a notorious thief and murderer was twice pardoned at a period (1770–5) when hanging was an everyday matter is rather startling. Or, at least, it would be startling, if we had not already remarked a similar instance in Galloway. And just as Billy Marshall lived under the protecting shield of the Selkirk influence, so had this James Baillie an advocate in the person of Mrs. Baillie, of Lamington ; to whose exertions he is said to have been indebted for the pardons referred to. A third case of this kind is also quoted by Mr. Simson, the offenders being "Captain" Gordon, the head of the Spittal gypsies, and his son-in-law, Ananias Faa. "They were convicted and condemned for the crime [sheep-stealing and threatening to kill] ; 'but afterwards, to the great surprise of their Berwickshire neighbours, obtained a pardon, for which, it was generally understood, they were indebted to the interest of a noble northern family, of their own name.'"

Owing to the alleged aversion to owning the charge of the possession of "gypsy" blood, one might have some diffidence in referring to particular families ; at any rate, when the date under consideration is not very far removed from our own. (When the period is more remote, such remarks cease to have the slightest tinge of personality. For, even in the rare cases in which a long pedigree is authentic from end to end, it only shows one particular line of descent. An early ancestor on such a tree is equally the ancestor of thousands of other people, who may or may not be aware of their relation to him, but who, in any case, would be as well entitled as any other of his posterity to regard him as personal property.) That the taint—if taint it be—is shared by a considerable number of people in the United Kingdom is shown by Mr. Huxley's statement, that the "dark whites" constitute the majority of our population.   And if, as some gypsiologists aver—and as there is every reason to believe—genuine "gypsies," of thorough "gypsy" descent (and not merely nineteenth-century men who have lapsed), can be found without the faintest indication of "dark" blood—and yet pure "gypsies" —then the unreason and absurdity of the "gypsy" prejudice is revealed.   For this would show, what everything in the foregoing pages tends to prove, that "British gypsy" is only an expression for "pagan" or "archaic Briton."   And that the most a man of cultured ancestry can say is—that his people ceased to be "gypsies" at an earlier stage than some others.

But, in the particular cases at present under discussion, it is hardly necessary to say anything in the way of apology. For the names of these "gypsies," and their friends, have been public property for some time past.

Although there is no proof that the celebrated Galloway *Faw* was a kinsman of the Selkirk family, and perhaps the actual chief (by blood) of one of its branches, this has been inferred : with what justice may some day be ascertained. But, in the instances of "Captain" Gordon and James Baillie, it is plainly stated that the two ladies of recognized position who exerted themselves to save these two "gypsies" from the gallows, did so *because* they were relations.   Namesakes, at any rate ; and relations in the case of Baillie.   It is diffi-cult to guess at any other motive that would prompt such people to become the champions of notorious thieves and cut-throats.   In the last of these cases, it is stated that the relationship was of an illegitimate kind, and that Baillie the "gypsy" was Baillie by surname, because he was the offspring of an intrigue between a Baillie of Lamington and a "gypsy" girl.   But, it has been already pointed out that, if this had been so, it would knock on the head the theory that the influential "gypsy" Baillies of the eighteenth century were the male descendants of the influential "gypsy" Baillies (or Bailyows—the name is admitted to be the same), of the sixteenth and seventeenth centuries, which would be manifestly absurd.   Besides, not only is it alleged that James

Baillie (of the Biggar Fair incident) "pretended" to be a natural son of a Baillie of Lamington, but so did "his fathers before him." It is incredible that such ties between the two families were formed in three or four successive generations, or that they would be regarded by the reputable side of the connection as so binding that everything must be done to obtain pardon—again and again—for the crimes committed by the morganatic branch. Nor is it likely, again, that if a relationship did not really exist at all, as the use of the word "pretended" suggests, the landed Baillies would ever lift a finger on behalf of a clan of alien "gypsies," merely because these *claimed* kinship with them.

Mr. Simson, the younger, arguing from his own standing-point, speaks to the same effect : (and, indeed, the above remarks are partly an unconscious reflection of the following) :—

I am very much inclined to think that Mrs. Baillie, of Lamington, mentioned under the head of Tweeddale and Clydesdale gipsies, was a gipsy ; and the more so, from having learned, from two different sources, that the present Baillie, of ——, is a gipsy. Considering that courts of justice have always stretched a point, to convict, and *execute*, gipsies, it looks like something very singular, that William Baillie, a gipsy, who was condemned to death, in 1714, should have had his sentence commuted to banishment, *and been allowed to go at large*, while others, condemned with him, were executed. And three times did he escape in that manner, till, at last, he was slain by one of his tribe. It also seems very singular, that James Baillie, another gipsy, in 1772, should have been condemned for the murder of his wife, and also had his sentence commuted to banishment, and been allowed to go at large : and that twice, at least. Well might McLaurin remark : " Few cases have occurred in which there has been such an expenditure of mercy." And tradition states that " the then Mistress Baillie, of Lamington, and her family used all their interest in obtaining these pardons for James Baillie. No doubt of it. But the reason for all this was, doubtless, different from that of " James Baillie, like his fathers before him, *pretending* that he was a bastard relative of the family of Lamington."

At the same place (pp. 470-1), Mr. Simson hints that the Duchess of Gordon, who obtained the pardon of " Captain " Gordon, was herself a "gypsy ; " and the existence of " gypsies," in great numbers, in all ranks of society, is a fact he repeatedly insists upon.

But, all throughout, Mr. Simson is clogged with the con-

ventional belief that "gypsies" are Orientals, who entered
these islands a few centuries ago (though there is no historical record of such an arrival) ; instead of being—as a fuller
examination of the question must inevitably prove them to
be—the un-christianized and un-modernized remnants of
various Oriental races, whose advent in this country, at a
much earlier period, is chronicled on a thousand pages of
history. Therefore, the most that Mr. Simson can urge, in
the case of "Captain" Gordon is that the Duchess of Gordon who befriended him was herself a "gypsy." Whatever
may be the ethnological history of her family (a well-known
division of the Maxwells) it is plain that the relationship
was much more likely to exist between the marauding chief
and her own husband, the nominal head of the Gordons,
than with herself. And the history of those Gordons
favours the idea. That they were once marsh-dwellers, or
"mossers," is seen from the fact that the oldest title of the
Duke of Gordon was *The Gudeman of the Bog ;* "from the
Bog-of-Gight, a morass in the parish of Bellie, Banffshire,
in the centre of which the former stronghold of this family
was placed." Another title of this chief was *The Cock of
the North ;* a style of name which, like *The Wolf of Badenoch,*
and others,* once borne by men of real power, is now

* Other such names have been already noticed. It was remarked that the
early *mormaers,* or earls, of the territory of Buchan, bore the name of *Mac
Dobharcon,* that is, "the children of *The Otter."* Also that one king of Alban,
in the tenth century, was known as *Cuilean*—in Latin, *Caniculus—The Whelp :*
that another was *Hundason, The Son of the Dog :* that the traditionary
Cuchullin was *The Hound of Cullin,* sometimes styled *An Cu—The Hound,* and
sometimes *Cu nan Con,*'*The Hound of the Hounds ;* and that Allan, the swarthy
pirate that ravaged the Hebrides in the fifteenth century, was known as "the
black-skinned *Boar."* The custom that gave rise to such titles was, it is
evident, the fashion of wearing the skins of various beasts, the animal chosen being
that which was the totem of the tribe. And that the whole tribe dressed itself in
one particular fashion was seen from an extract from a Gaelic poem, which stated
that—of three battalions in the army of the "King of Rualay"—one battalion
was composed of *Cat-heads,* and another of *Dog-heads,* and the third of *White-
backs* ("brown the rest, though white the back"). This *Dog-head* tribe is
known to have inhabited "*the marsh of the Dog-heads*" (Moygonihy) in County
Kerry ; and to have been always at war with the race of Fionn. Other such-
named tribes that can be localized are the *Calves* and *Heifers* (for so Mr. Skene
is inclined to render the *Lugi* and *Merta* of Ptolemy) of modern Sutherland, and
their neighbours the *Cats,* or Clan Chattan. Perhaps also the *Adders* of the
"black isle" in Ross-shire, as suggested by the name *Edderdale.*

relegated to the ranks of prize-fighting "gypsies" of the *Game Chicken* order, or "gypsy" minstrels like the *Soaring Eagles* and *Cooing Doves* of Wales. But the county of Banff was not the earliest-known residence of the Gordons. They are first found in Berwickshire, the district in which "Captain" Gordon and his band held sway. And we are told* that the descendants of the first great man of the family—those, that is, who remained in the earliest home of the clan—"continued to possess their original estates in Berwickshire till the beginning of the fifteenth century;" in which century, the era of the Black-Douglas overthrow, it is inferred that they became landless. But, though landless, they did not cease to exist. And, if they acted like other men of their time and station, they would continue to hold themselves as of as much consequence as ever, and take by force what had formerly been theirs by law. They would become *sorners*, or " masterful beggars," or (to use the more catholic term) *gypsies*. Which would account for such a statement as this—that " in Berwickshire, the original seat of the Gordons, the gipsies still retain the surname [Gordon]," and which would account also for the assistance rendered by the titular head of the Gordons to the chief of the Berwickshire division of his race.

So, also, in remarking on the conduct of the lady of Lamington, Mr. Simson assumes that *she* was of "gypsy" blood : which she may easily have been. But her maiden name was not likely *Baillie*. In this case, also, the kinship was evidently through the husband ; more especially as another squire of that blood was recognizably a gypsy. Here, again, the presumption clearly is that the marauding Baillies, who were gentlemen in manners, in dress and in education ; who bore themselves as men placed above " the common people," though their real tangible warrant for doing so had long been lost ; and who, in their worst moments, as robbers and murderers, were simply reproductions of the mediæval " noble ; " that these Baillies were lineal descendants of the chiefs of their race, and that it was for *this* reason that the more civilized branch of the family did so much to aid them.

* Anderson's " Scottish Nation," Vol. II. pp. 316–321.

Of all the "gypsy" clans, none is of more importance than that of the Baillies. Mr. Simson tells us that they and the Faas (a most provoking surname, as it points nowhere) are "the two principal families in Scotland;" "giving, according to their customs, kings and queens to their countrymen." This recognition—among gypsies—of varying degrees of rank is a fact of vital importance. That it is a fact, Mr. Simson repeatedly mentions. "Among those who frequented the south of Scotland were to be found various grades of rank, as in all other communities of men. There were then [in former times] wretched and ruffian-looking gangs, in whose company the superior gipsies would not have been seen:" (a statement which is quite in accordance with those made by Mr. Leland and others, regarding the greatly-differing racial characteristics of "gypsies," who appear capable of the most minute ethnological analysis). In referring to the Johnstones of Annandale (known popularly as "the Thieves of Annandale,") he further says—"These were counted a kind of lower caste than Baillie's people, who would have thought themselves degraded if they had associated with any of the Johnstone gang." Again, George Drummond, whose manner of dancing the Morris-dance, prototype of the harmless hornpipe and jig, has already been referred to, is spoken of as "a gipsy chief of an *inferior* gang in Fife," and as being, "in rank, quite inferior to the Lochgellie band, who called him a 'beggar Tinkler,' and seemed to despise him." Like Johnstone of Annandale, this Drummond was a *chief*, who never travelled without his harem and his followers. Nevertheless, though chiefs, there were "gypsy" castes higher than they.

That particular family of *faws* which latterly became known by the surname of Faa, Faw, or Fall, was apparently of nearly equal greatness with the Baillies. And in their case, as in that of the Gunns, the Gordons, the Marshalls, the Douglases, the Græmes, the Herons, and many others—their social rank is more elevated the farther back one goes. Prior to 1774, Henry Faa, a Border chief, "was received, and ate at the tables of people in public office," and "men of considerable fortune paid him a gratuity, called blackmail, in order to have their goods protected from thieves." In 1734,

"Captain James Fall, of Dunbar, was elected member of parliament for the Dunbar district of burghs." " The family of Fall gave Dunbar provosts and bailies, and ruled the political interests of that burgh for many years." " So far back as about the year 1670, one of the bailies of Dunbar was of the surname of Faa." A century earlier, " John Faw, Lord and Earl of Little Egypt," was recognized as a man of rank and authority, both by King James the Fifth, and by Mary Queen of Scots; and McLaurin, in his *Criminal Trials*, speaks of him as a " peer." And, in the same century, the *Herons*, whose descendant, Francis Heron, was king of the English-Border *Faws* in the middle of last century, were ranked among the most powerful clans on the Border.

From this last-mentioned fact, it cannot be concluded that Heron was necessarily the surname of this nameless " Faa" family, in every generation. The original meaning of *faw* having been gradually forgotten, it was confusedly interchanged with such surnames as Winter, Clarke and others ; as Wilson, in his *Tales of the Borders* has told us. The first-named of these is included by Sir Walter Scott as among " the most atrocious families " of the Borders, and by his time he believes them to have been wholly extirpated.* But " Faw " might have clung as a surname to any

* These Winters are referred to at pp. 96-7 of Mr. Simson's " History," and also in Sir Walter Scott's report of the gypsies in his shrievalty, transmitted to Mr. Hoyland. Scott's remarks upon the Border *græmes*, formerly quoted, tend to the same conclusion—namely, that the worst type of " Picts " has long ago disappeared. People like the cave-dwelling cannibals of St. Vigeans, Forfarshire, who—in the fourteenth century—were eventually captured and burned alive by the country people ; or, like those other cave-dwelling cannibals, " Sawney Bean " and his incestuous clan, who—in the following century—infested a certain district of the Galloway coast ; or, like the ferocious and untameable moss-troopers generally—have been quite exterminated. The incessant and relentless war between tribe and tribe, century after century, tells plainly of the continuous elimination of the fiercer elements of these races. Where two tribes, equally savage, lived in the same district, and in a state of continual antagonism, it is clear that their numbers would constantly be thinning. Or where one ferocious clan lingered on in a mountainous or marshy district—long after the surrounding country had been settled by people of peaceful tendencies (whether these were new-comers or the cream of the older savages) – then that clan had either to become civilized, or to be killed off as a league of criminals. So that, although modern " gypsies " are *tories*, as far as it is possible to be, yet they are not unaltered specimens of the earliest Picts. The hideous Moor of heraldry has

other family of Faws. Still, there is some ground for believing that the later kings of the Border Faws were the Herons of earlier history.

"I am inclined to believe," says Mr. Simson, "that the Faws and the Baillies, the two principal gipsy clans in Scotland, had frequently lived in a state of hostility with one another. . . , . At the present day the Baillies consider themselves quite superior in rank to the Faas ; and, on the other hand, the Faas and their friends speak with great bitterness and contempt of the Baillies, calling them 'a parcel of thieves and vagabonds.'" In spite, however, of this last remark, the Baillies must be regarded as distinctly the over-ruling caste of the "gypsies" of the South-Eastern half of Scotland (if not of the whole northern half of Great Britain, including Northumberland). This will become apparent presently.

Surnames do not form reliable supports in any genealogical inquiry, extending over a great stretch of time. A *dubh-glass* of Galloway may be the founder of a line of Scotts, or of Moors, or of Mac Dubh-Galls, or of any of the similar names already sufficiently reiterated. And from any one of these may branch off innumerable Robert's-sons, Dick's-sons, Tom's-sons, and Will's-sons. The same family may be, as Dr. Johnson learned, alternately called John's-son and Mac-Ian (which latter name is one of those popularly styled *Gaelic,* but which may be as fitly called *Old English* or *Old Dutch,* since it is *maga-* or *maag-Jan,* "the son of *Yan*") ; or the posterity of two brothers may become known, in the one line as Saunders, or Sanderson, and in the other as Mac-Alastair. While, again, a man may have received the surname of his feudal superior, without having the slightest relationship to his lord. A " Douglas' man " was not, of necessity, a " Douglas " (strictly so called).

Therefore, it would be somewhat rash to conclude that the Baillies derived their unsurpassed rank, from the unequalled position of the greatest man of their name. Nevertheless,

---

disappeared : partly by extirpation, partly by education, partly by intermarriage with more refined races. When Hugh Miller's colliers emerged from underground, after an isolation of some centuries, they had no nearer "marrows" than the savages encountered in the memorable voyage of the *Beagle.*

this is not unlikely. For the greatest (in rank) of the family
of Baillie, Bailyow, Balleul, Ballou, or Balliol, was once—as
everybody knows—the actual king of Scotland. The
Lamington Baillies,—those who identified themselves so
closely with the outlawed Baillies, and one of whom was, in
Mr. Simson's eyes, a veritable "gypsy,"—these Baillies (if
not all of that surname) believe themselves to be the descendants of John Baliol, the thirteenth-century king of Scotland. Which is quite in keeping with the exalted position
accorded to the *tory* Baillies, claimed by them, and admitted
by those of inferior castes, who repeatedly affirm that "kings
and queens have come of that family."

But Baliol is supposed to have been a Norman ? And the
outlawed Baillies, being " gypsies," must have been men of
dark complexion, which the Normans are not supposed to
have been. If a descendant of the ex-king had really been
a man of swarthy skin, there would have been nothing
extraordinary in the matter ; since his own niece was married
to John, the Black Comyn, Earl of Badenoch. That she
herself was white, is hinted by the fact that the son of this
marriage was styled the *red* Comyn ; *red* or *ruadh* having
then the signification of "tawny," and having been applied
to the half-breed branches of other black clans, such as the
Douglases and the Mercers. A daughter of this *ruadh*
Comyn—the Comyn slain by Robert Bruce—was also
married to the tenth Douglas chief, and so became the
grandmother of Archibald the Black. So that, at least, the
descendants of John Baliol's sister became *dubh-glasses*. But
it is not necessary to assume that his own direct posterity
mixed their blood with that of the " Moors." The nomadic
Baillies of this century are described as, " in general, of a
colour rather cadaverous, or of a darkish pale ; their cheek-
bones high ; their eyes small, and light-coloured ; their hair
of a dingy white or red colour, and wiry ; and their skin,
drier and of a tougher texture than that of the people of
this country." That is, of the people of this country *who
have lived civilized lives for many generations.* The
" Autocrat of the Breakfast Table " tells us that the possession of wealth for only four or five generations " *transforms
a race :* " and what is true of individual families is true of

societies. People who have never forsaken the wild life of our common ancestors cannot be expected to be identical, in body or in mind, with those who have made use of the accumulating culture of many centuries.

This elastic nature of the term "gypsy" (and its comprehensiveness is realized by few) allows us, therefore, to regard the outlawed Baillies as direct descendants of the powerful Baliol family. "Gypsies," we are beginning to see, are of the most diverse character. This is not only enunciated very distinctly by Mr. Simson; but, in a more indirect way, by Mr. Leland also. For, in spite of his various allusions to the "gypsy eye," and to the "black blood" that, beyond question, marks the great majority of "gypsies," he yet includes, in his list of their various tribes, such clans as the Bosvilles, Broadways, Grays, and Smalls, who are pure "gypsies," and, at the same time, of fair complexion.* Moreover, he says of the class generally (for one cannot, in the face of such statements, speak of the gypsy *race*):—"In the Danubian principalities there are at the present day three kinds of gypsies: one very dark and barbarous, another light brown and more intelligent, and the third, or *élite*, of yellow-pine complexion, as American boys characterize the hue of quadroons. Even in England there are straight-haired and curly-haired Romanys, the two indicating *not a difference resulting from white admixture, but entirely different original stocks.*" These two last divisions may be held to be fairly represented by the long-haired, cave-dwelling *ciuthachs* of West Highland tradition (the "glibbed" *tories* of Queen Elizabeth's time); and by the curly-headed Moors of British heraldry (historic specimens of whom are visible in the curly-haired, swarthy Silurian "Picts"). At any rate, it is easy to see why—on the ground of difference of race—the Lochgellie caste of Fifeshire "gypsies" should despise the alleged "inferior" race of Fifeshire Drummonds; or why the Baillies "would have thought themselves degraded if they had associated with any of the Annandale Johnstones;" or

---

* This is negative evidence. Mr. Leland does not characterize these clans as "half-bloods": therefore, it is to be presumed he regards them as pure. It is important, however, to observe that most of his "fair" families are labelled "half-blood."

why the Baillies should "consider themselves quite superior in rank to the Faws."

And this last parallel may perhaps start from a very important historical fact. For, let it be granted that the so-called "gypsy" Baillies are the posterity of the Norman king, and it will be evident that they had an ancestral reason for their self-conceit. Because the Balliols were of a race of successful conquerors; because their dynasty was for a while the ruling family in the country; because the Normans had achieved a higher civilization than the Picts, under which denomination the *Faws* must, of course, be classed. The clan that came to be known specially as that of "the Faws," being so high in rank that it rivalled that of the Baillies, must have been of a comparatively high caste; much above those "wretched and ruffian-looking gangs, in whose company the superior gipsies would not have been seen." But they were *Faws*. Therefore, of the race, or races, that the Normans overcame. There is great significance in this immemorial enmity of the Baillies. For the Normans are nowhere stated to have practised the customs of painting or tattooing. And the Balliols are supposed to have been Normans: therefore, they were not *Faws*, but the enemies of such.

This view of the ancestry of the *tory* Baillies, accords well with what we know of them. For, though daring and intractable outlaws, they have been always, so far as one may see them—men of brave presence and of good education: quite the equals, in every respect, of the highest classes of their neighbourhood; with whom they associated on equal terms, as stated on several occasions. The only differences between these and those were—and they were important differences—that, while the ordinary nobility and gentry of, say, William Baillie's time (about 1700), were believers in the spread of liberty, of education, and of peace, the *tory* Baillies, and others like them, adhered to the ideas of earlier times, when a "noble" or a "gentleman" was simply a robber on a very large scale, who took as much land, and money, and power as his weaker neighbours permitted him to take, and who paid no heed whatever to any assertion of individual right, where the individual had not a

backing of armed followers. (It is true that many kindly
and graceful acts are recorded of such *tories*, in the way of
giving to the poor what they had taken from the rich, but
these were the outcome of a generous impulse ; not the
acknowledgment of a demand.) Hence, though worthy
enough representatives of the eleventh century, such men
became less and less in harmony with the spirit of their time,
in each generation ; as the rights of all men, strong or weak,
became more fully recognized. Consequently, they who
were once *within* the law became *out*-lawed ; for, in the
modern estimation, what was once legal, or, at least, permis-
sible, is now *crime*. Thus, those Baillies who would not adapt
themselves to the newer ideas, and grow with the growth of
the nation, became, by degrees, a caste of landless outcasts,
without a fragment of that kind of power that the national
law recognized (though their ancient right of command was
still admitted by men of their own stamp).

It must be remembered that such *tories*, though faithful
reproductions of their ancestors, represent only one phase of
the ancestral life. They are, as it were, petrifactions. They
are some of the roots out of which the British nation has
grown. Just as *druidism* or magic, fortune-telling, juggling,
astrology, and superstition, still exist among "gypsies" and
charlatans ; while astronomy, science, and a high religion,
have been developed from the same fundamental source ; so
the aggressive characteristics of these stunted "gypsies" are
seen in the conquests of the British people : and so the
higher attributes of this or that "gypsy" tribe are displayed
in the civilized families who bear the same name and inherit
some of the same blood. The *tory* Baillies are certainly
reproductions of the mediæval noble, but not of *all* his
qualities. Those intractable robbers are suitable descendants
of the Norman invaders ; but the qualities of the founder of
Baliol College were most fully inherited by such a man as
Robert Baillie of Jerviswood, "the Scottish Sidney." Mr.
Simson may say, with all truth, "The nomadic gipsies in
general, like the Baillies in particular, have gradually declined
in appearance, till, at the present day, the greater part of
them have become little better than beggars, when compared
to what they were in former times." But these only con-

stitute the sediment of their race. What one loses another
gets. The *tory* Baillies have withered away : but the blood
of the same stock has flowed in the veins of thousands of
civilized and often eminent men.

In short, then, the claims of the "gypsy" Baillies to the
"gypsy" crown seem well-founded. Though, in one sense,
"the sediment of their race,"—it is by no means certain that
they are not its hereditary aristocracy. That is, by right of
primogeniture. This, indeed, is what they claim. When
Mr. James Simson speaks of "the presumptuous pride, the
overweening conceit of a high-mettled Scottish gipsy ; his
boasted descent—a descent at once high, illustrious, and lost
in antiquity ; his unbounded contempt for the rabble of town
and country "—he has in view that very class of "gypsies"
of which this particular clan is avowedly the chief. It is
their boast that "kings and queens" have come of their
family ; and their superiority is recognized by "gypsies" of
every degree of caste. To give every warrant to this assertion,—the very branch of civilized Baillies that made such
strenuous efforts to save the lives of their discredited namesakes, assert the same thing. The Lamington Baillies have
good reasons for believing themselves to be of a race that
gave at least *one* king to Scotland. An oral tradition,
handed down through centuries from sire to son is by no
means infallible ; but those who have studied such things
know how startlingly true such inherited beliefs sometimes are ; and how, after many generations, the discovery of
a lost document, or a lost fact, will demonstrate with absolute
certainty the truth of an unwritten tradition. It is impossible
to understand the attitude of the *tory* Baillies, or of any of this
type of "gypsy," without perceiving that they are cases in
point. No ordinary scamp, ignorant of grandparents, or
even of parents, could possible look down with contempt
upon those of his contemporaries who possess the wealth, the
education, and the authority of his day and generation ; the
men who may almost be said to hold his destiny in their
hands. It is incredible that such a man could hold the firm
conviction that his descent was "at once high, illustrious, and
lost in antiquity," and that all the magistrates and "swells"
throughout the land were so much "rabble." But such a

standing-point is perfectly conceivable in a man of really high descent, however degraded he may be himself.

This opinion, that the "gypsy" Baillies and the landed Baillies of that particular district of Scotland were, substantially, the same people, has received confirmation from an additional fact recently brought to light (and after the preceding sentences were written).

The English-speaking world has lately read and heard a great deal about the private life of one of these Baillies,— certainly not the least eminent of all that clan. In her *Letters and Memorials*, so recently published, Mrs. Carlyle states that . . . "my maternal grandmother was 'descended from a gang of gipsies;' was in fact grand-niece to Matthew Baillie who 'suffered at Lanark,' that is to say, was hanged there . . . . By the way, my uncle has told me that the wife of that Matthew Baillie, Margaret Euston by name, was the original of Sir W. Scott's Meg Merrilees.* Matthew himself was the last of the gipsies; could steal a horse from under the owner if he liked, but left always the saddle and bridle; a thorough gentleman in his way, and six feet four in stature!"

It is possible that Mrs. Carlyle's uncle may have mixed up the pedigree a little. The Matthew Baillie who married Margaret Euston (*Yowston;* sometimes *Yorstoun;* sometimes *Yorkston*) was certainly not "the last of the gipsies," even of those bearing his own surname. For he had a son, Matthew, and many other descendants, recognized as "gypsies." But we may accept as a fact that the Matthew Baillie, senior, was the great-uncle of that Jane Baillie, whose celebrated granddaughter has given an added interest to the Baillie lineage. Jane Baillie's grandfather, therefore, was a brother of this elder Matthew Baillie; and these two were sons of the celebrated William Baillie, king over all the gypsies in Scotland; accounted by one who knew him to be "the handsomest, the best dressed, the best looking,

---

* This adds one to the many "originals" of Meg Merrilees. Jean Gordon, Billy Marshall's wife Flora, his sister, and now Margaret (who, by the way, is sometimes called *Mary*) Yorstoun. At Gilsland, also, a belief has been developed that "Meg Merrilees" lived there, and they show you her cottage as a proof of it.

and the best bred man he ever saw:" "the stories that are
told of this splendid gipsy (says Mr. Simson) are numerous
and interesting." And Miss Baillie's grandfather was also,
therefore, an uncle of those four cavaliers who, throwing
off their scarlet coats, and rolling up the sleeves of their
shirts to give full play to the sword-arm, "furiously rode
up and down the fair" at Biggar, "with glittering swords
in their clenched hands,"—roused by an insult offered to
their mother, the celebrated Margaret Yowston, or Yorkstoun,
wife of the elder Matthew Baillie. With this part of her
lineage before our eyes, can we wonder that a personal friend
of William Baillie's eminent descendant should have said
of her, that "she was the proudest woman—as proud and
tenacious of her dignity as a savage chief"?

To speak of Mrs. Carlyle as "a Baillie" is not strictly
correct. But she was as much "a Baillie" as she was "a
Welsh." Had her connection with the Baillies come to her
through her father, she would have been spoken of as "a
Baillie"—though not inheriting any more of that blood than
she actually did. To speak of her as "a gypsy" would be
quite incorrect; unless one held, with Mr. Simson, that the
descendants of gypsies—though after generations of civilization—ought always to be regarded as "gypsies." But
Mrs. Carlyle was, by blood, as much "a Baillie" as any
other of her Baillie kindred; unless their fathers had married
back into the same stock.

Carlyle does not seem to have fully realized the exact
nature of his wife's Baillie lineage. He does not speak of
her kin as "gypsies." In the second volume of his *Reminiscences* (page 103) he says—"By her mother's mother, who
was a Baillie, of somewhat noted kindred in Biggar country,
my Jeannie was further said to be descended from 'Sir
William Wallace' (the great); but this seemed to rest on
nothing but air and vague fireside rumour of obsolete date."
Again (at page 128 of the same book)—"Walter [Welsh,
Mrs. Carlyle's maternal grandfather] had been a buck in his
youth, a high-prancing horseman, etc.; I forget what image
there was of him, in buckskins, pipe hair-dressings, grand
equipments, riding somewhither . . . . He had married a
good and beautiful Miss Baillie (of whom already) and settled

with her at Capelgill, in the Moffatt region . . . . From her my Jeannie was called ' Jane Baillie Welsh.' "

The impression derived from these remarks of Carlyle's is quite in keeping with the statements made by Mr. Simson, as to the fine manners, rich dress, and good education of this Jane Baillie's great-grandfather ("Captain" William Baillie) and the other near relatives of that "splendid gipsy." His great grand-daughter is remembered as " a good and beautiful Miss Baillie ; " she is regarded as the suitable wife of a dashing young squire ; and there is no word of her " gypsy " belongings. If we had learned these facts about her fore-fathers through some other source, who would ever have thought of calling her a " gypsy " ? We should probably have said that these Baillies, by their bearing, education, and dress, were nothing else than broken-down aristocrats,—the landless descendants of the cavaliers of the preceding (the seventeenth) century.

What may be regarded as the most important point—*the* point of the evidence brought forward by the Carlyles*—is the statement that Jane Welsh was descended from the Scotch hero of the thirteenth century *through these very "gypsy" Baillies*—through a race of assumed wanderers who "entered Europe about the fifteenth century." Not only does this fact show, by implication, that (like other Scotch-gypsy families) these Baillies have been associated with the history of Scotland from a very early period, but it also helps to clinch the connection between the landed and the landless sections of that race. For this alleged descent from Sir William Wallace is one of the articles of belief of the family who did so much to succour the "gypsy" Baillies when in distress,—saving them from death and banishment, on several occasions. " It is traditionally stated that the celebrated Sir William Wallace acquired the estate of Lamington by marrying Marion Braidfoot, the heiress of that family, and that it passed to Sir William Baillie on his marriage with

---

* Quoted from Mr. Froude's "Letters and Memorials of Jane Welsh Carlyle," Vol. II. p. 54 ; also from pp. 103 and 128 of the second volume of Carlyle's " Reminiscences." It is perhaps superfluous to add that the reference to Mrs. Carlyle's characteristics is found in the article contributed to the *Contemporary Review* (May, 1883) by Mrs. Oliphant.

the eldest daughter and heiress of Wallace. The statement,
however, is incorrect. Sir William Wallace left no legitimate
offspring, but his natural daughter is said to have married
Sir William Baillie of Hoprig, the progenitor of the Baillies
of Lamington."[*] So that, peaceable squire and robber-chief,
the same pedigree is claimed by each.

When one glances at these Baillies, in the mass, there
seems no reason why one should ever imagine that they
owned a differing origin. Biggar, Lamington, Lanark (where,
alas! Matthew Baillie was at last doomed to "suffer"),—all
these, and other localities connected with that name, are
situated within a radius of twenty miles or so. The favourite family-names of the two sections of the clan are the same.
The celebrated "Captain" William Baillie (who was killed
in November 1724, and of whom we have just been speaking)
was succeeded in his *tory* kingship, by his son Matthew (the
husband of Mary Yorstoun); and the four sons of this
Matthew that have been noticed in the incident at Biggar
Fair were named respectively— Matthew, James, William
and John. Hoprig and Lamington seem to be the names of
the oldest possessions accorded to this clan, and that chief of
the name who is said to have married the daughter of Wallace, and who is described as the lord of these places, was
a William Baillie. It must be through him that Mrs. Carlyle,
and other descendants of the "gypsy" William Baillie, claim
a descent from the hero of Scotland. It is through him that
the records of the other branches (not called "gypsies")
proclaim a like ancestry. The names of the four "gypsy"
Baillies, just named, may be found among the "civilized"
divisions of the same stock. *Matthew* Baillie, a boy of nine
years old at the time when his namesake, with his three
brothers, was scaring the peasants at Biggar Fair,—is known
to history as "a distinguished anatomist and the first physician
of his time." And his sister's name is more widely known
than his—the celebrated Joanna Baillie. These two—
brother and sister—were born in Lanarkshire (1761-2) and
were the children of Dr. *James* Baillie, a Presbyterian
clergyman, and latterly a professor of divinity in Glasgow
University. This James Baillie was believed to have

descended of the Baillie of Jerviswood line,—an offshoot
from the Lamington stock, which branched off in the person
of a *John* Baillie.   In looking at these Baillies from the
" stud-book " or Herald's Office point of view, we discover
" that Mr. Alexander Baillie of Castlecarry, a learned antiquarian, was of opinion that the family of Lamington were
a branch of the illustrious house of the Baliols, who were
lords of Galloway, and kings of Scotland."*   In viewing the
condition of those members of the clan who represented
toryism, we see that their eldest-born was held, by all men of
that kind in Scotland to be the *baurie rye, ard-ri*, or King of
all the "gypsies" in the country; that, therefore, being lord
of the lord of Galloway, he was himself lord of Galloway ;
and that his family was believed by all their archaically-disposed followers to have "given kings and queens to
Scotland."   What difference between the two varieties of
these Baillies was there but this—that the one, throughout
a constantly increasing civilization, adhered to the ideas and
manners of the remote ancestors common to both divisions,
—while the other continued, generation after generation, to
rise to the level of the tide of progress'?   A Baillie who
lived after the fashion of the horse-stealing "gypsy" who
" suffered " at Lanark was no rarity in that part of Scotland
a thousand years ago ; he was then the rule.   But a Baillie
who was born in a " manse," or who lived a quiet, harmless
life as a country squire, in a modern mansion, and in the
modern way, was a being who could not possibly have
existed under the conditions prevailing in Lanarkshire at the
date of the War of Independence in Scotland.   If there
could be no such thing as increasing culture ; if Scotland had
ceased to advance in the thirteenth century ; *all* of these
Baillies would have been " gypsies."   There would have been
no manse, and no mansion ; and, instead of the trim, sleek
ways of modern life, in the houses of the well-to-do, there
would have been the dingy, turf-built wigwam, or the rude
gypsy-tent, at one time " the common building of the country,"—without a chimney but the hole in the roof that served,
in windy weather, to blow the smoke downward into the
tent,—without any of the thousand household comforts of

* Anderson's " Scottish Nation " : name *Baillie*.

the eighteenth and nineteenth centuries,—and with the
primitive "gypsy" modes of cooking that were commonly
practised in the Scotland of earlier days.

It is not to be supposed that this divergence between the
two kinds of Baillies began at one easily-determined date ;
and that, from that period onward, the one division went
on its way "civilizing," while the other continued as steadily
to decay.   Nothing but a complete knowledge of all the
histories (not the *alleged* histories) of all the families of that
clan could enable one to realize the truth.   This is as impossible to obtain as it is superfluous.   But one can guess that,
in each generation, there was at least one conversion from
gypsydom to civilization.   Some Baillies have been "educa-
ting" themselves for centuries—others for generations only.
When Joanna Baillie's father was an inoffensive divine, Mrs.
Carlyle's ancestor was a fierce, marauding robber, a gentle-
man-of-a-very-old-school.   But it must only be necessary to
ascend Joanna Baillie's family-tree a little higher, in order to
discover that she, too, possessed forefathers of a like type to
Matthew Baillie, the "gypsy."   Even one of the best
specimens of her 'clan, Robert Baillie of Jerviswood, "the
Scottish Sidney" (a probable ancestor of Joanna Baillie),
belonged to a period when he might have lived as reckless
and wild an existence as his contemporary, Captain William
Baillie, without losing caste.   It does not require much
acquaintance with seventeenth-century ideas, to be able to
say this.   And, as a matter of fact, we know that the "distinguished gypsy" just referred to, used to associate on an
equal footing with "gentlemen of the first respectability in
the country."   And that he himself not only was a gentleman by education and in manners, but a very prince of
men : "the handsomest, the best dressed, the best looking,
and the best bred man I ever saw," says one of his local
contemporaries.   "He was considered, in his time, the best
swordsman in all Scotland :" and "his sword is still preserved
by his descendants, as a relic of their powerful ancestor."
Such a man, had he chosen, might have rivalled a Raleigh,
or a Drake : from whom he did not differ in any essential
degree.   If the eighteenth-century descendants of Drake
and Raleigh had lived as their great ancestors did—if they

had been genuine *tories*—they would have been little else than outlawed adventurers, as liable to be hanged as any "gypsy" Baillie. And, being *tories*, their way of dressing would have been that of their sixteenth-century ancestors—and of high-caste "gypsies." One reads everywhere that the gypsies wore dresses of scarlet and of green: what did the sixteenth-century Cavaliers wear? Certainly not the "sad-coloured" garments of the nineteenth century. The class that—eighty years ago—most resembled the Cavaliers, in dress—as in other traits—was assuredly our British "gypsies." When Mr. Borrow's friend, Jasper Petulengro, came in his best attire to visit the strangely-associated dwellers in "Mumpers' Dingle," he was dressed much more like a Cavalier, than any ordinary gentleman of that period: —"with a somewhat smartly-cut sporting-coat, the buttons of which were half-crowns—and a waistcoat, scarlet and black, the buttons of which were spaded half-guineas; his breeches were of a stuff half velveteen, half corduroy, the cords exceedingly broad." His shirt was of "very fine white holland." "Under his left arm was a long black whale-bone riding-whip, with a red lash, and an immense silver knob. Upon his head was a hat with a high peak, somewhat of the kind which the Spaniards call *calané*, so much in favour with the bravoes of Seville and Madrid." Among the articles of his wife's apparel was a necklace of "what seemed very much like very large pearls, somewhat tarnished, however, and apparently of considerable antiquity." She had inherited this "from her grandmother, who died at the age of a hundred and three, and sleeps in Coggeshall churchyard. She got it from her mother, who also died very old, and who could give no other account of it than that it had been in the family time out of mind."* These people when they took it into their heads to go to church, selected the (then vacant) pew of the lord of the manor as their proper place: and the fact that they could not read the

---

* Mr. Borrow's gypsy descriptions, though placed before us in a half-fictitious framing, are believed to be from life; and the eccentric doings of the "Romany Rye" are understood to be largely the experiences of the author himself. Therefore, the above quotations can be reasonably accepted as the descriptions of realities.

Prayer-Books which they held in their hands rather increases
than diminishes their affinity with the gentry of an earlier
period, who despised such attainments as only fit for
"clerics" and "scriveners." These were gypsies of *England*,
but Mr. Simson has much the same thing to say of the high-
caste gypsies of North Britain. " I have already mentioned
how handsomely the superior order of gipsies dressed at the
period of which we are speaking [more than a century ago].
The male head of the Ruthvens—a man six feet some inches
in height—who, according to the newspapers of the day,
lived to the advanced age of one hundred and fifteen years,
when in full dress, in his youth, wore a white wig, a
ruffled shirt, a blue Scottish bonnet, scarlet breeches and
waistcoat, a long blue superfine coat, white stockings,
with silver buckles in his shoes. Others wore silver
brooches in their breasts, and gold rings on their fingers."
The females of the Baillie clan "also rode to the fairs
at Moffat and Biggar, on horses, with side-saddles and
bridles, the ladies themselves being very gaily dressed. The
males wore scarlet cloaks, reaching to their knees, and
resembling exactly the Spanish fashion of the present day."*
They were also " dressed in long green coats, cocked hats,
riding-boots and spurs, armed with broadswords, and mounted
on handsome gray ponies saddled and bridled ; everything,
in short, in style, and of the best quality." Whether these
Baillies wore powdered wigs, like the Ruthven chief, is not
stated : but if they wore their natural hair only, it is likely
they wore it as the Cavaliers did. We get a hint or two
that comparatively-modern "gypsies" let their long tresses
hang down either cheek : we know that the earlier "Cavaliers" did so, tying a bright-coloured ribbon, sometimes, to a
favourite lock. "The Scottish Sidney" himself, "learned
and worthy gentleman " though he was, wore his dark, abundant hair in great masses falling down upon his shoulders—
just as a thousand of the best men of his time were accustomed to do. Had his own nature been fiercer, and had he
lived an out-door life for a few months, his general appearance
would have been quite as "barbarous "as that of the English
gypsy whom Mr. Simson saw at St. Boswell's fair. If his

* Or the Cavalier fashion of the sixteenth century.

kinsman, Captain William Baillie, was as fair of skin as some
of his descendants are pictured, a hundred years later,—
then "the Scottish Sidney" (supposing him to be of a wilder
nature than he really was) would have looked more like the
conventional "gypsy" than his redoubted cousin, the head
chief of all the "gypsies" in Scotland. For though not of
an actually *swarthy* hue, his complexion seems* to have been
rather dark than fair,—his eyes were apparently black,— and
his hair unmistakeably so. Joanna Baillie and her brother,
Dr. Matthew, though not particularly gypsy-like, yet resemble
the conventional dark gypsy, much more than do those fair-
skinned nomadic Baillies, of later times, described in the
Scottish *History*. The distinction between the two kinds of
Lanarkshire Baillies seems to have been purely one of *habit :*
there is no hint of a *racial* difference. Or if there is
(though one cannot argue from a few examples), the black-
haired individuals would appear to belong rather to the
civilized than to the predatory section.

This leads one to consider, in passing, the question of
gypsy *colour*. The statements made by the Messrs. Simson
(though not necessarily the theories deduced therefrom),
with regard to the Scottish gypsies of the last two centuries,
must always be accounted as of great value. In their book,
we get glimpses of an archaic state of society which no one
else has so fully described ; and which it is probably too late
for any one to attempt to investigate now, when gypsydom
is only "the shadow of a shade." It seems certain that, but
for this book, many valuable facts would have been wholly
lost. But, to turn to this question of the complexion of the
Scottish gypsies, it is plain that neither of these gentlemen
had very clearly formulated their ideas respecting the ethnological position of the people they wrote about. We are
told of the dark skin as being a gypsy feature, and that their
name for "us" (the general, sedentary population of these
islands, popularly assumed to be white people, though scien-
tifically asserted to be mostly *dark-white* people, or *Melano-*

---

* This is only based upon the woodcut in Anderson's "Scottish Nation";
but as the portraits in that work are carefully executed, and show the light and
shade sufficiently well, it is probable that an inspection of the original painting
would not contradict the above statements.

chroi) is *gorgio* (in the plural *gorgios*), or "white man:"
"gorgio-like" being rendered "like the white." But, in the
same book, we are told that there are pure "gypsies," who
are perfectly white people. For instance, we read such a
description as this, which is of a Fifeshire family:—"Not
one of the whole party could have been taken for a gipsy,
but all had the exact appearance of being the family of
some indigent tradesman or labourer. Excepting the
woman, whose hair was dark, all of the company had hair of
a light colour, some of them inclining to yellow, with fair
complexions. In not one of their countenances could be
seen those features by which many pretend the gypsies can,
at all times, be distinguished from the rest of the community.
The manner, however, in which the woman at first addressed
me created in my mind a suspicion that she was one of the
tribe."* The test applied was the putting a question in that
particular form of speech commonly used by such people;
and this family being accustomed to speak in that fashion
are, thereafter, conclusively *gipsies* in the estimation of
their interlocutor. Other such examples might be cited, but
this is enough to show the catholic nature of the term
"gipsy," as that word is used by the principal historian of
these people in Scotland. The vagueness of his creed is
seen in a single sentence (p. 341), relative to this subject:
"This question of colour has been illustrated in my enquiry
into the history of the gipsy language; for the language is
the only satisfactory thing by which to test a gipsy, let his
colour be what it may." Now, if there is one thing about
which there is more unanimity than about another, at the
present day, it is this, that language is the *least* satisfactory
thing by which to ascertain the ethnological position of a
people. Curiously enough, a most apt illustration of the
truth of this is furnished by Mr. Simson, the younger, who,
in his introduction, points out that an implicit belief in the
identity between language and race would lead one "to
maintain that the Negroes in Liberia originated in England
because they speak the English language."

A few pages back the Baillies and other Midlothian gypsies
of this century were spoken of as "in general, of a colour

* "History of the Gipsies," p. 299.

rather cadaverous, or of a darkish pale ; their cheek-bones high ; their eyes small, and light coloured ; their hair of a dingy white or red colour, and wiry ; and their skin, drier and of a tougher texture than that of the people of this country." This was quoted by Mr. Simson from a local account. On reflection this description seems of little value. It refers to a single generation (of the year 1839) of at least three families—Baillies, Wilsons, and Taits—in one parish of Mid-Lothian ; to any one of whom these physical peculiarities might be said to belong ; and there is no good reason why we should hold this representation as descriptive of the seventeenth and eighteenth century Baillie chiefs. If any of these Mid-Lothian Baillies of 1839 had inherited some drops of the blood of that line, it is quite evident that none of the good looks of the family had come down to them. Of the civilized branches, the three members who have been particularised—Robert Baillie of Jerviswood, Joanna Baillie, and her brother Dr. Matthew Baillie—are comely-featured people, Miss Baillie being, indeed, handsome. Of the *tory* division, its most celebrated representative, William Baillie, has already been referred to as one of the best-looking men of his day ; and it is said of his grandson, Matthew (son of Matthew Baillie and Mary Yorstoun, and one of the four heroes at Biggar Fair), that he " married Margaret Campbell, and had by her a family of remarkably handsome and pretty daughters." It is idle, however, to attempt to show that handsome features belonged peculiarly to that Baillie line : and it may easily be that the " remarkably handsome and pretty daughters " of the younger Matthew had inherited their good looks through the mother, Margaret Campbell. But this, at least, may be said, that if " Captain " William Baillie, who died in 1724, was as white of skin and as golden-haired as the Fifeshire " gypsies " just referred to, he was—being " the handsomest man," etc.—a very good specimen of the ideal aristocrat of the Norman era (a type of man whose existence in Western Europe may be vastly more ancient than that period), possessing, as he did, many of the chief characteristics of that extinct form of " gentleman." In his day the *cavalier* was still *chivalrous* (as many stories of him show). The declination of his kind of men had just begun.

A man could be a "gypsy" chief and yet, on the whole, as good a "gentleman" as most of his civilized brethren. Therefore, it is pleasant to think of this "splendid gypsy" as the descendant of one of the most courageous figures in history; and as, at the same time, the chief (by primogeniture) of another celebrated line. For it is pretty evident that the acknowledged head of all his tribe was the most probable seventeenth-eighteenth-century representative of the son-in-law of Wallace, William Baillie of Hoprig and Lamington. Which view is quite supported by the history of these estates; apparently often owned by junior and female members of the family: in the latter cases, the surname being artificially continued.

To recognize, however, that there are or were "gypsies" who did not, in the least, resemble the conventional dark-skinned "Egyptian," is to make a very important admission, with regard to which much might be said. For the present, then, the complexion of the gypsy Baillies need not be entertained. It is enough to point out that this redoubtable clan, like other Scotch-gypsy tribes already glanced at, possess several indications of an immemorial connection with Scotland. But as it would appear that the date of their supremacy over the robber-tribes was vastly later than that of other—and dark-skinned—clans, it will be better to defer the consideration of any other white-skinned "gypsies," and rather turn to those who were *Mauri* as well as *Picti*.

CHAPTER III.

THE supreme ruler of Alban during one portion of the tenth century was, we have been told, Kenneth (or Cinaed) *alias* "Niger" or "Dubh,"—"The Black." He seems to have reigned for some years over "white" provinces, as well as those inhabited by people of his own colour; but he is particularised as "*The Black,*—of the three black divisions." The names of these divisions,—"kingdoms," they were then called,—are given us in Gaelic, "the language of the white men," and in Latin. Being thus given, they tell us as little of the designations given to these kingdoms, by their own inhabitants, as do the words *Australia* or *Patagonia* inform us of the language of the aborigines; or the names which *they* give to their country, or to their kings. We have guessed that one division of the posterity of this powerful black king, of the tenth century, became known to Gaelic-speaking people as *Maga Dubh* (shortened into Mac Duff), or "the clan of The Black:" which race was for a long time paramount in the kingdom of Fibh (Fife)—itself, in all probability, one of "the three black divisions." And we noticed that, so recently as Queen Mary's time, a descendant of this clan (though bearing a different surname) was one of the ruling class in that district; and when spoken of was particularised as "black." And, further, that those of the natives of Fife who—two centuries after the death of Queen Mary—still continued to follow the fierce, marauding habits, and to display the haughty, overbearing disposition of the early "noble," were to be found among the confederacy of swarthy "gypsies," known as "the Lochgellie band:" who were precisely the kind of "gypsies" that their historian has in mind, when he dilates upon "the presumptuous pride, the overweening conceit of a high-mettled Scottish gipsy; his boasted descent—a descent at once high, illustrious, and lost in antiquity ; his unbounded contempt for the rabble of town and country." And, as the earlier Pictish language was un-intelligible to the Gaels and to the Normans, so the speech of those eighteenth-century Picts was described as " gibberish " and " jargon," by the civilized and modernized portion of the community.

The life of those painted Moors, or faws, therefore, has never been specially described until recent times. Or only described from the outside. The names by which their kings are remembered show this. Such names as that by which " Niger of the three black divisions " is generally known are purely *outside* names, or nick-names, given by another people. Kenneth, or Cinaed, when analysed, seems to mean nothing more than *The King,*—or, possibly, *The Chief of the race of Aedh.* At any rate, the *Cinaed vel Dubh* who reigned from 962 to 967, was succeeded by his own brother, also named Kenneth ; which seems to show that the name was more a designation than an individual cognomen : and that it be-longed to the occupier of a certain position, for the time being. This particular Niger would thus be *the* Black, in the sense that his chief rival was *the* White, and *the* Whelp ;—or as their contemporary, *Dubdon Satrapas Athochlach,* was *the* Black-Brown, Satrap of Athole ;—or as the chief of the Moraymen was *Dobharcu, the* Otter. The most notable of all those who bore this appellation of Kenneth, Kynadius, Kinat, or Cinaed,* was assuredly the son of Alpin who, " was the first king of the Scots who acquired the monarchy of the whole of Alban, and ruled in it over the Scots." This was in the year 844, " the twelfth year of Kenneth's reign, and the Chronicle of Huntingdon tells us that ' in his twelfth year Kenneth encountered the Picts seven times in one day, and having destroyed many, confirmed the kingdom to himself.' "†
Thus, by the year 844, " the black herds of Scots and Picts,

---

* A son of this Cin-aed, who reigned over the Picts for one year (877-8), was known as Aed, or Aedh. And the name is frequently introduced in Mr. Skene's last book. It is quite likely an appellative name, translateable into some such expression as " The Foreigner " or " The Moor." Generally, it is translated " Hugh·" ; but " Hugh " must have signified something, at one time. It is also, more rarely, rendered "king."
† "Celtic Scotland," Vol. I. pp. 308 321, 366

somewhat different in manners, but all alike thirsting for blood," had completely fallen out among themselves, and the former had conquered the latter. To use their alternative titles—the vagabond " Egyptians " had overcome the painted " blackamoors." The latter, it is believed, were half-exterminated ; though the year 844 did not put an end to the reign of *Picts* in Scotland. From that date, however, the customs of the Egyptians [*Scots Proper*] must have been paramount for a considerable time, in certain parts of North Britain.

Whatever the genealogy of this conquering Cinaed (and he is said to have descended from Swarthy Conall, son of Yellow Eochaid), he had apparently ruled over the Galloway district before attaining the supreme power. One writer (not of Mr. Skene's calibre, but at least the recorder of a tradition) states that " in 850, Kenneth was thane of Carrick." And he adds that " in that district and in Galloway [which really included " that district " at one time], where the Kennedys had, at one time, extensive possessions, the surname Kennedy is to this day pronounced Kennettie."* From which we see that the name of Kenneth, or Kynadius, or Cinaed, has come down to us in the form of Kennedy, as well as in that of Kenneth : (and that the *earliest* Kenneths and Kennedys were probably of the same stock as the race named MacDuff). The Clan of Kennedy, the son of Alpin, of the stock of Swarthy Conall and Tawny Eochaid, were thus the kings of Carrick a thousand years ago. They remained so for a long time. Scott tells† us that " the name of Kennedy held so great a sway [in that district] as to give rise to the popular. rhyme,—

> ''Twixt Wigton and the town of Air,
> Portpatrick and the Cruives of Cree,
> No man need think for to bide there,
> Unless he court Saint Kennedie.'"

This district—the south-western corner of Scotland—remained, therefore, under the dominion of the race of Kennedy from the middle of the ninth century onward to very recent times : the designation of the first Kennedy, Cinaed, or Kenneth, becoming gradually fossilized, in that quarter, into

* Anderson's " Scottish Nation," Vol. II. p. 600.
† In his preface to " The Ayrshire Tragedy."

a tribal name.   The chiefs of those south-western Kennedys
from 840–850 onward, were styled (it is stated) Thanes, or
Kings of Carrick.   A title, rooted so far down, naturally
became overshadowed in course of time by the later creations
of an incoming and successful Norman power,—until, at
length, the Chiefs of those Kennedys were only remembered
locally as Kings of Carrick.   So lately as the dawn of the
seventeenth century the holder of this position was known as
" King of Carrick ; " although there had only been one legitimate kingship in Scotland for several generations prior to
that.   The King of Carrick who preceded this one just
referred to, is chiefly remembered by an act that reveals his
ferocious nature.   His attitude is best understood and defended, by bearing in mind that he held his lands—or *believed*
that he held them—by right of a conquest preceding that of
the Normans by four or five centuries : and that, therefore,
deeds and grants proceeding from a race that did not come
into power till the fourteenth century were only respected by
him when it suited his arrangements.   We are told that,
"after he had, by forgery and murder, possessed himself of
the abbacy of Glenluce, he cast his eye on Crossraguel,"—a
neighbouring abbacy.   Securing the person of the Commendator of that Abbey, he conveyed him to his castle of Dunure ;
the earliest stronghold of the Kennedy chiefs.   In order to
compel him to sign a feu charter conveying the Crossraguel
lands to him—(the King of Carrick)—this savage chief caused
his servants " to convey the commendator to the ' black vault
of Dunure,' where a large fire was blazing, under a grit iron
chimblay.' "   " He then presented to him certain documents
to sign, and, on his refusal, he commanded ' his cooks,' says
the annalist, ' to prepare the banquet,' and so, first, they
stripped the unhappy commendator, to his ' sark and doublet,'
and next they bound him to the chimney, ' his legs to the one
end and his arms to the other,' basting him well with oil, that
' the roast should not burn.'   When nearly half roasted he
consented to subscribe the documents, without reading or
knowing what was contained in them."   "And thus the earl
obtained, in the indignant words of the describer of the scene,
' a fyve yeare tack ' [lease] and a 19 yeare tack, and a charter
of feu of all the landis of Croceraguall, with the clausses

necessaire for the erle to haist him to hell. For gif adulterie, sacriledge, oppressione, barbarous creweltie, and thift heaped upon thift diserve hell, the great king of Carrick can no more eschape hell for ever nor the imprudent abbott eschaped the fyre for a seasoune.' "

John Kennedy, the son and successor of this King of Carrick, was not very different in nature from his father. He "is remarkable chiefly for the slaughter of Gilbert Kennedy of Bargany." The Bargany branch was only second in importance to the Kings of Carrick themselves, and a constant vendetta seems to have been pursued, between these two septs. Hearing that the Bargany chief was about to go from Ayr to his house on the water of Girvan, with only a small following, the King of Carrick, attended by two hundred armed men "took his station at the Lady Corse, about half a mile north of Maybole." (This was in the year 1601.) Bargany soon appeared "at the Brochloch, on the opposite side of the valley ;" but, when he saw the strength of the enemy, he "said to his men that he desired no quarrel, and accordingly led them down the left bank of the rivulet by Bogside, with the view of avoiding a collision." But his relentless foe "followed down the south side, and coming to some 'feal dykes,' which offered a good support for the fire-arms of his followers, he ordered them to discharge their pieces at Bargany and his men." Thus brought to bay, Bargany and his few followers fought with great courage, but he and two of them were killed. One of those who escaped —Mure of Auchindrane, the brother-in-law of the slain chief,—then set about plotting an act of revenge. This was consummated a few months later, the victim being the guardian of the King of Carrick (during his minority) and the actors being Mure and another of his name, along with the brother of the slain Kennedy, and five or six followers. These, having waylaid this kinsman of the King of Carrick, "assaulted and cruelly murdered him with many wounds. They then plundered the dead corpse of his purse, containing a thousand merks in gold, cut off the gold buttons which he wore on his coat, and despoiled the body of some valuable rings and jewels." So the vendetta went on. During the same year, the King of Carrick bribed his brother, Hugh

Kennedy of Browns'-town, "commonly called the master of Cassillis," by the promise of a yearly payment, to undertake the murder of Mure, the ringleader of his enemies. But this villain, after skulking about the west country for several years, and committing at least one more murder, was finally beheaded at Edinburgh, and his lands forfeited.*

These two Kings of Carrick seem to have been examples of atavism, or "throw-back," upon the most savage line of their ancestry. For their immediate predecessors, and successors, were men of a much higher quality. It is because they were, in disposition, true representatives of that "Egyptian" Kennedy, or Cinaed, who, in the year 844, "encountered the Picts seven times in one day, and having destroyed many, confirmed the kingdom to himself," that I have preferred to regard them under the title which he and they were known by—that of "King of Carrick." But the Cinaed of the year 1509 had received a new title from King James the Fourth of Scotland ; one of whose advisers he was, and with whose ancestors his own forefathers had intermarried. The new title he received was not "Earl of Carrick ;" because his family were not recognized as thanes of that territory by the Stewart power. "Earl of Carrick" was a Norman creation, and had been borne by Bruces and Stewarts, through whom it became a title of the Prince of Scotland (and, on the erection of the new monarchy of 1603, of the eldest son of the reigning British monarch). Accordingly, the Early-Scottish Kings or Thanes of Carrick, became, in 1509, the Norman-Scotch "Earls of Cassillis,"—that name being taken from one of their possessions in Carrick. But, though nominal Earls of Cassillis, those two occupiers of that position, who have just been glanced at ; with their miserable clan-fights, their murders from behind "feal-dykes," and by hired assassins : their constant petty jealousies and wranglings, their treacherous robberies of land and goods, their "adulterie, sacriledge, oppressione, barbarous creweltie, and thift heaped upon thift," were in no way worthy of being regarded as noblemen and statesmen, but only as (what they were) the chiefs of a tribe of sixteenth-century Egyptians, or Scots Proper,—the kind

* See Anderson's "Scottish Nation," Vol. I. p. 604 ; and Sir Walter Scott's Preface to "The Ayrshire Tragedy."

of people that the Stewart kings, and the best portion of their countrymen, were endeavouring to put down by enactments of the severest kind. If these two Kings of Carrick ever did figure in a higher attitude, it was because they could not wholly evade the duties of their rank. But in nature they were truculent " Egyptians ; " and, *for that reason*, they ought to be regarded under their popular and traditional title. For, it must be remembered, they were not the actual possessors of the whole of the large district of Carrick. Their "kingship" had faded away long ago : though they were still called " kings." By the latter part of the sixteenth century—the date of these incidents—there was only one real king in the whole of Scotland. Those Kennedys were neither kings nor earls of Carrick : they were only the earls of Cassillis. But the first man ever distinguished by their name was King of the *Scots* of Carrick—then a race of conquerors. And, if those Kennedys were his descendants, they too were Kings of the *Scots* of Carrick,—by right of blood. But the Scots, as a distinct people, had long ago been overcome. The Scots of that very district of Carrick were those naked warriors, who, in the beginning of the fourteenth-century, had assailed the new Earl of Carrick, Robert Bruce, at the crossing of one of their own rivers : and, assailing, they had been vanquished. And, as in this one instance, so throughout Scotland. The early kingdoms of Picts, Scoto-Picts, Scots, and Black-Danes, gave way before the advance of the national Scottish movement, initiated (though not for the first time) by Wallace and Bruce : the motive power of which was newer, and better, than that of the early Scots. From the time that the Norman Earl of Carrick gained the Scottish throne, the decay of the Scots of Carrick had begun. And, by the close of the sixteenth-century, their power was fast approaching its end. The best part of the various races of Scotland had, by this time, become welded into one nation : and the Nationalists would not tolerate the survival of ancient sovereignties and barbarous usages (though these had really formed the foundation of the new system). Statutes were framed every year with the aim of wholly stamping out those expiring kingships ; and the system of force and oppression upon which they were

based. Scotland was, in short, becoming "respectable."
By the year 1612, the modernized and hybrid Scots of the
Borders who were distinguished by that name (Scott), finally
agreed to repudiate those of their kindred who came under
the designation of "common thieves and broken clans." By
the year 1662, civilized Scotchmen spoke of the "Scots" and
"mossers" as criminals and outlaws : as "felons—commonly
known, or called by the name of moss-troopers : " as murderers and thieves : as "gypsies."* Therefore, although it had
been once necessary for those living in the modern county
of Wigtown, and the south of Ayrshire, to "court Saint
Kennedie,"—in other words, to acknowledge the Kennedy
supremacy,—that supremacy became less and less felt as the
power of the Norman-Scottish Kings became consolidated.
And when the last of these kings became the first king of
United Britain, the blows dealt against such threadbare
"kingships," as that of the Scots of Carrick, were rapid and
decisive : resulting, as just observed, in the general outlawry
of all who followed the customs of the Early Scots. With
this effect, among others, that the threefold use of the term
"Scot" (as distinguishing the general Scottish nation,—the
mixed clan of "Scott,"—and the "mossers" of the south of
Scotland), became contracted so as to bear only two meanings,—the designation of all North Britons, and of "Scott"
families. While the marauding *Scot* became known chiefly
by the name he had apparently always given to himself, the
name of *Egyptian.*

Consequently, the "kingship" exercised by the Kennedys
over the district of Western Galloway was the kingship of its
"Egyptians," or "gypsies." But it was a kingship that had
been one of a genuine kind. And, just as the Earl of Angus
was admitted by the ruling party to have inherited the right
of leading the van of the Scottish army (he being nominal

---

* Simson's "History," pp. 113, 201, note ; and Scott's introduction to "The
Minstrelsy." The identity of "thieves" with "gypsies" has already been
shown. For example, when the chief of the Annandale Johnstones (*gypsies*) was
hanged at Dumfries—about the year 1733—it was necessary that the execution
should take place in front of the prison, and under the protection of a strong
guard, because it was reported that "the *thieves* were collecting from all quarters"
to effect a rescue. And it may be remembered that the severe statutes, formerly
quoted, were enacted against "common thieves, *commonly called Egyptians.*"

leader of the *dubh-glasses*, Moors, or Picts of Galloway, after the overthrow and outlawry of the real chiefs) so was the kingship of Carrick—quite an independent thing from the *ownership* of all that territory—held to be vested in that Kennedy line. In acknowledgment of which, the eighth Earl of Cassillis received the sum of eighteen hundred pounds in the year 1747, as compensation for the quasi-regal power possessed by his line ; which power was abolished, with all others of that nature throughout Scotland, by the Act of Parliament passed in that year—for the purpose of preventing a second Culloden.

But the Earls of Cassillis—considered as such—were in the position of the Earls of Angus. In each case the substantial privileges of the line were possessed by the nominal representative of the man who had gained those privileges. But in the Angus case (at least) the nominal head of that line was only a *dubh-glass* in a very slight degree. The real, inveterate *dubh-glasses*—the main stem of the tree—were underfoot. In such a case, family honours, or those of a royal dynasty, do not utterly lapse, until there is no one left to claim them—a rare circumstance. But it often happens—and, plainly, in the Douglas instance it did happen—that the oldest wearers of the title have to give place to those in whom the claim of blood is less strong, or wholly absent. That this had been gradually happening in the case of the Kennedy chiefs, seems clear from the records of their marriages ; and also from the characteristics of most of these chiefs, within historical times. For the two Kings of Carrick, who have been sketched, were quite exceptional Earls of Cassillis. Either that portion of the pedigree is at fault, or else they were, as suggested, reproductions of their earlier marauding Scot-Egyptian ancestors—those "shameless Irish robbers" who desolated the civilized portions of Early Britain. At any rate, the latter of these two was the last Earl of Cassillis who was a " King of Carrick "—in the earliest sense.

Who it was that took up the kingship of the Carrick Egyptians, when their nominal leaders rose to the higher duties of Scottish nobles,—cannot easily be ascertained. It is curious to notice that the Cassillis-Egyptian connection did not cease altogether with the death of the last " King of

Carrick." It was the wife of his successor, the sixth earl who eloped with the Faw leader, celebrated in the ballad. This event took place about the middle of the seventeenth century. But the lineage of the Countess's lover, John the Faw, has never been ascertained. It is important to notice how full of "gypsy" memories this Cassillis neighbourhood is.* The ford near the castle is called "the gypsies' steps :" and, from the word "steps," one may guess that it is not so much a ford as a crossing,—formed by large stones, placed at intervals,—a kind of crossing that antiquaries agree in ascribing to "Ancient Britons." Moreover, Cassillis is situated in the parish of Kirkmichael, and it was in that parish that the famous leader of the Galloway Picts of the eighteenth century was born,—"about the year 1671." And there was nothing in his history at variance with his birthplace. Because he was *specially* the King of the Scots of Carrick. The district that was particularly connected with one of his titles—"The Caird of Barullion "—lies in the south-eastern corner of Carrick, between "Portpatrick and the Cruives of Cree." He was more than King of the eighteenth-century Scots of Carrick : he was King of all the Scots and Picts in Galloway (of which Carrick is—or was—a part). And though Barullion was his most notable retreat,—he was (as Mactaggart tells us) almost as much in his own country when haunting the wilds of Cairns-moor, that lie to the south-east of the Cruives of Cree. While the extent of the territory over which he ranged—*sorning* for weeks at a time on the country lairds—was only limited by the limits of Galloway. Barullion, his peculiar haunt,—Kirkcudbright, the place of his burial,—and Kirk-michael, the place of his birth—denote, by their far-separated positions, the wideness of the territory over which he exercised

---

* And, therefore, of "black" memories. The district of Carrick teems with "black" localities, some of which have been previously given. Moors'-town, Morris-town, Dubh-glass-town, are in the centre of the Kennedy country ; and such names as these abound in the neighbourhood—Dunduff (the Black Dun), Craigdow (the Black Craig), Dalduff (the Black Dale), Blackdales (another form of the preceding) ; while there are very many Black Burns, Black Lochs, and Black Craigs. The Devils' Dyke, or Picts' Dyke (and, therefore, the Moors', Blacks', Carrs', or Grims' Dyke), crosses the south of Carrick from west to east and there is another Black Dyke at its northern boundary, besides a stretch of marsh, called Airds' Moss.

a certain kind of influence. And the closing years of his life (sufficiently enlarged upon, already) have shown us something of the peculiar rank he held. Whatever his connection with the seventeenth-century Kennedys, this man had all the characteristics of a king of the Galloway Scots.

Though holding the hereditary position of Kings of the Scots of Carrick, and showing—in two notable instances—the fierce disposition of that race, the Kennedys of Cassillis may have had little of the Early-Scottish blood. They may have had as little of the "gypsy" in them as some of Mr. Simson's scarcely-to-be-recognized "gypsies": (such as Wilson of Stirlingshire). But though the *Cassillis* Kennedys ceased to be "gypsies," it was not so with all of their name. "The Battle of the Bridge" at Hawick, fought in 1772-3, was between Kennedys and Ruthvens on the one side, and Taits and Gordons on the other. Like that Kennedy of Bargany who was shot at from behind a "feal dyke," in the previous century, the chief of the Kennedys in this fight was "a handsome and athletic man." He is placed, in rank, as above all of his party, including his own father-in-law, "the Earl of Hell." "Battle" is rather a large name to give to this struggle, though no battle could have been fought more desperately. And most of the weapons used were only bludgeons, though some of the Kennedys' foes were armed with cutlasses, and other deadly weapons. Like their predecessors —the *druidesses* ("witches," or "female gypsies") of Anglesey —the women of either party fought as savagely as the men: the chieftainess, Jean Kennedy, being slashed all over with cutlass-strokes. It is stated that every one of the combatants "except Alexander Kennedy, the brave chief, was severely wounded ; and that the ground on which they fought was wet with blood." Curiously enough, this battle was not decisive, although all of Kennedy's followers were beaten from the field, which he himself would not desert. "Posting himself on the narrow bridge of Hawick, he defended himself in the defile, with his bludgeon, against the whole of his infuriated enemies. His handsome person, his undaunted bravery, his extraordinary dexterity in handling his weapon, and his desperate situation (for it was evident to all that the Taits thirsted for his blood, and were determined to despatch him on the spot), excited a general and lively interest in his favour, among the inhabitants of the town, who were present, and had witnessed the conflict with amazement and horror. In one dash to the front, and with one powerful sweep of his cudgel, he disarmed two of the Taits, and cutting a third to the skull, felled him to the ground. He sometimes daringly advanced upon his assailants, and drove the whole band before him, pell-mell. When he broke one cudgel on his enemies, by his powerful arm, the townspeople were ready to hand him another. Still, the vindictive Taits rallied, and renewed the charge with unabated vigour ; and every one present expected that Kennedy would fall a sacrifice to their desperate fury. A party of messengers and constables at last arrived to his relief, when the Taits were all apprehended, and imprisoned ; but, as none of the gipsies were actually slain in the fray, they were soon set at liberty."

" The hostile bands, a short time afterwards, came in contact in Ettrick Forest, at a place on the water of Teema, called Deephope. They did not, however, engage here ; but the females on both sides, at some distance from one another, with a stream between them, scolded and cursed, and, clapping their hands, urged the males again to fight. The men, however, more cautious, only observed a sullen and gloomy silence at this meeting. . . . . In the course of a few days, they again met in Eskdale Moor, when a second desperate conflict ensued. The Taits were here completely routed, and driven from the district, in which they had attempted to travel by force."

" The country people were horrified at the sight of the wounded Tinklers, after these sanguinary engagements. Several of them, lame and exhausted, in consequence of the severity of their numerous wounds, were, by the assistance of their tribe, carried through the country on the backs of asses ; so much were they cut up in their persons. Some of them, it was said, were slain outright, and never more heard of. . . . . These battles were talked of for thirty miles around the country. I have heard old people speak of them, with fear and wonder at the fierce, unyielding disposition of the wilful and vindictive Tinklers."*

* Simson's "History," pp. 190–193.

These rather long extracts have been made with the purpose of showing those who have not read Mr. Simson's graphic descriptions, the exact nature of those tribal wars. And the sanguinary engagements of these eighteenth-century Kennedys do not differ, *in essence*, from those of their forefathers of the previous centuries by a single hair's-breadth. Kennedy of Bargany, keeping the stream between him and his foes, because they were in greater force, or Kennedy of Cassillis, firing at Bargany and his men from behind the shelter of a " feal dyke," are only prototypes of Alexander Kennedy and his vindictive enemies, the Taits, at the Bridge of Hawick, or on either side the water of Teema. There is no real difference between the two sets of men. The Kennedys of the sixteenth century where they were pure Scots, were *dubh-glasses*, or men of swarthy skin : all of them, except the very chiefs, lived in turf-covered, conical wigwams, and " gypsy" tents—" the common building of their country :" they cooked their food as " gypsies " : their superstitions, legends, and manners were those of " gypsies " : they *were* " gypsies." The only distinction between the men of the two periods is one of degree. By the eighteenth century the savage, high-handed ideas of those robber races were almost wholly out of fashion ; and the men who persisted in putting them into practice became degraded outlaws. Before their day the better qualities of their race had floated away from its most inveterate section, and were turned to higher and *national* uses. But the Kennedys, and such-like, of the sixteenth and those of the eighteenth centuries are almost identical. And, in either case, the forces of order eventually interfere, and measure out punishment to those offenders against civilization. In either scene there is a background of quiet, undemonstrative spectators,—" the country people " and " the town's people "—people who do not particularly care for bullying and cutting throats,—people who may possibly be styled poltroons and cowards ; but who, *from their very avoidance of warfare*, have necessarily been the progenitors of the great majority of our present population. And although it is " a far cry " from the ninth century to the eighteenth, and there is little light in those dim regions to guide us, it is by no means improbable that the men who wrote down the wars

H 2

of the *Scots and Picts*,—who tell us how the gypsy Kennedy of the year 844 "encountered the *Faws* seven times in one day, and having destroyed many, confirmed the kingdom to himself,"—were as little akin to those Kennedys and Faws as are many of our living "gypsy" writers to the people they write about.

CHAPTER IV.

IN speaking of "gypsies," however, one must discriminate. The greatest family of all the Scottish gypsies, says Mr. Simson, is that of Baillie. And the Baillies are white men : as their reputed ancestor, Baliol, King of Scotland, pretty surely was. Nevertheless, although more than one gypsiologist indicates that pure " gypsies " may be out-and-out white men, yet it is beyond question that the generally-accepted representative of that type of man is black-eyed, black-haired, swarthy-skinned. If we do not now say, like Penn, "as *black* as a gypsy," we at least say "as *dark* as a gypsy." And this—the main body of the class—is' divided by Mr. Leland into two distinct sections : the one straight-haired, the other curly-haired ; " the two indicating not a difference resulting from white admixture, but entirely different original stocks."

Those of us who are dark-whites, therefore, may represent —in a partial degree—either of these stocks ; or both. (" Represent," only,—because the British population has so long been mingled that, as already stated, dark-whites and fair-whites are, often enough, brothers : and, while the dark brother is the modified *representative* of a swarthy ancestor, his fair-skinned brother is equally that ancestor's *descendant*.) Accordingly, any dark-white—or any man owning a dark-skinned, or black-haired progenitor cannot be regarded as altogether *not* akin to the conventional "gypsy ; " whether of the ninth century or of the nineteenth. But it is probable that the men who wrote about the " *black* herds of Scots and Picts," and who designated the latter division, "nimble *blackamoors* " (as Claudian did), were themselves of almost—or wholly—white stock.

Whether the whites of Britain were always in the majority may be questioned. A mere handful of successful invaders

—being successful—might kill off the earlier races in great numbers: at first, in open warfare, and latterly by passing laws which awarded death to all those practising the religion and customs of the conquered people. Thus, although the British Islands, at the present day, contain many millions of fair-whites, and not a single pure black (of British descent), this fact does not predicate a similar distribution of colour at —say—the date of the Norman Conquest. At any rate, whatever the date of its ascendancy, and whatever the mode, it is clear that the white race (or races) gained the victory, *physically*, over the black. This is seen in the greater numbers of the former, at this time ; in certain words which make "black" a term of reproach or contempt ; and in the fact that the modern British tone is *white*. (Since the swarthiest Modern-Briton will talk of the Chinese as "yellow men," without reflecting that he himself is much darker than a Chinaman.) This *physical* ascendancy may, or may not, be the result of a white conquest. If the quasi-white conquerors of India—or, rather, if those of them now living in that Dependency—were to become wholly isolated from all other white races for five hundred years, the rulers of India in the twenty-fourth century might call themselves " British," and might speak something very like the present English speech, but the chances are that they would have lost many of the physical traits that now distinguish them. Indeed, this future ruling caste might be largely, or altogether, composed of one or other of the native races that at present occupy a subordinate position. Not by any sudden political movement, but by the bloodless victory that time and numbers bring about. An example of which we saw not very long ago, when an Indian Juarez ruled over the whole country that a semi-white race had conquered only three centuries earlier. What has' happened in Mexico may easily happen in the India of the future,* or may have happened in the Britain of the past. A conquering race—white or black—may gain a temporary ascendancy ; but, if numerically weak, it will certainly become quite lost in the subject race, in course of time ; if the latter be not exterminated, or diminished by violence.

* So long as India remains a dependency of this country it will not, of course, form a case in point.

But, whether the victory was political or physical, the prevailing British tone, at the present day, is *white*. And this too, was the tone of the educated men, in remote centuries, who have been quoted. Therefore, there are grounds for believing that the historians of " gypsies "—then and now—need not themselves be regarded as much akin (if at all) to the fierce, swarthy races they describe. Not although those races were actually the temporary rulers of the country.

" Gypsy " has, however, been used in its conventional sense,—in the last two or three paragraphs. That is, it has been taken to denote a dusky, black-eyed, black-haired people. But "gypsy" seems capable of infinite dissection. The royal Lochgellie, Fifeshire gypsies, hold their heads (or once did) above all other gypsies in their neighbourhood. These again were made up of layer under layer, each of which may represent a separate phase of history, and of race. And over-lording all the heterogeneous mass of conventional, dark-skinned gypsies, there is (in Scotland) the ruling caste of the Baillies—who are whites.

As these Baillies are apparently no other than the Norman Balliols, it seems unnecessary to call them "gypsies." Being Normans, they were certainly not *Egyptians*. Their supremacy is of a much more recent date than that of any Scot or Pict. The Baillie chiefs look down with the greatest contempt upon the dusky Pictish tribes that their ancestors subdued. The date of the Baillie supremacy is the date of the Norman Conquest, and the "gypsy" Baillies are stunted Normans. To admit this is to take the first step toward ascertaining the "gypsy" pedigrees, which are manifold and various.

There is thus really nothing—on consideration—to connect this tribe with the black-eyed, black-skinned sections of the "gypsy" classes ; the naked Picts of history. No kinship, that is to say. The common bond of outlawry has placed them all on the same level in the eyes of the Moderns ; and it is possible that, in course of time, they have also occasionally forgotten the restrictions of caste. But the pure *tory* Baillie is simply the embodiment of certain phases of the character of the Norman chief. The distinction between him (at his best ; not nowadays—when, if he exists,* it is as a poverty-stricken outcast,) and his kinsman, the civilized Baillie, is the difference between the meaning of the adjectives *cavalier* and *chivalrous*. Both have the same origin, but they have come to denote very different attributes.

After all, then, we do not get very far back by examining the Baillie lineage : if we want to learn more, we must look at the tribes that underlie them. These are really all comprehended under the denomination *Faws*. Or, at least, they ought to be.

The habitat of the Faws (so-called, latterly,) is delineated by Mr. Simson in these words : " It would appear that the district in which the Faw tribe commonly travelled comprehended East-Lothian, Berwickshire and Roxburghshire ; and that Northumberland was also part of their walk. " He adds—" I can find no traces of gipsies, of that surname, having, in families, traversed the midland or western parts of the south of Scotland, for nearly the last seventy years ; and almost all the few ancient public documents relative to this clan seem to imply that they occupied the counties above mentioned." As the statement of a man who has preserved a great deal of most valuable information, regarding the lapsed classes of Scotland,—information which was the result of close personal observation,—this statement has a certain value. But, unfortunately, it does not reach very far back. The name of the *faw kirk*, beside the *graemes' town*, in the fens of what is now Stirlingshire, indicates the presence of the Faws in that district also; which, from many other sources, we are aware was once Pictish territory. In fact, wherever the word *fah* signified " of various colours," there were the painted " gypsy " classes denominated " Faws." Moreover, we know that the " Moors " of Galloway were *Picts* up till the very close of the eighteenth century. It is possible that such ruddled tribes as those of Galloway were not painted " of various colours," and, therefore, were not *Faws* : (though

* Although the Scottish Gypsies are spoken of in these pages in the present tense, the remarks made with regard to them ought to be held to apply to the period at which the elder Simson wrote. An examination of any vestiges that may yet remain of Scottish Gypsydom would, in all probability, show that little is left of those characteristics and of that state of society which Mr. Simson described.

it has, hitherto, seemed scarcely necessary to make this distinction between the two terms). Be this as it may, it is clear that the *Faws* were not confined to the district limited by Mr. Simson.

The territory marked out by their historian as that within which the reigning Faws exercised jurisdiction includes the counties of Haddington, Roxburgh, Berwick, and Northumberland. There is no doubt that the last of these was distinctly a Faw district. Francis Heron, the Faw king who died in 1756, was buried at Jarrow, on the southern shore of the Tyne estuary. Wilson, in speaking of the bardic clan of the Allans, the gypsy bagpipers already referred to, tells us they were Northumbrians and Faws. If he does not distinctly say so in so many words, he does so inferentially. Besides, he gives as his impression that "the 'muggers' of the present day belong to the Faa aristocracy:" and the Allans were muggers; according to Dr. John Brown, whose dog "of the pure Piper Allan's breed" is styled "the mugger's dog." Wright, in his Provincial Dictionary, broadly defines a Faw as "an itinerant tinker, potter, &c.;" while Halliwell seems to limit the term to Cumberland. Wright's definition is the most correct, because even so lately as Grose's time, all "gypsies" were accustomed to "artificially discolour their faces." But, without farther hair-splitting as to whether the muggers (potters) constituted the ruling caste of all the Border Faws, or as to the exact date at which the term *Faw* died out in this or that district,—it is evident that Mr. Simson is mainly right in associating the name, in later times, with the territory he circumscribes.

The division of the country into various provinces is a feature of "gypsydom" that is more than once pointed out. When "the distinguished northern poet, Walter Scott, who is Sheriff of Selkirkshire," sent in his report to Mr. Hoyland, he made this remark, with respect to the Scottish "gypsies," generally: "They are said to keep up a communication with each other through Scotland, and to have some internal government and regulation as to the districts which each family travels." And he indicates something of this kind when he quotes the seventeenth-century author, Martin, (he who "conceived" the wandering Cairds, or Jockies of Scot-

land,—pipers and harpers—"to be descended from the ancient
bards ")—to this effect :—" One of them told me there were
not now above twelve of them in the whole isle ; but he
remembered when they abounded, so as at one time he was
one of five that usually met at St. Andrews." The *dubh-chis*,
or " black tribute " that they levied in their days of power is
another evidence of this. It is not to be supposed that John
Gunn and his Aberdeenshire " black watch " would permit
the Captain of an Argyleshire band to finger a penny of the
yearly " watch-money " that was paid by the lairds and
farmers of Aberdeenshire ; or that he would calmly allow the
Cairds of another district to encroach upon his territory. And
the Taits, we have seen, were ultimately expelled from the country of the Kennedys, " in which they had attempted to travel
by force." In speaking of the *horner* caste of " gypsies,"
Mr. Simson remarks :—" Some of the principal families of
these nomadic horner bands have yet districts on which none
others of the tribe [that is of the *tory* castes] dare encroach."
And, regarding the Scottish " gypsies " in general, he makes
the following most pregnant statements :—

    " These curious people stated to me that Scotland was at
one time divided into districts, and that each district was assigned to a particular tribe. The chieftains of these tribes
issued tokens to the members of their respective hordes,
' when they scattered themselves over the face of the country.'
The token of a local chieftain protected its bearer only while
within his own district. If found without this token, or
detected travelling in a district for which the token was not
issued, the individual was liable to be plundered, beaten, and
driven back into his own proper territory by those gipsies on
whose rights and privileges he had infringed. These tokens
were, at certain periods, called in and renewed, to prevent
any one from forging them. They were generally made of
tin, with certain characters impressed upon them ; and the
token of each tribe had its own particular mark, and was well
known to all the gipsies in Scotland. But while these passes
of the provincial chieftains were issued only for particular
districts, a token of the Baillie family protected its bearer
throughout the kingdom of Scotland ; a fact which clearly
proves the superiority of that ancient clan. Several gipsies

have assured me that 'a token from a Baillie was good over all Scotland, and that kings and queens had come of that family.' And an old gipsy also declared to me that the tribes would get into utter confusion were the country not divided into districts, under the regulations of tokens."

Here, then, is a most vivid illustration of what has been said on a previous page. By sheer force of tradition the modern Picts of Scotland have preserved the memory of a state of things which the eminent historian of the ancient Picts has lately presented to us. What the latter has ascertained by painful and scholarly research, the former could have told him as an indisputable, inherited truth. Scoto-Pictish Scotland, says Mr. Skene, was once partitioned off into various provinces. According to one account, Transmarine Scotland, or Scotland north of the Scythian Valley (the basin of the modern River Forth), was divided into seven provinces, each of which was made up of two districts. These had their respective kings and sub-kings. So lately as the tenth century three of these provinces were wholly " black ; " and the supreme ruler of these became, for a time, the paramount king of Transmarine Scotland : being known to history as *Kenneth, Cin-aed, Kennedy, Niger, Dubh,* or *The Black,* " of the three black divisions." Whether *The White,* who eventually displaced him, was in any way the ancestor of the royal, white-skinned Balliol line (who may at the same time have been Normans,—or earlier Nor'-men) can only be a matter of conjecture : though not an improbability.

These divisions do not include Southern Scotland. And, possibly, the long-standing rivalry between the Faw chiefs (whose country, as described by Mr. Simson, is very like ancient Northumbria) and the Baillies—for the kingship of the *tories* of Scotland—may be properly regarded as the clashing of " Transmarine Scotland " with the important kingship that stretched from the Forth to the Humber. While the Galloway confederacy may have had an origin independent of either. But these, being matters of speculation, need not be longer dwelt upon.

Of the use of these passes, or tokens, we have some interesting instances in modern times. (Of the *tory* passes—that is to say—the ordinary documentary passport being the modern

outcome of this custom.) In Mr. Simson's chapter on the
"gypsies" of the county of Linlithgow, we are told that two
local chiefs, "McDonald and Jamieson, like others of the
superior classes of gipsies, gave tokens of protection to their
particular friends of the community generally. The butchers
of Linlithgow, when they went to the country, with money
to buy cattle, frequently procured these assurances from the
gipsies. The shoemakers did likewise, when they had to go
to distant markets with their shoes. Linlithgow appears
even to have been under the special protection of these
banditti. Mr. George Hart, and Mr. William Baird, two of
the most respectable merchants of Bo'ness, who had been
peddlers in their early years, scrupled not to say that, when
travelling through the country, they were seldom without
tokens from the gipsies." Again,—it is said, that "the
gipsies gave passes or tokens to some of their particular
favourites who were not of their own race" (that is, of their
own way of living) ; and that one particular chief,—of a
Stirlingshire gang— not only "issued tokens to the members
of his own tribe," but, "besides these regular gipsy tokens,
he, like many of his nation, gave tokens of protection to his
particular friends of the community at large."

This chief, last referred to,*—a "principal gipsy" of
Stirlingshire, but "closely connected by blood with the Fife
bands,"—is stated to have been "of that rank that entitled
him to issue tokens to the members of his tribe." And the
two Linlithgowshire chiefs, above-mentioned, possessed the

* "The name of this chief was Charles Wilson, and his place of residence at
one time was Raploch, close by Stirling Castle, where he possessed some heritable property in houses. He was a stout, athletic, good-looking man, fully six
feet in stature, and of a fair complexion ; and was, in general, handsomely
dressed, frequently displaying a gold watch, with many seals attached to its
chain. In his appearance he was respectable, very polite in his manners, and
had altogether little or nothing about him which, at first sight, or to the general
public, indicated him to be a gipsy. But, nevertheless, I was assured by one of
the tribe, who was well acquainted with him, that he spoke the language, and
observed all the customs, and followed the practices of the gipsies. . . . . This
gipsy chief died within these thirty-five years [say, about 1810-15] in his own
house on the castle hill at Stirling, whither he had removed from Raploch. It is
stated that for a considerable time before his death he relinquished his former
practices, and died in full communion with the church."

This, again, is one of those "gypsies" of the Baillie order. A gentleman in
dress and bearing, and belonging to the class of "fair whites."

same privilege, "like others of the superior classes of
gipsies."

"But while these passes of the provincial chieftains were
issued only for particular districts, a token of the Baillie
family protected its bearer throughout the kingdom of Scotland." In other words, a Baillie token was a royal warrant:
the passes of the other ruling families were those of subordinate kinglets. "If found without this token, or detected
travelling in a district for which the token was not issued,
the individual was liable to be plundered, beaten, and driven
back into his own proper territory, by those gipsies on whose
rights and privileges he had infringed."

These tokens, it is said, "were generally made of tin, with
certain characters impressed upon them; and the token of
each tribe had its own particular mark, and was well known
to all the gipsies in Scotland." They were not invariably of
tin. There is a story told of a Dumfriesshire carrier of the
early part of last century, who encountered the head of the
royal Baillies one evening at a country inn. "This man,
once, in returning from Edinburgh, stopt at Broughton, and
in coming out of the stable he met a man, who asked him if
he knew him. Robert, after looking at him for a little, said:
'I think you are Mr. Baillie.' He said, 'I am,' and asked if
Robert could lend him two guineas, and it should be faithfully
repaid. As there were few people who wished to differ with
Baillie, Robert told him he was welcome to two guineas, or
more if he wanted it. . . . [The money being accepted,]
Baillie then gave him a kind of brass token, about the size of
a half-crown, with some marks upon it, which he desired him
to carry in his purse, and it might be of use to him some
time, as he was to show it, if any person offered to rob him.
Baillie then mounted his horse and rode off." The story goes
on to say, that some time afterwards this man was accosted
by two suspicious looking men, while travelling through an
out of the way district. "But recollecting his token, he said
a gentleman had once given him a piece of brass, to show, if
ever any person troubled him. They desired him to show it,
as it was moonlight. He gave it to them. On seeing it,
they looked at one another, and then, whispering a few words,
told him it was well for him he had the token, which they

returned ; and they left him directly." Now this was a
Baillie token, and good for the whole of Scotland ; so it is
possible that, being such, it was made of a different metal
from the ordinary counters, which were of tin. But the chief
feature of the token was the writing impressed upon it.
These circular counters were plainly the orthodox style of
pass,—but any other article could be transformed into one,
by the marking of certain characters upon it. This is
exemplified in two or three other incidents, similar to that
just related. And Mr. James Simson plainly states : "A
pen-knife, a snuff-box, and a ring are some of the gipsy passports. It is what is marked upon them that protects the
bearer from being disturbed by others of the tribe."

What *was* marked upon them ? It is too likely that not
one of these tokens is now extant. The unceasing persecution of "gypsies," generation after generation ; the
numerous statutes enacted against " sorners, masterful
beggars, and such like runners about ; " the belief, so often
acted upon, that they " might lawfully be destroyed, without
any judicial inquisition, as who carry their own condemnation
about them " ; all these—down to the milder laws of recent
days—have most effectually done their work. No civilized
man can regret the result, however harshly attained ; but
such a complete effacement of an ancient polity must be a
source of sorrow to all of the Dryasdust clan. That these
characters impressed upon the tokens of the Scoto-Pictish
kinglets were of the same kind as those which Bishop
Nicolson saw in the "book of spells, and magical receipts,
taken, two or three days before, in the pocket of one
of our moss-troopers,"*—may be regarded as extremely
probable. It is true that the bishop regarded these " barbarous characters" as derived from the black Danes, being
"very near akin to Wormius's Ram Runer, which, he says,
differed wholly in figure and shape from the common runæ."

---

* Referred to in a previous chapter, and quoted from the Introduction to
" The Minstrelsy of the Scottish Border." Bishop Nicolson cites this " book of
spells" as a proof that the Border mossers, or marsh-dwellers, or bog-trotters of his
day were not "utter strangers to the black art of their forefathers." It may be
remembered that, in this " book of spells," "among many other conjuring feats,
was prescribed a certain remedy for an ague, by applying a few *barbarous
characters* to the body of the party distempered."

Whatever they were, it is plain they were unintelligble to a man of mere *Latin* training. If they were black-Danish, their use in Scotland must have been more recent than the Pictish, or the later Scoto-Pictish dominion. But "Gypsydom" ranges from a quite recent period back to an undefinable limit ; and it is within the bounds of possibility that the "particular mark" of each tribe differed *in origin* from each of the others. But this is much less likely than that all the tribal tokens bore a legend, stamped in "common runæ," and that the "particular mark" was only the totem of the clan. And, since the bulk of the "gypsy" classes seem, by complexion and other characteristics, to belong to the race of Egyptians (Scots) and Moors (Picts), it is probable that the prevailing character of these symbols was of the kind intimated by Boece ; who, writing of the *Auld Mannieres of Scottis*, says—" In all their secret besiness they usit not to write with common letteris usit among other peplis, but erer with sifars, and figures of beistis maid in maner of letteris ; sic as thair epitaphis and superscriptions above thair sepulturis schew." And that the determined— and excusable—persecution of these Scottish Egyptians (whose alternative title of *Scot* gradually floated away from its original possessors, and became the national designation of the hybrid Scotch people) ;—and the attitude which the best part of the Scotch people eventually reached,—namely, the regarding of a "habit and repute Egyptian" as the equivalent of everything shiftless, savage, and irreconcilable ; —gave rise to the state of things that Boece indicates when he adds :—"noch-the-less this crafty maner of writing, be quhat slenth I can not say, is perist, and yet they have certaine letteris propir amang themself, quilkis war some time vulgar and common." That this assumption is correct, there is no reason to doubt. For Boece, born at Dundee, in the fifteenth century, of a family that had been landowners in Forfarshire for four or five generations, wrote as a *Scotchman*—not as a *Scot:* when he spoke of the Scots he used the third person (though his own family-tree may quite easily have contained pure *Scots*, as well as Normans, Angles, Danes, Moray-men, and all the ingredients that compose a *Scotchman*). And it is quite evident that he had in view

a distinct division of the people of Scotland ; the same
division—there can be no question—as that spoken of by the
Scotch writer in the *Mercurius Politicus* of the year 1662,*
when, writing from Edinburgh, he relates that "the Scots
and moss-troopers have again revived *their* old custom, of
robbing and murthering the English." That this man writes
in the broad spirit of a Modern Briton (using "English"
only as a convenient designation for the southern portion
of his fellow-countrymen) is proved by his added statement
that "a Scotchman, who was with them [the English],"
escaped from the clutches of these *Scots*, to tell the tale.
Therefore when Boece, and his fellow-Scotchman, Leslie,
described the ancient manners of the *Scots*, it is an absolute
certainty that they had in view the Egyptians of Scotland.
And, consequently, the "barbarous characters" that neither
Bishop Nicolson, nor the peaceful traders and hinds who
received those passes could read, must have been mainly
(if not wholly) those "sifars and figures of beistis maid in
maner of letters" that the Egyptian-Scots had made use of
from the earliest times. In short, they were Egyptian hieroglyphics.

Farther, the symbols and pictures that are carved upon
the well-known "sculptured stones of Scotland," must be
the work of the same Egyptian people. Boece distinctly
says so :—"In all their secret business, they (the Egyptians of
Scotland) used not to write with common letters used among
other peoples, but formerly with cyphers, and figures of
beasts made in manner of letters ; *such as their epitaphs and
superscriptions above their sepultures show*." That the "Sculptured Stones" are of a sepulchral nature is what all the best
modern antiquaries are agreed upon : and here is a fifteenth-
century writer stating as a matter of course that the sculp-
tors were the Early Egyptians of Scotland.

Whatever of uncertainty and error may attach to the conclusions reached in the foregoing pages, now, at any rate,
we are on solid ground. Ethnology tells us that one stream
of Modern British blood has come down from a common
source with that of the aboriginal people of Egypt. Tra-

* Formerly quoted. The extract is given by Sir Walter Scott in his Introduction to the "Minstrelsy" (Murray's reprint, London, 1869, p. 27, *note*).

dition states that our islands were overrun, at an early period, by swarthy marauding tribes;—of which one section alleged its descent from the daughter of a Pharaoh, from whom they took their name of *Scot*: that word, therefore, becoming synonymous with "vagabond,"—in the speech of the Celtic peoples who tried to repel these invaders. This name of *Scot* did not cease, until (at most) two centuries ago, to designate one particular division of the people of North Britain; although, by a common freak of nomenclature, it also became identified with the heterogeneous Scottish nation.* And that particular division was composed of those dusky, ferocious, pagan, and magic-working Egyptians, whose ideas and practices the more peaceable and civilized of the Scottish people have always regarded with abhorrence. For which reason, this element of semi-Christianity (though doing the greatest violence to its professed creed) continually fought against and eventually persecuted and hunted down all those who perversely remained "habit and repute Egyptians:" so that that title was at length equivalent to "outlaw" and "criminal," and its bearer liable to be killed without mercy. The name of "Egyptian"—loosely and erroneously given to a whole class—is still claimed by certain of the

---

* We still find it convenient to use the name of a long-defunct kingdom when speaking of *Scotland*, and to designate those of us who are born within its limits as *Scotchmen*, or *Scotsmen*. These are slightly-different pronunciations of *Scottish*-men or *Scottis*-men : the former being the equivalent of the modern sound of *Inglis*, which we now call *English*. When Archdeacon Barbour wrote of *Scottis*-men, and Boece of the *Scottis*, they may have pronounced the word as *Scottish*, *Scotch*, or *Scots*. That Barbour used "Scottis" in its widest sense is clear ; and when he spoke of the Scots (Proper) of Galloway, he called them "Galloways." But, like "Englishman" (of this century) and "American," the words Scottish, Scots, &c., must have meant very different things in different mouths. Mr. Skene ("Celtic Scotland," Vol. II. pp. 460–462) tells us that about the twelfth century "the name applied to the Gaelic language of Scotland was that of Scotic or Scotch"; but that, while Barbour denominated his language "the Inglis toung" (and it is almost identical with what we still call English), Gavin Douglas, writing in 1516, "in the same Lowland dialect," terms it "Scottés," or Scotch. And the miscellaneous natives of Galloway, who—referring to Barbour's "Galloways"—style them "the wild *Scots* of Galloway," lay claim to the general title of *Scots* themselves. There has, therefore, been a great diversity of meaning attached to this epithet, as there is to-day in the two parallel instances just cited. Nevertheless, the various references in the foregoing pages show very plainly that a distinction between the Scot Proper and the Scot General has long been observed.

Scottish "gypsies," who believe themselves to be "Pharaoh's folk." As *gypsies* and *faws*, they were—till quite lately—dictators of the whole of Scotland ; so far as concerned the safety of travellers passing through the various provinces into which they had divided that country ; each province the home of a certain tribe, and obeying the laws of its tribal chief,—and all the provinces and all those tribal chiefs recognizing the supremacy of one ruling family. As *Egyptians*, or *Scots*, and *Moors*, or *Picts*,—precisely the same thing is recorded of them : except, that, under these names, they had undoubted power and a historical position. As *gypsies*, we have seen that each tribe protected the infringement of its territory by a system of passes, issued by the higher castes ; and there may yet be proof that this custom was in full force during the historic age of the Scoto-Pictish kingdom,—as, manifestly, it must have been. The writing upon these tokens was illegible to men of modern English education,—and was only so many "barbarous characters" in the eyes of a bishop, of presumed latinity. "In all their secret business," these gypsies "used not to write with common letters used among other peoples." We do not actually know that the characters impressed upon such tribal tokens were "cyphers, and figures of beasts made in manner of letters :" though this is very probable. We do know, however, that the swarthy dwellers in the Hebridean wigwams of last century wore, upon their persons, broad plates of silver or brass, "curiously engraven with various animals, &c. ;" and we do know that, prior to the fifteenth century, the "cyphers and figures of beasts made in manner of letters," which the Scots Proper of that period made use of in their "secret business," were identical with those composing the "epitaphs and superscriptions" above their tombs. And this confronts us with the Sculptured Stones of Scotland.

These have been sketched, their inscriptions transcribed and deeply studied, and the result of these studies published —by men of great linguistic and antiquarian knowledge : who are, indeed, the only kind of men qualified to discuss such a subject. There are, of course, differences of opinion as to their meaning, and their probable age. On this last point, Colonel Forbes Leslie makes these remarks :* "The sandstone, on which so many of the Roman inscriptions taken from the walls of Hadrian and Antoninus are graven, is not to be compared in durability to Aberdeenshire granite ; yet Roman inscriptions carry us back sixteen or seventeen hundred years. There is therefore no limit within the historical or even the traditionary period to which sculptures in Aberdeenshire granite need be restricted, so far as depends on arguments founded on the wasting effect of atmospheric action on the surface of the stone. By far the greatest number, and those of most interest in the sculptured stones, in which there is no Christian emblem, are found in Aberdeenshire, and are of Aberdeenshire granite." Against this, however, must be placed the effects of time, in raising the superficies of the earth (principally through the agency of worms,— we have lately been told) : thereby rendering it improbable that an upright stone would be visible at the present day, had it been reared at a very remote period.

The sculptured stones of Scotland,—dotted here and there over the country, are found in greatest numbers in the north-eastern district. Of their inscriptions, it is said :† " Some of these emblems indisputably, and all of them probably, are of Oriental derivation." "The most remarkable of these are the double disc ; double disc and sceptre ; crescent ; crescent and sceptre ; altar ; altar and sceptre and hawk ; serpent ; serpent and sceptre ; elephant ; horse ; bull ; boar ; bird of prey ; human figure with dog's head ; fish ; dog's head ; horseshoe arch ; mirror ; mirror-case ; comb ; comb-case, etc." To these may be added lions, apes, camels, dragons and other "monsters," and the inter-linked loop known as "Solomon's Seal."

As these are admittedly sepulchral monuments, the most natural explanation of such devices is that they were the badges or totems of the dead. Thus the crescent would be the proper emblem for one of the many moss-trooping "thieves" or "gypsies" of the Border country ; of whom Scott says that the heavenly bodies formed their favourite crests. The dog's head would represent any one of that dog-headed battalion of the clan of the "King of Rualay"—

* "Early Races of Scotland," chapter xv.   † *Ibid.*

already noticed: the bull, such a man as the bovine-headed
figure of the Œland sculptures, or the cow's-skin-clad tinker
of Cornish tradition, or any one of the "Calves" and "Heifers"
of Sutherlandshire: the serpent, any native of Edder-dale:
the boar, such a warrior as the fifteenth-century "black-
skinned boar" of the Hebrides: and the horse, such a "giant
with horse's ears" as that one slain at the battle near Bally-
beg Abbey, County Cork, "in the time of all the battles."
In this way, the lion would indicate the grave of one of the
race of "*Dubh* of the three black divisions;" and the elephant, one of the progenitors of the Olifant clan; both of
these tribes having borne such cognizances.   And the dragon
might fitly be carved upon the tombstone of any one of the
"Sons of Uisneach,"—who are remembered as "the three
dragons of Dunmonadh."   The addition of the sceptre
might be taken to denote that a king was buried below:
while the altar may possibly bear reference to a priest.

It is doubtful to what extent the drawings of animals—
now strangers to Britain—are tests of the foreign extraction
of the artists.   Although camels were not familiar objects in
this country at the date of the Norman Conquest, or soon
after, they were not unknown.   The Irish Annals record
that, in the year 1105, "a camel, which is an animal of
wonderful size, was presented by the King of Alban to
Murcertac O'Brian."   And, no doubt, it was not the only one
imported.   Besides this, it is sometimes argued that, because
the elephants carved upon Scottish monoliths show, by their
grotesque outlines, that the artist had never seen a living
elephant,—*therefore*, the forefathers of such a man belonged
originally to a warmer climate than that of Britain.   This,
however, need not have been the case.   The artist may have
learned, incorrectly enough, the appearance of an elephant,—
and that by tradition,—although his ancestors had inhabited
Britain for an illimitable period.   Mr. Bonwick has some
remarks bearing closely upon this.   "A human skull, near
Falkirk (he states*), was discovered twenty feet below the
surface, and associated with the fossil elephant.   In Essex
such remains have been side by side with the hippopotamus
and rhinoceros, which then roamed about all England.   At

* "The Daily Life of the Tasmanians," pp. 219, 220.

Curragh, an older Irishman than the Celt hunted after what
we call the fossil elk. The Betages, or slaves of the Celts,
may have been his descendants." In the limestone caves of
Denbighshire, the skeletons of men are found beside those of
the hippopotamus, elephant, rhinoceros, lion, hyena, bear, and
reindeer. No one can tell at what date the last lion, elephant,
or hippopotamus of the British Islands was seen and slain.
If tradition is to be believed, the last-named of these was of
very recent date (comparatively speaking) : for the Celtic
legends are full of stories of water-horses and water-bulls.
(But as this may have another, and wholly different explanation—this point need not be pressed.) At any rate, it is not
impossible that descendants of the men who hunted the
living British elephant may have incised its likeness—though
not very faithfully—upon pillars of Aberdeen granite. There
is indeed a curious hint of such a traditional elephant, in the
form of the supporters of the Oliphant shield. The earliest
known chief of this tribe seems to have been a David *de*
Oliphant, one of those twelfth-century Scottish barons who
accompanied King David of Scotland in his unsuccessful
invasion of England. Likely enough, this David (of
Oliphant) was a Norman. But the people of the district
over which he ruled may have been British for countless
generations. At any rate, the supporters of that shield—
"two elephants proper"—are, according to a very carefully-
drawn representation of the year 1826,* delineated with tufts
of shaggy hair upon the haunch ; unlike any elephant that a
modern herald could have seen, though suggestive of some
animal that had not lost all resemblance to the hairy mammoth.

Accordingly, those creatures on the Scottish monuments
need not of necessity be exotic,—though strangers to this
country for a long period. But with regard to others of the
inscriptions, there is no doubt. "Some of these emblems
indisputably . . . . . are of Oriental derivation," says Colonel
Forbes Leslie. And a more recent authority,† speaking less
dogmatically, but with conviction, has expressed the opinion
that the inscriptions upon the "Newton Stone," in the Garioch,

* Given in "The Pocket Peerage of Scotland," Edinburgh, 1826.

† Lord Southesk, in a paper read before the Society of Antiquaries of Scotland, 11th December, 1882.

Aberdeenshire, form a compound of Oriental and Western
ideas, beliefs, and languages. And among these elements,
he includes the Egyptian.

Inscriptions of this variety are not emblematic, but are
written in various recognized characters. That one stone,
such as the Newton Stone, should bear on its surface an
inscription that unites Greek with Irish, Gothic, and Egyptian, is extremely probable. Whatever the *origin* of an incoming race, it could not possibly preserve its distinctive
features for several centuries, unaffected in the slightest degree
by the customs of those with whom it came in contact.
Though the Egyptian-Scots were at first " somewhat different
in manners " from the painted Moors who were their allies in
the invasion of South Britain, such an alliance would of
itself result in a blending of ideas, of manners, of speech,
and of blood. And this again would be affected by the invasions of later races. Therefore, when a man's investiga-
tions lead him to see a mixture of several languages and
creeds in one individual inscription, on a Scottish monument,
the likelihood is that his conjectures are pretty correct.

The belief in an Eastern origin of certain intra-British
languages and peoples is very old, and very old-fashioned.
There is, I believe, a mass of presumptive evidence in its
favour—in what is called the Gaelic language. Those of us
who know little or nothing of Gaelic can guess at its heterogeneous character, from the fact (already noticed) that when
Shaw's " Gaelic " dictionary was brought out a hundred years
ago, it was pronounced by others of his fellow-countrymen
to be something that was *not* Gaelic, whatever it was. And
it was also noticed that an eminent living student of Scottish
Gaelic has stated that that form in use a few centuries ago
was very different from that spoken and written at the
present day. In whatever part of the world—and at whatever epoch—" the language of the white men " reached
maturity, it is plain that it has become greatly altered, in
various places, and in varying degrees, by amalgamation
with other forms of speech. " Black speech," for example.
A last-century archæologist,* with what correctness I do not

* A contributor to the Transactions of the Royal Irish Academy for the year
1788.

know, makes these statements regarding this question : " If
they [the inhabitants of ancient Scotia, now Ireland] had not
an intercourse in former days with the Phœnicians, Egyptians
and Persians, how is it possible so many hundreds of words,
so many idioms of speech, so many technical terms in the
arts of those ages, could have been introduced into the old
Irish dialect ? . . . . . What people, the Egyptians and Irish
excepted, named the harp or music ouini, Irish Aine . . . . .
What people in the world, the Orientalists and the Irish excepted, call the copy of a book the son of a book, and echo
the daughter of a voice ? With what northern nation, the
Irish excepted, can the Oriental names of the tools and
implements of the stone-cutter, the carpenter, the ship-builder,
the weaver be found ? And with what people, the old Irish
and Egyptians excepted, does the word· *Ogham* signify a
book, and the name of Hercules or Mercury ? " If only one
half of these queries be grounded on positive truth, the connection between the old East and the later West is most
distinctly proved by the evidence of language.

These are questions that belong to *Egyptology* rather than
to *Gypsiology*—though it is difficult to say where the one
begins and the other ends. And as " gypsies " are of all
races, so are these references to Persians and Phœnicians not
out of place. For, like *gypsy*, *Egyptian* must be taken to include
a good deal : Assyrian, Jewish, Chaldean ; as well as Phœni-
cian and Persian. The " black art " (*dubh-chleasachd*) of the
conjurers and " magicians " (*druidhean**) of Early Britain,
was regarded by Pliny as almost identical with that practised
by the *magi* of Persia. And the " enchanters," " magicians,"
and " wise-men," attached to the court of the Pharaoh
mentioned in the Book of Exodus, were akin to both of
these, in custom. The *Liuth Messeath*, and the *Jodhan
Morain*, worn by the *druidhean* of Ancient Scotia, were—it
has been observed—identical with the breastplates and the
Urim and Thummim of Jewish and Chaldee priests : which

* The name of one of these magicians, *Dearg* or *Dargo*, indicates a history
similar to that of the word *ruadh*, which means both "red" and "dusky."
Dearg nan Druidhean, as he was called, was literally—*The Red One of the
Magicians*. In Gaelic dictionaries (as we have seen) this word is translated
"red"; but when it is called an Anglo-Saxon word, it is translated "dark":
and it is so spelled nowadays, and has this meaning, in what we call " English."

is not at all remarkable if those priests of Ireland were Early Scots,—that is, Egyptians. The hieroglyphical tablets of the Early Scots, their long "glibbed" tresses, and the ruddle with which they smeared their dusky faces, may all be matched in Egypt and Assyria. While such varieties of the "magic," just referred to, as sun-worship, serpent-worship, astrology, and soothsaying or fortune-telling ; and also the customs of passing children "through the fire to Baal,"* and the burying of the dead in sarcophagi,† are as much the property of the British Islands as of the East.

And most of these properties have remained longest in the possession of those *tory* classes,—commonly called gypsies. The divining-rod with which the magician at the court of the Pharaohs performed his incantations was swayed also by the British *druidh*.‡ And by the *ban-druidh*, female gypsy, or witch, also : and, just as this modern sibyl of the hedgerows refuses to prophesy unless her palm is crossed with silver, so have her kidney done in Britain as far back as the days of Cæsar.§ Like these also, she pretends to gain her prophetic knowledge from the stars. Thimble-rigging,—the peculiar property of those classes who, in Mr. Leland's opinion, are more or less of gypsy blood, and who, according to Mr. Simson, are distinctly gypsies,—is of Egyptian origin,—or, at least, was a practice

---

* Some modern authorities (both Mr. Skene and Dr. Hill Burton, I think, and perhaps others) agree in deciding that the word Beltane, Bel-teinne, or Beal-tine—popularly translated "Baal-fire"—is *not* connected with the name of the god Baal. If this be the case, the similarity of name is only a coincidence. But the *name* is of little importance : it is beyond question that the *ceremony* of passing children through the fire was quite commonly practised in Britain a thousand years ago, and survived in some parts of the country till last century. (For remarks upon this, and instances adduced, see, for example, Colonel Forbes Leslie's "Early Races," pp. 113-115.)

† How common this custom was in this country we cannot tell, the question-able practice of opening our ancient burial-mounds being yet in its infancy. But there is, at least, one instance of the discovery of sarcophagi—namely, in the neighbourhood—or at the base—of a hill in East Lothian, named Traprain Law.

‡ "It appears all the gipsies, male as well as female, who perform ceremonies for their tribe, carry long staffs." (Simson's "History," p. 272, *note*.)

§ "The fraud of the astrologers in taking money for predictions pretended to be derived from the stars is here compared to a similar imposition practised by the Druids, who borrowed money on promises of repayment after death." (Note to Bell's edition of "Hudibras," Part II. Canto III.)

of Ancient Egypt (*Simson*, p. 325, *note*). The Morris-dance, Moors'-dance or Blackamoors'-dance,—so distinctly a British dance that Handel regarded it as the national dance of our country,—was, even so recently as the era of the Fifeshire gypsies, described by Mr. Simson, scarcely one remove better than the degrading riot of the worshippers of Osiris.* Survivals of such worship may be seen (says Mr. Groome in his *Britannica* " gypsy " article) " in the honour paid by the three great German gypsy clans to the fir-tree, the birch, and the hawthorn . . . . and in the veneration in which Welsh Gipsies hold the fasciated vegetable growth known as the *broado koro*." The same low religion (Colonel Forbes Leslie points out in his chapter on *menhirs*) has been firmly rooted in Armorica and Brittany, and in portions of the British Islands. Of the serpent-worship with which this is inextricably mingled, traces " may be also found in various phrases, stories, emblems, and customs," belonging to " gypsies " in general,—says the article in the *Encyclopædia:* and a relic of this is also visible in the Gaelic language, in which there is one word for " serpent " and "father."† And, as the effect

---

* Mr. Tylor, in his "Anthropology," suggests that " the eye of Osiris, painted on the Egyptian funeral bark," is connected with all such "eyes" painted on the bows of boats from Valetta to Canton. It is possible that this "eye of Osiris," if used as a caste-mark, is the explanation of all Polyphemuses, Gaelic or Greek, whose huge, solitary eye in the middle of the forehead cannot be accounted for, either naturally or mythologically.

† The words given in Armstrong's Gaelic Dictionary as signifying "father" are—*athair, daidean* and *gintear*. The second of these is plainly a variation of the " gypsy " *dad* or *dada*, which is claimed by so many languages : being styled *Welsh* when it is *tad*, *Transylvanian gypsy* ("the Kolosvárer dialect ") when it is *dad, Modern-Slang* when it is *dad* or *daddy, Irish-Gaelic* when it is *dada, English-Romany* when it is *dadas. Gintear*, says Armstrong, is simply *genitor*. But the other word, *athair*, was once *nathair*. In an Irish-Gaelic Prayer-book of 1712, the Lord's Prayer begins with *Ar Nathair*. (Probably the feminine of this was *mnathair:* at least, this is suggested by certain cases of the word *bean*, "a wife, a woman;" which, in the genitive singular, is *mna*, in the nominative plural *mnai* and *mnathan*, and *mnathaibh* in the dative plural.) But *ar Nathair*, which, in the Lord's Prayer, must be translated "our Father," is literally "our Serpent." The modern Gaelic dictionaries give no other meaning but " serpent " to *nathair;* and *athair* with them means only "father." It is in what we call " English " that the former of these meanings has adhered to both variations of the word. In " English " we pronounce *athair* as *adder*. *Nadder* or *adder* is claimed as " Anglo-Saxon," *nathair* or *athair* as " Gaelic "; but they are clearly the same word. In Gaelic, *nathair* has become *athair*, just as *a nadder* has become *an adder* (or as, conversely, *an eke-name* became *a nick-name*, and an

of such beliefs, it has been shrewdly remarked by an observer, who has been already quoted, that the area which is most thickly studded with "the sculptured stones of Scotland," is that in which the Christian ideas of marriage have found least favour.

It is also worthy of notice that, in "the language of the white men," the word *dubh-chcist*—literally, "a black enigma" —is rendered (by Armstrong) not only as "a puzzle," "an enigma," but also as "a motto," "a superscription." In the first two instances, it might be understood as meaning nothing more than "a dark saying;" which expression may be derived with equal reason from the darkness or obscurity of the thing it expresses, and from the complexion of such people as those who were essentially adepts in "magic," or "black" art. But it is difficult to see why "a motto," "a superscription," should be designated "a *black* enigma" (*dubh-chcist*), unless one particular class of superscriptions was originally signified by this name : the class of superscriptions to which Boyce (or Bocce) refers, when he speaks of the epitaphs of "ciphers and figures of beasts made in manner of letters," inscribed on the grave-stones of the Early Scots, Scots Proper, or Egyptians of Scotland.

With regard to the dates of such inscriptions, there can be little unanimity of opinion— until the meaning of the legends has been thoroughly mastered by scientific men. Colonel Leslie's comparison between the hardness of the granite on which they are carved, and the less durable nature of the stone that still bears the impression of Roman graving-tools, would give a greater antiquity to the Aberdeen sculptures— were that required. But the tomb-stones of the Early Scots of Scotland may post-date the Roman invasion ; because the Scot invasion of Scotland was apparently subsequent to the days of Cæsar. The *supremacy* of the Scots in Scotland most certainly was : and their *arrival* in that country seems,

---

ewt or *eft, a newt*). In Middle English, says Mr. Skeat, *naddere* and *addere* are interchangeable forms.

It may be added that of these three so-called "Gaelic" words for *father*, the last-named, *gintear*, is probably the only one that belonged to "the language of the white men." For *gintear* is identified by Armstrong with *genitor ;* and it is likely the Latins were "white men," whatever the earlier Roman races may have been.

at the earliest, to have been contemporaneous with the arrival of the Roman legions in South Britain. Therefore those of the sculptures that Boece particularly refers to, are of comparatively modern date : some of them, indeed, only three or four centuries old.

We get little chronological information from the presence, on some of these monuments, of so-called "Christian" emblems. There are a good many sweeping statements made, with regard to this. Probably the emblem most of all in the minds of those who make this distinction between Christian and Pagan sculptures is the sign of the cross. There can be no doubt that this emblem has been, for many long centuries, closely associated with the Christian religion, with which it is now almost absolutely identified. (Though there are yet, I believe, certain "Pagan" races,—the Kabyles of Africa, for example,—who tattoo the cross upon their breasts, without the least reference to Christianity.) The fallacy of thus confusing this religion with the emblems that, at various times, became associated with its practice, is most clearly seen by considering this fact : that the founder of Christianity taught a *religion :* but that—if he taught the use of any religious emblems—the cross was not one of them. Nothing that was not taught by Christ can be distinctively Christian : consequently, the cross is not a Christian emblem.

Perhaps one of the best tangible proofs of this truth is found by regarding the form of the mediæval cathedral. The men who built and worshipped in these cathedrals were *essentially* Christian : though their Christianity was often clothed in pagan garments. But there is much in their ritual that, *of itself*, would argue them pagans. The cruciform cathedral of the middle ages was no more distinctively Christian than was the cruciform pagan temple from which it was evolved. A very perfect example of this early cathedral is seen in the temple of Callernish, or Classernish, in the district of Lewis—the chief division of the largest of all the "Islands of the Foreigners," or Deucaledonian Islands. The bird's-eye view of this temple (as given by Colonel Forbes . Leslie, in his *Early Races ;* Plate XXIII.) clearly shows us that in it—and others like it—we have the germ of the later cathedral. The Callernish stones are arranged exactly in the form of the so-called Celtic cross : and the circle that circumscribes the point of intersection seems to hint that the cross grew out of the circle ; and that, therefore, stone circles without any lines projecting from the circumference were places of worship at a date anterior to the formation of such temples as that of Callernish.

This confusion of Christianity with Paganism—resulting from the adoption of various Pagan emblems and ceremonies by people of the Christian faith, is more fully dwelt upon by Colonel Leslie, in the book already quoted from ; for exam- ple, in his chapter on Solar and Planetary Worship in Britain. To go over these various details, in this place, would occupy too much space, and would only be a repetition of what others with better information have told us.   It is enough to bear in mind that almost everything in the shape of outward ceremony,—whether sunk now into the abyss of " popular superstition,"—or whether still practised (as is the case all over the world) by men of the very highest kind,—is, of necessity, extra-Christian.   The worshippers of Osiris and the pagans of Rome honoured the " May-pole " ages ago : and as early an origin is assigned to the familiar " Hot Cross Bun." Easter eggs, Beltane cakes, and other dead or dying obser- vances, had no doubt a serious meaning to various heathen races, in Britain and out of it.   The lighting of fires on Beltane-day, or on Twelfthday-eve ; the forced-fire, or fire- by-friction, of the early British magicians (*druidhean*) ; the burning wheels that used to be rolled down hill-sides, on cer- tain annual occasions (a ceremony still extant in some parts of Scotland, I believe) ; are as distinctly traces of fire- worship as such customs as burying the dead with their faces to the east, the "orientation" of churches, the eastward posture when repeating a Belief,—are distinctly relics of the sun-worhip that was once almost universal.   These things, and others not referred to, though practised by some of the very best " Christians " in the world—now and formerly—are not themselves marks of Christianity.   The Buddhists of Asia ;—with their censers, incense, holy water, celibate monks (with tonsured heads), and celibate sisterhoods ; with their practice of confession to a priest ; with their chanted services and intoned prayers ; with their cathedrals—divided into nave, choir, apse,—entered from the west, and with the east as the most sacred extremity ;—the Buddhists of Asia, by all these tokens, proclaim their identity (*in outward things*) with the ritualistic sections of Christianity. If religion were a matter of form, and nothing else, the Asiatic Buddhists—the Greek Christians—the Roman Catholics—and the Ritualist-Anglicans, would all be merely sections of one corporate Church : and each and all of them be separated by a wide gulf from any sect of Christians—Methodist, or what not—that ignored such observances.

It is, therefore, evident that we cannot affirm that this or that inscription, burial, or temple belongs to the Christian Period,—merely because it bears the impress of some fashion that the Christians of such and such a date had adopted as their own. The cruciform "cathedral" of Callernish (being the merest rough, sky-roofed, skeleton of a cathedral) is probably of great antiquity. Even such a cathedral as that of Karli, situated in the Australioid Dekhan, was a complete, finished cathedral more than five hundred years before the birth of Christ.* Consequently, such a cathedral-germ as Callernish must either antedate such a finished cathedral as Karli by a long period ; or else it is the work of a people that separated from the (ultimate) builders of Karli long before that temple was built ;—they themselves never advancing (architecturally) after the era of their schism.

That—apart from the consideration just given—" the sign of the cross was in use as an emblem, having certain religious and mystic meanings attached to it, long before the Christian era," has been, for some considerable time, an article of belief among those who investigate such matters. And, in support of this belief, there are the facts just stated : the simplest and most forcible of which is, that as there is no evidence that Christ taught the use of such an emblem, it cannot therefore be regarded as Christian.

Of which long digression, the result is that nothing short of the translation of these inscriptions,—or the discovery of some fact that tells us, in the several instances, when and to

* 543, B.C., is the date given by Colonel Leslie, in his chapter on Solar and Planetary Worship in Britain, whence these facts are taken.

whom the monoliths were reared, can solve the question of
the Sculptured Stones. But this, at least, is certain—that
those of them that bear " ciphers and figures of beasts made
in manner of letters " were inscribed by the Scots, or Egyptians-of-Scotland, in or before the fifteenth century, when
Boyce wrote.*

The presumptive evidence that enables one to hold the
Early Scots and the Egyptians-of-Scotland as one and the
same people, cannot, I think, be gainsayed. Their traditional
descent from Scota, the daughter of a Pharaoh, may be
counted as worth little. But their origin has been indicated
in many ways. As regards their complexion—we saw that
they were slumped together with the Picts of Scotland,
whom Claudian calls " the nimble blackamoors, not wrongly
named 'the Painted People.'" And these Picts and Scots
were spoken of by a civilized South-Briton as so many
" *black* herds," " somewhat different in manners, but all alike
thirsting for blood." The earliest British home of these Scot-
Egyptians was Ireland ; and the conglomerate speech of that
country is full of words and expressions that are paralleled in
Ancient Egypt ;—while its soil has yielded up the emblems
of Chaldean priests. Whether there is a connection between
the "glibbed " locks of the Wild or Black-Irishman, and
those of the sculptured Egyptians may be questioned. But,
at any rate, the hieroglyphics of the Early Scots—if not
identical with the hieroglyphics of the Ancient Egyptians
(or one division of the people coming under that all-embrac-
ing term)—were, at least, based upon the same principle.
The Egyptian and British customs and attainments—religious and otherwise—sun-worship, fire-worship, serpent- and
phallus-worship, astrology, soothsaying, fortune-telling and
other forms of divination—all these have just been glanced
at. These were equally the property of the Magi of Britain,
the Magi of the Pharaohs, and the Magi of Persia : and Pliny,
on whose authority the last of these comparisons is made,

---

* This extract from Boece—now repeatedly made—is merely taken at second-
hand (from a pamphlet on the "Sculptured Stones," by Mr. Carr Ellison,
Durham). An examination of his remarks upon the "New and Old Manners of
the Scots," made on the understanding that *Scot* is therein used to signify *Scotch-
Egyptian*, must inevitably yield much important information.

states that the Early Britons (or a section of them) were as "black as Ethiopians." According to Mr. Skene, and other students, South-Britain contained, at the date of the Roman invasion, two very distinct types of men. And one of these—said to be the earlier—Mr. Skene regards as closely akin to the Deu-Caledones of Scotland; who were so far "Egyptians," in that they were Painted People, blackamoors, and probable *Australioids.* (For the Australioid skulls of Caithness were found in a district once known as Pict-land: and though this does not prove their owners to have been *Mauri* or *Picti,* there may be evidence yet forthcoming to warrant such a belief.) Indeed, the early *Scot* and the early *Pict* are, like their modern representatives, the *Egyytian* or *Gypsy,* and the *Faw,* not easily distinguished, the one from the other: the early *Scoti-Picti* (Pictish Scots; Painted Vagabonds) of Argyleshire belonging as much to the first division as to the second.

CHAPTER V.

THE period in which the powerful Scot-Egyptian began to lapse into the outlawed " Egyptian " cannot well be fixed. Assuming that *Scot* could be—and perhaps was—applied to *all* tribes that were "vagabonds" or nomadic ; that were swarthy of skin ; like the Scots Proper ; the painted Mauri, Moors, or Morays ; and the " black heathen " invaders, called Cimbri, or Dani ; then the decadence of the Scots of South-Western Scotland may fairly be said to have reached an advanced stage in the year 1445, when the power of the black section of the Douglases (who were once *all dubh-glasses*) was completely overthrown. This is the date at which *gypsy-dom* has hitherto been held to begin in Scotland (although it has been acknowledged that the Scotch *Tinklers* are spoken of as early as the twelfth century—in a document of the reign of William the Lion). To a certain extent, this may still be held as the beginning of "gypsydom" in that district of Scotland. Because by "gypsy" we do not understand (conventionally) anything of national and political import-ance. And it was at that date that the Moors, or Dubh-glasses, or Picts, of Galloway fell from their high estate into the position of outlawed and landless marauders : became, in short, *gypsies* and *faws* rather than (Scot-) *Egyptians* and *Picts*. It was about that period, also, that the laws against *sorners, Egyptians*, and such like began to be passed, by the Governmental party—which was the party of Norman, or semi-Norman ascendancy. These laws were continued, generation after generation, until all the *tories* of Scotland were either converted to Nationalism and Modernism, or were exterminated (except for the few and feeble specimens still visible here and there). It is plain that racial and quasi-religious feelings must have underlain this persecution.

Those *tories* were hunted down and banished because they were guilty of "sorcery, murder, incest, vagabondage, robbery, *sorning*, and heathenism," or non-Christianism, generally ; against which things the current of feeling throughout these islands had been setting strongly for a very long time. One who persisted in remaining a *Scot* (in the earlier sense of the word, as distinguished from the more modern and National *Scot*, *Scottish*, or *Scotch*-man), pure and simple, remained therefore a vagabond, a marauder, a mosser, a " habit and repute Egyptian : " until, at length, the name of *Scot* forsook him wholly. That such *tories* were, for the most part, descendants of the swarthy tribes of Britain, is seen from the fact that the "gypsy " of the popular imagination is indubitably a dark man : this being so much the case that Hume, a Scotch lawyer of two generations back, held that " black eyes should make part of the evidence in proving an individual to be of the gipsy race." Although this popular belief requires to be greatly modified, it seems that, of the many races of Britain, the slowest to accept the modern life have certainly been those of swarthy skin.

But, although 1455 may be taken as the date at which one important section of the Picts of Galloway became divorced from all connection with the party of progress, civilization (as we understand that term), and government ; yet no precise era can be fixed upon as that in which the black races of Scotland—or the "heathen " races of Scotland (to take an expression that includes " gypsies " of every hue)—degenerated into unimportant bands of marauders. That is to say —the era in which the *inveterate* sections of such races (their. *tories*) sank into this condition : (their other members added themselves, from time to time, to the mixed population that formed the Scottish nation). Powerful tribes and families were becoming "gypsies " in every century. When the Egyptian Kennedy of the ninth century conquered the powerful bands of painted Blacks seven times in one day, and so " secured the kingdom (a portion of modern Scotland) to himself,"—he was a man of great position and of historical influence. When the *Gypsy* Kennedy of the eighteenth century fought the Battle of Hawick Bridge against the Faws of Eastern Scotland, he was a (politically) insignificant outlaw. But, between these dates a great deal had happened : the whole of the authentic history of Scotland had happened. And, though this eighteenth-century " Egyptian " Cin-aedh, or the eighteenth-century gypsy Marshall, may be taken as the kings of the *tory* Scots of their districts, and therefore as representatives of King Kennedy or Kenneth of 844,—yet these are only the petrified specimens of their race. The higher qualities of the Scots Proper had animated the breasts of men who helped to change the whole life of Scotland,—of the British Empire,—of the world. In the doing of this, however,— in the making of Mediæval—and perhaps of Later—Scotland, innumerable dynasties had risen and fallen : innumerable combinations, physical and political, had been made between the various races, of whatever origin, that had entered Britain. From the earlier of these, it is plain we get the lower castes of "gypsies" : from the later—almost recent—dynasties, have come the "cavalier " families,—included by such writers as Mr. Simson under the designation of " gypsies."

That certain districts of Scotland retained their Faw (Pict) and Scot (Egyptian, or Gypsy) character up to quite recent times, we have seen. And it must be remembered that, in emphasizing such characteristics, it is by no means intended that these existed, *to the total exclusion of all others.* The others are not insisted upon simply because they do not belong to the present theme : which intentionally avoids all evidences of modern education and culture in Early Scotland, though these co-existed with the savagery that is more especially indicated. Because wigwams and gypsy tents formed the chief habitation of certain races in certain districts of Scotland, it is not to be forgotten that at the same period there were gracefully-carved churches and monasteries (the latter the homes and safeguards of all our learning and much of our refinement)—that there were strongly built castles, and fortified towns—that these towns were the nurseries of much of our present civilization.

But it has been shown, beyond question, that turf-covered wigwams and gypsy tents *did* form the chief habitation of important sections of the Scotch people within almost recent times : that, in short, these people lived as gypsies ; cooked, as gypsies ; dressed, or went naked, as gypsies ; painted their

skins, as gypsies ; sang the songs, and held the superstitions
of gypsies ; practised the religion, and lived the polygamous
(and more than polygamous) lives of gypsies ; in fine, were
nothing else but gypsies. That ideas so dissimilar as those
of Christianity and of various Paganisms should hold sway,
at the same period, within so small a territory as Modern
Scotland, is wonderful to us—who see the whole world united
by railways and telegraphs. It requires something of an
effort to realize the condition of this—or any other—country,
even a century ago : when districts, protected by natural
boundaries—of fen, or of mountain-ridge—were, to a great
extent, isolated from the national life ; so that Sir Walter
Scott was able to say that the carriage which took him into
Liddesdale was the first that had ever entered that valley—
through which the steam-engine now whistles fifty times
a-day. Under such conditions, it is really not so wonderful
that archaic customs should continue, or that kingships,
nominally dead, should retain their vitality, in various districts of Scotland, up to the very morning of the Modern
Age.

It is by remembering this, that we shall best understand
why the various recorded instances of arrivals of " gypsies,"
in certain towns or provinces, were regarded as the arrivals
of " foreigners," and allusion made to "their own country."
Even at the present day, there are English rustics who will
call any intruder into their parish " a foreigner." Rightly considered, the countries of Europe—a few centuries ago—were
confederacies of smaller kingdoms, rather than strictly unified states. This was certainly the case with Scotland,—the
country we have been most considering. The kingship of
Carrick was not formally abolished till after Culloden ; and,
even yet, Scotch people talk of the kingdom of Fife. The
Debatable land of the sixteenth century belonged to its
Graemes (black men, or gypsies),—and not either to England
or Scotland. When the whole of Great Britian was nominally under the rule of James the First, that monarch was
obliged to characterize one portion of the Hebrideans as
" wild savages, void of God's fear, *and our obedience*; "—one of
his bishops (the Bishop of the Isles) having also described
these people in a letter to the King—as " void of the true

knowledge of God, ignorant of the most part of your
Majesty's laws and their duty towards their dread Sovereign,
without civility or humane society."* An act of the Privy
Council, passed thirteen years after James had been pro-
claimed "the first monarch of this happy isle" (as Waller
afterwards puts it)—plainly states that, because the children
of Hebridean chiefs "see nothing in their tender years but
the barbarous and incivil forms of the country [that is, of the
Hebrides]—they are thereby made to apprehend that there
are no other forms and duties of civility kept in any other
part of the country [that is, the United Kingdom]."
What these last "barbarous and incivil," or, to phrase it
more fairly, those alien usages were—we have seen to some
extent. Those Hebrideans lived in turf wigwams, dressed in
a picturesque "gypsy" or "Red-Indian" fashion, wore
breastplates or brooches, engraved with hieroglyphics ;—and
the wilder natives of that archipelago, at perhaps a somewhat
earlier date, were known by such epithets as "the black-
skinned boar," "the one demon of the Gael ; " as "devils" ;
and as bearing such cognomens as *Green* Colin and *Blue*
Donald, significant of the appearance of their skins. We
saw that, at a period not much earlier than the Puritan settlement of Massachusetts, the Christians of the Hebrides—like
these same Puritans—required to go armed to church, "and
for the same reason, the dread of savages." That, in short,
the "plantation" of New-England was not far from being
contemporaneous with the "plantation" of the Hebrides.
To what extent the civilizing of these Islands affected the
blood of the "heathen" races need not be considered. The
fact stands, that this archipelago was fitly styled "the Isles
of the Foreigners," even at a time when James the First's
most illustrious subject was still writing his marvellous plays.
Whatever the *nominal* kingship of that monarch, he could
not be called *actual* king of even Great Britain (not to speak
of Ireland) so long as his laws were not acknowledged
throughout every inch of his apparent kingdom. And that
he realized the incomplete nature of his sovereignty is shewn
by those words of his quoted above. Their context, quoted

* These references have been made in a former chapter, and are extracted from
Collectanea de Rebus Albanicis, pp. 113, 115, and 121.

more fully, discloses the truth more clearly. The King states
—and this is in the year 1608—as his reasons for appointing
a Commission for " the Improvement of the Isles "—*" First,*
the care we have of planting the Gospel among these rude,
barbarous and incivil people, the want whereof these years past
no doubt has been to the great hazard of many poor souls,
being ignorant of their own salvation : *Next,* we desire to
remove all such scandalous reproaches against that state [by
which he means either the United Kingdom, generally, or,
more particularly Scotland—which by that date was a
province of the United Kingdom], *in suffering a part of it to
be possessed with such wild savages, void of* God's fear and *our
obedience :"* and, as a consequence of this, his third reason
(which, though he puts it last, was perhaps not the least important) is " herewith the loss we have in not receiving the
due rents adebted to us out of these Isles, being of the patrimony of our crown." Even so lately as 1635 (it was
noticed in a former chapter) a distinction was drawn between
" the Islanders " and " his Majesty's subjects." The former,
it was stated, used to " come in troops and companies out of
the Isles where they dwell, to the Isles and Lochs where the
fishes are taken, and there violently spoil his Majesty's subjects of their fishes and sometimes of their victuals and other
furniture, and pursue them of their lives." In all this, it was
previously observed, there was distinct proof that the various
kingships into which Scotland was once divided had not
wholly lost their power in the days of the last nominal King
of all North Britain. He, indeed, was not even so much as
the nominal king of what we call Scotland until thirteen
years prior to his becoming nominal King of the United
Kingdom. Until the year 1590, the Orkney Islands did not
form a portion of *Scotland*—but of *Denmark*. At a period
not much before this, the northern mainland of Scotland was
known to Gaelic-speaking people as *Gallibh,—The Country
of the Foreigners :* the whole of the Hebrides formed *Innse
Gaill,—The Islands of the Foreigners. Galloway* was (according to Mr. Skene) *The Country of the Gaels-and-Foreigners.*
The roots out of which these foreign kingships grew were
many and various : but it is enough to notice that they unmistakably existed.

Therefore, when we read the recorded instances of the arrivals of troops of "gypsies" in various Continental and British districts, we can understand how they were "foreigners "—to certain communities—and yet themselves of British or Continental nationality. The black-skinned, tattoed, and long-haired "gypsies" who entered Paris in the year 1427,—their women looking like "witches," and most of them, men and women, wearing silver ear-rings, "which they said, were esteemed ornaments in their country,"—may have come from no more remote district than the "marshes" of England and Scotland, or the Hebridean Islands. We saw that those Border "gypsies" were discovered, in several instances to be so irreclaimable, that "the evil was found to require the radical cure of extirpation." And, accordingly, they were banished the country—not to return under pain of death—or were enlisted as a kind of legion of *enfans perdus*, for the wars in the Low Countries and elsewhere. Whether from the Borders, or from the Hebrides, or from any other "out-land-ish" district (that is, any outlying district—remote from a township)—they contained in their ranks all the varied qualities that the vague designation "gypsy" comprises : they were "sorners," vagabonds, bards or minstrels, "jugglers or such like," otherwise styled "profest pleisants," or mountebanks ;—"the entertainment and bearing with" whom (it was stated in 1609), was "amongst the remanent abuses which, without reformation, have defiled the whole Isles :" and not "the Isles" only, as we have otherwise seen. The "band of 300 wanderers 'black as Tartars, and calling themselves *Secani*,'" that came to Lüneburg "late in 1417 ;" or the "troop of fully 100 lean, black hideous Egyptians," that entered Bologna in 1422,— whose queen (the wife of "Duke Andrew") was a druidess, witch, or sorceress, and "could read the past and future of men's lives ;" these, so far as complexion and characteristics go, may have come from any portion of the British Islands. It is not necessary to suppose that these had come so far ; for we have been told that—considered as *gypsies*—such people were known in Vienna, as well as in Scotland, during the twelfth century, "and that nowhere were they regarded as new-comers." And that, hundreds of years before the twelfth century, the whole of Europe was overrun with various races of conquering " Saracens." But it is quite possible that such wandering troops were simply the exiled tribes of Scotland, in many such instances.

We are not dealing with the Continent, however ; and scarcely with any other part of our own country than Scotland, in the meantime. The facts just pointed out ;—that Scotland, during the greater part of its history, was composed of a collection of separate kingdoms and chiefdoms,—whose existence could be prolonged wonderfully by physical aids, such as the barrier of a mountain-ridge, unpierced by any road ; these facts show how the natives of one portion of Scotland could be perfectly different from those of another in language, dress, complexion, custom,—everything. There can be no doubt that a nucleus of Scottish nationality existed in Central, Eastern, and part of Southern Scotland for a very long time : and that, from this centre, the national power was steadily spreading with every generation. But it is also clear —from the rough sketches previously made—that the Kings of Scotland were, to a considerable extent, only Kings of Scotland by courtesy. In the first half of the fifteenth century, the *dubh-glasses* of Galloway—the " Moors, or Saracens " of tradition—were its actual rulers. No one need think, at that time, of entering South-Western Galloway, unless he "courted Saint Kennedie." In other words, unless he acknowledged the supremacy of the Scot-Egyptian aristocracy, founded by a Cin-aedh, Kennedy or Kenneth of the ninth century. The latter half of that century (the fifteenth) saw the nominal King of Scotland assert his supremacy over one of those local kings—after much hard fighting : though the rule of the Scots of Carrick did not cease then. At an earlier date than this, Mr. Skene has shewn us that almost the western half, and all the north of Scotland, was under the dominion of invading races : Finn Galls and Dubh Galls— White Heathen and Black Heathen—North-men and East-men—Norse and Danes. One of these sovereignties was that of the Danish Prince or Leod, " Olave the Black "—the King of Sodor and Man (or Man and the South-Hebrides). Other foreign kingships there were, varying with every generation, and with the varying fortunes of their kings, or kinglets.

But none of these was the kingship that Bruce fought for. These were among his chief impediments in his difficult march to a supreme throne. It was those *dubh galls*, or "swarthy men of Lorne" that, in one instance, nearly cut short his career : it was against those painted "Moors" that he fought his solitary battle, on that moonlight night by the River Cree. And it was with the death-throes of such king-ships that the last nominal King of Scotland was struggling, when (after he had ascended the British throne) he sent his Commissioners to the Hebrides, for the purpose of making such arrangements as would "remove all such scandalous reproaches" against his sovereignty, as that a part of his nominal dominions should be "possessed with wild savages, void of God's fear *and our obedience.*"

One other instance of this feature (and it will be the last) is found in the Border ballad, known as *The Sang of the Outlaw Murray*. This ballad is known to every reader of the *Minstrelsy*. The identity of the hero of it is not regarded by Scott as fully established. "It is true, that the Dramatis Personæ introduced seem to refer to the end of the fifteenth, or beginning of the sixteenth, century ; but from this it can only be argued, that the author himself lived soon after that period." At any rate, whether the King of Scotland who figures in it was James the Fourth, or an earlier monarch, it is evident that his unquestioned sovereignty did not reach to the Cheviot Hills.

This outlaw is known as "Murray,"—like his namesake, "the black Murray" of Galloway tradition. In the latter case, we know that this name means nothing more than "the black Moor," or "the blackamoor." In the former case, there is no hint of complexion, *except* in the name. This, however, proves nothing ; since this outlaw's name may have reached the "fossil" stage, and himself have been a descendant of the earlier family of *de* Moravia. This outlaw is introduced as living in Ettrick Forest, with a "royal company" of five hundred men, clad in Lincoln green : himself and his lady "in purple clad." He dwells in a "fair castle" of stone and lime, with armorial bearings sculptured over the doorway (which renders it likely that he was descended from the Norman *De Moravia*). We are told that—

> Word is gane to our nobil king,
>   In Edinburgh, where that he lay,
> That there was an Outlaw in Ettricke Foreste,
>   Counted him nought, nor a' his courtrie gay.
>
> " I make a vowe," then the gude king said,
>   " Unto the man that deir bought me,
> I'se either be king of Ettricke Foreste,
>   Or king of Scotlonde that Outlaw sall be ! "

One of the king's nobles then advises him to send a message to the outlaw, desiring him to acknowledge the king's supremacy, and to hold his territory—not as absolute owner —but as a vassal of the king. " If he refuse to do that," adds this noble, "we'll conquer both his lands and himself."

All this is a distinct admission on the part of this king and his court, that this " outlaw " was as yet an actual, independent king ; and that modern Selkirkshire was not a part of Scotland. The following words quite bear out this impression. The king is laying his injunctions upon his ambassador :—

> Ask him of whom he holds his lands,
>   Or man [*i.e.* vassal], who may his master be,
> And desire him come, and be my man,
>   And hold of me yon Foreste free.

And say to him that—if he refuse—

> We'll conquess baith his lands and he.

The messenger reaches Ettrick Forest, and sees everything as described : the retainers in Lincoln-green, " shooting their bows on Newark Lee : " the knight himself armed from head to heel.

> Thereby Boyd [the ambassador] ken'd he was master man,
>   And served him in his ain degree.
> " God mot thee save, brave Outlaw Murray !
>   Thy ladye, and all thy chivalry ! "

To which the chief replies—

> " Marry, thou's well-come, gentelman,
>   Some king's messenger thou seems to be."

The answer to this interrogatory remark (which itself could never have been made by a vassal to the representative of his own sovereign) is conceived in the same spirit as the question :

> " The king of Scotlonde sent me here,
>   And, gude Outlaw, I am sent to thee ;
> I wad wot of whom ye hold your lands,
>   Or man, who may thy master be ? "

> " These lands are *mine !* " the Outlaw said ;
>   " I ken nae king in Christentie ;
> Frae Soudron I this Foreste wan,
>   When the king nor his knights were not to see."

The messenger then delivers the king's orders, adding the threat that, in the case of refusal,—

> He'll conquess baith thy lands and thee.
>   *   *   *   *   *
> " Aye, by my troth !" the Outlaw said,
>   " Then wald I think me far behinde.

> " E'er the king my fair countrie get,
>   This land that's nativest to me !
> Mony o' his nobles sall be cauld,
>   Their ladies sall be right wearie."

Murray's statement that he had conquered this territory from one or other of the sub-kings of Ancient Northumbria, and that it had not hitherto formed a part of Scotland, is endorsed by the king ; whose question, on the return of his messenger, shows that that district is a *terra incognita.*

> " Wellcum, James Boyd ! " said our noble king ;
>   What Foreste is Ettricke Foreste free ? "
> " Ettricke Foreste is the fairest foreste
>   That ever man saw wi' his e'e.
>   *   *   *   *   *
> " There the Outlaw keeps five hundred men ;
>   He keeps a royalle companie !
> His merryemen in ae livery clad,
>   O' the Linkome grene sae gaye to see ;
> He and his ladye in purple clad ;
>   O ! gin they live not royallie !

> " He says, yon Foreste is his awin ;
>   He wan it frae the Southronie ;
> Sae as he wan it, sae will he keep it,
>   Contrair all kingis in Christentie."

When the king receives this challenge, he at once gives

orders to raise the men of his kingdom; and the verse in which he does so seems to indicate that its limits were the limits of Early Scotia (not *Ancient* Scotia, or Ireland, but Scotia as it is defined by Mr. Skene;—being, roughly stated, the eastern half of Modern Scotland):—

> " Gar warn me Perthshire, and Angus baith ;
> Fife up and down, and the Louthians three,"
> *   *   *   *   *

It is unnecessary to quote much more. The Border chief —hearing

> That the king was coming to his countrie
> To conquess baith his landis and he,—

at once prepares for defence; and sends messages to the neighbouring chieftains who are his allies—some of them his kinsmen. In the references they make to the King of " Scotland," they undoubtedly recognize in him a much more powerful personage than any one of themselves: speaking of him as " *the* king," and as " a king wi' crown." But, nevertheless, they as clearly regard themselves as independent potentates : which the foregoing extracts show was, in a great measure, the opinion of the king himself. Eventually, the matter is compromised,—" Murray " agreeing to acknowledge the sovereignty of the king (and thereby adding all his territory—won from Northumbria, or perhaps Cumbria—to the increasing Scotch kingdom). In return for his homage, the king makes him Sheriff of Ettrick Forest,—and his posterity after him,—

> " Surely while upward grows the tree."

Like other ballads and legends, this is, no doubt, partly true, partly fanciful and untrue. As Scott states, a Murray certainly did become heritable sheriff of Ettrick Forest, "by a charter from James IV., dated November 30th, 1509," which continued in those of that name (the Philiphaugh family) till such jurisdictions were abolished, after Culloden. But some parts of this tale speak of an earlier time than 1509. And the traditions regarding this " outlaw" vary. " The tradition of Ettrick Forest bears, that the outlaw was a man of prodigious strength, possessing a batton or club, with which he laid lee (*i.e.*, waste) the country for many miles round." This account would give him a wilder aspect than that with which he is invested in the ballad,—and suggests rather the characteristics of the "Black Murray" of Galloway, of the "big, black giant with a club," who figures in the popular tales of the Highlands and Wales, of the "Black Oppressor," whom Welsh Peredur slew, of the Black Knight of Lancashire, and of that particular Black Dubh-glass who is remembered, locally, as "one of the most horrible devils that ever appeared in Scotland" (being, perhaps, no other than the Black Morrow of the same neighbourhood,—or of the same family). The club has always been a weapon of the "Moors" of Scotland—from the days of Severus down to our own ; when "the bludgeon tribe" is used—in Galloway, at least—as a synonym for "the gypsies."

Though none of the traditions seem to make reference to his complexion, beyond calling him a "Murray" (which may have been nothing more than a meaningless surname, in his case), yet the very spot in which the King's messenger is supposed to have found him, the locality of his stronghold has—in close proximity—a counterpart to the *Black Morrow Wood*, or *Blackamoor's Wood* of Kirkcudbright, namely, the *Black Andrew Wood*. Moreover, there are such names in the same immediate neighbourhood as *Black-house Tower*, situated on the *Dubh-glass Burn ;* the *Craig of Dubh-glass ; Duchar Law*, and *Duchar Tower ;* the last of which names signifies "*the Black Fort.*"* And a portion of the important rampart known as "*the Catrail*" or "*the Picts' Work*," that is, "*the Blackamoors' Work*,"—runs across the hills that overlook *Black Andrew Wood*. Therefore, it is not unlikely that "Black Andrew" was no other than the "outlaw" himself.

---

* This name of Duchar, Deuchar, Duchra or Duchray is given to many places in Scotland, and its recognized meaning is "the black fort." One would hesitate to make use of such a translation, if it were not recognized as the right one. Because *Dubh-Rath*, "the black fort," does not easily reach the stage of even *Duch-ra*. *Dubh-Rath* is naturally pronounced as if written *Doov-Ra* or *Doo-Ra* (which probably gives *Dura* as another form of the name) ; but the step from the labial *v* to the guttural *ch* is a pretty long one. However, it was likely by the way of *Doo-Ra* that this guttural sound was reached. At any rate, this etymology is the accepted one. And, moreover, it is stated by Mr. J. F. Campbell that this guttural pronunciation of *dubh* is by no means uncommon.

The Lincoln-green dresses of his followers are worth noticing. The terms " Lincoln-green," and " Kendal-green," must have had a connection with the lineage of those inhabiting these districts. This colour has been " British " from the earliest times—ever since woad, equally blue or green, was in use. We have seen that *gorm* is translated either "blue" or " green " : *uaine*, also, is "green": and both *gorm* and *uaine* were used as distinctive epithets. Woad, used as a dye for the skin, when no clothes were worn, would naturally be used as a dye for clothing, when the *gorm* tribes began to wear garments. *Gorm*, when translated "green," gives us the oldest colour of Ireland : when translated "blue," it gives us the *tory* colour throughout the country. That *red* was also a *tory* colour, is known from an anecdote of the seventeenth century : that it was a *tory* colour eighty years ago, is expressed by the ruddled faces of the Galloway "gypsies" : that red, blue, and white, form the colours of the British Standard, every one knows, and the reason of this may be guessed : but that *green* was the colour of a large section of the Early-Britons is beyond dispute. We know that *duine-dubh*, "a black man," in Scotch-Gaelic, is *duine-gorm*, "a green—or blue—man," in Irish-Gaelic: and that "a blue-skin" is the "cant" term for a mulatto. Therefore (without regarding the claims of other hues), one is not surprised to hear that green, according to the historian of the Scotch "gypsies," is "a favourite gipsy colour." And a more recent writer (Mr. C. G. Leland) corroborates this. " Till within a few years in Great Britain, as at the present day in Germany, their fondness for green coats amounted to a passion." " The male gipsies in Scotland," says Mr. Simson, " were often dressed in green coats. . . . . The females were very partial to green clothes." Like the followers of the Ettrick Forest chief, they wore "the Linkome grene sae gaye to see." Or, like the followers of the outlaw of Sherwood Forest : whose life was very similar to that of this Ettrick "outlaw," whose men are discovered " shooting their bows on Newark Lee." Either of these would have been styled "gypsies," by a fifteenth-century gypsiologist, had such existed.

It has been noticed that a swarthy skin is not necessary

to constitute a "gypsy." A "gypsy" is made, says one writer, by the living a certain archaic, "heathen" life, and speaking certain archaic languages. He may be a white man. The greatest "gypsies" in Scotland—the Baillies— are white men. The Scotch "gypsies" are, in short, only stunted Scotchmen: stunted at various stages of the national growth; and so, according to the length of the tory pedigree of each tribe, giving us examples of the various stages of " culture" in Scotland.

This Philiphaugh Murray, and his green-clad archers, were, therefore, "gypsies." Whether the leader was descended from none but white men—as the Baillies were—is immaterial. It is likely that his followers were, for the most part, genuine "Murrays." Because they formed part of the South-Scottish *Moravienses:* and the villages of their neighbourhood are still said to be " stocked" with "gypsies."

Like the Galloway Douglases—like the Baillies—like the Gordons—the Philiphaugh Murrays seem to have thrown out a *tory* branch. Or, more correctly, the main stem must have gradually lost hold of its possessions, *by being tory:* by not forsaking the wild and lawless life that was "the mode" some centuries ago: the following of which course—or *refusing* to follow the course of civilization—resulted in "out-lawry," as the land grew more peaceful and its laws more peace-helping. This assumption, with regard to the Murrays of Philiphaugh, is suggested by a statement of Mr. Simson's,* to the effect that "the chief of the Ruthvens (a "gypsy" family) actually wept like a child, whenever the misfortunes of the ancient family of Murray of Philiphaugh were men-tioned to him."

This Ruthven chief was one of the high-caste "gypsies." He is thus spoken of—

"I have already mentioned how handsomely the superior order of Gipsies dressed at the period of which we are speak-ing [the middle of last century]. The male head of the

---

* "History," pp. 187 and 213. The references in this book for the remarks made in the foregoing pages with respect to the division of Scotland into provinces, the limits of which were protected by a system of passes, are pages 121, 128-*note*, 130, 131, 157, 158, 159, 180, 181, 199, 200, 218, 219, 236, 237, 318-*note*, 341, 348, and 350.

Ruthvens—a man six feet some inches in height—who, according to the newspapers of the day, lived to the advanced age of 115 years, when in full dress, in his youth, wore a white wig, a ruffled shirt, a blue Scottish bonnet, scarlet breeches and waistcoat, a long blue superfine coat, white stockings, with silver buckles in his shoes."

This, then, was the outward appearance of the "gypsy" chief who bewailed the decadence of the Murrays of Philiphaugh. His brave exterior placed him among the "gentlemen" of his time, outwardly;—and as he belonged to "the superior order of gipsies," those who boast of their ancient and lofty lineage, and who look down with contempt upon "the rabble of town and country," it is evident that he was otherwise well entitled to the name of "gentleman." The clan of which he was chief was one of the three principal Tweed-dale castes, we are told: the other two being the Baillies and the Kennedys. "Gypsies" of this description were men of graceful bearing, and polished manners, who associated as equals "with gentlemen of the first respectability in the country," who could "discourse readily and fluently upon almost any topic," and who rode "the best horses the kingdom could produce." This was the kind of man indicated to us in the person of the venerable chief of the *tory* Ruthvens. All those "gypsies" were distinctly gentlemen (accepting this word in its conventional sense); dressed like other gentry of the day; the Baillie chiefs "attired in the finest scarlet;" they and such-like wearing "silver brooches in their breasts, and gold rings on their fingers," silver buckles on their shoes, powdered wigs, ruffled shirts,—in short, the full dress of seventeenth-century gentlemen. The wives of the Baillie chiefs, we are told, "rode to the fairs at Moffat and Biggar, on horses, with side-saddles and bridles, ... themselves being very gaily dressed. The males wore scarlet cloaks, reaching to their knees, and resembling exactly the Spanish fashion of the present day." If, therefore, the Murray of Philiphaugh, whose misfortunes the Ruthven patriarch wept over, resembled that chief himself, his attire was almost identical with that of his namesake of the ballad—"he and his ladye in purple clad;" and his followers in "the Lincoln green sae gaye to see."

So long as the regulus of Ettrick Forest held himself aloof
from his northern neighbour (the king of Scotia, or Scotland), refusing to pay him homage, then Ettrick Forest was
an independent kingdom ; forming no part whatever of
" Scotland." And Ettrick Forest, at that date, seems pretty
clearly to have been a *gypsy* kingdom. " Scotland," indeed,
extended a very little way to the south of the Forth basin,
only a few centuries ago. It is not a great while since people
spoke of going " out of Scotland into the Largs ;" Largs (or
" the Largs ") being situated in the district of Cunninghame,
and only about half-a-dozen miles to the south of the latitude
of Glasgow. Before the overthrow of the black Douglases in
1455, Galloway was not really a portion of Scotland. The chief
of those Douglases was an actual king, who held a court of
his own, created knights of his own, moved about the country
with a following of two thousand men, and possessed a
separate mint from that of the king of Scotland, in which
were struck coins of an order quite distinct from those of
Scotland. Some of these were popularly remembered as
" Douglas groats ;"* and it is most probable that "certain
peeces of silver, with a strange and uncouth impression
thereon, resembling the old Pictish coine," which Symson
chronicles as having been dug out of the ruins of an old
castle in the parish of Borgue (in Galloway), came out of
the Douglas mint. Whether called " Pictish " or " Douglas,"
such coins were, of course " Moorish,"—or, to use the alternative form, " Saracen." (Now-a-days, the word is " gypsy.")
That the chiefs of the black Douglases were attended by the
jugglers and mountebanks that are inseparable from " gypsydom " is seen from the carvings on an antique bedstead, taken
out of the castle of Thrave, and stated to have belonged to
the last of the black lords: and in these bas-reliefs such

---

* It is quite likely that another of these coins was that known as the *baubee ;*
which Mr. Halliwell says was " a copper coin, of about the value of a halfpenny."
He adds that " the halfpenny itself is sometimes so called ; " and it is well known
that this usage is quite common in Scotland ; being, indeed, popularly regarded
as peculiarly Scotch. But as Mr. Halliwell, and one (at least) of the " cant "
vocabularies, do not confine the word to any particular district, it may be assumed
that " baubees " were current in many other parts of the country. It is not improbable that the " inferior foreign coin," called the " gally-halfpenny," which
was prohibited by Henry the Eighth, was identical with the " baubee."

figures occupy a most prominent place. Of the actual appearance that a troop of fifteenth-century black-Douglases presented, one can only form an imperfect notion ; but, as a counterpart to the fact that they are remembered in tradition as " Moors or Saracens," and also to the fact that crescents and stars were the commonest emblems of families asserting a descent from them (or their kin), it may be stated that the curved sword which is so generally associated with the East was in use in the Douglas territory so recently as 1666. From which circumstances, it would seem that, although often acknowledging the superiority of Scotland Proper, the South-Western division of North Britain was, until modern times, so independent in its character and customs, and large sections of its people were of such an individual ethnic stamp, that the people and their country were as " foreign " to Eastern Scotland (Scotland Proper) as they could well be.

It has now been sufficiently insisted that "gypsies" of all kinds are only decayed aristocrats. The day when the most barbarous tribes (though these really do not exist nowadays) were in power, must be very remote. But *tories* such as these we have just looked at are of the most recent date. They are the people sketched by Professor Masson, in his remarks bearing upon the Register of the Privy Council of Scotland, during the sixteenth century. "In these old days the one and universal process in Scotland for intimating that a person was disobedient to the law, in any way or form, was to denounce that person rebel, and put him to the horn. . . . . Hence the highest personages in the land— earls, lords, lairds, and lawyers—found themselves again and again rebels to the king, and at the horn . . . . . the ' horners,' specially so-called, were those who obstinately and persistently remained in their state of rebellion, by not appearing to the charges, whatever they were, that had been issued against them, or by not paying the debts they had been decreed to pay, or finding the securities they had been decreed to find. The word ' outlaws ' defines their position accurately enough ; they were ' the King's rebels,' standing out in disobedience, and liable to very summary further process against them personally or in their goods. [Being, eventually, nothing less than ' pursuit with fire and sword as

enemies to God, His Majesty, and the common weal.'] This
was the theory and the law ; but, in fact, the country was
full of ' horners ' or ' King's rebels ' of all sorts, who laughed
at those summary processes of arrest or escheat of goods to
which they were liable, had no goods to be escheated, and
lived secretly with their friends, or went about openly, defying
arrest." And, as we have seen, in the cases of the Baillies
and the Gordons, the friends of such " outlaws " were even
powerful enough to save them from a well-merited death on
the gallows.

Such outlaws "going about openly, defying arrest," and
with " no goods to be escheated,"—plainly must have lived
by violence and the right of the sword, as their ancestors had
done : "enforcing a living on the common road." And, while
they did so, their relations quietly stepped into lawful possession of their titles and the lands which they had forfeited,
or dissipated. The banished Duke had always a "usurper " at hand, to take his place : a discredited Chief of the
Black-Douglases had always a Chief of the Tawny-Douglases
ready to sway the sceptre of the race. This is not to be
deplored ; nor are such terms as " usurper " or " time-server "
(applicable enough in such cases) to be understood in their
most offensive sense. No doubt, there were many cases of
unfair and gross usurpation ; but the "time-servers " were the
representatives of civilization. A loyal Earl of Angus, though
he succeeded in " feathering his own nest " very skilfully, was
a great improvement on a savage, marauding Black-Douglas ;
a wandering, irreconcilable " Moor or Saracen ; " whose
hatred of stone-and-lime was embodied in his saying, that he
" liked better to hear the lark sing than the mouse squeak."
Civilization had made a distinct stride in Scotland, when
"the Red Douglas put down the Black."

The references, made above, to the " gypsies " of very
modern date, are a little out of place. What we have been
considering is, that the earlier " gypsies " represented various
intra-Scottish kingdoms, that had been " foreign countries "
to Scotia, or East Scotland. When there were no roads—
to speak of,—and no means of locomotion except by riding
on horseback, or in a litter or palanquin ; and when the many
jarring forces, that composed even the most civilized commu-

nity, were still in a constant state of friction ; the King of the largest of all the distinct kingships of Scotland—that of " Scotia"—had enough to do inside his own realm, without attempting to make his way into this or that contiguous kingdom. *The Sang of the Outlaw Murray* says very plainly that the King of Scotia knew actually nothing of the country that lay to the south of the Lothians. It is only a ballad, to be sure, and it likely speaks of an earlier time than 1509,—but a glance at the maps in *Celtic Scotland* show us how several nationalities did co-exist in the small territory of North Britain. But, after all, this era need not antedate 1509 by *very* much. It was seen that so lately as the first quarter of the seventeenth century the Hebrides were still inhabited by people who did not own the Christian religion or the British law : and regarding whose language, laws, dress, customs, and complexion an ordinary burgher of Edinburgh or of Aberdeen must have been wholly ignorant. These differed as greatly from each other as if an Atlantic, and not only the breadth of Scotland, had separated them.

There is, positively, *no* exact date, that can be fixed as that in which this Border kingship finally ceased. When the *Graemes*, or *Gypsies* of the Debatable Land protested against the survey of their territory, by representatives of the central Government,—and when they backed up their protest by summarily ejecting the would-be " settlers," with all their belongings,—the independence of the Border Kingdom had not been wholly crushed. And this was only last century. The farther back we go, the larger is the size of this kingdom, and the greater the power of its rulers. The era of " the outlaw Murray " (whenever that was) marks the date at which the district of Ettrick Forest was added to the Kingdom of Scotia. But that only placed the boundary of Scotia about twenty miles to the south of its former limit. Between this new frontier and the Cheviot Hills there remained as wide a district still independent : and the country lying to the south of the Cheviots was not " England" either. 1509 is given as the period at which Ettrick Forest became formally a part of " Scotland." But, in 1529, James V. had to march an army of eight thousand men across the southern boundary of Ettrick Forest, and into the country of " the thieves" of

Teviotdale, Annandale, and Liddesdale. Indeed, so little
under his power was even Ettrick Forest itself, that the
"King of the Border" at this time (Adam Scott), lived at
his stronghold of Tushielaw, in the upper portion of the Vale
of Ettrick.* In this campaign—and during his brief reign—
James did much to enlarge the sway of the Modern-Scotch
monarchy. This King of the Border, and another "gypsy"
chief, Piers Cockburn, he hanged before their own peels, or
towers :† (as, it may be remembered, we noticed in a previous
chapter). A still more powerful "king," whose sway extended
more to the southward, met with a similar fate, on this occasion. This was the celebrated "Johnny Armstrong," of
whom it is stated, that "he always rode with twenty-four
able gentlemen, well horsed, and from the borders to Newcastle every Englishman, of whatever state, paid him tribute."
"He and all his followers, some accounts make them forty-
eight, were hanged (by the King's orders) on the trees of a
little grove at Carlinrigg chapel, two miles north of Moss
Paul, on the road between Hawick and Langholm." The

* ? *Aed-rik.*
† Wilson, in his "Tales of the Borders," associates those "peels" with the
faws. "In the wilderness between Keyheugh and Clovencrag . . . . stood some
score of peels, or rather half hovels, half encampments—and this primitive city in
the wilderness was the capital of the Faa King's people." The cattle which they
had carried off were seen "grazing before the doors or holes of the gipsy village,"
and "it was impossible to stand upright" in these huts themselves. ("The
Faa's Revenge.") The era of this legend is 1628, but (though the writer was a
Borderer) it cannot be relied upon in every particular, the relative positions of the
military and the *agricultural* castes being that of the second half of the eighteenth,
rather than the first half of the seventeenth century, at which period the former
was most distinctly the ruling caste (though time, and the operation of peace-
helping laws, gradually increased the power and importance of the latter till it
became paramount). But, in spite of this palpable and important misrepre-
sentation, Wilson's picture is of some value. It bears out the description given
by Æneas Sylvius—formerly quoted. "Upon the Borders he found [in the first
half of the fifteenth century] that most of the houses were not even huts, as they
were generally a small breast-work composed of mud, or such materials as were
at hand, and raised to a sufficient height by three or four poles meeting a-top,
and covered with straw or turf." Such were the wigwams of the Isles of the
Foreigners last century, and such were the dwellings of the "gypsies" "on
Yeta's banks" a little later.

It is also worth remarking that this application (by a Borderer) of the word
"peel" seems to denote a wider use of that term than the present. For it is now,
I think, applied solely to the square, stone-built tower that can yet be seen on the
Borders.

power of this latter confederacy—that ruled by the Armstrongs—was not finally broken till the following reign.* After which, the sovereignty seems to have passed over to the Herons,—since we saw that Francis Heron, who was buried at Jarrow in 1756, was the *faw* king of that period. His probable successor was Henry the *faw ;* of whom it was stated that he " was received, and ate at the tables of people in public office," and to whom " men of considerable fortune paid a gratuity, called blackmail, in order to have their goods protected from thieves." And " Will *Faa*," who died at Yetholm in 1847, seems to be the latest representative of this withered sovereignty.†

In the beginning of the sixteenth century, then, it is clear that the Border country,—as far north as the Vale of Ettrick,— was virtually an independent territory,—whatever may be the historical name of the nationality it represented (which perhaps was " Cumbria ": or " Northumbria "). No doubt at this, and an earlier period, the various Border Chiefdoms did not form one distinct, unified kingdom : or, if so, it was of a shifting nature. At one time this or that tribe of the Borders would form an alliance with the Scotch—at another

---

* The account from which I have been quoting (Anderson's " Scottish Nation ") states that "the hostile and turbulent spirit of the Armstrongs . . . . was never entirely broken or suppressed until the reign of James the Sixth, when their leaders were brought to the scaffold, their strongholds razed to the ground, and their estates forfeited and transferred to strangers ; so that throughout the extensive districts formerly possessed by this once powerful and ancient clan there is scarcely left, at this day, a single landholder of the name. Their descendants have been long scattered, some of them having settled in England, and others in Ireland." (In reference to one of these statements, it may be here repeated that the thoughtless custom of regarding the bearer of a modern surname as the representative of the race whence he derived it is an utter fallacy. Of the four great-grandfathers of a modern " Armstrong," two may have been Baillies and another Elliott. If so, this Armstrong is more an eighteenth-century Baillie than an Armstrong, though his surname has accidentally come to him from the latter. This is ignoring great-grandmothers, and all the thousand ancestors that went before them, who may have belonged to any one of the nations, clans, and families of Europe. To talk of a man being "a thorough Brown " or "a true Jones "—in a genealogical sense—is a misuse of language.)

† He was succeeded by Charles Blythe, who again was succeeded by his daughter, Esther Faw Blythe. But as Blythe was not of the swarthy Faw blood, and as his daughter (though inheriting some of that blood through her mother) was not very much more of a " Faw " than her father, these two were most imperfect representatives of this Border chiefship.

time with this or that other Border tribe—against whatever
foe it seemed convenient to fight. Moreover, the more important chiefs unquestionably did acknowledge the Scottish
King as their sovereign—after a fashion. But when (as with
the Galloway *dubh-glasses* and Island *dubh-galls* of the
fifteenth century) there seemed a chance of success in a united
attack upon the monarchy of "Scotia," their vassalage was
thrown to the winds. Indeed, it was chiefly because the
attitude of the Border leaders was formidable and threatening in the extreme, that the young king (James the Fifth)
had to act with such severity in his invasion of the Border
country. Those leaders, then, were "outlaws" and "King's
rebels" in a certain sense. In an exact sense, as we get
nearer our own time: in a very inexact sense, as we go back
to the period of the "outlaw Murray;"—who had conquered
his own territory for himself, from "the Southrons," and who
was therefore, least of all, a "rebel" to the King of Scotland.

The "Debatable Land," therefore, or the Border portions
of *Cumbria-cum-Northumbria*, maintained its integrity—as
a really important district—up till the end of the sixteenth
century: at which period James the Sixth of Scotland
finally rooted out the Armstrong aristocracy (whose place,
nevertheless, other and feebler clans of "mossers" continued,
in a manner, to fill). Not only did the chief of the Armstrongs refuse to acknowledge "either Henry or James" as
his over-lord ; but, on one occasion, when he and his tribe
had been out on the war-path in the north of England, the
English warden of the West Marches (Sir Robert Carey),
having "demanded satisfaction from the king of Scotland,"
"received for answer, that the offenders were no subjects
of his, and that he might take his own revenge." This was
in 1598; five years before the "King of Scotland" became
"King of Great Britain and Ireland." At that date—1598—
this "King of Scotland" had only been the undoubted
sovereign of the Danish Orkneys for eight years ; on his own
confession, the Hebrides were, for several years after this, not
under his rule (whatever they were *nominally*) ; and here also,
on his own confession, a large tract of country in the south
of Modern Scotland was possessed by tribes who "were no
subjects of his."

Sir Robert Carey, on receiving this answer from the king of Scotland, "accordingly entered Liddesdale, and ravaged the land of the outlaws." In doing this, he was assisted by those subjects of King James whom Carey styles "the foot of Liddisdale and Risdale;" and Scott states* that "the garrison of King James in the Castle of Hermitage" is included in this term. These statements, and further allusions to the "English side" of this territory, and "the high parts of the marsh towards Scotlande," leave no room for doubting its independent character. And "the garrison of King James in the Castle of Hermitage" may not inaptly be compared with a modern United States regiment, in a fort of Southern Arizona.

Because these, be it remembered, were our British "Indians:" from whom, or whose like, a large number of us are descended. The article on the *Minstrelsy*, in the *Edinburgh Review* of 1803, says :—" In these traits [of the Borderers], we seem to be reading the description of a Tartarian or Arabic tribe, and can scarcely persuade ourselves that this country contained, within these two centuries, so exact a prototype of the Bedouin character." One might echo Hamlet—" *Seems !* nay, it *is;* I know not 'seems.' " It *is* the description of Tartarian tribes : who were called by that very name, "thieving Tartarians," by their civilized contemporaries : whose complexion and customs can yet be paralleled in Arabia : who—geographically, chronologically, ethnographically—connect the "Old" World with the "New." These are the *Thieves, Scots, Mossers* and *Felons* referred to in the Edinburgh newspaper of 1662 ;—wherein they are spoken of as notorious robbers and murderers : who are characterized by Scott, on various occasions,† as "hardy and ferocious," "savage and licentious :" and regarding whom he has made many statements that fully justify the use of these terms. Of the "Southern Reivers" (or mossers south of the Cheviots) who captured the castle of Fairnihurst, during the sixteenth century, he states : "The commander and his followers are

---

* In his prefatory remarks to the ballad of "Johnnie Armstrong."

† See the "Minstrelsy of the Scottish Border," pages 19, 23, 27, 32, 96, and others (in the edition here quoted—Murray, London, 1869), for information of this sort.

accused of such excesses of lust and cruelty 'as would,' says Beaugé, 'have made to tremble the most savage moor in Africa.'" And when this stronghold was re-taken, in the year 1549, by a mixed force of Frenchmen and Northern " Reivers," the latter displayed the same savage qualities as their southern kindred (and enemies). The arrows of the besieged mossers having proved useless before the fire of the French musketry, and the savage archers themselves being driven from the walls ; and finally, the wall of the inner stronghold being shattered in one place, by a mine; the southern leader crept through the breach thus made, "and, surrendering himself to De la Mothe-rouge, implored protection from the vengeance of the borderers. But a Scottish marchman, eyeing in the captive the ravisher of his wife, approached him ere the French officer could guess his intention, and, at one blow, carried his head four paces from the trunk. Above a hundred Scots rushed to wash their hands in the blood of their oppressor, bandied about the severed head, and expressed their joy in such shouts, as if they had stormed the city of London. The prisoners, who fell into their merciless hands, were put to death, after their eyes had been torn out ; the victors [*not* the more civilized Frenchmen, who led the   attack] contending who should display the greatest address in severing their legs and arms before inflicting a mortal wound. When their own prisoners were slain, the Scottish, with an unextinguishable thirst for blood, purchased those of the French ; parting willingly with their very arms, in exchange for an English captive. ' I myself,' says Beaugé, with military sang-froid, ' I myself sold them a prisoner for a small horse [one of their "galloways "]. They laid him down upon the ground, gallopped over him with their lances in rest, and wounded him as they passed. When slain, they cut his body in pieces, and bore the mangled gobbets, in triumph, on the point of their spears.' " It is of these " Red-Indian " tribes that Scott is speaking, when he describes their gathering-song, with its savage burden of *a' a' a' a' a'*, " swelling into a long and varied howl ; " and when he states that, when raising their tribe for pursuit, or " the Hot trod,"—" they used to carry a burning wisp of straw at spear head, and to raise a cry, similar to the Indian war-whoop:" which similarity—apparent throughout all this paragraph—was still further increased when (like the "Galloways" of the twelfth century, in the army of William the Lion)* their bodies were naked from head to heel,—when they rode their little Indian-ponies without saddle or bridle,—and when their dusky skins were painted over with the "various colours" of the faws, or scarlet with the ruddle of the Wild Scots óf Galloway.

It is of these races that Fuller—at a date long subsequent to the twelfth century, and after many changes of custom, of blood, and of political position—writes as follows : † " These compelled the vicinage to purchase their security, by paying a constant rent to them. When in their greatest height, they had two great enemies,—*the Laws of the Land* and the *Lord William Howard of Naworth.* He sent many of them to Carlisle, to that place where the officer *doth always his work by daylight."* ,(Fuller, of course, refers more particularly to the Southern Borderers—whom he styles " English Tories "—and the laws he speaks of were those of England.) " After that they are outlawed . . . they lawfully may be destroyed, without any judicial inquisition [he is quoting from Bracton], as who carry their own condemnation about them, and deservedly die without law, because they refused to live according to [South British] law." These marauders, lurking in the marshes of Tarras, and "the Merse," are the *Scots* of whom the *Scotchman* Lesley, bishop of Ross, has given this sketch‡ :—" They sally out of their own borders, in the night, in troops,

---

* This reference—already given—is page 39 of Nicholson's " Historical and Traditional Tales" of the South of Scotland ; Kirkcudbright, 1843.

A distinct identification of these Picts, Faws, or Moors of Galloway with the gypsies of Scotland (of which the presumptive evidence already adduced is so strong that it may surely be regarded as incontrovertible) under the *name* of gypsies or of " Tinklers " (which, in Scotland, is the same thing), may, perhaps, be discoverable in that charter of William the Lion, in which (says the Encyclopædia writer) there is special mention of *Tinklers.* We know that the *Douglasses* of Galloway claimed the right that Mr. Skene accords to the *Picts* of Galloway : that is, to the *Moors* of Galloway : that is, to the *dubh-glasses* of Galloway. And we know that white Scotchwomen used to frighten their children with a song that threatens the appearance, in one version, of " the black *dubh-glass* "—in another, of " the black *Tinkler.*" But this charter may, perhaps, prove the identity more clearly still.

† Appendix to " The Lay of the Last Minstrel," note N.

‡ Already extracted : from the Introduction to the " Minstrelsy."

through unfrequented bye-ways, and many intricate windings.
All the day time they refresh themselves and their horses,
in lurking holes they had pitched upon before, till they
arrive in the dark at those places they have a design upon.
As soon as they have seized upon the booty, they, in like
manner, return home in the night, through blind ways, fetch-
ing many a compass. The more skilful any captain is to pass
through those wild deserts, crooked turnings, and deep preci-
pices, in the thickest mists and darkness, his reputation is the
greater, and he is looked upon as a man of an excellent head.
And they are so very cunning that they seldom have their
booty taken from them, unless sometimes, when, by the help
of bloodhounds following them exactly upon the tract, they
may chance to fall into the hands of their adversaries.
When being taken, they have so much persuasive eloquence,
and so many smooth insinuating words at command [" Gitano,
Gipsy, flatterer ; Gitanada, *wheedling* "], that if they do not
move their judges, nay, and even their adversaries . . . . . to
have mercy, yet they incite them to admiration and compas-
sion." These " moon-men " (as Grose states the " gypsies "
were called), mossers, or moss troopers, of whom Bishop
Nicholson, writing in the end of the seventeenth century,
said that they were not at that time " utter strangers to the
black art of their forefathers," are similarly described in that
act• of James the First (of the United Kingdom), which
states " that the thieves and limmers aforesaid, having for
some short space after the said act of parliament, (of 1609,
" anent the Egyptians," or " vagabonds, sorners, and common
thieves, commonly called Egyptians, ") . . . . dispersed themselves in certain secret and obscure places of the country
. . . . . . they were not known to wander abroad in troops and
companies, according to their accustomed manner, yet, shortly
thereafter, finding that the said act of parliament was neglected,
and that no enquiry . . . . was made for them, they began to
take new breath and courage, and . . . . unite themselves in
infamous companies and societies, under . . . . commanders,
and continually since then have remained within the country
[from which—either regarded as Scott's *moss-troopers*, or as
Simson's *gypsies*—they had been pronounced banished], com-

* Quoted in Mr. Simson's " History " (p. 114).

·mitting as well open and avowed rieffis (robberies) in all parts . . . . murders . . . . pleine stouthe (common theft), and pickery, where they may not be mastered ; and they do shamefully and mischievously abuse the simple and ignorant people, by telling fortunes, and using charms ["spells, magical receipts," and "other conjuring feats," as Bishop Nicholson says], and a number of juggling tricks and falseties, unworthy to be heard of in a country subject to religion, law, and justice."

These are the people who as "common thieves" were "commonly called Egyptians ;" and as commonly called "Tartarians," as we have previously noticed.* Either term— there is much reason for believing—correctly indicates the extra-British homes of certain marauding British castes (known to history as *Scots, Black-Danes*, &c.), though the changes of many centuries must, of necessity, have deprived those designations of their original correctness. The links of complexion, of custom, and of character, that unite the Black Dane with the Hun, seem to justify the use of the word " Tartarian : " the identity of the fifteenth century *Scot* with the fifteenth century *Egyptian* (as seen from the remarks of Boece and of Lesley, from the fact that *Scot* and *mosser* were interchangeable terms later on, and for other reasons already stated), and also the probable-identity of the *Scots* and *Ancient Egyptians*—tracing backwards from the fifteenth century to the third or fourth, and so to Egypt— seem to justify, with equal force, the use of the word "Egyptian:" both of which robber-nations, or the *tory* remnants of which, were styled "common thieves" so recently as the seventeenth century. (Their earlier and considerably remote Oriental connection with each other—if such connection existed—is a question with which we have nothing to do here.)

But before their "decay" and "ruine"—to quote Fuller

* The references were from "The Merry Devil of Edmonton "—"there's not a Tartarian, nor a carrier shall breath upon your geldings :" and from "The Wandering Jew" (1640), wherein the Hangman says, " . . . . and if any thieving Tartarian shall break in upon you, I will with both hands nimbly lend a cast of my office to him." And the Modern-Danish law denounces "the Tartar gipsies, who wander about everywhere, doing great damage to the people, by their lies, thefts and witchcraft."

again—those "common thieves" of the Borders—like their
fellows in Galloway and the Islands of the Foreigners, formed
one, or many, important communities. They "obeyed the
laws of neither" of the two chief countries that lay to the
south and to the north of the Debatable Land, *because* they
had laws of their own. They "went to church as seldom as
the 29th of February comes into the kalendar," *because* they
were not Christians, but heathens (*Heyden* being still used in
one *Teut-ish, Teutsch,* or *Dutch* country, as the term for a
Gypsy); with a religion of their own. Though latterly they
had degenerated, or their "irreconcilables" had degenerated,
into the position of "common thieves,"—they had once been
"thieves" in the same sense as the Modern-British are
"thieves" of Australia, or of India ;—and the Americans of
the territory of the United States.

During the indefinable period of which Scott mostly
treats, they were in their transition stage. At one moment,
you feel disposed to call them *Sorohen,*—at another
Sorners. Even the objectionable term, " Thief," was accepted
in a larger sense, in the days when James the Fifth of Scotland marched eight thousand men over his southern frontier,
"to daunton the Thieves of Liddesdale : " who were " no
subjects of his " (any more than of his grandson, the Sixth
James). Two of his most celebrated subjects—Sir David
Lindsay and Sir Richard Maitland of Lethington—regarded
Liddesdale as peculiarly the home of Falsehood, Common
Theft, and *Oppression :* the last of which qualities can only
exist with *Power.* " Sir David Lindsay, in a curious drama,
introduces, as one of his dramatis personæ, Common Thift,
a borderer, who is supposed to come to Fife to steal the earl
of Rothes' best hackney, and lord Lindsay's brown jennet.
Oppression, also (another personage there introduced), seems
to be connected with the borders ; for, finding himself in
danger, he exclaims—

> War God that I were sound and haill,
> Now liftit into Liddesdail ;

. . . Again, when Common Thift is brought to condign
punishment, he remembers his border friends in his dying
speech "—wherein, as once referred to before, he names

various "gypsy" tribes. And "when Common Thift is executed . . . Falsehood . . . pronounces over him the following eulogy :

> Waes me for thee, gude Commoun Thift !
> Was never man made more honest chift,
>   His living for to win :
> Thair wes not, in all Liddesdail,
> That ky mair craftelly could steil,
>   Whar thou hings on that pin ! "

Maitland's *Complaynt against the Thievis of Liddisdail*, written at the same period, tells us the same story. It complains that "the common thieves of Liddesdale" have "almost completely harrowed Ettrick Forest (by this time a portion of 'Scotland') and Lauderdale,"—and are now even extending their depredations into the Lothians. Not content with merely levying black-mail, they have so thoroughly cleaned out the country to the south of Edinburgh, that those who once had "meat, and bread, and ale," have now to be content with "water kale ;" which Scott renders "broth of vegetables." After recounting all their iniquities, and the names of some of their chiefs, he states that—

> " Of sum great men they have sic gait,
> That redy are thame to debait.
> And will up weir
> Their stolen geir,
> That nane dare steir
> Thame air [early] or late."

And he indignantly asks—"What, but want of justice among us, causes us to be so overborne by these robbers ? "

Even in the end of the sixteenth century those Thieves were not only "no subjects" of James the Sixth of Scotland,—inhabiting a country of their own, and fighting against Scotland on the north, and England on the south,—but they were virtually the rulers of Southern Scotland, up to the very walls of Edinburgh. Maitland's *Complaynt* says as much : and his statement that they were countenanced by "some great men," shows how important was their position. They were really the kinsmen and followers of the said "great men." But these—perhaps because they were con-

nected by blood with the National aristocracy, perhaps because they knew that barefaced marauding on the part of a
noble of Scotland (as in the earlier day of the *Dubh-glass*
power) could no longer be tolerated—for either, or both, of
these reasons, the "great men" took care not to identify
themselves openly with their own "thieves." Scott of
Satchells plainly says that they were actuated by the latter
motive. "He mentions, that the laird of Buccleuch employed
the services of the *younger* sons and brothers only of his
clan, lest the name should have been weakened by the
landed men incurring forfeiture." Of course, only those
inhabiting Scotland Proper required to protect their reputation thus. The *pure* Thieves, or Gypsies, of the Debatable
Land were wholly indifferent to the opinion of the Scotch
king,—for they were "no subjects of his," and he could not
therefore have forfeited their desolate territory, in any event.
Such independent chiefs, or kinglets, "had little attachment
to the monarchs, whom they termed in derision, the kings of
Fife and Lothian; provinces which they were not legally
entitled to inhabit,* and which, therefore, they pillaged with
as little remorse as if they had belonged to a foreign country:" *which was actually the case.*

At this period, and in this portion of Scotland, there were
therefore three chief divisions of society. There were the
civilized burghers, and the civilized Scotch, generally—there
were the half-civilized "nobles" of the country south of
Edinburgh, to the frontier—and there were the quite uncivilized followers of these "nobles," together with the
equally savage tribes of the Debatable Country—leaders or
led. The "half-civilized 'nobles,'" being part of the
aristocracy of the country, bore at this time, the two-fold
character of "noble" and "gypsy-chief." One result of which
was, as we see from Maitland, that a reign of terror existed
throughout southern Scotland: against which the peaceable
burghers and agriculturists could not lift a hand. These

* "By Act 1587, c. 96, borderers are expelled from the inland counties, unless
they can find security for their quiet deportment." The state of things thus
indicated, when referred to in another place, was likened to that existing in the
United States, and those "borderers" to the half-wild "Indians," who are not
allowed to leave their reservations without some such authority. (The extracts
given at this point are all taken from the "Minstrelsy.")

terms, "burghers" and "agriculturists," are not here used in a restricted sense; but rather as including all those whose power did not rest solely on force, and whose daily food was provided after a more civilized fashion than "thieving." Of this civilized element Sir David Lindsay and Sir Richard Maitland are good specimens,—whether we regard them as gentlemen, or as scholars, or as squires whose land was tilled by peace-loving peasants. The uncivilized element we see in its perfection, in the troops of armed and mounted gypsies that were the terror of this peaceable population, and whose outrages—murder, robbery, and fire-raising—form the theme of Sir Richard Maitland's *Complaynt.*

The immense importance of the gypsy castes at this period (it seems only yesterday—the reign of James the Sixth of Scotland), is evinced by an extract that Scott makes from Birrel's *Diary.* "This good old citizen of Edinburgh [Birrel] also mentions another incident, which I think proper to insert here . . . . as tending to show the light in which the men of the Border were regarded, even at this late period, by their fellow-subjects. The author is talking of the King's return to Edinburgh, after the disgrace which he had sustained there, during the riot excited by the seditious ministers on December 17, 1596. Proclamation had been made, that the earl of Mar should keep the West Port, lord Seaton the Nether-Bow, and Buccleuch, with sundry others, the High-gate. 'Upon the morn at this time, and befoir this day, there was ane grate rumour and word among the tounes-men, that the Kinges M[ajesty] sould send in *Will Kinmonde, the common thieffe*, and so many southlande men as sould spulyie the toun of Edinburgh. Upon the whilk, the haill merchants tuik their hail gear out of their buiths or chopes, and transportit the same to the strongest hous that was in the toune, and remained in the said hous, thair, with themselfis, thair servants, and luiking for nothing bot that thaye sould have been all spulyeit. Sic lyke the hail craftsmen and commons convenit themselfis, their best guidis, as it wer ten or twelve householdes in ane, whilk wes the strongest hous, and might be best kepit from spuilyeing or burning, with hagbut, pistolet, and other sic armour as might best defend themselfis. Judge, gentil

reader, giff this was playing.' The fear of the Borderers (continues Scott) being thus before the eyes of the contumacious
citizens of Edinburgh, James obtained a quiet hearing for
one of his favourite orisons, or harangues, and was finally
enabled to prescribe terms to his fanatic metropolis. Good
discipline was, however, maintained by the chiefs upon this
occasion ; although the fears of the inhabitants were but
too well grounded, considering what had happened in
Stirling ten years before, when the earl of Angus, attended
by Home, Buccleuch, and other Border chieftains, marched
thither to remove the earl of Arran from the King's
councils ; the town was miserably pillaged by the
Borderers, particularly by a party of Armstrongs, under this
very Kinmont Willie, who not only made prey of horses
and cattle, but even of the very iron grating of the
windows."*

Here we have that very King who did so much afterwards
—and previously—to crush these marauding habits, actually
employing his *tory* castes as a political engine. Kinmont
Willie, the gypsy chief, and all the savage "Tartarians" of
the Borders, threatening the security of his most civilized
subjects ; because, being alienated for the moment from
these subjects, he had absolutely no other weapon to rely
upon. At this crisis, the gypsies and semi-gypsies of
Scotland had a distinctly historical position.

The two-fold aspect in which those Border chiefs appear
to men of education, in this century—is what renders the
term "gypsy" only partially appropriate. The word now
signifies so degraded a caste, when used conventionally,
that it is not easy to realize that certain "gypsy" families
of one century back were richly-dressed, well-mannered,
and even well-educated people : and that the social importance of such families increases as one looks back in time.
Till we reach people who are not only fitted, by their
ferocious and heathen customs, to be the ancestors of the
most savage eighteenth-century *tories ;* but who also possessed
certain qualities that entitle them to be regarded as the
(unrefined and pagan) progenitors of all the civilized

* For this and other such extracts see "Minstrelsy of the Scottish Border,"
Murray & Son, London, 1869; pp. 29, 159, 232, 247, 264, 265, &c., &c.

Melanochroi of Britain. Black Agnes of Dunbar, directing
the defence of her husband's castle against the forces of the
Earl of Salisbury, was the prototype of the modern lady—so
far. But the modern gentlewoman, if one could fancy her
in such a place, would not have shouted over the battle-
ments, taunting and jeering at the besiegers. To find women
of this description, in modern times, you have to look at the
female-gypsies—Taits and Kennedys—on either side the
Water of Teema (in Ettrick Forest), "scolding and cursing,
and, clapping their hands, urging the men to fight." Ladies
with such proclivities are no longer regarded as ladies.
The "tory" *ranee* is a noisy *randy*, in the estimation of the
modernized Scotch : the "gypsy" *queen* is only a *quean* to
others. And this particular action of Black Agnes was
nothing exceptional in her day. "This sort of bravado
(says Scott) seems to have been fashionable in those times."
It is *now* one of the chief characteristics of Mr. Simson's
swaggering "gypsies." Just as the showy finery of the
Baillies and Ruthvens and other eighteenth-century "gypsies,"
scarlet and green, is paralleled with the gay attire of the earlier
"outlaw Murray," his consort, and his tribe. The prevalence
of which tastes is indicated by Scott, when he says : "Their
only treasures were, a fleet and active horse, with the ornaments which their rapine had procured for the females of
their family, *of whose gay appearance the Borderers were vain.*"
(The "fleet and active horse" was at last denounced by
statute ;* so that when the gypsy chief wished to divorce his
wife after the ancient *tory* fashion, he had to imitate the
ceremony by shooting one of the asses of his troop ; and
for every purpose, that useful animal took the place, as far
as it could, of the banished "hobby," "Galloway," or "Indian
pony.")

It is because Scott did not see his Border predecessors
in this light that his fancied representations of early Border
life are essentially false. Whatever his lineage—according
to the flesh—he was the intellectual descendant of men like

---

* "Minstrelsy of the Scottish Border," Murray's reprint, 1869, p. 27, note 1.
The use of fire-arms and other weapons was also prohibited to the Border gypsies
by this enactment, but Mr. Simson states that they continued to carry pistols in
their wallets for a long time after this, and even their amazons carried long heavy-
bladed knives.

Lindsay and Maitland ; in whose eyes the chiefs whose deeds he never tired of singing were simply "common thieves." If he had ever thought of describing an encounter between two opposing tribes of eighteenth-century moss-troopers—the Taits and the Johnstones, for example,—he would never have employed the respectful language which he used to their ancestors. In a mortal struggle between two chiefs the victor would have been styled a "murderer ; " and the whole moss-trooping population were " ferocious and vindictive " "vagrants." The aptness of these last expressions (Scott's own) cannot be disputed ; but, although he applied them to the eighteenth-century moss-troopers, he would never have thought of so characterizing their earlier forefathers,—who were equally "ferocious and vindictive," and 'equally "vagrant." This is how he describes an encounter between sixteenth-century gypsies :—" The only blood then spilt was in a duel betwixt Tait, a follower of Cessford, and Johnstone, a west border man, attending upon Angus. They fought with lances, and on horseback, according to the fashion of the borders. The former was unhorsed and slain, the latter desperately wounded." But, in writing of the same kind of people in his own day, he writes in this manner :—" By the by, old Kennedy the tinker swam for his life at Jedburgh, and was only, by the sophisticated and timed evidence of a seceding doctor, who differed from all his brethren, saved from a well-deserved gibbet. He goes to botanize for fourteen years. . . . Six of his brethren were, I am told, in the court, and kith and kin without end. I am sorry so many of the clan are left. The cause of the quarrel with the murdered man, was an old feud between two gipsy clans, the Kennedys and Irvings, which, about forty years since, gave rise to a desperate quarrel and battle at Hawick-green, in which the grandfather of both Kennedy and the man whom he murdered were engaged." When he writes of " Hughie the Graeme," unanimously sentenced by a Carlisle jury to "a well-deserved gibbet," his sympathies are all with the " kith and kin " in the court ; not with either jury or judge. Because the event happened long ago, and the thief and murderer occupied a vastly higher position than in his own day. When he writes of " Hobbie Noble" (another specimen of the

" ferocious and vindictive vagrant "), these are his words :—
" We have seen the hero of this ballad act a distinguished
part in the deliverance of Jock o' the Side, and are now
to learn the ungrateful return which the Armstrongs made
him for his faithful services,"—and so on. What this
" hero" had really done was to break into Newcastle Jail one
night, and rescue the said " Jock o' the Side " from an equally
" well-deserved gibbet." The contrast between the two
forms of phraseology is ludicrous : since they were applied
to the one set of men and by the same individual.
" Hero," "distinguished," "faithful services ": " ferocious
and vindictive vagrants," " a well-deserved gibbet,"
—" I am sorry so many of the clan are left." The
utter falsity of Scott's attitude is seen when we realise that
he had neighbours living *precisely* the life of those earlier
marauders—identically that life, in every particular, so far as
the times would allow—and yet he had to be told by Mr.
Simson that they were very fond of the ancient Border
ballads, and that "they were constantly singing these compositions among themselves." His visitor could have told
him—if he did not know—that the Minstrels of the Scottish
Border* were not extinct, as a caste ; but half-merryandrew,
half-musician (jongleur-juggler), formed the life of every
country-wedding among the humbler classes—the classes
which adhere the longest to ancient customs. But, no—
Scott's love of gypsydom was purely sentimental and archaic.
He glorified the robber-tribes that were the terror of fifteenth-
century scholars, burghers, and husbandmen : but when their
least-altered descendants came before him in their hereditary
character (comparatively harmless and insignificant by his
day)—he did not know them ! Sir Walter Scott of Abbots-
ford regarded them precisely as Sir Richard Maitland of
Lethington had done—as " common thieves :" the instincts
of the modern squire were aroused in him—not those of
the robber-chief represented by the gypsy *captain :* " it appeared to me (says Mr. Simson) that the mind of the great
magician was not wholly divested of the fear that the Gip-

* The identity of " Border Gypsy " with " Border Minstrel " has already been
pointed out. For Mr. Simson's confirmatory remarks see pages 226, 229, and
307 of his " History."

sies might, in some way or other, injure his young plantations."

It matters little what Scott's precise pedigree was. He
himself has told us that, though it took the civilized forces of
Scotland a hundred years to do it, the marauding castes of
the Borders were at last schooled into Christian civilization :
though, in the process, the most intractable sections had to
choose between death and banishment. Consequently, a
great number of civilized and refined modern Scotchmen
must be (as Mr. Simson continually preaches) the descendants of those ferocious gypsies. So that, for that matter,
Scott's people might have been pure " pagans " not very long
ago. But, in reality, it seems that he had comparatively
little of this blood in his veins. It was his boast (the author
of Waverley's boast) that his birth " according to the preju-
dices of his country," " was esteemed *gentle ;* " that his lineage was that of the aristocracy of the Border Scotts. And
that aristocracy had, for many generations, been identified
with the Anglo-Norman and Dutch * element, whose power
superseded that of the earlier *Scots :* the leaders of those
Border Scots being little more than *Scotts* by name. No
doubt, this aristocracy—as we have just seen—was closely
bound up with the commonalty of the Borders, in many
ways ; but, slowly and surely, the civilized and civilizing sections of these tribes came to repudiate all connection with
the " common thieves." The heads of families would not allow
their names to appear as leaders in those plundering expeditions (which they secretly countenanced), for fear of incurring
forfeiture. And, at last, they had to wholly cut the connection.
In 1612, the chiefs of the clan particularly named " Scott "
(as the chiefs of many other clans did), formally bound themselves by contract " to give up all bands of friendship, kindness, oversight, maintenance or assurance, if any we have,
with common thieves, and broken clans, &c." Possibly, they

---

* No doubt this "element" included many others of kindred nature, which
might be called Norse and Celtic, Latin and Greek. Perhaps it would be better
to call it the " English-speaking element." For the " English " tongue was the
language of the Governmental party—the party of Bruce and his successors—from
at least the fourteenth century onward. It was in "the English tongue " that
the fourteenth-century Barbour wrote ; and though Gavin Douglas and others
afterwards called that language " Scotch," it was still the same speech.

did not at once adhere to the terms of this contract, and may have been among the Border gentry complained of in the proclamation of 1616, which sets forth that, not only do these "common thieves" "wander abroad in troops and com‐ panies," committing outrages of all sorts, but that "great numbers of his majesty's subjects, of whom some outwardly pretend to be famous and unspotted gentlemen, have given and give open and avowed protection, reset, supply and maintenance, upon their* grounds and lands, to the said vagabonds, sorners and condemned thieves and limmers, and suffer them to remain days, weeks and months together thereupon, without controlment, and with connivance and oversight, &c." His descent being therefore deduced from this—not the *toriest*—section of the clan Scott : the party of expediency and compromise : Scott himself was little of a "gypsy" by descent. Had he been descended from those who were nobles prior to the success of the Anglo-Norman or English speaking party he would have been himself a gypsy-minstrel. He *was* a minstrel : but his lays are full of a spirit that the earlier minstrels did not know : the spirit of refinement, of civilization, of Christianity ; by which he saw even while he sung them, that the deeds of his moss-troopers were the deeds of savages. None of *his* ballads tell us that the women of the Borders fought with a bravery and fury not inferior to that of the men. The genuine moss-trooping songs do so, as we are told :† but *his* lays tell us only of "gentle maidens" and "fair ladies"—whose existence is very doubtful.

Charles Kirkpatrick Sharpe, whom Scott regarded as a Scot-

---

* "*Their* grounds and lands." This is the "root of bitterness" out of which have grown half the troubles of this country. By craftily remaining in the back‐ ground, and leaving the "younger sons and brothers" to risk the doom of "rebels" and "thieves," the heads of these tribes found themselves in course of time the *absolute* owners of what had once been small kingdoms—the common property of each little "nation." So long as the "younger sons and brothers," with the humbler *tories* of the tribe, brought in plunder, or conquered fresh terri‐ tory, without falling under the ban of the central government, their kinship was duly recognized. But, when the day came in which it was declared unlawful to retain such followers, these were calmly repudiated, and the tribal chief became proprietor, *in fee*, of the territory of his disowned clan.

† "Simson," p. 193; and compare the Border virago in "The Fray of Suport" (in the "Minstrelsy").

tish Horace Walpole ; as a "very remarkable man ; " and as
having "a great turn for antiquarian lore ; " has left us his
impression of Scott's antiquarian abilities—in very plain and
uncomplimentary language.　Dr. Daniel Wilson, in his interesting sketches of Sharpe,* tells us that—as a marginal note,
referring to some of Scott's statements—Sharpe has written
these words : "Sir Walter knew nothing of antiquity, though
he pretended to understand it.　In that he was the greatest
dunce and liar I ever knew." Dr. Wilson appropriately adds :
" Browning has entitled one of his poems, ' How it strikes a
contemporary ; ' and here we have the very thing,—we who
have since seen, and shared in, the world's celebration of a
Scott Centenary ! "

To echo Sharpe's ungracious words would be unpardon-
able in any man now living : pardonable least of all in one
whose scattered antiquarian facts have chiefly been taken from
Scott himself.　But this angry snarl over the dead lion is not
without excuse ;—proceeding, as it did, from a man of real
learning and considerable talent : who, though miles behind
Scott in *greatness*, was—considered as an antiquary—distinctly his superior.　That Scott should have attempted so
often to realise the life of the past, is a thing to be for ever
regretted.　To realise the past is impossible.　A few stray
facts come down to us out of various ages : and, when some
of these facts are contemporaneous, we can indeed form
some dim and hazy idea of the life of that period.　But, at
the best, it is guess-work.　We know a few things as positive
certainties—"so dim, yet so indubitable ; exciting us to endless considerations :" firing an imagination like Scott's to the
consideration of things that never happened ; to the supposition of ways of life and thought of which he could know
nothing.　What can a few isolated certainties tell us about
the myriad other certainties of their day ?　" Jerusalem was
taken by the Crusaders, and again lost by them ; and Richard
Cœur-de-Lion ' veiled his face ' as he passed in sight of it :
but how many other things went on the while ! "

Therefore, it is a most unfortunate thing that Scott wasted
his genius in attempting the unattainable.　His weakness
consisted in the fact that he was not a good antiquary.　He

* "Old Edinburgh," Vol. I. p. 42 (D. Douglas, Edinburgh, 1878).

collected a great mass of floating traditions—gave them to the public—and, in doing this, made the public appreciate antiquity ; as no mere Dryasdust could ever have done. And for this he cannot be sufficiently thanked. But his miserable error lay in this—that he didn't even make a proper use of such " isolated certainties " as he possessed ; that, while some of the figures in his canvas are undoubtedly correct, the *general effect* of the picture is as plainly untrue. His moss-troopers are not his only mis-creations. But the false conclusions which he arrived at regarding them—he, a man intimately acquainted with the modern social life of the Borders—are quite sufficient of themselves to damn him as an antiquary. The provoking part of the thing is, that he did not *require* to write about the past. The Author of "The Antiquary," of " Redgauntlet," of "Guy Mannering," might have written such books all his life, and only made himself more famous ; and have left an infinitely richer legacy to us. For, of course, it is only as an antiquary that he failed. Setting that aside—one can admit everything else that is said of him. It is impossible not to admire him otherwise : not to feel the strong, virile humour that runs throughout his writings—the exquisite tenderness of some of his touches—the splendid swing of his verse : to recognize, in short, the whole *genius* of the man : and yet to know that—as an antiquary—he failed. For he did fail—greatly. And his mediæval romances cannot possibly be accepted as the fictitious presentment of a real state of society. Hardly any more than *Cymbeline* or *Macbeth*.

CHAPTER VI.

SCOTT, then, had he lived three centuries earlier—as Poet and Author—would have regarded those who, he says, were among his own ancestors, as "common thieves" or "gypsies." There might have been this additional modification, that he himself might have been a trifle less refined. Perhaps this modification is dubious : but this, at least, is certain, that the gypsy tribes that were his aversion would assuredly have been much more powerful—their chiefs, in many cases, having a historical position and great social influence,—a position and an influence vastly superior to that of the best-bred Baillie or Faa of the eighteenth century.

It is really doubtful whether Scott, as a sixteenth-century Man of Letters, would have been less refined ;—extremely doubtful. The idea that he might be so presented itself to my mind rather in connection with Beaugé, the historian-soldier, than as associated with the cultured men of Scotland, at that period ; in the mass, or individually. And Beaugé was, of course, a soldier. Still, he represents the civilized section of the combatants, in the siege of that Border tower, previously sketched. The question is, did he fairly represent the civilized Scotchmen* of his day ? If so, then the civilized men of to-day—American, British, French, or what not—are not so savage as those of three centuries ago. When Beaugé tells us how the Border Indians tortured their prisoners—" contending who should display the greatest address in severing their legs and arms before inflicting a mortal wound "—killing them *after* their eyes had been torn out—laying one of them, pinioned, upon the ground, and

* Though a Frenchman, Beaugé was there as a civilized Scotchman. And besides, the early-modern French element in the blood, the manners, and the speech of Scotland, is not inconsiderable.

utilising his prostrate body as their butt, in a kind of bloody
tent-pegging ; and, after the unfortunate wretch had suc-
cumbed under the lance thrusts (cautiously though these
were given), galloping to and fro with pieces of his quivering
flesh upon their spear-points :—in recounting all this to us,
Beaugé merely observes, dispassionately,—" I cannot greatly
praise the Scottish for this practice." And he frankly tells
us that the victim of "this practice," a prisoner captured by
him, was sold to those savages for "a small horse" (one of
their "Galloways" or "Irish hobbies"). Moreover, he adds
that, as the mossers of the Southern or English Border had
behaved with the greatest barbarity to their Northern foes,
in their hour of triumph, "it was but fair to repay them,
according to the proverb, in their own coin."

The outrages of the English savages, being such "as
would have made to tremble the most savage Moor in
Africa," went far to justify the pitiless revenge of their
Scottish neighbours. The insulted husband who, "at one
blow," struck the head of his worst enemy "four paces from
the trunk," must have many sympathisers, at the present
day, and among civilized men. But the *way* in which the
"Northern Rievers" paid back their Southern kidney—
though the payment was made in the same coin—how many
modern men would extenuate that ?

At the first thought, one would say that no civilized man
would regard such barbarities, except with disgust ; and that
Beaugé is a long way behind any modern military officer or
war-correspondent : that—to continue the comparison formerly made—no American officer would sell a prisoner to a
tribe of "friendlies," for the sake of an Indian pony ; and
aware of the fate in store for the captive.

But, then, one remembers barbarities on the part of
"civilized" people, of very recent date. It will be long
before men forget the horrid death of the Kabyles in the
caves of Dahra ; or the superfluous savagery attending the
execution of the Sepoys—blown from the cannon's mouth—;
or the wholesale massacre of the Piegans of America. The
last example, like that of Dahra, means the slaughter of
women and children : and I have heard it said that, when
one of these American soldiers—with some strange touch of

pity—asked his commander if the Indian baby was to follow
its murdered mother, he received an oracular response, to the
effect that an Indian man-child—if let alone—would one day
be an Indian man.

These things are, fortunately, exceptional at the present
day. But if some one, many generations after this, ascertained that such barbarous deeds were done—in the middle
of the nineteenth century, and by the representatives of
three of its most civilized nations,—he might hastily assume
that these "civilized nations" were so many hordes of heart-
less savages. And, therefore, though a civilized Frenchman
of the sixteenth century *did* hand over a prisoner to the
horrors of Red-Indian torture ; and although, at the close of
that century, the King of Scotland made use of his
"Tartarian" subjects in order to enforce his will against that
of "the contumacious citizens" of Edinburgh and Stirling ;
yet it does not follow therefrom that the most refined people
of that day endorsed such acts. Consequently, had Scott lived
as a sixteenth-century writer, he might not have differed in
any degree from what he actually was.

It is important to bear in mind that Scott—apart from all
his "vain imaginations"—was, in everything but blood (and,
perhaps in that, too, to a greater extent than he knew), the
descendant of such sixteenth century men as the scholars
Maitland and "Davie" Lindsay.* Because these were on
the winning side. Although,—owing to the national importance of their leaders (though these kept in the background),
the Common Thieves of Liddesdale were permitted to
terrorise all the south-east of Scotland, and to *sorn* upon the
husbandmen of the Lothians, till the latter had been despoiled of everything—clothes, household goods, everything
but the actual necessaries of life—this did not continue for
ever. (At Maitland's date, indeed, this state of matters—
brought about by the extreme youth of the King—was distinctly a *relapse* into the rule of violence, so far as concerned
the agricultural districts.) His consolatory prophecy, that—

---

* Maitland and Lindsay themselves may, of course, have descended from
"gypsies" of a certain era. Whether that era was only a century before their
day, or a whole millenary, is of little moment. They are here taken as representing the educated men of their time.

or [ere] I dee,
Sum sall thame see,
Hing on a tree
Quhill thay be deid——

may not have been so completely fulfilled as he could have wished, during his lifetime. But such a death became more and more the fate of those who persisted in living the lives of " common thieves, commonly called Egyptians," for whose suppression statute after statute was enacted. The process was a slow one. The agricultural inhabitants of the Vale of Ettrick, in the latter part of the sixteenth century, were—as described by Maitland—completely under the sway of the Common Thieves ; to whom they not only paid black mail, but were also forced, most unwillingly, to render up nearly everything that their dwellings contained. But the descendants of these husbandmen, even so recently as the first half of the eighteenth century, were—as we are told by the most famous of all the Ettrick Shepherds*—by no means free from this galling yoke : and when one energetic farmer was at last roused to a distinct protest against those *sorners* (a branch of the Kennedy clan), refusing point-blank to suffer them to live at their pleasure in his own out-houses, and on his own sheep, poultry, and " all superfluous and movable stuff, such as hams, &c.," he was forced in the long-run to admit the folly of his insubordination ; and, " after a warfare of five years' duration," " he was glad to make up matters with his old friends, and shelter them as formerly." Moreover, it can scarcely be said that the yeomen or farmers—with their labourers—constituted the majority of the population of certain Border districts, even in the eighteenth century. A *Blackwood* correspondent, writing in 1817, and referring to his schoolboy days (which could not have been earlier than the middle of the previous century), recalls "the peculiar feelings of curiosity and apprehension with which we sometimes encountered the *formidable* bands of this roaming people, in our rambles among the Border hills, or when fishing for perch in the picturesque little lake at Lochside." When "a gang of them came to a solitary farm-house, and, as *was* usual, took possession of

* *Blackwood's Magazine*, Vol. I. p. 53.

some waste out-house ; " and when " another clan," arriving
there on the same day, contested the possession of the place
until the ground " was absolutely soaked with blood ; " which
constituted " the population " of that district—the dwellers
in the " solitary farm-house," or the " common thieves " ? To
repeat the Transatlantic simile—whether was Kentucky an
" Indian territory," or the country of the (*soi-disant*) white
man, in the time of Daniel Boone ?

The importance of remembering that Scott—whatever his
pedigree—was, in all his tastes, habits, and ways of thought,
a representative of the civilized scholars, burghers, and
yeomen of sixteenth-century Scotland ; and not of the
Common Thieves of sixteenth-century Liddesdale, or Debatable-Land ; cannot be too strongly insisted upon.
Because these, as just said, " were on the winning side."
The ultimate victory, long-delayed, of the party by whom
those statutes against *sorners* were enacted, means the victory
of those scholars, burghers, yeomen, and peaceably-disposed
aristocrats ; who were the resolute opponents of that rule of
violence. And there is clearly an ethnological fact under-
lying this.

Those enactments of the sixteenth century (and the earlier
part of the seventeenth) directed against the people of the
Hebrides, or Isles of the Foreigners, which have been several
times noticed, were " raised at the instance of the whole
inhabitants of The Burghs of this Realm ; "* otherwise
spoken of as " the free burghs." Such burghers were denominated " his Majesty's subjects," and " the lieges ; "
whereas the greater part of the island-population was described as composed of " wild savages, void of God's fear
and our obedience," and as following " the barbarous and
incivil forms of the country " (*their* country) ; at so recent a
period as the closing years of Shakespeare's life,—the words
quoted being those of Shakespeare's sovereign. The British
monarch's relation to the Hebrideans had plainly been
hitherto more that of a *suzerain* than of a *sovereign*. And,
during the time of his several predecessors in the kingship of
" Scotland," that kingship had not even exercised a *suzerainty*
over various parts of North-Britain : then divided into wholly

* *Collectanea de Rebus Albanicis,* pp. 102, 115, 121.

separate nationalities. Of which the chiefest* were—the Kingdom of Sodor and Man (or the South-Hebrides and Man)—the Kingdom of Carrick, being the western portion of Galloway—the Kingdom of Innse-Gaill, or the Islands of the Foreigners (the Northern Hebrides)—Gallibh, or the Foreigners' Country, which is now best indicated by modern Caithness and the archipelagoes lying north of the Pentland Firth —and, lastly, the independent stretch of territory that latterly shrunk into the Debatable-Land Proper, but that formerly included all the south-east of Modern Scotland, and the north of Modern England ; which territory was itself sub-divided into various provinces, such as Ettrick-Forest, Liddesdale, Annandale, Nithsdale (the Dale of the Niduari), and The Waste. These were all quite distinct countries from "Scotland," though they were absorbed by that power, one after another. And the people who made them to be "foreign" countries were "foreigners" in the eyes of those who spoke the forms of speech which we call "Gaelic" and "English." Other kingdoms, *within* the pale of early-Modern Scotland, continued also to exhibit signs of individual life, long after they had become portions of "Scotland ;" but the countries just specified distinctly retained their independence for a longer period. Of these, the Kingdom of Carrick, or West-Galloway, may be regarded as standing mid-way between the wholly-independent and the nominally-extinct countries : for although the Kings of Carrick came gradually to be known by titles emanating from the Kings of Scotland, yet the rhyme which tells us that one need not attempt to live in Carrick without "courting Saint Kennedie"—or the power founded by Kenneth—is a rhyme composed by men who spoke the Scotch (or English) tongue. To the same speech belongs the saying, "Out of Scotland into the Largs," which was "at one time a common expression ;"† the town of Largs being situated in the north-western corner of Ancient Gallo-

---

* Those, at any rate, that catch one's eye in a hasty glance at North Britain in early-modern times ; and which seem to have maintained their individuality the longest. For actual scholarly information on the subject of the earlier kingdoms of North Britain, "Celtic Scotland" is, I presume, the unsurpassed authority. But it is enough, for our purpose here, to cite the few kingdoms mentioned above.

† Mackenzie's "History of Galloway," Vol. I. p. 146.

way. And it is in the same "Inglis toung" (as the fourteenth-century Aberdonian, Barbour, calls it) that the painted Moors, or Gypsies of Galloway, are known as "the wild Scots of Galloway" and "the Galloways;" *Picti qui vulgo Galwey-enses dicuntur*, as sixteenth-century Camden puts it, in the less "vulgar" speech.

It is quite evident, then, that the main current of Scotch history has come down to us from those people who, in the fifteenth and subsequent centuries, were "his Majesty's sub-jects," "the lieges," "the whole inhabitants of The Burghs of this Realm:" and that the laws (promulgated at Edinburgh or Stirling, Falkland or Linlithgow) which eventually became current throughout the whole of North-Britain, were made *on behalf of* "his Majesty's subjects;" and *not* of those "wild savages, void of our obedience," who inhabited the various half-dying kingdoms just indicated. Such "wild savages"—living according to their own ideas—were offered the choice of conversion to Modern-Scotch ideas of life and religion, or of extermination. They were treated precisely as such races are now treated by modern colonizing races: certainly not *less* mercifully. The earliest distinct movement of this sort, it may be remembered, seems to have been "the plantation of Moray," or Moravia, or "the Moors' country," in the latter part of the twelfth century. This "plantation" was effected by King Malcolm of "Scotland," grandson and successor of David, Earl of Northamptonshire and King of "Scotland." This David was the youngest son of the gentle and pious Margaret—sister of Eadgar Aetheling and queen of Malcolm *Ceann-mor*—who did so much to civilize her husband, and her husband's people. Her youngest son,—the future King of "Scotland,"—in addition to the gentle training which he must have received from his mother, had also been "polished from a boy by intercourse and familiarity with" the Anglo-Norman nobility. And his reign—says Mr. Skene —"is beyond doubt the true commencement of feudal Scot-land;" and marks the adoption, in Scotland proper, of Norman ideas and usages. Whatever may have been the condition of North Britain prior to David's accession to power—*Fionn* (white) contending with *Dubh* (Black) for the sovereignty of the chief kingdom; and whatever the ethnological distribution of the population; it is clear that a fresh start was made in this twelfth century—the impetus of which is still felt at the present day. The remonstrance made by Robert Bruce (ancestor of the famous King) to this semi-Norman monarch, at the date of his invasion of England,—is plainly that of one of a conquering race; few in number, probably, but holding the country by right of conquest. This Norman noble speaks of "the Scots" and "the Galloways" (the latter a more special term) as the subdued natives of the country; against whom he and his kindred had fought "so often," "because of thee and thine" (addressing the King),—and whom "we have . . . . deprived . . . . of all hope in rebelling, and altogether subdued . . . . to thee and thy will." That they had not "altogether subdued" these races is seen from the revolts and wars that took place afterwards, but it is evident that these twelfth-century Normans (and others) were in Scotland as a ruling caste: and this Robert Bruce, lord of Annandale, was ruler of that district much in the same way as a British magistrate is ruler of an East-Indian territory (though with various apparent differences). And, moreover, that "the English"—or, more correctly, the Anglo-Norman nobles—were the friends of the twelfth-century Scoto-Normans, is as clearly seen from this speech of Bruce's: although they gradually became estranged, afterwards.

The "plantation of the Moors' country"—or "the settlement of the Indian territory"—did not take place until 1160, after King David's death. But that territory had really been added to the Kingdom of "Scotland," in the year 1130; having been conquered by King David's commander-in-chief—Edward, the son of Siward, Earl of Mercia, a cousin of his own—who had defeated the Moors, under "their King Oengus,* son of the daughter of Lulag," in a decisive battle. And, consequently, King David was enabled to make use of the conquered *Muravenses* at the Battle of the Standard, eight years later.

* This name is elsewhere spelled *Ungus*, which is really very like *Uncas*. *Ungus*, *Oengus*, *Anagus*, or *Angus*, is said to have been originally *Æneas*. But there is no reason against its identification with either *Æneas* or *Uncas*—separated as these are by such a vast stretch of time.

The statements here made are from "Celtic Scotland," Book I. Chapter IX.

It is worth while to waive for a moment "the plantation
of the Moors' country," in order to glance at this northern
army—whose motley character may be dimly seen. The
van was composed of the painted Galloways, or *dubh-glasses*
—who took that position as their acknowledged right: their
chiefs, it is stated, being "Ulgrice and Dovenald [Domh-
vall?], who were both slain." These "Picts of Galloway"
were, in the opinion of Mr. Skene, the probable descendants
of the second-century *Novantæ*, spoken of by Ptolemy. And
the same author "does not doubt" that these *Novantæ* were
no other than the Pictish *Niduari,* or Faws of Nithsdale.
From the second century to the twelfth is a long period, and
it is pretty certain that—if derived from those Nithsdale
Faws of a thousand years back—the *dubh-glasses* that
formed the vanguard of King David's army had likely
changed somewhat since the days of those remote ancestors.
However, if we look at them as they appeared when heading
the army of William the Lion, forty years later, we shall
probably receive a correct impression of the figure they
presented at the Battle of the Standard. It is likely that
they were all mounted men—as these moss-troopers seem
always to have been ; as they were, at any rate, when they
came against the Norman Bruce beside the river-ford, about
two centuries later. These fierce warriors were entirely
naked, and their swarthy skins were gleaming with war-
paint, or covered over with the "rude figures, iron-graved,"
that distinguished their savage ancestors, in the days of the
Roman invasion. The little mustangs they bestrode had no
better saddle than "an unshorn hide ; " and their riders,
innocent of stirrup or of spur, guided them by a rough
bridle of "rope or thong," held in the left hand. The left
arm bore a skin-covered wooden shield ; and, at the left
side, hung a small dirk or "black knife." The right hand
grasped a long spear ; which was used either as a lance, or
hurled at the enemy as an assegai—when required ; these
warriors being "very expert in throwing and aiming their
javelins at great distances." To these weapons were probably added the tomahawks that have been found in the
territory of the Galloways, within recent times. If they

* "Celtic Scotland," Vol. I. pp. 132–3.

resembled their kindred in Ireland, two centuries afterwards, these Galloway *dubh-glasses* had plaited their long black tresses into manifold plaits or " glibbes ; " forming a natural thickset, stout enough to bear off the cut of a sword. When they galloped to the charge against the English host at Northallerton, they raised the " loud, horrid, and frightful " war-whoops of their race.*

The formation of the rest of the Scotch army was, we are told, as follows :—The second body, led by Prince Henry, was composed of " soldiers and archers " (race not specified), with the natives of Strathclyde and Teviotdale—who were " Welsh." The third body consisted of the Anglian Lothian-men, and the Islanders and Men of Lennox. King David, surrounded by " many of the Norman and English knights who still adhered to him," commanded the rearguard, which was largely made up of the conquered Scots and the quite-recently-conquered natives of " the Moors' country."

Of all this heterogeneous army, it is probable that the " soldiers and archers " of the second body, and perhaps the Lothian-men of the next battalion, were most akin to the Celtic-Norman king and his Anglo-Norman officers. But the more savage element was very strong. The " black herds of Scots (gypsies) and Picts (Faws) " that had ravaged the civilized districts of South Britain many centuries before, appear to have constituted the greater part of this Northern army : though acting under the direction of a ruling caste that was strongly imbued with Norman ideas ; and whose blood seems to have been chiefly Celtic, Norman, Anglic, and Flemish.

To return, then, to the " plantation " of that "Indian territory "—which comprised (approximately) the eastern halves of the modern counties of Ross and Inverness, together with the counties of Nairn and Elgin, and those detached

---

* The references on which these statements are founded have, in some instances, been already given. One or other of these particulars may be seen in Mackenzie's " History of Galloway " (Vol. I. pp. 27, 236 and 237) ; Nicholson's " Historical and Traditional Tales " (pp. 37 and 39) ; the Appendix to " Rokeby " (Notes 2 R and 3 C) ; and, of course, "Celtic Scotland," Book I. Chapter IX. There can be little doubt but that the *Tinklers* mentioned in the charter of William the Lion (referred to in the "Gypsy" article of the Encyclopædia Britannica) formed one division of his *Faw* auxiliaries.

parts of Cromarty that are surrounded by Ross-shire, or
project from that county on the east. Although defeated
by King David's general in the year 1130, and made to
fight in the ranks of his army at the Battle of the Standard, in
1138, these northern " blackamoors " do not seem to have been
wholly subdued at that date. In the year 1160, Malcolm,
the grandson and successor of David, found it necessary to
march into this nominally-conquered country in order to
quell a revolt of the natives ; and to follow up his invasion
with a proceeding that was calculated to put an end to any
further trouble in that quarter, from these people. In that
year (it is stated by Fordun), he " removed them all from
the land of their birth, and scattered them throughout the
other districts of Scotland [not *modern* Scotland, but twelfth-
century Scotland], both beyond the hills and on this* side
thereof, so that not even a native of that land abode there,
and he installed therein his own peaceful people." And
this settlement of " his own peaceful people " is known to
history as " the plantation of Moray ; " just as a similar
movement, at a later period, was styled " the plantation of
Virginia."

Mr. Skene does not regard Fordun's description as wholly
accurate ; and Fordun, be it remembered, did not write until
two hundred years after this event. Since the north-eastern
corner of this twelfth-century " Moors' country " has continued to bear the name of " Moray " down to the present
day, and as another portion of that large territory is still
known as " the Black Isle ; " it would appear that various
" reservations ". were left to the native tribes, after the conquest ;—or that such scraps of their original country were
retained by them against the will of their enemies. However, Mr. Skene endorses Fordun's statement to this extent
—that Malcolm certainly granted large tracts of the more
fertile regions† of " the Moors' country " to certain of his
followers (two of whom were Flemings, named Berowald and

---

* It seems that Fordun wrote from Aberdeen or from St. Andrews.

† One of the fertile districts particularized by Mr. Skene is in that very portion
that longest retained the name of " Moray ; " which seems rather to contradict the
theory that that corner was longest inhabited by " Morrows " or " Morays."
Perhaps, as in the case of the adjoining inlet—" the Moray Firth "—the name
lingered on more by accident than because it conveyed any special meaning.

Freskine, understood to be the respective ancestors, *inter alia*, of the north-country Inneses and the modern dukes of Athole). But, though these Flemish colonists, and others of "his own peaceful people," supplanted the intractable "Moors" in certain districts of that northern "Moravia," yet Mr. Skene seems to think that considerable numbers of the earlier inhabitants continued to inhabit their fatherland, even after the ownership of it had been given to others. And that these were perhaps the mountain-gypsies (" Highland Scots") that—with the Galloway Faws—formed the main part of William the Lion's army, in his invasion of England, in 1173. Fordun says that this army was chiefly composed of "Galloways" and "mountain-Scots, whom men call *Bruti ;*" and another writer of the same date speaks of King William's "Scots and Galloways."* All through this twelfth century, indeed, these half-suppressed races appear to have been in a state of ferment: now acting as auxiliaries in the armies of their over-lords ; and again asserting their rights as distinct nationalities. Particularly these Faws or *dubh-glasses* of Galloway. It may be questioned, however, whether these mountain-Scots, or *Bruti*, ought to be regarded as Scots Proper—Scots of Ancient Scotia (Ireland). The Scots Proper, invading North Britain from Early Scotia, had overcome the native *Mauri* many centuries before this ; and, even in the middle of the ninth century, those earlier *Mauri* had begun to be styled *Scoti.†* It is generally believed that the conquering Scots nearly exterminated the native‡ North-Britons—those "nimble blackamoors," or "painted men," whom the Romans had previously encountered. But if any of them retained some fragments of

* These particulars are taken from Book I. Chapter IX., of "Celtic Scotland."

† "Celtic Scotland," Vol. I. p. 328.

‡ This word "native" must necessarily be used rather loosely. The "nimble blackamoors" of Claudian were "natives" to the incoming Scots. These Scots, again, with all other ex-foreigners ("black heathen" and "white heathen") of ante-Norman times had become "natives" to later colonists, such as the Normans and Flemings. The "native men" of the various Highland tribes— spoken of in the *Collectanea de Rebus Albanicis*—may have been of the most varied and once-foreign origin, their rulers being (as so many individual pedigrees show) of *Continental* extraction, at various dates subsequent to or contemporaneous with the Norman Conquest.

their former independence, these would most likely be found
among the mountains—the last refuge of all conquered
peoples.   Therefore, it is not unlikely that those "mountain-
Scots" of the twelfth century, distinguished from other Scots
by that qualifying designation, and, more particularly, by the
term " Bruti," represented—in a partial degree, if not wholly
—the earliest known inhabitants of North Britain.   And
their designation of "Scot" would therefore have no racial
meaning whatever ;—as it apparently had not when first
applied to their kindred in the ninth century (as just noticed).
Thus it would seem that the term " Scot" was employed
in a non-racial sense a thousand years ago ; and was applied
equally to conqueror and conquered,—much as " American "
was used a few generations ago, and as "Australian " and
" New Zealander," at the present day.   And yet, concurrently
with this loose practice, we have seen that certain particular
tribes among the Scots-general were remembered as Scots
(*Proper*) up till the close of the seventeenth century.

As already stated, the remonstrance made to King David
of " Scotland " by Bruce, the Norman lord of Annandale,*
clearly shows that the speaker and his king were much more
nearly related to the party that had conquered South Britain
than to the Scots Proper of North Britain and their subject
Mauri.   To this ruling caste David belonged wholly by
breeding, and partly by blood.   Whether his pedigree—on
the North-British side—may be assumed to indicate a descent
from races *akin* to this Anglo-Norman caste (such as Northmen, or "Gentiles of pure colour," and Gaels Proper, or those
whose particular speech was once "the language of the
white men," and to whom "Scots" were *scuits*, or vagabonds) ; or whatever may be the ethnological meaning of
the incessant warfare that had agitated North Britain prior
to his time ; it is quite plain from this speech of Bruce's
that the people vaguely styled " Scots" were not so much
the friends and kinsmen of their king as his half-alien *subjects.*   "Against whom dost thou this day take up arms and
lead this countless host ?"—says Bruce to the Scotch king,
on the eve of his English invasion.   " Is it not against the
English and Normans ?   O King, are they not those from

* "Celtic Scotland," Vol. I. pp. 465-466.

whom thou hast always obtained profitable counsel and prompt assistance? When, I ask thee, hast thou ever found such fidelity in the Scots that thou canst so confidently dispense with the advice of the English and the assistance of the Normans, as if Scots sufficed thee even against Scots? This confidence in the Galwegians ["the Picts (or faws) who, in the common speech, are styled Galloways;" who, in Gaelic, were known as *dubh-glasses*, or *Mauri*; and who formed the vanguard of the North-British army] is somewhat new to thee who this day turnest thine arms against those through whom thou now rulest.* . . . . . With what forces and by what aid did thy brother Duncan overthrow the army of Donald and recover the kingdom which the tyrant had usurped? Who restored Eadgar thy brother, nay more than brother, to the kingdom? was it not our army? . . . . Recollect last year when thou didst entreat the aid of the English in opposing Malcolm, the heir of a father's hate and persecution, how keenly,—how promptly,—with what alacrity, Walter Espee and many other English nobles met thee at Carlisle; how many ships they prepared,—the armaments they equipped them with,—the youths they manned them with; how they struck terror into thy foes till at length they took the traitor Malcolm himself prisoner, and delivered him bound to thee. Thus the fear of us did not only bind his limbs but still more daunted the spirit of the Scots, and suppressed their tendency to revolt by depriving it of all hope of success. Whatever hatred, therefore,— whatever enmity the Scots have towards us, is because of thee and thine, for whom we have so often fought against them, deprived them of all hope in rebelling, and altogether subdued them to thee and to thy will." This appeal undoubtedly indicates—what modern historians agree in telling us—that the greater portion of Great Britain, during this twelfth century, was dominated by Normans and semi-Normans. And this lord of Annandale—Norman and North-

* The words which follow " whom thou now rulest," are "— beloved by Scots and feared by Galwegians." The expression "beloved by Scots" is hardly in keeping with the general tenor of this appeal, referring as it does—again and again—to "the Scots" as King David's unwilling vassals. Perhaps the explanation of this seeming inconsistency is that Bruce—like other "Scotchmen" after him—did not invariably employ "Scot" in its strictest sense.

man—clearly regarded "the Scots" as conquered aborigines.
That this ruling caste, to which the King of " Scotland " and
his nobles belonged, was composed chiefly, or altogether, of
white-skinned men, may be regarded as almost certain. And
it is equally certain that a considerable portion of the North-
British army at this period (the middle of the twelfth century)
was made up of " gypsy " tribes :—the vanguard being wholly
composed of the painted "Indians" of Galloway ; and the
main portion of the rearguard consisting of the newly-
conquered "Moors" of northern "Moravia" (Moor-, or
Morrow-, or Murray-Land), together with other " Scots,"—
this rear battalion being under the immediate supervision of
the King and his Norman or semi-Norman nobility.

The "Scotland" of this period—we have been told *—" was
limited to the districts between the Forth, the Spey, and
Drumalban,"—which last name denotes "the range of mountains which divides the modern county of Perth from that of
Argyll." This kingdom only began to be known by that
name in the tenth century ;† and for three centuries after
that date " Scotland " was confined within these narrow limits.
This twelfth-century Scotland was nothing more than that
territory which is represented on modern maps by the coun-
ties of Banff, Aberdeen, Kincardine, Forfar, Perth, Clack-
mannan, Kinross, and Fife : a mere fragment of Modern-
Scotland.   "The Moors' Country," on its north-western side ;
Cathanesia, or Gallibh, to the north of that ; The Islands of the
Foreigners ; all the Western Highlands ; and the whole of
Modern-Scotland lying south of the fen-country of the
Forth‡ (now called Stirlingshire) ; all these countries were

* By the author of "Celtic Scotland."

† Prior to which, "Scotia," or "Scotland," "was Ireland, and Ireland
alone." To avoid confusion, Ireland up till the tenth century may be regarded
as "Scotia ;" and the small North-British kingdom (indicated above) as "Later.
Scotia," or "Early-Scotland."

‡ The greater part of the Forth basin is now solid, cultivated ground ; though,
in its north-western extremity, there are still large stretches of bog-land. But
even so recently as the end of the thirteenth century, the high ground on which
the Castle and Old Town of Stirling is built was surrounded by "carse-land" of
so marshy a nature that it was "impracticable for cavalry," at certain seasons (as
Dr. Jamieson, quoting from Lord Hailes, pointed out—under the word "Carse"
in his Dictionary). Some centuries earlier, it must have been one of those districts of which it was said that "being constantly flooded by the tides of the
ocean, they become marshy." ("Celtic Scotland," Vol. III. pp. 9 and 10.)

quite *outside* of twelfth-century Scotland. Edinburgh—afterwards the capital of the later kingdom—was no more a town, or stronghold, of the " Scotland " of William the Lion, than is Dublin a city of Wales. It was situated in the kingdom of Laudonia, or The Lothians ; whose kings, or kinglets, were contemporaneous with the kings of " Scotland," to the north of them ; and with the many other kings or kinglets that ruled over the various countries of North-Britain—all of which were "furth of Scotland " (*outside* of it).* Therefore the forces which David and William the Lion led across the Cheviots during the twelfth century were rather confederacies of allies (allied for the time being) than *national* armies. Early-Scotland was clearly regarded as the principal among these twelfth-century kingdoms of North-Britain ; and—more than that—as occupying a higher position than any other of these kingdoms. For not only was the leadership of such hosts assigned to the Kings of " Scotland," but the right of these monarchs—during the twelfth century—to exact homage and military service from the lesser kingdoms, was clearly acknowledged, in several instances. But, nevertheless, this particular period was emphatically one of transition. The hold which the Norman nobles had upon various territories must have been very slight. For example, after Bruce, the Norman lord of Annandale, had in vain tried to dissuade King David from his impending invasion of England, he—being to a much greater extent an *Anglo-* than a *Scoto-*Norman (in virtue of possessions and dignities)—had found it necessary to resign his lordship of Annandale in favour of his second son, *because* that lordship was tributary to the crown of " Scotland." (And, oddly enough, in the subsequent Battle of the Standard, Bruce the elder, fighting as an Anglo-Norman against the northern army, took as prisoner his own son, fighting in David's host as Scoto-Norman lord of Annan-

Indeed, when these particular words were written—namely, in the third century, —the Forth basin, up to Aberfoyle, can scarcely have reached the category of *marshy* districts : for this was the " Scythian Vale " across which the "nimble blackamoors " of the north ferried themselves in their skin-covered canoes. And there is further testimony to show that this level district (not wholly dried-up even yet) was the bed of the Firth of Forth not very long ago, in the fact that skeletons of whales have been discovered in various parts of that neighbourhood, at no great distance from the surface, during the present century.

* This is proved most distinctly in the Introduction to " Celtic Scotland."

dale.)   But it is questionable if many of the "native men" of Annandale accompanied their Norman lord to battle.   Or whether they recognized his supremacy at all ; except when forced to do so.   At any rate, when the most famous of all these Bruces of Annandale began his memorable resistance to the rule of the English Edward, the *men* of Annandale refused to help him at the very outset.   That they would have followed a chief of their own race is most likely : it is not improbable, indeed, that the men of Annandale were among those very "Galloways" that were the King's bitterest enemies.   And although the Bruces became, later on, the Earls of Carrick, yet the people of that territory recognized as their *kings* the representatives of a dynasty ante-dating the Norman Conquest by many centuries,—of a dynasty founded by Cin-aedh, the Picto-Scot.

Unquestionably, the power of the kings of Early-Scotland (the outlines of which country have just been indicated) in-creased tremendously during the twelfth century.   In that century, the great territory known as "The Moors' Country" was annexed, its natives half-exterminated, and the remnant placed upon various reservations throughout "Scotland,"— their most fertile districts being handed over to such "peaceful people " as the Flemish colonists.   Moreover, the same kings that subdued this northern territory, directed their arms against various other nationalities in the south and west of North Britain, reducing them to—at least—a nominal subjection. And this century, Mr. Skene assures us, is the period from which we . ought to date the successful assertion, in North Britain, of Norman ideas and usages.

It is clear, then, that Early-Scotland of the twelfth century —the North-Eastern portion of Modern-Scotland—is the germ out of which the later Scotch nationality was developed. And if the laws and customs of Early-Scotland were largely Norman, and the blood of its aristocracy also Norman to a considerable extent, it is equally clear that the Flemish ele-ment was largely represented too.   Not only is this to be surmised from the fact that the Normans were assisted, everywhere, by Flemish allies,—and from the fact that various North-British pedigrees prove the same thing,—but also because the *ways* of the townspeople of North-Eastern

Scotland (as elsewhere in Britain) are—very plainly—Flemish. It is stated that, in the early part of last century,—and probably there is no appreciable difference at the present day, —"the Flemish style of building was common in all the towns on the Murray Frith."* The steady influx of Dutch immigrants—into various parts of Britain—during many centuries after the Norman Conquest; and the fact that this immigration—because silent—has been greatly overlooked by historians; has been pointed out by a living authority.† And this immigration cannot be overlooked. For these very people—being traders, agriculturists, burghers,—are precisely the people who ought to be most considered in any question affecting the pedigree of Modern Britons. Such people do not figure in "gypsy" battles, of the kind we have been glancing at. Soldiers they have shown themselves to be, at various dates; but not mere fighters for fighting's sake. It must be of this kind of Scotchman that the saying arose—"a Scot will not fight until he sees his own blood." Such a proverb could by no possibility have ever been applicable to the *wild* tribes of Scotland; call them Scots, or moss-troopers, or Egyptians, or Tartarians, or whatever name may seem most suitable—according to locality and epoch. Men of this kind were roused to anger and bloodshed by a single word: they lived for nothing else but fighting. They drew their sustenance, not from the soil or from peaceful barter and manufacture, but from the spoils which they gathered by violence from others. They carried on a constant vendetta with like-natured tribes—their neighbours and rivals; never forgetting an injury, and handing down their blood-feuds from father to son, interminably. Therefore, when you have two *kinds* of people, occupying one country for many centuries; —the one living as peacefully as possible, encouraging industry and learning and religion, and making laws to foster the growth of these;—the other continuing, generation after generation, to rob and murder at every opportunity; and when you know (as we do know with regard to Scotland) that the former party gained more and more, century after century, the direction of the government of that country; you

---

* The description of house to which these words relate is referred to by Captain Burt in his "Letters" (Letter III.).

† Mr. Skeat, in the Introductory Notes to his Etymological Dictionary.

cannot but see that the ultimate ascendency of their ideas
and laws denotes a *racial* victory. Since the people who
believed in settled laws, in order, in education, in agriculture,
and in the advance of civilization, eventually became the
victors—it is clear that the people who did not believe in
any of these things must have waned as the others increased,
and have only saved themselves from extermination by re-
nouncing the life of their ancestors. But when we first dimly
see this conflict of opinions in Scotland—namely, in the
twelfth century—the winning party was, pretty clearly, composed of white races. And the people whom they overcame,
and whose lands they appropriated for the uses of civilization,
were—more distinctly—of black complexion : being the
" nimble blackamoors " of Claudian ; with their conquerors,
"somewhat different in manners " but also "thirsting for
blood," the Scot-Egyptians or gypsies ; and—in the Border-
lands, as elsewhere,—various clans descended from " the black
heathen " Danes.

It is important to consider this. Because, although we
have seen that various British " gypsies," regarded as unmixed "gypsies " by more than one modern gypsiologist,
are quite void of any trace of " black blood," yet there can
be no doubt that the great portion of the unreclaimed sections of the British people—popularly called "gypsies "—are
of swarthy skin : that, in the estimation of most men, to be
" like a gypsy," is to be black-haired, black-eyed, and of dark
complexion. Therefore, in whatever way the white " gypsy "
may be accounted for, it is plain that the orthodox "gypsy "
is descended from, at least, two of the black races of Britain.
" At least, two,"—because a diligent student of such people
has told us that "even in England there are straight-haired
and curly-haired Romanys,* the two indicating not a difference resulting from white admixture, but entirely different
original stocks:" because, also, with regard to Scotland, we
have seen that not only "at least, two," but, at least, *three*

* Mr. Leland applies this term " Romany " to all "gypsies." But we have
seen that they are known in Europe by many names—such as *Saracens, Tartars,*
Heathens, Ishmaelites, and *Tinklers*—while in Scotland (of which we are at
present, almost exclusively, speaking) the name of " Romany " seems to be little
known. Scotch people, generally, apply to the *tories* of Scotland such titles as
Cairds, Tinklers, and (formerly) *Jockies ;* and Mr. Simson says that they style
themselves *Nawkens* and *Tinklers.*

black races have entered that country,—"the nimble blacka-moors, not wrongly named the Painted Folk;" the "black herds" of Egyptians, or Scots; and the "black heathen" pirates from the Cimbric channels. None of these races were the ultimate rulers of any part of Britain. And although *nowadays* the "dark whites" and "fair whites" of our country have long been inextricably mingled; yet the white element is beyond a doubt numerically the greater;* and the prevailing Modern-British sentiment is distinctly *white;* while the popular speech is full of expressions that render "black" a synonym (whether justly, or from mere racial hatred) for everything that is objectionable.†

NOTE.—The argument advanced in this chapter—" that the main current of Scotch history has come down to us from those people who, in the fifteenth and subsequent centuries, were 'his Majesty's subjects,' 'the lieges,' 'the whole inhabitants of The Burghs of this Realm';" as opposed to the turbulent races that formerly ruled the country districts and the provinces of North Britain that lay outside of Early-Scotland—this argument receives confirmation from a statement recently made by one whose opinion is worthy of consideration. The "Convention of Royal Burghs" of Scotland has been defined by Lord Rosebery (in a speech made at Sydney on 10th December, 1883) in these terms :—It "is a body which sits in Edinburgh. . . . . It is an ancient body—some three centuries old—and entirely represents the feeling of Scotland." Now, any "feeling" that may be peculiar to Scotland at the present day is quite of a provincial character; because, ever since the year 1603, "Scotch history" has been a part of Modern-British history, and many Scotch people have been making their homes in other parts of their country than Scotland. So that, since that date—in some degree—and since 1707, beyond question, any assertion of local feeling in Scotland (as distinguished from the rest of the country), or in England (as distinguished from the rest of the country), has been of a purely provincial and archaic nature. Scotland, *qua* Scotland, has no "feeling" that deserves to be represented; although, as an aggregate of British counties, it forms an important division of the country. Nevertheless, this statement of Lord Rosebery's reveals to us the fossil of Scotch nationality; and that nationality was "entirely" represented by a convention of the royal burghs of Scotland.

* For, although the *Melanochroi* of Britain are said to outnumber the *Xanthochroi*, yet, according to Professor Huxley, the former are half-bloods—descended from earlier *Xanthochroi*.

† Notably in Ireland, where "a wild Irishman" was once "a black Irishman;" and where, at the present day, such expressions abound as "a black villain," "a black rogue;" and where "a nagur" is one of the commonest terms for "a scoundrel."

CHAPTER VII.

WHEN the children of Ettrick-dale farmers, exploring among the Border hills,—about a hundred years ago,—encountered most "formidable bands of this roaming people ; " or when some remote farm-house entertained a gang of such wanderers, for the night,—repaid by an evening of *Border Minstrelsy*, and the knowledge that they had made friends of possible foes ; at the period when the state of things indicated in the first volume of *Blackwood* constituted the life of the Scottish Border-land ;—at that time we can distinctly see that Southern-Scotchmen were divisible into two wholly different sections.   The one composed of prosaic, hard-working, sedentary yeomen and shepherds : the other of unresting clans of fighters, minstrels, and hunters.   The entirely op-posite character of either class was tacitly admitted by each. The shepherds and husbandmen did not court the society of the "gypsies," whom they stood in considerable awe of : the "gypsies" looked down upon the "bucolics" with the most lordly contempt—though often utilizing their dwellings and substance for their own uses.   To what extent this difference was one of *blood*, is a problem that is most difficult to solve.

This, at least, is certain : that those fierce, marauding "gypsy" clans were no other than the "Borderers" of whom Scott has written so much.   Their very surnames tell us this. Border history (and when not solely "Border" then *British* history) is interwoven with their names for many long cen-turies.   Excluding altogether the deductions of the foregoing chapters, and accepting as "gypsies" *only* those who have hitherto been popularly accepted as such,—here are some of the names of "gypsy" or "Egyptian" tribes :—*Douglas, Gordon, Lindsay, Ruthven, Montgomery, Shaw, Irving, Heron, Fenwick, Allan, Rutherford, Young, Baillie, Fetherstone, Simson,*

*Arington, Kennedy, Stirling, Keith, Wilson, Tait, Graham,
Jamieson, Geddes, Gray, Brown, Robertson, Anderson, Yorkston,
Faw* or *Fall, Johnstone, Blythe, Fleckie, Ross, Wallace, Wilkie,
Marshall, Miller, Halliday, Gavin.** All of these names—
the names of supposed interlopers of three centuries back—
are of distinctly British association, and some of them are
the oldest in these islands. And although, in some of these
examples, the owners of the names appear as isolated individuals, others are mentioned as *clans*—as " gypsy " clans.
Such as the Kennedys, the Douglases, the Herons, the Gordons, the Ruthvens, the Johnstones,—and so on : the very
clans that have been the most prominent in North-British
history. That such names have been borne by men who have
been civilized,—and whose individual line has been civilized
for as many generations as they can prove,—we all know. But
individual families do not make a *tribe*. Individuals whose
habits and manners are those of the ever-changing Present
are of no use in studying the Past. When one wishes to
learn what the manners of an earlier period were, one does
not look to the men and women who follow the fashion,—
changing from generation to generation. One must look at
the people who do *not* change. The Douglas who—in the
fifteenth century—became the follower of King James of
Scotland, was a sensible man who understood " the spirit of
his age." But, for that very reason, he was not a representative man of the *past*. He was ready to adapt himself to any
change that might come. It was the Douglases who would
not change that represented an earlier day, and a previously
existing polity. Those Douglases continued to live on as
they had always done : not adopting newer customs ; not
acknowledging an alien king ; not intermarrying with those
of other races, but continuing their tribal life (and, consequently, maintaining their own individuality of type). And
such men were *gypsies*.

Apparently, the first recorded instances of particular
Borderers being styled " Egyptians " was only three hundred
years ago ; when, on the 8th of August, 1592, " Simson,
Arington, Fetherstone, Fenwicke, and Lanckaster, were

---

* Most of these names will be found in the "gypsy" contributions to the first
volume of *Blackwood*, or in Mr. Simson's " History of the Gipsies."

hanged [at Durham], being Egyptians."[*]   By what means a
Borderer was recognizable as " an Egyptian," is a matter
that could be very easily decided, if we were sure that
"gypsies " were invariably swarthy.   That a " Borderer "
differed distinctly, in appearance, from the people of other
districts, is quite clear.   When (as Scott tells us) a Borderer
was prohibited from entering, or dwelling in, the central
parts of Scotland without a passport, it is evident that something in his appearance prevented him from travelling
through those districts, undetected.   If one were not
hampered by this tremendously-loose application of the
term "gypsy " (a term applied to men of all complexions),
one would say he was recognizable because he was a
" gypsy."   Indeed, they *were* so recognized—whatever the
term may be held to include.   In the latter part of the
seventeenth century, the Annandale Borderers — " the
Thieves of Annandale "—were known to the burghers of
Wigtown by a rather odd variation of one of the Scotch
equivalents for *Caird, Tinker,* or *Gypsy*—namely, *Jockey.*
We are told, by a writer of the year 1684,[†] that "they [the
people of Wigtown] have a market for horses and young
phillies, which the Borderers from Annandale, and places
thereabout, (the stile the countrey calls them by, is Johnnies,)
come and buy in great numbers."[‡]   Now, there can be little
doubt but that those " Borderers of Annandale " were
Jockies," that is " *Gypsies ;* " whether the writer just quoted
had altered the name for the sake of euphony, or whether
those Wigtown people really did use another form.   So that,
if those Wigtown burghers and agriculturists understood "a
black man " by "a gypsy "—as William Penn, at exactly
that period, certainly did—then those Annandale Borderers
were " gypsies" of the orthodox, black-skinned kind.   And
if so, then it is likelier still that " Simson, Arington, Fetherstone, Fenwicke,§ and Lanckaster," who were hanged at

* *Blackwood's Magazine,* September, 1817.
† Andrew Symson, in his "Description of Galloway."
‡ It will be remembered that it is stated in the "History of the Gipsies" that
the "gypsy" dialects are still much used by Scotch horse-dealers,—whether
nominal gypsies or not.
§ In May, 1714, a John Phennick [Fenwick] was convicted at Jedburgh of
being a "notorious Egyptian," and, with others, was "sentenced to be tran-

Durham a hundred years earlier (1592), for "being Egyptians," were also "gypsies" of the orthodox, swarthy type. Moreover, it would appear that the south-western corner of Scotland had not developed a caste of dark-whites in the year 1684 ; or, at any rate, that there was still a considerable part of its population that had refused to mingle its blood with that of the opposite—the white—party. For the same writer of 1684 tells us that at that date the parish of Portpatrick (Wigtonshire) was "yet called the black quarter" of the parish of Inch ; of which parish Portpatrick had once formed a part. And this Portpatrick was one of the boundaries of the " Kennedy " kingdom : and it was at this port—at various times in his career—that Will Marshall and his band of swarthy Picts—embarked, in " the ships of the Piccardach," to encounter their Irish kindred of the opposite coast. Thus, granting that *all* the "gypsy" followers of Billy Marshall were dark-skinned men, there is plenty of reason why not only one but many districts of Galloway should be fitly known as "black,"—so recently as 1684.

The "black quarter" of the parish of Inch was one of the boundaries of the kingdom founded by Kennedy, Kenneth, or Cin-aedh. Simson does not tell us whether the Kennedies were black-skinned gypsies or not, though he includes them among the "three principal clans" of Tweed-dale gypsies (the other two being the Baillies and Ruthvens). When the Kennedies had retreated to the wilds of Tweeddale, they—like the Black Douglases—had been driven some distance from their earlier home. But a son of one of the " Kings of Carrick "— Walter Kennedy, a celebrated minstrel,—was plainly of tawny skin. He was of the latter part of the fifteenth and the beginning of the sixteenth centuries ; and is remembered chiefly for his " Flyting " with his contemporary Dunbar (a kind of rhyming battledore-and-shuttlecock ; the language on either side being Billingsgate of the most pronounced description). In this " Flyting," his opponent taunts Kennedy with his complexion,—using such expressions as these :—" Thy skolderit [scorched] skin, hued

sported to the Queen's American plantations for life." (*Blackwood*, September, 1817.)

like ane saffron bag ; " "blackenit is thy blee " [" your complexion is black "]; "blae [blackish], barefoot bairn ; "
"loun-like Mahoun " [*i.e.* "Saracen "]; " Fy ! fiendly
front ! " [" devil-like visage "] ;—all of which denote that
this "Irish thieving minstrel " (another of Dunbar's pretty
epithets) was of "gypsy " blood : which quite bears out his
reported descent from the Egyptian-(*Scot*) Kennedy, of the
ninth century.

[As Kennedy retorts upon Dunbar in similar terms, it
would seem that both of them,—like a contemporary royal
minstrel, *Peter the Moryen,*—were of the same race as those
earlier black *jongleurs* of the John-of-Rampayne anecdote.
Kennedy speaks of Dunbar as—"Lucifer's lad, foul fiend's
face infernal," "Saracen," "juggler," and "*jow* " ; which last
title, it appears, means nothing else than *tinker* or *gypsy.**]

Therefore, if this Kennedy was a good representative of
his tribe, the Kennedies were *gypsies* of the genuine kind.

.   .   .   .   .   .

These remarks have been rendered necessary by the fact—
which has forced itself forward—that the term "gypsy " has
certainly been applied of late years, if not earlier, to people
who do not belong to either of the two black stocks that
Mr. Leland regards as making up the Gypsies Proper. Mr.
Simson gives us many instances of "gypsies "who were fair-
skinned, blue-eyed, yellow-haired ; the very opposites of the
conventional "gypsy." And unquestionably, if one looks at
any gathering of Scotch nomads, such as that seen annually
at St. Boswell's Fair (which Mr. Simson characterizes as
"an Asiatic encampment, in Scotland,") one sees that not
only a few, but *the great majority* of those "campers " are
Xanthochroi. If such people are to be called "gypsies,"
then the word has completely lost its original signification.
And it really has done so,—in Scotland, if not elsewhere.
Not only does Mr. Simson speak of the white-skinned
Baillies, and others, as "gypsies," but the celebrated colony
at Yetholm was composed of tribes of perfectly-opposite
stock. One who visited that neighbourhood fifty years ago

---

* At page 84 of "The Yetholm History of the Gypsies " (by Joseph Lucas,
Kelso, 1882), it is pointed out that *Jow*, as used by Chaucer and others, does not
signify a *Jew*, but a juggler or gypsy.

writes thus of the inhabitants :—"The principal names of
the gypsies residing at Yetholm are Faa, Young, Douglas,
and Blythe. The two latter are the most numerous, but
they are evidently not of the same race. The Douglases,
the Faas, and the Youngs, are generally dark-complexioned
with black hair ; while the Blythes mostly are light-haired
and of fair complexion."* If, then, "gypsy" is to be held
to mean nothing more than "heathen" (as in Dutch *heyden*),
or "tory," or "nomad"—although at one time it bore special
reference to those "gypsies" who were swarthy *Egyptians*—
then it becomes a matter of great difficulty ever to determine the ethnological position of the various tribes of
Borderers. It both simplifies the question, and complicates
it. It renders it easy to understand how an ordinary fair-
white might be able to prove a descent from a genuine
Border "gypsy," and to prove that none of that lineage were
anything else than fair-whites, and yet to know that there
was no contradiction between the physical appearance of all
the clan and their title of "gypsy" or "Borderer." The
point that needs to be ascertained is the date at which
"gypsy" first became indiscriminately applied.

But, at least, those turbulent, marauding, non-agriculturist
clans of "Borderers" were clans of "gypsies ;" forming as
distinct a species in the time of Maitland of Lethington as
in the time of the Ettrick Shepherd. The "Borderers of
Annandale" were "the gypsies of Annandale," whether we
regard them as *Jockies* ["Johnnies"] or under their well-
known designation of *The Thieves of Annandale.* They were
"common thieves, commonly called Egyptians ;" and when
one of their most daring leaders, *Jock Johnstone*, was hanged
at Dumfries last century as a notorious *gypsy*, it was still
the *thieves* that attempted a rescue. It was against the denomination of those "common thieves, commonly called
Egyptians," that Sir Richard Maitland of Lethington (in
the sixteenth century) "complained" so bitterly ; ending his
complaint with the fervent prophecy—

---

* Oliver's "Rambles on the Scottish Border." He discriminates still more
closely—"The Douglasses (he says) may be distinguished from the other dark-
complexioned families, in consequence of most of them being rather in-kneed."
[Perhaps because they were pre-eminently moss-troopers, or riders.]

O

Yet, or I dee,
Sum sall them see
Hing on a tree
Quhill thay be deid—

a prophecy that was fulfilled in his own and subsequent
generations. Those sixteenth-century "common thieves,
commonly called Egyptians," not only exacted a "black
tribute" from the non-combatant people of "Ettricke forest
and Lawderdail," and even of the Lothians, but they had so
sorned upon those unfortunate people that their houses were
"harried" of food and chattels, and themselves almost
reduced to famine.

As already pointed out, the position of those sixteenth-
century "Egyptians" was that of a fierce, idle, marauding
aristocracy: employed, sometimes, by the Scotch king to
overawe his citizens ; fighting, occasionally, on the King's
side against England ; fighting, incessantly, amongst each
other. Such "Egyptians" as those hanged at Durham in
1592,—Simson, Arington, Fetherstone, and Fenwick ;—or
such as "Francis Heron, King of the Faws," who was buried
at Jarrow nearly two centuries later ;—may be taken as
representing those of the Southern Border—"our English
Tories," as they were once called :—while, on the northern
side were the Gordons, Douglases, Johnstones, Irvings, and
other tribes—whose latest battles, and whose ways of living,
are pictured to us in Mr. Simson's History.

From what period "the Borders" presented this scene
of strife and rivalry between people of that sort, one cannot
definitely say. We have seen that we may go back a
thousand years—at the least—to find anything different.
"There is no doubt that not long before the accession of
Kenneth MacAlpin to the Pictish throne, the kingdom of
Northumbria [*i.e.*, "the Borders"—and a great extent of
territory stretching south and north of that district] seems
to have fallen into a state of complete disintegration, and
we find a number of independent chiefs, or "duces" [dukes]
as they are termed, appearing in different parts of the
country and engaging in conflict with the kings and with
each other, slaying and being slain, conspiring against the
king and being conspired against in their turn, expelling him

and each other, and being expelled." * And such expelled "dukes"—whether *Picts* of the earlier "Moorish," or of the Egyptian-Scottish, or of the Black-Danish division,—or of a jumble of all three—must have been people like the swarthy "Duke Andrew" with the Druidess, his wife,—who are recorded as having entered Bologna in the year 1422, and of whom, or whose like, it was said that "the men were black, their hair curled ; the women remarkably black, and all their faces scarred." Duke Andrew's era was the beginning of the fifteenth century, while that of Mr. Skene's Northumbrian Faw dukes was about the ninth century : but those of the latter who were expelled—not killed—must have left representatives in one part or other of Europe ; and, conversely, Duke Andrew and his following of " lean, black, and hideous Egyptians" must have had ancestors during the ninth century, who were as likely to be living in Northumbria as in any other part of the world.

Just as the thieves of the northern side of the Borders were distinctly recognizable as " Borderers " or " Gypsies " (whether we ought to accept the latter term in its strictest sense or not), so were those of the Southern districts. Herons, Fenwicks, and others, — they were dubbed " Egyptians ; " and hanged as such. The English "Borderer " was quite as much an object of aversion to the burghers of the North-of-England towns, as his brother of Scotland was to the Scottish burghers. We are told that there existed formerly " a by-law of the corporation of Newcastle prohibiting any freeman of that city to take for apprentice " a native of the territory known as the Waste of Bewcastle—the home of those Mossers ;—which again indicates a racial difference. That (in spite of the modern white-gypsy usage) this difference was one of colour is most probable ; since in this quarter also, the tax exacted by those marauding chiefs was known by the peaceable castes as " black tribute : " one of the latest distinct specimens of those chiefs (Henry the Faw, who—circa 1700–1750—" was received and ate at the tables of people in public office ") being a member of that clan whose Yetholm representatives, a century after, are pictured to us as " dark-complexioned, with black hair."

* Skene's " Celtic Scotland," Vol. I. p. 373.

This Henry the Faw was accustomed—it will be remembered
—to receive from " men of considerable fortune " a "gratuity,
called blackmail, in order to have their goods protected
from thieves ; " a " gratuity " which their forefathers had
paid to another " common thief" of an earlier day—the
notorious Jock Armstrong. In the Scotch Highlands this
tax, paid to a similar caste by a similar caste, was called by
the same (or a similar) name ;—being known as *dubh-chis*,
or " blackmail," and otherwise as "watch-money." The
chiefs to whom such tribute was paid were, in the Highlands,
styled "captains" of "watches ; " which, when composed of
"gypsies," were " black watches." There is a hint that a
kindred term was in use in the Border districts,—in " the old
tune, 'Black Bandsmen, up and march ! ' "*

It is interesting to notice how this " blackmail " became
gradually and insensibly legitimized. When, in the beginning
of last century, Henry Faw "was received and ate at the
tables of people in public office," he was tacitly recognized
as holding a position that, if not actually official, was semi-
official ; the guardian, namely, of a certain district, conditional
on his receiving a certain "gratuity" (which no one was
foolish enough to withhold). But Will Faw, who probably
succeeded him, and who was buried at Yetholm in 1783-4,
occupied a position that was even less equivocal. " Will

---

* Sir Walter Scott's *Auchindrane*, Act III. scene I.

It is stated with regard to a fifteenth-century Borderer, named Cuthbert Blackadder, and styled " Chieftain of the South " [of Scotland], that " on his expeditions against the English, who crossed the borders for plunder, he was accompanied by his seven sons who, from the darkness of their complexion, were called
the ' Black Band of the Blackadders.' "   In this instance the " Black Band " was
distinctly so called on account of the black complexion of its members. And it
, is worth remarking that the district in which they lived was called " Blackadder,"
from the name given to a river flowing through that territory (a portion of the
Merse, or *Marsh*, of Berwickshire). On one bank of the Blackadder there is
"an ancient camp," known as " Blackcastle ; " and an entrenchment on the other
side of the river is called the " Black Dikes." " Black*adder* " itself is said to
mean " Black*water ;* " (and it is a tributary of the Whiteadder which drains the
country lying to the north-east of the Blackadder valley). Here, then, we have
a small district containing at least *three* "black " names of a topographical
nature. It cannot be supposed that the camp, the entrenchment, and the river
are all *black*. But the rulers of that district in the fifteenth century were spoken
of as a "black band," on account of "the darkness of their complexion." (They
are referred to in Anderson's " Scottish Nation," Vol. I. p. 309.)

exercised the functions of *country keeper* (as it was called), or restorer of stolen property; which he was able often to do, when it suited his own inclination or interest, very effectually, through his extensive influence among the neighbouring tribes, and his absolute dominion over his own."* What Henry Faw was in reality Will Faw was in name—as well as in fact. And, by the latter half of the eighteenth century, this *official* position of the "gypsy" chiefs was acknowledged in other districts. One of them, Patrick Gillespie, who was "keeper" for the county of Fife, has been figured to us as mounted on horseback, "armed with a sword and pistols," and "attended by four men, on foot, carrying staves and batons." Another—"Robert Scott (Rob the Laird)—was keeper for the counties of Peebles, Selkirk, and Roxburgh." And a friend of Mr. [Walter] Simson's stated that he was present when several "Gypsy constables, for Peebles-shire," were sworn into office. (That, in this last instance, the "gypsies" possessed certain racial characteristics may be gathered from the added comment, that "he never saw such a set of gloomy, strange-looking fellows, in his life."†) That, in all these instances, the men were installed formally into such offices *because* of their "extensive influence among the neighbouring tribes," there can be no doubt. Thus, the wages which the county paid to them for maintaining order in the district, and safe-guarding the goods of the inhabitants, was virtually a modified form of "blackmail."

The Peebles-shire farmer who "never saw such a set of gloomy, strange-looking fellows" as those Border chiefs, may have been of the same race as—and certainly was of one mind with—the sixteenth-century Ettrick-men whose lands and houses the ancestors of such "common thieves, commonly called Egyptians," had "neirhand herreit hail" ("almost wholly harried"). But had he expressed to them the surprise he felt, that such offices should be held by men of whom "not one . . . . . had a permanent residence within the county," they might have answered him that, since they and their forefathers had controlled that district for many centuries, no one was better entitled, or

* *Blackwood's Magazine*, May, 1817.   † Simson's "History," p. 344.

better fitted, to control it than they. And that, although
it was not the regular custom of their race to have a *permanent* residence anywhere, yet that territory—and that
territory alone—had been the home of their people for many
generations. And that—although a newer race, or newer
fashions, or both combined, had made it the custom to dwell
in towns of stone-built houses, and to live plodding, sedentary
lives—yet, at one time, "the common building of their country" had been those turf-built wigwams which they still
reared, and the common way of living had been the predatory existence which many of them still continued to follow.

CHAPTER VIII.

DURING the past year (1883), two interesting figures have vanished from Border life: interesting beyond a doubt, although the attention paid to them was perhaps in excess of their merits. These two were David and Esther Blythe, the nominal heads of the Yetholm "tories." They were brother and sister; having inherited through their father the blood of the white-skinned "gypsy" Blythes,—and, through their mother, that of the dusky Faws. Their Faw lineage is traced back to the "Will" who is mentioned in the previous chapter: their "Blythe" pedigree was, apparently, of less note.

In complexion, these two Blythes were not so dark as many Scotch people who are never thought of as "gypsies;" and the character of their features was that of many other Scotch folk. They were both born in the closing years of last century; and it is probably more than fifty years since Esther was married to "John Rutherford, chief of one of the many gipsy tribes." (His occupation was, I believe, that of a mason: if so, and if he really was—by descent—the chief of the Border clan of Rutherfords, he only offers one example out of many of the social decline of an old stock; a decline that has been brought about, in all such cases, by the refusal to fall in with new ideas.) In 1861, after her husband's death, Esther was promoted to the vacant position of "Queen of the Border Gypsies"—being thus the latest representative of that "King of the Borders" (Scott of Tushielaw) who was hanged by King James the Fifth in the year 1528. Her brother, David, had previously declined the office. As there must be many of her kindred, now in America and the Colonies, her right to the position was probably of a very dubious nature; but at least none could have been found

who was better fitted to fill it. Were it not for the sentimental halo that, during the past few generations, has been
thrown around those people who have longest continued to
live after the once-universal fashion of their neighbourhood,
it is probable that she would never have been known by any
more poetical name than that which she was entitled—by
her marriage—to bear. But the real kingship exercised by
the sixteenth-century " King of the Borders " could not have
faded away into unreality and anachronism under a gentler
personification. For this woman—while a true " gypsy " in
her wit, her vivacity, her graceful bearing, and her love of
the songs and traditions of her fatherland,—seems to have
been delightfully free from any of the unpleasant attributes
with which those of her kind, in former days, are often
credited.

She and her brother were essentially, and in all respects,
"tories : " and this dear old woman did not speak with much
respect of those people whom she sometimes spied from her
poor little room in Kelso—those who "*called* themselves
'ladies and gentlemen.'" And she had still some of the
moss-troopers' contempt for the farming classes. "*My* folk "
were the oldest families of the district : and in what sense
they were "hers," she herself was perhaps best fitted to
explain. " I ken naething about thae new folk "—her
brother David is reported to have said, referring particularly
to some of this despised class—" they come frae goodness
kens whaur ; there's naething o' the bluid o' the auncients in
them." They themselves, at least, were not " new folk : " as
any one might learn from their own lips. To the query—
" Your people have been settled at Yetholm for a very long
time, I believe ? "—Esther's answer came, with a world of
force, " *For generations !* " Whether those *Faws* were of the
stock of Francis the Faw who was buried at Jarrow in 1756,
does not appear. If they were, then the patronymic of their
mother was properly " Heron." And the Flodden sword*

---

* The Flodden sword is evidence of a rather ambiguous nature. One account
says it was "*found* on Flodden Field." On the other hand, Esther distinctly
told Mr. F. H. Groome that it had belonged to one of her *ancestors*. These
extracts are chiefly taken from "The Yetholm History of the Gypsies," by
Joseph Lucas ; and "David Blythe," by C. Stuart, M.D. (both published by J.
& J. H. Rutherfurd, Kelso).

which had belonged to their ancestors may have been wielded by that Heron whom Scott speaks of in *Marmion.*

But though her people had been settled at Yetholm "for generations," she disowned all kinship with the present dwellers in that place. "'The inhabitants were,' she said, 'maistly Irish, and nane o' her seed, breed, and generation.'" She insisted strongly that the *muggers* and *trampers* going about the country, and "passing themselves off as 'gypsies,'" were not of her kind at all. (Nor were those Yetholm people recognized as "gypsies" by a genuine English "tory"—of the swarthy type—who had looked in on them, out of curiosity, some years ago :—" They're not *gypsies*," he said with great emphasis, " they're *muggers*, that's what they are : goin' about with pots and pans, and caravans. *They* ain't gypsies. When we was near Yetholm,—at a place about five miles off, —me and the boys went over there with the horses. And when we tried one o' them fellows with Romany, he didn't understand a word: just opened his mouth and gaped. Yah! *they* ain't gypsies! ")

This David Blythe seems to have been a wonderfully good specimen of the old Borderer. "In nature a true wild man, he was fond of sport, and had a profound contempt for the game laws, which he considered the most unjust statute in the calendar. 'Lang syne, when I walked owre the moors, and cam to a Moorfowl on her nest, I stept aside, thinking I wad get a crack at the covey some day. But noo naething but watchers and keepers, ... ' On one occasion his son was seen to lift a dead fish by the water-bailiff, and was summoned to the court at Duns for doing so. Old David was in a state of great indignation, and went with his son to the court, who, when fined in the usual penalty, or go to jail, the audience was electrified by David getting up and shaking a bag of sovereigns, saying, 'I hae plenty to pay the fine wi', but ye'll jist get him to keep.' "

In maintaining this defiant attitude, David Blythe acted precisely as any unaltered Border moss-trooper should do. The Game Laws, as now intensified, are entirely modern. Some one or other of Scott's characters is made to say that, to take a deer from the hill, or a salmon from the river, is a deed that no man need be ashamed of. And these must be the

sentiments of all "true wild men," in whatever locality they
may be found.   In the Border Country of past times, there
could be no such thing as "poaching"—unless when the
hunters trespassed upon the lands of a neighbouring tribe.
For example, *any* "Annandale Thief" was free to hunt the
game of Annandale : whether he was the chief of the clan
that ruled that district, or merely one of his followers.   The
wild animals of a certain independent territory were no more
the sole property of the chief who ruled over that territory,
than are those of this United Kingdom the sole property of
the reigning monarch.   Consequently, any Borderer adhering
to the ideas of his forefathers must necessarily regard all
"watchers and keepers" as impertinent intruders, and the
laws that give them authority as outrageously unjust.   It
would be hopeless to attempt to make such a man understand
that the Game Laws have reason upon their side : that, however it may have been three hundred years ago, it is now
absolutely necessary that there should be laws for the protection of wild animals, if such are to exist in a thickly-popu-
lated country.   But, as in everything else, the "true wild man"
—the true "gypsy"—is the true "tory ;" and what we
moderns style "poaching" is as natural to him as sleeping
and waking.   For this manner of supporting life—by hunting
and fishing, or by stealing from the herds of his neighbours
—made up the chief part of the existence of the Borderers of
three hundred years ago.   So that, when we say that a
"gypsy" is an inveterate "poacher," we simply say that he
is an inveterate "tory."

David and Esther Blythe were both married in the old
Border fashion ; that is, by one of their own kind, and not by
any Christian priest.*   After the birth of his first child,

---

* David Blythe states that "in 1817 Patie Moodie tied me and ma auld
neebour [his wife] at Coldstream Bridge ; " and it is added in a foot-note [p. 16
of Dr. Stuart's "David Blythe "] that "his sister, Queen Esther, was also 'tied'
at Coldstream Bridge."   In a sketch of Border Life, called "Fastern's E'en in
Scotland Forty Years Ago " (by P. Landreth, 1869), it is further stated that
Coldstream Bridge was "a refuge for lovers which was only less famous than
Gretna Green ; " the priest is a bibulous blacksmith ; and the lovers who are
united in marriage by him are sedentary Scotch Borderers, following peaceful
avocations.   If those Patie Moodies were *invariably* blacksmiths (as they often
were), one might say that the term "tinker" would describe them more accurately.   But one thing is clear : that Gretna Green and Coldstream Bridge did not

David Blythe acknowledged the existence of the local clergyman, by getting him to baptize the infant; but the marriage itself does not appear to have been homologated by any Christian ceremony. Which is just what one ought to expect of the descendants of those Border moss-troopers, who " came to church [a Christian church] as seldom as the twenty-ninth of February comes into the calendar ; " and who never travelled without " books of spells,"—written in a character which was apparently not English, nor Latin, nor Greek—but which may easily have represented the speech of the " Romany."

Whether or not the ability to speak the language of the " Romany," constitutes a Gypsy Proper or Egyptian, it is plain that both Esther the Faw and the English gypsies referred to previously,—all of whom spoke this tongue,— regarded themselves as " gypsies," and quite denied the right of ordinary trampers and campers to make use of this designation. The consideration of the languages used by " gypsies " is a large question, and cannot be more than referred to in this chapter. But the fact just stated, that the late Esther Blythe and her brother regarded themselves as different from the modern inhabitants of Yetholm—who could not speak their speech—is quite clear. And also that they looked down with contempt, not only upon certain vagrant classes, but also upon many who are now accounted " highly respectable : " these being " new folk," from " goodness kens whaur," with 'naething o' the bluid o' the auncients

attain to matrimonial celebrity, *because* (being situated on the Border line) they were the respective points at which English runaways entered Scotland. They were so situated ; but this fact alone will not explain the presence there of non-Christian priests. For this reason : both of these places were utilized by *Scotch* as well as by English people. The villagers in the book just referred to were *Scotch* villagers, who might easily have been married by the parish minister, had they chosen. And David Blythe, though born at Wooler, in Northumberland, was apparently living at Yetholm (in Scotland) when he and his " auld neebour " were married at Coldstream Bridge. Esther, also, was presumably living there, too, on a like occasion ; and both she and her brother were accepted as *Scotch* Borderers. Thus all of these villagers, sedentary or half-nomadic, passed *out of* Scotland into England (or, at least, to the very confines of England) in order to get married by this blacksmith-priest. The explanation of which fact seems to lie in the assumption that the *attributes* of those priests (who correspond with Mactaggart's Galloway "auld boggies"), much more than the situation in which they lived, formed the original reason for their being sought after. .

in them." That they regarded *themselves* as of "the blood of
the ancients "—and the "ancients" of that particular district,
is to be inferred in more ways than one. And, farther, that
they also looked upon certain modernized local families as
being, to some extent, "their folk :" although these had
adopted the manners in vogue during each changing generation,—and had subscribed the laws of British nationality.

These latter, when their pedigrees are avowedly derived
from earlier "mossers" or "moss-troopers," are descended from
those of whom Scott (in his Introduction to the "Minstrelsy ")
says that "numbers . . . . . were executed [during the sixteenth and seventeenth centuries], without even the formality
of a trial ; and it is even said, that, in mockery of justice,
assizes were held upon them after they had suffered. . . . . .
By this rigour, though sternly and unconscientiously exercised,
the border marauders were, in the course of years, either
reclaimed or exterminated ; though nearly a century elapsed
ere their manners were altogether assimilated to those of
their countrymen." In reality, a much longer time elapsed
before this consummation was reached ; if the time has come
even yet. It is only the other day (as Leyden's lines remind
us) that the "tories" of the Debatable Country were
inhabiting the same kind of dwellings that all of "their
countrymen "—the people of ancient Northumbria—had
lived in, a few centuries earlier. But, of course, when Scott
speaks of "their countrymen," he means the people whose
attitude toward the Borderers was that of *enemies;* who
hated them for their religion—or *ir*religion—their "handfast-
ing" and other un-Christian unions, their "sorcery," their idle,
plundering habits, and their whole way of living : whether or
not they also hated them out of the lower instinct of racial
difference.

But Esther Blythe, Faw, or Rutherford was apparently as
good a specimen of the Border chieftainess as could possibly
exist in these degenerate days. Those who knew her personally tell us of her deep attachment to the ancient life, her
intimate acquaintance with the genealogy of the Borders,
and with its traditions, songs, and music. Had it not been
for the continual tightening—year after year—of the cord
that has almost strangled "gypsydom" in the British Islands,

it is likely she would have lived and died as her forefathers.
To one who saw her on what proved to be her death-bed,
she said, "I never was happier than when lying on the
heather—by the corner of my tent—and the sky above me.
I don't like these clothes over me [thrusting at the bed-
clothes, and perhaps half-unconscious of what she was saying—for, by this time, body and mind were nearly worn out,
and she seemed to wander a little]—I don't like these clothes
—I like to be nätteral-like. . . . . I've lived a gypsy, and I'll
die a gypsy." And, as a "gypsy" she had traversed the Faw
territory again and again, though apparently never quitting
it; never, for example, going farther west than Dumfries, the
boundary, on the eastern side, of the country of the Galloways. Though she had approximated, in many ways, to
the modern standards, she was yet at heart "a true wild
woman;" or (if the phrase may pass) "a true wild *lady*"—
for there was nothing of *gaucherie* in her, either in her
physical or her mental structure. In one respect, she fell short
of the typical *Egyptienne*, for she only admitted one occasion
on which she had descended to personal strife: which was,
when, hustled by some inquisitive plebeians at a railway
station, she had "lifted her bit nievie [fist]" and struck the
nearest offender, a woman, in the face—giving her a black
eye, she contritely owned (though the laughter that lurked
in her countenance as she made the confession made one
doubt whether her repentance was very deep). She must also
have been truly a Borderer in her ideas on the subject of
"mine and thine;" although it does not appear that she was
ever punished for any transgression of the modern laws.
Possibly, the "tribute" that was—chiefly from sentimental
reasons—paid to her by casual visitors and by those local
families of note, among whom she periodically made what she
called "voyages" (something very like the coshering of an
earlier day); and the earnings of her husband prior to her
elevation; preserved her from the necessity of following the
ancestral custom of living upon the goods of others. But
she must, at least, have tacitly countenanced the doings of
all those "common thieves, commonly called Egyptians,"
over whom she reigned. As she was an old woman when
she died, she had lived when the old Border ideas were still

in force among all "tories." The idea, of gaining a livelihood by ploughing and sowing and reaping, or by shopkeep-
ing, could find no favour among Borderers of the old school,
so long as it was possible to obtain food by hunting, or by
moonlight raids upon farm-yards. If Esther Rutherford's
husband really worked as a mason, it is not likely that she
ever hinted the readiest way to fill her empty larder by some
modern adaptation of the " pair of clean spurs," served up as
" dinner." And if so, she also failed in this respect to represent the true "tory " spirit.

But if Esther Blythe was not strictly a "gypsy" in this
detail, another noted Borderess, who has been previously
mentioned, supplies the deficiency—and in an era that probably overlapped Esther's youthful days. Mary Yorkston,
Yorstoun, or Youston, the wife of Matthew Baillie, the celebrated Tweed-dale chief, is thus pictured to us :—" In height
she was nearly six feet, her eyes were dark and penetrating,
her face was much marked with the small-pox, and her
appearance was fierce and commanding." Another writer
represents her in these words—" She was fully six feet in
stature, stout made in her person, with very strongly-marked
and harsh features ; and had, altogether, a very imposing
aspect and manner. She wore a large black beaver-hat, tied
down over her ears with a handkerchief, knotted below her
chin, in the gipsy fashion. Her upper garment was a dark-
blue short cloak, somewhat after the Spanish fashion, made
of substantial woollen cloth, approaching to superfine in
quality. The greater part of her other apparel was made of
dark-blue camlet cloth, with petticoats so short that they
scarcely reached to the calves of her well-set legs. [Indeed,
all the females among the Baillies wore petticoats of the
same length.] Her stockings were of dark-blue worsted,
flowered and ornamented at the ankles with scarlet thread ;
and in her shoes she displayed large, massy silver buckles.
The whole of her habiliments were very substantial, with
not a rag or rent to be seen about her person. [She was
sometimes dressed in a green gown, trimmed with red
ribbons.] Her outer petticoat was folded up round her
haunches, for a lap, with a large pocket dangling at each
side ; and below her cloak she carried, between her shoulders,

a small flat pack, or pad, which contained her most valuable articles. About her person she generally kept a large clasp-knife, with a long, broad blade, resembling a dagger or carving-knife ; and carried in her hand a long pole or pike-staff, that reached about a foot above her head." Mr. Simson further states that she "went under the appellation of 'my lady,' and 'the duchess';" and that "she presided at the celebration of their barbarous marriages, and assisted at their. equally singular ceremonies of divorce "—a true _ban-druidh_.

What rendered her a fit consort for a Border chieftain was, more especially, the peculiarity dwelt upon by the writer* first quoted. Mr. Simson has told us how she was known to have stripped a shepherd's wife—whom she encountered among the Tweed-dale hills—as naked as the day she was born, leaving her to find her way home in this condition. And Dr. Brown writes in the same strain :—" She was even more dreaded than her husband, as she was more audacious and unscrupulous. Few persons cared to give her offence, because, if they did, they were sure in the end to suffer some loss or injury. . . . She was, like her husband, a dexterous thief and pickpocket . . . Many stories of her sayings and exploits were at one time prevalent among the peasantry of the Biggar district. We give a specimen or two. One day Mary arrived at the village of Thankerton, with several juveniles, who were usually transported from place to place in the panniers of the cuddies [donkeys]. She commenced hawking her commodities amongst the inhabitants, when some of the children of the village came into the house where she was, and cried, 'Mary, your weans are stealing the eggs out of the hen's nest.' Mary quite exultingly ex-claimed, ' _The Lord be praised ! I am glad to hear that the bairns are beginning to show some signs o' thrift._'"

One is disposed to question whether the heroine of this amusing little incident was the dreaded "duchess" or not. But her words reveal the attitude of the genuine "tory," "gypsy," or (in this instance) "Borderer." Because, when a moss-trooper's children began to walk in the way they should

* The late Dr. John Brown of Edinburgh, in his review of "Biggar and the House of Fleming."

go, they began to *steal.* And, according to Border ideas,
this was "to show some signs o' thrift : " for no Borderer of
the old school could expect to thrive if he did not know how
to steal. And of this class, generally,—not only in the
Border districts, but elsewhere,—it is worth noting that "to
work" and " to steal " are expressed by one word. That is
to say, what *we* call "stealing " *they* call "working." When
a "gypsy" speaks of *choring*, he means what modern people
know as *stealing :* when modern people use what is clearly
the same word, slightly altered, as *charring* and *chores* (a
provincialism for daily drudgery), they indicate innocent
manual labour.

Thus, if Esther Blythe did not wholly sustain the character she professed to act, Mary Yorstoun certainly did.
She, however, was of an earlier generation ; and had she
lived in the present century without, in some degree,
" assimilating her manners to those of her countrymen," it is
extremely probable that she would have " suffered " like her
unreclaimed ancestors of the previous centuries, or have been
banished to Botany Bay, like many of her kindred. It was
impossible for a Mary Yorstoun to flourish in nineteenth-
century Scotland ; though less-pronounced " Egyptians,"
such as Esther Blythe, contrived to retain a good deal of
their ancient manners.

Esther, then, was only *faute de mieux* the " Queen of the
Borders." There must have been many Borderers who had,
by right of blood, a better title to the position ; but who—
and whose immediate ancestors—never dreamt of limiting
their nationality to a small "country," whose boundaries
were being obliterated every year. Such people had taken
their position as " Scotchmen " and, latterly, as " Modern-
Britons ; " and, when compared with this newer and nobler
citizenship, the territory and the nationality of their forefathers seemed alike paltry and mean. If the sixteenth-
century Scott of Tushielaw was represented by any civilized
descendants (as it is very probable he was) when the Border
throne became vacant in 1861, it is not likely they panted
for the ancestral title of " King of the Border Thieves." No
doubt, too, there were others—Faws, Herons, and what not,
—who were entitled, both by blood and by adherence to

archaic notions, to claim the position occupied by Esther Blythe ; but these, again, were living in America and Australia, to which places they or their fathers had, in most cases, been sent by the British Government. And, at any rate, the attractions of the position were nearly all gone : so much so, that he who should have been "King"—David Blythe—does not appear to have troubled his head about the matter. Indeed, a considerable amount of modern humbug seems to have clustered round "Queen Esther,"—of which her own "royal proclamation" has a distinct flavour. Nor is it to be wondered at that a person who, though not uneducated, was certainly not highly educated,* should have assumed some of the mystery and romance that were popularly attached to those of her description ; or that, after being "interviewed" by every tourist that came to Yetholm, she should have, in some ways, accepted herself at their valuation.

But, whatever their claim to the leadership, she and her brother were distinctly old-fashioned Borderers ; and that before everything else. As with the "outlaw Morrow" of the song, that Border country was the "land that was nativest to them ;" and they cherished all its oldest customs, songs, and legends, as only children of the soil can do. Nor were they solitary examples. In the Yetholm of fifty years ago, when the inhabitants were chiefly Black-Douglases, Faws, Youngs, and Blythes, these people are described by a passing visitor† as identifying themselves with the traditional Fastern's E'en—or Shrove Tuesday—festivities of that neighbourhood ; of which a football game (ending sometimes in bloodshed) was one of the chief features. This is only one particular: but Mr. Simson gives many others—most of which have already been pointed out. This special observance, however, was intimately associated with the gypsies of Yetholm—and, probably, of other places. "Kirk Yetholm ball on 'Fastern's E'en' is one of the keenest that can be played ;" says one writer. And it is also stated that

---

* Esther was certainly not uneducated, and had received good schooling in the days of her girlhood, *Latin* being included among her studies. She states that "one Trumbull" had been one of her teachers at Yetholm, and that she had altogether received a "very good education."

† See Oliver's "Rambles in Northumberland, &c." p. 270.

the late Faw chief, "Will *Faw*," who died at an advanced age in 1847, was " a great football player " in his youth. This same writer* further states that Kirk Yetholm "is, perhaps, the only place where females engage in the game of football, and they still play as eagerly as any man." Some ancient heathen rite seems to underlie this particular game upon this particular day. We are told that, on Fastern's E'en, " all over the [Scotch] Borders, this game was played not only vigorously, but also with a fierceness quite unknown in the contemporary matches between any two English parishes, and often led to serious fighting at the time and to worse-blooded feuds afterwards."† It is, apparently, still the practice of the mixed and modernized population of these localities to celebrate Fastern's E'en in this way. But it was never more keenly played than by the "tories" of Yetholm.

So many extracts have been made from Mr. Simson's valuable book, that it seems scarcely pardonable to quote from it again, unless for the sake of additional information. But the following paragraphs, although in a great measure the repetition or confirmation of former statements, present so graphic a picture of archaic Border life that their introduction here (even when not strictly germane to the subject) may not be out of place. The writer is the elder Mr. Simson, and as he is picturing the " gypsies " of Tweed-dale, it is to be presumed that those of the Yetholm district are included in the description :—

I will now describe the appearance of the gipsies in Tweed-dale during the generation immediately following the one in which we have considered them ; and would make this remark, that this account applies to them of late years, with this exception, that the numbers in which the nomadic class are to be met with are greatly reduced, their condition greatly fallen, and the circumstances attending their reception, countenance and toleration, much modified, and in some instances totally changed.

Within the memories of my father and grandfather, which take in about the last hundred years, none of the gipsies who traversed Tweed-dale carried tents with them for their accommodation. The whole of them occupied the kilns and out-houses in the country ; and so thoroughly did they know the country, and where these were to be found, and the dis-

---

* Mr. Lucas, in his "Yetholm History of the Gypsies," p. 131.

† Mr. Landreth's " Fastern's E'en in Scotland," p. 8.

position of the owners of them, that they were never at a loss for shelter in their wanderings.

Some idea may be formed of the number of gipsies who would sometimes be collected together, from the following extract from the *Clydesdale Magazine*, for May, 1818 : " Mr Steel, of Kilbucho Mill, bore a good name among ' tanderal gangerals.' His kiln was commodious, and some hardwood trees, which surrounded his house, bid defiance to the plough, and formed a fine pasture-sward for the cuddies, on a green of considerable extent. On a summer Saturday night, Mary came to the door, asking quarters, pretty late. She had only got a single ass, and a little boy swung in the panniers. She got possession of the kiln, as usual, and the ass was sent to graze on the green ; but Mary was only the avant-garde. Next morning, when the family rose, they counted no less than forty cuddies on the grass, and a man for each of them in the kiln, besides women and children." Considering the large families the gipsies generally have, and allowing at this meeting two asses for carrying the infants and luggage of each family, there could not have been less than one hundred gipsies on the spot.

My parents recollect the gipsies, about the year 1775, traversing the county of Tweed-dale, and parts of the surrounding shires, in bands varying in numbers from ten to upwards of thirty in each horde. Sometimes ten or twelve horses and asses were attached to one large horde, for the purpose of carrying the children, baggage, &c. In the summer of 1784, forty gipsies, in one band, requested permission of my father to occupy one of his out-houses. It was good-humouredly observed to them that, when such numbers of them came in one body, they should send their quarter-master in advance, to mark out their camp. The gipsies only smiled at the remark. One-half of them got the house requested ; the other half occupied an old, ruinous mill, a mile distant. There were above seven of these large bands which frequented the farms of my relatives in Tweed-dale down to about the year 1790. A few years after this period, when a boy, I assisted to count from twenty-four to thirty gipsies who took up their quarters in an old smearing-house on one of these farms. The children, and the young folks generally, were running about the old house like bees flying about a hive. Their horses, asses, dogs, cats, poultry, and tamed birds were numerous.

These bands did not repeat their visits above twice a year, but in many instances the principal families remained for three or four weeks at a time. From their manner and conduct generally, they seemed to think that they had a right to receive, from the family on whose grounds they halted, food gratis for twenty-four hours ; for, at the end of that period, they almost always provided victuals for themselves, however long they might remain on the farm. The servants of my grandfather, when these large bands arrived, frequently put on the kitchen fire the large family *kail-pot*, of the capacity of thirty-two Scotch pints, or about sixteen gallons, to cook victuals for these wanderers.

The first announcement of the approach of a gipsy band was the chief female, with, perhaps, a child on her back, and another walking at her feet. . . . . This chief female requests permission for her *gudeman* and *weary bairns* to take up their quarters for the night, in an old out-house. Knowing perfectly the disposition of the individual from whom she asks lodgings, she is seldom refused. . . . .

Instead, however, of the chief couple and a child or two, the out-house, before nightfall, or next morning, will perhaps contain from twenty to thirty individuals of all ages and sexes. The different members of the horde are observed to arrive at head-quarters as single individuals, in twos, and in threes ; some of the females with baskets on their arms, some of the males with fishing-rods in their hands, trout creels on their backs, and large dogs at their heels. The same rule is observed when the camp breaks up. . . . .

A considerable portion of the time of the males was occupied in athletic amusements. They were constantly exercising themselves in leaping, cudgel-playing, throwing the hammer, casting the putting-stone, playing at golf, quoits, and other games ; and while they were much given, on other occasions, to keep themselves from view, the extraordinary ambition which they all possessed, of beating every one they met with, at these exercises, brought them sometimes in contact with the men about the farm, master as well as servants. They were fond of getting the latter to engage with them, for the purpose of laughing at their inferiority in these healthy and manly amusements ; but when any of the country-people chanced to beat them at these exercises, as was sometimes the case, they could not conceal their indignation at the affront. Their haughty scowl plainly told that they were ready to wipe out the insult in a different and more serious manner. Indeed, they were always much disposed to treat farm-servants with contempt, as quite their inferiors in the scale of society ; and always boasted of their own high birth, and the antiquity of their family. They were extremely fond of the athletic amusement of " o'erending the tree," which was performed in this way : The end of a spar or beam, above six feet long, and of a considerable thickness and weight, is placed upon the upper part of the right foot, and held about the middle, in a perpendicular position, by the right hand. Standing upon the left foot, and raising the right a little from the ground, and drawing it as far back as possible, and then bringing the foot forward quickly to the front, the spar is thrown forward in the air, from off the foot, with great force. And he who " overends the tree" the greatest number of times in the air, before it reaches the ground, is considered the most expert, and the strongest man. A great many of these gipsies had a saucy military gesture in their walk, and generally carried in their hands short, thick cudgels, about three feet in length. While they travelled they generally unbuttoned the knees of their breeches, and rolled down the heads of their stockings, so as to leave the joints of their knees bare, and unincumbered by their clothes.

Many practised music ; and the violin and bagpipes were the instruments they commonly used. This musical talent of the gipsies delighted the country-people ; it operated like a charm upon their feelings, and contributed much to procure the wanderers a night's quarters. Many of the families of the farmers looked forward to the expected visits of the merry Gipsies with pleasure, and regretted their departure. . . . .

To these extracts, it is as well to add the following from *Blackwood's Magazine* (of April, 1817)—to which casual reference has more than once been made. In the above passages, Mr. Simson has not dwelt upon the savage conflicts between rival tribes—although he does so in other pages of the history. The *Magazine* article, in referring to such combats, goes on to say—

Such skirmishes among the gypsies are still common, and were formerly still more so. There was a story current in Teviotdale,—but we cannot give place and date,—that a gang of them came to a solitary farmhouse, and, as is usual, took possession of some waste out-house. The family went to church on Sunday, and expecting no harm from their visitors, left only one female to look after the house. She was presently alarmed by the noise of shouts, oaths, blows, and all the tumult of a gypsey battle. It seems another clan had arrived, and the earlier settlers instantly gave them battle. The poor woman shut the door, and remained in the house in great apprehension, until the door being suddenly forced open, one of the combatants rushed into the apartment, and she perceived with horror that his left hand had been struck off. Without speaking to or looking at her, he thrust the bloody stump, with desperate resolution, against the glowing bars of the grate; and having staunched the blood by actual cautery, seized a knife, used for killing sheep, which lay on the shelf, and rushed out again to join the combat. —All was over before the family returned from church, and both gangs had decamped, carrying probably their dead and wounded along with them; for the place where they fought was absolutely soaked with blood, and exhibited, among other reliques of the fray, the amputated hand of the wretch whose desperate conduct the maid-servant had witnessed.

The village of Denholm upon Teviot was, in former times, partly occupied by gypsies. The late Dr. John Leyden, who was a native of that parish, used to mention a skirmish which he had witnessed there between two clans, where the more desperate champions fought with clubs, having harrow teeth driven transversely through the end of them.

*   *   *   *   *   *

The crimes that were committed among this hapless race were often atrocious. Incest and murder were frequent among them. In our recollection, an individual was tried for a theft of considerable magnitude, and acquitted, owing to the absence of one witness, a girl belonging to the gang, who had spoken freely out at the precognition. This young woman was afterwards found in a well near Cornhill, with her head downwards, and there was little doubt that she had been murdered by her companions.

We extract the following anecdotes from an interesting communication

on this subject, with which we have been favoured by Mr. Hogg, author
of the " The Queen's Wake " :—" It was in the month of May [this event
is placed about the year 1717] that a gang of gypsies came up Ettrick ;—
one party of them lodged at a farm-house called Scob-Cleugh, and the
rest went forward to Cossarhill, another farm about a mile farther on.
Among the latter was one who played on the pipes and violin, delighting
all that heard him ; and the gang, principally on his account, were very
civilly treated. Next day the two parties again joined, and proceeded west-
ward in a body. There were about thirty souls in all, and they had fine
horses. On a sloping grassy spot, which I know very well, on the farm of
Brockhoprig, they halted to rest. Here the hapless musician quarrelled
with another of the tribe about a girl, who, I think, was sister to the latter.
Weapons were instantly drawn, and the piper losing courage, or knowing
that he was not a match for his antagonist, fled—the other pursuing close
at his heels. For a full mile and a half they continued to strain most violently,—the one running for life, and the other thirsting for blood,—until
they came again to Cossarhill, the place they had left. The family were all
gone out, either to the sheep or the peats, save one servant girl, who was
baking bread at the kitchen table, when the piper rushed breathless into
the house. She screamed, and asked what was the matter ? He answered
" Nae skaith to you—nae skaith to you—for God in heaven's sake hide
me ! "—With that he essayed to hide himself behind a salt barrel that
stood in a corner—but his ruthless pursuer instantly entering, his panting
betrayed him. The ruffian pulled him out by the hair, dragged him into
the middle of the floor, and ran him through the body with his dirk. The
piper never asked for mercy, but cursed the other as long as he had breath.
The girl was struck motionless with horror, but the murderer told her
never to heed or regard it, for no ill should happen to her. . . . . By the
time the breath was well out of the unfortunate musician, some more of the
gang arrived, bringing with them a horse, on which they carried back the
body, and buried it on the spot where they first quarrelled. His grave
is marked by one stone at the head, and another at the foot, which the
gypsies themselves placed ; and it is still looked upon by the rustics as a
dangerous place for a walking ghost to this day. There was no cogni-
zance taken of the affair, that any of the old people ever heard of—but
God forbid that every amorous minstrel should be so sharply taken to
task in these days !

It is needless to quote more. Everything that is said by
these chronicles brings out more and more clearly that of the
two castes inhabiting the Borders last century—the warlike,
haughty, domineering moss-troopers, and the peace-loving,
industrious shepherds and farmers—the former were those
who were, beyond any doubt, identified with all the oldest
Border customs. And their surnames bear out the identity.
When it is stated that " above seven of these large bands,"

numbering not less than forty and sometimes a hundred people, frequented the district of Tweed-dale last century, and quartered themselves upon the submissive husbandmen whenever they chose, it is at the same time stated that forty, fifty, or a hundred of the clan Ruthven—of the clan Kennedy —of the clans Douglas, Rutherford, Tait, or Gordon (as the case may be) were roaming at large in that territory. For these, and many others, were the surnames of the Border "gypsies." And these are the surnames immemorially associated with the Borders. Clan-life in that district—clan-life in any district—had not utterly faded away so long as those "tory" bands maintained something of their ancient system. There has been much said about "clans" (which, by some unaccountable process, are popularly regarded as peculiar to the Scotch Highlands,—though it is known they existed all over the British Islands) ; and much has been written about them ; but they are nowhere *visible* except as *gypsies*. These people, and only these, are distinctly recognizable as living the tribal life ; having laws, customs, and chiefs of their own ; and obeying these, to the ignoring of all other laws, customs, and chiefs,—so long as they could. And the clans particularly described in the pages immediately preceding were those of the Border moss-troopers.

And the elder Simson, faithfully delineating the ways and manners of those moss-troopers—just as they were fading from sight,—was doing far greater service to history than Sir Walter Scott, with all his genius. Simson pictured them *as they were:* Scott as he *fancied* they were. What Simson and his contemporaries, writing of the Border "gypsies," have preserved for posterity, is the actual daily life of those Borderers in all its varying aspects : with its endless feuds, its sickening scenes of bloody combat, its revelry, its sports and pastimes, its minstrelsy, its heathen religion and observances. These Border "gypsies" were distinctly the people of whose ancestors Scott has said :—" Their only treasures were, a fleet and active horse, with the ornaments which their rapine had procured for the females of their family, of whose gay appearance the borderers were vain." They are the people who, in recent times, could—while galloping along a river-bank—transfix the salmon in the river with a thrust of

the long lance they still carried ; and who, in earlier and
bloodier days, would use this lance, after the same fashion,
to torture a helpless prisoner, lying bound upon the earth.
These are the tribes whose customs and ideas have justly
been compared to those of "Arabians and Tartarians:" the
tribes whose midnight forays, and stealthy retreats through
the intricacies of their vast "mosses," have been pictured to
us : and who, when scouring the territory of their own clan,
in order to gather the warriors for the pursuit of a retreating
war-party of invaders, "used to carry a burning wisp of straw
at spear head, and to raise a cry, similar to the Indian war-
whoop." They are the people who, as *Borderers*, were prohibited from entering the Lothians and certain other parts of
Scotland, without a permit : against whom the most stringent
laws were enacted again and again, for their crimes of robbery,
murder, sorning, fire-raising, incest, sorcery, fortune-telling,
buffoonery, and for a whole system whose nature we do not
yet thoroughly apprehend ; but which was utterly opposed to
the ideas now paramount among Western races, and existing—if not always paramount—in portions of the British
Islands, during a period that stretches back into the dimness
of antiquity. And these *Borderers* were punished, expelled,
and executed, for "being *Egyptians*."

NOTE.—On reflection, it seems unfair to give Mr. Simson full credit
for his pictures of ancient Border society, and to debar Scott from any
share in these descriptions. Because, on the one hand, the former did
not recognize the importance of the people he wrote of ; and, as regards
the latter, *he himself* contributed much of the *Blackwood* information
that has been cited. The chief thing to be said in favour of the former
writer is, that he contented himself with the description of *facts :* the
latter did not. Or rather, he did not place his facts in the proper light.
He knew, and he has told us, that two or three hundred years before his
birth, the people known as "Borderers" were fierce savages ; who,
eventually, were "either reclaimed or exterminated ; though nearly a
century elapsed ere their manners were altogether assimilated to those
of their countrymen." It never occurred to him that if any were *not*
reclaimed—even in his own day—their names, their manners, their ideas,
would correspond exactly with those of the "marauders" whom, as Sheriff,
he must often have passed judgment upon. From him, and from others,
we can form some idea of the *morale* of those early Borderers. But, either
because these early Borderers were, in some sense, his own ancestors ;
or, because they were at that time people of importance; or for both
reasons ; his pictures of them half-extenuate their vices, which he speaks

of in courtly phrases. When he regards their unchanged descendants in his own day, it is as a stranger. They " commit many crimes "—" murders of singular atrocity "—and are " great plagues to the country :" expressions which are identical, in sentiment, with those used by men of *his own* mental stamp, at an earlier date, with reference to those same " early-Borderers," who were their contemporaries.

CHAPTER IX.

WHEN, in the reign of Queen Elizabeth, "black-tribute" was "paid unto some inhabiting near the Borders, being men of name and *power;"* and when, at the same period, the Armstrongs who ruled over Liddesdale and the Debatable Country were declared by James of Scotland to be "no subjects of his;" it is clear that, on either side of the Cheviots there existed a territory that was neither England nor Scotland—(whether or not it be right to regard it as the wreck of Ancient-Northumbria). When, after Elizabeth's death, the Scotch king became the nominal ruler of all Britain; but had nevertheless to admit that much of North-Western Scotland was inhabited by "wild savages, void of his obedience;" there existed another portion of Great Britain that did not own allegiance to the British monarch. And when, in the district that stretched "from Wigtown to the town of Ayr—Portpatrick to the Cruives of Cree," no man could dwell in safety unless he acknowledged the supremacy of the Kings of Carrick, there was a third territory that was neither Scotland nor England.

It is impossible to fix the exact dates at which these kingdoms—and others like them—ceased to be. It was immaterial that a certain man, called George, should be styled "King of Great Britain;" so long as another man, named Henry, and styled " King of the Faws," was virtually the ruler of a portion of the same Great Britain; recognized as such by the nominal subjects of King George, and receiving—with great regularity—his royal dues from year to year. So long as Henry was not put down, George was not really King of Great Britain. When the provost of Linlithgow, and other traders of that town, did not attempt to travel through Linlithgowshire without an engraved token, granted by the local "tory" chief,—then Linlithgowshire was not absolutely under British rule, but was still—in some degree—an independent province. When Will Marshall, and his own particular following of "tories," regarded the whole province of Galloway as bound to keep them in meat and drink, and to give them shelter when desired,—and succeeded in obtaining what they desired,—Galloway was not under the protection of Modern-British law.

There can be no doubt that the "tory" rulers of those various provinces were firmly persuaded of their right to rule : and, also, that they clearly understood the limits of each dominion. We are told of Billy Marshall that "he well knew the Braes of Glen-Nap, and the Water of Doon, to be his western precincts." As soon as he crossed that boundary—the River Doon—he was met by "a powerful body" of the "tories" who dwelt in the territory lying farther north : who, after a fierce battle, sent him back, beaten, into his own country. Indeed, it is a feature of "gypsydom" more than once pointed out by Mr. Simson, that the various tribes had each their separate "walk" or country, into which no other dared to venture, except at the peril of their lives. And he also adds that they inherit the belief that the whole of Scotland was once divided into separate provinces,—of which these were the remnants,— and we know from Mr. Skene's researches that the truth of their tradition is borne out by facts. Another unmistakable example of this feature, in addition to those just given, is that of the territory in Kinross-shire, which was at one time under the sway of Peter Robertson,—one of those "gypsies" who combined the characters of *chief* and *druid* (or medicine-man). "Peter was a tall, lean, dark man, and wore a large cocked hat, of the olden fashion, with a long staff in his hand. . . . . He was frequently seen at the head of from twenty to forty gipsies, and often travelled in the midst of a crowd of women. Whenever a marriage was determined on, among the Lochgellie horde, or their immediate connexions, Peter was immediately sent for . . . . . . to join them in wedlock." Added to these attributes, he possessed great skill as a physician. But the point to be attended to here, in connection with him, is that he was the ruler of a certain district in Kinross-shire ; so much so, that when his children set up in life for themselves, he allotted particular divisions of that territory to each (like any *Lear*, real or imaginary), reserving only to himself the portion known as *The Braes of Kinross.** It is not likely that any parchment recorded these gifts : and it is certain that the arable portions of the lands so given away were sub-divided into various modern "estates," which *were* held by parchment-rights,— the holders of which would be recognized to-day as the undoubted proprietors. But this "tory" chief, and all his kind, knew nothing of paper-rights. They really belonged to a period when there was no title to land except the strong arm. People who lived quietly, and regarded *law* as superior to *force*, were only so many eccentric and inoffensive fellow-beings, of totally different ideas and, perhaps, of totally different race ; but whose existence was a matter of in-difference to the "tory" tribes so long as they did not in-terfere with their old way of living—their fighting and drinking, their hunting and fishing, their wild minstrelsy and wilder dances, their heathen ceremonies of marriage and burial, and their once-unchallenged right to scour their own territory at will.

Such people, ignoring the changes that time had wrought and was still working around them, regarded North-Britain as though it was still what it once had been. They had their pro-vinces, ruled over by chiefs who had the right to grant passes to travellers through their respective territories ; and these chiefs were subject to a Supreme Chief, or King ; who was all-powerful, and whose passes allowed a traveller to traverse the whole of Scotland,† unmolested. These passes, as we have seen, were called in, and new ones issued, at stated in-tervals, in order to avoid a mis-use of them ; the engraved characters, at each issue, being presumably different from those on the previous tokens ; and, in all cases, being only intelligible to those who understood the "tory" language, or languages. Mr. Simson does not, I think, specify any place as the annual rendezvous ; but Martin mentions ‡ that, during

* Simson, pp. 264-6.
† It may be doubted whether the Baillie supremacy extended over the whole of Scotland, but Mr. Simson seems to indicate as much.
‡ See the "Advertisement to 'The Antiquary.'"

the seventeenth century, one of those meeting-places was the town of St. Andrews (and it is not unlikely that the "Faw-Kirk Tryst"—once a notable annual gathering—was originated for political and religious, as well as social purposes). And in Galloway, the Fair of Keltonhill seems to have been the recognized rendezvous for all the "Tories" of that territory. In England, a similar state of things existed. "The Rogues of the North used to meet, at night time, once every three years," at the celebrated cavern known as the Peak's Hole (near Castleton in the Peak of Derby): and another trysting-place, farther south, was "by Retbroak at Blackheath."* And, even in Mr. Borrow's day, they mustered "from all parts of England" at the annual fair held at Fairlop, in Epping Forest.

It may yet be possible to ascertain the various "tory" districts in these islands; and to guess at the story their boundaries tell. But it seems almost too late. "Gypsy-dom" has been so completely broken up by the movements of the past century. Even if the tribes still held something of their former power, how could they preserve the integrity of their frontiers with railways crossing their territory at every angle? If Will Marshall and his painted army could be supposed to exist to-day; and if they wished to make a raid into Ayrshire; they could reach the heart of the enemy's country, unopposed, in the course of an hour or two. But a hundred other causes have worked to the same end. The steady persecution of "rogues and vagrants"—the appropriation by individuals of territory that was once common to all (by which all travellers, of every kind, have been pushed off and off the land—until only the roads are left)—the increasing strictness of the Game Laws, which have deprived the "wild man" of one of his chief means of sustenance—all these causes, and many more, have brought about the complete downfall of genuine "gypsyism." Although, in newer and sparsely-peopled countries, the "gypsy" life may be lived for many years to come by the descendants of British "gypsies," yet the overthrow of the *system* is complete.

* Viles' and Furnivall's "The Rogues and Vagabonds of Shakspere's Youth," page xvii. of the *Preface* of the 1880 edition. Also *Blackwood's Magazine* for April, 1817.

And this means that Nationalism has triumphed over ex-Nationalism, or Provincialism. The game laws—the laws against local autocrats, known as *sorners*, &c.—the laws by which (with doubtful wisdom) men have been given absolute possession of land which their predecessors merely *governed*, thus enabling them to confine all wayfarers to roads and "rights-of-way"—all these laws have been framed by the supreme Government, and endorsed by all the Nationalists in the country. In place of twenty kingdoms in these islands, we have now only one.

NOTE.—That archaically-disposed castes should continue to live as though those various small nationalities had *not* gradually been rolled into one ; and instead of, with wider vision, seeing only one monarch and one monarchy, should continue to confine their gaze to the petty kingdoms of their forefathers ;—this is not surprising, when one realizes that political divisions of vastly newer date than those early heptarchies (but, nevertheless, as obsolete as they are), do even yet present themselves as *realities* to many people—and these sometimes of the best education. For at least eighty years, the British Islands have been under one Government. For nearly a century longer, Great Britain has been one country : for two hundred and eighty years it has formally acknowledged only one supreme power : its principal divisions have been nothing more than provinces since the year 1707—and, rightly regarded, since the year 1603. And yet how constantly are those extinct nationalities spoken of as if they really existed ! There is a book from which some facts, cited in these pages, have been taken—and it is a book of very considerable interest and value—which is named " The Scottish Nation." If it treated only of Scotchmen who were born before the accession of James to the British throne, the book would be correctly enough named. But it does not : it comes down to our own day. And, therefore, the title is inaccurate. There has certainly been no Scottish Nation for a hundred and seventy-six years : and, properly speaking, that nationality (ill-defined as we have seen it to be) came to an end in 1603. When James ascended the British throne, he became the first of Modern-Britons,—of " Englishmen " (to use the latest and more euphonious—if less accurate—designation). When others of his extraction flocked southward in his train, they were not alien adventurers—as the provincially-minded section of South-Britons esteemed them to be. They were merely British subjects, coming up to the capital from the provinces, like any of their fellow-countrymen in Yorkshire or in Devon. Had Scotland been the richer country, as it was the poorer,—and had James selected his ex-capital as the seat of British government,—the movement would have been reversed ; but the South-Britons, trending naturally to the centre of wealth and power, would not have been " adventurers." Although red-tape and provincialism did not admit this new citizenship till 1707,—and then reluctantly,—

it was certainly represented by James the First and his government ; which was neither " English " nor " Scotch,"—but *British.* After that period, to talk of *Englishmen* or *Scotchmen,* except in a geographical sense (or using the former term in its modern and extended acceptation), was to commit an anachronism. But the error is made every day : and most of us are guilty of making it. It may be a trivial inaccuracy to designate England Proper, Ireland, and Scotland as " countries," but it is an inaccuracy, nevertheless. For these are merely provinces of the United Kingdom—whether we call that kingdom the British Islands, Great Britain, Britain, or England. The title of the book just referred to shows that, in the estimation of many people, the inhabitants of Scotland constitute a " nation." And many other examples of the same usage might be cited, to denote that this is no solitary instance. In Scotland, and also in England Proper, there are religious societies which are very frequently spoken of as " national " churches. But the expression is incorrect. Although every inhabitant of either of these provinces held the religious tenets of those respective " national " churches, that would not render those churches national. There cannot be two national churches in one nation. No doubt, each of the divisions referred to represents (if only in a partial degree) certain religious organizations that were once formally recognized as national. But, as the *nations* which so recognized them have been *provinces* for, at least, a hundred and seventy-five years, the modern representatives of those *ci-devant* national churches must be now provincial. This altered attitude is perhaps most clearly seen by regarding the relative positions of the British Premier and the English Primate—of which the first is national and the second provincial. The position of the British Premier is like that of the Royal Academy, or the National Gallery : it is national. The members of the Royal Academy are from every part of the United Kingdom : those of the Academies of Ireland and of Scotland are almost solely local men. In the ex-capitals of Ireland and of Scotland, there are people who lament over the social " decay " of these two cities. But there has been no decay in either of these portions of the empire. The centre of government has been shifted to London : and the territory governed is vastly greater than before. There has been anything but decay. Carlyle, who (I think, invariably) employed the term " Englishman " in its widest sense, was equally an Englishman whether he lived at Edinburgh or at Chelsea. Sheridan may be called an Irishman or an Englishman with equal accuracy (the latter being, of course, accepted in its sense of " British "). Scott, who is somewhere stated to have protested against the modern application of " Englishmen " to all inhabitants of the British Islands, was as much a Modern Englishman as any native of Sussex or of Kent.

The fitness of the usage which has given to a new country the name which properly belongs to only one of its sections, may be questioned. It is, indeed, probable that from this loose nomenclature has arisen much of the confusion of ideas with regard to nationality, which is plainly so widespread. So widespread is this error that almost none of us are free from it. Even the twelfth representative of British monarchy was trained as though her kingdom had been no larger than Elizabeth's. On the occasion of her first visit to the northern parts of her dominion, she remarked that "the Scotch coast" was "totally unlike *our* coast." And the same feeling is latent in such an incident as this : In one of our illustrated papers, not long ago, there had appeared some humorous sketches of the doings of the Provincialist party in Ireland, which had given offence to certain members of that party. To atone for this, a courteous and conciliatory paragraph was inserted in a subsequent number of the journal, in which the following sentence occurred—" As for the sketches of the National Convention, we made no more fun of its members than we have frequently made of our own House of Commons." This remark was addressed by one subject of Queen Victoria to others of his fellow-countrymen ; but the words " our own " could never have been used had the author realized that they *were* his fellow-countrymen. The House of Commons is quite as much " our own " to a native of Tipperary as to a native of Middlesex. And, although quite unintentionally, this writer was placing himself in the same attitude as those who talk so foolishly about "English rule" (sometimes called "tyranny") in Ireland. The power that governs Ireland and Great Britain is quite as much Irish, Scotch, and Welsh, as it is English. Ireland really *has* "home rule" : like any other part of the United Kingdom. The government of our country is "English" in the catholic sense of that word—and only in that sense. Its members are not composed solely of natives of the *province* of England. Indeed, far from this being the case, the House of Commons is so constituted that every member in it *might* be a man of Irish birth. Although some of the people of Ireland have not yet understood this, it is nevertheless the case : and those who have not understood it are still in the bonds of Provincialism. Such people do not see that they—as much as the natives of Great Britain, and those of Ireland who *do* see it—are members of a power that rules half the world ; compared with which the defunct nationalities of Ireland or of England are contemptibly insignificant. And that to revive the extinct life of the individual provinces—East-Anglia or Connaught, Scotland or Wales—out of which this empire has grown, is a feat as difficult and undesirable as reviving a corpse, or transforming a grown man into a child.

But the point to be emphasized here is this—that, although our country is primarily the British Islands, and, in a less-defined sense, the whole British Empire, there are many well-educated British people now living who do not fully realize this fact ; but still see, in imagination, the boundary-lines of countries that no longer exist. And, if modernized people have not succeeded in forgetting the nationalities of two or three centuries back, it is no wonder that those "tories" we are speaking of—who wilfully adhered to their hereditary ideas—should have represented the nationalities of a period—or periods—still more remote.

CHAPTER X.

It is hardly necessary to recapitulate what has been said regarding the higher castes of Scotch " tories : " that they rode horses of the finest breeds, were armed with swords and pistols, wore riding-boots, ruffles, fine coats of scarlet or green, watches, rings, silver buckles, and all the other adornments of the "nobility and gentry" of their time ; that their women were similarly dressed ; and that either sex, when so dressed, *looked* the character they assumed. Moreover, that they were accustomed to associate with, and be received into the houses of people holding positions that were recognized as important and honourable by the community at large : and that (though this was perhaps not specified before) they themselves—though living the nomadic life—enjoyed the same luxuries of diet as any of the more sedentary gentry. " The gipsies in Tweed-dale were never in want of the best of provisions, having always an abundance of fish, flesh, and fowl. At the stages at which they halted, in their progress through the country, it was observed that the principal families, at one time, ate as good victuals, and drank as good liquors, as any of the inhabitants of the country. A lady of respectability informed me [Mr. Simson] of her having seen, in her youth, a band dine on the green-sward, near Douglass-mill, in Lanarkshire, when, as I have already mentioned, the gipsies handed about their wine, after dinner, as if they had been as good a family as any in the land." Such people, we have been told, were intensely proud—claiming for themselves an ancient and illustrious lineage—and regarding themselves as quite superior to either the low-caste gangs of "gypsies," or the *bourgeoisie* and yeomanry with whom they came in contact.

From whatever races he may have been descended, Mr.

Simson plainly regards the gypsy castes from the burgess-and-yeoman point of view : what may be called the *modern* point of view. It was a most puzzling thing to him, that people who had no fixed place of abode, and whose ways were so totally at variance with those of his own kind, should yet be treated with something very like respect by people of staid and settled habits. " Instead of endeavouring to repress the unlawful proceedings of the daring Tinklers, numbers of the most respectable individuals in Linlithgowshire deigned to play at golf and other games with the principal members of the body.* . . . . The honourable magistrates, indeed, frequently admitted the presumptuous Tinklers to share a social bowl with them at their entertainments and dinner parties. Yet these friends and companions of the magistrates and gentlemen of Linlithgowshire were no other than the occasional tenants of kilns, or temporary occupiers of the ground floor of some ruinous, half-roofed houses, without furniture, saving a few blankets and some straw, to prevent their persons from resting upon the cold earth."

But his adjectives are wholly misplaced. If the " gypsies " he is here speaking of were—as they plainly were—those accomplished horsemen and swordsmen, finely attired, and of graceful bearing, whom he has shown to us in several places, and who could " discourse readily and fluently on almost any topic,"—on which side was the condescension ? Which were " honourable " and which " presumptuous "—those cavaliers, or the burghers at whose houses they dined ?

In the same page, he places the two castes in a light that shows their respective positions more clearly :—" The children of these gipsies attended the principal school at Linlithgow, and not an individual at the school dared to cast the slightest

---

* "The proficiency which the gipsies displayed on such occasions (continues Mr. Simson) was always a source of interest to the patrons and admirers of such games. At throwing the sledge-hammer, casting the putting-stone, and all other athletic exercises, not one was a match for these powerful Tinklers. They were also remarkably dexterous at handling the cudgel, at which they were constantly practising themselves." These statements serve farther to emphasize what is pointed out by Mr. Leland and others—that the races, or castes, known as " gypsies " are inseparably connected with all those exercises and pastimes which we regard as peculiarly " Old English : " and that the perfunctory interest taken in those sports by non-gypsies is " as moonlight unto sunlight " compared with the ardour evinced by the " tory " castes.

reflection on, or speak a disrespectful word of, either them or their parents, although their robberies were everywhere notorious, yet always conducted in so artful a manner that no direct evidence could ever be obtained of them. Such was the fear that the audacious conduct of these gipsies inspired, that the magistrates of the royal burgh of Linlithgow stood in awe of them, and were deterred from discharging their magisterial duties, when any matter relative to their conduct came before their honours." But "their honours" were merely brewers and bakers, while "these gypsies" were mediæval "gentlemen."

This is unmistakable. It is a fact that seems to have been somewhat lost sight of in recent times; but the previous pages have been written to little purpose, if they have not shown the existence of a caste of nomadic *nobles* (that word, like "gentlemen," being here used to denote a ruling class—without reference to its etymological fitness). Those people formed "the upper class" in certain neighbourhoods. When Sir John Sinclair referred to the village of Eaglesham (in his Statistical Account), he said that it was "*oppressed* with gangs of gypsies, commonly called Tinklers, or sturdy beggars." The enactments against them style them "*masterful* beggars" and "sórners." In the Eaglesham instance, they were the actual over-lords of that particular district. There was "no magistrate [*except* the gypsy chief] nearer than four miles" from that last-century village. And the villagers paid "black tribute" to their rulers: whom they feared and dared not offend. Although it is Mr. Simson who calls those gypsies "presumptuous" because they played golf with the tradesmen of Linlithgow, it is himself who tells us that those tradesmen did not venture to travel throughout the country without one of the orthodox "tokens" granted by those predatory nobles. It is he himself who tells us that certain castes of such people possessed all the manners of gentlemen, with the bearing and style of dressing suited to that character. He, and others, tell us that they were not penniless outcasts; but men and women who not only wore fine apparel and ornaments of gold and silver, and jewelry, but who also carried well-filled purses with them —the contents of which they often lavished on the poor.

Even so recent a specimen as David Blythe of Yetholm
could afford to flourish a bag of sovereigns in the face of the
court that condemned his son for what they called "poaching," but what he and his ancestors regarded as legitimate
sport. It was not *poverty* that made him refuse to pay the
fine, but a dislike and contempt for modern laws and legis-
lators. The last-century "King of the Beggars," named
Andrew Gemmell, could afford to play for high stakes at his
favourite games of draughts, dice, and cards : and the minister of Galashiels informed Sir Walter Scott "that many
decent persons in those times would, like him, have thought
there was nothing extraordinary in passing an hour, either in
card-playing or conversation," with this particular gypsy
chieftain. Sir Walter Scott was so utterly different from
those early Borderers about whom he wrote, that he could not
understand how such a man as this Gemmell could ever be
regarded as an equal—not to say a superior—by men who
slept under roofs and followed prosaic callings. He expects
you to regard with amused surprise Gemmell's statement
that "begging was in modern times scarcely the profession
of a gentleman." He had so little sympathy with those old
Border marauders that he did not see how Gemmell's
"begging" and their "sorning" were, radically, one and the
same thing : and that, if they were "gentlemen," Gemmell
was a "gentleman" also, as he (and all such gypsies) emphatically asserted themselves to be. Their purses were
replenished by robbery, and by "begging" that was "demanding" rather than "entreating." But this was the
immemorial fashion of that particular type. As a contemporary of Scott has said, "these borderers seemed to have
considered all this as honourable, or, at least, not disgraceful."
Scott thought, as Sir Richard Maitland of Lethington thought,
and as most of "us" think at the present day, that the custom
of taking by force what was not one's own was "Common
Theft." But neither those early "sorners," nor their modern
representatives, regarded that as dishonourable or criminal,
whatever name they gave it. Those ideas form a portion of
the "peculiar *morale*" that Mr. Leland states is the characteristic of "gypsies."

Thus these high-caste gypsies of Mr. Simson's clearly con-

stituted a nomadic aristocracy. And although (to judge
from his book) the yeomanry did not always regard them
with respect, it is evident that they were inspired with a
wholesome dread of the " gypsies." Let them come by fifty,
or by a hundred, the farmer's chimney smoked for their
dinner, and the farmer's larder supplied their chief families
for four-and-twenty hours. It is true they lightened the
evening with their dances, and the music of their violins and
bagpipes ; and that, after the first twenty-four hours, they
seemed to hold themselves bound to cater for themselves.
But, unless the yeomanry of the eighteenth century differed
greatly from their successors to-day, it cannot have been a
matter of indifference to them that a whole clan should squat
upon their premises, uninvited, and that the farmers and their
servants should toil to feed this crew of hungry hunters and
fishers. It is indeed quite apparent—from the same book—
that had this forced hospitality not been granted, the peaceful
farm would have seen the " brandished swords " and " furious
looks" with which such gypsies were accustomed to resent
an affront, or enforce a demand.

In short, those people were the remnants of an earlier
nobility. It is told us, again and again, that they looked
down with the utmost contempt upon the agricultural classes,
and that they were permeated through and through with the
pride of high descent. Their way of living was assuredly
not that of serfs and labourers. If idleness be regarded as
an essential of " aristocracy " (as, in the eyes of vulgar
people, it still is), then those were surely aristocrats. Their
only attempt at real work was that involved in the commission
of some robbery. When they came strolling in to a Border
homestead, on a summer evening, it was with fishing-rods
and fowling-pieces, " and large dogs at their heels : " and they
varied the monotony of sport by minstrelsy, " cudgel-playing,
throwing the hammer, casting the putting-stone, playing at
golf, quoits, and other games." Whether the "tamed birds "
that formed a part of their large *impedimenta* were falcons, is
not stated by Mr. Simson. But it is likely they were. In
fine, these wandering bands were composed of idle and
haughty " nobles," of a quite old-fashioned type : whose ideas
with regard to almost everything,—and whose racial qualities

(it may be) also—rendered them the very antipodes of the people who have described them.

These " gypsies " have been pictured to us *from the outside.* Thus pictured, we have seen them to be nomads ; but, nevertheless (in the higher instances), nomads who were finely apparelled, who were warriors rather than workers, who possessed horses of the finest breeds, who exacted tribute from all the sedentary castes within their territories, and who bore themselves toward those castes *du haut en bas.* Farther, "at the stages at which they halted, in their progress through the country," they were accustomed to " eat as good victuals, and drink as good liquors " as any in the neighbourhood ; it being particularized, in one picture of such a " gypsy " banquet, that they " handed about their wine, after dinner, as if they had been as good a family as any in the land."

But such people must have had *their own* view of things. And as they, too, were Britons ; and Britons occupying positions that were distinctly notable ; they must, also, have left us some record. They had their castes of minstrels and bards (who, indeed, seem to have been *the* minstrels of the country), and it was pointed out that two of these were very probably the dark-skinned fifteenth-century minstrels, Kennedy and Dunbar. It is not proposed to cite their evidence here (if they have left any), but that of their contemporary, Barclay.

None of the published descriptions of the manners of Scotch "gypsies" seem to go farther back than two centuries. Therefore, when we look as far back as the fifteenth and sixteenth centuries, we must expect to find them occupying positions that were more distinctly exalted. Because they —the superior castes of the eighteenth century—" always boasted of their own high birth, and the antiquity of their family ;" looking down with contempt upon "the rabble of town and country." And, consequently, if that haughty attitude was warranted by facts (as we may say, with some confidence, it was in the instance of the black Douglases), then we must look for the forefathers' of the eighteenth-century " tories" among the castes that were *supreme* two or three centuries earlier ; and whose position was much more clearly defined than that of their later descendants.

Now, Barclay (sometimes styled a native of Scotland,

sometimes of England), in giving a sketch of the every-day
life of a "courtier" of his own time, describes a state of
things that corresponds very closely with the picture given
by Mr. Simson of the high-caste "tories." In recounting
their experiences " at the stages at which they halted in their
progress through the country," Barclay says, of these
courtiers—

> They oftentime sleepe full wretchedly in payne,
> And lye all the night forth in colde, winde, and rayne;
> Sometimes in bare strawe, on bordes, ground, or stones,
> Till both their sides ake, and all their bones.

When it is their fortune to

> lye within some towne,
> In bed of fethers, or els of easy downe,

their condition is hardly improved, since they are surrounded
with the most noisome companions, human and otherwise.
After entering into all the disagreeable details which give
those courtiers, under such conditions, " worse easement than
if they lay on ground,"—Barclay, in the person of his representative " courtier," continues :—

> but heare more misery,
> Which in their lodging have courtiers commonly ;
> Men must win the marshall or els herbegere,
> With price or with prayer, els must thou stand arere ;
> And rewarde their knaves must thou if thou be able,
> For to assigne the a lodging tollerable,
> And though they promise, yet shall they nought fulfill,
> But poynt the place nothing after thy will :

the lodging assigned being often—as with their descendants
—in a stable or out-house.

This courtier goes on to say that, while one may put up
with the indifference of the marshall or the "herbegere ; " to
whom, indeed (being men of rank in this travelling court),
it was a courtier's duty to be polite; there remained a necessity that was almost intolerable—the showing of politeness
to people of a wholly different order,

> But yet for certayne it were thing tollerable
> To becke and bowe to persons honorable,

As to the marshall, or yet the herbegere,
Or gentle persons which unto them be nere ;
But this is a worke, a trouble and great payne,
Sometime must thou stoupe unto a rude vilayne.
Calling him master, and oft clawe his hande,
Although thou would see him waver in a bande.*
For if thou live in court, thou must rewarde this rable,
Cookes and scoliens, and farmers of the stable,
Butlers and butchers, provenders and bakers,
Porters and poulers, and specially false takers :
On these and all like spare must thou none expence,
But mekely with mede bye their benevolence.
But namely of all it is a grievous payne
To abide the porter, if he be a vilayne ;
Howe often times shall he the gates close
Against thy stomake, thy forehead, or thy nose ;
Howe often times when thy one fote is in,
Shall he by malice thrust thee out by the chin.
Sometime his staffe, sometime his clubbish feete
Shal drive thee backward, and twine thee to the streete,
  *   *   *   *   *   *
Without thou standest in rayne and tempest sore,
And in the meane time a rascolde or vilayne
Shall enter while thou art bathed in the rayne.

Of all this description, that given by the gypsiologists is
merely an echo : and, like all echoes, it comes from the
opposite side.   In these sixteenth-century rhymes, we have
the picture of a ruling and *nomadic* caste : of sorners who
were still *sorohen*, or nobles, going *a-coshering* throughout
the territory which their king ruled over ; and demanding
harbourage from all and sundry.   Regarding themselves as
" gentle persons," they—or, at least, the humbler among them
—are often obliged to show an outward respect to men whom
they utterly scorn, and would fain see " hanged in a halter ; "
who are " rude villains "—butchers and bakers.   As often as
not, they are made to sleep in filthy out-houses, and sometimes are refused entrance altogether (at the gates of the
inn or house at which they apply),—being thrust and kicked
into the street.   And while such a " courtier " is ignomini-
ousiy shivering in the rainy street, the porter who turned
him away admits, without hesitation, a fellow-"villain."   All
this is but a copy of the same strange picture—a tribe of

* " Hang in a halter."

wandering nobles ; counting themselves as nobles, and despising the dwellers in towns and farms ; exacting " black-mail" in one shape or another from such people ; feared and disliked by these people, who ill-use them as much as they dare ; and who regard as "robbery" that which the *sorners* take from them with or without their leave.

The *villain* here is pretty clearly a *town's-man:* and our modern "tories" still call their chief aversion a *town's-man (gav-moosh).* And, as clearly, the "courtier" is *not* a *town's-man.* This representative courtier says so, distinctly, himself—

> And of these cities talke we a word or twayne,
> In which no man can live avoyde of payne,
> For whither soever the court remove or flit
> All the vexations remove alway with it.
> If thou for solace into the towne resorte,
> There shalt thou mete of men as bad a sorte,
> Which at thy clothing and thee shall have disdayne,
> If thou be busy† the club shall do thee payne ;
> There be newe customes and actes in like wise,
> None mayst thou scorne, nor none of them despise,
> Then must thou eche day begin to live anewe.
> As for in cities I will no more remayne,
> But turne my talking nowe to the court agayne,
> After of this may we have communication
> Of cities and of their vexation.

These lines breathe most emphatically the spirit of the "tory" (to use that word in its *unchanging* signification) : and also the spirit of the provinces. These people, clinging most tenaciously to the ideas and manners of their forefathers, abhor the "new customs and acts" of the dwellers in cities—who never halt in the onward march, never rest on their oars for a moment, or say "this will suffice ; " but who have learned something more by each successive sunset, and "each day begin to live anew." And these same wandering "courtiers"—"gentle persons" though they be —discover, when they come into the towns, that the "rude villains" and such despised "rabble" look down upon *them* in turn, "disdaining" both them and their archaic dress.

* Mr. Leland makes use of this term several times ; but it appears that *gav-engro* is better Romanes. Either form, however, signifies " town's man."
† ? *Choring.*

It is Linlithgow over again : the "honourable magistrates"
are only "honourable" in the eyes of the burghers: they
are merely "rabble" to the marauding "tory" lords. And
vice versâ.

In every essential, this unresting "court" that Barclay
pictures, is the prototype of those portrayed by Simson.
Ever "removing or flitting," and carrying its "vexations"
along with it, one of the chief duties of its courtiers is to
follow the banner of their leader. In other words, these
"courtiers" are not only nomads and sorners, but marauders
too.

> Nowe would I speake of paynes of the warre,
> But that me thinketh is best for to defarre ;
> For if thy lorde in battayle have delite,
> To sue [*pursue*] the warre be paynes infinite.
> For while he warreth thou mayst not bide at home,
>   *   *   *   *   *
> To sue an army then hast thou wretched payne
> Of colde or of heate, of thirst, hunger and rayne,
> And mo other paynes than I will specify,
> For nought is in warfar save care and misery,
> Murder and mischiefe, rapines and cowardise,
> Or els crueltie ; there reigneth nought but vice.

These fierce "tory" courtiers of the provinces, then, were
much given to fighting: their chiefs, in many cases, "having
delight in battle." And the people against whom they
fought—the "armies" that they "sued"—were presumably
of the same kind as themselves, and not the "rude villains"
of the towns. And all this—these attacks and reprisals—
these "murders and mischiefs, rapines and cowardice, or else
cruelty"—took place in various districts of Great Britain.
Just like the clan-battles that the gypsiologists describe—
the only battles (excluding the Jacobite struggles) that have
been fought in Britain, during times that are comparatively
recent. And these eighteenth-century gypsy battles give
peaceable people some idea of what that warfare of an early
day really was:—"murders and mischiefs, rapines and
cowardice, or else cruelty ;" men hacking each other's limbs
off—stabbing a hunted enemy to the death—breaking-in
one another's skulls with heavy clubs, transfixed with
harrow-spikes (the "maces" and "morning-stars" of history).

There are fine words that can be used to describe such combats, so that the truth is almost hidden from our eyes ; but
it was bloody work at the best, as all warfare is.

The extracts just made* have indicated, as plainly as any
more modern statements, that the "rude villains," or
burghers, and the "gentle," nomadic "courtiers" of the
fifteenth and sixteenth centuries, were people of quite
opposite characteristics. And their differences are precisely
the differences that distinguished the high-caste eighteenth-
century "gypsy" from the rest of his fellow-countrymen.

There is one other feature of those wandering "courts"
of the fifteenth and sixteenth centuries which it is necessary
to refer to. The term "gypsy" has been seen to be so
comprehensive that it has included every variety of the
marauding "tory"; many of these varieties suggesting
quite separate racial origins. And one result of this is that
some statements made by the "gypsy" writers *appear* to
flatly contradict others. For example, in the particular about
to be noticed—the relation of the sexes. On one page
"gypsies" are said to be monogamists : on another polygamists of the most pronounced kind. The probable explanation being, that quite different tribes were described.
But many of the Scotch "gypsy" chiefs are portrayed by
their historian as invariably accompanied by a *seraglio*.
(And it was conjectured that, for this reason, most of the
words that are equivalent to "a female gypsy," or a "gypsy
queen," whether in "gypsy" or in "cant," have come to be
applied to women of a degraded kind.) Now, the kings,—
or kinglets,—whose vagrant habits have just been glanced at,
were distinguished by the same practice. The "courtier,"
who is the spokesman for all his caste, tells us that the
"marshal" was, like himself, a "gentle person,"—and one
possessed of much authority. The etymology of "marshal,"
it has been observed, is *mare chal*, or "horse man :" which,
when the position was one of importance, may better be
rendered by "Master of the Horse." But the same word
also denoted the holder of an office that is now obsolete in
this country, but was quite common in the fifteenth and

* Which are taken from Mr. Fairholt's outline of Barclay's "Cytezen and
Uplondyshman" : printed for the Percy Society, July, 1847.

sixteenth centuries ; that of *marescallus de meretricibus.**
The position seems to have latterly been occupied by
gouvernantes ; but the females under the charge of this
" marshal " are always described as *" suivant la cour du roy "*
—" *suivant ordinairement la cour."* And those female
" courtiers " are remembered as *courtezans.* So that, in this
respect—as in others—the "gypsy" kinglets of the
eighteenth century are identical with the nomadic kinglets
of the fifteenth.

The eighteenth-century "gypsies"—or some of them—
alleged that their lineage had always been exalted, and that
they and their ancestors were kings, or dukes, or lords.
Mary Yorkstoun, the wife of one of those "tory" nobles,
was styled " my lady " and " the duchess," even by the non-
gypsies of her territory. To what extent such people were
rulers of the district they terrorised is, of course, a matter of
opinion. Viewed in the light of some centuries ago, they
really were " nobles." They formed a caste of whom "the
common people " stood in awe ; they lived upon these
" common people," exacting by force whatever they desired
—clothing, or food, or money. When the peasantry and
yeomanry of southern Scotland refused to harbour those
sorners, they were made to feel that they had offended a
superior power. As when Hogg's acquaintance—the
Ettrickdale farmer—threw off the yoke of the Kennedys.
" A warfare of five years' duration ensued between Will and
the gypsies. They nearly ruined him ; and at the end of
that period he was glad to make up matters with his old
friends [or *quasi*-friends], and shelter them as formerly."
When that fiercest of *faws,* the swarthy chief of the Winter
gang, came into some little Northumbrian village, his appear-

---

* See an article ''On the Nature of the Office of Mareschal," which was
communicated to *Blackwood's Magazine* of May, 1817.

It may be pointed out that this phase of a *mare chal's* office does not at all interfere with the meaning of the word, if Mr. Borrow is correct in saying that *mare,*
at one time, denoted either "a horse" or "a woman," "all women being considered mares by old English law, and, indeed, still called mares in certain
counties where genuine old English is still preserved." And, as "mares," led to
the cattle-market (chattel-market) with a halter round the neck, and sold.
(Borrow's "Romany Rye," Vol. II. Chap. XI.) The word "jade," it may be
observed, has also borne this two-fold meaning.

ance "was a signal for the inhabitants to close their doors ; while he, as if proud of the terror which he inspired, would keep walking back and forward, with his arms a-kimbo, on the green." The submissive people paid *rent* to him, and such as he : he was their over-lord, governing them by force and cruelty—a "black oppressor." And if the celebrated Chief of Galloway was more amiable, in many respects, than this gloomy savage ; and if he lived on friendly terms—generally —with the people on whom he sorned ; he was none the less dreaded throughout the whole of Galloway. In districts where the rule of violence had not been overthrown, such men were assuredly the lords of the neighbourhood. When, at last, the central power became much too strong for them, and their exactions required to be "conducted in so artful a manner that no direct evidence could ever be obtained of them," then their position was more equivocal.

But they claimed an "illustrious" (and *not* exotic) lineage. And when we look back, as they invite us to do, we see that, in those earlier times, *their* ideas and manners prevailed in certain districts—if not throughout the country. Consequently, the people holding such ideas occupied the most prominent places in this country ; and were its nobles, dukes, and "kings :" or "kinglets" as we should nowadays term the rulers of what were comparatively small territories—so small that those battles in which one army of "courtiers" pursued another, of a different nation, were for the most part conducted in an island that is little more than one-third the size of Madagascar. And this little island contained two separate "kingdoms" not very long ago ; and many separate kingdoms in remoter periods. The warfare that Barclay's nomadic gentry found to be so full of "murder and mischief, rapine and cowardice" was only enacted in the southern (though larger) portion of the island : and yet it was between two confederacies so equally matched that it went on for thirty years. And the combatants, as described by Barclay, possessed the ideas, moral and social, of "gypsies :" and were treated by the town's-folk of their time very much as the Scotch burghers treated the same castes during last century—with a curious mixture of respect and aversion.

When the tory tribes of recent times are written about,

their leaders are referred to as "so-called" "kings," and
their claims to distinction are dismissed, off-hand, as "pretensions." But just let us try to realise the magnitude of the
position held by the wandering, polygamous, marauding
"courtiers" of Barclay's youth. They are much better
known to history than the townspeople who were their contemporaries: for the same reason that makes Captain
William Baillie, and William Marshall of Galloway, stand
out above the nameless tradesmen and farmers whom they
lived upon—because they were constantly doing some deed
—good or bad—that gave them prominence; while the
quiescent classes lived and died unknown to any but their
immediate friends. Those fifteenth-century bands of
marauders, then, traversed the provinces of England, each
led by a "noble" or "king"—who, like the similarly-
disposed Scotch chiefs of last century, carried along with
him a completely organized harem. Such nomadic "nobles,"
during a whole generation, towards the end of the fifteenth
century, were employed in killing each other—their forces
being massed into two confederated armies. And a supposititious follower of theirs is made, by a contemporary writer,
to define their warfare as nothing but murder, mischief,
rapine, cowardice, cruelty, vice, misery, and care. After
Southern Britain had been sickened with slaughter—at the
end of thirty years—this huge vendetta came to an end with
the triumph of one side and the overthrow of the other. It
was then found that a large number of those *sorners* had
been killed off: no fewer than "eighty princes of the blood,
and the larger proportion of the ancient nobility of the
country." The number of "nobles" is not given in this
estimate; but if eighty "princes" were killed, the number
of "nobles" could not well be less than eight hundred.
That is, somewhere about a thousand nomadic, marauding
"princes," "dukes," and "earls" killed each other between
the years 1455 and 1485, in the southern and central districts
of Great Britain. Supposing that one-half of the original
number came out of this long feud alive,—we have about
two thousand as the number of wandering "dukes" engaged
in the conflict. And all this took place in a territory not a
quarter the size of Madagascar. If an island of that extent

were discovered to-day, containing (by inference,) not less than a hundred "princes of the blood," and about two thousand "nobles," we should be inclined to smile at the exalted rank claimed by such very petty "princes." And, all the time that this was going on in England Proper, Ireland and Scotland had each a similar story to tell.

"The larger proportion of the ancient nobility" of the southern and central parts of Great Britain, were slaughtered in the latter part of the fifteenth century : the period in which the swarthy Douglases, and the Gordons of southern Scotland, ceased to be formally recognized as landowners and nobles. If, in any of these cases, the vanquished survivors of this "ancient nobility" continued (in spite of defeat) to live after the fashion of their forefathers, then they continued to live as wandering, polygamous "dukes ; " and, at least in southern Scotland, their "common dwellings" were the tents and turf-covered wigwams of the "gypsies." As long as possible, they would support themselves in the ancient fashion—by the sword, and by hunting and fishing. The last thing they would think of doing would be to hire themselves out as the servants of "rude villains," or as · labourers on the gradually-increasing areas of cultivated ground. Remembering their ancestral power, and even trying to regain it, they would still maintain a haughty attitude toward "the rabble of town and country." They would not come down to the level of selling the manufactures, and working at the handicrafts, that were peculiar to certain early British tribes (much in the same way as the vanquished "dukes"* of North America have done), until they and their followers were wholly restrained from appropriating the goods of others, and from killing a deer, or hooking a salmon, whenever they felt inclined to do so. They would still remain "dwellers on the heath "—*heathen*. They would still be averse to the ever-renewing fashions of the towns ; and the townspeople, careless—or ignorant—of ancestral fashions, would stare with surprise at their appearance, "disdaining

---

* The fact is, perhaps, scarcely worth noticing ; but the aristocracy of the earlier inhabitants of North America (described as " Indians " and " Moors " by the settlers) are designated " emperors," " kings," and " dukes " by the writers of the sixteenth and seventeenth centuries.

both themselves and their clothing." They would, in short, become " English gypsies."

And, whatever may turn out to be the proper definition of this loosely-applied term, this at least can be said : that, while the " gypsy " tribes of Scotland are known by names that are famous in Scottish history—the Douglases, the Gordons, the Ruthvens—those of England are distinguished by surnames that are equally illustrious. For there are no more typical " gypsies " in England than the clans of Stanley, and Lovel, and Lee.

.   .   .   .   .   .

Such surnames as these just given are, no doubt, more closely associated with the days of the Cavaliers than with the earlier era of the Wars of the Roses. But the notables of the first-named period were in many cases descended from the notables of the latter. And the days of " gypsy " supremacy were not nearly over in the times of the Cavaliers. Indeed, Mr. Simson's picture of the life of the Baillie caste of the eighteenth century is the picture of a supremacy that was alike " gypsy " and " cavalier." For such people were pre-eminently "cavaliers." That name must have been first used seriously ; and it signifies " horsemen " or " riders." And this is precisely what we have seen the " gypsies " were : or, at least, certain tribes of such people. Whether we look at Tawno Chickno and his swarthy comrades at Borrow's horse-fair, or regard Simson's equestrian highwaymen in Scotland, we see those "gypsies" to be the most perfect horsemen. And, in appearance, they correspond more closely than any of their contemporaries with the traditional " Cavalier." They have the same long tresses, the same haughty, " magnificent " manner, the same dashing style of dress. When Jasper Petulengro attired himself in a " smartly-cut sporting-coat, the buttons of which were half-crowns—and a waistcoat, scarlet and black, the buttons of which were spaded half-guineas," he presented a figure that was certainly unusual in nineteenth-century Britain. But one, or two, or three hundred years earlier such a way of dressing would never have attracted attention on the score of magni-ficence. Certainly not among the chiefs of the Ayrshire Kennedies of the sixteenth century ; one of whom is

pictured* as wearing, like Jasper, gold buttons on his coat,—
and at least as many "valuable rings and jewels" as Mrs.
Petulengro herself.

Mr. Simson's unlimited application of the word "gypsy"
("unlimited" in an ethnological sense) renders it impossible
to arrive at any distinct ethnological conclusion, in this
respect, without further information. While Mr. Leland em-
braces within the term "gypsy" only our dark-skinned "tory"
compatriots, who themselves (he tells us) are plainly descended from two "entirely different original stocks,"—the
Scotch writer goes much farther, and includes many clans of
"fair whites" in this designation. In the meantime, therefore, "gypsy" cannot well be held to denote much more than
"tory" or "heathen."

But in spite of the fair-whites of the one gypsiologist, and
the curly-haired *melanochroi* of the other, there does seem
evidence that Mr. Leland's straight-haired "Romany" occupied the highest positions in Britain not very long ago.
Scott tells us that the famous Earl of Leicester was spoken
of as "the gypsy," by his rival, Sussex "on account of his
[Leicester's] dark complexion." The dark-grey skin that distinguished more than one of the later Stewart kings is
characterized as "of sable hue," by Marvell—in his descrip-
of Charles II. It would be easy enough to adduce other
instances of men of rank, within comparatively recent times,
who were distinguished by the epithet "black":† easier to
do this than to show the exact meaning that that expression
conveyed at the time. When, more than a century ago,
Forbes of Culloden made use of these words—"If any one
Scotsman has absolute power we are in the same slavery as

---

* In the Preface to "Auchindrane: or, The Ayrshire Tragedy."

† Such as Thomas Rutherfurd, "the black laird of Edgerston;" "black
Ormeston, an outlaw of Scotland;" "Black Mr. John Spens;" "Black
Arthur," brother to the Master of Forbes, killed in a tribal fight between the
Forbeses and the Gordons at Tillyangus, Aberdeenshire; Hugh Rose of Kilravock, "the black baron;" all sixteenth-century men: and another Hugh Rose
of Kilravock, also "the black baron," in the seventeenth century. And other
similar examples, of various dates, some of which have been already given, *e.g.*,
that fifteenth-century Border clan "who, from the darkness of their complexion,
were called the 'Black band of the Blackadders,'" "the black knights of Lorne,"
and the *Dubh* divisions of the important clans of Mercer, of Cumming, and of
Douglas.

ever, whether that person be a fair man or a black man,"
he perhaps did not mean more than we should now do if
we used the word "dark." But, at an earlier period than
Forbes's, we seem to find visible proof of the exalted position of this "Romany" element. It is the opinion of a
modern student of men* that the " English [type] has changed
much within a few generations. 'The features of men
painted by and about the time of Holbein have usually high
cheek-bones, long upper lips, thin eyebrows and lank, dark
hair';" a cast of countenance that is found among many
Red Indians and Gypsies. And these gypsy-like people were
of course, the notables of their day—the first half of the sixteenth century. We are told that "eighty-seven sketches of
persons belonging to the court of Henry VIII. by Holbein are
still extant;" and the physical attributes of these courtiers
have just been described. The *moral* attributes, and the
mode of living of the courtiers of that very period—or say
a generation earlier—have been pictured to us in Barclay's
Eclogues. And from these we have seen that their ways
were the ways of *gypsies :* polygamous, unresting, sorning,
and marauding *gypsies,* with innumerable "princes of the
blood," and all the show and glitter that is now called "flash."
If, therefore, Barclay's and Holbein's courtiers were at all
related to each other—even though they were not identical—
it is plain that the porter who refused admittance to a
nomadic "courtier," while welcoming a brother "villain,"
was partly actuated by racial feelings. He was putting out a
man who, to some extent or another, was of "gypsy" blood.

The question that most requires to be settled is this—"Of
what composition were the townsmen of our chief cities at
this period?" "Villains," we know, were once serfs. Were
these "Villains" the descendants of early Britons of peaceful mould; or were they incoming traders of almost recent
centuries; or were they a blending of both? The
question is of great importance; because these "villains"
are the people whose ideas are much more prevalent in this
country to-day than the ideas of the ex-nobility. Whatever

---

* The quotation that follows is taken from an article on " Heredity," contributed to the *Atlantic Monthly* of October, 1883, by Mr. II. W. Holland : the
opinion is Mr. Francis Galton's.

the exact ingredients of the blood we have inherited, all of us who are supposed to be "civilized" are in the position of the burgher rather than in that of the marauding lord. We do not nowadays acquire landed estates by force, but by purchase,—that is, by peaceful barter. The man who tries to acquire property by force is called "a burglar;" and he is punished by the laws of a peace-loving nation. When the "courtier" tries to thrust his way into a house, uninvited, he is "twined to the street" as a "vagrant" and a "beggar." If a "gypsy" shoots a hare on the hunting-grounds of his forefathers, he is imprisoned as a "poacher." And all these laws are on the side of the people who, in earlier times, were *citizens;* or, if countrymen, then tillers of the ground, not "dwellers on the heath," or "moss-troopers." They are the same kind of laws as those enacted in favour of "the free burghs of this realm," and against the "wild savages" of the Hebrides. Those "free burghs" have spread out and out into the uncultivated country; converting moors and fens into farms, and restricting the limits of the "heathen" more and more, until there is scarcely any camping-ground remaining for them. Or, where there is, laws have been passed forbidding these waste places to be occupied as formerly. So that, whereas you might once have seen a dozen tents of the wandering people in an afternoon's stroll across Hampstead Heath, you are now confronted only by the placards announcing the law that prohibits them. There is no longer a visible community of Norwood *Gypsies*, though we have not yet heard the last of the Norwood *Roughs*.

Let it be granted that our tendencies, during the past few generations, have been in the direction of peace,—and it will easily be seen that any caste or castes with "gypsy" proclivities must either have dwindled away during that period, or else gone over to the side of the peace-lovers and workers. "A man who is violent and pugnacious will, as a general rule, be more often imprisoned or slain in the prime of life than his more pacific neighbours, and will therefore leave fewer children to inherit his fighting spirit. Thus the constant process of elimination of combative men will continue, without any compensating advantage in the struggle for existence arising as heretofore from success as a warrior. The man of

the future, therefore, will . . . . be particularly averse to engaging in personal conflict—a lover of peace at any price."
So says Mr. Kay Robinson, looking forward from to day.
But the truth of the principle he lays down has been illustrated in these islands already. When, in the twelfth century, North-Eastern Scotland was colonised by "peaceful
people," and the turbulent "Morrow-men" expelled or killed,
"the man of the future" was the peaceful colonist, and not
the savage. Or, let us take for example the period of the
Wars of the Roses. No doubt the many kinglets, and their
followers, who took part in these clan-fights, were possessed
of various qualities that counterbalanced the fiercer side of
their nature. But they were "combative men." During
their celebrated thirty-years' struggle, they succeeded in
exterminating "the larger proportion of the ancient nobility
of the country." These, certainly, were not "the men of the
future." But, all during this thirty-years of warfare, the un-
warlike traders of the towns were pursuing their ordinary
avocations—and multiplying.

Whether there is more "honour" in killing one's fellow-
men than in trading with them, is a matter of no importance
here. But what *is* important is—that the trader, or the yeo-
man,—the peace-lover, let us say—is immeasurably the most
important person in the genealogy of nations. The "combative men" have left their mark in history : but their ideas
have now fallen into disrepute, and the number of their pure-
blooded descendants is necessarily small. The non-combat-
ants, dying quietly in their beds, have in each generation
more than doubled their numbers. The result of which is
that, from whatever date peaceably-inclined people were
enabled to follow out their peaceable inclinations, from that
date they became the chief progenitors of "the man of the
future,"—that is of the present. While, on the other hand,
the fighters—killing each other, dying in early life, and (latterly) persecuted for their combativeness by the now-prepon-
derating body of "peace-lovers"—have decreased* in an
inverse ratio to the increase of the opposite class.

---

* Such men as Marshall of Galloway must undoubtedly have left numerous
descendants. But polygamy, while it greatly increases the number of the children
of one particular man, must obviously tend to diminish the increase of the *tribe.*

If we ought to set aside the white-skinned "gypsies" altogether, and accept " gypsy " in its popular sense of a dark-skinned, black-haired, black-eyed man ; then we might obtain something tangible from a consideration of the statements just made. Although our population is said to be composed very largely of dark-whites, it is quite clear that we are vastly more white than black : that while an immense number of us are pure blondes, there is not one Modern-Briton who is as black as a negro : that, although certain black divisions of our ancestry have affected the white stock to a tremendous extent, we are a nation of whites and darkened *whites*. If, then, gypsy supremacy meant a " *black* oppression," of which the latest *important* phase was faintly visible in Holbein's pictures, the final overthrow of that supremacy meant a victory of white people. The ideas now paramount are, in a great measure, opposed to those of the " common thieves " who once ruled the provinces, and who were " gypsies ; " and the non-gypsies were burghers. Therefore the burghers were white people.

Whatever else the town-populations of Britain comprised (during the past five or six centuries), it is plain that the Dutch immigrants formed an important portion.   These immigrants, Professor Skeat* has told us, have been greatly overlooked by historians ; perhaps because their entrance was quiet and bloodless. " We may recall the alliance between Edward III. and the free towns of Flanders ; and the importation by Edward of Flemish weavers." And again— " After Antwerp had been captured by the Duke of Parma, ' a third of the merchants and manufacturers of the ruined city,' says Mr. Green, ' are said to have found a refuge on the banks of the Thames.' "   And Early Scotland—which afterwards spread out into Later Scotland ; and which was, in the twelfth century, merely a small area on the north-eastern side of North Britain,—this germ of Later Scotland was in a great measure a Dutch colony. If such people were allowed to live in their own way for five or six hundred years—ploughing, and weaving, and trading, but *not* fighting (except in self-defence)—their posterity at the present day must be very numerous. So numerous that all the blondes, and (on one side)

---

* In the introductory remarks to his " Etymological Dictionary."

all the dark-whites of the British Islands might be the descendants of those "peaceful people ;" while the "gypsy' races that preceded them—spending their hot lives in un-ending feuds—might have so thinned out their own numbers as to have left comparatively few representatives of their type.

No doubt, many instances could be found of the overthrow in particular districts, of "black princes." The case of the fifteenth-century Black-Douglases is a case in point. So also is that of the eighteenth-century Winters of Northumberland. Their chief, William Winter, has already been spoken of. "This man belonged to a family which was one of the worst of a bad gang of *faws*, itinerant tinkers, who formerly infested this part of Northumberland [Elsdon] in considerable numbers, robbing and threatening the small farmers, who would not allow them to lodge in their out-houses, and who did not, either in provisions or money, pay them a kind of *black mail.* Winter is described, by the country people who remember him, as a tall, powerful man, of dark complexion, wearing his long black hair hanging about his shoulders, and of a most savage countenance. The appearance of this ruffian in a small village was a signal for the inhabitants to close their doors ; while he, as if proud of the terror which he inspired, would keep walking back and forward, with his arms a-kimbo, on the green."* This man was at last brought to justice, and executed at Newcastle in the year 1792 : and of his family, Sir Walter Scott says, "I have little doubt they are all hanged."

Winter, of course, lived at a time when the supremacy of such as he was almost quite over. *Cavaliers* had become known as *thieves, rogues,* and *roughs,*† and Winter only

* Oliver's " Rambles in Northumberland," p. 113.

† As "Satchells" points out, the definition—"a freebooter's a cavalier that ventures life for gain" did not hold good upon the Borders after "King James the Sixth to England went." "He that hath transgress'd since then (he says) is no *Freebooter* [or Cavalier], but a *Thief.*" And, whatever may have been his ethnological position,—and although his own son and grandson had all the attributes of Cavaliers,—it was assuredly during the reign of James the Sixth of Scotland that some of the most severe enactments were passed against *sorners,* or "cavaliers"—"commonly called Egyptians."

With regard to the word "rogue"—an equivalent of "sorner"—it has been stated that one of its primary meanings is "haughty" or "cavalier." It is probable that *rough.* which is still pronounced *roch* (*ch* guttural) in Scotland, is virtually the same word.

represented the sediment of that caste. But he and his family stand out as specimens of a race of dark-skinned tyrants, who were at last exterminated, root and branch. And yet, had he lived two or three centuries earlier he would be remembered in history by some such title as " Lord of Elsdon ; " which he virtually was.

Another example of " gypsy " oppression is seen in the pages of "Lorna Doone." Mr. Blackmore's novel is only in part true : but in it he tells us of a clan of high-born tyrants, who, dispossessed of their lands in the North of England, settled among the fastnesses of Exmoor, about the middle of the seventeenth century. Like any of Mr. Simson's high-caste " gypsies," they looked down with the most lofty contempt upon the country-people around them. Like these " gypsies," the Doones regularly attended the local fairs with a view to plunder : like them they were cruel and vindictive. One incident in the novel reveals to us their savage nature as clearly as if every page had described such a scene ; and the incident is vouched for as "strictly true." A gang of these Doones making one of their usual raids upon a lonely farm-house, and obtaining little booty except the hapless farmer's wife, amused themselves before leaving by taking her infant child out of its cradle, flinging it up to the kitchen ceiling, and then—without a grain of pity—letting it come down on the stone floor smashed and lifeless, before the very eyes of its mother. After which, they addressed the tiny corpse in a jeering couplet, still remembered by the local peasantry. Such raids were made at night-time, according to the custom of the " mossers " of that Border country from which these Doones came ; and we are told in the novel, that they "had a pleasant custom, when they visited farm-houses, of lighting themselves towards picking up anything they wanted, or stabbing the inhabitants, by first creating a blaze in the rickyard." [On one such occasion, however, they got worsted ; for the farmer-widow, who lived there alone, had trained a heavy shot-gun for their reception, and, just as " five or six fine young Doones came dancing a reel (as their manner was) betwixt her and the flaming rick," they got the full contents of the shot-gun hurtling among them.] Not only were those "Doones of

Badgeworthy" notorious murderers, thieves and ravishers ; but they had the further " gypsy " characteristics of gambling and polygamy. One of their chiefs, *The Carver*, is said to have had " ten or a dozen wives." They had also a priest, or medicine-man, remembered as *The Counsellor*, a miracle of craft and jugglery.* And the district in which they lived— the wilds of Exmoor—is still famous for a breed of small horses akin to the "Galloways" and "hobbies" of other districts associated with similar people : from which fact it is natural to infer that, if the Doones were the first "mossers" who inhabited that locality, they had ridden southward from the Borders on the ancestors of the present " Exmoor ponies."

The fate of this heathen aristocracy was similar to that of the Winter clan of the Faws of Northumberland. As the Reedsdale yeomanry rose up against the oppression of that "marked and atrocious family," so the yeomanry of Devonshire rebelled at last against the unendurable insolence of the Doones. With the triumphant result so powerfully described by the author of " Lorna Doone."

That book, however, does not profess to be history ; and we can only lean upon it here so far as it states uncontradictable facts. The Doones are nowhere in it styled "gypsies ;" though it is certain that the Scotch writer would have so designated them, had he lived in that particular time and place. Beyond giving them black hair and black eyes, Mr. Blackmore does not make these marauders appear to us as *conventional* " gypsies." Indeed, he speaks somewhere of the white skin of one of their leaders. But it is probable that he did not obtain that particular from any local tradition, and even if white-skinned, that did not make them different from the Baillies, the Blythes, and many other North British "gypsies." Certainly according to the loosest usage of that word ; and perhaps, also in its strictest, conventional

* " The Counsellor" is a very good specimen of the *rogue*, in the more modern sense of that word. The pronunciation *rough* conveys to us one of the impressions that *rogue* conveyed to the civilized classes of a few generations ago. But *rogue*, as we now understand it, hits off a peculiarity of those "mossers" who could *talk* their captors into freeing them, by sheer force of " blarney " ; a peculiarity still possessed by the " Romany " fortune-tellers and gypsified cheap-Jacks, &c., of the present day.

acceptation; those "Doones of Badgery" were "gypsy" lords.

They, furthermore, have many of the characteristics of the early Black Danes, from whom they were, no doubt, partly descended. Assuming, like those historical tyrants, an attitude of the most brutal haughtiness toward the classes beneath them, they also—like those early *dubh galls*—were intensely ferocious, grotesquely savage in nature. The men who—heathens in morals and in religion—could dance a reel by the light of the burning haystacks of the people whom they were about to pillage and murder, and who could regard as a practical joke the slaughter of a helpless child,—would have been (as probably they were) most fit descendants of those swarthy satyrs whose attacks upon civilized Britain, a thousand years ago, are dimly remembered in tradition, oral and written; who thought that a humorous ending to a heavy debauch was to pelt each other with the bones remaining from the feast,—and who, dancing " round the great fires of pine-trees," are said to have " danced with such fury holding each other by the hands, that, if the grasp of any failed, he was pitched into the fire with the velocity of a sling."[*] And of whom it has been said that " a common practice among these barbarous pagans " was " to tear the infants of the English from the breasts of their mothers, toss them up into the air, and catch them on the point of their spears as they were falling down." Nor does the comparison end here. The worst form of the oppression of the Doones, as well as of the Danes, was not robbery, nor even murder, but the irretrievable insults to the honour of the country people.

But we need not " hark back " to the period of the early Black-Danish supremacy. During the passing of many centuries a hundred causes must have tended to make the least-altered descendant of a tenth-century Black-Dane a very different being from his remote ancestor: such causes as mixture of races, and of ideas—and the never-ceasing elimination of the more savage clans.

What we have been most considering, in this chapter, is the period—rather undefinable—at which the " tory " clans, of the superior kind, were still actually *rulers;* the period which

---

[*] See note 4 C, in the Appendix to " Marmion."

justifies their latest representatives in asserting that they are
descended from "dukes" and "kings." And we have seen
that this period is not *very* remote : that the fighting-men of
the fifteenth century—and even later—who are remembered
in history by various titles, were much more allied to the
castes that we call "gypsy," than to the generality of Modern
Britons. If Mr. Simson's catholic use of the term be understood, the difference between those fifteenth-century notables
and us (or between them and the contemporay burghers and
yeomen ; or between modern "gypsies" and "us") was *not*
a difference of blood, but simply of ideas, religious and social.
If on the other hand a "gypsy" be considered as—of necessity—a dark-skinned man, then the difference was one of
race : and the triumph of *bourgeoisie* and *yeomanry* meant a
"white conquest." The fact that the notables of Henry the
Eighth's time were, generally, possessed of physical attributes
that distinguish no particular Modern-British caste, except
that caste whose habits—even yet—faintly suggest the habits
of the "nobles" of earlier days,—this fact not only leads us
to believe that those nomadic classes are perfectly warranted
in boasting of their high descent, but it also explains why the
nominal aristocracy of the present day is not distinguished
by the "high cheek-bones, long upper lips, thin eyebrows, and
lank, dark hair" of King Henry's courtiers. Had these
"courtiers" not been attached so firmly to the morals and
ideas of their ancestors, they and their descendants would
not have sunk in the social system as they have done—from
the possession of power to the *questioned* possession of power
—from that to the position of men whose power was wholly
repudiated by the nation—and from that to the level of mere
outcasts and criminals (for it is now regarded as "criminal"
to acquire property by force, or to follow polygamous prac-
tices*). That they did so sink we have seen from several

---

* Of the modern exponents of "gypsyism," Messrs. Groome and Leland are
(I think, altogether) silent as to the practice of polygamy. And the former of
these, with Mr. Borrow, supplies evidence which reveals that none of her sex
throughout the world are more virtuous than the gypsy woman—of a certain
caste. But Mr. Borrow, though saying little or nothing of polygamy, represents
one of his genuine gypsies as the husband of two wives. This man, Ryley
Bosvil, "was a thorough Gypsy, versed in all the arts of the old race, had two
wives, never went to church, and considered that when a man died he was cast

particular examples, from the fact that their features are best represented by our still-existing nomads, and from the fact that these features do not particularly belong to our modern people of title. And this is as it should be. Because modern people of title are not, as a rule, the descendants of the "courtiers" of the fifteenth and sixteenth centuries. In some cases, they are the posterity of people who were quite unknown to history at these periods : in others, of people who, if notables, did not possess the racial characteristics that prevailed at and before the time when Holbein painted : and, in other cases, if descended from one or more of the "notables" of the Holbein order, they are also the posterity of other people who, at that date, did not belong to that order. It is plain that, if a certain physical type belonged to those sixteenth-century courtiers, and if they and their offspring refused to intermarry with other castes, the existing posterity of such people, in whatever rank of life they may now be, must have preserved the ancestral characteristics intact. But this could not happen with people who desired to identify themselves with the growing life of the nation. It *could* happen with those who reverenced their own caste above

into the earth, and there was an end of him." Mr. Simson's remarks, and those of other Scotch writers, tell us plainly that polygamy was quite common among many of the northern tribes. And Grose says as much of his "gypsies."

It must, however, be remembered that one of these writers—the one who has probably the best right to pronounce upon the subject—refuses to recognize as "gypsies" any but the comparatively few families of unmixed blood ; in whose eyes Grose's "gypsies" are merely mongrels, with as much of the *gaujo* in them as the gypsy.

But *all* the gypsiologists show us that "gypsies," both pure and mixed, are at heart the enemies of modern law. It is impossible not to perceive this in reading any of the books relating to them. Even those pleasant people whom one encounters in the pages of "In Gipsy Tents" have very archaic notions on the subject of stealing ; and one of the characters in that book states that most of his pure-blooded kinsmen are in America. That many of these went there against their will may be assumed for many reasons. And Mr. Leland, who has studied the class on both sides of the water, indicates very clearly that their "peculiar *morale*" means antagonism to modern laws ; and that horse-stealing is not even a peccadillo in their eyes, while "killing a policeman" is within the bounds of possibility. "In Gipsy Tents" has been of great value in showing us the lovable side of gypsyism ; and it might be shown that a certain set of graces and virtues have been more at home among gypsies than among *gaujos*. But the belief in the rule of force—once so common throughout the country—is still, if in a modified form, a characteristic of gypsydom.

every other, and who regarded with aversion the introduction
of any new element into "the blood:" and the British
people in whom this feeling is most distinctly shown are those
wandering "cavalier" castes described by Mr. Borrow.   In
the ever-changing society that is somewhat vaguely known
as "the aristocracy" there is no such exclusiveness.   There
is, indeed, a semblance of such a spirit, but it will not bear in-
vestigation.   Present wealth, and almost that alone, is what
constitutes modern "aristocracy."   A man may have a really
genuine pedigree of "notables"—stretching back, in every
line, for many centuries,—but if he should happen to become
quite destitute of means, "aristocracy" knows him no more,
and yesterday's butcher takes his place.   Such a body, though
insisting upon certain qualifications of manner, of education,
and—as far as possible—of birth, is not *radically* a caste ; for
caste implies a connection of race as well as custom.   It is
only in such a community as that pictured by Borrow—in
which the mother would drive her daughter out of her tent
for ever on account of an intrigue with a *gaujo* (not because
of the intrigue, but because the lover was a white man)—it is
only in such a community that this pride of blood is eminent.
Therefore, we need not expect to find, nor shall we find, in
the "notables" of our own time, the racial stamp of those of
the fifteenth and sixteenth centuries.   Individual instances of
that type there may be—as of others ; but, if it occurs, it
does not occur in sufficient strength to characterize the whole
body.   And the ruling classes of Britain must have become
less and less identified with particular *castes*, in proportion
as modern ideas became more and more powerful.   The
increasing sway of wealth, as opposed to the decreasing sway
of force, must soon have put an end to government by
dynasties : and the intrusion of wealthy traders into the
highest ranks must have been common for many generations.
It would not require a *Sir Mungo Malagrowther* to cite
illustrations of this, if the ungracious task were necessary.
But if the name of the occupation of each ancestor had
descended as certainly as the title that adhered to one
particular line of descent, it would be seen that many
bearers of ancient titles are quite as much *bourgeois* as *gentil-
lâtre*.   Indeed, it could only be by intermarriage with rich

traders, or with yeomen, or (an unlikely event) by the adoption of habits of peaceful industry, that members of an order founded on force, averse to daily labour, and contemptuous of everything but fighting and *soming*, could prolong their existence as aristocrats into the newer era of industry and peace.

It was always "an unlikely event" that people of "cavalier" tendencies should attempt to support life by peaceful industry, when they were thrown upon their own resources. Cromwell, when not appreciated by his country, devoted himself to farming and the reclamation of the Fens. The alternative that presented itself to Prince Rupert, when finally defeated by the Parliamentary party, was to go and follow, for several years, the idle and lawless life of a West-Indian buccaneer. Had he not been so famous a man, it is not improbable that, in place of going into exile in this way, he would have supported himself in a similar manner in England. That is, he and his followers would have lived by the sword, exactly after the fashion of his contemporary, the celebrated Scotch cavalier—Captain William Baillie.* And, of these two, Prince Rupert would have been much more like the orthodox "gypsy." William Baillie is described as belonging to the class of fair-complexioned "gypsies" (although the heavy, black tresses of his cultivated kinsman, "The Scottish Sidney," do not help to bear out this description). Prince Rupert, on the other hand, though not so dark-skinned as his cousin—the "sable" monarch, Charles II.—was yet of sallow complexion ; and his swarthy hair, hanging in great masses on either shoulder (according to the

---

* This, it will be remembered, was the most famous member of the "tory" section of the Baillies. It may be convenient to repeat Mr. Simson's sketch of him here : "The extraordinary man Baillie, who is here so often mentioned, was well known in Tweed-dale and Clydesdale ; and my great-grandfather, who knew him well, used to say that he was the handsomest, the best dressed, the best looking, and the best bred man he ever saw. As I have already mentioned, he generally rode one of the best horses the kingdom could produce ; himself attired in the finest scarlet, with his greyhounds following him, as if he had been a man of the first rank. ["The right to possess greyhounds was a proof of gentility." "Chambers's Encyclopædia."] . . . . He was considered, in his time, the best swordsman in all Scotland. With this weapon in his hand, and his back at a wall, he set almost everything, saving fire-arms, at defiance. His sword is still preserved by his descendants [one of whom was the late Mrs. Carlyle], as a relic of their powerful ancestor." ("History," p. 202.)

custom of his race)—with one tress kept together by the usual brightly-coloured ribbon—must have given him an appearance that (using the term in its *strictest* application) would stamp him as a "gypsy" prince. Except that Prince Rupert was possessed of many qualities that made him a really distinguished man, he did not differ one whit—in his buccaneering days—from the notorious Northumbrian gypsy of last century; who "is described, by the country people who remember him, as a tall, powerful man, of dark complexion, wearing his long black hair hanging about his shoulders, and of a most savage countenance."* In their ideas, in their way of living, in their physical attributes, and in their dress,† the two were alike. And, of all nineteenth-century Englishmen, none more closely resembled such "cavaliers," in outward appearance, than the Durham chief, whom Mr. Simson the elder encountered at St. Boswell's. "At St. Boswell's Fair I once inspected a horde of English gipsies, encamped at the side of a hedge, on the Jedburgh road as it enters St. Boswell's green. Their name was Blewett, from the neighbourhood of Darlington. The chief possessed two tents, two large carts laden with earthenware, four horses and mules, and five large dogs. He was attended by two old females and ten young children. . . . This chief and the two females were the most swarthy and barbarous looking people I ever saw. . . . [He] was a thick-set, stout man, above the middle size. He was dressed in an old dark-blue frock coat, with a profusion of black, greasy hair, which covered the upper part of his broad shoulders. He wore a high-crowned, narrow-brimmed, old hat, with a lock of his black hair hanging down before each ear. . . . He also wore a pair of old full-topped boots, pressed half way down his legs, and wrinkled about his ankles, like buskins. His visage was remarkably dark and gloomy. He walked up and down the market alone, without speaking to any one, with a peculiar air of independence about him, as he twirled in his hand, in the gipsy manner by way of amusement, a strong bludgeon, about three feet

---

* Oliver's "Rambles in Northumberland," p. 113.
† Assuming Winter to have been dressed like Mr. Simson's "superior" gypsies.

long, which he held by the centre." Whether "Blewett" is
a surname that has any history in that neighbourhood, or
whether this man inherited his "tory" blood from other
ancestors than the one whose patronymic distinguished him,
he is clearly a nineteenth-century representative of the
Northumbrian Faw, who is sketched above ; and also of the
ordinary Cavalier of the century preceding Winter's. The
fashion of his dress and hair, his complexion, his isolated
attitude, and his lofty bearing, all attest his descent from
earlier cavaliers. And, if his occupation was out of keeping
with the popular conception of such people, it is to be
remembered that the laws of his country had long branded as
a "thief" "a cavalier that ventures life for gain ; " that to
exist by no other ostensible means than the levying of "black
mail" was to be "a robber," and therefore a criminal, liable
to be executed any day ; and that, in his day, the surviving
remnant of that "Border-banditti," from whom were descended "some rich and noble families on the borders," were
reduced to "travel the country in the character of tinkers,
horners or spoonmakers, and occasionally steal sheep and
plunder houses."*

That this "cavalier," Blewett, regarded the ordinary people
whom he encountered at St. Boswell's as his inferiors, was
evinced by his manner. And Borrow recognized distinct
reasons for such a feeling, among the gaily-dressed cavaliers
with whom he connected himself. His statements cannot
possibly apply to the *whole* class that is vaguely included
under one title, because these—it is evident—are possessed
of the most varied characteristics. But this is what he says
of them :—"Their complexion is dark, but not disagreeably
so ; their faces are oval, their features regular, their foreheads
rather low, and their hands and feet small. The men are
taller than the English peasantry, and far more active,
they all speak the English language with fluency, and in
their gait and demeanour are easy and graceful ; in both
respects standing in striking contrast with the peasantry,
who in speech, are slow and uncouth, and in manner
dogged and brutal." Such people,—who are known by surnames such as Lovel, Bosville, Stanley and Leigh ; and who

* In the words of the writer of the article "Banditti," in Pyne's "Microcosm."

(even so lately as this century) were attired in the gold-buttoned scarlet or green riding-coats of an earlier gentry—are surely the least-altered descendants of those who sat to Holbein : such a peasantry has surely inherited the blood of those stolid Dutchmen who "sprad all England over."

Indeed, the little sketch that Mr. Simson gives* of the "tories" of Cambridgeshire seems to realize, more than anything else, the appearance of a royalist party before Edgehill ; or one of those wandering "courts" described by Barclay. The description is embodied in the following anecdote :—

A man, whom I knew, happened to lose his way, one dark night, in Cambridgeshire. After wandering up and down for some time, he observed a light, at a considerable distance from him, within the skirts of a wood, and, being overjoyed at the discovery, he directed his course toward it ; but, before reaching the fire, he was surprised at hearing a man, a little way in advance, call out to him, in a loud voice, " Peace or not peace ?" The benighted traveller, glad at hearing the sound of a human voice, immediately answered, " Peace ; I am a poor Scotchman, and have lost my way in the dark." " You can come forward then," rejoined the sentinel. When the Scotchman advanced, he found a family of gipsies, with only one tent ; but on being conducted further into the wood, he was introduced to a great company of gipsies. They were busily employed in roasting several whole sheep—turning their carcases before large fires, on long wooden poles, instead of iron spits. The racks on which the spits turned were also made of wood, driven into the ground, cross-ways, like the letter X. The gipsies were exceedingly kind to the stranger, causing him to partake of the victuals which they had prepared for their feast. He remained with them the whole night, eating and drinking, and dancing with his merry entertainers, as if he had been one of themselves. When day dawned, the Scotchman counted twelve tents within a short distance of each other. On examining his position, he found himself a long way out of his road ; but a party of the gipsies voluntarily offered their services, and went with him for several miles, and, with great kindness, conducted him to the road from which he had wandered.

It would thus appear that the likeliest way to arrive at something like a true conclusion as to the habits and every-day appearance of the "cavaliers" of the seventeenth and previous centuries, is by studying the habits and appearance of the only "cavalier" caste that was visible in the eighteenth

* In his chapter on "English Gipsies," out of which the foregoing extracts have been taken.

century—and even later. People there were, no doubt, at these later periods, who kept horses and knew how to ride them; but the only distinct *caste* of "cavaliers" was that described by Mr. Borrow as "gypsies," and pictured by him as "jockeys"—one of the commonest names given to them in the northern parts of Great Britain. The examination of them, in this aspect, must necessarily destroy many preconceived ideas; but it cannot contradict established facts— although these facts may require to be re-constructed.

Whether the use of war-paint, and the practice of tattooing, *prevailed* among the fighting-classes of Britain, so lately as the seventeenth century, is not likely. But we know that the former custom *existed* in Galloway at that time, and that the latter practice was at least a usual thing among seamen. Prince Rupert's piratical crew, in his West-Indian days, must unquestionably have been *blueskins;* and it is not unlikely that some of his land-forces were so, too. In short, the "Red-Indian" features of the Galloway chief and his tawny, painted army, must have been quite visible in certain sections of the English population, a century earlier. Even in the earlier part of this century, those most inveterate "tories," discarding all modern ways of communicating with each other—though this was before the days of the penny post— actually discovered the whereabouts of their friends, by following their "trail" across the country—like any other "Indians."* And it must have been in this way, also, that a gang of the "courtiers" of Barclay's era was enabled to follow in pursuit of a retreating tribe; or to ascertain the direction taken by members of their own clan, if defeated, or "on the war-path" in front of them.

One is strongly tempted to believe that the struggles of

---

* In Chapter XI., Book I., of "The Romany Rye," reference is made to the "patteran"—"the gypsy trail, the handful of grass which the gypsies strew in the roads as they travel, to give information to any of their companions who may be behind, as to the route they have taken." It is explained that "patteran" signifies "a leaf"; and that "the gypsies of old were in the habit of making the marks with the leaves and branches of trees, placed in a certain manner." And one of Mr. Borrow's friends is stated to have tracked her husband half the length of England by means of this "patteran." (This custom has been already referred to—in Chapter III. of Book II. It does not appear to have wholly fallen into desuetude even yet; though modern gypsies communicate by letter, like other people.)

the seventeenth century were, in a great degree, of a racial nature. The regiment commanded by the notorious Colonel Kirke, at the time of Monmouth's rebellion, was distinctly composed of "gypsies " of the popular type—if we are to rely on the description given of them by the eminent novelist who has been already quoted in this chapter. The hero of " Lorna Doone," encountering a party of " Kirke's Lambs " after the fight at Sedgemoor, says of them—" I disliked those men sincerely, and was fain to teach them a lesson ; they were so unchristian in appearance, having faces of a coffee colour, and dirty beards half over them. . . . Moreover their dress was outrageous, and their address still worse. . . . These savage-looking fellows laughed at the idea of my having any chance against some twenty of them." Now, these " coffee-coloured," " savage-looking fellows " are not spoken of as *foreigners,* either by the novelist, or when ordinarily mentioned by other writers ; and, in this fictitious encounter, they converse in English, and bear such names as " Dick the wrestler," " Bob," &c. Kirke and his followers had been engaged for a long ti.me in Tangiers, " fighting the infidels ; " and the leader's ferocious disposition is explained by his having become " savage by the neighbourhood of the Moors there." But these statements are surely quite insuffi-cient to explain the " coffee-coloured " complexion, the " unchristian " appearance and " outrageous " dress of " these savage-looking fellows." The nick-name of " Kirke's Lambs" is said to have been given to them by the people of Somersetshire, and perhaps the tradition as to their com-plexion was received from the same source. If so, and if those Somerset people formed one of the many compara-tively-modern Dutch colonies in England, it is easily under-stood that (supposing this tawny gang to have come from another district of England, and to be composed of the descendants of earlier Britons than those Dutch immigrants) the difference in complexion, dress, and manners, between these two sets of men might be extremely great : bearing in mind there were then no railways, and very few roads, to bring together and blend into one the motley nationalities that co-existed in the same island.*

* A critical examination of the Somersetshire dialect would easily determine whether it approached more nearly to the Dutch of a certain period, or to some

And it seems a peculiar coincidence, also, that the Hebridean Macleods,—the descendants of "the black prince of Man," some of whose posterity, last century, were compared by Boswell to "wild Indians,"—should have been found fighting at Worcester under the banner of the "black prince," Charles ; in which engagement they were nearly all killed. It would appear as though the examination of tribal histories, like the examination of that of the aggregate of tribes, would show—in very many cases—a division styled *dubh*, or black, and another styled *ruadh*, or tawny,—and a third by some adjective signifying "white-skinned."

It is, at least, a fact deserving of very special attention that we are told by writers of the sixteenth and seventeenth centuries that the provinces were then overrun by bands of people whom *they* called *gypsies, moon-men, blueskins, greenmen, jockeys*, &c., who lived by plunder, who terrorised the farmers, who were polygamists and heathen, and who (as a quite modern Scotch writer tells us) were in absolute command of the country, as distinguished from the town ; who were, in short, British people occupying a position that was most distinctly of importance. These large companies did not consist of so many *nameless* units. People who lived as they did, must have impressed their personality most strongly upon the memories of those on whom they sorned. And in any

other variety of speech belonging more particularly to people then residing in Britain, *not* immigrants. That such forms as *Jan* and *Jänkin* should be common on either side of the Bristol Channel, and that *s* should take the place of *s* in Somersetshire, would lead a casual observer to conclude that the people who first used these forms were comparatively-modern Dutch. The specimens that Longfellow gives, in his essay on "Dutch Language and Poetry," might easily pass for provincial English ; and, possibly, of that district in particular. Such as—

Wanneer de wijn is in den man,	*Whene'er the wine is in the man,*
Dan is de wijsheid in de kan :	*Then is the wisdom in the can.*

And—

Als April blaast op zijn hoorn,	*When April blows on his horn,*
Is't goed voor hooi en koorn :	*It is good for hay and corn.*

Indeed, certain parts of Great Britain seem to have had a closer connection with the Continent—about this period—than with other parts of the island. When it was customary for young Scotchmen to attend the university of Leyden, and when one of them (Rutherford) was offered a professorship in that place, it is a question whether they had to contend with the difficulty of acquiring a *foreign* language.

feuds of that period they must have taken most important and even the most important parts. So far as can be perceived from the transient glances we have cast on these times, the party known in history as the Royalist or Cavalier party is closely akin to such predatory nobles, if it did not include them all within its pale. And, if those "cavaliers" were the seventeenth-century forerunners of existing "gypsies," so were the Parliamentarians, to a very great extent, the forerunners of "us." Of these two great divisions there can be no doubt as to which contained "the men of the future." Of the two great leaders who have just been com-pared with each other, Cromwell was distinctly the "modern Briton." Spending the years of his retirement, as he did, upon his estate in the country; and reclaiming the waste lands of that neighbourhood; he was what we should now call "a model country-gentleman." Whereas his distinguished opponent, employing *his* leisure in brigandage and murder, would, with the common consent of the British people, be summarily executed as a "criminal." Prince Rupert, like others of his time and caste, was the possessor of many high qualities that have long ago floated away from the body of which our modern "gypsies" and "roughs" are the sediment;* but in his ideas, his way of living, and his physical characteristics he was merely a magnified "gypsy" chief.

* The above sentence was written before a perusal of Mr. Groome's "In Gipsy Tents," and a casual acquaintanceship with one or two gypsy families, had convinced the present writer that it is still too soon to speak of *all* of our nomadic fellow-countrymen as constituting a "sediment." It is unquestionable that if there are any nomadic descendants of the Scotch William Baillie still in existence, they are as likely to be inferior to him as his cultivated descendant, the late Mrs. Carlyle, was his superior. And the same rule would probably apply to other such families throughout these islands. But, nevertheless, it is equally certain that some of our nomadic families do still retain various graces of mind and body that render them the superiors of large masses of their house-dwelling compatriots. And if this recognition be held to contradict any previous remarks on the subject of gypsy vices, it can only be said that the science of "gypsiology" is yet in its infancy; and that although two opposing statements might be made with regard to the people called "gypsies," neither of them need be untrue. Gypsydom is a country that has been very partially explored; and one of the most distinguished authorities on its language has admitted that "once only in his life had he spoken with living Gipsies." No man who wished to write a book upon the language of Fiji would content himself with secondhand information, or with one solitary interview with Fijians. But this is the attitude of many of the gypsiologists. One or two have really lived in the country, and associated as

What, perhaps, most of all, brings home this cavalier-gypsy identity to modern people is the fact that the principal *clans* (not mere individual families) among our English gypsies to-day bear surnames that are most intensely "cavalier." Some of these are Bosville, Stanley, Roland, Lee, and Lovel ; while, formerly—if not now—others bore such names as Featherstone, Fenwick, Chilcott, Richmond, and Lancaster. Names like Lancelot Lovell and Sylvester Bosville—the names of two representative gypsies—have a peculiarly "cavalier" sound ; nor would they be out of place in any page of English history—back to the Norman conquest.*

But a closer examination of the aspect of bye-gone gypsy life, in England and Wales, reveals these people to us in the same light as those of Scotland. Two things become chiefly apparent ; the one, the decadence of " gypsyism " within comparatively recent times—the other, the wide differ-ence between the various castes of "gypsies " (so-called). It may be remembered that the elder Mr. Simson, in speaking of the wandering castes of North Britain, has informed us " that the numbers in which the nomadic class are to be met with are greatly reduced, their condition greatly fallen, and the circumstances attending their reception, countenance and toleration, much modified, and in some instances totally changed." The suitability of these remarks, if applied to the nomadic system of England and Wales, is rendered still more evident after the perusal of one or two "gypsy" books, which had not been examined when the immediately preceding pages were written.

friends with the natives ; other have occasionally visited its shores ; and some have never been there at all. With such imperfect data, then, one may allowably make statements which would seem to contradict each other, but which would be reconciled by a fuller knowledge of the subject. In every country there are people in whom the higher national qualities predominate, and others in whom these qualities are almost absent. And yet the tie of nationality—which is partly of blood and partly of custom—unites them together. So is it with gypsies and gypsydom.

* Mr. Leland gives a list of the tory clans of England and Wales, in which the following names occur :—Ayres, Buckland, Dickens, Draper, Herne, Ingraham, Loveridge, Mace, North, Pinfold, Taylor, Wheeler, and Woods. (He, of course, also includes the Bosvilles, Rolands, Lees, Lovells, and Stanleys.)

The subjoined dialogue is between the author of *In Gipsy Tents*, and an elderly gypsy—Silvanus Lovell—who is thus described :—" A hale old man, he stands over six feet two ; his merry nut-brown face is lighted up by dazzling teeth and a pair of glittering hazel eyes ; his grizzling hair curls round the brim of a high-crowned ribbon-decked hat. A yellow silk neckerchief, brown velveteen coat with crown-piece buttons, red waistcoat with spade-guinea dittoes, cord breeches, and leathern leggings, make up his holiday attire ; his left hand wields a silver-headed whalebone whip ; and from a deep skirt-pocket peeps forth the unfailing violin." He and his visitor have been talking of the old days of his boyhood which he characterizes as " merry times." And, in answer to the query if they were " better than now ? " he replies—

" Better ! ay, sure enough. You might go where you liked, and stop where you liked : none of these blue-coat gentlemen about. First time, I mind, as ever we seen a policeman, was at Brompton Bryan June fair. There was a lot of us going, twenty belike or more, my grand-father and all the rest on 'em. And that was a curious thing, too, his own sons would never call him 'daddy,' but always nothing but plain ' Henry.' Forty pounds he brought with him to spend on horses, and we had come up all the way from Limer's Lane ; but soon as ever he sees this mounted policeman (they all were mounted at first starting), he turned back, wouldn't go anighst the fair. We'd heard some talk of 'em before, but never put much hearkenings in it. Why. you'd see the lanes then crowded with Romané—Lovells and Boswells and Stanleys and Hernes and Chilcotts. Something like Gipsies they were, with their riding horses, real hunters, to ride to the fairs and wakes on ; and the women with their red cloaks and high old-fashioned beaver hats ; and the men in beautiful silk velvet coats and white and yellow satin waistcoats, and all on 'em booted and spurred. Why, I mind hearing tell of my grand-father's oldest sister, aunt Marbelenni, and that must have been a hundred years and more. She was married to a very rich farmer in Gloucester-shire, so she was very well off ; and one day some of her brothers, Henry including, went to call on her, and when she seen 'em, she wouldn't allow them into her house, for she said, ' Now that I am married, I shall expect you all to come booted and silver-spurred.'* · Gipsies ! there aren't no Gipsies now."

* This incident seems to hint that the gypsies of England—like those of Scotland—reserved their fine dresses for high-days and holidays ; wearing very plain clothes on ordinary occasions. This is stated by Mr. Simson to have been a custom with Scotch gypsies ; though other passages of his show that other sections were *invariably* dressed in the bravest style.

" What do you call yourself, then ? "

" What do I call myself? why a crab in a coal pit. But what I mean, it's different from how it used to be. All the old families are broken up, over in 'Mericay, or gone in houses, or stopping round the nasty poverty towns. My father wouldn't ha' stopped by Wolverhampton, not if you'd gone on your bended knees to him, and offered him a pound a day to do it. He'd have runned miles if you'd just shown him the places where some of these new-fashioned travellers has their tents."

" Yes, I have often thought what a poor exchange brickyard or build-ing-plot must be for lane or common. I remember one patch of ground near the Addison Road Station, close to London, that only five years back was covered with tents and waggons, but now is all built over. There were some of the Norths stayed there ; and one of them, a very old old woman, told me a story about those Boswells you were speaking of. How, when she was a little child, she fell over a stile in Wales one day, and made her nose bleed ; and how two beautiful ladies, dressed all in silks and satins, picked her up. Their grandeur awed her, though they spoke to her in Romanes, for they were two of the great Boswell tribe ; and still she spoke of them with deep respect, as I might speak of some high-born stately countess. Yet gorgios fancy all gipsies are the same— Lovells and Taylors, Stanleys and Turners, Boswells and Norths."

Those English Lovells and Chilcotts and Stanleys, then, were of precisely the same description as the finely-attired cavalier families in Scotland—such as the Baillies, Ruthvens, and Kennedies. Not necessarily of the same description, *ethnologically* (in the case of the fair-skinned Baillies certainly not), but in all other characteristics the same. And in either case, the existence of a variety of castes is most evident.

The style of dressing that Silvanus Lovell remembered, and which he exemplified in a slight degree in his own fashions, is referred to by Borrow several times. The appear-ance of his Jasper Petulengro has already been spoken of, and how Mrs. Petulengro glittered over with jewels and rings, which had been "family jewels" since her grandmother's time, and likely for much longer. Mr. Borrow, again, in speaking of a certain horse-dealer who had married a Herne (though not himself a gipsy) says—" it is a pleasure to see his wife, at Hampton Court races, dressed in gipsy fashion, decked with real gems and jewels and rich gold chains, and waited upon by her dark brothers dressed like dandy pages." His Ryley Bosville is another kindred specimen. " Ryley Bosvil was a native of Yorkshire, a country where, as the gypsies say, ' there's a deadly sight of Bosvils.' [And both

his parents were of that clan.] He was above the middle
height, exceedingly strong and active, and one of the best
riders in Yorkshire, which is saying a great deal. . . . His
great ambition was to be a great man among his people, a
gypsy king. To this end he furnished himself with clothes
made after the costliest gypsy fashion ; the two hinder buttons
of the coat, which was of thick blue cloth, were broad gold
pieces of Spain, generally called ounces ; the fore buttons
were English 'spaded guineas'; the buttons of the waistcoat were half-guineas, and those of the collar and the wrists
of his shirt were seven-shilling gold pieces. In this coat he
would frequently make his appearance on a magnificent
horse, whose hoofs like those of the steed of a Turkish sultan,
were cased in shoes of silver. . . . He was very fond of hunting, and would frequently join the field in regular hunting
costume, save and except that, instead of the leather hunting-
cap, he wore one of fur, with a gold band around it, to denote
that though he mixed with Gorgios he was still a Romany-
chal."*

Another picture of English gypsy fashions is that given
by Mr. Simson, junior (in a note to the "History," p. 510):
" There are two gipsies, of the name of B——, farmers upon
the estate of Lord Lister, near Massingham, in the county of
Norfolk. They are described as good-sized, handsome men,
and swarthy, with long black hair, combed over their
shoulders. They dress in the old gipsy stylish fashion, with
a green cut-away, or Newmarket, coat, yellow leather
breeches, buttoned to the knee, and top boots, with a gipsy
hat, ruffled breast, and turned down collar. . . They are
proud of being gipsies."

The conventional stage "gypsy" dress was found by Mr.
Crofton, some years ago, to be as follows:—"A broad-
brimmed wide-awake, from which drooped a dissipated pea-
cock's feather ; a yellow doublet, a frowsy red cloak to be
thrown over the shoulders ; loose maroon knee-breeches and
coarse sacking gaiters to be crossed with red-and-yellow
garters far from new."† It may be added that the great-
grandfather of one of Mr. Groome's gypsies, who—when in

---

* "Lave-lil," pp. 282, 291, 294, and 295.
† See "The Academy" of 15th April, 1876 (p. 356).

full dress—used to wear "a high hat," and brown gloves,
"always wore breeches and leggings." Mr. Leland corroborates Mr. Simson as to the gypsy love for green coats :
"Till within a few years in great Britain. . . their fondness
for green coats amounted to a passion." The same writer
states that all true gypsy men " delight in a bright yellow
neckerchief, and a red waistcoat." He also says that they
are equally fond of velveteen coats : and when wearing himself " a broad, soft felt hat," he encountered one of the Lees
at Aberystwith, that gypsy patriarch said to him. . . .
"When I was still young, a few of the oldest Romany *chals*
still wore hats such as you have ;' and when I first looked at
you, I thought of them."

These descriptions vary a little ; and they probably portray
the fashions of many grades of gypsydom. The battered
Roger Wildrake who figures as the gypsy of the stage, differs
considerably from those " booted and silver-spurred " cavaliers
who, mounted on high-bred horses, and wearing cloaks of
scarlet or green, and dressed in all the bravery of the seventeenth century, thronged our English lanes on the day of
some great gathering. And those two Romanes-speaking
Bosville ladies of last century, " dressed all in silks and
satins," must also have belonged to the very highest caste.

Their manner of dressing is quite a suffcent proof that
those tory cavaliers carried full purses. A man who—like
the grandfather of Silvanus Lovell—rode to the race-course
with forty pounds in his pocket (equivalent to a much larger
sum now), to be lost or doubled in betting, must have been a
man of some substance. People who buttoned their
garments with gold coins must have carried a good many of
such coins loose in their purses. And Mr. Leland gives
direct evidence of considerable wealth when he records what
one of his gypsy friends told him. They were speaking of
a custom which it seems that some of those " tories " have
not even yet given up—a custom that is one of the oldest in
our islands—that of burying the valuables of the dead along
with them. (Our antiquaries speak of them as " grave-
goods," and they are disinterred, at intervals, from our
ancient places of sepulture.) " Dighton told me the other
day," says this gypsy, " that three thousand pounds were

hidden [buried] with one of the Chilcotts. And I have heard of some Stanleys who were buried with gold rings on their fingers." The latter sentence, though not quite irrelevant, does not speak to the possession of great wealth ; but a Chilcott who had three thousand pounds was plainly a man who could afford to dress in the finest cavalier style (assuming, of course, that the idea of merely using the *interest* of his money had never entered into his calculations). The "gypsy" Ingrams and Woods who settled in Wales in the beginning of last century were assuredly rich people ; ". . . near Aberystwith some of them bought little estates. . . They were supposed to be in possession of abundance of gold, when taking these places ; they were thought gentlefolks of in those days." One of the Lees, who died at Beaulieu, Hampshire, in 1844, at the age of eighty-six, "and who some years before had given his grandchild Charity one hundred spade-guineas and much silver plate for dower," 'must certainly have been possessed of a good deal of wealth in his lifetime, whether or not any of it was buried with him.✱ And when a modern writer, speaking of the custom of destroying the goods of the dead, immediately after the funeral, states that everything is destroyed *with the exception of coin or jewels*, he indirectly testifies that coins and jewels are not even yet dissociated from gypsydom. We have seen how far back this association reaches in North Britain ; since John [the faw], Earl of Little Egypt, was possessed—in the year 1540—of "divers sums of money, jewels, clothes and other goods, to the quantity of a great sum of money." A century before him, again, we recognized a veritable gypsy king in the chief of the black Douglases ; who was not only the most powerful man (at one time) north of the Borders, possessed of an army and a court of his own—but who minted "Douglas coins" for the use of himself and those of his nationality.

However, we are at present considering the gypsies of Central and Southern Britain ; during recent times ; times as recent as the early part of this century, when—on the occasion of some great gathering—the lanes were "crowded

---

✱ For notices of these facts, see Mr. Leland's "English Gipsies," page 59 ; and pages 126 and 198 of Mr. Groome's "In Gipsy Tents."

with Romané—Lovells and Boswells and Stanleys and Hernes and Chilcotts." And the costly nature of their dress, with its gay appearance, is recorded by one of them still living ; now an old man. That this magnificent style of dressing should have been reserved for special occasions seems evident. It was characteristic of many of Mr. Simson's high-caste Scotch gypsies of last century that they dressed plainly—even meanly—on ordinary occasions ; carrying their fine clothes·in a "pad" strapped to the back, and exchanging these for their commoner garments when they thought fit to do so. An example of this practice is afforded by a southern Scotchwoman of the seventeenth century, whom Mr. Simson, senior, would most likely have denominated a "gypsy," had he been born a century earlier. This was a Lady Margaret Jardine, who is thus described by a descendant of her sister* :—" She generally wore rags ; but carried, when visiting, articles of finery in a napkin, which she would slip on before she entered the house." That this was akin to the usage of the families spoken of above (although "rags" is not likely a term that would have described their every-day dress)—is most likely, for two reasons. The one is that those features of their dress which so emphatically indicate their pedigree would not have permitted their pedigree to be lost sight of, if they had been accustomed to wear such attire every day of their lives. The other is that the gypsy writers—by several passages—show that it was by no means the custom of these people to "dress up" unless when about to pay a visit or attend some great festival—whether a fair, a race meeting, or a wake ; and that their descendants seem still to act upon this principle. The representative gypsy who is introduced upon the first page of *In Gipsy Tents* did not wear his "yellow silk neckerchief, brown velveteen coat with crown-piece buttons," and "red waistcoat with spade guinea dittos" except as "holiday attire ;" although his every-day dress perhaps included one or other of these articles. And those gypsies (mentioned in the *Encyclopædia*) who turned out to do honour to the Queen when she visited

* See Mark Napier's "Memorials &c. of John Graham of Claverhouse," Vol. I. p. 253. The "descendant" referred to was Charles Kirkpatrick Sharpe.

Dunbar some years ago—the men in scarlet coats, the women
in silk and velvet—assumed these dresses for that exceptional
occasion ; returning them to their wardrobes thereafter, as
being too good for daily wear.

Had the attire that old Lovell speaks of been the *daily*
dress of his near ancestors, their pedigree could never have
been lost sight of. There is only one caste in English history that distinctly claims them as its members—and them
in preference to any other division of modern Englishmen—
the "Cavaliers" of the seventeenth century. That section
of the nomadic classes which bears the name of "Romané "*
is little else than a society of seventeenth-century Englishmen projected into this present age,—or, at any rate, into
the dawn of this present century. Those Lovells, Boswells,
Stanleys, Hernes, and Chilcotts, who—booted and spurred,
and with gay-coloured cloaks and doublets of velvet and
satin, and with feathers waving in their high-crowned
sombreros, beneath which streamed the long tresses of their
race,—clattered along our English lanes to attend those old-
fashioned race-meetings with which they are even yet
identified, were living embodiments of the men who followed
the Charleses and Prince Rupert, at Edgehill or at Worcester.
And if the ideas of the Second Charles and his kinsmen
were paramount in this present year, then the "gentle
Romané" would still be "thought gentlefolks of," as some
of them were in Wales last century. That the ideas of
Charles II. were the ideas of the people whom we call
"gypsies," and who were called "tories" by an earlier
generation, is quite evident. The Parliamentarians, whose
ideas have mainly triumphed in the long run, enacted laws
against all those things with which "gypsies" are most
identified :—cock-fighting, bull-fighting, bear-baiting, dicing,
itinerant acting, and minstrelsy. All these things were the
delight of the Cavaliers ; and with the Restoration the laws
against them were rescinded or ignored. One who writes of
this period states that "England, during the reigns of

* It is most necessary to discriminate in speaking of "gypsies." And the
people called Romané or Romani, although forming the very essence of gypsydom, must not be confounded with the thousands of unmodernized hybrids who
only possess a slight trace of that blood.

James I. and his immediate successors, presented two different forms of national life, character, and customs, as if they had belonged to two entirely different and even hostile races."* And this statement strikes deeper than its author knew.

It cannot be assumed or maintained that, at so recent a period as the seventeenth century, the British Islands formed the scene of a struggle between two " entirely different " races. But it does seem most likely that, on either side, there was a *background* which was totally dissimilar from that of the opposite side ; and not only dissimilar in ideas, but in blood as well. Such a man as Rochester, although he is said to have publicly performed as a mountebank on a stage at Tower Hill, and to have gone " a-roaming" on several occasions along with his king, may not have been at all a "gypsy" by blood, and only partly one by habit. But if not one himself, his vassals were of " the black breed " (to use Grose's words) ; as the " Black Will " incident, in his episode with Dryden, clearly shows. If the pure Romani were not Cavaliers, in the highest acceptation, they were Freebooters ;—at a time when a " freebooter " was " a cavalier who ventures life for gain." If the majority of the Cavalier leaders were " fair whites " (although Charles the Second and Prince Rupert were at least *Melanochroi*), the majority of their followers must have been genuine gypsies. It seems necessary to go back a hundred and fifty years from the era of the Civil Wars, to find a uniform tendency towards gypsyism in the features of the ruling class of England. That we do not see this likeness, in an intensified form, at an earlier period, is only the effect of the shortness of our vision. If Holbein had lived a century earlier, and had left us the portraits of the aristocrats of Galloway who would have been his contemporaries, we should then have the actual canvas representation of a gypsy aristocracy. But, if the whole Cavalier section was not composed exclusively— or only partially composed—of genuine gypsies, at least its ways and sympathies were entirely gypsy. Had the country never adopted any other ideas than those which Charles the Second favoured, old Lovell would have had no cause to

* "The Comprehensive History of England ;" Vol. II. p. 620.

lament the advent of the policeman, and the social laws which he carries out.

That those Chilcotts, Lovells, and others are the least-altered descendants of the Cavaliers—and, through them, of that "ancient nobility of the country" which filled the fifteenth century with bloodshed and rapine—is evident from all their ways. And the gypsy writers who have so placed them before our eyes give us a representation of archaic life that is infinitely more lifelike and picturesque than those which we have hitherto possessed. For those gypsy cavaliers are *real men ;* compared with whom the fictitious "cavaliers" of *Kenilworth, Woodstock,* and the stage, are so many blood-less marionettes. In regarding the high-caste gypsies, we must dismiss all the lower orders from our minds, for the moment. And those pure-blooded Romanys are distinctly a handsome race. "Their complexion is dark, but not dis-agreeably so ; their faces are oval, their features regular, their foreheads rather low, and their hands and feet small. The men are taller than the English peasantry, and far more active, they all speak the English language with fluency, and in their gait and demeanour are easy and graceful ; in both respects standing in striking contrast with the peasantry, who in speech, are slow and uncouth, and in manner dogged and brutal." This is how they appeared to Borrow, whatever they may be like at the present day. And it is evident that, like their horses, they were thorough-bred. If there is one thing more apparent than another, it is the racial pride of the genuine gypsy. A man like Grose, speaking as one of the successful party—the white section—might talk of them as " the black breed ; " but it is this very " black blood " that the true Romani are so proud of. So invincible is this pride that it has survived generations of defeat and persecution ; so that, even in this century, such a gypsy could be found as Ryley Bosville who " used to say that if any of his people became Gorgios he would kill them." If Grose himself had ever heard his special division of Englishmen spoken of as plainly by their opponents as these were characterized by him, he would have learned with surprise that the blood which *he* possessed was regarded as the inferior strain. And certainly, to an unbiassed onlooker, Grose—who was the

personification of the "slow and uncouth" Englishman—
was a vastly poorer specimen of the human animal than
those "easy and graceful" cavaliers described by Borrow.

These, then, were the kind of men that the belated Scotchman encountered in the woods of Cambridgeshire. And if
that night-scene was not a realization of a Cavalier camp in
the seventeenth century, it is difficult to conceive another
nearer the truth. In all England there was no more
thoroughly English scene than that. The men themselves,
their names, their dresses, their songs, their dances,—all were
as completely "old English" as they could possibly have
been. And most genuinely "cavalier." Whether throughout
that night of revelry, or as they appeared at other times—
backing a prize-fight or a race—or acting the chief parts in
either—these were typical Cavaliers.

Borrow's sketch at the horse-fair makes one feel how it is
that those men were remembered as "Riders ; " men who
sat their horses "like gulls upon the waves." This knowledge
—and all the knowledge we possess regarding these people
—fills this "Cavalier" picture with life and colour. A lithe
and graceful race, full of the wildest impulses—fierce and
vindictive, yet generous and brave,—passionate and proud,
but often melting into laughter and music—altogether the
strangest compound of good and bad that ever any human
society presented. But—good or bad—they are real, warm-
blooded men, and not lay-figures, as with waving feathers
and silken vests, brilliant garments and costly jewels, black
eyes flashing from dusky faces, and long tresses floating out
behind, they go jangling along, with much racket and
laughter, through the green lanes of England.

What has been said with regard to the Douglases, Ruthvens,
and others of Scotland, is equally applicable to the Cavalier
surnames of England. It is not until we look at the black
Douglases of modern Yetholm, or those of many centuries
back, that we see the name of "Douglas" indicating an
actual national, or family type. And the distinct inference
is that such people are the purest specimens of their race ;
their modernized and hybrid namesakes being representative
of no special British type. So also with their more southern

kindred. " A Lovell," " a Stanley," "a Leigh,"* conveys no
ethnological meaning whatever, unless one regards the tory
sections of these clans. It may be necessary, in individual
cases, to go back three, five, or ten centuries, to find the date
at which a particular Leigh, Stanley, or Lovell lost caste
among his kinsfolk by intermarrying with the despised white
race, and adopting their ways. The people who regard the
" cavalier " tribes as " pariahs," and interlopers of a few centuries back, have assumed that they *borrowed* their famous
names from the people whom they used to detest (and are
scarcely reconciled to even yet). The idea is manifestly
absurd. That a Ryley Bosville, or a "black Lovel," permeated through and through with the pride of race and the
memory of bye-gone power, should adopt the surname of
the inferior caste, was the unlikeliest thing in the world. But
the facts already stated prove that their claims to such surnames are trebly stronger than those of any mixed-blood
bearing the same name. It may, or may not be that the
settled and modernized families who bear such names are
accustomed to regard themselves as of " Cavalier " origin.
If they do, the two or three centuries suggested will bring
them to an ancestor who was a typical representative of his
name. Dickens says that the farther back a pedigree goes,
the more do its members show themselves addicted to
" violence and vagabondism." In some families it may be
necessary to go back the whole ten centuries suggested, to
find this resemblance. But all history bears out the truth of
Dickens' statement ; and even in the seventeenth-century
" violence and vagabondism " were among the characteristics
of one division of British aristocracy.

.   .   .   .   .   .

Although many of the most prominent features of extinct
aristocracies are more clearly seen in the physique and the
habits of our nomadic, and even criminal classes, than in any
more respectable section of the community, it must be re-

---

* This spelling seems to be the more correct. It has been pointed out by one
or other of the gypsy writers that the equivalent of " Lee " in Romanes signifies
a " leek." And that, consequently, this translation dates from
the time when " Leigh " was pronounced with a guttural termination (still surviving, in a modified form, as " Leake "). " Lee," indeed, appears to be generally
regarded as a modern spelling of " Leigh," or " Legh."

membered that these nomads and others represent little more than the frame-work of former systems. "Gypsydom" is like a half-dried river-bed, out of which the main stream has long been turned,—to flow with increasing strength along a newer channel : it is a heap of skeleton-leaves, strewn upon the ground, retaining the original structure, but without the original life,—while overhead the growing tree is throwing out a fuller foliage every spring. So that these people re-mind us both of what we *have been* and of what we *are*. For, if the term is to include the Xanthochroic type, as well as one or more of darker hue, then even the presumably-white citizens, scholars, and farmers of a previous time were only early-civilized "gypsies." And, again, if that word ought to signify the dark-skinned types alone, then our modern "gypsies" still show us what we have been. For we are mostly Melanochroi. And the many varieties of the dark-skinned stocks are seen, not only under tents and in caravans, but among all the ranks of civilized people. Even the least picturesque variety of all—that of the prize-fighter, the "old-fashioned gypsy ' bruiser ' "—may be seen, again and again, refined and civilized as highly as any other type, among the heterogeneous masses of educated Britons.

And our whole atmosphere is impregnated with gypsyism. The scarlet cloaks that even Washington Irving regarded as peculiar to a limited few had been common in English coun-try districts so lately as 1782, and are still, I believe, worn by the peasantry of some parts of Ireland. That colour is still the distinctive colour of the British army : the scarlet coats of the "gypsies" may be seen any day in the hunting-field and on the golf-links—as if to remind one that these people were the passionate lovers of these as of all other "Old English" sports. "Lincoln green" and "Kendal green—supposed also to be "gypsy"—is the uniform colour of many of our oldest societies—" Scottish Archers," "Ancient Orders of Foresters," and others. Plain as our style of dressing now is, we yet retain a lingering love of showy dress—even in men—which we reserve for occasions of high ceremonial. We still keep up a slight distinction between City and Court, and the latter is still so far nomadic that wherever the mon-arch goes there is the Court. We hold it a crime to take by

force the goods and lands of *individuals ;* but to "annex" the
territory of other *nations,* by right of superior strength, is
quite justifiable. "Prince Rupert's Land" is strong enough
evidence that we have inherited some of Prince Rupert's
ideas. We do not go to war with each other in armies of a
few hundreds, or a few thousands ; but we occasionally fight
other nations with armies of tenfold magnitude. We are as
ready to resent the infringement of a frontier as ever any
eighteenth-century Pict of Galloway. Only our frontier is
immensely wider. We have, in short, *expanded :* in power,
in knowledge, in ideas. But many of our qualities—though
modified—are those of earlier *Faws* and *Cavaliers.* In a
thousand peculiarities of feature and of custom, we prove
ourselves to be only modernized "gypsies."

CHAPTER XI.

THE effects that heathen domination has had upon the early Christianity of Europe are too numerous and of too intricate a nature to be entered into here, or to be enlarged upon by any but one who has studied the matter. Since, however, the supremacy—within recent times—of "gypsy" castes must have signified also a supremacy of this kind in the world of religion, it becomes necessary to refer, however slightly, to this point.

We learn, accordingly, that this very "gypsy" domination in religion was one of the causes that strongly influenced the Reformer Knox, in his movement of revolt. We are told that, in sixteenth-century Scotland, "inferior benefices were openly put to sale, or bestowed on the illiterate and unworthy minions of courtiers; on dice-players, strolling bards, and the bastards of bishops." Now, three, at least, of these designations—*courtiers, dice-players,* and *strolling bards* —indicate the very gypsies of whom we have been speaking. More than this, the short description of the *quasi*-religious world of that time and place, as given in the book just quoted from (McCrie's *Life of John Knox*), would lead an ordinary observer to suspect that the Scotch expression, "*black* prelacy," was something more than a mere phrase. Indeed, in a letter which was written to Henry the Eighth by a Caithness "clerk," named John Elder,—the main theme of which is a proposal to drive out, or exterminate, the Scotch bishops and their adherents; and to add Scotland to King Henry's dominions—in this letter the writer speaks of those "bishops, monks, Rome-rykers, and priests" as though they were of quite a different stock from himself, a large section of his compatriots, and the English king to whom he was writing. And he points out the lineage of those bishops and others in these words: they "derive Scotland [the word] *and them-*

T 2

selves from a certain lady, named Scota, which (as they
allege) came out of Egypt." That is to say, he plainly
classifies a certain ruling caste (chiefly, though not wholly,
composed of priests) as Scots Proper or Egyptians. This
letter, which was written to the Tudor king, "knowing what
true faithful hearts the most part of the commons of Scotland (if they durst speak), beyond the water of Forth, have
to your highness," is included in the *Collectanea de Rebus
Albanicis* (pp. 23–32) : and it is interesting in many ways ; of
which not the least interesting is this indication of community of feeling, if not of blood, between two widely separated
sections of British people, at a period that ante-dated the
elevation of James of Scotland by fully sixty years. And
equally important is the recognition of Scotland *south* of the
Forth as a country not in sympathy with Scotland Proper :
while the formal admission that the priestly hierarchy was
composed of men descended from quite another race than
the writer,—and that race " Egyptian,"—is a statement of the
greatest significance. Here it is distinctly asserted that the
sixteenth-century priesthood of Scotland (*not* that priesthood
of which Elder himself was a member, but an over-ruling
order, whose ranks were recruited from gypsy-minstrels)—
derived its descent, by right of blood, from the Scots of Early
Scotia (now Ireland), who drew *their* descent from " Scota,
the daughter of a Pharaoh."

It is unnecessary to repeat what has formerly been said as
to the links that unite the Early Scots with the Egyptians.
But, in regarding more especially the religious side of the
question, the following remarks made by Mr. Moncure D.
Conway are not out of place. In an article on *The Saint
Patrick Myth*, and referring to the tradition that " Gadelas,
grandson of the Pharaoh who pursued Israel," had conquered
Ireland, and established therein his posterity (thenceforward
known as the Gaidheal, or Gaels)—in referring to this and
other relative legends, Mr. Conway says : " It appears incredible that this vast mass of traditions, many of which are
not Biblical, but nearly all pointing to Egyptian and Jewish
regions, could have been invented since the introduction of
the Bible into Ireland. It seems tolerably certain that, anterior to the Christianization of Ireland, there were in Ireland

eastern myths closely resembling those of the papyri, and that the stories of the Bible found there a congenial soil." *
This opinion is quite in accordance with the statements made in a former chapter with regard to the existence in Early Scotia (Ireland) of emblems, rites, and words whose origin must be looked for in the East. This, however, is a question which can only be alluded to in these pages.

But what Elder leads one to infer is, that the Scotch bishops of the year 1542 were not of his own or Henry Tudor's (Theodore's) race: and that they themselves derived their descent from "Scota, an Egyptian lady,"—the traditional ancestress of those Scots Proper, who, along with the Painted-Moors ("black herds of Picts and Scots"), are seen "committing depredations" in various parts of Great Britain during the earlier centuries of the Christian era. If the majority of those prelates of three hundred years ago were really descended from the invading hosts of Early-Scots, it is probable that they were also the posterity of other British races, of various dates ; and that their resemblance to the conventional "Egyptian" did not extend much farther than the high cheek bones, long upper lip, and lank, black hair, that characterized the South-British "courtiers" of the same period. And that each of these classes, priests and courtiers, were only connected "on one side of the house" with the gypsy-minstrels and irreclaimable "Egyptians" of their time.

As if to bear out this view, it is affirmed by other writers that *Mendicant Friars* and *Abraham-men*—both of which orders are included under the title *gypsy*—are not visible as a source of public annoyance until the dissolution of the Monasteries by Henry the Eighth had thrown them upon the country for support.† Grose's *patricoes* or *patter-coves*,

* "The Saint Patrick Myth : " *North American Review*, October, 1883.

It may be remarked here that to admit the identity of the Gaidheal with the Ancient Egyptians is to admit the correctness of Dr. Skene's statement that the Early Scots and the Early Gaels were one and the same people : which was called in question on an earlier page.

† At first sight, this insinuated kinship between Henry the Eighth and a class or community that was antagonistic to those self-styled "Egyptian" bishops, may appear to conflict with the statement that the aristocracy of England, during Henry the Eighth's reign and prior to it, bore a certain resemblance to the orthodox "gypsy" type : with which type their way of living connects them, if

who are classed by him as part of " the canting-crew," and whose ceremonial is that assigned by Simson to gypsy-priests, are *Mendicant* Priests. It is true that their rites do not appear to be connected in any way with Christianity. But are we to say that Carleton's Irish gypsy-priest was " a Christian" because he used to ensure the safety of his followers, here and hereafter, by the simple expedient of tattooing a cross into their skin : that emblem being now-a-days regarded as peculiarly Christian? Whatever may have been the original belief and practice of the early Roman mendicant-priests, it is at least certain that the latest visible members of such a nomadic order were the *Romany* mendicant-priests : who, like those beneficed clergymen against whom Knox *protested*, were also " dice-players and strolling bards."

Indeed, the distinction between Christianity and Heathenism seems to have been rather ill-defined at the period of the Reformation, and previously. We have been told that, in thirteenth-century Norfolk, the nominally-Christian priests of that district used to regard as one of their most sacred duties that of keeping alive "the eternal flame " in a small lamp which hung above the altar, and which was never suffered to go out. That such priests, though avowedly celibates, made no more pretensions to sustain that character than any of Mr. Simson's Scottish gypsy-priests may be accounted to be a fact of comparatively little moment. But this duty of sustaining a sacred flame, night and day, while it connects this priesthood with those of Persia and Peru, has really no connection whatever with Christianity. And the people of the district in which those thirteenth-century priests officiated are described as living precisely after the fashion of gypsy tribes.*

it does not prove them to have been of genuine "gypsy " stock. But Henry the Eighth did not belong to the same *breed* as his courtiers, if the popular portrait of him is anything like the original. Besides, he is stated to have been a near descendant of a brewer in Beaumaris, Anglesey (of the name of Owen Theodore) : and his family only rose into importance in the fifteenth century—the era in which the Black-Douglases and Gordons of Scotland became landless " gypsies," and "the larger proportion of the ancient nobility " of England were killed or overthrown.

* " Village Life in Norfolk Six Hundred Years Ago : " Rev. Dr. Jessopp ; *Nineteenth Century*, February, 1883.

Even in the seventeenth century the professed teachers of Christianity do not seem to have freed themselves altogether from pagan notions; if one is to accept as a faithful likeness the sketch of a Jesuit priest which is given in a recent study of that period—*John Inglesant.* In that book it is stated that Father St. Clare (a fictitious character, but intended to represent the Jesuit order of his day) was a master of the science of astrology, in which he instructed his pupil. Now, no modern clergyman of that order, although he might take up the study of *astronomy*, would ever think of teaching the art of divination by the stars. Neither did an early British apostle of Christianity, such as Columba, preach any such belief: although it formed an important feature of *druidism*, the creed of the Pictish Magi. Again, in one of the folk-tales of the south of Scotland, it is mentioned that the mode by which the pastor of a parish—in one instance—defended himself and one of his flock from the Powers of Evil was by drawing a circle around them, praying as he did so; much as any "gypsy" Magus might have done. And, though the precise date of this traditional story may not be known, there would be nothing extraordinary in a Scotch clergyman of the sixteenth century, although nominally Christian, following this or any other "gypsy" ceremonial, if he happened to be one of those "dice-players and strolling bards," whose appointment as teachers of the Christian religion was so strongly objected to by the Scotch Reformers.

The fact seems to be that at no time in their history have these islands been exclusively Christian (even using that term in its least exact acceptation). To what extent British Druidism has affected British Christianity may be left an open question. But Druidism, pure and simple, has maintained its hold upon the British people with the most wonderful tenacity. It is more than thirteen hundred years since Columba began his campaign against the paganism of the "Moorish" Magi (or Druids); and yet that paganism is not extinct yet, but asserts itself every now and then—though in an attenuated form—among the more ignorant classes. When Patrick and Columba attempted to gain over to Christianity the heathen kings of Ireland and of Scotland, these chiefs sought counsel of their "*Magi* and enchanters and soothsayers and doctors," who—"with many incantations" sought to overcome the teachers of the newer faith. Some of the beliefs of these "enchanters and soothsayers" are alluded to in the poem attributed to Columba, in which he says—

> " I adore not the voice of birds,
> Nor the *sreod*, nor a destiny on the earthly world,
> Nor a son, nor chance, nor woman ;
> My *Drui* is Christ the son of God."

And yet these very things,—omens, such as the flight of birds and the *sreod* (sneezing), and "luck,"*—are still believed in by many people ; and in every newspaper one reads of servant-girls who have been entangled in the meshes of the dusky "soothsayers" that still foretell events by the aid of "the host of heaven." We have seen† that, in the first century of the Christian era, the swarthy, curly-haired, and painted Silurians were described as a people who "worshipped the gods, and both men and women professed a knowledge of the future ;" and that the Druidesses of the Isle of Sena, off the French coast, "had power over the winds, which they were in the practice of selling to credulous mariners." And although "these unfortunate damsels fell at last victims to the sanguinary system of persecution to which the votaries of bardism were everywhere subjected" (after Christianity, so-called, had become paramount), yet the crusade against "witchcraft" did not begin or end with them. Scott has told us how—only last century—a Druidess in the Orkneys earned a livelihood by exactly the same means as those earlier

---

* One obtains several glimpses of those heathen "Magi" in the second volume of "Celtic Scotland" (Chapter III.) ; out of which these brief extracts are taken. In that chapter, the identity of *Druid* with *Magus* (i.e. *wizard*) is clearly shown : an identity already indicated in these pages. Such omens as the flight of birds, and sneezing, are still believed in, to some extent, by the uneducated portions of the community : the latter, notably, in Ireland ; and the former in Scotland, where the signification of "the flight of birds" (more especially, of crows) is expressed in a popular rhyme—

> *One's joy :*
> *Two's grief :*
> *Three's a marriage :*
> *Four's death.*

† Book I., Chapter III., *ante.*

sisters of hers in the Isle of Sena. And James the First
(of Great Britain)—in whose reign a "cavalier"* became
equivalent to a "thief"—waged a most bitter war against
"sorcerers," whom he classed with these same *cavaliers* or
sorners, and *bards* and *Egyptians*.

Between the Druidess of the first century, who prognosti-
cated by the aid of the planets (on the understanding that
she was to receive payment for her divination), and the
Druidess of the present day, who foretells by the same aids
and on a like basis, there is a great distance of time. But a
racial connection is quite visible between them. The former
were of the swarthy, curly-haired, and painted race that is
known as Silurian. The latter belong to a swarthy, *ci-devant*
painted people—one division of which is described as "curly-
haired." And, although the space that intervenes between
these is very great, it can no doubt be filled up. The Druids
of the North-British kinglets, who figured in the Columban
episodes, belong to the sixth century. Those Druidesses
of the Isle of Sena are said to have been burned at the stake
by "Conan, Duke of Bretagne;" whose era was, apparently,
mediæval. And Mr. Borrow tells us that a celebrated Welsh
bard, Dafydd ab Gwilym, was married by a Druid priest of,
probably, his own race; the time being the fourteenth
century. We are informed that the poet was married "beneath the greenwood tree by one Madawg Benfras, a bard
and a great friend of Ab Gwilym. The joining of people's
hands by bards (continues Mr. Borrow), which was probably
a relic of Druidism, had long been practised in Wales, and
marriages of this kind were generally considered valid, and
seldom set aside."†

This incident brings into view one of the surest tests of the
longevity of Druidism. The marriage ceremonial is one of
those things that bring out the innate conservatism of one's
nature, where that is found in any appreciable degree.
People, as a rule, prefer to be married after the same fashion
as their forefathers. Now, the above paragraph has told us
that "the joining of people's hands by bards" "had long been
practised in Wales" at the date of Ab Gwilym's marriage

---

* Or rather, the "cavalier who ventured life for gain."

† "Wild Wales," Vol. III. Chapter XVIII.

—some time in the fourteenth century. And *the* bards of Wales (not to speak of the bardic caste in general) are the "gypsies" of Wales.* That the authority of such gypsy-priests has survived into this century may be seen in the references already made to the priest of Coldstream, "Patie Moodie," who performed the ceremony of marriage in the case of the late David Blythe, and perhaps also in his sister's; as well as in many other instances,† among the neighbouring peasantry. The preference shown by the southern Scotch and Borderers for such a mode of marrying, is further seen in the reference made by the Galloway writer to a caste of priests known in that district (and about the same period as Patie Moodie), as "auld boggies." "People are said to be married in an *owre boggie* manner, or to have an *owre boggie wedding* when they do not go through the regular forms prescribed by the national kirk. . . . Those who plot in secret are called *auld boggie fowk;* and displaced priests, who used to bind people contrary to the canon laws, . . . were designated *auld boggies.*"‡ And, again, we are told that—"In the upper part of Eskdale, at the confluence of the White and Black Esk, was held an annual fair, where multitudes of each sex repaired. The unmarried looked out for mates, made their engagements by joining hands, or by *hand-fisting*, went off in pairs, cohabited till the next annual return of the fair, appeared there again, and then were at liberty to declare their approbation or dislike of each other. If each party continued constant the *hand-fisting* was renewed for life ; but if either party dissented, the engagement

---

* "The Eisteddfods of Wales have witnessed the triumphs of gipsy harpists ; and hundreds have been charmed by the concerts of the Roberts family, not knowing they were hearing a gipsy band." (*Encyc. Brit.* 9th edition, art. "Gipsies.")

† "A report, however, had only that afternoon reached the ringleaders, to the effect that Jock Telfer, a young tailor, had on the previous evening made a run-away marriage at Coldstream Bridge—a refuge for lovers which was only less famous than Gretna Green." (*Fastern's E'en in Scotland Forty Years Ago ;* a sketch of local manners in the *Merse* [once the *marsh*-lands] of Berwickshire, in the early part of the present century.)

‡ *Scottish Gallovidian Encyclopedia,* p. 369. Mactaggart adds (somewhat pro-vokingly)—"There was an ancient song, I believe, of the name of the *Owre Boggie* burned at Edinburgh in the turbulent times ; this song is lost, so think the antiquaries."

was void, and both were at full liberty to make a new choice."*

Such priests as Mactaggart's "auld boggies" were likely akin to the *patricoes* or *patter-coves* of Grose : who are described by him as "strolling priests that marry people under a hedge without gospel or common prayer book." And Grose's priests belong to "the canting crew," or gypsydom. The more sedentary "Patie Moodie," of Coldstream Bridge, might have been accounted less distinctly a "gypsy," had it not been for the fact that he officiated at the wedding of the late Faw chief, David Blythe ; whose sister, Esther, was also "tied" at the same place, whether by the same "Druid" or not. This man Moodie seems to resemble closely such a priest as the fourteenth-century Madawg Benfras of Wales, who is remembered as having "tied" the celebrated minstrel Ab Gwilym to his spouse. The *patricoes*, again, may have gone through a ceremony more like that detailed by Mr. Simson, in his *History*. While the hand-fasting (or hand-*fisting*) custom, referred to above, appears to have been independent of any priesthood ; and to be very much like the marriage ceremony of Mr. Borrow's favourite tribes, the Smiths and their connections. When Ursula is married to Lancelot Lovel, the pair simply "take each other's words" (which is really the kernel of all marriage ceremonies).

These marriages, it must be remembered, were quite serious compacts ; and people so united were united almost indissolubly. Ursula, in "The Romany Rye," regards the usual Christian form as something not to be spoken of in the same breath with that act of "taking each other's words" which she and her tribe regarded as constituting the most sacred union. And Mr. Simson tells us of a Fifeshire gypsy, Thomas Ogilvie, who viewed such ceremonies in much the same light. "On one occasion, when a couple of respectable individuals were married, in the usual Scottish Presbyterian manner, at Elie in Fife, Ogilvie, gipsy-like, laughed at such a wedding ceremony, as being, in his estimation, no way binding on the parties. He at the same time observed that, if they would come to him, he would marry them in the Tinkler manner,

---

* Jenkinson's "Guide to Carlisle, &c." The statement is quoted from "Hutchinson."

which would make it a difficult matter to separate them again."

" The joining of people's hands by bards . . . . . had long been practised in Wales [prior to the fourteenth century], and marriages of this kind were generally considered valid, and seldom set aside." And although the example cited, Ab Gwilym's, happened to be one of those exceptions to the rule, it is probable that the officiating bard, and others of that race never admitted the validity of the divorce. It is important to notice that such marriages were evidently regarded as valid by *all* fourteenth-century Welshmen ; not only by those of earlier stock, but by the later Norman and Dutch colonists who, presumably, observed different rites. And this recognition of the validity of "gypsy" marriages, even by non-gypsies, has continued down to the present time—if the Border marriages should be found to be based upon gypsyism. It appears that people are even yet married at Gretna, and that there were—in 1875—"half-a-dozen people who had acted the part of priests" in that particular locality ; of whom one "seems to have married more than all the rest put together." This man's father and grandfather had occupied the same position ; which would lead one to inquire into their ancestry. It would also be interesting to know what *kind* of people availed themselves of this ancient custom, so recently as 1875.*

Not only have ceremonies of this nature "been long practised in Wales," and on the Borders, and in Galloway, but they have also been common in other parts of Great Britain, and are probably still existent. Grose tells us of those

* The statements regarding Gretna are made in Mr. Jenkinson's " Guide to Carlisle."

There can be no doubt that Gretna, like Coldstream and Lamberton Toll, was often used by run-away lovers from the south, merely because it was north of the Borders, and because such marriages were recognized by Scotch—though not by English law. But this does not explain why the peasantry of *The Merse*, which is *not* in England, travelled to Coldstream Bridge, in order to get " tied " by Patie Moodie—in place of their parish minister ; or why the Faws of Yetholm did the same thing. The real explanation seems to lie in the fact that these places were all situated on the Border line ; and that, *therefore*, they represent the last vestiges of the religion of that Border Kingdom, regarding whose inhabitants it was said : —" They are called *moss-troopers*, because dwelling in the mosses, and riding in troops together. They dwell in the bounds, or meeting, of the two kingdoms, but obey the laws of neither."

"strolling priests that marry people under a hedge [or "beneath the greenwood tree," as Borrow more poetically puts it]
without gospel or common prayer book"; but he also tells
us that, in the army—or, in certain regiments of the army—
a marriage ritual of a like nature was in vogue. Now, the
army has its archæology, like any other society of old standing; and those of its regiments that have anything of a
pedigree are the lineal representatives of certain *races ;* *
some of whose customs probably still cling to the regiments
or class of regiments that have succeeded them. So that when
Grose informs us that in the army (or a portion of it) a ceremony, of which the chief feature was "leaping over the
sword," † was held to constitute an irrefragable marriage
between the two chief parties, he points to what in all likelihood was a *tribal* rite. It is most probably the same ceremony that in less war-like portions of the community, took
the form of " jumping over a broom-stick," or a pair of
tongs ;‡ and in all these cases it was beyond doubt a ceremony of real and lasting importance, although the *meaning*
of this now-eccentric performance has very likely been lost.

These are some of the many obsolete, or almost obsolete,
marriage ceremonies that belonged to various British tribes.
Scott tells us of another when he states that "the troth-
plighting of the lower classes" in Orkney was observed by
"joining hands through a circular hole in a sacrificial stone,
which lies in the Orcadian Stonehenge, called the Circle of
Stennis;" and as this ceremony was "considered as peculiarly binding," it was probably never followed by another,
homologating it. Indeed, Norna of Fitful-head is made to

* This is more particularly pointed out in the Note appended to this chapter.

† There is a reference to this ceremony in a Scotch ballad of the eighteenth
century—or earlier. The heroine of the ballad sketches the wedding scene in
these words (the bridegroom being " a gentleman dragoon ") :—

> " He led me to his quarter house,
>   Where we exchanged a word, laddie,
> We had no use for black gowns there,
>   We *married o'er the sword*, laddie."

This ballad—known as " No Dominies for me, Laddie "—is given by Mr. W.
H. Logan, in his " Pedlar's Pack of Ballads and Songs " (Edin. 1869).

‡ This employment of the tongs (and perhaps also of the sword and the
broomstick) is popularly identified with "Tinkler" marriages in Scotland.

assert that this form (exemplified in her own case) constituted
a wedding. And the original of Norna having been the
Druidess who lived only a few miles from "the Orcadian
Stonehenge," and from whom Scott gained the story of "The
Pirate," she may have informed her illustrious visitor
that her own wedding ceremony had been conducted
in such a way. This ancient Druidess, who "sold winds"
to sailors, like her mediæval prototypes in the Isle of
Sena, or like her contemporaries, the "witches" of Lapland,
is thus pictured by Sir Walter Scott :—" She herself was, as
she told us, nearly one hundred years old, withered and dried
up like a mummy. A clay-coloured kerchief, folded round
her head, corresponded in colour to her corpse-like complexion. Two light-blue eyes that gleamed with a lustre like
that of insanity, an utterance of astonishing rapidity, a nose
and chin that almost met together, and a ghastly expression
of cunning, gave her the effect of Hecate."* If the colour of
this woman's eyes was not the opaque black of the Romany
"witch," she was at least as much a "gypsy," in this particular, as the late Esther Blythe ; whose skin was also no darker
than that of this "clay-coloured" Druidess, and whose features, moreover, bore less resemblance to the " Meg Merrilies"
type than those of this Northern sibyl.

Perhaps the marriage tie was never looser than among
those tribes who had one name for "woman" and "mare,"
and who led their wives—with a halter round their necks—
to Smithfield, where they sold them like cattle. The
memory of this period is still preserved in every-day English
by the twofold meaning of the word "jade" ; and that this
nomenclature also survives among the tory classes is illustrated by two of Mr. Groome's gypsies (" In Gipsy Tents ; "
pp. 175 and 180). The place that is most celebrated as a
wife-market, Smithfield, is one of those districts which were
the special abode of "Tinkers, called also Prigs," in the
sixteenth-century (and before and after)†; and it is likely
among such people that this custom is still kept up. For it

---

* See Note G. appended to " The Pirate."

† The Smithfield of two or three centuries ago is spoken of as "Smithfield,
with its world of cut-purses, drolls, and 'motions';" which may be rendered
"its world of ' prigs,' mountebanks, and merry-go-round men ; " and, these, we
have seen, are all, to some extent, of "gypsy" blood.

is not quite obsolete. Not that the halter, or a particular locality, seems now necessary; but the custom of selling wives is still occasionally recorded in our newspapers. And it is likely that there are many other cases which are not so recorded. The newspapers do not, perhaps, specify that the wife-buyers and wife-sellers are "gypsies;" but it is probable they are so. The practice of wife-beating is one that "Ursula," in "The Romany Rye," holds up as a "gypsy" custom; and she maintains that a man has— according to the ideas of her people—a perfect right to maltreat his wife, and that it is her duty to submit humbly to such maltreatment. From which one may infer that, in those districts where wife-beating is a common practice, and recognized as a marital right, the natives are, in a great measure, of gypsy blood. And it is not unlikely that the men who buy and sell their wives are also of the same lineage. It is often by chance that the newspapers record the "gypsy" blood of the perpetrator of actions of this kind. A recent incident that came under the notice of the present writer—the arrest of a young Aberdeenshire gypsy for bigamy (which was *no* crime to one of his ideas)—was only chronicled in *some* of the journals that took notice of it as the arrest of a "gypsy." And the omission of this particular made a vast difference in the character of the act. Had the bigamist been a man professing Christianity, and acknowledging unreservedly the laws of the United Kingdom, he would have been a "criminal." But if he belonged to such a clan as Marshall's, of Galloway; and since his attitude towards the laws of Modern-Britain was the attitude of the "tory"; then his act was perfectly justifiable in the eyes of those of his own caste.

Those several marriage customs * are so diverse in character that it is evident their origins are various. Between those

---

* It is probable there were many others. One of which, it has been already suggested, is still visible in the make-believe marriage that Scotch children are familiar with; referred to in Dr. Jamieson's *Dictionary* under the name "Merry-metanzie," and also referred to in these pages as "Jing-ga-ring"; both of which words, or combinations of words, occur in the chanted rhyme that accompanies the dance.

(The description given by Dr. Jamieson of this dance is very incomplete; and he confuses it with others of a like nature.)

of Borrow's "Romany," and the "Tinklers" of Simson, the difference is great. Those Lovels and Smiths (Petulengres) "take each other's words," without any priestly interposition ; and the union is thenceforth regarded by each as inviolable. Moreover, such "gypsies" are monogamists ; and, according to Borrow, the women certainly—and the men almost as certainly—evince the purest fidelity to their vows. With such "gypsies" as Marshall of Galloway, or some of the Fife-shire tribes, or those whom Grose describes, the case is different ; and among these polygamy, or an intercourse vaguer still, is the rule. And in these latter instances the presence of a priest seems necessary, both in marriage and in divorce ; although the husband himself could sometimes fill that office—when he happened to be of a particular caste.* Again, while some have been satisfied with "the greenwood tree" as a temple, others have required a sacred circle, such as the stones of Stennis. Ursula Lovel regards "a church" with contempt ; but the moss-troopers of the Borders thought differently. "It is, or rather was, the custom of the tribes on the Borders of England and Scotland to attribute success to those journeys which are commenced by passing through the parish church ; and they usually try to obtain permission from the beadle to do so when the church is empty, for the performance of divine service is not con-sidered as essential to the omen." From which latter feature, Sir Walter Scott (who makes the foregoing state-ment in a note to "Quentin Durward") infers that these "tory" Borderers are "totally devoid of any effectual sense of religion ;" although there are better grounds for arriving at the opposite conclusion, since such a form would never be gone through by people who did *not* regard a church with reverence. That they should prefer to make this procession when the building was not occupied by people of a different religion from their own was most natural and consistent.

* The Scotch word "dominie "—applied to teachers of religion as well as of secular knowledge, and signifying (radically) "a lord "—seems a survival of the rule of a Druidical or Brahminical caste. And the most recent Scottish examples of such a caste are found among Mr. Simson's eighteenth-century gypsy chiefs and chieftainesses. For many of these were not only priests and teachers—as the civilized "Dominies " were—but they were also secular rulers and hereditary nobles.

Of course, it may be doubted whether such a church as that through which the "tories" of Sir Walter Scott's youth were accustomed to pass, before starting upon an expedition, was such a "church" as that in which their own forefathers worshipped. This may be doubted: though the lineage assigned by Elder to the Scotch bishops of three hundred and forty years ago—the lineage of the "strolling bards" whom they enrolled into their priesthood—does not tend to dispel such doubts. Whether such churches were Christian or Heathen is a question that may be waived at present. But the earliest temples through which a "gypsy" tribe would pass, on the eve of battle or foray, was pretty surely of the same kind as that in which the Druidess, Norna, was supposed to have plighted her troth; namely, a sacred circle. The very word *circle* is assumed by some to be the progenitor of the word *church* (thus, *church, chirch, circ* or *kirk, cirque*): and a similar origin was assigned to the word *llan* or *lawn*, on a previous page. Such a church the "faw kirk" of the "painted blackamoors" of the Forth marshes most probably was. And such a "church" was that in the marshes of Cavan, in Ireland, in the centre of which, surrounded by his twelve subordinate idols, stood the golden figure of the *Crom Cruach*, who "was the God of all the people which possessed Erin till the coming of Padric." It was a church of this kind that those High-landers had in view when they asked each other, of a Sunday, "Are you going to *the stones?*" Or rather, it was such a church that was intended *when the phrase originated.* For, if the origin assigned to the word *chirch*, or *kirk*, be correct, then those Highlanders who said, in Gaelic, "are you going to *the stones?*"—within recent times—are as little to be identified with the earliest worshippers among such "stones" as are those people who say "Are you going to *church?*" Since the two words (granting the correctness of the etymology) originally represented the same thing. And, as those stone circles were most probably used for that worship of the heavenly host, of which there are many evidences; and as one day was specially set apart for the worship of the sun; it would appear that the mere act of "going to church on Sunday" is a practice which is not distinctive of Christianity.

Indeed, the earlier apostles of Christianity in Western Europe avowedly adopted many of the pre-existing heathen customs; and other such customs, introduced at later dates by later pagan invaders, have not yet lost hold of the British people. It has just been noticed that various marriage ceremonies, that are quite unconnected with Christianity, have been adhered to—in preference to others—by a large number of almost-modern Britons. And, even yet, it has never been satisfactorily explained why certain seasons are "lucky" or "unlucky" for the celebration of this rite. The month of May is still studiously avoided, and the eve of the New Year as carefully selected, in many districts of the country. Two hundred years ago Mr. Andrew Symson, the minister of the parish of Kirkinner, in Wigtownshire, noticed this preference for particular days and seasons among the peasantry of that district. "Their marriages (he says*) are commonly celebrated only on Tuesday or Thursdays. I myself have married neer 450 of the inhabitants of this countrey; all of which, except seaven, were married upon a Tuesday or Thursday. And it is look'd upon as a strange thing to see a marriage upon any other days; yea, and for the most part also, their marriages are all celebrated *crescente luna.*" That these observances were founded upon lunar-worship, and the worship of Tyr and Thor, is most obvious. Similarly, the appearance at certain seasons of such things as the once-sacred plants of mistletoe and holly, and of emblems such as "Easter eggs" and "hot cross buns," argue a like origin. And the spring moon regulates the movable feasts of large sections of the Christian community.

The wandering *patricoes*, or hedge-priests, described by Grose are included by him as part of "the canting crew,"† or gypsydom. If gypsies of the orthodox complexion, those men were not only "mendicant friars" but they were also "*black* friars." If the dice-players and strolling minstrels who received "inferior benefices" from those Scotch bishops who drew their own descent from the Early-Scots, or Egyp-

---

* In his "Description of Galloway."

† Grose plainly regards "the canting crew" and "gypsies" as one. And the author of "The Yetholm History of the Gypsies" states (at p. 141) that "the Gypsies at Yetholm do not use the word Romany as the name of their language, but they call it simply The Cant." In Gaelic, *cainnt* means "speech"; and this form of speech is *dubh-chainnt*, "black speech."

tians,—if those strollers belonged to the " idle people calling themselves Egyptians " (as the statutes enacted against them prove pretty clearly), then those Scotch monks of the six-teenth century were " black friars," *by complexion.* And the higher prelates who—for no visible reason, unless that of kinship,—befriended them so materially (claiming *themselves* a far-back descent from " Egyptians ") ; those higher prelates were most likely more allied to them by the ties of blood than to Henry the Eighth or " the most part of the commons of Scotland " north of " the water of Forth " (who if Elder's letter speaks truth, were quite in sympathy with the English king, and violently antagonistic to this priestly caste). Thus, if this were the case, the term " black prelacy " conveyed a certain racial meaning ; although it is not to be supposed that the whole of this order consisted—at that period—of one unvaried type. How far the name of " black friar " applied to the complexions, rather than the dress, of the divisions so designated, may be questioned. Yet it is worthy of note that the community which received, as a kind of friendly prisoner, the captured chief of the outlawed Black Douglases, in the latter part of the fifteenth century,[*]—this community, the brotherhood of Lindores, in Fife, was a com-munity of " black monks." (Knox, writing seventy-one years after the death of the captive gypsy noble, refers to his asylum as " the abbey of Lindores, a place of black monkes.")

The dark-skinned, curly-haired Silurians who " worshipped the gods," who " professed a knowledge of the future," who wore " black cloaks " and " tunics reaching to the feet," and who " walked with staves," " leading for the most part a

---

[*] After the Black Douglases had been dispossessed of their lands, and had become outlaws and " gypsies," the last of their earls (formally recognized as such by the Stewart party)—who had not been present at the crowning defeat of Langholm—continued to haunt the fastnesses of the Border country for thirty years. In 1484, with a following of five hundred moss-troopers, he (who used to traverse the country with two thousand followers, holding a "court" of his own, and creating nobles of his own) advanced as far as Lochmaben ; but the king's-men of the neighbourhood having assembled to bar his progress, he was defeated by them at Birrenswark, in Dumfriesshire. " The King (James the Third) con-tented himself with confining him to monastic seclusion in the abbey of Lindores in Fife, while the earl muttered ' He who may no better be, must be a monk.' " (Anderson's " Scottish Nation," Vol. II., pp. 44-45.)

wandering life," were very distinctly "black monks" (as well as "mendicant friars") both by dress and by complexion. And the witches of Anglesey, who encouraged their kinsmen to resist the attack of Suetonius and his soldiers, were not only "arrayed in black garments," but they were also most probably of the same dusky hue. It is quite conceivable that such orders as these might have been prolonged, century after century, receiving into their ranks men and women of a wholly different complexion, until such a title as that of "black friar" became applicable chiefly, or solely, to the garment. This is conceivable. And at the present day the black garments of the druidical orders are worn quite ir- respective of lineage, by the modern representatives of those orders, of whom, however, a very large proportion are—on Professor Huxley's hypothesis—the descendants of brown- skinned people.* But it does not appear, on the one hand, that those friars of the sixteenth and earlier centuries, who were known as "black friars," were the *only* priests who wore a black dress ; and, on the other hand, there seems much reason for believing that certain quasi-religious bodies, at these periods, were composed chiefly, or altogether, of dark- skinned men. The latest "mendicant friars" visible to us moderns are those people known as patricoes, or gypsy- priests. Whether they wore a certain distinguishing dress is not stated by those who write about them ; but it is known that they "led for the most part a wandering life," like their early forerunners in these islands ;—and that (like them) they "walked with staves" is shewn by the statement that "all the gypsies, male as well as female, who performed cere- monies for their tribe, carried long staffs."† And these people were mainly, or altogether, of the dark-skinned races. And whether as unrecognized *patricoes*, or as the holders of "inferior benefices" in sixteenth-century Scotland, they were at once "mendicant friars" and "black friars," by custom

---

* There is no reason—except that of inherited custom—why black should be regarded as peculiarly appropriate to clergymen, doctors, lawyers, and other representatives of the druidical system : a system which included "doctors" (teachers) of many branches of knowledge. The first of these just named is the division that, in modern days, adheres most strictly to this colour ; although the others do so in a slight degree.

† Simson's *History*, p. 272 (note.)

and blood. And with such Egyptians the Scotch bishops of that period identified themselves, both by bestowing favours upon them, and by asserting for themselves a like lineage.

While it is probable that those prelates—of so late a day —were of hybrid ancestry; and, therefore, only partially related to their wards, the "strolling-minstrels and dice-players" (whose habits, be it remembered, were much the same as their own *) ; yet it is evident that, outwardly, they did not differ from the earlier heathen priesthoods that each, in a measure, represented. If those Scotch bishops and abbesses were attired in black garments, so were the Druids and Druidesses of Anglesey and Brittany. If they wore white surplices, they did not differ, in that respect, from the " Magi " who opposed St. Patrick in his Irish mission.† Or, if the *rochet* formed any part of their attire, it only served to connect them with those Egyptian Druidesses who visited Paris in 1427. If these various articles constituted their apparel, they did not serve to dissociate them from heathenism. If they shaved their heads, or practised certain ceremonies referred to in a previous chapter, these forms did not of themselves help to identify them with Christianity ; since they were also the property of non-Christian religions. And, as their own lives were recklessly non-Christian, they seem to have possessed few claims to be regarded as the teachers of Christianity.

That the influence of such gypsy-priests was visibly stamped upon at least one British church, seems to be proved by a fact recently pointed out by Mr. Joseph Lucas,‡ in these words :—

It is probable that Walter Simson's remarks upon divorce ceremonies

---

* The references made in the first chapter of McCrie's " Life of John Knox " disclose the fact that those orders against whom men like Knox were violently opposed were largely composed of men whose tastes and ideas were almost entirely those of " gypsies." One might think that the rancorous spirit of par-tizanship might have induced the writer of that book to magnify the failings of those bishops into vices of the first magnitude. But his statements are all well founded. And although these do not hint at nomadism among the higher ecclesiastics, they show that their lives were *openly* at variance with all that is supposed, in the present day, to characterize the ideal teacher of the Christian religion : and that many of their habits and ideas were shared by " gypsies."

† Skene's " Celtic Scotland," Vol. II. p. 112.

‡ " Yetholm History of the Gypsies," p. 138.

(*Hist. of Gypsies*, pp. 273–5) explain the following mysterious discovery recorded in the *Gentleman's Magazine*, 1777, p. 416, in a letter signed " T.M." : " A workman employed in repairing and whitewashing the church of Frecknam, in the county of Suffolk, in the spring of 1776, struck down with his hammer a piece of alabaster—it was fixed in the inside of the church, in the wall near the north door of the nave. It appeared then a plain stone about fifteen inches long and twelve broad ; but, on its falling down, the other side was discovered to be carved in relievo and painted. The carving represents a bishop or some mitred personage, *in pontificalibus*, holding in his left hand the whole leg and haunch of a horse recently torn off, and striking the hoof with a hammer which he holds in his right hand. Near him is the horse in a rack, standing on three legs, having the shoulder whence the other was torn off bloody. He is held by a person with a round cap on, not unlike a Scotch bonnet. The legs of this person appear under the horse having on long picked shoes. In the background there is a furnace, and round it in various parts horse shoes and other implements belonging to a smith." . . . . " The carving is now in the possession of the rector of Frecknam. It seems worthy the attention of our antiquary readers." Opposite p. 416 is a plate illustrating the carving.

The whole account of the ceremony in Simson is too long to quote, but one or two sentences will suffice :—" When the parties can no longer live together as husband and wife, . . . a horse without blemish, and in no manner of way lame, is led forth to the spot for performing the ceremony of divorce . . . . The gypsies present cast lots for the individual who is to sacrifice the animal, and whom they call the priest for the time. . . . . The individuals who catch the horse bring it before the priest, ... the priest takes a large knife and thrusts it into the heart of the horse, and its blood is allowed to flow upon the ground till life is extinct."

Although the sculptured ceremony does not coincide with that observed in Mr. Walter Simson's days, there can be little doubt that the two are cognate. And there can be no doubt that the tearing off of a horse's leg forms no part of the duty of a teacher of Christianity ; although it, or a kindred custom, was of great significance in the eyes of gypsies. Thus this " mitred personage," clad " in full pontificals," was plainly an Egyptian priest, whether or not he claimed for himself the same lineage as those Scotch bishops of the sixteenth century who " derived themselves from a certain lady, named Scota, which (as they alleged) came out of Egypt." And if this was the kind of man who undertook " the cure of souls " in a Norfolk parish " six hundred years ago," it is no wonder that he regarded the keeping alight of the sacred fire above the altar as a most important and serious duty.

Mr. Leland, in his " English Gipsies " (pp. 129-130), makes
the following statements :—" The gipsy eats every and anything except horse-flesh. Among themselves, while talking
Romany, they will boast of having eaten *mullo baulors*, or pigs
that have died a natural death, and *hotchewitchi*, or hedgehog,
as did the belle of a gipsy party to me at Walton-on-Thames
in the summer of 1872. They can give no reason whatever
for this inconsistent abstinence. But Mr. Simson in his ' His-
toy of the Gipsies' has adduced a mass of curious facts, indicating a special superstitious regard for the horse among the
Romany in Scotland, and identifying it with certain customs
in India. It would be a curious matter of research could we
learn whether the missionaries of the Middle Ages, who
made abstinence from horse-flesh a point of salvation (when
preaching in Germany and in Scandinavia) derived their
superstition, in common with the gypsies, from India."

There may be many different opinions, at the present day,
with regard to the precise meaning and teachings of Christianity ; but it must be universally acknowledged that those
" missionaries of the Middle Ages, who made abstinence from
horse-flesh a point of salvation," were not apostles of Christianity. Or if so, then only in a partial degree. It is quite
likely that, although their nineteenth-century representatives
" can give no reason whatever " for this observance, those
mediæval missionaries were actuated by some now-forgotten
belief in preaching this peculiar abstinence : but that belief
has no place among the doctrines of Christianity. Whatever
else they may have taught the people of Germany and Scandinavia, those " missionaries of the Middle Ages "—viewed
in this particular aspect—were distinctly the prototypes of
Mr. Simson's eighteenth-century gypsy-priests, and also of
Mr. Leland's " English gypsies " of the present day. That
they were the prototypes of those "dice-players and strolling
bards " who were beneficed clergymen in sixteenth-century
Scotland is almost certain : that they were also the prototypes of the higher orders of that Scottish hierarchy—whose
members "derived themselves " from Scota, the daughter of
a Pharaoh, and who were the avowed guardians of strolling
Egyptian dice-players—is also, in some degree, probable.
And it is also probable that all of these castes—Scandi-

navian priest, sixteenth-century stroller or "beneficed clergy-man," Pharaoh-descended bishop, strolling-priest of eigh-teenth-century Scotland, and "English gypsy" of the nine-teenth-century—are all connected by a kindred belief, and perhaps by kindred blood, with the "mitred personage, *in pontificalibus*," sculptured on the walls of the church at Frecknam, Suffolk.

It was not only in pre-Reformation Scotland that the pro-fessed teachers of Christianity exhibited a strong if not prevailing tint of heathenism (which in the diction of the Netherlands, is "gypsyism"). We have noticed that in six-teenth-century Scotland, "inferior benefices were . . . . . bestowed on the illiterate and unworthy minions of courtiers [who were then semi-nomades], on dice-players, strolling bards, and the bastards of bishops." Of these, one division, clearly,* and the others less clearly, were the people known in Scotland as *Sorners, Cairds, Jockeys, Tinklers,* or *Gypsies.* And on the Continent a similar state of things is indicated to us. "In the rural districts [of Germany], says Wimphe-ling, the persons selected for preachers were miserable creatures, who had been previously raised from beggary, cast-off cooks, musicians, huntsmen, grooms, and still worse." " A profane spirit had invaded religion, and the most sacred seasons of the Church . . . . were dishonoured by buffoonery and mere heathen blasphemies. The 'Easter Drolleries' held an important place in the acts of the Church. As the festival of the resurrection required to be celebrated with joy, everything that could excite the laughter of the hearers was sought out, and thrust into sermons. One preacher imitated the note of a cuckoo, while another hissed like a goose. One dragged forward to the altar a layman in a cassock ; a second told the most indecent stories ; a third related the adventures of the Apostle Peter, among others, how, in a tavern, he cheated the host by not paying his score. . . . . The Churches were thus turned into stages, and the priests into mountebanks." " The rural districts became the theatre of numerous excesses. The places where priests resided were often the abodes of dissoluteness. Corneille Adrian at Bruges, and Abbot Trinkler at Cappel, imitated

---

* Dr. Jamieson's definition of " a bard " would of itself prove this.

the manners of the East, and had their harems. Priests associating with low company frequented taverns and played at dice, crowning their orgies with quarrels and blasphemy. . . . . . In several places, each priest was liable to the bishop in a certain tax for the female he kept, and for every child she bore him. One day, a German bishop, who was attending a great festival, openly declared that, in a single year, the number of priests who had been brought before him for this purpose amounted to eleven thousand. This account is given by Erasmus."*

These extracts most assuredly do not describe a society of Christian apostles : and it is easy to understand how one of those priests, " Thomas Linacer, a learned and celebrated ecclesiastic," who " had never read the New Testament" until the last year of his life, should have affirmed, on that occasion, " Either this is not the gospel, or we are not Christians." There seems to have been little or nothing in the doctrine they taught, and certainly nothing in their own way of living, to connect them with the earliest teachers of Christianity. But they showed, in many ways, their connection with strolling minstrels, mountebanks, and " the idle people calling themselves Egyptians."

Monumental tablets in various Continental churches— erected " at Steinbach in 1445, 'to the high-born lord, Lord Panuel, Duke in Little Egypt, and Lord of Hirschhorn in the same land '; at Bautma in 1453, 'to the noble Earl Peter of Kleinschild,' [and 'of Lesser Egypt']; and at Pforzheim in 1498 'to the high-born Lord Johann, Earl of Little Egypt '"† —all attest to the authoritative position of " Egyptians " in the religious as well as the social world of fifteenth-century Europe ; and a tombstone in the churchyard of Weissenborn, Saxony, in memory of " Dame Maria Sybilla Rosenberg, Gipsy, and wife of the honourable and valiant Wolfgang Rosenberg, Cornet in the Electoral and Brandenburg army," shows that this gypsy supremacy survived in Middle Europe even in the seventeenth century. Of a similar nature was

* D'Aubigné's *History of the Reformation* (Beveridge's Translation), Chapter III. of Book I. Vol. I.

† It seems quite clear that these "Little Egypts"—like those of Scotland— were European ; although the names preserved the memory of an ancient connection with Egypt Proper.

the interment of a gypsy noble in the abbey of Malmesbury, in the year 1657 ; and there are various other records of the same kind in British history, of which Mr. Groome gives many specimens, (in the fifth chapter of " In Gipsy Tents ").

It is true that some of these inscriptions—German and British—point to the probable Christianity of the gypsies they commemorate. And, when Wolfgang Rosenberg gave a silver flagon to Weissenborn church ; or, in the tradition that "a gypsy king" had "aided in repair of East Winch church," Norfolk ; in such cases one would, at first, assume the Christianity of those "heathens " (as the Dutch call them). But then—what is Christianity, and what Heathenism ? Under which heading are we to place those " missionaries of the Middle Ages who made abstinence from horse-flesh a point of salvation ?" And was the " mitred personage " on the walls of Frecknam Church a Christian ? And " Corneille Adrian at Bruges, and Abbot Trinkler at Cappel," were these Christians, like Paul and Peter, or heathens like those polyga- mous gypsy-priests described by Simson ? When churches were the scene of " Easter Drolleries " and general buffoonery ; when the officiating priests were drawn from the gypsy castes ; when such men proved their origin by their way of living and of preaching ; were such churches and churchmen Christian or Pagan ? A gypsy noble might well repair one of these temples, or give a silver flagon to another, without laying himself open to the charge of being called a Chris- tian.

It may be that many pre-Reformation ideas are even yet existent among the gypsy castes. Mr. C. G. Leland states that "they are all familiar with " one, at any rate, of those monkish legends—that which has made the owlet become known among them as "the baker's daughter."* That one or more monkish legends, of which the general British popu- lation knows nothing, should be preserved by the caste that is *the most closely connected* with those mediæval priests, is a most striking fact.

One other resemblance between these two sets of men may be pointed out. Grose talks of gypsies as "the canting crew ;" the Yetholm tribes are said to style their language

* "English Gipsies," p. 16.

The Cant; and a mongrel dialect often confounded with Romanes, is denominated "cant." Of course, this word signifies "speech": it does so, at any rate, in Gaelic, and it did so in Latin. But it seems to have been associated with a particular *kind* of speaking. The Latin *cantare* is said to mean—"to speak often of a thing; to praise; to rhyme; to chaunt; to celebrate by song; to sing of; to repeat an incantation; to call up or raise by spells or charms; to enchant; to bewitch." Now, this is the kind of speaking with which those "gypsies" of former days were invariably associated. "To bard" and "to flatter" were synonymous terms in Scotland: those Bards, or Gypsies, used to "celebrate by song" the deeds of their leaders in the most flattering terms. The connection between the *jongleur* and the *juggler*—or their absolute identity—has already been pointed out. And "witchcraft" and "gypsyism" go hand-in-hand. The same union is seen in the various meanings of the word *cantare*. "The canting crew" were always celebrated for their "spells or charms"; that portion of them specially known as "Borderers" were, at one time, never without a "book of spells," relating to "the black art of their forefathers." But, while *cantare* signifies "to speak," it more especially signifies a particular *way* of speaking. A way of speaking that is so closely allied to singing that *cantare* is often translated "to sing." This special form of singing or speaking is best known to us by our other form (in modern English) of *cantare*,—that is, the word *chaunt*.

No instance has come under my notice in which gypsies—known by that designation—have made use of this peculiar recitative utterance. But Mr. J. F. Campbell records that one of his Highland tale-tellers distinctly *intoned* the legend he was relating. And it may be asserted as a probability that is most likely to develop into a certainty, that this rhythmical measure was characteristic of the bardic, druidical, or "gypsy" castes. It seems to have, beyond a doubt, characterized those castes in Ireland. An eighteenth-century bard of Ireland, who is spoken of as "the last of that Order of Minstrels called *Tale-Tellers*," and who combined in his person more than of the one special qualities of his class—since he was Bard, Historian, and Genealogist—is spoken of in these words :—

"Poetry was the muse of whom he was most enamoured. This made him listen eagerly to the Irish songs and metrical tales which he heard sung and recited around the "crackling faggots' of his father and his neighbours. These, by frequent recitation, became strongly impressed on his memory. His mind being thus stored, and having no other avocation, he commenced a *Man of Talk* or a *Tale-Teller*. . . . . He was now employed in relating legendary tales, and reciting genealogies at rural wakes, or in the hospitable halls of country-squires. . . . . Endowed with a sweet voice and a good ear, his narrations were generally graced with the charms of melody. . . . . He did not, like the Tale-teller mentioned by Sir William Temple, chant his tales in an uninterrupted *even-tone ;* the monotony of his modulation was frequently broken by cadences introduced with taste at the close of each stanza. ' In rehearsing any of Ossian's poems, or any composition in verse (says Mr. Ousley) he chants them pretty much in the manner of our Cathedral-service.' "*

This man is represented as one of the last of that order of Irish Bards of whom it was said that their language differed so much from "the true Irish " that "scarce one in five hundred could either read, write, or understand it." In the reign of Queen Elizabeth those people were described as "idle men of lewd demeanour, called Rymors, Bards, and dice players, called Carroghs, who under pretence of their travail do bring privy intelligence between the malefactors inhabiting in these several shires [Cork, Limerick and Kerry] ;" and this same monarch, who enacted laws for their suppression in Ireland, also put down their fellow-minstrels in England and in Wales. That those itinerant minstrels were so suppressed *because* they belonged to "the idle people calling themselves Egyptians," has virtually been asserted already, and this assertion will be repeated more distinctly in another chapter. But, since this individual member of that class, who was regarded as a true representative of that bardic caste in the eighteenth century, was accustomed to chant his legendary stories "pretty much in the manner of our Cathedral-service," it is to be presumed that this was the common custom of his forerunners in office. That they formed, liter-

---

* Walker's *Historical Memoirs of the Irish Bards*, &c., Appendix, pp. 56–7.

ally, a "*canting* crew." Which is equivalent to saying "a gang of gypsies ; " according to Grose. And, indeed the term "canting crew," as applied to gypsies, seems singularly inappropriate—without this explanation.

A consideration, then, of the statements made in the present chapter renders it apparent that the boundary-line between what is called "Christianity" and what is called "Gypsyism" is very ill-defined : so badly defined, indeed, that it is very difficult to say where the one begins and the other ends. And if European gypsyism be assumed to denote European Heathenism (and the word "gypsy" has plainly been applied in a most general and inexact fashion), then the position of matters, stated roughly, seems to be this. Leaving out the comparatively small* number of "Christians" who ignore—or almost ignore—anything of a ceremonial or ritualistic nature, we find in the religious societies called "Christian" an immense number of practices and beliefs (the latter perhaps obsolete now) that are also claimed by "Heathens." Under this term "Heathen" may be included not only the non-Christian element in the byegone history of Europe, but also one or more non-Christian religions still existing. For example, it was noticed in a previous chapter, that much of the outward ceremonial of Buddhism resembles very closely, or is identical with, the ritual of the Christian churches. (Incense, chanting, and tonsured monks being among those things that Colonel Forbes Leslie indicates as common to Buddhism and Christianity.) But we are more concerned with European—and particularly British—Heathenism, as that has existed in the past. And it is among the people called "gypsies" that we find most resemblance to the "Christian" priests of pre-Reformation times. The only orders of mendicant priests

---

* By far the most important, numerically, of all the divisions of Christendom is that division known as the Roman Catholic ; which, in the tabular view before me (that given in *Chambers' Encyclopædia*, in the article "Religion"), is stated as numbering nearly twice as many as the division called Protestant. The first of these divisions is pre-eminently ritualistic ; and the bulk of the second is ritualistic also, in the same direction, though in varying degrees. The Greek Church, whose followers number something like three-fourths of the Protestant, is also eminently ritualistic ; its ritual, however, differing in many ways from that of the rest of Christendom.

distinctly visible to our modern eyes are those whom Mr. Simson describes under the name of "gypsies." Those men carry "pastoral staves;" they possess secular as well as religious power; like the Abbot Trinklers of the Continent, they openly practise polygamy; like the Father St. Clares of even post-Reformation date, they study the pseudo-science of divination by the stars; like the Scotch prelates of Henry the Eighth's day, they "allege" their descent from Egyptians; like the mitred pontiff in the Suffolk church, or like the mediæval missionaries of Scandinavia, they regard the horse with peculiar reverence, sacrificing it in their most impressive ceremonies, and abstaining from the use of it as an article of food (and this from no gastronomical fastidiousness, as the gypsiologists very clearly show); like the nominally-Christian actors in the "Easter Drolleries," those gypsies were "canting" minstrels and mountebanks; and either caste, for some mysterious reason, held it necessary to shave the head * after a peculiar fashion: in short, the resemblance between certain sections of the Christian priesthood, prior to the Reformation, and the gypsy-druids of later times, is so strong that one can apprehend, in some measure, why the writers of last century should have asserted that gypsyism in England began with the dissolution of the monasteries by Henry the Eighth. After which date the only visible "mendicant friars" were the "black friars" belonging to "the idle people calling themselves Egyptians;" with which Egyptians the Scotch prelates had also declared themselves to be identified. And it is the "Egyptians" of the present day who "are all familiar with" one, at least, of those monkish legends which we—the hybrid and modern British population—are only aware of through the medium of books.

Only some of the resemblances between British Heathenism and British Christianity have been enumerated above: but there are many others. It is enough, for the present purpose, to point out that such a resemblance, or identity, exists. And this must mean one of two things. Either those

* It has been seen that the prize-fighters of last century, and the mountebanks of that, or an earlier date, were accustomed to shave the head; while an act of Henry the Eighth's shows that it was, in his reign, a very common custom in Ireland. And prize-fighters and mountebanks belonged to the castes we style "gypsy;" while Ireland was originally the special home of the Egyptian-Scots.

observances were originally Christian, and have been adopted by non-Christian races—European and Asiatic—without the accompanying acceptation of the fundamental beliefs of Christianity ; or else—they have originated in a far older system of religion than that which is called Christian, although the teachers of Christianity have—whether voluntarily or not—accepted them as the outward habiliments of their faith. That the latter of these two assumptions is the more feasible seems to be asserted alike by history and by reason. In the book which is the mainstay of Christianity— that which relates the history and teachings of Christ—there is little or nothing laid down as to ceremonial. On the other hand, a good deal is known of the ceremonies of Pagan Europe and Pagan Asia : and many of these are now the property of Christianity. The apostles of Christianity in Early Britain *may* have practised all the ceremonies that are still observed by " ritualistic " Christians : but, at any rate, those same ceremonies were practised by the British " Magi," whom they came to convert. With this important difference. That, whereas those rites have, in many cases, no apparent connection with the Christian religion, they were of the most vital importance to the followers of an earlier paganism. To people who worshipped the sun, " orientation," whether in burial or in worship—was the natural attitude of reverence : to fire-worshippers, it was imperative that the sacred flame which burned above their altars should never be suffered to go out : priests who—like those of early Britain and modern Wisconsin—regarded various evergreens as " sacred," would make use of these plants on occasions of high solemnity : and a race that, for some forgotten reason, attached great importance to the shaving of the head, might be expected to illustrate that peculiarity in the persons of its teachers. But the religion that was taught by Christ does not appear to demand the observance of any of these forms. That many such ceremonies are observed by the great majority of modern Christians is certain ; but such usages seem to be rooted in inherited custom, and not to embody any special Christian ideas. Nor do they appear to be regarded as of much importance by those who present themselves to the outside observer as the most characteristic specimens of their faith.

When one regards the modern Christian apostle, either as he appears in the slums of London or as an exile among the most degraded races, the most salient features of his character are not those which connect him (if he be a "ritualist") with the non-Christian religions of the East; they are those which make him indistinguishable from the least ritualistic of all his fellow believers. When men sacrifice talents and fortune (each, in many cases, of the highest magnitude), health, worldly comfort and pleasure, and everything that one naturally likes, in a continuous endeavour to make others emulate the self-denial and purity of which they themselves are no bad examples,—then the special "religious denomination" of each individual retires into the background, or is even lost to sight. Such men prove their "apostolical succession" by their lives; whichever of the Christian sects—from Jesuit to Methodist—they may nominally be identified with. The various sectarian differences that may be said to constitute the "red-tape" of ecclesiasticism are of no importance whatever when compared with the noble uniformity that marks the lives of those nominally-different "Christians." If Christianity means anything, such men are its truest representatives. The mere ceremonies which many—which the majority—of them practice, do nothing to establish the individuality of their religion. Because these ceremonies are almost identical with those of other faiths.

Imperfectly as we know it, we do know that when Christianity invaded these islands it found there a religion similar to that of Persia and of Egypt; and there are many reasons for believing that its devotees were of the same section of humanity as the priesthoods of those countries of the East.* To what extent the British Islands became Christianized during the first few centuries of our era is uncertain. But we know that, after this period, the country was again in-

---

* In this connection, it may be remarked that one of the peculiar offences of the "vagabonds," &c., of Scotland—in past centuries—was, that the closest consanguinity was no bar to marriage. Now, this also characterized the "Magi" of ancient Persia and Egypt; who married their very nearest female relations, with the express purpose of retaining the priestly authority in the hands of one special Levite caste. What would be the effects of this, continued generation after generation, is a question of a physiological nature. But it can scarcely have failed to cause a marked physical and mental deterioration in the race.

vaded, and conquered by non-Christian and Oriental races. Thus, Christianity had not only to contend with the probable reflex action of the earlier religions of Britain, but it was subsequently smothered by later heathen domination. Of the later pagan immigrations, only that composed of the *nigræ gentes*, or "black Danars," has been emphasized ; (though much may be said with regard to others of earlier periods). But it is enough to remember that British Christianity had to encounter, first, the natural reaction of early British Heathenism, and then the later paganism of a race of conquerors. Now, a race cannot well conquer another without imposing its religion upon the natives, in some degree or another. (The religious condition of Hindustan in 1784, as compared with 1884, is evidence enough of the correctness of this self-evident proposition.) As long, therefore, as those heathen conquerors formed any part of the aristocracy of this country, so long would their inherited ideas continue to modify the social and religious life of the nations they governed. It is a fact that ought to have been enlarged upon prior to this chapter, that—with, perhaps, the exception of the Northmen and the Latins—*all* the races that have invaded these islands have been Orientals. And those Oriental races have, in varying degrees of time and locality, all occupied the position of ruling castes. That such heathen conquerors should, as soon as they became " Britons," have discarded their ancestral ideas and taken up, unreservedly, those of their Christian serfs—whom they treated with the loftiest contempt—is most unlikely. The probability rather is that, so long as the Oriental races remained visibly on the surface, so long would Oriental ideas also predominate. And, even so recently as the fifteenth century, a struggle between the East (as represented by the " Saracen " Douglases) and the West (personified by the Normans) seemed to divide North Britain ; resulting in the triumph of the Western faction. While, in England of the same period, there are many indications of a similar movement. In the following century, in Elder's letter to the Tudor king, there is a distinct ring of *insular* feeling ; an expressed desire for united action among certain British communities, with the purpose of throwing off the shackles of a foreign priesthood ; that priesthood identifying itself with the "gypsies" of the country—and itself virtually regarded as Egyptian by this same North British writer.*

But it is not necessary to go farther back than the Reformation, in order to see this " gypsy " ascendancy in the religion of Europe. The facts that have been referred to in this chapter,—added to many other similar facts in the quasi-religious life of that period,—make it evident that the movement, so well known by that name, was a genuine Reformation. And that those who facetiously talk of it as a de-formation have not the faintest conception of the previous condition of things. Not only was there a re-formation, but it seems quite an inaccuracy to speak of the modern Roman Catholic Church as though it were not one of those that were thus Reformed. Abstinence from horse-flesh a point of salvation—the teaching of astrology—"Easter Drollery"—and such like, form no portion of the belief or practice of any modern Christian church. The great religious movement of the sixteenth century was assuredly a reformation ; and one that reformed the whole of Christendom.

What concerns us here, however, is the apparent fact that it was a revolt against gypsyism. Just as the glimpses we have obtained of the Stanleys, Bosvilles, Lees, Lovels, Ruthvens, Baillies, and other Cavalier clans, of the eighteenth and preceding centuries, have shown us a caste of gypsy *aristocrats*, possessed of many bodily and mental attributes that (apart from the material wealth which they also possessed) constituted them a distinct section of British nobility ; so the fragmentary instances pointed out in this chapter have disclosed a contemporaneous rule of gypsyism in British religion.

NOTE.—Since a reference has been made in this chapter to the archæology of the army, the following remarks do not constitute a very wide digression.

Where a regiment is of very old standing, and has inherited certain peculiarities of dress or custom, which render it quite distinct from other

---

* It is worth noticing that, in the reign of Elizabeth Tudor, "on the 17th of April, 1571, an Act was drafted, but was not passed, that ' preists and other popisly affected ' lurking ' in serving mens or mariners apparaile or otherwyse dysguised ' were to be ' demed judged and punished as vachabounds wandering in this realme called or calling theym selves Egiptians.' " (Crofton's " English Gipsies under the Tudors," pp. 10-11.)

regiments, or many other portions of the community, it may be reasonably assumed that that regiment—though now composed of men of all
varieties—was once a particular *tribe.* That one or many dragoon
regiments should regard a certain marriage ceremony ("leaping over the
sword") as inviolable ; and that the same form should be observed by
tribes of "lancers"--such as those Borderers who could spear a salmon
as they galloped by the river-bank—is more than a coincidence. Palpably, the inference is that the regiment following that particular custom
was originally composed of men taken from the tribe or nationality to
whom that special ceremony was a genuine solemnity. And the tribe or
tribes who practised such a ceremony are known to us as "gypsies"
[certainly Scotch gypsies, and probably those of England also]. Marriage by "leaping over the sword" is not, it may be assumed, a custom
of any modern British regiment. But it was seriously practised last
century, and earlier ; as Grose and the ballad tell us. At so recent a
date as the eighteenth century it is probable that the members of such
a regiment were of no special British race, and only followed the custom
because it had come down to them from the men who first composed the
regiment. And that, therefore, if "a gentleman dragoon"—like him of
the ballad—did not marry until after he had left the army, he would
never dream of going through a ceremony such as that which his brother-
soldiers still regarded as valid : but would follow the conventional
custom. Even at the present day we see this distinction between the
soldier and the *man.* When an officer has retired into private life, his
funeral is that of a private gentleman ; and although he may possess
twenty horses, not one of them — nor any of his possessions—follow him
to the grave But if he dies as a soldier, his horse, servant, and
accoutrements *do* follow him to the grave ; the reason of which—as
archæologists very rationally explain—being that the traditions of
British warriors (or, perhaps, of a section only) go back to the time
when the horse, slave, and other possessions of a chief were buried with
him. Which shows how much more conservative a special society is
(whether we call it Army, Navy, Church, or Bar) than that concretion of
individual (and ephemeral) families that make up society in general.
And this funeral custom—like the marriage one just referred to—brings us
again to our "tory" castes. (For these are *castes;* inheriting a special
blood as well as special ideas.) Among them, we find that ancestral
custom, which our army gives a hint of, still in full force. When the Yorkshire chief, Ryley Bosville,—a man of this present century—died, his horse
was killed, and all his possessions destroyed, by his surviving relatives.
So also, in 1773, "the clothes of the late Diana Boswell, Queen of the
Gipsies, value £50, were burnt in the middle of the Mint, Southwark,
by her principal courtiers, according to ancient custom." In fine, it is
stated as still applicable to the "tories" of this century that, "when a
gypsy dies, everything belonging to him (with the exception of coin or
jewels) is destroyed."

Hussars, generally, are deduced from the *Chazar* tribes (the *ch* in this
name being, of course, guttural). The earliest French hussars (the

"hussars of the Marshal de Luxembourg") are thus described :—They "were habited and equipped in the Turkish fashion. [And Mr. Howorth has pointed out that the Black Chazars, or Ugres, or Hungarians, used to be known as 'Turks.'] An enormous moustache drooped over the chest ; but, with the exception of a long tuft on the crown, their heads were closely shaven [like Chinamen, or American Indians, or various British races]. On their heads they wore a fur cap, surmounted by a cock's-tail plume. Their uniform consisted of a scanty tight-fitting tunic, with breeches that were very large at the top, and tight below the knee, where their boots were drawn over them. This was their complete costume, and it was worn without any kind of under-garment whatever. For protection against the inclemency of the weather they were provided with tiger (or panther) skins, which they wore suspended about their necks (prototypes of more recent hussar pelisses with their fur lining) ; and these they adjusted in such a manner as would best oppose them to that quarter from which the wind might be blowing upon them. They were but inferior shots ; but with the curved sabre they exhibited a dexterity that was truly wonderful." (*Quoted at pages* 181-182 *of Mr. C. Boutell's* "*Arms and Armour.*") That these particular "Hussars" slew the horse of a dead chief above his grave we may well believe : because they were Huns, and that was the fashion of Attila's burial. And, since the same kind of people, known not only as Saracens and Moors, but also as "Huns," have invaded the British Islands, it is not difficult to understand why such customs should still survive among our official "Chazars," and the most "Saracen"-like division of our fellow-country-men.

One special British regiment—"The Black Watch"—has already been spoken of. When there was "paid in *blackmaill* or *watch-money* openly and privately, £5,000" to the "cateran" tribes of the Scotch Highlands, every year ; when the chief of such "caterans" styled him-self "the Captain of the Watch," "his banditti" being known as a "watch" ; it is evident that, if those "caterans" were at all like the "getrins" against whom certain Tweeddale gypsies fought, in the seventeenth century, then they were so many "black watches." And if any of these were formed into a regular regiment—as many were—it would be appropriately designated a "Black Watch." That this was the origin of the distinguished regiment now bearing that name can scarcely be questioned. The "dress" theory,—in the face of such facts, —would be by far the least probable of the two, *even if* there were such a thing as a black tartan. But there is no black tartan ; and the "Black Watch" wore red coats so far back as the War of Independence in America, at which period the regiment was only forty or fifty years old. There does not appear to be any regiment of "Borderers" bearing a similar title to this ; though there must have been such in the days when "the old tune, 'Black Bandsmen, up and march !'" was a familiar Border air : and we have Scott's statement that the Border gypsies were gathered into regiments and sent to fight in the "Low Country" wars. One or more of such regiments might easily have continued to bear the

title of " Black Bandsmen " long after ceasing to be composed exclusively of " Egyptians " ; and even down to the present day, when the
only " Egyptian " element visible would be the *Melanochroic* section,
represented by all grades. Whether or not the " Black Brunswickers "
were originally one with the *Schwarz-reiters* of Germany, it seems
evident that the latter title was given not only because those cavaliers
rode black horses and wore black clothes, but also because their faces
were black. This certainly does not seem to have been the natural
colour of their skins, and Fynes Morrison says, " I have heard Germans
say, that they do thus make themselves black to seem more terrible to
their enemies." But many brown-skinned races have blackened their
faces artificially,—*e.g.*, certain Fijians of the present day, and the
" Moors " of North America in the days of William Penn ; and the
" Black Act " of George the First's reign was directed against the
" Waltham Blacks," a league of freebooters who mustered strong in
Epping Forest at that date. These " Waltham Blacks " were so called
because they were accustomed to blacken their faces : and, although
not popularly remembered as gypsies, it seems very likely that they were
so. Mr. Borrow says of the English gypsies, " there is not such a place
for them in the whole world as the Forest : . . it is their trysting-place
. . and there they muster from all parts of England." And if the forefathers of Mr. Borrow's " tory " fellow-countrymen did *not* assemble in
Epping Forest, in George the First's time, it is difficult to find a reason
for their descendants doing so in the present century, and on very short
notice, since the " Black Act " was only repealed in 1827. Thus, the
probability that the " Waltham Blacks " were Epping Forest Gypsies is
very strong. And, while they followed a custom that is still practised
by the Romanes-speaking minstrels of our fairs and watering-places, and
that has been practised by Morris-dancers, minstrels, and mountebanks
for many centuries, they—like all of these people—were connected by
blood with races of brown complexion, though in differing degrees.
Thus, those German *Schwarz-reiters* may have been " Black Hussars "
by custom, and " Brown Hussars " by complexion.

Generally, it may be assumed that all regimental peculiarities that are
known to be of very old standing were once the peculiarities of certain
races. The tiger and other skins of the earlier Hussars are still represented in hussar uniforms ; but, though now nothing else than a picturesque and useless detail, their genuine ancestors were the skins of
actual wild animals, killed by their wearers, and worn by them for the
most simple reasons. So also with the " facings " of regiments (when
not of modern creation). The very word " facings " is significant. The
ruddled clans of Galloway wore red " facings :" certain Cambridgeshire
tribes, even in this century, wore blue " facings "—unalterably punctured
in. And these colours, red and blue, are still the commonest " facings "
in the British Army.

CHAPTER XII.

IT is now evident that, in viewing the "gypsydom" of these islands, we are confronting not one but many obsolete systems ;—not one variety of "Briton" only, but several. Such people, for example, as those who constituted the Scotch "cavalier" clan of Baillie, Bailyou, or Baliol, might be more appropriately styled "tory"-Normans than anything else— if one could feel justified in using a race-name of the eleventh century to describe a family of the seventeenth, in a country wherein so many different nations have intermingled in every possible combination. These and other "white gypsies" might, perhaps, be fairly enough classified under such a heading, in the meantime. Others, of darker hue, have been assumed to be the descendants of such races as the Black Danes, the Egyptian-Scots, and the painted Mauri or "black-amoors." So far as the modern students of such people have been relied upon, there would seem to be only three or four existing divisions in this country : the white-skinned (which might be sub-divided into the blue-eyed, flaxen-haired variety, and those having the rough skins and wiry, reddish hair ascribed to some of the Lothian tribes)—the dark-skinned, black-eyed, curly-haired "Romany" of Mr. Leland—and those to whom he gives the same complexion, but who have the lank, black hair of the English "notables" of three hundred years ago, and the American "Indians" of to-day.

If the difference between these two latter divisions arises "not . . . . . from white admixture," but because such "gypsies" are descended from "entirely different original stocks," it is clear that the name of "Romany" cannot be fitly applied to *both ;* if that name has a facial meaning. Borrow uses this term indiscriminately with "Egyptian," in speaking of his tawny comrades of the camp, the race-course, and the ring; while his American successor appears, gene‧rally, to discard the latter form, in its unabbreviated shape. And with him, as with many members of the race itself, the ability to speak the language of the Romany constitutes "a gypsy." Or very nearly so. It was formerly noticed that one of the most genuine of English "gypsies" pro‧nounced the present dwellers at Yetholm to be nothing else than "muggers," *because* they could not answer him in his own language. As for the author of *The Gypsies*, it is pro‧bable that he, too, had made this distinction, until he disco‧vered the "Shelta Thari;" which is *the* "Tinkers' Language," and which he describes as "purely Celtic,"—but which he now classes "with the gypsy, because all who speak it are also acquainted with Romany." This, he believes, was the language chiefly spoken to Mr. Simson; and although that author assuredly assigns the Romany Jib to the people of Yetholm, it is notable that his Scottish gypsies are not known to each other as "Romany," but as "Nawkens" and "Tinklers."

Whether it be true or not that all those who speak the *Shelta Thari* are also acquainted with the Romany tongue; and whether or not these two are the only "gypsy" lan‧guages spoken in the British Islands;* it seems to be quite clear that the orthodox, conventional "gypsy" of England Proper (and, of course, of Australia and the United States), regards this "Romany Tschib" as his mother-tongue. There seems to be an agreement among those who have studied the matter that *Rom* is the earlier form; though

---

* It must be remembered that while one gypsiologist regards the Romany Jib as a form of speech that is common to all "gypsies," another states that the variety spoken in Wales is "nearly unintelligible" to the Romany of England. It may be that what is called "Welsh" is much mingled, in some places, with what is called "Romanes;" just as the latter tongue intrudes into the partly-Celtic *Shelta Thari*. It seems certain that "Romanes" and "Welsh" have each got an element that is also *Persian*. Mr. Leland points out the connection of that language with Romanes, in several places; and a statement made not long ago shows that a similar tie links Persian with Welsh. Mr. G. A. Sala (in the *Illustrated London News* of 21 April, 1883) states that, at a luncheon given in Wales a few years ago, the then Persian Ambassador "enumerated no less than seventy Welsh words, which were also Persian words expressing the same signifi‧cation as their Cymric congeners." That is, there are a great many words in Persia, in Wales, and in the tents of the Romany, that are identical in mean‧ing and in sound: whatever name may be given to them.

there is less unanimity as to its origin. But most will agree with one writer* that "the general name for a gypsy [of the 'conventional' type] is *Rom ;*" from which, some say, has come the verb to *roam* (and certainly, to go a-gypsying is to go *a-roaming*). The writer last quoted states, on the authority of Sir Gardner Wilkinson, that *Romi* signified "a man " among the ancient Egyptians : which gives a pretty early date for the Egyptian-Romany connection, and which offers the simplest solution of the apparent contradiction. *Rom* or *Rum* (continues this writer) "still means 'noble and good' among our gypsies. 'Rum Roy' [Romany Rye] is a gentleman, but every gentleman is not by any means a Rum Roy among the gypsies." It is only among the Romany themselves that this word retains its sense of "noble and good ;" for, like many of their words, and like themselves, it has lost caste, entirely, with the general public. This has been so for the last two or three generations. Pierce Egan, in his Preface to the third edition of Grose's *Dictionary of the Vulgar Tongue*, states (what any one acquainted with "slang" is well aware of) that "the word *rum*, which, in Ben Jonson's time, and even so late as Grose, meant *fine* and *good*, is now generally used for the very opposite qualities." Thus, even in Grose's day, a *rome*, or *rum, mort* was "a great lady ;" and then, or earlier, *rum bouse* was "good drink"—a *rum chant* was "a fine song"—a *rum cove* was "a dexterous or clever rogue" ("rogue," itself, having anything but a contemptuous meaning). And, as the country districts were quite under the sway of such "cavalier" clans, "the highway" was known as the *Rum pad*, or *Romany path ;* while *Rum padders* were "highwaymen well mounted and armed." And it is significant of the totally different attitudes of the "cavaliers" and the non-"cavaliers," that while a *Rum Duke* must have been an expression of great respect among the Romany (being an equivalent of *Rum* or *Romany Riah*), it is rendered "a grotesque figure" by a representative of those classes that despised the odd dresses of the "courtiers" of three centuries ago.† The fate of such words corresponds

* Mr. Joseph Lucas, author of *The Yetholm History of the Gypsies.*

† Wright and Halliwell both refer to " Rum Duke," in their dictionaries, and in similar terms. That it means a " Romany Duke " is, of course, evident from

most precisely with the decline of the power and social value of the class of people (*race*, let us say) with whom they are identified. If such a representative of that class as the one recently selected—Prince Rupert—was ever spoken of as *a Rum Duke* by his contemporaries (which was very probable), the expression conveyed, as Pierce Egan tells us, the highest possible respect. That is, if it was used by men of his own stamp. If used by their opponents, the term bore an inimical rendering, which in a later day, and after the social triumph gained by these opponents, degenerated into the contemptuous and scornful. Nowadays, it is hardly necessary to observe, the adjective *rum* is not regarded as classical English ; and those dictionaries that deign to notice it make the qualifying observation that it is " a cant term." (That its meaning should be defined as " old-fashioned," is only another testimony to the fact that the *Romany* are *tories*.) *Rum*, therefore, as an adjective, has had its day. And its enlarged form of " Romany " does not take high rank in modern society. Mr. C. G. Leland lays down as an axiom that " whenever one hears an Englishman, not a scholar, speak of gypsies as 'Romany,' he may be sure that man is rather more on the loose than becomes a steady citizen, and that he walks in ways which, if not of darkness, are at least in a shady *demi-jour*, with a gentle down grade." He adds—" I do not think

the identity of *Rum*, or *Rom*, with *Romany*. (The same verbal identity is seen in the word *Romanie*, which is the Scotch-Gypsy name for *whisky*, when compared with the kindred term, *Rum*.)

That a " Rum Duke " should ever mean anything else than " a grotesque figure " is rather difficult for us to realize. *Because* our attitude is, in the main, that of Parliamentarians : and the ideas they fought against have mostly fallen into disrepute—as well as the people who adhere the most tenaciously to those ideas. But it must be remembered that the " Rum Duke " had—and has—his own view of things : and perhaps he does not think so highly of " us " as we do. The two sides of the question can best be seen by comparing the " courtier's " description, in Barclay's *Eclogues*, with that given by the " rude villains," as embodied in the well-known lines—

> *Hark ! hark ! the dogs bark,*
> *The beggars are coming to town ;*
> *Some in rags and some in tags,*
> *And some in silken gowns.*

For that is exactly how those " courtiers " (as described by Mr. Simson, pp. 214-5) appeared to the plebeian classes upon whom they *sorned ;* in the days when a " beggar " was a " gypsy," and a " gypsy " a " lord."

there was anybody on the race-ground who was not familiar
with the older word ; " the race-ground being Molesy Hurst,
"famous as the great place for prize-fighting in the olden
time," and the race in question being "one at which a mere
welsher is a comparatively respectable character, and every
man in a good coat a swell."

And although the most out-and-out "Romanys" did not
probably form anything more than a fraction of the assem-
blage, there is every reason to believe that at such a gathering as the one just spoken of the *Xanthochroic* element was
represented in a far less degree than at any ordinary meeting
of British people. Moreover, that with the excess of the *Melanochroic* element, there was also a prevailing tone of the
" Old English," "Tory," or "Cavalier" description. For, if this
kind of thing is Cavalierdom run to seed, it is Cavalierdom
nevertheless. Mr. Leland says you can tell the Romany
men by the "rake" or "slouch" with which they wear their
hats. To wear one's hat with a slouch is not a mark of
"respectability" at the present day. Neither did the Parliamentarians of the seventeenth century regard this fashion
with favour ; though it distinguished their enemies the Cavaliers. According to Mr. Leland, it denotes the "gypsy" : it
also denotes the "jockey," or "horsey" man, and the
"rough." All of which terms are synonyms for "cavalier."
But enough has already been said with regard to the Cavalier-
Romany identity. It is necessary to continue the consideration of the word " Rom " or " Romany" ; and also its derivative " Romanes."

Grose says that "a Romany" is " a gypsey ; " and that "*to
patter romany*, is to talk the gypsey *flash*." This, we have
seen, is vague ; both as regards the people and the language.
But, whether "Romanes" is spoken with greater purity in
Wales or in England, there can be no doubt that there is such
a tongue ; although it, and the race of the Romany, may
have become as "dreadfully mixed" as Mr. Simson's "gypsies" averred themselves to be. If the language spoken by
Roberts, the Welsh harper, is really the best kind of Romanes,
then a study of the old Welsh bards would throw most light
upon the subject. The tongue of the old Welsh bards appears
to be in a great measure a foreign language to those who speak

what is called "Welsh ; " and it is probable that the mother-
tongue of the minstrel Roberts is as little understood by such
people. "The works of Taliesin, Llywarch Hên, Aneurin
Gwawdrydd, Myrddin Wyllt, Avan Verdigg . . . are hardly
understood by the best critics and antiquarians in Wales."*
But, if the testimony of this gypsy-minstrel has any significance at all, it cannot be doubted that such critics and antiquaries have only to add to their knowledge of "Welsh"
the mastery of the language still spoken by the bards of
Wales, namely Romanes, in order to understand every poem
composed by those earlier minstrels. Indeed, Mr. Borrow himself says as much. These are his remarks while studying
"Welsh : "—" And here I cannot help observing cursorily that
I every now and then, whilst studying this Welsh, generally
supposed to be the original tongue of Britain, encountered
words which, according to the lexicographers, were venerable
words, highly expressive, showing the wonderful power and
originality of the Welsh, in which, however, they were no
longer used in common discourse, but were relics, precious
relics, of the first speech of Britain, perhaps of the world ;
with which words, however, I was already well acquainted,
and which I had picked up, not in learned books, classic books
and in tongues of old renown, but whilst listening to Mr.
Petulengro and Tawno Chikno talking over their every-day
affairs in the language of the tents." †

Whatever may be the language of the wandering minstrels
of Scotland,‡ it is not understood either by those who speak
what is called "English," or by those who speak "Gaelic."
And the same thing could be said of the Irish bardic tongue,
at one time, if not now. The "gypsies" of Ireland have not
received one tithe of the attention that has been paid to
those of the larger island ; and, therefore, one cannot say

---

* See the Preface to *Specimens of Ancient Welsh Poetry*, by the Rev. Evan
Evans. "Reprinted from Dodsley's Edition of 1764 : " Published by John
Pryse, Llanidloes, Montgomery.

† *Lavengro*, Chapter XIX.

‡ The existence of gypsy bagpipers and fiddlers in *modern* Scotland has been
indicated in Mrs. Craik's little story of *Two Little Tinkers ;* which refers more particularly to the Highlands of Scotland. That "gypsies" were the Minstrels of
the Scottish Border—and of all the other parts of Scotland—in *former* times, has
already been made tolerably clear.

much about them, for lack of information. But we have
already noticed that the ancient bards and *seanachas* of Ireland (who combined the various offices of bard, genealogist,
and rhapsodist) did not speak the " Gaelic " language. Of
this caste, or castes, it has been said—" The tongue is sharp
and sententious, and offereth great occasion to quick apoph-
thegms and proper allusions. Wherefore their common
jesters and rhymers, whom they term Bards, are said to
delight passingly these that conceive the grace and property
of the tongue. But the true Irish indeed differeth so much
from that they commonly speak, that scarce one in five hundred can either read, write, or understand it." The author who
introduces this statement into his description * of this ancient
system—a system which included many orders of " doctors "
or " medicine-men " [there is no appropriate modern word
to describe these archaic *teachers*]—says of one division
of this collegiate order—" The OLLAMHAIN RE DAN [' *doctors* of poetry and song '] . . . . . were Panegyrists or Rhap-
sodists, in whom the characters of the Troubadour and
Jongleur of Provence seem to have been united."

The professional characteristics of these people are everywhere the same—in the British Islands, or on the Continent
of Europe. Genealogists and historians (of a kind), who
were accustomed to " bard and flatter,"—bards and rhymers
who were also jesters and mountebanks,—whose name of
jongleur or *jougleur* has now (like other of their titles and
qualities) little enough respect among us. That, wherever
they were found in Western Europe, they were connected by
the ties of a common language, if not by kindred blood,
seems most patent. And, in the one glimpse we get of their
physical appearance—a single lightning-flash dividing the
darkness of accumulated centuries—in the traditional story
quoted by Sir Walter Scott, we see that those *jongleur-jug-
glers* were a black-skinned race.

And what was the language of those dusky "Troubadours and Jongleurs of Provence," and elsewhere? Was it
Romance? Or, was it Romanes? Or, is there any difference
between the two?

So far as concerns the pronunciation of the name, there is

* " Historical Memoirs of the Irish Bards ; " Joseph C. Walker, Lond. 1786.

no real difference. To us who have thrown back the accent in *Roman'-us*, making it *Ro'-man*, the natural pronunciation of *Roman'-es* (Romance) is *Ro'-manes*. All that can be said about the accentuation seems to be, that while the one form, *Romance*, has apparently preserved the emphasis in its proper place—or nearly so—the other form, *Romanes*, has preserved the proper number of syllables; since the word is apparently trisyllabic—the original pronunciation having been, presumably, *Ro-man'-es*. There is as little real difference, also, between the "gypsy" adverb, *Romaneskas*, and the form, *Romansque*. Indeed, it would seem that, in this case, the tradionary accent of the people has proved more faithful to the original than the voiceless symbol of literature : and that *Romanesque*, or *Romanesques*, was—and is—a word of four syllables. There is, therefore, no reason for supposing that the word which the Romany call "Romanes"* is anything different from the word that has come to be spelled "Romance" in books.

But it is clear that the language popularly known as "Romance" is not "Romanes;" or, if so, only in a partial degree. The former word, however, has had a very wide application. We are told† that "the name of Romance was indiscriminately given to the Italian, to the Spanish, even, in one remarkable instance at least, to the English language." And then it is added :—"But it was especially applied to the compound language of France." And, if there is really any particular form of speech that is "popularly known" by this name, it is this "compound language of France"—as that existed in mediæval times.

One sometimes hears such languages as Spanish and French classified as belonging to the Latin *or* Romance division. Now Latin *and* Romance were two wholly different tongues ; or, at any rate, so far different that a man who spoke Latin was unintelligible to a man who spoke Romance. "At a period so early as 1150 it plainly appears that the Romance language was distinguished from the Latin, and

---

* The names of the *people* and of the *language* have been confounded with each other for a long time ; and Grose talks of speaking *Romany*. But this is clearly an error, although often perpetrated by the Romany themselves.

† In the Eighth edition of the *Encyclopædia Britannica* (article "Romance") from which all of these statements, in this particular, are taken.

that translations were made from the one into the other; for
an ancient romance on the subject of Alexander, quoted by
Fauchet, says it was written by a learned clerk,

> ' Qui *de Latin* la trest, et *en Roman* la mit.' "

Thus, whatever shape that language, or one of its offshoots,
may have taken in France, at a later date, it is clear that the
Romance of 1150 was quite distinct from *Latin*. And as it
is with the former speech that we are at present concerned,
we need not regard the latter as at all connected with the
question.

With regard to the " one remarkable instance at least," in
which " the English language " is termed *Romance*, it is
stated :—" This curious passage was detected by the industry
of Ritson in *Giraldus Cambrensis*, '*Ab aquâ illa optima,
quæ Scottice vocata est* FROTH ; *Brittanice*, WEIRD ; Romane
vero *Scotte-Wattre*.' Here the various names assigned to the
Frith of Forth are given in the Gaelic or Earse, the British
or Welsh ; and the phrase *Roman* is applied to the ordinary
language of England. But it would be difficult (adds this
authority) to shew another instance of the English language
being termed Roman or Romance."

The significance of this single instance, however, is very
little affected by its isolated character. At the present day
the continent of Australia is still occasionally spoken of as
" New Holland ; " but one may safely predict that that name
will soon be quite obsolete. But if five hundred years hence,
an antiquary should discover one solitary instance of this
name being seriously applied to Australia, he would be quite
justified in assuming that, although only one example of
the usage had come down to him, it had at one time been
quite common. And we know his conclusion would be correct. Therefore, although no other instance should ever turn
up to parallel that which Ritson has recorded, we must accept
it as a fact that one of the languages spoken in Great Britain
during the twelfth century was known as "Roman or
Romance." The statement was made in the most natural
manner by a Pembrokeshire man,—the son of a Norman (De
Barry) and a South-Welsh " Theodore ; " and when he applied the term " Roman " to " the English language," it is to

be supposed that neither he nor any of his contemporaries saw any inconsistency in the expression.*

In the twelfth century, then, Latin and Roman, or Romanes, were two distinct languages. And the latter was the tongue of the "Troubadours and Jongleurs of Provence," and elsewhere. This conclusion, indeed, has been almost reached by a recent writer on "gypsies;" who makes such remarks as these†:—

"De Bezers, a Languedoc poet in his ' Breviari d' Amor,' dated 1288, in a passage cited by Tyrwhitt (*Notes to Cant. Tales,* v. 11, 453), says ' that the *Joglar* sings and dances, plays instruments, or enchants people or does other *joglayria.*'

"Gilfillan relates that ' in 1328, during the siestas at the coronation of Alonzo IV of Aragon, "el *Juglar* Ramaset" sang a villanesca (comic song) composed by the Infanta (Don Pedro), and another *Juglar* called "Novellet" recited,' etc. In the *Chron. d'Aragon* the *Juglar* ' Ramaset' is called ' Romanset *Jutglar.*' *Romanset* smacks strongly of the Romany, while *Ramaset* comes very near the Scotch name of Ramsay. . . . .

"About the middle of the 13th century a great change of meaning takes place in the word. Dr. Burney (*Hist. of Music*) says, ' William de Girmont, Provost of Paris, 1331, prohibited the *Jungleurs* and *Jungleuresses* from going to those who required their performances in greater numbers than had been stipulated. In 1395 their libertinism again incurred the censure of the Government.'

    *   *   *   *

"S. R. (Samuel Rid), writing in 1612, says, ' The true art of *Juglers* consisteth in legerdemain—that is, the nimble conveyance and right dexterity of the hand, the which is performed divers wayes, especially three—(1) Hiding and conveying of balls, (2) alteration of money, (3) shuffling of cardes.'"

The identity of such people with those against whom the Scotch enactment of 1579 was directed hardly needs to be pointed out. In order "that it may be known what manner of persons are meant to be strong and idle beggars, and vagabonds, and worthy of the punishment before specified, it is declared" that such consist of "all idle persons going about

---

* The words selected, viz. *Scotte-Wattre*, do not, certainly, assert themselves as Romanes. But, then, are the other examples any happier? Is *Froth* the Gaelic, and *Weird* the Welsh for *Forth*? The *examples* do not appear to illustrate anything: but the existence of the use of "Roman or Romance," as applied to one of the twelfth-century languages of Britain is most apparent from the passage.

† Mr. Joseph Lucas, "Yetholm History of the Gypsies," pp. 86–88.

in any country of this realm, using subtle crafty and unlawful plays, as jugglery, fast and loose, and such others ; the idle people calling themselves Egyptians, or any others that feign themselves to have knowledge of prophecy, charming, or other abused sciences, whereby they persuade the people that they can tell their weards, deaths, and fortunes, and such other fantastical imaginations . . . . . and all minstrels, songsters and taletellers, not avowed in special service by some of the lords of Parliament, or great barons, or by the head burghs and cities, for their common minstrels." Everybody knows that " the idle people calling themselves Egyptians " are, and have been, wholly identified with the various callings and attributes enumerated above ;* and the game of " fast and loose " is as much their property as thimble-rigging. It is thus described : " Fast and loose, formerly called pricking at the Belt or Girdle, a cheating game still in vogue amongst trampers and impostors at fairs. A leather strap is coiled up tightly, and placed standing on a table, the folds being so artfully arranged that one of them is made to resemble the central roll of the strap. The player pricks in that particular fold with a stick, believing that he has thus made *fast* the strap ; but the strap being in reality *loose*, the trickster detaches it at once. There are numerous allusions to this game (continues this writer†) in the dramatic writings of the sixteenth and seventeenth centuries." And, as an example of these, Mark Antony's words are quoted :—

This foul Egyptian hath betrayed me :
 *   *   *   *   *   *
O this false soul of Egypt ! this grave charm—
 *   *   *   *   *   *
Like a right gypsy, hath, at fast and loose,
Beguiled me to the very heart of loss.

That all these people were of the same kind as those *Juglars*, or *Jongleurs*, mentioned in Mr. Lucas' extracts (just

* This statute is quoted in the April number of *Blackwood's Magazine* for 1817 ; in the " gypsy " article frequently referred to.

† Robert Bell, in a note to *Hudibras* (Part III. Canto II.). " Fast and Loose " is also referred to by Mr. Lucas, at page 145 of his " Yetholm History of the Gypsies." He calls it " a well-known Gypsy trick," and states that it was practised, during the thirteenth century, by the nomadic class in France.

quoted,—whose "true art" consisted in thimble-rigging, card-sharping, and "alteration of money"—is unmistakeable. In London, as we saw in an earlier chapter, they found a home in Southwark; "Smithfield, with its world of cut-purses, drolls [mountebanks], and 'motions' [Punch-and-Judy-shows —or else, merry-go-rounds and swings] ; Moorfields, where ballad-mongers and cudgel-players abounded, and the rook-eries of the Bermudas, reeking with ale and tobacco."[*] Corresponding, thus, with those earlier *Jouglers* or *Jongleurs,* their language (if they possessed one that was peculiarly their own) must have been that of those *Jongleurs.* That is to say, it must have been *Romance* (to adopt, for a moment, the conven-tional spelling of the speech of the Troubadours). But these people exist in our own time ; though in a greatly decayed condition. And one who has studied them very closely has told us "that among all these show-men and show-women, acrobats, exhibitors of giants, purse-droppers, ginger-bread-wheel gamblers, shilling knife-throwers, pitch-in-his-mouths, Punches, Cheap-Jacks, thimble-rigs, and patterers of every kind there is always a leaven and a suspicion of gypsiness." And the language that, in the estimation of this observer, appertains peculiarly to such people, is called—*Romanes.* It is impossible to avoid seeing that pure *Romance* (not "the compound language of France," but *pure* Romance) must be exactly the same thing as pure *Romanes.* And it may be regarded as a matter of almost absolute certainty, that when one of the black-skinned *Jongleurs* of the time of John-of-Rampayne encountered a brother-troubadour he greeted him, like any of the modern Romany, with the words *"Ne rakesa tu Romanes, miro prala?"* ("Don't you speak Romanes, brother?")

Of the truth or error of which deduction there is tangible proof lying to hand, in the compositions of the early bards of Wales ; which are only imperfectly understood,—or not at all—by those who only speak what is called "Welsh ;" but which must be almost wholly intelligible—perhaps altogether intelligible—to those who speak Welsh *and* Romanes. This Romanes is the language of the best minstrels in Wales at

---

[*] Extracted from the Memoir prefixed by Bell to his edition of Ben Jonson's poems.

the present day : "the Eisteddfods of Wales have witnessed
the triumphs of Gipsy harpists ; and hundreds have been
charmed by the concerts of the Roberts family, not knowing
they were hearing a Gipsy band."* And this language, like
the people whom we call "gypsies," is pre-eminently associated with the minstrelsy of Europe.

If once the language of the bards of Wales, as far back as
it can be traced, is indubitably proved to be Welsh-Romanes,
then it may legitimately be assumed that the language
spoken by the minstrels of the other portions of the British
Islands has been closely allied with it, from a very early
period. That the "Romany" and "the idle people calling
themselves Egyptians" were one and the same people, seems
beyond doubt. And we find it on record that the Egyptians
of Scotland "danced before the king in Holyrood-house,"
on at least one occasion during the year 1530 : and that, in
the books of the Lord High Treasurer of Scotland this
entry was duly made—"Apr. 22, 1505. Item, to the Egyp-
tianis, be the kingis command, vij lib." Also, "that, in
1501, one of the [Scotch] king's minstrels was 'Peter the
Moryen,' or Moor." Also, that "in 1504, two blackamoor
girls arrived, and were educated at court [the Scotch court],
where they waited on the queen. They were baptized Elen
and Margaret. In June 1507, a tournament was held in
honour of the queen's black lady, Elen More,† which was
conducted with great splendour." And, at this particular
period,—the very beginning of the sixteenth century, the
minstrel Dunbar (himself styled a "Saracen" by his equally

* It is the misfortune of a roughly-sketched outline such as this, that—to a
merely superficial reader—an apparent identity is established between some of
the finest castes of Modern Britons and some of the most degraded. This arises
from the fact that the races chiefly dealt with in these pages have a most ancient
lineage ; that the civilization—or civilizations—they represent have long ago
decayed ; that castes originally compact have split up into divisions of the most
various character—the distance between each growing wider and wider with every
century ; and that, consequently, it is possible to see a race-connection, very
remote in its point of union, between people of the most refined nature and
others of a greatly different description.

† This Ellen More offers an unmistakeable example of this surname (More)
having been given because the person distinguished by it was a *Moor, Morrow,* or
Murray. "Peter the Moryen" is a kindred specimen : and it is probable that
he became ultimately "Peter Morgan" (for this is apparently only another form
of that word).

swarthy rival, Kennedy), in describing the amusements of
the upper classes in the Edinburgh of that day, says :—

> "Some sings, some dances, some tell stories ;
> Some late at even brings in the *Moreis*."

which last word is usually construed " Morris-men ; " and
that is equivalent to saying " Moors."

Of the existence of this minstrel-mountebank, jongleur-
juggler class, in the Scotland of the above period, there is
abundance of evidence. " In 1489, the year after he [James
IV. of Scotland] ascended the throne, a band of English
pipers [bagpipers*] came to Edinburgh, and they played at
the Castle gate, where his majesty heard them, and rewarded
them with twelve *demyes* ["twelve shillings Scots"]. In
1491, three English pipers were heard by the king at
Linlithgow, and paid seven unicorns. . . . . Among the
' musicians, menstralis, and mirrie singaris', mentioned by
Dunbar, the Treasurer shews that there was one Nicholas
Gray, who played ' on the dron '—the drone bagpipe. In
1505, besides ' Jamie Wederspune,' the fiddler, there was
' Jamie that playes on the drone'. . . . The Treasurer's
accounts shew that harpers of various nations attended the
court ; and that something like competitions occasionally
took place between the English, Irish, Highland and Lowland harpers. Frequent gratuities are entered as having been
given to the performers. Of the ' oratouris,' and ' Frensche
flingaris,' of whom Dunbar speaks, many proofs could be
adduced from the Treasurer's accounts. By orators the
poet, no doubt, means storytellers. Richard Wallace, a
courier, or bearer of letters, was at times a teller of tales
or ' geists ' to the king. There was also ' Widderspune the
foulare, that told tales and brocht foulls to the king,' together
with ' Watchod the tale tellare,' all of whom occur between
1496 and 1497. ' Hog the jestour,' and ' Thomas the jestour '
are frequently mentioned. ' March 5, 1507-8. To the
Frenche menstrallis, that maid ane danss in the Abbay,
be the kingis command, 12 French crowns, £8 8s.'" "The
same king, on the 1st January, 1505-6, granted to Ronald

---

* It has already been shown that bagpipes and bagpipers were not peculiar
to any one part of the British Islands ; though now popularly identified with the
Scotch Highlands.

Makbretun, *clarschawner* [harper], six marks worth of land of Knockan, in Wigton-shire, for his fee [as one of the king's musicians] during his life. . . . On passing through Wigton [in 1502], the king gave 14*sh.* to the pipers of that town, who usually had such gratuities for their music ; . . . [and while at Whithern, in Wigtonshire, in 1505–6], he gave an unicorn [18*sh.*] to two tale tellers." And, among the figures cut in bass relief upon "an antique bedstead or buistie of the Black Earl, who was assassinated in the Castle of Stirling " (the brother of that black Douglas who was overthrown in the year 1455), "the piper is a conspicuous person," while "a variety of sword and morrice dancers " are "represented in all the zany and buffoon attitudes of such performers."

These Jongleurs and Jugglers belong to the fifteenth and sixteenth centuries; but "Reid the mountebank and his blackamoors " show us the same people in the latter part of the seventeenth century, and in the same district (southern Scotland). And their existence, in that district, and at those periods, is attested by Scott. "About spring time, and after harvest, it was the custom of these musicians to make a progress through a particular district* of the country. The music and the tale repaid their lodging, and they were usually gratified with a donation of seed corn." This last reference bears more particularly upon the minstrels attached to certain burghs. "These town pipers, an institution of great antiquity upon the borders, were certainly the last remains of the minstrel race. Robin Hastie, town piper of Jedburgh, perhaps the last of the order, died nine or ten years ago [1802] ; his family was supposed to have held the office for about three centuries. . . The town-pipers received a livery and salary from the community to which they belonged ; and, in some burghs, they had a small allotment of land, called the Piper's Croft."

The above extracts† refer mostly to those divisions of this class who were recognized and authorized by law,—down to

---

* This "particular district " is quite in keeping with Mr. Simson's statement that each gypsy clan had a certain territory, into which others dared not venture.

† Which are taken from Mr. James Paterson's edition of Dunbar's Poems (Edinburgh, 1860), pp. 108–111 and 275 ; as well as from Mackenzie's "History of Galloway " (Vol. I. pp. 417–8, and Vol. II. pp. 68–9), and also from Scott's Introduction to "The Minstrelsy of the Scottish Border."

quite recent times. But, while those " minstrels, songsters, and taletellers," who were " avowed in special service by some of the lords of parliament, or great barons, or by the head burghs and cities, for their common minstrels."—while these are specially exempted from the penalties laid down in the Scotch Act of Parliament of 1579 (enacted during the minority of James the Sixth), that statute strikes most forcibly at those " strong and idle beggars," who were not so attached ; and who are characterized as " idle persons," " using subtle, crafty and unlawful plays, as jugglery, fast and loose, and such others—the idle people calling them-selves Egyptians "—and " any others that feign themselves to have knowledge of prophecy, charming, or other abused sciences, whereby they persuade the people that they can tell their weards, deaths, and fortunes,"—and " all minstrels, songsters and taletellers " who (as just remarked) were not attached to certain barons and lords, or to burghs and cities.

And it is with the *nomadic* divisions of these castes that we are most concerned. It is probable that those individuals who settled down in the towns (as the Jedburgh Hasties) gradually lost their race characteristics, and mixed their blood with that of other citizens. Indeed, when Dunbar wrote his poem " to the merchants of Edinburgh " (the date of which is placed at " about the year 1500 "), he referred contemptuously to the " common minstrels " or " mowars " (jesters) of the city, as being such very poor specimens of this class. " Cunninger men (he says) maun serve Sanct Clown." But the nomadic divisions are those that longest retained their individuality. And this in spite of the most bitter persecution : relentless and almost* continuous, and ending nearly in their extermination. But " Reid the mountebank " and " his blackamoors " show us that, in the seventeenth century, the *jongleurs* still continued to be iden-tified with the black-skinned races ; while Mr. Simson's sketches, which relate chiefly to the eighteenth century, prove that, at that period, " Egyptian " and " Jongleur " were interchangeable terms. " The violin and bag-pipes were the instruments they commonly used. This musical

---

* Not wholly continuous : for the laws against them were only enacted and enforced when their opponents were in power.

talent of the gipsies delighted the country-people. . . and contributed much to procure the wanderers a night's quarters. Many of the families of the farmers looked forward to the expected visits of the merry gipsies with pleasure, and regretted their departure." At "penny-weddings" and other rustic feasts, these "gypsies" continued to be the "minstrels of the Scottish Border" down to the present century; and it is likely enough they are so at the present day—if railways and newspapers and telegraphs have not utterly killed out all local life.

It was not only in Scotland that these things were. The scattered instances quoted above could certainly be capped by many others, not only in Scotland but throughout the British Islands. At the Scotch "Eisteddfods" of the fifteenth and sixteenth centuries, the minstrels were "English, Irish, Highland and Lowland"—and this must assuredly have included Wales as well. The English statute-books, as well as the Scotch, contain enactments against those nomadic minstrels. "In the thirty-ninth year of Elizabeth, a statute was passed by which 'minstrels, wandering abroad,' were included among 'rogues, vagabonds, and sturdy beggars,'— 'tramps' is now the word (remarks the writer* I am quoting from),—and were punishable as such. Cromwell (1656) renewed the ordinance . . . including 'fiddlers' in the musical category." And the historian of the Irish bards of the same, or an earlier period, has told us that in them "the characters of the Troubadour and Jongleur of Provence seem to have been united."

All these people are most visibly of the same nature. And it seems equally certain that they were mainly—or wholly— of the same dusky complexion. The John-of-Rampayne anecdote is perhaps the only *vivid* glance that we get of these "troubadours and jongleurs;" but the other references made to them in later times are almost as convincing. The books of the Lord High Treasurer of Scotland, which tell us that "harpers of various nations attended the court of James the Fourth," and that—in the year 1505—one of his minstrels was "Jamie Wotherspoon the fiddler," or (for the same man

---

* Mr. J. S. Dwight; "Our Dark Age in Music," *Atlantic Monthly*, December, 1882.

is probably meant by either designation) "Jamie that plays
on the drone," or bagpipe ; these same Accounts also state
that, in that very year there was paid "to the *Egyptians* be
the kingis command, vij lib." And the poet who describes
the Edinburgh life of that same period states that to "bring
in the Moors" was an ordinary finish to an evening's gaiety.
So that, although "Peter the Moor" is perhaps the only one
of the royal minstrels whose complexion is plainly visible to
us, yet we may quite reasonably conclude that "Jamie
Wotherspoon," "Hog the jester," "Thomas the jester,"
"Watchod the tale teller," and also (in Wigtonshire)
"Ronald Makbretun, harper," and the two unnamed "tale
tellers," who received the royal "tip" of nine shillings apiece,
that all these were as much "Moors" and "Egyptians" as
any of their contemporary *jongleurs*, or Reid's "blackamoor"
mountebanks of a later day. There is not the least dubiety
as to the minstrels and "flingers" who danced before King
James the Fifth, at Holyroodhouse, in the year 1530; for
these are styled "Egyptians." And when a sixteenth-century Englishman, Marlowe, says that

> *Every Moorish fool can teach*
> *That which men think the height of human reach;*

or, when Barclay—in the same century—wrote these lines :—

> *No faute with Moryans is blacke dyfformyte,*
> *Because all the sorte lyke of theyr favour be ;*

in either of these instances it may be regarded as certain
that the "Moorish fools" and "Moryans" whom the writers
had in view were of the same kind as "Peter the Moryan"
and the other "Moors" who entertained the citizens of
Edinburgh with their music, dancing, tale-telling, jugglery,
and buffoonery, three or four hundred years ago.

And thus, since those "mowars," or jesters, who "served
Sanct Clown" in the Edinburgh of *circa* 1500, and those
"profest pleisants" and "fancied fools" who were "suffered
to *vaig* and wander throughout the whole country," were
really of the race of "Egyptians" or "Moors," it does not
become necessary to look back to an astonishing distance in
order to see that the *Picti* of the circus and the pantomime

were also *Mauri.* If such "Moorish fools" resembled, in
feature, the thick-lipped "Moors" of heraldry or the
"blubber-lipped" *ciuthachs* of the Hebrides, or those
Lothian colliers described by Hugh Miller (who were
probably, Mr. Simson indicates, "of gipsy extraction"), or
the ugly "giants" caricatured in Welsh tradition; or if—to
put it ethnologically—this section of the ancestry of the
British *Melanochroi* possessed the "remarkably coarse and
flexible" lips that Mr. Huxley assigns to the *Australioid*
division of humanity (to which the ancient Egyptians belonged); then the "fancied fool" of that period did not
require to paint a huge, grinning mouth around the margin
of his own. For it was as wide and thick-lipped as heart
could wish. And he did not require to wear a skin-tight
cowl, showing an apparently bald or partially-shaven head.
Because to shave the head "like a fool," or "after the fashion
of a roguish fool," has been a proverbial expression in the
Highlands, as well as the Lowlands, of Scotland from time
immemorial.* Nor was the *white* paint upon his face a
superfluity (as it now is); for his complexion was that of
the swarthy Egyptian-Moors.

This Picto-Moorish identity has become less and less
visible during the lapse of time. "Reid the mountebank
and his blackamoors" show us that, two centuries ago, the

---

* This has already been referred to (Vol. I. p. 76). From the remarks made
by Mr. J. F. Campbell (" West Highland Tales," Vol. II. p. 474, and Vol. III.
p. 205), it is clear that the custom was once quite common in the Scotch Highlands and Isles. Scott, in "*The Doom of Devorgoil* (Act II. Scene I.) refers to
the same practice when he speaks of "clipping the hair after the fashion of a
roguish fool." Douce states that the heads of fools were "frequently shaved,"
and that the practice "can be traced to the twelfth century;" and he produces
an example of this in the person of "the Duke of Suffolk's fool in the time of
Henry VIII." (See Douce's *Illustrations of Shakspeare*, Vol. II. pp. 323 and
331.) When the strolling-harper, Tristram of Lyonesse, wandered among the
Cornish woods in a crazy condition, and "fell into the fellowship of herdmen
and shepherds," it is said that "they clipped him with shears and made him like
a fool." (Malory's "Morte Darthur," Book IX. Chap. XVIII.) And, during
the late disturbances in Ireland, it was seen that to "make a fool of" a man by
clipping his hair, is not even yet an obsolete custom in that part of the country.

(This portrait of the Duke of Suffolk's fool shows a considerable resemblance,
in outline, to that of the juggler whose portrait is given on page 342 of Mr.
Morley's *Memoirs of Bartholomew Fair*. The head of the latter is not shaved;
the hair being drawn up into a tuft at the top; but either head shows the same
curious conical shape.)

painted clown of Southern Scotland was a " Moor ; " and the brown-skinned, painted *Mignon* of Goethe suggests that the strolling tumblers and jugglers of Germany were dark-skinned gypsies, in the eighteenth century. That the strolling *players* of Germany, at the same period, were also gypsies has been assumed from another passage in *Wilhelm Meister ;* and that those of seventeenth-century Scotland were " Egyptians," we know from the statement that these people acted plays yearly, during May and June, at " the stanks of Roslin." One would, at first, think that the social revolutions of the past few generations must have utterly destroyed all traces of the connection that has once existed between certain occupations and a certain race. And yet, a student of gypsy life has plainly told us that there is a distinct leaven of " gypsiness " among our nomadic actors, mountebanks, and musicians. The last of these, in many instances, are accustomed to blacken their faces artificially, "that they might the better pass for Moors ; " while those who act as clowns presumably paint their faces "of various colours." And the language called " Romanes " is more or less familiar to all of these. Whether the same connection is at all visible in our more sedentary circuses and theatres can hardly be settled at present Mr. Leland, certainly, has told us that "there are several stage words of manifest gipsy origin ; " but the traditions and language of the modern circus do not seem to have been studied.

But these are side issues. The features of the early " clown " have long disappeared from British faces : chiefly no doubt, because the race, or races, to whom those "clowns " belonged, have been subjected to almost ceaseless persecution, and have been hunted down and killed like animals. In other words, because the process of evolution has never ceased to operate ; and men of high attributes (physical and otherwise), intolerant of those beneath them, have stamped them out. And, as the real features of those clowns have disappeared, so have their worst moral characteristics. A " buffoon " is not nowadays " bold ; " nor is he distinguished for his " jests obscene ; " as was once the case. Nor, again, is the mere clown (the mock-clown of modern days) united to the *actor*, as he seems to have once been. To separate such people, in these days, is a simple matter. But they were more closely connected in past times,—when a single word (*Jongleur, Jougleur, Juglar, Juggler*) was used to denote minstrel and buffoon. To show the dividing line between the archaic strolling bard and strolling priest; strolling mountebank and strolling player; is no easy feat—though the gap between each of these professions is wide enough now.

Still, it is curious to notice that, even in modern times, various walks in life—those most removed from the prosaic, dull, and unimaginative—are not utterly dissociated from "gypsydom." It is only a generation ago that artists, actors, poets, were represented as wearing long, flowing hair,—dressing in an individual fashion,—and living a free-and-easy kind of life. Why should such people have been called "Bohemians:" and why should certain "gypsy" characteristics have attached to them? One doesn't naturally figure a ploughman or a brewer as a man with long black curls, flashing black eyes, and a jaunty manner; yet those things seem quite appropriate to the *artist* (of whatever kind) as he used to be portrayed. And the castes known as "gypsies" are castes of *artists*. A writer upon gypsies, in the aggregate, writes to this effect :—" Many famous artists . . . . . have issued from their ranks ; and their own melodies sounding over the wide Hungarian pushtas, the steppes of Russia, or through the streets of Jassy, are not easily forgotten. Some of them have indeed become the much-valued property of other nations, or are embodied in some of our favourite operas. No less wonderful is the grace and charm of their wild dances. Altogether, the gypsies are one of the most gifted races, the lost genuises, so to say, of humanity."* But if from such people have come all the poetry, the grace, the *romance* of Europe, they are "the geniuses," and not "the *lost* geniuses," of European humanity.

A word in the last sentence recalls us to the particular class of "gypsies" we are considering in this chapter. For it must be remembered that under this title of "gypsy" is comprised so many different types, that it looks as though we ought to regard it as meaning nothing more than "wild

* "Chambers's Encyclopædia ;" art. "Gypsies."

man," or "tory." Between the graceful, handsome cavaliers described by Borrow, and the "Moorish fools" whose hideous features have just been glanced at, there is such a wide difference that a similar complexion seems the only connecting tie. And those "clowns" may safely be set aside, at present, as belonging to those "inferior gangs" with whom the Scotch "gypsies" of last century—and previously—acknowledged no kinship whatever. What we have to continue to regard is that class of "gypsies" whose ideas, and traditions, and language, are those of *Romance.* And the class with which these ideas, traditions, and language, are most identified, is the class thus described by Mr. Borrow:—
" Their complexion is dark, but not disagreeably so ; their faces are oval, their features regular, their foreheads rather low, and their hands and feet small. The men are taller than the English peasantry, and far more active. They all speak the English language with fluency, and in their gait and demeanour are easy and graceful ; in both respects standing in striking contrast with the peasantry, who, in speech, are slow and uncouth, and, in manner, dogged and brutal." These people, who (according to Mr. Simson, and Mr. Borrow), are imbued with that feeling of "contempt for agriculturists so striking in the poems of the *trouvères*,"* are the people who are even yet identified with minstrelsy, and whose speech is that of the *trouvères* of the Middle Ages—the language known as *Romanes* or *Romance.*

The identity of *Romanes* with *Romance* is almost asserted by Mr. Lucas in his "Yetholm History." He therein tells us that "Gypsies call their language not only Romani, but much more frequently *Romanis*, and sometimes (as Mrs. Eliz. Lee) *Romanish*, which come to the well-known form *Romance* (languages), about which no doubt exists."

Speaking of this word "Romance," Mr Skeat says:—" This peculiar form is believed to have arisen from the late Latin adverb *romanice*, so that *romanice loqui* was translated into

* It is perhaps incumbent upon one who has not made himself acquainted with "the poems of the *trouvères*," to acknowledge that the above statement is made in a Note appended by Mr. Fairholt to Barclay's "Cytezen and Uplondyshman ; " and that that gentleman refers to "some curious instances [of this gypsy-pride] . . . given by Mr. Wright in his paper on the Political Condition of the English Peasantry during the middle ages."

Old French by *parler romans*." All these are clearly so many different spellings (and accentuations) of the same word.

Although British Romanes, as spoken at the present day, differs greatly from "the compound language of France," yet it approaches it more closely (at some points) than any other form of speech that belongs to the British Islands. An entire ignorance of mediæval French, or of French Romanes, prevents me from comparing British Romanes with the form known under that name in French. But the kinship just referred to will be seen clearly enough from a comparison between certain words in modern British Romanes, and the corresponding words in Modern French as given below.

MODERN FRENCH.	BRITISH ROMANES.
Londres	Lundra.
Angleterre	Anglaterra.
Couronne	Coraunna.
Tasse	Tass.
Roi	Roy.
Royal, *adj*.	Ryally, *adv*.
Tu	Tu.
Ne	Ne.
Boutique	Boutika.
Mendier . ⎫	⎧ Maund.
Demander ⎭	⎨ Mong. ⎩ Mang.
Mille	Mille.
(Thousand)	
Mille	Meéa.
(Mile.)	
Poche	Poachy.
Lâche	Laj.
(Cowardly.)	(Shame.)
Lire	Lil.
(To read)	(A book.)
Dent	Dan.

In the British-Romanes word for "to beg," we have plainly a modern phonetic rendering of the nasal *n* ; or rather that caricature of the nasal *n* which asserts itself in the French of those modern Britons who are not regarded as masters of the French language. Borrow and his successors quite ignore the *d* in their spelling of *maund* ; and, from this, one may assume that the *d* sound has really disappeared from the British-Romanesque pronunciation of this word, during the present century. For the modern writers always seem to spell it either *mong* or *mang*. But in the older Cant* vocabularies it is *maund;* and the song of "The Canters' Holiday," "sung on the electing of a new *Dimber Damber*, or King of the Gypsies," begins with the words:—

> Cast your nabs and cares away,
> This is *Maunders'* Holiday ; "

and, indeed, the verb "to maunder" is still found in English dictionaries, with the definition "to beg." A parallel example of this twofold orthographical expression may be seen in the word *mandi* or *mendi* (signifying "me "), which is alternately spelt *manghi, menghi,* or *monghi*. The spelling of *meťa*, "a mile," is nothing else than the French *mille* expressed phonetically. Thus, we see that the *jongleurs* of the British Islands, identical with those of Provence in many ways, were not (and are not) wholly different from them in speech.

But the connection between the "Troubadours and Jongleurs" of this country and of France is of very old date, and such resemblances as those given above are very probably few in number. Perhaps the first recorded instance of the arrival of French gypsy-minstrels in England,

---

* It must be remembered that "cant," though apparently a mere jargon, yet contains many words that are common to Romanes. Moreover, the last-century writers—such as Grose—seem to have been satisfied with characterizing as "cant" and "gibberish," all the forms of speech which belonged to the nomadic class ; and of course they included pure Romanes under this term.

As the words quoted above have all been taken from the works of modern writers, it may be as well to refer to Borrow's *Lavo-Lil* (particularly, pages 6, 65, and 132), Mr. Leland's *English Gipsies*, p. 50, and the works of Mr. Groome and Messrs. Crofton and Smart. It may also be necessary to refer to one of the words, specially. This is *roy*, which is almost invariably written *rye, rei, rai, riah, rayah,* &c. But Mr. Lucas records that the Yetholm form is *roy :* and Mr. Borrow states that Yetholm Romanes, though meagre, is purer—in some respects—than that of any other part of this country. *Roy*, of course, is only *rye*, pronounced with a broader vowel sound. The transition from *rah-ee* to *raw-ee* is not very great after all. The *roy* spelling has been chosen in the above list merely to show the French connection more clearly. *Ryally* (or *royalls*) is spelt *reiali* by Messrs. Crofton and Smart ; but there is no reason why the one spelling should be preferred above the other.

is that of the juggler* Taillefer (or Tulliver, as we now pronounce it) ; who rode before the Norman army at Hastings, singing the *Song of Roland* as he rode, and throwing up his sword into the air, and catching it again, after the dexterous fashion of his caste.

Apart, however, from all questions of a philological kind, it is enough to insist that "gypsyism" and "romance" are synonymous terms. It may reasonably be doubted whether the past was *actually* more "romantic" than the present. Some people regard our present civilization—with its machinery, factory-chimneys, plodding, regular habits, and general "philistinism"—as the essence of all that is prosaic. While the past, in their eyes, is dominated by poetry. The accurateness of this view may be questioned, with success. It is a mere truism to say that there have been deeds done, in this "prosaic" century, by very matter-of-fact people—grimy engine-drivers and "pointsmen," miners, life-boat-men, and other products of modernism—which, for bravery and high self-sacrifice, have never been surpassed by any action of the "romantic" age. And the things that can be done by means of steam and electricity are supremely poetical. Whereas, on the other hand, the brutality, the swagger and self-laudation, the utter disregard for the sanctity of human life, that characterized the heroes of "romance ;" and the probability that their daily life con-tained at least as much that was harsh and monotonous as can be found in any phase of modern existence ; all this has been softened down by time, or overlooked in the natural tendency to seek for poetry anywhere but in the present scene. But, while this is true, our conventional notions of romance do not cluster round chimney-stalks or railway-stations. Modern romance is either too near us, or of too new a kind, to be generally recognized as such. What we conventionally know as romance is the irregular, unfettered life of gypsydom—with its colour and motion, its minstrelsy

---

* "That jugglers, sleight of hand performers, dancers, tumblers, and such like subordinate artists, . . . were also comprehended under the general term of minstrel" has been proved "very successfully" (it appears from the article on *Romance*, in the eighth edition of the *Encyclopedia Britannica*) by Mr. Ritson. This identity has already been sufficiently dwelt upon in these pages.

and its bloodshed. It is human nature in its wild state.
" The gypsy is one of many links which connect the simple
feeling of nature with romance," says one writer,* in a
chapter which illustrates the sentiment I am referring to.
And this statement (true enough) might be very much
amplified ; for gypsyism is *the* link which connects us with
the romance (so-called) of this and past ages.

The popular notions with regard to mediæval romance are
all based upon works of fiction ; written long ago, and re-
flected in the pages of modern novelists and poets. That the
" tales of chivalry " have some real foundation cannot be
doubted. But if the "Idylls of the King," and the books
out of which these incidents are taken, truly describe a real
system of society, then Cervantes did not know what he
was about, and *Don Quixote* ought never to have been
written:

It is not likely that many people really do accept those
romances as genuine history, whether they read them in the
older collections, or in the exquisite version by which they
are chiefly known in this century. Perhaps, however, the
chief—if not the only—fault of those old romances is the
halo of false sentiment that surrounds them. Let us accept
their facts as true, and what is it that they describe? There
cannot be a better interpreter of those old tales than
Cervantes himself, and his whole book is meant to show how
"knight-errantry " really appeared to modern men. Whatever a " knight " may once have been, a " knight-errant " was
simply a "nomadic horseman," who lived by plunder. " 'I
have heard your worship say,' quoth Panza, 'that it is usual
for knights-errant to sleep on heaths and deserts the greater
part of the year.' . . . . 'What then, is this an inn ?' replied
Don Quixote [on a certain memorable occasion] . . . since
it is so, that it is no castle, but an inn, all that can now be
done is, that you excuse the payment ; for I cannot act
contrary to the law of knights-errant, of whom I certainly
know, having hitherto read nothing to the contrary, that
they never paid for lodging, or anything else, in any inn
where they have lain. ' " These are precisely the manners of
those *sorners*, " masterful oppressers," who were " suffered to

* Mr. Leland, in the Introduction to his book on " Gypsies."

vaig and wander throughout the whole country," until their power became less and less as the successive statutes of post-mediæval times (enacted by sedentary and civilized communities) were enforced against them.   Prior to these statutes, their power was unbounded ; and the timid towns-folk and yeomen permitted them to levy blackmail and to live upon the goods of others whenever and wherever they pleased.   Even in the eighteenth-century Scotland, there were " knights-errant " who were so much dreaded that when (as in the cases of Will Marshall and the Baillie chiefs) they were known to be guilty of numerous murders, no one was bold enough to bring them to justice ; or, when it did happen that they were judicially tried and sentenced to death or banishment, the sentence was afterwards repealed.   " Where have you seen or read (asks Don Quixote) of a knight-errant being brought before a court of justice, let him have committed ever so many homicides ? "   But, although the knight-errant of the Middle Ages, and—in rare instances—of the eighteenth century, was permitted to kill his fellow-men with impunity, things are somewhat different now.   He is called by the prosaic name of "criminal," and his fate is either capital punishment or penal servitude.

It is most apparent that the "gypsy" of last century and the "knight-errant" of earlier days, were imbued with the same ideas and actuated by the same motives ; and it is extremely probable that they were closely connected both by language and by blood.   In either case, we have mounted men, scouring the country in search of adventures and of plunder, "sleeping on heaths and deserts the greater part of the year," exacting house-room and food without any offer of recompense ; and fighting—always fighting.   It cannot be a mere accident that has made "pugilist" one of the synonyms for "gypsy."   And not only were those mediæval "knights-errant" the most inveterate fighters, but they must also have belonged, physically, to the "bruiser" or "bull-dog" type.   It may be incorrect to regard the conventional "bruiser" as a full-blooded gypsy, for he appears to be a hybrid.   But it has been already shown that, while many pure gypsies have been thoroughgoing "bruisers," the conventional prize-fighter has the side-locks, the language (to some extent) and the complexion (also in a partial degree) of the conventional gypsy. Now, if there is anything in heredity, it is obvious that a distinctly pugnacious nineteenth-century caste is more likely to be descended from a pugnacious caste of the Middle Ages than from any peace-loving race of that period. And those wandering fighters of the earlier period are thus the most probable ancestors of a similar race in modern days. Or, again, if it be a truth that a man's facial expression, and (in course of time) his physique, can be greatly modified by his own manner of living, not to speak of his father's and grandparents'; it is plain that a race of men who devoted themselves to a life of combativeness must have developed the aggressive physical features of the professional fighter. Thus, viewed in either light, the " knights-errant " of the Middle Ages—or earlier—were, by hypothesis, either full-blooded gypsies, or else cross-bred " half-and-halfs " or " mumpers."

If we try to realize their daily existence, we must perceive this likeness more and more. Those early romances have been so beautifully rendered in the present century, by one writer before all others; and by all modern writers they have been made the groundwork of so much that is high and noble; that it seems essentially barbarous to tear aside these films of poetry which obscure our view. But what kind of men were those " knights-errant " in reality? They were men who would not be endured now-a-days. If they lived in the present day, they would be found in such places as Dartmoor and Millbank. They were eternally fighting. And not only were they prize-fighters, but they were prize-fighters whose battles ended fatally, as often as not. It is probably a considerable time since a British prize-fight has resulted in the death of one of the combatants, though it is on record that this happened at Brighton about a century ago; George IV., then Prince of Wales, being one of the spectators. But, whatever the result of the individual contest, or the nature of the weapons, those combats of the " romantic " period were nothing else than prize-fights. The combatants fought with two objects in view—the defeat of a rival, with the consequent increase of the victor's fame—and the receipt of some more tangible prize, such as the diamonds referred to in the story of *Elaine*, or some other "badge" that entitled the victor to be called a "champion"—until he got beaten by somebody else. And the conqueror in such a fight, like all other "champion" prize-fighters, went swaggering about the country, defying all and sundry. There is no substantial difference between the two sets of men. If we seek for a caste in this century corresponding to those pugnacious nomads of early times, we find them among our modern prize-fighters. In either case, the object is self-glorification and the defeat of an opponent; the "champions" are assisted by "squires;" the scene is a "ring," against whose "barriers" it is a humiliation to be driven; and the peculiar language of the combatants and their friends is that form of speech which is known as Romanes. The arena of such combats was not always the diminished "ring" of this generation. One of the celebrated fighters of last century had a regular "amphitheatre" (situated in Oxford Road), which was the scene of many an encounter; "and a larger one was erected in the same locality in 1742 for one Broughton, the funds being subscribed by some eighty noblemen and gentlemen." It is also curious to notice that the language used by one of these fighters—the celebrated Sutton—in speaking of his rival (Figg), is of the same grandiose character as that employed by the earlier heroes of "romance." He taunts his foe with having "by 'sleeveless pretence' shirked a combat with him, 'which I take [he says] to be occasioned through fear of his having that glory eclipsed by me, wherewith the eyes of all spectators have been so much dazzled.' He further assures the said Figg, that if he can muster courage enough to fight with him, he (Figg) 'will have the advantage of being overcome by a hero indeed!'" Moreover, the names by which such warriors are known among their friends are all of the *Cœur-de-Lion* and *Front-de-Bœuf* order; the descriptive or semi-poetical kind of nomenclature. And the whole terminology of the "amphitheatre" teems with expressions of an imaginative and periphrastic nature.*

---

* The kinship between the "bruiser" and the burglar has already been spoken of. A recent event in the annals of Paris house-breaking seems to show that the French burglars employ nick-names of this same order; by which

The kind of language just spoken of is, of course, more "English" than anything else; although it has been shown that "Romanes," pure and simple, is the mother-tongue of many famous British prize-fighters—who, indeed, seem to be *the* representatives of their order. But the "imaginative" terms referred to are nearly all to be found in modern English dictionaries; and are, therefore, independent of Romanes. Still, it is impossible to wholly separate "English" from "Romanes," or either of these from "Cant." More than one example of "Romanes" and "Cant" that is identical with "English" might easily be cited; but one is enough for the present purpose. And, though the word to be taken is not included in the vocabularies of *Romanes*, it is at least *Cant*, and is identified with the classes at present referred to. This is the word *Kid*, or *Kiddy;* with regard to which Grose says, that it is "particularly applied to a boy who commences thief at an early age; and when, by his dexterity, he has become famous, he is called, by his acquaintance, *the kid* so and so, mentioning his sirname." But this word *Kid* or *Kiddy* is just another spelling (and accent) of *Child* or *Childe;* the causes which have given rise to this twofold spelling and accent being the same as those which have made the word *circ* become *kirk* in one district and *chirch* or *church* in another. And the "tory" pronunciation has this advantage over the other that it has preserved the dissyllabic sound; which its more reputable twin-brother has lost. Accordingly, when a young thief has become a hero in the eyes of his friends, and has established a right to be styled "*the kid* so and so;" and when he is of Romani stock (as many thieves are), he is, in reality, *The Child* Lovel, Roland, Leigh, Bosville, or whatever else his patronymic may be. Of course, a distinguished thief is not a "hero" in the eyes of educated modern people; but it must be remembered that great districts of Northern England and Southern Scotland were dominated by "Common Thieves," only two or three centuries ago,—at which time the definition of "a thief" was "a

they are known to themselves and the police. Two of this interesting caste at present in Paris bear the respective titles of *Cœur-Vaillant* and *Couche tout-nu* (and, although the latter of these is not poetical, it belongs to the same class of names as the former).

cavalier who ventures life for gain." We, who are, in one degree or another, "educated people," do not hold a leader of thieves in high esteem; but one division of our ancestors certainly did so; and, indeed, this division was nothing else than a conglomerate of robber-tribes. And it is of importance to notice that while "we" know nothing of "Childe So and So," except from books; the gypsified classes make use of the term, *by inheritance.* From which the plain inference is that they are purer representatives of those castes than "we" are; an inference which has now been drawn for a considerable number of reasons.

Thus, the "knight-errant" is distinctly the progenitor of the "knight of the road," with whom he is connected by the ties of custom, of ideas, of language, and (inferentially) of blood. One cannot applaud the one without applauding the other. Sympathy with "Lancelot of the Lake" (not the Lancelot of Malory and Tennyson, but the real man behind him) cannot be separated from sympathy with Dick Turpin and Joseph Blake. If the earlier nomad-robber was a "hero," so were those of the seventeenth and eighteenth centuries. And an examination of all of their peculiarities shows that they belonged to the "gypsy" castes: Tristram of Lyonesse was a vagabond-minstrel and a *sorner;* and "Sir Gawain" was "Sir Tinker," not only when regarded etymologically, but in many other ways. One thing is evident, that men who were accustomed to ride about the country in quest of plunder and strife—like the knight-errant, the "banditti" described in Pyne's *Microcosm,* the "moss-troopers" of Scott, the "knights of the road," and the modern "gypsies"—and who (like all of these, except the two last) are represented as wearing defensive armour made of metal,—it is evident that such men must have thoroughly understood how to solder and "tinker;" or otherwise, they must have been, over and over again, at the mercy of the nearest foe.

The identification of one division of the gypsy castes with the knights-errant of Romance, however, implies a good deal that requires fuller consideration. For example, it may be erroneous to regard the Norman invasion as an inroad of *Xanthochroi.* The Northmen are remembered as "white strangers" and "gentiles of pure colour;" but it may be more correct to regard the Normans as a comparatively dark race—"dark, but not disagreeably so," as Borrow says of the Lovels, Bosvilles, Rolands, and others. It may be that the Normans were a cross between the white-skinned Northmen and the Moors of Picardy—or some other dark-skinned race. But it is enough for the present to point out that the mediæval knights-errant were the prototypes of our modern gypsies—or of one division of these—without going further into the subject.

One of the modern names for the knight-errant, then, is "prize-fighter." Of course, his fighting was usually of the deadliest kind ; he was both soldier and prize-fighter. Indeed, the word for "prize-fighter" in Romanes is also the word for "soldier." The modern prize-fighter has to be content with merely disfiguring his opponent (and himself) ; and were he to attempt to go to extremes—as his predecessors did—he would be executed as a "criminal." At least, it is regarded as a crime to kill one's fellow-countrymen ; although, in certain circumstances, it is quite a proper thing to kill people of another nation. We have clearly advanced a stage since the days when our islands were ruled by the Romanesque castes.

But the "amphitheatre" of the pugilist was unmistakably the latest representative of the mediæval "lists." And the spectators were, quite recently, men of high rank. The decline of pugilism has been so rapid and so recent that young men in the present day cannot easily realise how "respectable" it was not very many years ago. It has been lately remarked that if the fight between Sayers and Heenan (or between similar "champions") were to take place to-day, the lookers-on would scarcely be of the same social value as those of 1860, and the fight itself would be described in less respectful terms. And the farther back one looks, the higher is the position accorded to prize-fighting. In 1817, the Czar of Russia witnessed an English prize-fight, and shook hands with the victor. In 1814, Lord Lowther treated the Allied Sovereigns and their generals to " a series of boxing-matches in his drawing-room, which were so highly relished that they were repeated a few days afterwards." George IV., when Prince of Wales, attended a fight at Brighton, in which one of the combatants was killed. Broughton's amphitheatre in the Oxford Road was erected at the expense of "some eighty noblemen and gentlemen." And, in a much earlier day, Richard the Third—and, earlier still, Alfred the Great—are spoken of as "patrons" of pugilism (though they were probably something more than patrons). Tournaments, so conducted, only differ from those that the poets write of in one particular—they were fought on foot. But they often ended fatally. And the combatants seem chiefly to have belonged to a race of "cavaliers;" whose speech was the language called Romanes or Romance.

The account from which the above facts are taken* does not make special mention of Charles the Second and his times. But his Restoration witnessed the restoration of all such things. That period is interesting, because it might well be taken as the date at which the Romanesque word, *kooromengro*, began to have the twofold meaning of "soldier" and "prize-fighter." Those seventeenth-century cavaliers—like their prototypes, the knights-errant—were certainly something more than mere prize-fighters. Although "prize-fighter" is one of the modern names of the knight-errant, one must think of him as a "soldier" also. The "champion prize-fighter" undoubtedly embodies many of the characteristics of the Lancelots of mediæval times; and either of these went about the world challenging every fighter to prove himself a better "champion." But then, the modern prize-fighter is not allowed to kill; and he is not acknowledged as a leader of warriors. The mediæval "champion" is represented in this century by the "champion" soldier, as well as the "champion" prize-fighter; and it is, of course, the first of these who embodies his highest attributes.

The Restoration, however, seems about the period when this divergence fairly began. That the Cavaliers were soldiers everybody knows. But they were also prize-fighters and jugglers. All the kind of thing that we now regard as the property of "gypsies" and "jockeys" and "welshers," all that kind of thing was the amusement of the seventeenth-century "cavalier." Pugilism is not a "drawing-room recreation" at this date, whatever it was in the beginning of this

* An article on "Boxing, or Pugilism," in *Chambers's Encyclopædia.*

century. But pugilism, cock-fighting, bear-baiting, gambling, and so on—these were the amusements of those Cavaliers. The Restoration is spoken of as an age "when jugglers and conjurers came into extraordinary request." "Sleight-of-hand tricks . . . . . by which a single piece of money was multiplied *ad infinitum*, were much encouraged by the nobility, who frequently hired show-men and professors of magic to entertain their guests." And these things were the accomplishments of the dusky *jongleurs* of the Middle Ages, as well as of our gypsified castes to-day. And the distinguishing language of either is Romanes.

If a mediæval knight-errant, or a seventeenth-century cavalier, were to come to life at the present day, these are the things that he would seek out, if he wanted amusement. And he would find what he sought among our gypsy and semi-gypsy classes. It was just the other day that the British "champion" made a progress through the country; giving entertainments, at which he exhibited his various trophies, besides showing off his pugilistic powers. In an account of one of those meetings it is stated :—"The champion of the P. R. was supported by a company of artists, consisting of vocalists, violinists, jugglers, and negro buffoons, who did their best to amuse and fill up the first part of the programme." When the champion visited London his meetings were, of course, held in the East End (because the West is not mediæval). And this is the place and the company that this hypothetical knight-errant, or cavalier, would feel most at home in ; if he came suddenly into nineteenth-century life. If the former culture and *vivacity* were gone, he would still see the unchanged *form*. At such a meeting as this he would find the people paying homage to a man who was a "hero" in his eyes ; and whose only fault was that he did not kill the enemy he fought against. He would find that the other actors in the scene were those "jugglers, sleight-of-hand performers, dancers, tumblers, and such like subordinate artists" who were "comprehended under the general term of minstrel," in his own day ; and some of these would have their faces blackened, "that they might the better pass for Moors." It is not uncharitable to suppose that many of the ladies present would—like that "miracle of women," referred

to in " The Princess," or like Mr. Simson's **Border queans**—
be accustomed to do their own fighting, when required. And
I venture to think that this supposititious hero of " Romance" would be thoroughly conversant with the language
which he would hear occasionally spoken around him ; and
also, that he would find there a larger proportion of his
kindred than in any ordinary assembly of the same size in
London.

CHAPTER XIII.

WHEN one attempts to show that British *Romanes*, at the present day, is the sediment of British *Romance*—in the "Middle" and "Dark" Ages—it is plain that one cannot stop there. Because the Romanesque languages are derived from something that is akin to *Latin;* and, consequently, to connect the language of the modern Romani with the Romanesque tongues of the days of "chivalry" is to do everything but state that the modern Romani have received their language, if not their blood, from their famous historical namesakes.

It is, of course, an accepted belief at present that the Romanesque languages (as the expression is generally understood) are all derived from the historical *Romans*, and have nothing to do with the *Romani* tribes at all. Now, one of the first things that must strike any one who takes up this subject with an unbiassed judgment, is the curious fact that while a historical race of *Romani* has affected the condition of Europe to an immense degree, and although an existing race of *Romani*—possessed of many distinct individual traits—is yet found all over Europe, no attempt to connect the two has ever been made. Gypsiologists, instead of looking to Italy for the origin of this name, go further afield even than that —to Roumania, to Egypt, and to Hindostan. That the *Rom* of India and of Europe have come from one common source need not be disputed. But why should we look to such a distance—in time and space—to find the origin of our Romani, when we know that their namesakes have made themselves famous at a period, and in a territory, that (comparatively speaking) is near our own—nearer, at least, than Ancient Egypt or India? It is wrong to say that *all* gypsiologists have ignored this resemblance. Borrow, for instance, speaks of his gypsies as "Romans;" and tells us that they

call themselves so. They do things " Romanly" and " in the
Roman fashion : " and he soliloquizes over their names—
Ursula, Lucretia, Lydia, Lavinia, Clementina, and so on.
Those women, he says, " appeared to be as faithful to their
husbands as the ancient Roman matrons were to theirs.
Roman matrons ! and, after all, might not these be in reality
Roman matrons ? . . . . . Might not they be of the same
blood as Lucretia ? . . . . . It is true their language was
not that of old Rome ; it was not, however, altogether different from it. After all, the ancient Romans might be a tribe
of these people, who settled down and founded a village with
the tilts of carts, which by degrees and the influx of other
people, became the grand city of the world. . . . . Why,
after all, should not the Romans of history be a branch of
these Romans ? " And again, he remarks, " Rome, it is said,
was built by some vagabonds ; who knows but that some
tribe of the kind settled down thereabouts, and called the
town which they built after their name ? "*

To prevent confusion, it is well to remember—before going
further—that the language called *Romanes*, and the people
called *Romani*, only belong to one division of the "gypsies"
of Britain. Setting aside Xanthochroic gypsies altogether
(though this is what Mr. Simson refuses to do), there are still
two distinct *kinds* of dark-skinned gypsies,—though Mr.
Leland, while recognizing this " entirely different" origin,
gives them the one common name of *Romani*. The handsome cavaliers described by Mr. Borrow have, at least, no
near relationship with those " lean, black, and hideous Egyptians," referred to in Continental annals. The followers of
" John the Faw," in the ballad, were " black, but *very bonny* " :
while, on the other hand, Mactaggart and Simson give hints
of a thick-set, squat race of "gypsies." Accordingly, any
conclusions we may arrive at with regard to the origin of the
Romany Proper need not be held to contradict, in any degree,
the statements already made in these pages on the subject of
British " gypsies."

Mr. Borrow, then, thought it not unlikely that his English
gypsies were descended from, and received their name from

* See his soliloquy in " Mumpers' Dingle," in *The Romany Rye :* also *Lavengro*, Chapter XVII.

the historical Romani. (The spellings of *Komany* and *Romani*, it may be remarked, constitute a distinction that is not a difference ; and such gypsiologists as Groome, Smart, and Crofton give the preference to the *Romani* form. This latter form, therefore, we may adhere to henceforth.) Following Borrow, Mr. Lucas—in his "Yetholm History of the Gypsies" (pp. 68-76)—upholds the belief that a portion of the earlier population of Italy was made up of what we now call "gypsy" tribes ; and that the city of Rome derived its name from them. Whatever may have been the ethnic position of the Latin-Roman invaders of Britain, it seems likely that our British Romani of to-day would never have been known by such a name, had the historical Romani never entered our islands. Dr. Skene, in considering the Southern-Scottish people, states that "we must turn in the first instance to the Cymric legends," to obtain any facts, or traditions, with regard to them. These legends, he says, "tell us that this [South-Scottish] population may be referred to three races, the Brython, the Romani, and the Gwyddyl. Thus in a poem contained in the Book of Taliessin we find them thus alluded to :—

> Three races cruel from true disposition,
> Gwyddyl and Brython and Romani,
> Create discord and confusion.

. . . . . Of the last two races, the Brython and the Romani, we have an account in an old document. 'The Descent of the Men of the North.' . . . . . After noticing the three tribes under which the supposed descendants of Coel were ranged, The Descent of the Men of the North proceeds to give the pedigrees of those said to be of Roman descent . . . . . These were obviously the Romani of the poem, and can be mainly traced in connection with the central districts of Annandale, Clydesdale, and Tweeddale."* And these districts—Annandale, Clydesdale, and Tweeddale—were, says Mr. Simson the elder, virtually governed, up till the eighteenth century, by "races cruel from true disposition," who spoke the language known as *Romanes*. At the present stage of our information it is impossible to

* *Celtic Scotland*, Vol. III. pp. 100-103.

speak with decision upon the matter.   But it is a much more
rational and less credulous thing to believe that those
eighteenth-century "gypsies" of Clydesdale, Tweeddale,
and Annandale, spoke the language of the Romani *on account
of* the invasion of these dales by the historical Romani, ten
or fifteen hundred years before ; than to believe that the
historical Romani, having been there, vanished altogether
from sight, and were succeeded, at a distance of a thousand
years, and in precisely the same localities, by tribes possessing very similar characteristics, speaking a language
known as Romanes, calling themselves Romani, but of quite
another race and origin from their earlier namesakes.   The
modern theories that would derive those South-Scotch
Romani from straggling bands of immigrants of the fifteenth
and sixteenth centuries are not only quite at variance with
those ancient traditions, but they make far larger demands
upon one's credulity than the conjectures hazarded by Mr.
Borrow and supported by the various statements made in
the present chapter.

It must, again, be borne in mind, that what is here said
with regard to the Romani of any particular part of the
United Kingdom does not apply to the whole of British
gypsydom, but only to a portion of it.   And that, although
we may temporarily ignore the Picto-Moorish origin assigned
to certain tribes of British gypsies—while pursuing the
Romani division of such people—the conclusions drawn with
regard to the latter need not affect (unless indirectly) the
lineage and history of the former.   Though in this chapter
the British Romani are specially glanced at, that does not
cancel the fact that in one particular district of our country
(as probably in others) there were once " *three* races cruel
from true disposition," and that the Romani were only one
of these three.   In the comparatively small territory to
which these Welsh legends refer, the Romani were rivalled
in fierceness by the " Gwyddyl and Brython."   Indeed, it is
most likely that it was owing to a *racial* difference such as
this that those "gypsy" clans of Annandale, Clydesdale,
and Tweeddale, described by Simson and others, were forever engaged in mutual struggles and vendettas.   The
bloody encounters between eighteenth-century Kennedys

and Taits and Shaws were probably nothing else than the outcome of remoter feuds—in the same district—among those "three races cruel from true disposition, Gwyddyl and Brython and Romani."

It may further be premised, incidentally, that what has been said in relation to the accentuation of the word Romance or Romanes, bears also upon the pronunciation of Romani. We who have made *Ro'man* of *Roman'us* are the very people who would transform *Roman'i* into *Ro'mani*. There is no verbal difference whatever between the British " Romani " of one century and of another.

Thus, although the South-Scottish clans of Kennedys, and Marshalls, and Black-Douglases and others, may have been originally descended from invaders of Scot-Egyptian stock, or from other races of *dubh galls* not belonging to the Romani family, it may easily have come about that clans belonging to this last division impressed their language—and perhaps their physical attributes—very strongly upon many of those whose lineage was vastly different from theirs. For example, the Black-Douglases, whom we noticed as still retaining, in a faint degree, their ancestral nationality or clanship—so recently as the year 1835—those Black-Douglases were ranged under the leadership of the Yetholm Faws, and their language was, presumably, the Romanesque "cant" of Yetholm. It is evident, to the most ordinary observer, that the "cant" of Yetholm is Romanes ;[*] and, although the nineteenth century Black-Douglases of Yetholm *may* have inherited certain peculiarities of speech that distinguished them from other Yetholm families (just as their dark skins distinguished them from the fair-complexioned "gypsy" Blythes), yet it is likely that they—and all the modern Yetholm families—made use of the Romanesque " Cant " of Yetholm, with few deviations, or none at all. Whether the Galloway clans, and those of other parts of the country, understood Romanes, or spoke languages quite different from it, may be left an open question. But Romanes was,

---

[*] This is clearly shown by various gypsiologists, and it proves that Mr. C. G. Leland is in error in assuming that what Mr. Simson learned was the *Shelta Thari*. He may have acquired that too,—but when he conversed with the Yetholm gypsies, he must have spoken Romanes.

and is, spoken in the South of Scotland : and it is probable that such surnames as Romanes and Romanno,* connected with that district, have come down from the Romani invaders. (In other parts of the country one finds names which suggest a similar origin,—such as Romsey, Romney, and Romford,—and the " cant " name for London, " Romeville.")

Those people who, at the present day, call themselves Romanys, and their speech Romanes, belong distinctly to one of the darkest-skinned sections of our population. Now, if the early Romani invaders who became the progenitors of certain British-Romani clans were men of white skins, we should account for the dark colour of our modern Romani by assuming that they represent a hybrid race, and that their non-Roman ancestors were among those ante-Cæsarian British races which were " as black as Ethiopians " (in Pliny's words), or " blackamoors " (in those of Claudian). And that the darkest of all our modern Romani .are quite light in complexion as compared with their " Moorish " ancestors. But then, to confute this hypothesis, there is the fact that such people call their language both the *Romani Jib* and the *Kaulo Jib* (that is, *black speech*, or *dubh chainnt*) ; and " the blood" which it is their pride to possess is the *Kaulo Rat* (or *black blood*). Thus it would seem that the purer the " Roman " the darker his skin† : and that, therefore, those early Romani invaders were not white men.

The composition of the mixed nation whom we may distinguish as Historical Romans is a matter that cannot be dealt with in a single paragraph, or by one who has only paid a transitory attention to the modern British people bearing that name. But it is important to notice that, in the twelfth century, *Latin* and *Roman* were two separate languages ; it being necessary to translate from the one into the other. It is also important to remember that the *Latins* were not the *Romans Proper ;* between which races there

---

* This name is perhaps extinct, as a surname, though it once belonged to a family known as the Romannos of Romanno, in Tweeddale.

† One of Mr. Borrow's most ultra-Romanesque acquaintances was a certain Mrs. Heron ; and she is remembered by her relatives as having been of a most swarthy complexion—" almost black," to use their own words.

may have been an immense ethnological difference. It has been remarked that more than one scholar is agreed as to "the presence of a large Turanian admixture among the ancient Romans." What "Turanian" implies is perhaps not easily defined ; but at least it is an expression that does not denote the Xanthochroic type. If applied to a Red-Indian or "Gypsy" stock, it would not be regarded as wholly unsuitable. Now, it may be remembered that, at the outset, we took notice of the opinion held by Signor Gennarelli, an Italian archæologist, to the effect that among the earlier inhabitants of the Italian peninsula there were certain tribes, spoken of as Aborigines, Siculi, Liguri, Umbri, and others, who—in his estimation—were very probably European Red-Indians. His various reasons for this belief were briefly indicated when his theory was referred to : * and he ascribed to this hypothetical red-skinned race many attributes common to the Ancient Egyptians and the Mexicans. Gennarelli is not the only writer who has assigned to the Liguri of Italy the physical attributes of the Red-Indian. For the author of "The Yetholm History of the Gypsies" (at p. 73 of that book) expresses the opinion that at least one Ligurian tribe, the *Salassi*, was composed of a distinctly "gypsy" race : and the statements which he makes, in that connection, indicate very clearly the presence of a dusky, fortune-telling, "Indian" people, among the inhabitants of ancient Italy. He quotes Juvenal to show that, in ancient Italy—as in ancient and modern England—there were soothsayers who told fortunes, on consideration of receiving a sum of money ; and that those Italian soothsayers (like their congeners of ancient England and of Persia) interpreted by such means as the lines of the hand, and the entrails of animals (and, presumably, by the stars and by dreams). And the complexion of such people is indicated by Juvenal when he states that "the hired Phrygian, or Indian Augur, will give an answer to the rich ; " and that "the rich Roman requires at his table the Indian of duskier hue than the Moor." † What proportion those races bore to the entire

* See *ante*, Book I., Chap. I. p. 13.

† This is quoted from Mr. Lucas' "Yetholm History," p. 72. The word "Roman"—in the phrase "the rich Roman"—must here be accepted in its comprehensive sense, and be held to have no more racial significance than the word "Briton" at the present day.

population of ancient Italy is, of course, quite uncertain ; but it seems evident that, to find a period at which castes of swarthy *Magi, Druids,* and *Soothsayers* (akin to those of ancient Assyria, Persia, and Egypt) did *not* inhabit the West of Europe, inclusive of the British Islands, we must look far beyond the period of Cæsar's conquests.

The consideration of " Roman " in what appears to be its earliest recognizable sense gives us the clue to the identity of " Egyptians " or " Gypsies " with " Romani." Because the word *Rom* or *Romi* signifies "a man," both·in Coptic and in Romanes. That is to say, among Ancient Egyptians as among later Italians and British, there were people to whom a *Rom* or *Roman* was " one of ourselves,"—one of our " men." In other words, certain Ancient Egyptians were Romi or Romani. The writer from whom the foregoing facts are chiefly taken (Mr. Lucas) distinctly draws the founders of Rome from Ancient Egypt : in doing which he goes a step farther back than Mr. Borrow. The name of " Egyptian," it is quite clear, could never have been persistently given to a certain race, or to certain races, without any reason for this designation. But if it is once admitted that a red-skinned Coptic people called themselves *Romi* or *Romani,* then it is easy to see how—if they emigrated from Egypt— they would be *Egyptians* (afterwards shortened into '*Gypsies*) to other people. That the British Romani do—or did— call *themselves* " Egyptians " is stated by Mr. Borrow. He also says (in Chapter XVII. of *Lavengro*) that Jasper Petulengro is the " Pharaoh " of the English Gypsies : there are other *kings,* " but the true Pharaoh is Petulengro :" a usage which implies the most correct knowledge of the proper application of the word " Pharaoh." Mr. Simson again states that his Scotch gypsies—or some of them—style themselves " Pharaoh's people ;" and when he says that they also call themselves " Ethiopians " there is not, of necessity, any contradiction in the use of these two terms by the same people—if the same people used them. The name of " Ethiopian " must, of course, have been quite inapplicable to the white-skinned tories of Scotland ; and perhaps not applicable, either, to one or more of the dark-skinned divisions. But it is plain that certain Scotch-gypsy clans called themselves—and were called— " Ethiopians." Mr. Simson says of some of them, "they persisted in their own tradition, that they were a tribe of *Ethiopians ;*" and John the Faw, "in a pardon dated Feb. 15, 1615," is formally styled "Joannis Fall, *Ethiopis,* lie [in law] *Egiptian.*" "I think it must be conceded [remarks Mr. Lucas,—from whose "Yetholm History" (p. 31) the foregoing clauses are extracted] that some, at least, of the Scottish gypsies did come, as they aver, through Ethiopia and Egypt, having made a long enough stay in Nubia or Ethiopia to have forgotten India." Of course, the writer just quoted is one of those who have not contemplated the possibility of such Nubians and Ethiopians having arrived in Britain prior to the Christian era. But, as both Pliny and Claudian have told us that there were tribes of Ethiopians and Moors in these islands at the time of Cæsar's invasion, it is possible to agree with Mr. Lucas in this supposition of his, in every portion of it except that which relates to the date of such a migration, or migrations. And, to corroborate Pliny, not only have we one (or many*) British tribes of the eighteenth and nineteenth centuries "persisting in their own tradition that they were a tribe of *Ethiopians ;*" and such people were "in law, *Egyptians ;*" but we have the same tradition asserted at a far earlier period by those British clans who derived their descent from Gadelas, an Egyptian chief, and from "Scota, the daughter of a Pharaoh :" from which names those tribes were then known as Gaels and Scots.† The island which was the earliest British home of those (alleged) descendants of a Pharaoh was Ireland ; and that island was once full of a race that possessed many Egyptian qualities, even in recent times.

* Mr. Simson says that "all the Scottish Gipsies" believe themselves to be of Ethiopian descent. In saying this, he manifestly contradicts his own statement that many Scotch gypsies are "fair whites." But it is to be assumed that, at least, *several* clans of gypsies assured him of their Ethiopian (traditional) descent.

† It seems necessary to believe that the early Gaels and Scots were the same people : and consequently, *not* Xanthochroi. And that "the language of the white men," spoken to Captain Burt last century, though called "Gaelic," was very different from that spoken by the "Gaidheal" of fifteen centuries before. And, as an authority on the subject (Dr. McLauchlan of Edinburgh) has said that, even three or four centuries ago, the language called "Gaelic" was very different from that spoken now ; it may be assumed that a thousand years earlier the difference was greater still, and that the introduction of other races and other languages have so altered one division of Gaelic that it is now little more than "Gaelic" in name.

When we regard the Scots of Ancient Scotia (Ireland) as
" Egyptians," we do not necessarily assume that they were
in Egypt at the same time as the Italian Romani, or that
they were akin to them. But, on the other hand, they may
have inhabited Egypt at exactly the same period as the
Romani of Italy ; who may have been of precisely the same
stock as themselves. In the fourth century the Scots of
Ancient Scotia swarmed across St. George's Channel into
Wales ; and that territory is still celebrated for the coracles
and the harps which such people used. And it is further
celebrated as being that part of the British Islands in which
the purest Romanes is spoken at the present day ; while the
compound language known as "Welsh " also contains, we
have been told, a large number of words that are pure
Romanes and pure Persian.* The name of "Wales " (like
those of " Galloway " and " Inchegall ") means nothing more
than " The Foreigners' Country." Its natives, like those of
the rest of our country, are descended from the most various
stocks ; and it is not easy to say which of them caused it
to be called " The Foreigners' Country." But it is among
those "Welshmen " who speak the language of the Romani, that we find the ancient traditions of Merlin and of
Trinali—of great wizards and witches, *Magi* and *Druids,*—
and these legends not read out of printed books, but even
yet handed down from father to son, as portions of a genuine
unwritten history. And, since the custodiers of the oldest
traditions of Wales are those hereditary bards whom we call
gypsies, and who call themselves Romani, they are the people
whom we ought to regard as among the very earliest known
races of Wales. If they are the descendants of the fourth-
century Scots who overran the district known as Wales, then
those Scots—being the alleged posterity of " the daughter of
a Pharaoh," and of another royal Egyptian, and (of course)
of many others of the same race—must have called themselves *Egyptians,* and perhaps *Romani.* And the reason why
the Romanes of Wales is so much purer than that spoken in
any other part of the United Kingdom may be because the
hereditary bards of Wales—the *gypsies* of Wales—have pre-

* See *ante,* pp. 311 and 315.

served an isolated attitude longer than the other sections of their British kindred.

It is not unlikely that the Early Scots have fewer living representatives in their first British home (Ireland) than in Great Britain itself. The first accounts of them reveal them as invaders of Great Britain *from* Ireland—"shameless Irish robbers"—and they must have settled in considerable numbers in that portion of Scotland which became known as "Scotia."* What with these emigrations, and the intrusions of other races, Ireland may have gradually lost the greater part of its Scot-Egyptian population. But, still, it seems clear that Romanes belongs even yet to Ireland. A closer examination of this question shows that Mr. Leland's impression as to the *Shelta Thari* being the language spoken by Mr. Simson's Scotch gypsies is not endorsed by facts. The latter-mentioned writer gives more than one list of Scotch-Gypsy words which plainly prove that those gypsies spoke Romanes. And when Mr. Borrow conversed with Esther Blythe at Yetholm, he found that (although her vocabulary was very limited) she spoke the language of the Romani: and, more than that, that she possessed several Romani words that he had never heard used in England, although his wide-spread acquaintance with that variety of speech told him that those Scotch-Gypsy words were genuine *Romanes.*† Thus, although the Scotch historian may have known something of the *Shelta Thari* (regarding which name, however, he says nothing), there can be no doubt that when he spoke to gypsies he—and they—employed a variety of Romanes. Moreover, Mr. Simson shows us that the gypsies of Ireland (of his period) also spoke Romanes. (See

---

* The movement that made the North-British *Scotia* spread out into *Scotland* was (it has been pointed out) originated by later immigrants than the Early Scots.

† Mr. Borrow also accuses her of calling several words "Romanes" that (he says) do not belong to that form of speech. "She called a donkey 'asal,' and a stone 'cloch,' which words are neither cant nor Gypsy, but Irish or Gaelic." To which (had she known) she might have retaliated with the *tu quoque* that the "*cromes* or bends" in the framework of the tents which his "Wandsworth Gypsies" made, were also "Irish or Gaelic" in name. As for "asal," he might, with equal justice, have styled it "German and Latin" (*esel* and *asella*). But no word can be *accurately* ticketed with any race-name, except the name of the race who first used the word ; when that is known.

pp. 328-9 of his *History.*) And this fact is also proved by Mr. Leland. The Irish tinker who gave him so many examples of the *Shelta Thari* was also able to "rakker Romanes." Nor was he an exceptional case. In speaking of this language (*Shelta*), which is apparently a blending of "Gaelic" with "Romanes," Mr. Leland says—"I class it with the gypsy, *because all who speak it are also acquainted with Romany.*" Thus Ireland, which was the early home of the Scot-Egyptians, still retains, in some measure, the speech of the Egyptian-Romani. And Scotland, into which, "as early as the beginning of the sixth century" (says Dr. Skene), those Scot-Egyptians passed ; the memory of which migrations their descendants have not forgotten, since, (as Mr. Simson tells us) "almost all the Scottish Gypsies assert that their ancestors came by way of Ireland into Scotland ; " Scotland, also, has retained the language of the Romani. Thus, those Irish gypsies, who are even yet in possession of Romanes, must be regarded as the modern representatives (and probable descendants) of those eleventh-century "common jesters and rhymers," in connection with whose speech it has been said that "the true Irish" was so different from it that "scarce one in five hundred" could "either read, write, or understand it." And the wandering gypsy-minstrels of the Scotch Highlands, whose language, whatever its exact form, is not "Gaelic," must also be regarded as the modern Scotch representatives of the same order.

Although the word "Gaelic" has just been used to designate a particular form of British speech, it is not necessary to regard that title as the correct one. Probably "Gaelic," is as much—or as little—the language of the early Gaels as "English" is the language of the early Angles. Modern "Gaelic" is, to a great extent, the speech of Northmen. And, if the early Gaels were really descended from a Gadelas and a Scota of Egypt ; and if those tribes left Egypt at a time when *Rom* meant "a man," and *tem* "a country" (as in ancient Egyptian and in modern Romanes) ; then the language of the early Gaels is more likely to be nearer that used by the remnants of the Highland nomadic tribes than the speech of the settled classes, in much of Ireland and in north-western Scotland.

But the assumption that the early Egyptian-Scots were really a branch of the Romani takes us quite outside of the traditions and history of the British Islands ; and points to a period far too remote to be considered in these pages. Let us return to Romanes at a time when it is more within our reach.

"At a period as early as 1150 it plainly appears that the Romance language was distinguished from the Latin, and that translations were made from the one into the other ; for an ancient romance on the subject of Alexander, quoted by Fauchet, says it was written by a learned clerk,

'Qui *de Latin* la trest, et *en Roman* la mit.'"

Mr. Skeat, also, informs us that "by the ' Roman ' language was meant the vulgar tongue [what the Scotch-Highland gentry of a particular period called *dubh-chainnt*, or "black speech "] used by the people in everyday life, as distinguished from the ' Latin ' of books." Thus, when the translator of the tale just spoken of " drew it out of Latin and put it into Romanes," he was transmuting *Latin* into *Thieves' Latin*.

" The Roman language," although distinguished from " the ' Latin ' of books " in many ways, is not (says Mr. Borrow) " altogether different from it." This may be seen from the Romanesque words cited in the previous chapter——*Angla-terra, Mille, Tu, &c.* It may be seen also in the tendency of the modern British " Roman " to add the affix " 'us " to his nouns ; and also from the fact that he forms many of his plurals by adding *ia* to the singular.* If " Cant " is to be

* Some of these words are subjoined. It is necessary to premise that the spellings are not those usually given ; and for this reason. It is well known that certain sounds do not impress every listener in the same way ; and two people, hearing a word distinctly uttered by the same speaker, may easily write it down differently. An examination of two or three "gypsy" books shows several instances of this, particularly in the use of the letter " r." This letter conveys various degrees of force to various sections of English-speaking people ; and this is noticeable both in the United States and throughout the British Empire. The difference is perhaps most marked when the letter " r " occurs after a vowel and at the end of a word. (There are some instructive remarks on this point in a monograph " On the letter *r*," by Mr. R. F. Weymouth ; which may be seen in the Transactions of the Philological Society, 1862-3, Part II.) An American, of " Northern " breeding, will express the accent of a Southerner, in the words " before the war," " never," &c., as " befoah the wah," " nevah," &c. And the same kind of American finds fault with the Southern-Englishman's accent, for

regarded as being "Romanes" (and it is to be remembered
that the Yetholm Romani called their speech "The Cant "),
then we get such semi-Latin words as *Romeville* (London),
pannam (bread), *grannam* (grain), *togeman* (a gown or cloak ;
that is a "toga"—whence "togs"), and the verb to *fake*,
• which "signifies to do any act, or make anything": "to
fake a screeve is to write any letter or other paper."•

There is one word which shows the identity between
modern Romanes and early "Roman" as plainly as one could
desire. This is the word *caapa* (variously spelt *capa, gappa,
kappa, koppa, kopper*, and *coppur*). This word is used by our
modern Romani to denote "a blanket," or "the covering of
a tent;" and, with other complements, to denote various
kinds of "coverings." Pott makes the distinction that *kappa*
is "a woman's cloak," and *coppa* "a bed-cover." The radical
meaning of the word is clearly "a cover." Now, this is what
we call modern Romanes. But Mr. Skeat informs us that
this word belongs to "Low Latin "—" the Roman language "
—" the vulgar tongue used by the people in everyday life, as
distinguished from the 'Latin' of books." He tells us that
the words *cap, cape,* and *cope,* which we find in our Modern-

---

the same reason. On the other hand, those who think that the final *r* ought to
be *hinted*, rather than pronounced, or even altogether ignored,—such people,
wishing to express in print the accent of an American Northerner. or an Irishman, or a Scotchman (when these are of distinctly provincial breeding) will write
rr in place of *r*. To what extent the letter *r* ought to be sounded, in certain
circumstances, is thus clearly a matter of taste, or of association. But this difference exists. And where one gypsiologist writes *gorgio, corlo, plarshta, parner,
baryor, ranyor, yackor,*—another will write *gaujo, kaulo, plashta, pawnee, baria,
ranya, yacka.* What seems to the one the sound of *r* after a vowel is to the
other not *r* at all. Consequently, since the plural of *ran* (a rod) is distinctly
ranya or *rania*, according to the hearing of many English-speaking people, it
may be assumed that *ranyor* is a less correct spelling of this plural. Assuming,
then, that the final *yor, ior, or* and *ar* of various Romanesque plurals, ought to
be written as *ia* and *a*, we get such plurals as these :—*baria, busnia, cania, dania,
durilia, gavia, juvia, kaunia, lavia, millia, mahlia, mutzia, naia, pappia,
pattina, puvia, poria, palia, pala, rania, sainia, scunia, shockia, scraunia, spinia,
truppia* and *yacka.* These are all plural nouns, and although (except in such a
case as *puvius,* "land ") the singular is generally a monosyllable, it is to be
remembered that some of the Romani have still the habit of adding *us* to the
singular noun, even when that is a modern word. So that these singulars had,
likely enough, the *us* termination at one time ; or, perhaps, *ius, ium,* or *um.*

• Some of these words will be found in Grose's *Dictionary ;* others in Logan's
Pedlar's Pack of Ballads, &c.

English dictionaries, "were all the same originally." And that the original word (so far as it may be traced) was the Low-Latin *capa* or *cappa;* whose various meanings, at one time or another, are "cap; cape; cope; cover; hooded cloak." Among other things, we are told that "this Low-Latin *cappa,* a cape, hooded cloak, occurs in a document of the year 660 (Diez) ; and is spelt *capa* by Isidore of Seville, 19. 31. 3." Thus the "frauenmantel" of Dr. Pott, which is *Romanes* of the nineteenth-century, is identical with the *Roman* "hooded cloak " of the year 660.

Probably many other words could be adduced by those who are proficient in Romanes and the various " Cant" dialects, which would prove that they are "not altogether different from " Latin. Indeed, one or other of these dialects is known as *Latin ;* sometimes as *Thieves' Latin.*

It is of great importance to keep in view that the early Latins were not the early Romans. The early Latins appear to have been Northmen (not necessarily of the same breed as those who are so known in history, but still " Northmen " in the eyes of the early Romans). That they eventually became known themselves as " Romans " is no stranger than that the conquerors of Australians and Americans should become known by these names. To consider the race-history of Italy in pre-Christian times, or to speculate upon the probable proportions of *white, black,* and *brown* in the armies of Cæsar and Agricola,—these are questions of a very extensive nature. But it is beyond doubt that the pure Latins and the pure Romans belonged to different races ; that the Latin language, even in the twelfth century A.D., differed very considerably from the Roman ; and that the Latin-speaking classes of the time of Agricola—though calling themselves Romans—amused themselves after dinner by " bringing in the Moors," much in the fashion of the Edinburgh citizens of three or four centuries ago. These same dusky, fortune-telling, juggling " Moors " of the time of Juvenal and Agricola being quite likely of the more aboriginal "Romani " races—such as the gypsy-like Salassi, and other Ligurians, as well as the Siculi, Umbri, &c. ; being, in effect, the " Turanians " of some writers, and the " Ancient-Egyptians " of Signor Gennarelli.

That Egyptians should have colonized Italy, Iberia, the Islands of the Oestrymnides, and the British Islands, long ages before the days of Julius Cæsar; and that all of these should have originally called themselves *Rom*, *Romi*, or *Romani* (from the Cophtic word for "a man"); this is a theory which is supported by a considerable number of facts. It seems unquestionable that castes of *Magi*, of precisely the same *kind*, can be seen in Ancient Persia, Ancient Egypt, Italy, and Britain, as far back as our present vision reaches. And that British "druidism" was no novelty to Cæsar's soldiers. Whether the customs of tattooing and painting were unknown to—or, at least, not practised by—any of Cæsar's army, may be questioned. The fact that Cæsar spoke of certain British natives as "Blueskins" and "Green-Men" does not prove, of necessity, that some of his followers had not earned the same titles. Our own sailors—though in a very modified way—were given to the practice of tattooing, when they took our troops out to New Zealand; but officers, or authors, writing of the Maori customs, did not probably reflect that the practice of tattooing, though much more observable among the New Zealanders, was not a custom that wholly separated them from our own countrymen. One thing is clear—that whether the name of "Romani" was used by the Scot-Egyptians or the ante-Cæsarian Magi of Britain, or whether these people had other names ("the sons of Gadelas," "the sons of Scota," &c.)—an important line of the Romani ancestry in Britain was brought in with Cæsar, or by his successors. The Romani that Dr. Skene tells us were dominant in Annandale, Clydesdale, and Tweeddale, are all made to derive themselves from Romani of post-Cæsarian date.

It is thus imperative that we should regard one division of British Gypsydom—and, perhaps, even one section of the British Romani—as of Cæsarian and post-Cæsarian date. It may be that Romanes is the most important speech (though not by any means the *only* speech) of British Gypsydom, on account of the conquests of Cæsar and his successors. Whether or not prize-fighting, the amphitheatre, and the Romanesque languages existed in pre-Cæsarian Britain, they certainly existed in the Italy of Cæsar; and they have, presumably, never ceased to characterize the Britain of post-Cæsarian days. Horse-racing, practised almost precisely as at Epsom, with the accompaniments of stud-books and the distinguishing colours of the various jockeys, was one of the features of Roman life. And there seems much reason for believing that Yorkshire has been a " horsey " district ever since Cæsar's invasion. It is stated by one writer (Dr. Burton of York, in his *Anecdotes of Horse-Racing*) that " in Aurelian's time or before," York or its neighbourhood was famous for horse-races ; and it does not appear that this chain of custom was ever broken. Yorkshire is still famous for its jockeys ; and in this county, " where, as the gypsies say, ' there's a deadly sight of Bosvils,' " Romanes is not only spoken by those who call themselves gypsies, but such people admit that there is also a widespread (if very fragmentary) knowledge of Romanes among the mixed and sedentary classes of the same shire.

Whatever may have been the ethnic composition of the Roman armies of about two thousand years ago, it is evident that, when the Roman Empire fell to pieces, a portion, or portions, of its nationality must have remained in Britain. Of these, Dr. Skene's Tweeddale and Clydesdale Romani form a distinct section ; and there must have been many others. What right—outside of England—could a thirteenth-century Cornish chief have to be styled " King of the Romans " ? That this Richard, who is called " earl of Cornwall," was the king of the British Romani, or of the South-British Romani, is no doubt true enough. But he was not " King of the Romans " in the sense that Cæsar was ; for Cæsar's empire was nowhere in the thirteenth century. That this Richard of Cornwall was the head-chief of a confederation of British Romani is quite likely. Indeed, it is worth noticing that among the many people who assert a descent from this Romani king there is a Cheshire family— a sedentary and modernized family—that is still distinguished by the surname of a well-known Romani clan. It is also notable that this Richard is remembered, among other things, as the founder of an abbey of *black* priests—the abbey of Burnham (of " beech " celebrity). When a " King of Romans " founded a religious establishment, in an age when various rival nationalities co-existed in our islands, the probability is that the men whom he placed in charge of it were of his own race ; and that, in addition to being "black monks," they were also " Romani." So that, when such establishments were broken up by Henry the Eighth, about three hundred years after the time of this " King of the Romans," the disbanded priests of his monastery formed one addition to the crowds of gypsy-priests that thronged the highways. There are many reasons for believing that the statement which places the beginning of English " gypsyism " at the date of the break-up of " black prelacy," is a statement founded upon fact.

Difficult though it is to understand the intricacies of this connection, there has evidently been a certain Romanesque influence felt throughout Europe for the last two or three thousand years. Much of this influence, and all of this blood, has been absorbed by various modern systems and nationalities ; but there is still a Romanesque language that is common to various castes throughout Europe (though none but a scholar could overcome the barriers of differing dialects). In the Dark Ages the same castes possessed the same language ; though, at that period, the language and the people occupied a most important position ; and, before the beginning of our era, a race, bearing the same name, speaking (or some of them speaking) the same language, and possessed of many of the same characteristics, were identified with the power that exacted homage from the greater part of Europe.

CHAPTER XIV.

It has been stated that the United Kingdom, "during the reigns of James I. and his immediate successors, presented two different forms of national life, character, and customs, as if they had belonged to two entirely different and even hostile races." The parties who represented these two "entirely different" societies were the Cavaliers and the Parliamentarians. And their chief social differences were these. The first section was that of a caste of *horsemen*; the others, inferentially, were not. The "Riders" were prodigal in their habits, splendid in their attire—which was of costly nature, and of brilliant colour;—they wore the hair long, with one tress fastened by a bright-coloured ribbon; feathers waved in their wide *sombreros*, which they wore in a "rakish" fashion; their conversation was much garnished with oaths, and their manner was so overbearing that "cavalier" became an adjective that is almost synonymous with "rough" (the two terms being still more alike, when regarded etymologically). Their opponents wore the hair short; they were plainly dressed, in "quiet" colours; they wore little jewellery, and their garments were not—like those of the other section—of velvet, and satin, and silk. Their hats were set straight on the head, as is now the fashion among the "respectable" classes; and not with a "slouch," after the manner of modern "gypsies," and "jockeys," and "roughs." This Parliamentarian caste was not given to swearing; and they have the reputation of being vastly more sober and moderate than their rivals. The recreations of the "Horsemen" were—horse-racing, betting, cock-fighting, bear-baiting, prize-fighting, sleight-of-hand, jugglery, minstrelsy, buffoonery, and general "vagabondism." When their opponents were in power all these things were frowned at. When one of the chief leaders of the first caste was, temporarily, in the shade, he lived as a highwayman of the seas. When the leader of the other side lost credit for a time, he lived as a modern country-squire. The two societies were totally dissimilar ; and there is much reason for believing that this difference was, to a great extent, a matter of race.

An examination of the statutes of various periods must necessarily suggest a good deal that is ethnological. Why should Cromwell legislate against itinerant fiddlers, if it was not that then (as now—in a much less degree) they consisted of Romanes-speaking and Romani-blooded people ? And why should "strolling players" have come under the ban of the Parliamentarians, if not for the same reason ? The dislike of the Puritans to Actors and Minstrels is often ascribed to a feeling of a quasi-religious nature. But it is inconceivable that dramatic taste and a love of music were qualities that the Parliamentarians did not possess. The party that was influenced, to a great extent, by John Milton, cannot have been a society that lacked either of these attributes ; although bitterly opposed to *certain castes* of players and musicians.

One writer tells us that "the Bards and Minstrels of Scotland, as well as those of Wales and Ireland, incurred the reprehension of Government at certain periods." But then, *at what periods ?* And of what kind of men were such "governments" mainly formed ? In the fifteenth century a struggle was going on in Scotland between two rival confederacies, one of which was that headed by the " Moorish " Douglases. And it may be remembered that, in a wood-carving belonging to those Douglas princes, a most prominent place was given to "fancied fools," minstrels, "and such like runners about." Of these two confederacies, that which favoured the Minstrels, &c., was overcome ; and its armies dwindled down into bands of marauding "Moors or Saracens." And the *conqueror* in this struggle, James the Second of Scotland, forthwith enacted laws for the "away putting of sorners (forcible obtruders), fancied fools, vaga-bonds, out-liers, masterful beggars, bairds (strolling rhymers), and such like runners about." The people who passed these laws and tried to enforce them ; and those who continued to defy them ; were, in reality, continuing the war that had *apparently* come to an end in 1455.

During this period, and in this locality,—fifteenth-century Scotland—the game of "tables," which seems to have included chess, draughts, and backgammon, is said to have been "popular." And we have seen that more than one traditionary story connects this game, or games, with dark-skinned people. As pointed out in another place,* there are other reasons besides the evidence of tradition to make us believe that these games, and others, were peculiar to one or more nationalities ; of which nationalities our modern "gypsydom" is the shadow. Now, while such games were "popular" in Scotland at a period when that territory was as much a dominion of *dubh-glasses* as of their ultimately successful foes, they were legislated against and pronounced "unlawful" in the succeeding century ; when this "Moorish" confederacy had become more and more sub-divided into bands of marauders and rebels. There can be no rational explanation of a statute that declared such games as cards, dice, tables, golf, &c., to be "unlawful" in Aberdeenshire, in the year 1565,† except the reason that such games were played chiefly by people of a certain race ; and that to allow them to congregate for purposes ostensibly innocent was to countenance meetings among people who were antagonistic to the ruling powers. It is true that such people were wholly abandoned to the passion of gambling, and that cards and dice are even yet intimately associated with this vice ; but it can hardly be supposed that those law-makers of 1565 were swayed by a pious horror of gambling when they enacted this law. If so, they were a great deal more "proper" than we are. So very "proper" that they would not permit even the innocent recreations of golf and chess. But it is absurd to suppose this. Mr. Simson's descriptions of Scotch "gypsies" have shown that they were masters of the game of golf, which their abundant leisure allowed them to play to

* *Ante*, Vol. I. pp. 328-331.

† This statute is quoted by Dr. Jamieson, in his Dictionary, under the word "Biles." This word "bile" is, he says, the same as the French *bille*, a billiard-ball ; and he defines "biles" as "a sort of billiards,"—being played by four persons. The games decreed to be "unlawful," by this statute, are "specially cards, dice, tables, golf, kyles (?), biles, and such other plays."

their heart's content ; and the other games referred to were also peculiarly theirs. The sixteenth-century enactment that made such games "unlawful" was only a variety of the statutes against "the idle people calling themselves Egyptians."

When a certain game was almost, or wholly, identified with a certain race, it is evident that meetings connected with such a game were virtually tribal gatherings ; whether the players assembled purely for the sake of amusement, or with ulterior motives. Scott points this out, when speaking of the gypsy clans of the Scotch Borders. "Their warlike convocations were, also, frequently disguised, under pretence of meetings for the purpose of sport. The game of foot-ball in particular, which was anciently, and still continues to be, a favourite border sport, was the means of collecting together large bodies of moss-troopers, previous to any military exploit. When Sir Robert Carey was warden of the east marches the knowledge that there was a great match of football at Kelso, to be frequented by the principal Scottish riders, was sufficient to excite his vigilance and his apprehension. Previous also to the murder of Sir John Carmichael, it appeared at the trial of the perpetrators that they assisted at a grand foot-ball meeting, where the crime was concerted."*

Queen Elizabeth, who (in spite of her attachment to "the gypsy" Leicester) passed enactments for the suppression of English gypsydom, was also the enemy of the same castes in Ireland. One of her acts runs thus :—"Forasmuch as no small enormities do grow within those Shires (*i.e.* the counties of Cork, Limerick, and Kerry), by the continual recourse of certain Idle men of lewd demeanour, called Rhymers, Bards, and dice-players, called Carroghs, who under pretence of their travail do bring privy intelligence between the malefactors inhabiting in these several Shires, to the great destruction of true subjects, [it is hereby ordained] that orders be taken with the said Lords and Gentlemen [followers of the Earl of Desmond], that none of those sects, nor other like evil persons, be suffered to travail within these Rules, as the Statutes of Ireland do appoint, and that Pro-

* See the Introduction to "The Minstrelsy of the Scottish Border."

clamation, &c., &c." We have already seen how those Car-roghs, or Carrows, were described ; " wild Irishmen " (or " Black Irishmen," in the language that is most intimately associated with Ireland), whose only garment was the " mantle," which they wrapped round the left arm as a shield when fighting, and which they would often gamble away, " and then truss themselves in straw or in leaves." " They wander up and down," says Spenser, " living upon cards and dice ; the which, though they have little or nothing of their own, yet they will play for much money, which, if they win, they waste most lightly, and if they lose they pay as slenderly." (Whence it may be seen that "welsher" is one of the modern equivalents for "carrow.") When, therefore, Elizabeth framed a law against those people, she was warring against a certain *race*.

In the case of the Irish Bards and Dice-players, and also in the case of the Border football-players, it is distinctly seen that movements of a political nature were carried on under the veil of ordinary amusements and avocations ; and it has been surmised that the Aberdeenshire enactments against golf and dice were also blows struck at a similar political system. Mactaggart points to a parallel substratum of nationality in Galloway, when he says that "displaced priests, who use to bind people contrary to the canon laws . . . . . were designated *auld boggies ;*" and that " those who plot in secret are called *auld boggie fowk.*" " Plotters in secret " —that is what all those people were ; the dice-players and minstrels of Ireland, the football-players of the Borders, and the strolling-priests of Galloway. And, in each case, they must have " plotted" with some object in view ; a " Restor-ation " of one kind or another.

Though attached to a gypsy noble, Queen Elizabeth was one of those monarchs who legislated against gypsies, both in England and in Ireland ; and Dr. Walker tells us that " the Welsh Bards likewise gave offence to Elizabeth." Now, as Elizabeth herself belonged to a Welsh* dynasty that rose

* It is almost unnecessary to remark, at this stage, that the terms *Welsh, English, Irish,* and *Scotch,* are used throughout in their geographical sense ; ex-cept in the rare cases when *English* and *Englishman* have been used as equiva-lents for *British* and *Briton.* The last-named words are, of course, also used in the same " geographical " fashion. Indeed, they can be used in no other fashion.

into power over the heads of the "ancient nobility" of England, during the fifteenth century, it is pretty likely that the
Welsh bards whom she persecuted were not the same *kind* of
Welshmen as those from whom she was partly descended.
Her father before her was also the enemy of the minstrels of
Ireland, against whom he passed prohibitory laws. In the
twenty-eighth year of his reign, also, "an act was made respecting the habits and dress in general of the Irish [? of
some sections of the people of Ireland], whereby all persons
were restrained from being shorn or shaven above the ears,
and from wearing Glibbes or Coulins (long locks) on their
heads, or hair on the upper lip called a Crommeal "* which
custom of shaving the head was practised in England so
recently as last century, by Sutton and Figg, the prize-
fighters,—who most probably belonged to the class of people
called "gypsies."

All these references relate to laws made *against* gypsies.
Before the fifteenth century, in Scotland, there were apparently no laws made against them ; and the reason of this
seems obvious. Because, in the fifteenth century and earlier,
large portions of North Britain were under the sway of
"gypsies" ; who were themselves rulers and law-givers. And
the whole system which (in its decayed state, and enforced
against people who were either aliens or moderns, or both)
rendered them so obnoxious to communities actuated by
different social ideas,—this system of *sorning*, or, more correctly, *coshering*, may be fully examined in Mr. O'Donovan's
"Book of Rights," as it existed in its prime.

While, therefore, there were periods when laws were
enacted for the suppression of gypsy characteristics, there
were also periods when these characteristics gave the tone to
large communities of British people—which were virtually
nationalities, of various sizes, and degrees of importance.
Moreover, although James II. of Scotland did overcome the
black Douglases and enacted severe laws against people of
their description, that monarch (James) died in early man-

The swarthy Silurians of Wales, or the Black Danes who exacted tribute from
white-skinned "Welshmen," all these became "Welshmen" by residence. And
mixtures of the same description, though possibly in varying proportions, have
rendered the names of the other divisions equally valueless to ethnology.

* Walker's "Irish Bards," p. 134.

hood ; and it does not appear that any of his immediate successors maintained the position which he had gained. On the contrary, it seems that, for more than a hundred years after his death, North Britain was mainly ruled by chiefs whose names and proclivities suggest that the factions opposed to James the Second recovered a good deal of their former power, after his death. And Mr. Simson states that during the following century (the sixteenth), and for " a period of about seventy-three years," the gypsies of Scotland were quite unchecked by any ordinance against them (with one brief exception). The probable reason being that such government as existed in North Britain at that period (a very tempestuous one) was largely controlled by their own nobles.

But with the Sixth James of Scotland began a series of enactments against gypsyism. These are quoted by Simson and others ; and they have been sufficiently referred to in these pages. It is enough to repeat that they were not only directed against " Egyptians," under that name, but they banned all the national usages of gypsydom. Sorners, strolling-minstrels, mountebanks, jugglers, players at fast-and-loose, fortune-tellers, and nomads of every calling,—all these were struck at by James VI. of Scotland. Though the name of " Egyptian " may not have appeared in every one of these statutes, it amounted to the same thing if the habits and practices of " Egyptians " were the things legislated against. And these laws were very severe ; such laws as a conqueror imposes upon a conquered race. What these statutes demanded was nothing less than this—that large North-British populations should become converted to the ideas represented by James the Sixth, under pain of death or transportation. The nomads were to " be compelled to settle at some certain dwelling, or be expelled forth of the country:" if sorners could not show that they had "goods of their own to live on," they were not to be allowed to take those of others ;—and the choice before them was to follow some honest occupation, or to be sent out of Scotland for life, or to be summarily executed.

Not only did this James wage a muffled warfare against Egyptians under the various designations just enumerated, but he also fought them for their religious opinions, and also (it is to be feared) for their superior scientific attainments, which—under such names as "sorcery and witchcraft"—he denounced unceasingly. It may be affirmed with some confidence that, at this period, for every "witch" and "magician" that was hanged, burned, or drowned, a "gypsy" was put to death. The peculiarities of the "witch" were largely of a physical or *racial* nature ; and a recent writer speaks of the "peaked eye" of one class of gypsies as the eye of the "witch." In one account * on this subject, reference is made to the *stigma* impressed upon proselytes to "sorcery ;" and we are told that "this mark is given them it is alleged, by a nip in any part of the body, *and it is blue*." The effects of such "nips" were once visible all over the bodies of certain British people ; and they are not wholly out of fashion yet. Incidents such as these examples of "bewitching" are only repetitions of the old Gaelic tale of the girl who was brought up by (*educated by*) the "Magi," "who coloured her skin as green as grass." The fortune-telling that James suppressed was one of the characteristics of a nation versed in astrology, which is the half-brother of astronomy. Scott tells of a gypsy who "cast his glamour" over some people at Haddington ; and the well-known ballad says that the Earl of Little Egypt influenced the Countess of Cassilis after the same fashion. If these things were chronicled in our newspapers to-day, they would be spoken of as the effects of mesmerism, or "electro-biology." The "books of spells" that the "felons, commonly known or called by the name of moss-troopers"—the "common thieves, commonly called Egyptians"—used to carry about with them, these books are witnesses to a civilization of a perfectly different kind from that which James of Scotland owned. When the Egyptians of Scotland "used not to write with common letters used among other peoples, but with ciphers, and figures of beasts made in manner of letters ; such as their epitaphs and superscriptions above their sepultures [in Scotland] show ;" and when "this crafty manner of writing . . . perished" by reason of the relentless persecution of the people whose national character it was ;—then a race that, in some respects, was highly civilized, had

* "A History of the Witches of Renfrewshire :" Paisley, 1877, p. 17.

been wholly subjugated by a comparatively-ignorant people. The reasons that must make most modern people sympathize with the conquerors rather than with the conquered are these—that with the possession of much real knowledge and scientific development, this Egyptian nature contained much that was also savage and base. The social and religious ideas of their somewhat stupid conquerors were vastly more in unison with those now prevalent, than were those of the subjugated race. Whatever graces may have once clustered round this particular Egyptian religion, there seems to have been none remaining at the period spoken of. Their meetings —" Witches' Sabbaths," and suchlike—were wild orgies of the most degrading kind ; and every archæologist knows the meaning of monoliths, and May-poles, and hot-cross buns. It was imperative that the manners of a race swayed by such ideas should be "assimilated to those of their countrymen." But, at the same time, the hints that one receives from an examination of the question seem to say that the conquered races of Britain have been, in many ways, the instructors of their conquerors.

This, however, is too vast a question for discussion here. It is enough to notice that James the Sixth of Scotland waged war against the Egyptians of Scotland, not only by enacting laws against them *as Egyptians ;* but also by severely repressing, and almost stamping out, all the characteristics that distinguished them from himself and his followers.

This sixteenth century seems unmistakably to mark a revolt against gypsyism all through the British Islands. It was then that Henry the Eighth and Elizabeth endeavoured to suppress strolling minstrels (who used " to nobbet about the tem, bosherin'," as their modern representatives say) ; and it was then that Henry the Eighth received a letter from a North-Briton, stating that large populations in that part of the main island were sympathizers of the Tudor king, and entreating him to rid the country of priestly castes who "derived themselves from a certain lady, named Scota," who, " as they alleged, came out of Egypt." It is certain that, at this period and from whatever cause, Henry the Eighth did break up a religious system that was called

" Roman," and that thenceforward the country swarmed with
" black monks" and Romani "patricoes." This Henry
Tudor is also remembered as having cancelled "an inferior
foreign coin," then current in his dominions, and popularly
styled a "gally-halfpenny ;" though there seems no account
of its origin or the reason for its prohibition. *. And in this
sixteenth century, laws were passed in various parts of the
British Islands against Egyptians and Romani (under their
former name), and against everything that particularly distinguished them. It was at this era of gypsy persecution
that one of their favourite instruments—the bagpipe—is said
to have "retired to the hills;" which seems to be the same
thing as saying that the gypsy castes were driven to the
mountains at this period.

James VI. of Scotland, whatever the amount of his self-
conceit, and stupidity, and whatever else his faults and
failings may have been, was apparently the consistent
opponent of gypsyism all his life. And he was a really important personage. Because, when, with the death of
Elizabeth, the kingdoms of England and Scotland also died
natural deaths, this ex-king of Scotland was the man appointed to be the first representative of the monarchy which
we now acknowledge. Its outlines were not then so clearly
defined as now ; but still it was, substantially, the Modern-
British monarchy. There were still other kingdoms in the
British Islands, but these were of no importance whatever
compared with his ; and they speedily·became undistinguish-
able. But we have already noticed that parts of north-
western Scotland were not actually under his rule ; and that,
between England and Scotland there lay a considerable
stretch of territory whose people were "no subjects of his,"—
and which territory, along with the districts that lay near but
outside of it, owned the sovereignty of a line of Faw Kings,
even down to the eighteenth century. In addition to these
independent provinces, there must have been at that time
(particularly in Ireland) many other districts that did not
acknowledge the sovereignty of James ; and a closer examination of the question would no doubt reveal their extent
and nature.

* See note appended to this chapter.

But, in the sixteenth-century Debatable Land, there were no laws *against* gypsies; though many such edicts were framed every year in England and Scotland. Because the rulers of the Debatable Land were themselves gypsies. And this party—the gypsies and the philo-gypsies—must have gradually come to the front again after the death of James the First. For, paradoxical though it may sound to say that Cromwell was more fully the representative of James I, than his own grandson Charles II. was, this is nevertheless true in several respects. It was Cromwell, and not Charles, who emulated Henry VIII., Elizabeth, and James I., in his enactments against gypsyism. When Charles II. and his followers were in power, gypsyism was in fashion. During the Commonwealth it was under a cloud; but with the Restoration it re-asserted itself. And, as has been already remarked, if the ideas that were dominant at the time of the Restoration were still in vogue to-day, the policeman would never have existed to be the aversion of the "tory" castes, whom he, and the laws that back him up, have almost completely annihilated—or converted to modernism.

To follow the successive "see-saw" movements of these two "entirely different and even hostile races," and to say which was up and which was down, in this or that locality at such-and-such a period, would be a task beset with many difficulties. Only a few things, here and there, have been chronicled by "history;" what has been preserved is a mere fraction of what has been lost. Nevertheless, it may be said that the educated portions of the modern British people are much more in sympathy with the Parliamentarians of the seventeenth century than with their opponents, although by no means wholly swayed by the ideas of the former, or wholly antagonistic to the ideas of the latter. The question is not one of romantic sentiment. Whatever people may *fancy* their feelings to be, in this respect, it seems quite evident that the ordinary Modern-Briton, if he could be transported into the seventeenth-century, would find himself much more at home among the men of the Commonwealth than among their opponents (though differing from each party in many ways). That is to say, those Modern-Britons —peers, squires, bankers, tradesmen, and labourers—who believe in bank-accounts, orderly streets, and the rule of the policeman. If any Modern-Britons would hail with delight a second "Restoration" (could that happen), it would be the kind that throng the race-course at Molesey Hurst.

. . . .

. . .

It has gradually become apparent to the writer that to dwell upon the savage and objectionable features of gypsies (particularly of *Egyptians* and *Romani*), to the exclusion of their better qualities, is to fall into a great error. From their once-high position--Magi, "black monks," "black princes," and so on—it is quite clear that, though falling to ruin as successive nationalities and religious systems, all their best blood and most of their learning, have done a vast deal to build up the present British Empire. Without considering, at present, the problem of white-skinned "gypsies," it seems plain that the dark-skinned British have contributed much to the sum of British knowledge. This is partly apparent from various facts referred to in the foregoing pages ; and the writer is still more convinced of the truth of the proposition by various facts subsequently learned, but that cannot be further enlarged upon here.

And yet civilizations of one kind or another have co-existed with much that is savage. People who were masters in the working of metals ; who possessed hieroglyphic writing, science and semi-science ; who made chessmen and chess-boards of costly material, and played at many games akin to chess ; these people were highly civilized, in some respects. But they were naked (as often as not) ; they used war-paint, and followed many savage customs,—cannibalism included ; their religion seems to have led to a vast amount of what is now called immorality ; and human life was of little value in their eyes ; consequently they were savages.

But a detailed examination of various periods ; and not a general survey of this sort ; is the only way by which any-thing like justice can be done to the races chiefly spoken of. Besides, even fierceness of disposition requires to be looked at impartially. If it is an enemy who has chronicled the fierceness, his testimony is that of a partisan. One can see that easily enough. The modern British soldier, when at home among his friends, is a peaceable fellow-citizen, and, in all his private relations, as amiable as the rest of his fellow-countrymen. But the same man, in the enemy's trenches, with a naked sword or a bayonet, doing his best to mutilate and kill,—what does he look like to his foe? If he is not then what we understand by "a savage," he might as well be one,—for all the difference it makes to the man whose heart's blood is streaming down his weapon. It is not likely that he and his comrades will be remembered thenceforward by their foes as being of a "highly-civilized" race, and the models of amiability that they are to their wives and children. They will go down in the chronicles of their enemy (supposing that enemy to be some small unknown nation, ignorant of the other side of British nature) as ferocious warriors; and such chronicles will have nothing to say of British literature, religion, or art. A very good illustration of the effect of prejudice and ignorance may be seen in the picture sketched by Mr. Hepworth Dixon of a Cherokee chief; which was quoted in an early chapter of this book, and which—since the picture was palpably one-sided—ought to be rectified now. This "Billy Ross," whom Mr. Dixon took as an example of the intractable "savage," is spoken of by another writer* as "William P. Ross, a cultivated and accomplished gentleman." As Hepworth Dixon had himself visited the Indian Territory, the glaring inaccuracy of his portrait seems indefensible, and one can only express regret that his remarks should have led to the error of taking one of the many specimens of the educated Indian as an example of the ferocious savage. Still, if this Cherokee chief ever did go on the war-path (although the Cherokees are nearly all civilized hybrids), he and his followers may be assumed to have followed the old fashions of painting and scalping. And yet, at home, the leader was "a cultivated and accomplished gentleman!"

These remarks are rendered necessary by the fact that much of our information regarding Egyptians Proper seems to have been originally recorded by the people who knew least about them—their enemies—and that these enemies were almost quite ignorant of the internal polity of the "gypsies"; whose hieroglyphics they called "barbarous

* Mr. Edward King; in his "Southern States of North America," p. 208.

characters," whose science was " magic," and whose religion
was "sorcery and witchcraft."

NOTE.—Reference has already been made to Pictish coins, Douglas
Groats, and the Gally-halfpenny, conjectured to be the "baubee." With
regard to "Moorish" coins, generally, it may be stated that in a
" hoard " found at Skaill, in Orkney, several years ago, a large number
had been minted at Samarcand, bearing dates of (I believe) the eighth
and ninth centuries. (They are referred to by Dr. Joseph Anderson, in
his "Rhind Lectures.") The presence of Asiatic coins, in considerable
numbers, would naturally suggest the presence of Asiatic people ; the
date leading one to infer that they had been brought by the latest Oriental
invaders—the Black Danes. In speaking of certain English "Egyptians" of the year 1542, one writer states that "there money is brasse
and golde." (Referred to at p. 14 of Mr. Crofton's " English Gipsies
under the Tudors.") As for the " Douglas groats " of Galloway ("Moorish groats "), they are likely enough the same as the " tinkler's-tippence "
(" gypsy's twopence ") which Mactaggart defines as " useless cash, money
full of harm." Since Mr. Halliwell rates the *baubee* as of lower value
than a halfpenny, a twopenny-bit of the same *nationality* would be less
than the value of twopence ; although it would not become "useless
cash" until the overthrow of the Douglas power had rendered " Douglas
groats," and all other money of Douglas minting, quite valueless. That
the money belonging to " John Faw, Lord and Earl of Little Egypt," in
1540, was of brass and gold, like that of the Egyptians mentioned by
Andrew Borde in 1542, is most probable. And that one or other of their
brass coins was "the inferior foreign coin " prohibited by Henry VIII.,
and known as a "gally-halfpenny" (and perhaps as a "baubee") is also
very probable.
Grose makes a curious suggestion, in this respect. He states that
there is —or was—" a small Indian coin, mentioned in the Gentoo code
of laws," which is called a *dam*. And he hints that a slang expression,
supposed to be of a profane nature, is connected with this coin ; that,
in short, " not worth a dam" means "not worth a farthing." What gives
an air of soundness to this suggestion is the fact that this piece of
" slang " sometimes assumes the enlarged form of " not worth a *tinker's*
dam." If the word referred to a malediction, the phrase—especially in
its latter shape—would be of little meaning. But after the enactment of
Henry VIII., the "gally-halfpenny" was not worth anything. And
if it was one of the brass coins of which Borde speaks, it was a "tinker's
halfpenny." Consequently, a phrase might easily arise at that date
which would compare anything that was worthless to "a brass farthing"
or "a tinker's halfpenny"—a thing of no value whatever after the passing
of the prohibitory law.

CHAPTER XV.

JUST as there are many varieties of British "gypsies"—and *two* divisions, at least, of the black-haired, black-eyed, dark-skinned kind—so there are many varieties of "gypsy" speech.

There is Romanes Proper. There is the *Minklers' Thari, Shelta Thari*, or Tinkers' Language, which Mr. Leland "classes with the gypsy, because all who speak it are also acquainted with Romany;" and which seems to be a jumble of Romanes, Cant, and Gaelic. The Romanes of England (England Proper) is sub-divided by Mr. Sylvester Boswell into six varieties; "1st, that spoken by the New Forest Gypsies, having Hampshire for its headquarters; 2nd, the South-Eastern, including Kent and the neighbourhood; 3rd, the Metropolitan, that of London and its environs; 4th, the East Anglian, extending over Norfolk, Suffolk, Cambs, Lincolnshire, Northampton, and Leicestershire; 5th, that spoken in the 'Korlo-tem,' or Black Country, having Birmingham for its capital; 6th, the Northern." The writers* who quote this classification (which they do not wholly endorse) mention in addition the Romanes of Wales, and that of Yetholm. As Ireland and Scotland seem to have been scarcely examined at all by students of the nomadic or "tory" classes, and their speech, these districts are most likely capable of being partitioned off as England has been.

The above paragraph refers chiefly to Romanes and Shelta. Other dialects, which seem to belong mainly to the "Cant" family, are mentioned by Mr. Lucas.† "There is the *Parvie's Cant*, spoken in the north by hawkers and chap-

---

* Messrs. Smart and Crofton. See the Introduction to their "Dialect of the English Gypsies."

† "Yetholm History of the Gypsies;" Chapter XIII.

men [which may be the *Pedlars' French* of an earlier day]*
. . . . .; the *Buskan Cant*, spoken by the *Buskers*, or travelling musicians,"† also in the north ; the *Manchester Thieves'
Cant* [probably the very language spoken by the " Rogues of
the North," referred to by Harman],‡ which is quite distinct
from the *Patter* of the London thieves, 'Thieves' patter ' ;
Latin, the name of a cant ; *The Fly Language, Fly, or Flash* ;
. . . . . the *Welshers' Cant*, spoken by horse-dealers, who
have a cant of their own ;" and " the ' Backslang,' spoken by
Irish costermongers, in which words are written or spoken
backwards." The *Fly*, or *Flash* Language is regarded by
Mr. Lucas as similar to, or identical with, *Vlach, Wallach*, or
Welsh,—the last word being used in its meaning of *Roth-
Welsch.*

It is likely that the various gypsy writers would each have
several words to say for or against the various classifications
here quoted. But that many unstudied dialects—if not
languages—are still in use by certain sections of Modern
Britons, is what none of these writers would dispute. The
fact that some of these dialects can be limited to particular
stretches of territory seems significant.

A most superficial and random examination of the " tory "
languages, styled *Romanes* and *Cant*, shows that many such
words are only separated from what we call " English " by
their "tory" pronunciation. Pronunciation is a point that
seems to be very often overlooked. People who have divided

* The fact has been overlooked in the foregoing pages, but it will likely
become apparent that "nomadic-tradesman" cannot be separated from "nomad."
Autolycus was first-cousin to Christopher Sly, if not brother. Indeed, since
"gypsydom" is the ghost of nomadic *nationality*, it must contain fragments of
all the component parts of a nation ;—trade, manufacture, knowledge, and
religion. And that the *trader* and the *robber-noble* can be one and the same
person (odd though it seems), has been shown by the late Mr. John Richard
Green, in his last book.

The writer has somewhere seen a notice of the "Chapmen of the Lothians ; "
an existing brotherhood, which seems to hold an annual—or periodical—social
meeting, at Edinburgh : at which meeting they address one or more of their
members by the title of "lord" So-and-so.

† This word *busker* seems only another form of the Romanes *boshero*, "a
fiddler,"—who, of course, is an itinerant musician.

‡ In Harman's case, "the north" signifies nothing more northern than the
Borders ; and probably the modern writer quoted above uses the term with the
same limitation.

the British nation into two large sections of *Saxon* and *Celt* (quite oblivious of the fact that, if these two terms had ever a racial signification, that must have disappeared ages ago)— such people are more or less under the impression that "English" is one language and "Gaelic" another. The Gaelic vocabulary abounds with words that *look* different from English ; but, when pronounced, they are simply "English." Sometimes they are identical in accent with what we call "English"—sometimes they differ slightly. And these are not modern English words to which a Gaelic twist has been given (of which kind of words there are several). Indeed, the farther one looks back upon "English," the more does it resemble "Gaelic." What is called the "Irish brogue" is to a considerable extent, the "English accent" of Spenser and Shakespeare. To read Shakespeare with our modern accent is not to read "Shakespeare" as its author pronounced the words ; and that Shakespeare's accent was largely what we now call "Irish" is strongly maintained by an eminent Shakespearian scholar; who, to give one illustration, asserts that Shakespeare and his London contemporaries must have pronounced "dream" as "dhrame." We can all *read* the English writers of one or more centuries past, but it does not follow that we pronounce the words as they did. Even a man who can recall the early years of this century must remember many words whose pronunciation has altered, although the spelling remains the same. And, in several aspects, the older pronunciation tends to what we call a "Gaelic" or "Irish" accent. When a man of this day pronounces "tea" as "tay," and "sea" as "say," he is popularly regarded as speaking with an Irish accent (though this enunciation of the *ea* is not confined to Ireland). But, for how long a time has "tea" been pronounced as "tee"? Certainly it was not so pronounced in the London of Queen Anne :—

> "Thou, great Anna, whom three realms obey,
> Dost sometimes counsel take, and sometimes—*tay.*"

And this "Irish" accent in "English" becomes more and more frequent as one recedes from the days of Queen Anne. "That the speech of educated Irish gentlemen represents

the pronunciation of the English language at its best,—in the
Elizabethan period, the period of Shakespeare and Bacon, and
of our translation of the Bible,"—is the emphatic belief of
(at least) two students of the English Language, Professor*
Newman and Mr. Richard Grant White.* The phrase
"educated Irish gentlemen" is perhaps a trifle misleading ;
because it is quite likely that Irishmen coming under that
description would disclaim (with reason) the possession of an
accent so marked as that ascribed to the Elizabethans. Still,
there are—throughout the English-speaking world—peculiarities of accent which distinguish one community from another ;
and there are many places in the British Islands, and elsewhere, where one can detect a local accent in the speech of
men who are thoroughly "educated" and as thoroughly
"gentlemen"—slight though that accent may be. Without
discussing the probable educational and social grade of the
supposititious Irishmen referred to, it is enough to say that
an accent, belonging more to Ireland than to any other
place, at the present day, is stated by these writers to have
been the accent of Shakespeare and Bacon. And that,
when they—or Spenser, or Raleigh, or Elizabeth herself—
uttered the words *dream, sea, seat, conceit, either, neither, suit,
soul, distraction*, and others of like kind, they pronounced
them as if (according to our modern orthoepic ideas) they
had been written *dhrame, say, sate, consate, ayther, nayther,
shoot, sowl,* and *deesthraction.* In effect, the modern pronunciation of these words is an innovation—or a series of inno-
vations ; and the reason why the older accentuation is more
connected with Ireland than elsewhere is identical with the
reason which makes Dublin people talk of "jarveys," after
that name has been forgotten in London. But the "Irish
accent" belongs also to other parts of the United Kingdom :
the Galloway "tory" who has been spoken of in these pages
pronounce *deal* as *dale*, and one of Mr. Groome's English
gipsies says *rale* for *real ;* while *old* and *gold*, may be heard
as *ould, owd, gowd, &c.,* in many districts of the larger
island. The *ea* sound is, indeed, plainly in a state of transition just now. It is counted a provincialism to pronounce
sea and *seat* in the way that Bacon and Shakespeare did ; but

* See Mr. Grant White's "Every-Day English," London, 1880, pp. 82-4.

it is quite correct to give that very accent to *yea, break, great, steak, &c.* And the old-fashioned pronunciation is still given to such proper names as *Reay, Keay, Threave, Sleat, O'Shea,* and *McLean.** Now, all these old-fashioned pronunciations tend in the direction of "Gaelicism." And, when the best English accent was that which gave "*born* instead of *bawn, car* instead of *cah, arms* for *alms, order* for *awduh,* and *lord* for *lawd;*" and when the "1" was pronounced in such words as *calm, talk, walk, &c.;* then the enunciative tendency was also in the direction of "Gaelic."

Although one writer asserts that our "slang" words are nearly all Romanes, while another—with equal emphasis—ascribes their origin to Gaelic; and although Mr. Borrow found that the oldest Welsh words were every-day Romanes; and although the early Gaels, like the modern Romani, are stated to have come from the same country, namely Egypt; yet the above remarks are not intended to show a connection between Romanes and Gaelic (so-called). These remarks merely serve to illustrate what has been said with regard to *pronunciation;* that modern "English" is (as many people know) something that never existed before, and that almost certainly will be represented next century by a slightly different form of speech. And that the earlier pronunciations of many "English" words are to be found in "Gaelic" dictionaries. It is true that the words supplied by the author of "Every-Day English" were not intended to be examples of this class (although two or three of them are). But the *tendency* of their earlier pronunciation is in accordance with the phonetic principles of modern "Gaelic": which seems to indicate that the resemblance would increase more and more if one could learn the pronunciations given to "English" in the various centuries that preceded the Elizabethan era. Spelling is a matter of little moment, until one knows the

---

* One often hears the name of O'Shea pronounced *O'Shee;* and this is, of course, wrong. When a man refuses to speak with the accent that most of his educated fellow-countrymen acknowledge as *the* accent of their time, he is a provincialist. But every man is entitled to have his own surname pronounced in the ancestral fashion (whatever may be the newer accents of the day). And to pronounce O'Shea as anything else than *O'Shay,* is to be guilty of the same kind of blunder as the mis-pronunciation of such names as Cholmondeley, Colquhoun, and Grosvenor.

phonetic principle upon which that spelling is based. The (so-called) Gaelic words *beithir, claidheamh, crabhat, dragh, drabh, dre, geola, glaodh, lagh,** plaugaid, rainnsaiche, siucar, stiubhard,* and *tasg,* are represented in "English" dictionaries by the words *bear, glaive, cravat, drag* and *draw, draff, dray, yawl, glue, lag** and *law, blanket, ransack, sugar, steward,* and *task.* These "English" words give the meaning of the "Gaelic" ones ; and very nearly give their exact pronunciation. At any rate, the resemblance is close enough to let one see that the former list reveals to us the earlier accent of certain "English" words ; whose etymology they help to ascertain. Thus the chief difference between these two lists is that of phonetic principle.

The great difference between modern "English" and its earlier forms would be seen more visibly if the latter were written according to modern orthoepic rules. For example, any modern Englishman bearing such a name as "Yahdweena" would be suspected to be of "foreign" extraction ; whereas, if he were styled "Edwin," he would be regarded as the bearer of "a good old English name." But (if we are to believe those who know most about them†) the Anglo-Saxons would have stared at any one who addressed one of their number by such a name as "Edwin"; although one of their favourite names was "Eadwine," or "Yahd-weena" (as we should now write it, if we heard it for the first time). When we write the name of some Red-Indian chief, we spell it according to *our* ideas of spelling ; but the names of early Britons we spell according to *their* ideas ; which is somewhat confusing. And when our novelists describe the life of our peasantry in various parts of Ireland, they write down their speech *phonetically.* While if they attempt the impossible feat of placing before our eyes the every-day life of Shakespeare and his contemporaries, they make them speak with the accent of the educated nineteenth-century Londoner ; instead of showing us, orthoepically, that their speech was

---

* The "lag" pronunciation is what is called *Cant* or *Thieves' Slang.* But this word *lagh* seems to show that the *x* in *lex* was a guttural ; which would make the gradual transition to *law* more easily accounted for. There is, at least, one distinct example of the guttural accentuation of the Latin *x*—in the word *salax,* which is pronounced "sala*ch*" in the (so-called) Gaelic of the Scotch Highlands.

† See Mr. Grant Allen's "Anglo-Saxon Britain."

i

akin to that of the modern Irish provincialist, and akin also to that of the existing provincialist in the district delineated —whether Warwickshire or Middlesex.

The bearing of this upon the present subject will be seen if we examine a few English "gypsy" words. Mr. C. G. Leland has a chapter (in his " English Gipsies ") upon " Gipsy words which have passed into English slang." Had these words been described as " English words which have lost caste, or whose pronunciation has altered," they would have been perhaps more accurately named. But it will be of more use to add to Mr. Leland's list of English words that are "gypsy," than simply to repeat that list here. The following are taken from vocabularies of " Romanes " and "Cant"; those words which are Romanes being indicated by the letter R.

Boutika. (R.). A Shop. *Booth.* A house. One list gives " the booth being raised " as a cant expression for " the house being alarmed." But *booth*, although generally used in modern English to denote something that is more of " a shop " than " a house," was used in what is called " Middle English " in the latter signification. It was also then spelt *bothe*, the pronunciation of which was probably *bothy.* In those parts of the British Islands which are furthest removed from the centre of modern British civilization, *booth* and *bothy* are still every-day words for " a house." (In these latter cases, modern nomenclature styles the words " Gaelic " and " Welsh.")

Bor. (R.) Mate, friend. (As pointed out in Messrs. Smart and Crofton's vocabulary, this word is as much " English " as " Romanes.")

Cappa or *Caapa.* (R.) A covering. *Cap, Cape, Cope.*

Caulo or *Kaulo.* (R.) Black. *Collied,* in the sense of " blackened," is used by Shakespeare ; in the line (*Mid. Night's Dream*)—

" Brief as the lightning in the *collied* night."

" Collied " is derived by Professor Skeat from the same root as A.S. *col*, " a coal ;" and " coals " are occasionally spoken of as " caulos " (lit. " blacks ") in Romanes. Another form given by Mr. Skeat is *cholo* (*ch.* guttural) ; which is pretty nearly the same as *caulo.* Thus, when we talk of " coals " and the Romani of " caulos " we use what is really the same word, to denote the same thing.

Chor or *chore.* (R.) To steal. It has previously been pointed out that " the great distinguishing feature " of gypsyism (formerly, if not now) was to appropriate the goods of others. This was their *work* ; and *char, chares,* and *chores* are " English " words relating to work.

Cumbo. A hill. (R.—Bryant.) Common all over England in such names as *Edgcumbe, Wycombe, Morecambe.*

Chúri. A knife. (R.) *Chive* also given by Leland as Romanes. *Chive* is also included in a collection* of Cant words ; with the definition " a knife." And *Shive* is still an English pronunciation ; signifying " a slice," *i.e.* " something cut off." While *shave* is evidently a variant of *shive.* The Anglo-Saxon *shivere,* " a slice," seems to connect all of these words.

Chal. (R.) Fellow : *e.g. Romani-chal = Romani-man.* So also, in " English," *marshal – mare man* or *horse-fellow.*

Chabo or *chavo.* (R.) Boy. ? Chap and Chappie. Professor Skeat derives *chap* from the same source as *chap*man, namely *cheap.* On the other hand, Mr. Leland suggests that " shavers, as a quaint nick-name for children " is from the Romani *charies.* It seems likely enough that both *shavers* and *chaps* have come from *chavies* and *chabos.* If this be so, then a Lowland-Scotchman, when he speaks of " a little boy" as " a bit chappie " (which is a common Scotch expression), is " talking gypsy." Because *bit* or *bittie* means " little " both in " Scotch " and in Romanes." Its real meaning is, of course, " a bit of," " a piece of ;" from which it has come to mean something *little,*—being used in such ways as " Wait a *bittie*" (Wait a *little*), " a *bit* bairn " (a " bit " of a child, a little child), " a *bit* callant,"† or, as above, " a *bit* chappie." This last phrase is taken in preference to the others, because it shows an every-day‡ Scotch expression which, both in the adjective and the noun, is also every-day " Romanes " or " Gypsy."

Fams, or *Fambles.* Hands. The same words as *palms* and *fumble.* *Folm* is the Anglo-Saxon spelling of *palm;* and *fumble* is one of its derivatives.

Ful, Full, Fool. (R.) Excrement. This word is seen in Icelandic, Anglo-Saxon, Lowland Scotch (obsolete, probably) and in our modern dictionaries—under the spelling *ful* or *full, fulyie* or *foulyie,* and *foul.* In some cases, it is used adjectively, and with slightly-different shades of meaning. The " gypsy " pronunciation is identical with the " Anglo-Saxon " and " Icelandic ;" but the precise meaning is not identical in these cases. To find the same *meaning* as that attached to the " gypsy *ful,* one must look to the forms given in Jamieson's Scotch dictionary— *fulyie* and *foulyie.*

---

* That appended to Logan's " Pedlar's Pack of Ballads ; " from which, and from Grose's Dictionary, these various *Cant* words are taken.

† " A bit callant " is said to signify " a very young *girl,*" in the district of Galloway ; but it seems to have a masculine application throughout the greater part of the Scotch Lowlands. In Ireland, as *cailin* (modernized into *colleen*), it is feminine ; and in the Scotch Highlands and Western Isles it is used in the same way—*cailinn,* a girl ; *caileanta,* girlish. But in the districts last named it is solely masculine when used as a proper name, viz., *Cailean* (Colin). This double usage is again seen in the word *caileanta,* which not only means " girlish " but also " fond of girls " : whence it would seem that *caileanta* is the word that is spelt " gallant " in " English " dictionaries.

‡ It is, at least, a Scotch expression. Perhaps one or other of the kindred phrases given above might be found to be more " common " and " every-day " than this one.

Foki. (R.) Folk.

Hotchiwitchi. (R.) Hedgehog. An examination of the earlier forms of *hedge* and *hog* renders it at least a *possibility* that this is only a phonetic spelling of an archaic pronunciation of *hedgehog.*

Kid, Kiddy. Child. Anglo-Saxon *cild.*

Laund. Field. Like the preceding this word is not claimed as Romanes; bnt is included among "Cant" terms. It is evidently the Anglo-Norman *launde,* "a lawn"; and virtually the same as the modern *lawn, llan* and *land* (the last of these being a farmer's word, applied to the unploughed divisions of a field.)

Matto or *Matti.* Drunk. (R.) This is the same word as *Mad.* Mr. Skeat states that *mad* is "not connected with Sanskrit *matta,* mad (pp. of mad, to be drunk)." But while our dictionaries usally define *mad* as synonymous with *insane* or *crazy,* the word is used in Gloucestershire (see Halliwell) to signify "intoxication," and in the tents of the "tories" it has the same meaning. In the United States (more than in this country) *mad* has still the meaning of *angry.* Thus, although a scholar has stated that *mad* is "not connected with Sanskrit *matta,*" it seems most apparent that it is. And that it has been, and is applied to various kinds of *insanity.*

Mang, Mong, Monger. (R.) *Maund, Maunder.* (Cant.) To beg : a beggar. Still found, as *maunder,* in modern English dictionaries ; and, in French dictionaries as *mendier* and *demander.*

Mindj, mintsh. (R.) Used by Mr. Groome's Hungarians (" In Gipsy Tents," p. 40) in the sense of "woman ;" that is *minx.* Assuming that the Hungarian *minj,* the modern *minx,* and the "tory" *mindj,* are virtually one word ; this would give to *minx* an origin similar to that ascribed by Borrow to *rom,* "a husband or man."

Mongeri, Mengro, &c. (R.) This word has several forms, and it is not easily rendered into modern English. This may be seen by glancing at a few of the many words into which it enters. From the words *nasher,* to run —*kester,* to ride—*matcho,* a fish—*bosho,* a fiddle—and *katsi,* a pair of scissors,—are made the compound words, *nashermengro, kestermengro, matchomengro, boshomengro* and *katsimengro* ; which signify "a runner, a rider, a fisher, a fiddler, and a scissors-grinder." The word has many shapes, and many applications, being used in relation to inanimate objects as well as to men. But one of its equivalents is clearly *monger,* as used in such a word as iron-*monger* or iron-*master.* (Another word would perhaps show more clearly that *monger* and *master* can be used as synonyms.) Now, the word which we pronounce *monger* was once written *mangere* and *mangari.* And the "tory" pronunciation is thus much nearer those forms which we call "Anglo-Saxon" and "Icelandic." The modern *monger* seems to be merely an evolution from the "tory" *mengro, mengery, mengere, mongeri, &c.*

Naam, nav. (R.) Name. Simson (p. 300) gives the first form ; the second is more common. This is simply *name;* which, in Anglo-Saxon was *nama,* in Dutch *naam,* and in Danish *navn.*

Pand. (R.) To bind. ? *Band* and *bind.*

Pad. Path. *Padder.* A highwayman. *Rum-pad.* **The highway** (lit. Romani-path, or Roman-road). **This word seems to be regarded as "Cant."** It appears in modern English in the compound word **"foot-pad,"** (which is itself a curious instance of divergence in meaning, from the one word, since *foot, path,* and *pad* are radically one). Thus *pad,* in the sense of "road," is only a "tory" pronunciation of *path.*

Siv, Soov. (R.) To sew. A needle. This is Sanskrit *su, siv,* "to sew"; in Anglo-Saxon, *siwian.* Thus the "gypsy" *sivomengro,* "a tailor," is really "sew-monger." There is no modern English word to denote "a man who sews clothes;" because a *tailor* is radically a *cutter.* In Somersetshire, there is a word *sewster,* which means a "sempstress;" but there is apparently no masculine form extant,—*except* that in use among the "tory" castes. If *siwian-mangare* was good Anglo-Saxon for a "dealer, or worker, in sewing," then *sivomengro* is nearer the Anglo-Saxon pronunciation than *sew-monger* (which is the shape which it would take if used by modernized people).

Thus it appears that the earlier English pronunciation of *sew,* and also a derivative from that word (not found in modern dictionaries), may yet be heard "in gypsy tents."

It will therefore be seen that some—if not all—of the words given in the above list "are only separated from what we call ' English ' by their ' tory ' pronunciation." And it is this "tory " or old-fashioned accent that distinguishes, generally, the speech of "gypsies " from that of modern people of education ; when the language employed is what we call " English." When one looks at certain peculiarities of utterance ascribed to "gypsies," one sees that the peculiarity is solely of the " tory," or " extremely-conservative," or " very old-fashioned" description. For example, one reads that " English Gypsies . . . hardly ever employ any other [definite-article] than the English word *the,* which they, like other foreigners, often pronounce *de.*" And a specimen of this is afforded by another of the gypsiologists : " Dere now, boy, goand meet your sister. Dere's de bull a roaring after her. She will fall down in a faint in de middle ob de ribber. . . . Dey do say dat dat is a very bad bull after women." But " English Gypsies " are *not* the only existing English people who speak in this way. Here is a specimen of the ordinary Sussex dialect, as submitted to the Philological Society,* by one of its members ; the passage supposed to be spoken being (as every one knows) from the Song of Solomon :—" I

---

* See the Society's " Transactions " for 1862-3 (Part II. p. 263.)

be *de* roaz of Sharon, and *de* lily of *de* valleys": "O my
dove, *dat's* in *de* clifts of *de* rock, in *de* secret plaüces of *de*
stairs." This is the ordinary dialect of Sussex. And Kent
possesses the same characteristic. "Dat dere pikey is a
reglar black-tan," is a sentence that Mr. Halliwell* put into
the mouths of the Kentish peasantry. This same feature is
also noticed by many of those who render the "English" of
the Irish peasantry phonetically ; such words as *with, without,*
&c., being written *wid, widout,* &c. : (and perhaps *the, that,*
there, &c., are similarly spelt by such writers). Shetland,
also, still retains this archaic sound. In the seventeenth-
century "Description of Galloway," it is stated that "some
of the country people, especially those of the elder sort, do
very often omit the letter h after t, as ting for thing ; tree for
three ; tatch for thatch ; wit for with ; fait for faith ; mout
for mouth." This *t* sound is somewhat sharper than that
just spoken of, but it is another form of the same kind of
enunciation. And, at the present day, the *t* sound (in place
of *th*) is probably much more common throughout the
British Islands than the deeper *d*. In the Highlands and
Western Isles of Scotland, in Cumberland, Westmoreland,
Yorkshire, and in Lancashire, this substitution of *t* for *th* is
prevalent.

What all this really means is that *th* being a comparatively
new sound in the British Islands, all British people have not
yet learnt its use ; some being at the *t* stage ; and others,
farther behind, at *d*. It is true that "gypsies" are "like
other foreigners" when they say *de* instead of *the;* but the
"foreigners" with whom they are most connected are their
(and our) forefathers, who entered these islands a thousand
years ago—and at other periods still farther back. Those
early "East-men" and others were, in this as in other respects, vastly more like "gypsies" than like "us" : like Mr.
Groome's Lovell family, they had "hardly a *th* among them,"
—in some cases, none at all. When *path* was pronounced
pad there was no *th ;* although *d* became gradually aspirated
afterwards into þ and ð.

Similarly, the accent which gives "*ob* de *ribber,*" instead of

* In his "Dictionary ;" under the word "Black-tan."

"of the river,"* is merely old-fashioned. *B* is simply an older form of *v* and *f.* In Spanish, *b* is actually *v;* as may be learnt from the pronunciation of *Caballero, Sabado,* and *Habana* (in each of which words *b* has the sound of our *v*). In Gaelic, *v* is unknown—as *v;* but it is heard again and again as *b aspirated* (and also as *m aspirated,* but with a more nasal sound). Such words as *oval, carve, grave* (the verb), and *livre* (French) are expressed in what is called "Gaelic" by the spellings—*ubhal, cearb* and *corbh, grabh,* and *leabhar;* the pronunciation of the consonants in the latter list being identical with that of the former. The Gaelic *sgriobh* is nothing else than *scrive* or *scribe,* which is still pronounced *screeve* in "Cant;" and from which came the word *scrivener.* The word *Gawain, Gawn, Gavin,* or *Govan* is written *Gobhainn* in Gaelic; and its other form *Gow* is written *Gobha.* But, although *written* "bh," the modern Gaelic accent is always *v* or *w.* Nevertheless, as its presence indicates, and as an able archæologist has already stated, "the *b* was pronounced in old time." So that, to say "*ob* de *ribber*" is to speak with an Old-Gaelic accent. And that (according to the Gadelas-and-Scota tradition) is to speak with an *Egyptian* accent.

The "gypsy" vocabularies show yet another evidence of "toryism." This is furnished by the interchangeable nature of the letters *v* and *w.* I believe, this is popularly regarded as a cockneyism; probably because it characterizes such men as the "Wellers" of Dickens. That it forms a striking feature of Romanes, has just been observed: it is also an accent of Norfolk—and of many other parts of the country. The "Description of Galloway" (in the seventeenth-century) has already been referred to, in this connection; and, speaking of those "country people, especialy those of the elder sort," who "do very often omit the letter h after t," this writer goes on to say:—"So also, quite contrary to some north country people, (who pronounce v for w, as voe for woe; volves for wolves,) they oftentimes pronounce w for v, as serwant for servant; wery for very; and so they call the months of February, March, and April, the *ware* quarter, w

---

* Mr. Borrow also gives an instance of this in "Wild Wales" (Vol. III. p. 346), where he has "*Dibbel*" for "*Duvel.*"

for v, from *ver*."[*] This writer draws a distinction between
those who use *v* for *w*, and those who use *w* for *v*. Whether
he is right in doing so or not, it is clear that the letter *v* has
no place in " Gaelic " and " Anglo-Saxon " vocabularies ;
and it seems that in Latin (as in the well-known *veni, vidi,
vici*) its *pronunciation* is that of *w*. (And if this was its in-
variable sound in Latin, then—if the paradox may be
allowed—the Latin *v* was not a *v* at all, but a *w*.)   In such
books as Barbour's *Bruce* (written in "the Inglis toung ")
and the *Wallace* of Henry the Minstrel, one looks in vain
for *v* ; *waley, wencusyt, weng, wer, werray, werytê, wyser,
wictailyt, woce* and *woyd* being the spellings of *valley, vanquished, 'venge, ver, very, verity, visor, victualled, voice* and
void. But it is unnecessary to take particular instances.
One has only to go back a few centuries to find the " Weller "
accent prevailing through English literature.   The Galloway
parson of two centuries ago expressed that particular accent
in the same fashion as Dickens did,—namely, by substi-
tuting *w* for *v*, and writing " serwant for servant," and " wery
for very."   This also is the plan adopted in Barbour's *Bruce*.
How general that orthographical fashion may have been,
and in what districts, is unknown to the present writer.
But if the *w* was not always used where we now require *v*,
the letter *u* was employed instead ; which gives the same
result.   When it was not " serwant " and " wery," it was
" seruant " and " uery."   And as *u* was really *oo* (and not
yew) it did not affect the sound of " serwant," in the least,
though spelt " seruant."   Thus, this " gypsy " indifference to
the modern distinction between *v* and *w* is simply another
" tory " feature.   In this, as in so many other things, it is
they (and not *we*) who are " so English."

   Indeed, their old-fashioned accent crops up every here and
there.   It was a " gypsy " who said " priestés," as Chaucer
did, not " priests," as *we* do.   Modernized Englishmen speak
of " alocs " as " ayloz "; but " tory " Englishmen talk of

---

[*] This transposition is still represented by the common Scotch spelling of the
surname *Vere*, namely *Weir*. Although really the one name, the *w* pronunciation (as well as spelling) is generally that preferred by Scotch families bearing
that name.   However, one instance has come under the notice of the present
writer, in which a Scotch family—one in very humble circumstances—has preserved the pronunciation *Vere* while adhering to the spelling *Weir*.

"aloways." Norfolk people who live in houses may say
" Low'stoft " ; but those who still live as the people in Norfolk did "six hundred years ago" give full effect to the
original meaning of the word and pronounce it " Low-es-
toft."

But it is unnecessary to enlarge upon these toryisms of
speech. There are people who believe that " English
Gypsies" are " foreigners" who landed in England three or
four centuries ago ; but who, although known as formidable
marauders quite recently, had entered the country so quietly
that history has no word of their arrival. These people talk
of them as " Orientals " and " Asiatics ; " and we are informed that " any one desirous of viewing an Asiatic encampment, in Scotland, should visit St. Boswell's Green, a day or
two after the fair." And it is shown to us that their language
is closely connected with Sanskrit ; and that many of their
customs are of " Eastern " origin. But the scholars of the
past century have been preaching to us that *we* are " Asiatics "
(whichever " wave " may have borne our individual ancestors
hither) ; that *our* language is also closely connected with
Sanskrit ; and that *our* ideas and customs are largely of
" Oriental " origin. If Scotland has ever, in all its history,
contained people who did not come from "the East," such
people must have " viewed an Asiatic encampment in Scotland" when that portion of Great Britain was invaded by
the Black Danes, or East-Men, and also when it was invaded
earlier by the races known by the title of " Saxons." And
although the Egyptian-Scots were not precisely " Asiatics,"
they were assuredly of " Eastern " extraction. It seems to
have been assumed that all the motley colonists of the
British Islands have advanced in civilization at almost precisely the same rate. The probability that pride of race—
political differences—and the natural aversion to a code that
is based upon peace and industry,—the probability that such
causes might retard the development of one or many of
these warring castes seems hardly to have been considered.
Had any section or sections of those early " Eastern "
immigrants adhered more tenaciously than others to the
warlike, nomadic ideas, the earlier forms of speech, and the
various non-Christian and non-European customs of our

Asiatic forefathers, they would resemble no other British people so closely as the various "tory" castes, who are "commonly called Egyptians." That this name "Egyptian" eventually came to mean little more than "Tory" has already been noticed ; and the several British nations who were orginally "Orientals" will be briefly glanced at in the next chapter.

CHAPTER XVI.

THE statement made by one writer, that, eventually, "the name of *Ægyptians* was wholly lost in that of *Rapparees* or *Tories*," may be true of one particular period ; but the converse seems to hold with regard to the era of which the two Simsons wrote. For in their book it is quite clear that all Rapparees (or Robbers, as we now pronounce the word) and Tories were included under the name of "gypsy." Although the Messrs. Simson remind us that John Faw, Earl of Little Egypt, was an Ethiopian, and "in law" an Egyptian ; and although they tell us that many of the Scotch tribes asserted their descent from Ethiopians and Egyptians ; yet they nevertheless regard large clans of nomadic *Xanthochroi*, —fair-skinned, blue eyed, yellow-haired — as out-and-out gypsies. And at the place to which we are directed if we wish to see an Asiatic encampment in Scotland, at St. Boswell's Green, the preponderating element among the modern campers is distinctly that of the "fair white." Moreover, such *Xanthochroic* nomads used (we are told) to speak the language, or languages, and follow the social and religious customs of gypsies. And thus, according to this mode of reasoning, all of those tribes—white, brown, and black—were gypsies.

Instead of using "gypsy" in this vague fashion, it is evidently much better to employ the word "Tory"; accepting it in its early sense of *Sorner* and *Ultra-Conservative* (from which second meaning has, of course, come the nickname applied to the more Conservative division of modern politicians). That certain clans are, or were, distinctly Moorish or Ethiopian in complexion, and probably Egyptian by origin, is unmistakable ; and these dark-skinned clans are said by a modern writer to be divisible into two sections "of entirely different original stock." The same writer applies one name—that of Romani—to this compound people ; though it is obvious that the name can only properly belong to one of these types. But, whatever their title to this name, these dark-skinned people are the inheritors of "Moorish" blood ; and it may be that both stocks have an ancestral right to the name of "Egyptian." These, then, are Gypsies Proper: and it is likely they represent, if only in a partial degree, two primitive Egyptian types. In addition to these Gypsies Proper, who (in the British Islands) are said to number "only a few hundreds," at the present day, there are the nomadic mixed-bloods, of whom there are "many thousands." This calculation, however, takes in both the half-breeds and those "who have only a very slight trace of the dark blood ;" and the latter kind are supposed to form the great majority of this nomadic mixed-blood population. Although some writers talk of the members of this large class as "gypsies," the Gypsies Proper (and those gypsiologists who know most about their subject) do not recognize them as anything but "half-and-halfs" and "mongrels" of various degree. And, since the half-bloods among them are distinctly in the minority, it is plain that this large roaming population of "many thousands" belongs more to the Xanthochroic section than to any other ; though containing a strong dash of the blood of Gypsies Proper. The tribes of purely Xanthochroic "gypsies," spoken of by the Scotch writers, would (if not already included in the above list) add still more to the white element in this division.

Besides the "few hundreds" of Gypsies Proper, and the "many thousands" of nomads who share the genuine Gypsy blood in one degree or another, there are also many *millions* of sedentary British people, whose physical attributes attest a like descent. Some of these are (ethnologically) Gypsies Proper, more of them are "half-breeds," and the rest of them (probably the majority) only show by their black hair, or by black or hazel eyes, or by a pale skin, that one or more of their forefathers owned a different pedigree from that of the typical red-and-white skinned, blue-eyed or grey-eyed, and yellow-haired "fair white." Of this same

sedentary population, the other portion (said by one writer
to be the lesser) has no hint whatever of this "gypsy" blood.
This sedentary population—in other words, almost the whole
Modern-British people—is so intermingled that although the
separate *types* are quite visible they do not separate family from
family ; since all the varieties may be found in one family-con-
nection. And any lines of demarcation that are visible in this
population are the effect of money and good-breeding (or the
want of these attributes) : there is no division of *caste*. A *Melanochroic* lady does not refuse to marry a man because he has
blue eyes and yellow hair : one man does not "cut" another
on the ground of differing complexion. There is no racial
antipathy whatever in this body—the British people, *minus*
its nomads. To be the darkest of the *Melanochroi*, or the
fairest of the *Xanthochroi*, neither tells for or against a man's
social position. It is only when one gets among the "tories"
that this ancient grudge of race is felt. The more of the
"dark blood" that the gypsy has, the prouder he is : he
despises the *gaujos*, or white men, and asserts that "the breed
of 'em is bad." On the other hand, the tory *gaujo* taunts his
swarthy rival with "the black devil in his face." The Faws
(who seem to have been once distinctly black) are always
fighting the Baillies, whom the recorder of this fact proclaims
to have been white.

It seems quite plain, then, that those people whom many
speak of as "gypsies" can only be called "tories ;" although
one or two divisions of the "tories" may be accurately denominated "gypsies." Thus, the white blood that is the
predominating element among British nomads, represents
the least-modernized portions of the white-skinned races of
Britain : and the dark blood of the genuine gypsy is that of
the "tory" division of the dark races.

To say that the white blood preponderates among our
modern nomads is not to contradict the statement that nearly
all these nomads (at least, in England Proper) have "a suspicion of gypsiness" in their blood and in their speech. It
only serves to show that the genuine gypsy was of a ruling
race ; a race that impressed itself most strongly upon the
whites. So strongly, that although the really *black* gypsy of
two centuries ago seems to have quite vanished (by inter-

marriage, exile, and execution), yet this modern floating population of "many thousands" takes its tone from the minority of a "few hundreds"—this minority, itself, being far from pure-blooded. That the white blood preponderates throughout the British population—settled or not—is quite evident. The dark-whites are said to be in the majority ; but they themselves are mixed-bloods ; and, consequently, the *dark* blood only forms a proportion of about one-fourth to three-fourths of white.

It has been occasionally suggested in these pages that the tory tribes and confederacies were the remains of various conquering robber races, whose fierce natures had, in course of time, placed them among the "criminal classes," in a population whose main desire is to live quietly and safely ; and that this latter population was made up chiefly of people who had once been enslaved by those savage invaders, but had gradually—century after century—asserted themselves more and more ; until, at length, by actual fighting, and subsequently by enactments which embodied their own ideas, they had succeeded in conquering their conquerors, many of whom they had absorbed into their own society. The "irreconcilable" or "tory" sections of these conquering races had, it was supposed, thus become our modern "gypsies."

But, to support this theory properly, it is necessary to assume that the British Islands contained a population, at a very remote period, that was not of "Oriental" or "Asiatic" extraction. And that everything that characterized them *except their physique*, had been quite destroyed and submerged by the successful and successive invasions of various Eastern nations, who had impressed upon them their languages, their ideas, their religion, their amusements, and, in short, everything that can distinguish one people from another. And if the conventional idea that the white skin marks the European, as distinguished from the Asiatic or the African, if this idea be founded upon facts of a very old date, it would be necessary to believe that *Frank, Frangi,* or *Feringhee,* is a name that has been bestowed upon West-Europeans for a period almost illimitable. That it is the name given to West-Europeans by Asiatics at the

present day is well known ; and, for that reason, it seems
likely that the first occasion on which a West-European
people received the name of "Franks" was when it was
given to them by a race of invading Asiatics.*

It is popularly believed that our white blood is all of
Asiatic origin ; and that the first "Feringhees" were
Orientals. There can be no doubt that there are, and have
been, plenty of white Asiatics ; and the belief referred to,
although resting to a considerable degree upon the treacherous support of language and laws, has many reasons in its
favour. But a good deal might be said in support of a
theory of white invasions from the North and West. At
one important period of their history the British Islands
were simultaneously overrun by two nations ; the one known
to the then " British " as North Men, and the other as East
Men. And the *North* Men were called "gentiles of pure
colour," while the *East* Men were "black foreigners." It is
true that those North Men are believed to have been themselves of Asiatic descent ; and this may be incontrovertible.
But, at any rate, it is certain that a colony of those North
Men, starting from Iceland, settled in Greenland during the
tenth century ; and that, when some of these Icelanders
explored a portion of the North American continent (in the
year 1000 and subsequently), they found not only a population of an Eskimo and Samoyed character, in the territory
now known as New England, but they also discovered a
country adjoining this district, which they named *The Land
of the White Men.* This Land of the White Men is assumed
by some to mean the whole extent of territory that stretches
between Chesapeake Bay and the Gulf of Mexico. Whatever its exact situation, it received its name from the complexion of its inhabitants. Its alternative title (among the
North Men) was " Great Ireland ; " and it is stated that the
language of the people "resembled Irish." Moreover, these
same records speak of an intercourse at this period—the
tenth century—between " Great " Ireland and our own island
of the same name. It is, of course, impossible to say what
kind of language was called " Irish," eight or nine centuries

* The name of *Frangipani* is at least twelve hundred years old in Italy ; and
the words *Frangi Pani* signify " The Frankish Sea."

ago. In the century preceding this discovery of a trans-Atlantic "White Man's Land" the kings who ruled at Dublin were Northmen; the first of this line being Olave the White, who conquered Dublin in 852, "and founded the most powerful and permanent of the Norse kingdoms in Ireland." And it is said that, five hundred years before this, the "supreme King of Ireland" was a man bearing the Icelandic name of Neil, Nial, or Njal (remembered as "Nial of the nine hostages"). Of course, during these very periods, Ireland contained populations other than Norse: for example, the Scot-Egyptians, from whom it received its name of "Scotia." Thus, when the band of Icelanders, who penetrated to the trans-Atlantic "Land of the White Men," stated that the language of these white men "resembled Irish," it is difficult to know what form of "Irish" speech they had in view. But these Norse records plainly speak of a White-Irish population on either side of the Atlantic, in the tenth century and previously. Not the least important point is, that the *trans*-Atlantic Ireland was the one named "Great:" which fact is quite opposed to the idea that its people were merely colonists from Little Ireland. It may be that those who have identified Great Ireland with the greater part of the Eastern and Southern States have been in error in assuming that the configuration of the Atlantic sea-board was the same at that period as now. In eight or nine centuries many changes in the earth's surface may take place. And the "White Men's Land" of the tenth century may be now wholly covered by the Atlantic Ocean. However, without speculating as to its probable connection with "the lost Atlantis," it is enough to emphasize the fact that *Great* Ireland lay on the western side of the Atlantic in the tenth century; and that, therefore, the white races of Ireland were more likely colonists *from* "Great Ireland" than the founders of a western empire vastly greater than Ireland.* It is well to remember, also, that from the sixth century onward, the Scots of Ireland were leaving that island and settling in the northern parts of Britain (and in some of its other portions also): which might mean that they were ex-

* These particulars regarding the Norse discoveries in America are taken from the standard work on the subject,—*Antiquitates Americanæ*; published in 1837.

pelled by immigrants from the White Man's Land that lay somewhere to the west of Ireland. That the Atlantic should have been much narrower then than now is quite possible. The fact that illiterate peasants all along the western shores of Europe and the British Islands have traditions of submerged territories lying to the west, is very significant. Geology can say nothing for or against the truth of the tradition ; since geologists know nothing of the sub-Atlantic stratifications. But it is inconceivable that such a belief could have been preserved among unlettered people, and yet be without any foundation in reality.

Therefore, a theory which would identify the British " Franghees " of pre-historic times with white nations living in the countries bordering the Atlantic, rather than with the Asiatic robber-tribes that established various temporary sovereignties in these islands ; such a theory might be found to have a good deal to say for itself. But it would be necessary to believe that such a hypothetical " Feringhee" nation had been so long conquered that everything that characterized it (except racial qualities) had been wholly lost. Because it seems that all our " Old English " customs, languages, &c., are traceable to the East. Or, otherwise, it would have to be assumed that such early " Feringhees " had no civilization or learning of their own at all : for these, also, seem to have come to us from the East.

But it scarcely seems worth while to differ from the accepted theory of an Eastern origin of *all* British people. In reviewing the points of difference between British gypsies (so-called) and other British people, what seems most apparent is that the essence of that difference has chiefly been custom, disposition, and ideas,—rather than *race.* That, in short, the word "tory" is the best explanation of gypsyism. And that the people who, at all periods, have regarded the nomadic castes as different from themselves, have simply been people who (and whose *immediate* ancestors) have forgotten their ancestral customs, religion, and forms of speech ; and who have gradually developed those independent characteristics which we call "Western " or " European." The never-ceasing flux and re-flux of races in Western Europe, during the past two thousand years, have made it possible for one section of men— become rapidly civilized in one locality, and then migrating to another—to regard the natives of their new home as aliens, for no better reason than that these natives had adhered to the ancient manners that the immigrants had given up two, three, or four centuries earlier.   Of course, there have also been racial differences of the most marked character, but these are quickly disappearing by intermixture.   Even yet there is a most visible contrast between a fair-skinned, blue-eyed, yellow-haired Briton, and the darkest of all living British people (probably a " Roman ").   But though the difference between these two is very great, yet the whole British population is connected by blood with both.

It must be remembered that this is a nation of hybrids. It has not *one* origin and *one* history ; but many origins and many histories.   Actual *British* history—the history of the British Islands as one country—is very brief.   The Modern-British have scarcely had time to acquire a history and traditions.   Of their early origins, the educated British people have no tradition whatever ; because these origins are separate.   Last century, when Cowper wrote " Boadicea," he and his readers believed themselves to be descended from the British of ante-Caesarian days.   This century, when Kingsley wrote his " Ode to the North-east Wind," the same kind of people believed that their forefathers were the invaders who conquered those earlier races.   As a matter of fact, the Modern British people know nothing certain about their remote ancestors.   The majority of them know nothing at all about their ancestors, near or remote ; and as for the few who have tolerably good grounds for believing that this or that man was an " ancestor " five, ten, or fifteen hundred years ago, none of them can actually *prove* the connection. Before a man can succeed to land or honours, at the present day, he is required to give incontrovertible proofs that he really is the man he professes to be.   And it is quite as necessary that his proofs should be equally clear and incontrovertible before he can be accepted as one of the descendants of a remote ancestor.   Unless the chain that appears to join him to the man of a thousand years ago is one unbroken series of links, the reputed pedigree is no pedigree at all. Moreover, even though such a pedigree should be clearly established, it is almost of no use to ethnology. Randolph of Roanoke was the legitimate descendant of a Red-Indian (and the distance was only a tithe of a thousand years), but that did not make *him* a Red-Indian. Thus, the people who really have some shadowy right to be regarded as the posterity of one or other of the figures in early history, cannot, by reason of their own physical attributes, furnish us with a genuine clue to the outward appearance of that ancestor. Because it is likely that no instance exists of such indisputable kind of pedigree (of a thousand years or more) ; and because, if such case does exist, it only relates to one ancestor, and the hypothetical modern may have no outward resemblance whatever to this particular progenitor.

There can be no doubt that the difference between "gypsies" (so-called) and other people has been, to a great extent, the difference between the "tory" and the modern. So that the darkest of the educated *Melanochroi*, outwardly a Gypsy Proper, or, at least, a half-breed, might visit such a scene as Mr. Simson's "Asiatic encampment" at St. Boswell's, and see many families of *Xanthochroi*, who were living the lives of "gypsies,"—while he and his whole kindred for many generations had been always in the van of British civilization. Using "gypsy" in this loose fashion "gypsy" signifies no distinction of race.

But it is also beyond a doubt that the dividing lines between the various sections of British people are more and more distinctly marked as one recedes from the present. And that certain attributes, of body and mind, have been closely associated with certain nations of dark-skinned magic-workers, this connection being discernible even yet.

The historical names for these people (so far as concerns the British Islands) have been assumed to be these :—the painted "Moors" of ante-Caesarian Britain, known by such names as Silurians, and spoken of as Druids or Magicians, whose customs caused the nickname of "Blueskin" or "Green-Man" to be applied to them by Caesar ; also the Scots of Ancient Scotia, or Ireland, who seem to have left that island for Great Britain at various periods, beginning so early as the fourth century ; also a section of the Italian

" Romani," who—though forming part of the Latin nationality—seem still to have preserved much of their individual
blood, customs, and speech (the latter being styled Low-
Latin by the Latins Proper) ; and, lastly, the Cimbri, or
Dani, or East Men, of the ninth century, who are remembered by various British provincialists as " black heathen "
and " black Danars," or " Danes," and whose tribute, in one
particular instance, was called " the tribute of the black
army."

That all of these were black-skinned, or brown-skinned
races there are many reasons for believing ; and there are
also many reasons for believing that some (at least) of them
were the darked-skinned progenitors of the modern British
Melanochroi, — inclusive of those families still retaining
many ancient characteristics, and known as Gypsies Proper.
It may be that all of these swarthy races have branched out
from one parent stem, in Egypt or Assyria ; and, though
passing through the most varied experiences, in various
countries, have still retained some of the features by which
their kinship to one another can be recognized.   It is certain
that the surest proof of kinship is that of physical features :
and that language, though a most important witness, cannot
be wholly relied upon, in trying to ascertain " the pedigree
of nations " (whatever may have been the opinion of Dr.
Samuel Johnson).   In this special instance no clearer proof
of the fallacy of trusting exclusively to language can be
found, than in the fact that very many British "gypsies,"
past and present, have been proficients in the language of
the " Romani," though themselves belonging to a wholly
opposite ethnical type ; while a nation such as the " Black
Mountaineers," or Montenegrins, whom an authority on this
subject regards as a nation of Gypsies Proper,—these people
are perfectly ignorant of the Romani speech.

Let us then glance hastily at the several historical invasions that may be regarded as invasions of Gypsies Proper.
And the natural thing to do is to look back from where we
now stand.

Captain Burt's allusion to the " German refugee women "
and the " Moors " in London, one of whose fashions he
compared to that in use among certain classes in the north

of Scotland; and the fact that the Gypsies Proper of Germany were then suffering persecution and banishment; also the existence of some words in *Romanes* and *Cant* that seem to be of modern German connection (*esel*, *von*, &c.); these things render it almost certain that some families of Gypsies proper arrived in this country only last century.

It is likely that occasional arrivals of the same unimportant description took place during the period stretching from the eighteenth century back to the Norman Conquest. Although the Flemings have been taken in these pages as exclusively Xanthochroic, it may be necessary to modify this belief considerably. We are told that "the fourteenth century was remarkable for the numbers and excellence of the Flemish *Sprekkers*, *Zeggers*, and *Vinders*, or wandering poets;" and a class of this kind is very suggestive of those "strolling bards" who, in our own islands, were identified with "the idle people calling themselves Egyptians." Moreover, pedlars cannot be well dissociated from gypsies; and it may appear that many traders of gypsy blood entered the British Islands as "Flemings." As for the Norman Conquest, it is clear that that signified the introduction of much that was genuinely "gypsy." The foremost "Norman" in the charge at Hastings was Tulliver the juggler: and it may be that such clans as the Rolands and the Bosvilles have not been British for more than eight hundred years. An element in British-Romanes that is more suggestive of *French* than of any other form of speech has already been noticed. And the connection between the Normans and the *Jugglers* or *Jongleurs* has also been referred to. Although John of Rampayne was of such a complexion that he required to "stain his hair and his whole body entirely as black as jet" in order to sustain his assumed character, he was, nevertheless, "an excellent juggler and minstrel" himself. Though not one of the Romani by birth, he was a good specimen of the *aficionado*. Another kindred example is that of James V. of Scotland (1512–1542); who was a most pronounced Bohemian, in nature, although described as yellow-haired, and blue-eyed, with an aquiline nose and oval face, and as being a typical representative of his family— the Stewarts—who "came in with the Conqueror." This

James spent much of his brief existence in the society of North-British Egyptians : one of their nobles being styled by him "our loved John Faw, Lord and Earl of Little Egypt ;" and James himself being presumably well acquainted with "the beggar's tongue," although it does not appear that the love of *language* was his primary reason for going a-gypsying.* Indeed, there is a singular consistency in Mr. Simson's statements, that "old Charles Stewart, a gypsy chief, at one period of no small consequence among these [Fife, Stirling, and Linlithgow] hordes," was a man of fair complexion, and that "he affirmed, wherever he went, that he was a descendant of the royal Stewarts of Scotland."

Again, although "The Song of Roland," relates to the achievements of one who fought against

> the cursèd heathen folk,
> As black as ink—all black except their teeth,

yet we find a notice, in the year 1549, of "John *Roland*, oon of that sorte of people callinge themselffes Egiptians ;" and "Roland" is still the surname of a (so-called) "half-blood" clan, said to live "chiefly about London." Altogether, it seems likely that a great fusion of races was going on during the centuries that are called "mediæval." The mail-clad Norman Bruce was momentarily seen defending himself against a swarm of naked "Moors :" the Teutonic League (which is equivalent to saying "the Frankish League," since *Frankish = Tudesque*) was formed to repel the attacks of the "Saracenic" invaders of West Europe : the legendary knights fought against "felon" knights and Paynim knights, or "Heathen" (in token of which the "Moor's head" became a frequent heraldic bearing) : "to tilt at the Saracen" was the preliminary exercise for the young Western warrior, before he had learned to face the veritable Paynim in the flesh ; "to fight like a Turk"; "to catch a Tartar ;" to

* Mr. Simson points out that this same James latterly passed a very severe law against those Gypsies who lived within that part of North Britain which was then "Scotland"; but he keeps in view that (whatever may have given rise to this enactment) he was otherwise a strong friend to North-British Egyptians.

It may be as well to mention that the reference to "the beggars' tongue" is made by James himself, in the ballad of "The Gaberlunzie Man" (of which he is admitted to be the author).

be subjected to the depredations of "thieving Tartarians ; " all these were the experiences of certain sections of British people. But, in spite of this, the two opposite confederations seem to have greatly affected each other,—in blood and manners. The "knight-errant" seems plainly to be the child of the "Saracen" as well as of the "Frank"; and to have passed from "knight-errant," or "cavalier-who-ventures-life-for-gain," into the position of "thieving Tartarian," or "common thief," "commonly called Egyptian."

Whatever may have been the various race-combinations in Britain, at and after the Norman Conquest, the arrival of the Black Danes seems to mark the first important inroad of Asiatics (if we look backward from the nineteenth century).

These people are remembered in Gaelic records as Black-Lochlinners (Black Scandinavians), *Dubh Galls*, or *Dubh Gennti* (black foreigners, or people), and also as "black Danars." Another account speaks of them as "Dani or Cimbri," and they are called *latrones*, pirates, or robbers, "in the Gallic tongue." They are remembered as Ost-men, or East-men. "They make their first appearance [in the British Islands] in the year 793 in an attack upon the island of Lindisfarne ; " and they are said to have overrun the Hebrides in the same year. "Simeon of Durham tells us that in 875 the host of the Danes who had ravaged the east coast of Britain divided itself into two bands, one of which under Halfdan marching into the region of the Northumbrians laid it waste, and wintering near the river Tyne brought the whole country [Northumbria, presumably] under their dominion, and destroyed the Picts and the people of Strathclyde." One division of them was defeated at Luncarty, Perthshire, in the year 970. In 986-7, it is recorded that "Godisriç the son of Harald, with the black nations, laid waste Menevia (St. David's, in Wales) ; and did so much hurt in the country besides, that to be rid of them, Meredyth was faine to agree with them, and to give them a penie for everie man within his land, which was called, ' The tribute of the blacke armie ' ; " a like tribute, in other districts, being known as "Dane-gelt" (the popular names for such a tax being the Gaelic *dubh-chis*, and the English *black-mail*). About the same period, the supreme king of Ireland, Brian Boroimhe, incessantly opposed himself to their inroads ; and it is stated that "he defeated the Danes in upwards of twenty pitched battles, restricting their influence to the four cities of Dublin, Wexford, Waterford, and Limerick alone,"—and that he " gained a signal victory " over them at Clontarf, in 1014, in which battle he himself was killed. In 1014, also, the Danes are said to have made a treaty with Malcolm of Scotland ; and even to have nominally retired from his territories. But the dates of the various Danish onslaughts are well known to historians ; and also the territories over which they ruled. Even after the victories of Alfred they retained a large slice of the larger island ; "the whole eastern country from the Tweed to the Thames, where it washes a part of Essex," being under their dominion. And this over and above their other British possessions.*

" The cruelty of the Danes is painted in the strongest colours by our most ancient historians, who lived near this time. ' The cruel Guthrum,' says one of these historians, ' arrived in England, A.D. 878, at the head of an army of pagan Danes, as cruel as himself, who, like inhuman savages, destroyed all before them with fire and sword, involving cities, towns and villages, with their inhabitants, in devouring flame, and cutting those in pieces with their battle-axes who attempted to escape from their burning houses. . . . All the towns through which they passed exhibited the most deplorable scenes of misery and desolation, . . . old men lying with their throats cut, . . . the streets covered with the bodies of young men and children, without heads and arms, and of matrons and virgins, who had first been publicly dishonoured, and then put to death. It is said to have been the common practice among these barbarous pagans to tear the infants of the English from the breasts of their mothers, toss them up into the air, and catch them on the point of their spears as they were falling down :' . . . The horrid operation of scalping, peculiar [?] to the North American savages, was occasionally performed by these nations on their enemies. . . . ' Earl Godwin,' says an ancient

* These dates, &c., are taken from Dr. Skene's " Celtic Scotland," Vol. I. pp. 302 and 325 6 ; and from other accounts which, if less notable, seem quite reliable.

historian, 'intercepted Prince Alfred, the brother of Edward
the Confessor, at Guildford, in his way to London, seized his
person, and defeated his guards, some of which he imprisoned,
some he sold for slaves, some he blinded by putting out
their eyes, some he maimed by cutting off their hands and
feet, *some he tortured by cutting off the skin of their heads*, and,
by various torments, put about 600 men to death.'" Of
their ravages and cruelties, history has many records; and
monasteries and churches shared the fate of towns and
villages.   It is stated by one writer that the Abbess of
Coldinghame actually cut off her nose and upper lip, in order
to render herself repellant to the " black heathen " victors ;
who had no respect for any attribute except superior strength.
They were so notoriously treacherous that they became
known to the English as " the truce-breakers."

Not the least important features in the above description,
are those which link the Black Danes with "Tartarian"
races.   Their manner of levying a money - tax upon
the vanquished was precisely that of the Black Huns
in Italy, many centuries before : and it is unnecessary to
emphasize the fact that they scalped their enemies like any
modern " Red Indians." The Tartar features of these
Black Danes are visible again and again : (the word " Tartar "
being here used much as it was done when "as black as
Tartars " was a proverbial expression).   For example, when
the Danish Tartars of the year 1237, "headed by their Khan
Batto, or Battus, after ravaging great part of Poland and
Silesia, broke suddenly into Russia, where they committed
the greatest cruelties.   Most of the Russian princes [this
account* continues] . . . were made prisoners, and racked
to death ; and, in short, none found mercy but such as
acknowledged themselves the subjects of the Tartars.   The
imperious conqueror imposed upon the Russians everything
that is most mortifying in slavery ; insisting that they should
have no other princes than such as he approved of ; that
they should pay him yearly a tribute, to be brought by the
sovereigns themselves on foot, who were to present it humbly
to the Tartarian Ambassador on horseback.   They were also

* The article " Russia " in the *Encyclopædia Britannica* (Third Edition).

to prostrate themselves before the haughty Tartar ; to offer him milk* to drink ; and, if any drops of it fell down, to lick them up." These are the ways of a thirteenth-century horde of Tartars, emerging from the Danish or "Cimbric" peninsula. Let them be compared with the manners of the Black Danes of the eighth, ninth, and tenth centuries, as exhibited toward the people of the British Islands. "The martial spirit of the Danes was attended with the most ferocious insolence. . . . So abject was the submission of the English to Danish insolence, that when an Englishman met a Dane on a bridge, or in a narrow path, where he could not avoid him, he was obliged to stand still, bareheaded, and in a bowing posture, as soon as the Dane appeared, and to remain in that posture till he was out of sight. . . , If an Englishman presumed to drink in the presence of a Dane, nothing but instant death could expiate the offence." Truly, a race of "Black Oppressors" — "Black Knights," "holding the people in vassalage, and using them with great severity."

That those Tartars of the Baltic, whose insolent bearing towards the conquered Russians has just been pictured, were descended from those Black Danes whose yoke had been partly thrown off by the British Islanders, some centuries before, can hardly be doubted. Whether they were connected with the "Saracens" against whom the Frankish king, Charles Martel, fought during the eighth century, may be questioned ; but it seems likely they were of the same stock as those "Pagans of Saxony" that the same king and his grandson, Charlemagne, were continually engaged in combating. (And that, had it not been for the victories of Charlemagne, the Black Danes might not have been so persistently the invaders of the British Islands.) When, in the fourteenth century the Teutonic Order (Tudesque, or Frank-

---

* One does not, perhaps, naturally associate a milk-diet with a savage nature ; but this was one of the characteristics of Lemprière's Sarmatians. He calls them "a savage, uncivilized nation, . . . naturally warlike, and famous for painting their bodies to appear more terrible in the field of battle. They were well known for their lewdness. . . They lived upon plunder, and fed upon milk mixed with the blood of horses." The Concani, of the "Basque Provinces," also "lived chiefly upon milk mixed with horses' blood ; " and of the people of the Deucaledonian Islands (Hebrides), during the first century of our era, "it was reported that they . . . lived upon fish and milk."

ish* Order) overcame the "Pagans of Prussia," and cleared large districts of their presence, it is probable that these "Pagans of Prussia" were the same as those "fiends" whom Sir Walter Scott tells us are pictured on a fifteenth-century map ; "dressed in caftans and armed with scimitars," and contesting the possession of that portion of Europe with the "Frankish" nations. And it is equally probable that the "band of 300 wanderers, 'black as Tartars and calling themselves *Secani* [*Zigani*],'" who arrived at Lüneburg in 1417, formed a small division of these "fiendish" warriors. In short, when it is stated that "the Scandinavian and Low-German [word] *Tatare* identifies Gipsies with the Mongolian hordes, the terror of Europe in the thirteenth century," two words are employed, which, though very comprehensive, are still precise enough to denote the ethnological and political position of these races. These words are "Tartar" and "Gypsy"; and these terms seem to be applicable with equal fitness to the sections known as Cimbri, or Black Danes.

There is some temptation to parody the title of Mr. Crofton's instructive pamphlet, and to speak of those fourteenth-century "Pagans of Prussia," when overcome by the Teutonic or Tudesque League, as "Continental Gypsies under the Tudors." But there are two objections to this : the one being the manifest error of using "Teutonic" or "Tudesque" in an exclusively racial sense, at so late a period ; the other being the fact that the "Continental Gypsies" were by no means *under* the Tudesque Order at the date referred to. When these Continental Gypsies, "under Udislaus Ingello," besieged Dantzic, in the year 1389, they and their opponents were pretty equally matched. It is true that the besieged "Tudors" eventually "made a furious sally, cut the besiegers to pieces, and cleared the district"† of them ; but the affair might have terminated in a

---

* "The court language of the Franks was the *Francthcuch*, called also the *Thiotique*, or *Tudesque*." (Longfellow.) This seems to indicate that *Frank* (Feringhee) = Teuton.

† The account from which this is taken (Anderson's "Scottish Nation," Vol. II. p. 43) gives us a proof that the "Teutonic Order" of the fourteenth century was by no means composed exclusively of *Xanthochroi*; whatever "Teuton" or "Frank" may have signified at one time. For one of the heroes of the successful sortie from Dantzic was himself a "Black Douglas." The pro-

Saracenic victory. And, long after this event, they remained
a terror to Middle Europe. Only last century, it is said of
them—in this locality—"they often marched as strong as
fifty or a hundred armed men ; bade defiance to the ordinary
police, and plundered the villages in open day ; wounded
and slew the peasants, who endeavoured to protect their property ; and skirmished, in some instances successfully, with
parties of soldiers and militia, dispatched against them."
One reads that some of them who, in 1724, had been captured "near Hirzenhayn, in the territory of Stolberg,"
" escaped to a large band which lay in an adjacent forest ; "
and that, even yet, such forests (the *Black* Forest, for
example) contain the same kind of people, though in a
decayed condition. In Hungary they long maintained their
right to the ownership of the soil ; and, either in that
territory, on in those districts out of which, as " Pagans of
Prussia" they were at last driven, they styled themselves
" the band of Upper Saxony, of Brandenburg, and so forth,"
resenting "any attempt on the part of other Gipsies to in-
trude on their province." These Inter-Tartarian battles seem
to have been frequent and bloody ; and, so recently as last
autumn, one of these encounters took place in the Hungarian
Commitat of Weissenburg, resulting in a considerable amount
of bloodshed, and several deaths. In Modern Denmark, as
throughout Europe—after the re-assertion of Frankish power
—those Tartarians have been legislated against for many
centuries ; being characterized as " The Tartar Gipsies, who
wander about everywhere, doing great damage to the people,
by their lies, thefts, and witchcraft."

But our aim is rather to show how the Black Danes of a
thousand years ago were Tartar-Danes, or Danish-Tartarians,
than to follow the fortunes of their " Irreconcilable " or
" Tory " fragments, in later centuries.

The " Tartarian " origin of the Black Danes is nowhere
more clearly seen than in the fact that the Baltic seaboards
have yielded up immense numbers of Eastern coins, struck

---

bability is that if—like his grandfather, "the good Sir James"—this particular
Douglas was also "of a black and swart complexion," he was also, like his
grandsire, a Christianized West-European by training and in all his ideas ;
although actually a " Moor or Saracen " by descent.

in Asiatic mints at various dates during the Black-Danish supremacy. " Hoards of Eastern coins and ornaments are almost annually discovered in Norway and Sweden, and occasionally in Orkney and the North of Scotland. The museum of Stockholm possesses a collection of more than 20,000 Cufic coins found in Sweden, dating from the close of the 8th to the end of the 10th century, and vast quantities of those silver ornaments of peculiar forms and style of workmanship, which are also believed to have been brought from the East." In the month of March, 1858, a "hoard" of silver ornaments and coins was "unearthed in the Links at Skaill, in the parish of Sandwick, Orkney." "One of the coins was a St. Peter's penny of the tenth century, struck at York ; another was a penny of King Athelstane, A.D. 925, struck at Leicester. But these were the only European coins in the hoard. All the others, ten in number, were Asiatic, and ranged in date from A.D. 887 to A.D. 945. *The places of mintage were Bagdad and Samarcand."* *

Now, the finding of 20,000 Kufic coins, in the Baltic countries, in modern days, signifies a great deal. When twenty thousand can be *found*, eight or nine centuries after the latest of them was coined, it may be assumed that a hundred thousand (at the very lowest computation) were in circulation, in these districts, between the eighth and tenth centuries. That some of that obsolete currency has been lost, and that most of it exists to-day in the form of modern European coins and ornaments, is a conjecture that scarcely requires to be supported by argument. What meaning can these discoveries have ? If some Africander antiquary of the twenty-eighth century should discover a " hoard " of Victorian sovereigns and half-crowns in a cellar at Cape Town ; and if 20,000 kindred coins were found in the southern portions of Africa, at the same time, what would be the natural conclusion of this hypothetical archæologist ? Of nineteenth-century British conquest and colonization he would probably have some dim knowledge ; and perhaps he would be disposed to regard himself as, in some degree, a

---

* These statements have been made by Dr. Joseph Anderson, in his *Orkney-inga Saga* (p. 127, note), and also in his " Rhind Lecture," delivered at Edinburgh on 17th October, 1881.

descendant of that nation of colonists. And his first conclusion would be that the presence, in his fatherland, of these 20,000 coins bearing the London mintage, was a proof that the nineteenth-century power which had its centre in London extended its sovereignty over Southern Africa as well. This would be his first conclusion ; and it would probably be his last. If he ever thought it necessary to hold a contrary opinion, we know he would be completely wrong. But it is not likely his original conviction would alter. Because it would be the most natural and reasonable conclusion he could arrive at. South Africa may become an independent country ; with one or many systems of coinage, and many South-African mints ; and the Africander of the twenty-eighth century may be a man with little or no British blood in his veins ; but all that would not alter the fact that Cape Colony is at present a part of the British Empire ; and any Victorian coins found at Cape Town nine centuries hence would be silent witnesses to the fact. The prevalence of a certain national coinage, in certain districts, means the presence of the race to whom these coins meant *money*. Therefore, when the countries bordering on the Baltic, and those portions of North Britain which were overrun by the " black heathens," are found even yet to contain an immense number of coins bearing Kufic inscriptions ; and when some of these coins bear the stamps of Bagdad and Samarcand ; and when the era of these coins corresponds *exactly* with the era of " black heathen " supremacy in these very territories, the unavoidable deduction is, that the sources from which the " East Men " drew their wealth, and the centres of the allegiance they owned, were situated as far East as Bagdad and Samarcand. That the prevailing character of these inscriptions was Kufic would indicate that Bagdad was the principal centre. But they are of many varieties ; " presenting more than a thousand different dies, and coined in about seventy towns in the eastern and northern districts of the dominions of the Caliphs. Five-sixths of them (continues this writer*) were coined by Samanidic Caliphs." Thus, although Charles Martel had checked the Arabian or " Saracenic " invaders at Tours, in the year 732 ; and,

* Mr. Worsaae, in his " Danes and Norwegians ; " London, 1852 ; p. 104.

although the Califate of "Aaron the Just," as distinctly
defined, did not extend so far north-west as the Baltic Sea ;
yet it seems clear that, when the *nigræ gentes* made their
appearance at Lindisfarne in 793, and overran the Hebrides
in the same year, Asia had virtually extended itself to the
very western limits of Europe.

Though the Black Cimbri were not actually subjects of
the celebrated Calif just spoken of (and better known to
most of us as " Haroun al Raschid "), yet it is probable they
were among those nations living near his north-western
border (Chazars, Huns, &c.), against whom he was often fighting, and whom he reduced to the position of tributaries.
We are told that when the King of the Franks, Charlemagne, was engaged in repelling the attacks of these very
Black Danes and their allies, he was at peace with the great
Sultan of the East, who owned the same tribes as enemies ;
the friendly understanding between these two great
monarchs being indicated in the mention of the fact by a
modern writer,* that an elephant "had been sent [at this
period] to Charlemagne by Aaron, the King of the Saracens,
i.e., by Harun ar Rashid." Probably the countries of what
is now Middle and Eastern Europe were in a condition that
alternated between peace and war all through this particular
period. That much trading was then carried on, all over
Modern Europe and the East, is evident from the statements
of authorities ; but, difficult to comprehend though it be, the
trader and the *robber-chief* were often one. So that, when
Mr. Worsaae states (as he does at page 103 of his " Danes
and Norwegians ") that there are " still existing Arabian
accounts of merchants who in those days visited the coasts
of the Baltic for the sake of trade, where considerable
trading places, such as Sleswick and many others, are mentioned," it does not follow that these are the accounts of
peaceful expeditions. The silken garments, gold-studded
spears, and golden helmets, that various British traditions
assign to the " black heathen " pirates, may have been
gained by them after the most peaceful fashion ; or they
may not. But, at any rate, the connection between the
masters of the Cimbric Peninsula and of large parts of the

* Mr. H. H. Howorth ; " Early Intercourse of the Danes and Franks," p. 30.

British Islands, with the great and powerful Empire of the Califs, is distinct : whether the former ought to be regarded as tributaries or not. And after the Black-Danish conquests of 793, at Lindisfarne and elsewhere, it must have been a matter of ordinary conversation in the bazaars of Bagdad and Samarcand, that such-and-such a race (Black Chazars or what not) had succeeded in making conquests and settlements throughout the most western of the islands of Frangistan. And this connection is quite sufficient to account for the fact, frequently commented upon, that unlettered British peasants—in many districts—possess many tales that are akin to, or identical with, those of the " Arabian Nights." Whether such tales are oftenest found among the swarthier sections can hardly be known ; but one of those collectors who has given us many stories of dusky warriors, with Eastern characteristics, has more than once passed a remark upon the tawny complexions of the people from whom he got those " Popular Tales : " such people forming part of the population of the " Isles of the Foreigners," and often claiming a descent from the *dubh galls* referred to.

Of these inroads, and settlements, and conquests, there are numberless traditions in these " Islands of Frangistan." The *nigrae gentes,* or *dubh galls,* or " black Danars," are remembered by many other names in British speech ; as " thieving Tartarians," as " marauding companies of Moors or Saracens," and, very likely, as " Turks." When the word Turk occurs in Gaelic it is translated " a boar ; " and the sculptured figures in the Baltic island show the fashion of wearing armour shaped to resemble such an animal (examples of which are occasionally found in these islands also). Whether or not the word has signified " boar " longer than " Turk," it seems to have often been used to denote the *man* who resembled the animal ; and not the animal itself. There is a " Bridge of Turk " in Wales, and another in Scotland ; and there are several mountains and glens in Ireland and Scotland whose names are translated into " the mountain (or glen) of the black boar (or pig)." But it seems quite as legitimate to translate the word " Turk " as to translate it " Boar " (or sometimes the feminine name). Because *Tuirc* signifies equally " of or belonging to a Turk," and " of or belonging to a Boar." In the *Story of Conall Gulban*, Conall and his comrades are warring against *Turcaich*, properly translated "Turks" by Mr. J. F. Campbell. But it would be as reasonable to use the word "Boar" in this story, as to use it in the song of Allan Mac Ruari (Roderick, or Roderigo, or Rory, or Ruy). He is spoken of as "the black-skinned *boar;*" but we should probably understand his position better as "the black-skinned *Turk.*" That, there-fore, the "Moors or Saracens" who are remembered in British tradition as "making depredations" in various quarters, were also known as "Turks," is very probable. Indeed, a meaning which this word, *Torc*, bears in Ireland, shows that it has been used to designate a race of rulers. Because, in Ireland, *Torc* not only means "a boar," but it also means "a sovereign; a lord."* Now, Ireland could never have been governed by four-footed boars; though much of it felt the power of the Black Tartarians of the Baltic. And these must have been the kind of "black boars" whose rule is still remembered in British topo-graphy.

In Galloway, also, which is a district celebrated for the inroads of "Moors or Saracens," from whom have come many clans distinguished by the Saracenic emblem of the crescent moon, there were people who, so recently as the year 1666, were armed with "crooked swords, like Turks."† And the curved blade known as a "gully" was probably of the same origin. Indeed, one particular "gully,"‡ is assumed to have been "some blacksmith's work in Fife;" having probably issued from the "gypsy" foundry, called "Little Carron." We are told that this kind of sword was "a common weapon with the [Black] Danes;" to whom it was known as an *atcgar;* being "the same scythe-shaped weapon as . . . . the Turkish 'yataghan.'" Indeed, the descriptions given of Black-Danish arms and armour are consistently Oriental; scale-armour, damascened battle-axes, gilded helmets and hilts, and "the same scythe-shaped weapon as the Turkish 'yataghan:'" (this special descrip-

---

* This definition is given in McAlpine's Gaelic Dictionary.
† "History of Galloway," Vol. II. p. 164
‡ In Skinner's poem of "The Christmas Ba'ing."

tion being taken from " The Comprehensive History of England," p. 116).

Another memory of this period is the word *Mahoun* or *Mahound.* It is stated to have been a form of Mahomet ; and to have been latterly " transferred to the devil : " " all over the western world (says Lord Hailes) *Mahoun* came to be an appellation of the devil."* According to Mr. Halliwell, Mahound, or Mahomet, was also " a character in old mysteries ; " though in later days it became synonymous with " a bugbear "—as in the kindred cases of " the black Douglas," and " the black Tinkler." In short, *Mahoun* was only an equivalent of " Saracen : " and it was used in this sense by the poet Dunbar when he called his rival, Kennedy, a " loun-like Mahoun ; " (which was an instance of " the pot calling the kettle black," as both of these minstrels seem to have been of swarthy hue). When Kennedy threw back the epithets—" Lucifer's lad, foul fiend's face infernal," " Saracen," " juggler," and *"jow,"* he was employing various synonyms for that word which " came to be an appellation of the devil," " all over the western world." And, just as *Mahoun* signified " Turk," so did another name for the same kind of people gradually come to signify a female Turk. Unlike *Mahoun,* this word survives at the present day ; being no other than " termagant." When Scott speaks of " the turban'd race of Termagaunt," he means the " Saracens." Thus, it would seem that the masculine bearing of that term has gradually been discarded ; until " termagant " has become used in the same way as " randy " is in Scotland ; and it may be added that Mr. Simson's opinion of the latter word is that it is only a variant of " ranee," or " gypsy queen." It may be that this rendering does an injustice to many " gypsy queens," past and present ; but from what Scott has told us of such gypsy queens as Black Agnes of Dunbar, and the Borderesses of about her era ; and also from what Mr. Simson has told us of the Borderesses of the eighteenth century, it is evident that the expression " termagant," if applied to them, would not be wholly inappropriate.

In addition to these particular titles, however, there are

---

* See Jamieson's Scottish Dictionary.

numerous traditions, all over the British Islands, of "black men" of fierce disposition ; and certain British sea-boards still retain legends of "devils" who attack coasting vessels, and either kill the mariners, or rob them of all they possess. There is no doubt that a large detachment of such "Saracens" hailed from the port of Algiers ; and that they had a remote political and ethnical connection with the northern "Saracens ;" but many of these traditions clearly relate to the latter division of those people.

One phase of this question cannot be passed over. It seems quite evident that "Saracens," "Moors," and "Egyptians" were utterly obnoxious to several Western races (whom it may be convenient to speak of as "Franks"), on the ground of their religious practices and their scientific knowledge ; which, in the eyes of their opponents, was a compound of "sorcery," "witchcraft," and gross evil. These "Franks" may have appeared equally obnoxious to their enemies, for *their* "infidelity," and for other practices that appeared to them objectionable. But the superior knowledge of those Eastern nations becomes most apparent, when one examines their characteristics ; though it seems equally clear that, with many "civilized" attributes, those Oriental races were otherwise most savage and cruel. And this invasion of Black-Cimbrians, or Danes, places both of these sets of qualities before us. That they were fierce, intolerant, and over-bearing ; that they burnt, plundered, killed and ravished without mercy ; and that they practiced such barbarities as scalping, impaling babies upon their spear points, and every form of torture that could be devised ; all this cannot be questioned. But they also possessed much material civilization ; silks, jewels, gold and silver, the games of chess, cards, dice, &c., the use of money—in short, many, if not all, of the attributes of the great Eastern Empire whose coinage was theirs, and whose supremacy they may have occasionally acknowledged. But, most of all, they practised *Magic ;* that is to say, they were acquainted, in some degree, with the immemorial system of the *Magi.* And that means the possession of knowledge. The very sentence that introduces those "black heathens" to modern Britons—the sentence which describes their first appearance off the coast of England—suggests that they were masters of a certain branch of knowledge which (though without good reason) is popularly believed to have been unstudied by any European races at that date.

"Simeon of Durham tells us* that their approach was heralded by 'fearful prodigies which terrified the wretched nation of the Angles; inasmuch as horrible lightnings and dragons in the air and flashes of fire were often seen glancing and flying to and fro';" and, in the description† of a naval engagement between two fleets of such corsairs, off the British coast, about three centuries later, the advance of the one party is referred to in these words—

> " Nearer went the daring Eastmen
> To the unexampled *fire-rain*."

Now, although all this was mystery and "magic" to "the wretched nation of the Angles," it would not be so to any civilized modern people. "Horrible lightnings and dragons in the air and flashes of fire. . . glancing and flying to and fro," accompanied with "fire-rain," that is by no means "unexampled,"—these are the ordinary adjuncts of modern warfare.

"Whatever obscurity may hang over the early history of gunpowder (says a recent authority‡), it seems most probable that its employment as a propelling agent originated among the Moors or Saracens,—whose civilization for several centuries contrasted forcibly with the intellectual darkness of Christendom." "The researches of all authorities seem to point to the Far East as the birthplace of an explosive mixture of the nature of gunpowder." "The most ancient reference of all is in the Gentoo code of laws (Halhed's translation), supposed by some authorities to be coeval with Moses. It runs thus: 'The magistrate shall not make war with any deceitful machine, or with poisoned weapons, or with cannon and guns, or any kind of firearms.' The translator remarks that this passage may 'serve to renew the suspicion, long

---

* Skene's "Celtic Scotland," Vol. I. pp. 302-303.

† Dr. Joseph Anderson's "Orkneyinga Saga," p. 45.

‡ The author of the article "Gunpowder" in the *Encyclopædia Britannica* (9th edition); whence the above information is taken.

since deemed absurd, that Alexander the Great did absolutely meet with some weapons of that kind in India, as a
passage from Quintus Curtius seems to ascertain.'"   "The
Saracens used it [Greek fire] against the Crusaders. Maim-
bourg, in his *History of the Crusades*, describes its effects ;
and Joinville, who was an eye-witness, says 'it was thrown
from a petrary, and came forward as large as a barrel of
verjuice, with a tail of fire as big as a great sword, making a
noise like thunder, and seeming like a dragon flying in the
air."

It will be seen that Simeon of Durham's description, and
that given by De Joinville, are much alike ; and the latter
assuredly pictures a discharge of artillery, very much akin to
the modern bomb-shell and mortar. Both of these writers,
also, compare this fiery missile to a "dragon." Now, the
word "dragon" has had many meanings attached to it ; and
there is a Gaelic word (*beithir*) which not only denotes "a
prodigiously large serpent," but also "a thunder-bolt." And
the ideas that attached to a "thunder-bolt," two centuries
ago, may be seen from this definition of *fulmen* in a Latin-
English dictionary of 1693 : "*Fulmen*. . . . A Flash of
Lightning, which when it is hurtful is called a Thunderbolt :
a shot or arrow. 'Tis commonly thought to be some stone
or solid body, but that is justly questioned. . . The Poets
ascribe *Fulmen* to the Boar, because of its cruel tusks and
his blasting breath." It may be only a coincidence that
Boars (which, in Gaelic, are *Turks*) are associated with these
"shots or arrows," accompanied by "flashes of lightning."
But it is evident that no mere animal has a "blasting breath."
This peculiarity ascribed by "the poets" to boars, brings
us back again to the word "dragon." Because our traditions
are full of stories of "fiery dragons ;" who vomited forth
fire and smoke ; who protected treasures ; who were covered
with steel scales ; and who carried off maidens. Now, if
those "dragons" were any species of saurian (as some suppose), it is impossible to understand what interest they could
have in the protection of treasure, or in the abduction of
virgins. But, if they were no other than the scale-armoured
Black Danes, who fashioned their armour to resemble bulls
and boars and other animals ; whose advent in these islands

was heralded by " horrible lightnings and dragons in the air
and flashes of fire. . . glancing and flying to and fro ;" who
both possessed treasure of their own, and took that of others ;
who were justly dreaded by the maidens of Britain (some
of whom remembered the " shelly-coated cow " as a cause
of terror, even in Allan Ramsay's day) ; if *these* were the
" fiery dragons " of our legends, then it is easy to understand
the allusions to virgins and treasures.   There is, indeed, a
distorted record of the attacks of such " dragons ; " in the
chronicles of the Abbey of Croyland, in the Isle of Ely,—
wherein there is mention of tribes of black-skinned and
" blubber-lipped " " devils," with " scaly faces " and " fiery
mouths " who infested the Ely marshes, and made desultory
raids upon the monastery there : the period in question being
at or prior to the Norman Conquest.

Besides, it is difficult to believe that gunpowder could
have been in use among Asiatic peoples for several thousands
of years, and yet be quite unknown in Europe until a few
centuries ago.   All the more difficult to believe, if Europe
has been largely, or wholly, peopled by migrations from
Asia ;—the most of which are placed at periods subsequent
to the era of Moses and the Gentoo law forbidding the use of
" cannon and guns, or any kind of firearms."   It is to what
we regard as the *oldest* group of British dialects that we must
look, to find the etymology of the word *gun* itself.   And this
assumes a knowledge of firearms, in British territory, long
anterior to the Black-Danish inroads.   This, indeed, is
asserted by one of the writers on the subject of the " Magic "
of Early Britain ; more commonly known in connection with
that period and place under its name of *Druidism* (Gaelic,
druidh, " a wizard ; " German, *drud,* " an enchanter, a wizard,
a sorcerer, a witch, a magician)."[*]   Of course, this takes us
back to a far earlier epoch than the one just under consideration : but the resemblances between the British *Magians* of
two thousand years ago, and those of the East, have already
been referred to.   And the immemorial acquaintanceship
with gunpowder, among Asiatic nations, leaves us free to

---

[*] Smith, in his " History of the Druids " (p. 73), says that " there are many
presumptive, if not positive, proofs for placing the art of gunpowder " " among
the *arcana* of nature which our Druids were acquainted with."

assume the possibility of one or other of the races of Europe being also acquainted with it at various remote periods. We have seen the definition of a "thunder-bolt." And, although it is true that Jupiter and his "thunder-bolts" represent, in one aspect, an all-powerful Deity and the artillery of heaven, yet many of the legends connected with Jupiter are " of the earth earthy." These, it may well be believed, are the memories of real events among men ; however jumbled together afterwards. It is significant to observe that when Vulcan started his foundry in the Isle of Lemnos, he and his Cyclops were chiefly engaged in forging "thunder-bolts" for his father. Does *real* lightning require to be forged in an iron-work ?—or is it only earthly artillery ?

Thus, the knowledge of this—and of many arts and sciences—may have been a property of the Europeans of various ages and various stocks ; and political revolutions, and the entrance of other races, may have caused these arts and sciences to be quite smothered for a time ; or nearly so ; —to be revived, again and again, by races of new-comers, or by a few descendants of the older *illuminati*.

However, we are dealing with the Tartarian Danes of the eighth, ninth, and tenth centuries. If these were the same people as the Tuatha De, or Tuatha De Danann, of " Gaelic " tradition, then their "magic" comes again to the front. Because the descendants of these people, in comparatively modern times, are described as "adepts in all Druidical and magical arts ; " and a legend announcing their landing in Ireland says that "the Tuatha De arrived, *concealed in their dark clouds*;" * which again suggests the smoke of gunpow- der. But if the Black Danes are to be regarded as the *only* race remembered as " devils," then there are the popular stories also to fall back upon. Because the "devils" of folk- lore are much given to disappearing with a flash of fire, a report, a cloud of smoke, and the odour of *sulphur*. And if such " devils " were of the race of Mahound, or Mahomet, who latterly became known as a " devil " " all over the western world ;" or if they were of the same breed as the fifteenth- century " fiends " of Courland, wielding scimitars and wear- ing caftans ; or, if they were as real as Robert, the " devil," •

* " Celtic Scotland ; " Vol. I. p. 178 ; Vol. III. p. 93.

of Normandy, or the "devil" who begot Merlin the Mage, or that other one whom Geoffrey Plantagenet married ; or as real as those "devils" who are remembered in British topography as the builders of bridges, "dykes," mills, and (in one instance) of a cross ; or as real as the "devil" who is said to have been the architect of Cologne Cathedral; then it is likely that their demoniacal qualities were simply those bodily and intellectual attributes that appertained to "the turban'd race of Termagaunt." And all "magic," "witchcraft," and "dealings with the devil," were really various forms of scientific knowledge ; of which the races who so denominated them were utterly ignorant. So that the traditions regarding "devils," and "fiery dragons" which guarded the castles of black "magicians," may be modernized into "Saracens," "fire-arms,"* and the strongholds of the Black Danes ; who either were themselves the possessors of much scientific knowledge, or who included in their ranks large numbers of the "Magi" of the Eastern cities where the coins which they used were minted.

That the civilization of "the Moors or Saracens" "contrasted forcibly with the intellectual darkness of Christendom" has long been recognized by moderns. And the mere fact that so many of our scientific words are Arabian—such words as *algebra, alchemy, alembic, elixir, alkali, alcohol,* and *almanac†*—this fact is most significant of the presence and influence of the Arabians in Europe. But they were

---

* "Dragons" may have been either the actual fire-arms or the men who used them ; or they may have signified the ships (" dragons") that spouted forth their "unexampled fire-rain." The word "dragon," in fact, was once very comprehensive in its application. Armstrong, in his Gaelic Dictionary, gives *duine borb* as one of the equivalents of "dragon" ; and *duine borb* means "a fierce, tyrannical man." Again, we are told by the author of "Northern Antiquities," in explanation of the dragons of romance, that "as the walls of the castles ran winding round them, they often called them by a name which signified *serpents* or *dragons.*" And, further, a (so-called) Gaelic word for a dragon, namely, *beithir*, which according to "English" orthoepy is spelt *bear*, this word is defined by Armstrong as "any wild beast" (which shows that *bear* was even more comprehensive than *deer* and *cattle*). This same word *bear* or *beithir* is also rendered "a dragon" and "a thunderbolt." "Dragon," therefore, seems to have denoted anything terrible : and fiery dragons may have been the men, or their weapons, or the missiles propelled therefrom, or the dragon-ships themselves.

† To these may be added the less "scientific" words—*albatross, alcove,* and *alligator.* It ought to be stated that Professor Skeat does not admit the claims of *almanac* to be regarded as Arabian.

"sorcerers," "wizards," and "magicians" to the ignorant nations whom they partly conquered and greatly influenced.

It is apparent that the wisdom of the *Magi* was not known to every kind of "Oriental," though it seems to have emanated from "the East." Even a tenth-century Persian, the poet Firdousi, while describing "what were doubtless the effects of rockets and wildfire discharged upon the enemy," "ascribes the whole to magic." Of course the word "magic" may have borne a meaning to him very much akin to our "science ;" because *Magi* were known to be *Wise Men.* Therefore, the Persian poet was very likely in the same position as that of a modern poet, when referring to some effect of chemistry or other branch of science, of which he avows himself to know little or nothing. But the Magian wisdom was "magic ;" and one form of "magic" was the knowledge of the uses of gunpowder. So that, when one hears of "an extract from the Georgian 'Life of Giorgi Mtharsmindel' (eleventh century), which describes how at Constantinople certain descendants of the race of Simon Magus, *Atsinkan* by name, sorcerers and famous rogues, slew wild beasts by their magic arts in the presence of Bagrat IV.," then one may reasonably assume that those wild beasts were shot after the usual fashion of our own times.

There can be no doubt that the long-continued persecution of "magicians" has signified the suppression (perhaps the extinction) of a great deal of real knowledge. The difficulty is to understand the *cause* of this persecution. It is not merely a question of ignorant races trying to stamp out all the knowledge that rendered their "magic-working" foes so formidable to them. No doubt, those enactments made by the successful faction in Scotland—against such things as "witchcraft" and "sorcery"—were intended to render their half-vanquished enemies altogether powerless. But other reasons than those of race and nationality seem to enter into the question. At a period that ante-dated those Scotch enactments by fifteen centuries, we see this same opposition to "magic ;" and in this instance the foe of "sorcery" was neither a half-ignorant monarch, nor the avowed enemy of any nation of men. We are told that one of the effects of the preaching of the Christian apostle, Paul,—when at Ephesus—was this, that "not a few of them that practised magical arts brought their books together, and burned them in the sight of all" (the value of these books being then estimated at "fifty thousand pieces of silver"). Now, if this had been the act of a victorious enemy of those "magicians," one could only lament over a temporary triumph of brute force over intellect. At the best it seems to have been a barbarous deed—though the sacrifice was voluntary. What language and character was impressed upon those volumes ?—what "arts" did they treat of ?—*why* were they destroyed ? No definite answer can ever be returned to these unavailing questions ; but, in the *cause* of the holocaust seems to lie the explanation of the whole continuous warfare against the learning of the *Magi*. St. Paul was not a con-quering savage or an ignorant fanatic ; and it is inconceivable that he, of all men, should have believed that his religion demanded the *ignorance* as well as the innocence of children. Moreover, the act was done willingly by those ex-Magi ; after the apostle had turned them to his own views. Therefore, the inference is that, although they possessed much genuine knowledge, their learning was greatly mis-applied ; and the sacrificed volumes were contaminated with an element that was utterly repugnant to Christianity. It is well known that a high civilization and much knowledge have co-existed with qualities that would not commend themselves to any civilized modern people : and various ancient systems are often particularly cited in illustration of this. The mere fact that the Magi of Persia and of Egypt (as well as those of the British Islands) confined their knowledge within the narrowest possible limits, by systematically ignoring the restrictions of consanguinity in the marriage relation, this alone makes one understand why people who were imbued with the feelings of Christianity should abhor a religion which was represented by such a priesthood : and, no doubt, other "magian" creeds and practices seemed equally obnoxious to those of the newer faith. The whole question of "gypsyism," in fact, resolves itself into a struggle between Christianity and Heathenism. Though the "Teutonic Order" was a league against "Pagans," yet it contained many Christianized "Saracens" within its own ranks ; and the Scotch statutes did

not affect those "gypsies" whose manners had become "assimilated to those of their countrymen." Racial antipathies did
a great deal, no doubt, to cause and to prolong such struggles:
but the chief point of difference seems to have been the
possession of antagonistic *codes*, resulting in wholly antagonistic ways of life. Thus, the most offensive features of
" magic " appear to have been those which encouraged and
inculcated practices that were essentially opposed to Christianity : and this must be the justification of so much that
was otherwise unjust and inexplicable in the persecutions of
'' witchcraft."

There can be no doubt that the "wizards" and
" magicians " of tradition have always been (as their names
imply) "wise men ;" whatever may have been the nature of
their moral attributes. We are told by one writer (Mr.
Wirt Sikes) that the people of South Wales long regarded
North Wales as the home of enchantment ; and North
Wales was certainly the home of *Druidism* for a very long
time. " The chief philosopher of that enchanted region was
a giant who sat on a mountain peak and watched the stars."
Mr. Blackmore, again, speaks of an Exmoor "magician"
who possessed a " magic book," of which the distinctive
property was, that, when he pointed it at any man who may
have been crossing the moor (no matter how far from the
magician's tower), that man was obliged to come to the
wizard, whether he wished or not. We, too, have " wizards "
who watch the stars, and who can bring distant objects quite
close to us (apparently), simply by levelling a certain
" magic " instrument at such objects. But, in our phraseology,
such men are "astronomers," and their magic instruments
"telescopes."

It has been remarked that Pliny regarded the early
Magianism of the British " Druids " as almost identical with
that of Ancient Persia. These " Magi " of Wales and of
Exmoor may have belonged to any period anterior to our
own ; and the existence of the traditions regarding them
does not necessarily prove these traditions to be of very old
date. But the following remarks of Dr. Armstrong's, in his
Gaelic Dictionary, help to endorse the belief of Pliny :—

" The word *gloine* [glass] seems to be *glaoth-theine*, glued by fire.

From the composition of this vocable, Dr. Smith infers, with much reason, that the Druids [Early Magi of Britain] were no strangers to the making of glass ; the knowledge of which art, he observes, they might have obtained from the first inventors, the Phoenicians [who were, perhaps, *themselves*]. Dr. Smith presumes further, that the Druids were so perfect in the art, and so well acquainted with the properties of glass, as to apply it, with the most eminent success, to the purposes of astronomy. Mr. Huddleston, the very ingenious editor of ' Toland's History of the Druids,' touching this opinion, is somewhat sarcastic on Smith. He remarks that the telescopic hypothesis rests on a mistaken meaning of a quotation from Hecateus, who says, that the *Boreadæ bring the moon very near them ;* and that the Boreadæ, even granting they were Druids, only asserted a prerogative which was common to all magicians, namely, ' to bring down the moon ' ; and, consequently, that the allusion is made to incantation, and not to telescopes. All this does not in the least repel the opinion of Dr. S., which derives additional strength from Diodorus Siculus, who makes mention of an Hyperborean *island,* from which the moon was to be seen, *apparently* at a small distance from the earth, and exhibiting several inequalities and eminences on its surface. This is not the language of incantation, but a just description of the moon as seen through glasses of very considerable power."

Now, when Huddleston objected to the " telescope " theory, on the ground that " to bring down the moon " was " a prerogative which was common to all magicians," he was really doing a great deal to strengthen the argument which he despised. He was saying that this prerogative was common to all " wise men ; " or, rather, to all " men of science " (for the terms are not quite synonymous). He has not recorded his own definition óf " magician " and " magic ; " but it may be assumed that he, like many of his contemporaries, had not wholly shaken off the ideas of the more ignorant sections of our ancestry. It is probable that he *believed* himself to be a disbeliever in the possession, by any of his fellow-men, of supernatural power ; but " magic " must have been a word that possessed a certain meaning to him—although he may never have tried to analyze his impression. If he did not believe that anything but superior knowledge could enable one man to do what others could not do, then (without realising it) he must have understood " magic " as " knowledge." If he thought otherwise, then he was—like the more ignorant sections of his ancestry—a believer in the possession of supernatural power by ordinary mortals. But, whatever he believed, he was virtually stating

that the power " to bring down the moon " was "a prerogative which was common to all men of science." And this
" prerogative " has always belonged to astronomers and
astrologers ; besides being shared by many other people.

Sir John Maundevile, in describing his visit to the court
of the Great Khan of Tartary, speaks in similar terms of
similar " Druids." " And than," he says, " comen Jogulours
and Enchauntoures, that don many marvaylles : for thei
maken to come in the Ayr, the Sonne and the Mone, be
semynge, to every mannes sight." The phrases employed
by men of the non-scientific castes, when speaking of such
things, are always the same : they are the result of " the
black art," " magic " (the science of the Magi),* and "enchantment " or " incantation."

The periods just glanced at are, of course, widely
separated by time ; and the localities referred to are also
widely separated by space. But the people under consideration possess the characteristics " common to all magicians ; "
and, therefore, the more modern " magicians " may fairly be
held as representing the same *system* as those of older date
—if they ought not also to be regarded as racially descended
from the same stock. The *Magi* of early Britain were
regarded by Pliny as stewards of the same mysteries as
those known to the *Magi* of Persia : and it is to be remembered that Pliny styled some (at least) of those early Britons

---

* " Magic " must, of course, have included much more than the few depart-
ments of knowledge referred to in these pages. For example, when Scott
delineates the famous scholar, Michael Scott, as

> " A wizard, of such dreaded fame,
> That when, in Salamanca's cave,
> Him listed his magic wand to wave,
> The bells would ring in Notre Dame ; "

when citing this evidence of Michael's power, he is hinting at something very like
telegraphy. Sir Walter was, of course, aware that Magic *included* Science, if
he did not regard the terms as synonymous. And he himself remarks, in this
connection :—" Spain, from the relics, doubtless, of Arabian learning and superstition, was accounted a favourite residence of magicians. Pope Sylvester, who
actually imported from Spain the use of the Arabian numerals, was supposed to
have learned there the magic, for which he was stigmatized by the ignorance of
his age. There were public schools where magic, or rather the sciences supposed to involve its mysteries, were regularly taught, at Toledo, Seville, and
Salamanca." (Appendix to the " Lay," Note 2 D.)

"Ethiopians"—although it does not appear that he applied that term directly to the British *Magi*. When Patrick was preaching Christianity in Ancient Scotia we are told that, on one occasion, "the Gentiles were about celebrating an idolatrous solemnity, accompanied with many incantations and some magical inventions and other idolatrous superstitions; their kings being collected, also their satraps with their chief leaders, and the principal among the people, and *Magi* and enchanters and soothsayers and doctors, inventors of all arts and gifts." "And again we are told that St. Patrick 'came to Muada; and behold the *Magi* of the sons of Amolngid heard that the Saint came into the country, a very great crowd of *Magi* assembled, with the chief *Magus* named Recrad, who wished to slay Patrick; and he came to them with nine *Magi* clad in white garments, with a magical host.'"* Thus, although the early British "magicians" may have become nearly extinct (or converted to newer ideas, religious and social, as well as altered in physique by miscegenation) at the period when the "black heathens" of the Baltic ("black Lochlinners," or black Scandinavians) invaded the British Islands, yet this eighth-century inroad of Eastern "pagans" and "magic-workers" may have been, in many respects, little more than a variation of the Scot-Egyptian migrations, or those of still earlier date.

All these people, then, were masters of "magic," or the science of the *Magi;* otherwise spoken of as "the black art," "enchantment" and "incantation." And the literal meaning of these last two words enables us to understand why the "irreconcilable" remnant of those "*Magi* and enchanters and soothsayers" should have been known last century as "the canting crew."

And "the canting crew" were "gypsies:" "incantation," or "enchantment," or "sorcery," is inseparable from "the wisdom of the Egyptians." That the fourteenth-century "Jugglers and Enchanters," who "brought down the moon" at the court of the Great Khan of Tartary, belonged to the same stock as those eleventh-century "descendants of the race of Simon Magus," who "slew wild beasts by their magic arts in the presence of Bagrat IV.,"—this we have every

---

* Skene's "Celtic Scotland," Vol. II. pp. 111-112.

reason to believe. And the latter of these were called *Atsinkan ;* and are identified with the *Zingani*, or Gypsies Proper. The " Tartar gypsies " of modern Denmark were persecuted by the sedentary and Christianized castes for their " witchcraft : " the " black Danars," or *nigrae gentes* of Denmark, of a thousand years ago, were distinguished by the same characteristic when they overran the British Islands. And, long after the supreme power had slipped out of their hands, the moss-trooping " Tartarians " and " Egyptians " of these islands continued to practise " the black art of their forefathers."

It does not appear that the existing "tories" of these ancient systems have preserved many fragments of their ancestral knowledge. They do profess a kind of astrology, and arrogate to themselves an innate prophetic power : and they may still possess a peculiar knowledge of the art of healing. And Borrow tells us that " some few " of their words are Arabic.* But the Arabic words that belong to real science have long ago passed into the composite " English " speech ; and with them must have come a distinct addition to British learning, and a contemporaneous accession to the ranks of the *Melanochroi* of Britain. Nevertheless, although British " gypsies " (considered as such) may only possess the merest scraps of the " magic " of their (and our) ancestors, yet it is not a great while since the connection between certain arts and this special race could be dimly seen. The likelihood of such a connection has presented itself to (at least) one living authority on the subject of " gypsies : " and this quite apart from the considerations dwelt upon in these pages. The chief argument advanced by M. Bataillard in proof of an ancient European-Gypsy connection is the familiarity of Gypsies Proper with the metallurgical arts, and the fact that these arts have been practised in Europe from immemorial times. The authority just referred to is not, however, the French scholar, but an

---

* One of these words is "*tass* or *dass*, by which some of the very old Gypsies occasionally call a cup." Mr. Borrow cites this as a French word. It is, of course, French (*tasse*) ; but it is also Spanish (*taza*) and Lowland-Scotch (*tass* and *tassie*). Probably, it has been " Arabic " and " Romanes " for a longer period than it has been " French," " Spanish," and " Lowland-Scotch."

English writer ;* to whom this remote European-Gypsy connection, and also the immemorial connection between Science and Gypsydom, present themselves in the light of *probabilities ;* if insufficient evidence prevents them from, as yet, becoming settled *convictions.* Mr. Groome has noted that there are various indications that, both on the Continent and in the British Islands, *Gypsies* and *Artillery* have, in some way, been identified with each other. It is worthy of remark that one tradition connects " Mons Meg " (the antique cannon that forms a distinct feature in the Castle of Edinburgh) with the " Saracenic " district of Galloway. The accuracy of this legend has been called in question ; but whether or not that is the particular cannon referred to, there is certainly a tradition that, when James the Second (of Scotland) was besieging the Black-Douglas stronghold of Thrave, in the year 1455, he was materially assisted in his operations by the use of a huge cannon which his vassal, Maclellan, presented to him ; and which had just been forged by a family of local smiths (the head of the family being remembered as " Brawny McKim "). Moreover, those Maclellans of Bombie bore " a mortar-piece, or bomb, with the motto *Superbo Frango,*" in their coat-of-arms ; at an early date— though it seems uncertain whether this was before the time when the Black-Douglas overthrow enabled Maclellan to wear the " Moor's head," with the motto *Think on.* The tradition is, as all traditions are, vague ; but it is important to notice that there were " smiths " in Galloway, in the year 1455, who were able to cast cannon. This is quite in keeping with the statements made by Dr. Johnson's critic (Mc Nicol) as to the antiquity of iron-working in Scotland ; and it also accords well with Mr. J. F. Campbell's and Mr. Cosmo Innes' testimony to the existence of numerous floating legends (in Scotland) with regard to smiths who possessed " magical " powers. Of course, it is necessary to assume that the McKim family had become renegades to the Black-Douglases, when they forged cannon in aid of the Stewart

* Mr. F. H. Groome ; whose views in this matter are quite independent of those expressed in these pages. While Mr. Groome may not be disposed to endorse the theories here advanced, it is of much importance that his own opinions have been formed independently of such theories.

forces. But the story shows, at any rate, that, in the territory which was lorded over by "Moors or Saracens," there,
existed also the ability to manufacture and to use artillery.

Mr. Groome further calls attention to the "gypsy"
foundry of "Little Carron" in Fife; and to the fact that
while the church-bells of Edzell, Forfarshire, were cast by
"a band of Tinkers" in the year 1726, the bells of Kirkwall
Cathedral had been cast at Edinburgh by the *master-gunner*
to James V., in the year 1528. It might thus be inferred
that since church-bells were forged by an artillery-maker in
1528, the people who forged church-bells in 1726 were probably adepts in the art of making cannons also. If this
were so, then the master-gunner of James the Fifth appears
as a member of the same brotherhood as the Forfarshire "band
of tinkers" of the year 1726: the founders of either century
being consequently "gypsies." It is certainly worthy of
remark that this master-gunner, though living in North
Britain, and presumably of North-British lineage, thought it
necessary to style himself a "Scot." That title was not
used as a surname; because the man's name was Robert
Borthwick. But he inscribed upon all the cannon which he
cast, that they were fabricated by "Robert Borthwick, *Scot*."[*]
Now, as those pieces of ordnance were cast in Edinburgh
Castle, and were not intended to be captured by any enemy,
it seems clear that the designation "Scot" was chiefly meant
to meet the eye of North-British people. Inferentially, then,
all North-British people were not "Scots" at that date
(1509–28). We know from Elder's letter of the same period
that there existed at that time a North-British priesthood,
deriving itself from "Scota, the daughter of a Pharaoh"
(the alleged ancestress of the Early Scots of Ireland). And
we know, from an allusion in an Edinburgh chronicle, that,
more than a hundred years later, the moss-trooping "Scots"
were distinguished from contemporary "Scotchmen." We
have also seen that, soon after the Norman Conquest, the
Bruces and their comrades did not regard themselves as
"Scots"—though they did much to form a North-British
nationality which became known as "Scottish." Thus, there
is a strong presumption that this "master gunner" knew

* See Anderson's "Scottish Nation," Vol. I. p. 340.

himself to be descended from the ante-Norman race of Scots
—whose traditions were drawn from Egypt. And that, consequently, the inscription on his cannon was meant to denote
that he was " Robert Borthwick, *Egyptian.*"

This is, to a certain extent, conjectural. But (though
it relates to a different art) there is no dubiety in the
statement that the gypsies of the south of Scotland
" practised copper-plate engraving " so recently as the
eighteenth century. There is also a record of a " Mr.
William Sympsoune " of the year 1586, who, " when about
eight years of age, was taken away by ane Egyptian into
Egypt . . . where he remained ten years and then came
home." This Sympsoune is described as a great scholar, a
doctor of medicine, and (which is notable) as the *King's
smith.* It is further noticed that, in the year 1592, a *Simson*
was hanged at Durham " for being an Egyptian." The re-
currence of this name, at this place and time, and in this
character, is a little suggestive. Of course, the man who,
after ten years of Egyptian training, had developed into an
accomplished scholar, and an artificer as well, may have only
been " an Egyptian " by education.* The country in which he

---

* It appears evident that, at no very distant date, many British people of fair
complexion were accustomed to blacken their faces artificially, " that they might
the better pass for Moors." And this custom is probably the explanation of the
term " counterfeit Egyptians," which occurs in the Scotch Acts. In a " Process
against the Egyptians, at Banff—1700—" (*Miscellany of the Spalding Club*,
Vol. III.) it is argued for the defence that the people " comonlie called Egyptians,
. . . are onlie interpret to be idle beggars, *blakeing their faces*, fortune-tellers,
cheating of the people by waine superstitiones," &c. The attempt to exonerate
the accused (the famous minstrel, McPherson, and a man named Gordon) proved
of no avail ; and the prisoners were declared to be " habit and reput wagabonds,
soroners, and Egiptians," and—as such—were hanged at the Cross of Banff, 16th
November, 1700. But the reference incidentally made shows that the " Waltham
Blacks," if not pure-blooded Gypsies, were at least what the Scotch Acts called
"counterfeit Egyptians;" not only because they were "habit and reput wagabonds and soroners," but also because of their custom of simulating the dusky
complexion of the Egyptians Proper. This practice alone, then, would connect
the "counterfeit Egyptians" of Scotland, the Waltham Blacks of Epping
Forest, and the modern Morris-men of our race-courses and fairs, who (Mr.
C. G. Leland tells us) speak a broken Romanes. And the *need* of artificially
blackening the face suggests a mixed race of people—Egyptians, in some degree,
but not swarthy enough by nature to pass for genuine Egyptians.

An example of the adopted Egyptian, then, is seen in the Sympsoune of 1586 ;
whether or not he ever found it desirable to imitate the hue of his preceptors.
Although not a "counterfeit Egyptian " in the popular sense,—that term was
nevertheless quite applicable to him.

was educated, it may be observed, need not have been situated
outside of Great Britain, and the "Egyptian" who trained
him may have been a North-Briton as well as himself,—
though not necessarily living in "Scotland."[*]
Indeed, many such men of science may easily have been
of this stock, even although the fact is not recorded. When,
in the year 1501-2, James IV. of Scotland sent "iiij hary
nobles . . . *to the Leich to Multiply*," the said coins being
of the total value of £9, it would seem that this doctor of
medicine of 1501-2 was fooling this simple monarch with
the famous "great trick" of the Egyptians (past and present), who pretend " as how they can make money breed
money, all along of a charm they've got." Deceived by
which pretence, many confiding people have entrusted their
money to an Egyptian wizard ; with the result that neither
the sum so lent, nor its mythical progeny, ever find their way
into the repositories of the expectant lender. Whether or not
" Mr. William Sympsoune " of the year 1586 ever attempted
this well-known piece of Jugglery, it is certain that he must
have known how to go about it—after his ten years' education among Gypsies. That men of real scholarship should
ever have utilised their talents in such a way shows that a
code of honour then existed that was quite at variance with
that which is now obeyed ; and it also reminds one that such
words as *crafty, artful, knowing,* and *cunning* have a twofold
meaning, which does not at all combat the theory that the
men who practised the "great trick" of the Egyptians were
also famous as teachers of many arts and sciences. And the
important point of this incident of 1501-2 is that the "code
of honour " which characterized this " Physician in Ordinary "
of James IV. of Scotland was precisely that which our
modern gypsies frankly confess they obey (as one may see,
for example, at pages 371-381 of " In Gipsy Tents ").
The considerations just touched upon make it evident that
no race or class of men (whether discredited, as now, or respected, as in the year 1501) who avowedly repudiated the
doctrine laid down in the law " Thou shalt not steal,"—such
men, it is clear, cannot be regarded as attempting to put into
practice the precepts of Christianity. The law referred to is,

[*] I am indebted for all these particulars to Mr. F. H. Groome.

of course, vastly older than Christianity, but that religion accepts it as one of its most important rules. And this fact —that the " magic-working " castes had no respect whatever for this law—makes it more apparent that " the wisdom of the *Magi* " embodied principles that were radically opposed to Christianity. And that—as already suggested—this is why " Magic " has always been persecuted. This antagonism to the law " Thou shalt not steal " is inseparable from gypsy-dom. We have been told that " *the great distinguishing feature* in the character of the gipsies is an incurable pro-pensity for theft and robbery." And that they were far from denying the truth of the statement. Stealing was (and, to some extent, still is) a *virtue* with them: "thou shalt not steal " was a law which had no meaning to them. This fact alone helps one to understand why severe laws were passed against " Egyptians," by people who believed that stealing was a crime ; and an impediment in the way of civilization. And it tends to show how the laws against " gypsyism " were laws against " heathenism," made in the interests of what is either " Christianity " or something akin to it. Moreover, the consideration of this fact shows that it offers a strong argument in favour of a national code (in morals and society). " A state religion " is a phrase that has different meanings to different people ; but it is obvious that no nation can keep together without some kind of national "code." If all British people were at liberty to act as they thought right, then it would be utterly unjust to prosecute for such things as theft, poaching, bigamy, murder, or (as a recent occurrence suggests) burning the bodies of the dead ; for all of these things have been, and some still are, regarded by certain people as quite justifiable. Whence it appears that the laws made against " Egyptians " denoted a battle between antagonistic *principles* even more than a struggle between rival *races*. And that "gypsydom " was virtually the " Heathenesse " of tradition.

. . . .

While, therefore, recognizing an ancient connection between the " Magus " and the " Egyptian Proper," it is nevertheless clear that "gypsy " has usurped the place of "tory " to a great degree. In the first place, the really *black*-skinned

gypsy has quite disappeared ; thereby showing that the
darkest modern gypsy is a semi-white hybrid. Such phrases
as "as black as Tartars " (applied to the self-styled *Secani*
[*Zigani*] on one occasion), or "as black as gypsies " (a comparison made by early New-Englanders, in speaking of the
"dark Americans "),—such phrases do not tell us *how* black
the people referred to were. The "Gaelic" words that
signify *black Danes, black Scandinavians, black Irishmen,* and
black heathen ; and such terms as " the black army," or *nigra
gentes,* are more exact, if the word " black" was used in its
proper sense. In the *Song of Roland* and in the traditional
John-of-Rampayne story, the phrase " as black as ink " leaves
no room for doubt ; neither does the Welsh story of the girl
whose skin was " blacker than the blackest iron covered with
pitch." And, although the *Maurus* of Claudian denotes,
according to some writers, a *dark-brown* rather than a *black*
complexion, Pliny's adjective, which signifies " black as an
Ethiopian," may be held to denote the darkest of all dark
skins. No modern gypsy, therefore, can be regarded as the
pure-blooded descendant of any Black-European race. It
is true that the Ancient Egyptian of Professor Huxley is not
" black as an Ethiopian," but this is a distinction which may
be waived at present.

Not only does the darkest modern gypsy appear to be of
lighter complexion than the Ancient Egyptian, but many
of the customs which render him " peculiar" among modern
people are the customs of races that have been assumed to
be white.

One of these races is that called " Saxon." The people to
whom this name was first applied are popularly believed to
have been "fair whites." The name is said by some to be
an abbreviation of " Saka-suni ; " and if they were " the sons
of the Sakas " of ancient Tartary, they were certainly descended from *Xanthochroi.* Professor Max Müller refers to
the Sakas in these words : " They are best known by the
name of *Yuch-chi,* this being the name by which they are
called in Chinese chronicles. These Chinese chronicles form
the principal source from which we derive our knowledge of
these tribes, both before and after their invasion of India.
[They " took possession of India, or, at least, of the govern-

ment of India, from about the first century B.C. to the third
century A.D."] . . . They are described as of pink and white
complexion, and as shooting from horseback ; and as there
was some similarity between their Chinese name *Yueh-chi*
and the *Gothi* or *Goths*, they were identified by Remusat
with those German tribes, and by others with the *Getæ*, the
neighbours of the Goths." " Between the years 139–126 B.C.,"
the *Yueh-chi* inhabited a territory situated " 7,000 li north of
India. . . They were herdsmen and nomads, and resembled
the Hiung-nu [the "Huns" of De Guignes and Gibbon] in
manners and customs. Driven out of their seats by the
Hiung-nu, they fell on the Tochâri from the West, and
defeated them."* Thus, the Sakas, or early Saxons, appear
as the otherwise-styled "White Huns ; " and if any scrap of
early-Saxon nationality is still surviving, it will probably be
represented by some such people as the "pink and white "
Tekke-Turcomans, who, as "herdsmen and nomads," still
occupy a territory not far removed from that of the Sakas,
and whose physiognomy is that of the "Tartar."

The recognition of the fact that a Xanthochroic race resembled a swarthy people such as the Black Huns "in
manners and customs ; " and many other reasons which could
be adduced ; renders it necessary to admit the error of assuming that kindred practices—such as painting or tattooing—
must necessarily denote kindred blood. Nothing in these
pages has proved that such practices have belonged exclusively to dark-skinned people ; and it is probably as well to
abandon any such half-formed proposition. As, however, the
question of *complexion* does not seem to have been solved, it
may not be right to assume that difference of colour means
difference of stock. Swarthy Samoyeds and fair-skinned
Eskimos seem to be *structurally* alike ; and there may have
been little or no difference in the physique of the White Hun
and the Black. Thus, kindred customs may have denoted
kindred blood, *even though* the complexions varied.

The Sakas are also remembered as the rulers of northern
Afghanistan and Southern Turkestan, at about the same
period as their government of India—the second century
B.C. But the name "Saka" (which is also rendered

* Max Müller's "India," pp. 85-6 and 275.

" Scythian ") is applicable to so many periods, and probably to so many races, that—like " Asiatic "—it may have been used to denote men with white, and brown, and yellow complexions. However, as it is undoubted that one, or many, divisions of "Sakas" found their way to these islands, their history and characteristics are " British." The date of their arrival seems uncertain. It is, at least, known that they, along with the Scots, Attacotts, and Picts, were the terror of the civilized Britons in the *fourth century* ; and that " the invading tribes penetrated so far into the interior, and the extent and character of their ravages so greatly threatened the very existence of the Roman Government, that . . . the most eminent commander of the day, Theodosius the elder, was despatched to the assistance of the Britons." " The Picts (says Claudian) he drove into their own region, to which he (Claudian) gave the poetical name applied to Caledonia of Thule. The Scots he pursued across the sea to the country from whence they proceeded—the Island of Ierne ; and the Saxons he indicates had formed their headquarters in the Islands of Orkney."[*] Thus, while we see the Sakas ("before Christ") associated with the swarthy, tattooed Huns, we see them again—in the fourth century of the Christian era—as the invaders of the Christianized parts of Britain, contemporaneously with the Egyptian Scots, and the "nimble blackamoors, not wrongly named ' The Painted Folk.' "

That the Saxons (to give them the usual name) were really some kind of Huns may be seen, for one reason, from their use of the term " Hun " as signifying something equivalent to " a bold warrior." Mr. Karl Blind, who points out this usage, is not disposed to regard it as proving a Hun descent, his reason being that they pronounced the word " Hune " and not " Hunn." But this objection tells the contrary way. Because the sound of " Hune " was probably the same as *Chuni* (*ch* guttural) or *Ounnoi*,—that is " Hun." Moreover, just as we have come to speak of the " Huni " of history as " Huns," so have the names of places which record their residence in Britain also become pronounced " Hun." " In England there are a vast number of place-

* Skene's " Celtic Scotland," Vol. I. pp. 99-101.

names, from Kent and Suffolk up to Shetland, all pointing
to settlements of those German Hunes ; such as Hunton,
Hundon, Hunworth, Hunstanton, Huncote, Hungate, Huncoat,
Hunslet, Hunmanby, Hunwick, the Head of Hunna, and
Isle of Hunie [as also Hun-gill, in Nithsdale]. Old English
personal names, too, like Ethelhun (Noble Hune), have the
same origin."*

This last name—Ethel-hun—confirms the belief in the
Hun kinship of the " Saka-suni." *Ethel-hun* may easily
have meant "noble warrior" to the race over whom this
particular man was chief. But to their enemies it signified
"Attila the Hun." The word "Attila" has been identified
with the (so-called) Hungarian word "Aethele," *noble ;* and,
indeed, the celebrated "Attila the Hun" is spoken of in the
Nibelungen Lied as "Etzel, king of Hunland." *Attila,
Aethele, Etzel, Ethel*—all these are recognizable as so many
different forms of the one word. Of course, the "Ethel-
hun" who appeared in England need not have been the
most famous "Attila" of all the Huns. "A Hune" would
mean "a bold warrior" to one race ; just as "a Rom" meant
"a man" to another, without any individuality being denoted by the name. (To their foes they would be, respectively, Huns or Hun-men, and Roms or Rom-men, in the
same general sense.) So that the Ethel-huns referred to by
Mr. Karl Blind may have been *any* chiefs of the Huns ; and
the term "Ethel-hun" or "Etzel-Hun" may have been used
by their enemies in a similarly loose way (much as the parallel
term *Cean-aedh* [Kenneth or Kennedy] seems to have
been employed).

It may be noted, at the same time, that while the celebrated fifth-century Ethel-Hun, or Attila the Hun, had a
brother bearing the name of Bleda, so was Bleda the name
of one of the fifth-century Saka-suni who invaded Britain†
—having been one of those who besieged the Christianized
Britons at Mount Badon, near Bath. And as the Black

---

* Mr. Karl Blind ; in the *Gentleman's Magazine* of May, 1883.
† A brother of this Bleda is called "Kenric"; which seems to be only
ceann-righ, "a head chief," and does as little to tell to us the name by which
he was known to his friends as the title of *Cin-aedh, Kennedy,* or *Kenneth* denotes
the names of the men so known in history. The father of this Kenric and Bleda
is known as *Cerdic.*

Huns "scarified their faces," so did the Saka-suni, or Saxons. Indeed, the Saka-suni appear to have resembled the Black Huns "in manners and customs," during the earlier centuries of our era, much as the Sakas of Tartary had resembled the Hiong-nou many centuries before.

A modern writer, making use of the modern* title of "Anglo-Saxon," and the somewhat vague designation "Aryan" (which, if it really signifies "ploughman," can scarcely apply to a race of "herdsman and nomads"), informs us that "our Aryan ancestor in person, as Mr. McLennan and Mr. Lang have shown, was a most undoubted totemist; and even our far later Anglo-Saxon progenitor, when he first landed in Britain, was a very fair specimen of an untamed barbarian indeed. He tattooed his face, like the æsthetic New Zealander; he captured his wife by main force, like the unsophisticated Australian; and he lighted the need-fire with a wooden drill, like the primitive Hindu. It was only at a later date, when missionaries from civilized Rome and civilized Ireland had introduced a little southern and Celtic culture, that the gentler Christian Anglo-Saxon took to buying his wife with so many head of cattle, like the commercial Zulu, instead of stunning her with a club, like the simple-minded Australian; and to painting his face in stripes, like the intelligent Redskin, instead of pricking it with a needle, like the amiable Polynesian: and therefore there is nothing out of keeping with Anglo-Saxon culture (or want of it) in the fact that many clan-names were derived from obvious totems."

While accepting the facts introduced in the above paragraph† it is not necessary to assume that they are viewed in the truest light. "Civilization" and "barbarism" are difficult to define. When of two races, otherwise alike, the

---

* The late Mr. J. R. Green remarks (at page 193 of "The Conquest of England"): "It may be well to note that the word 'Angul-Saxon' is of purely political coinage, and that no man is ever known, save in our own day, to have called himself 'an Anglo-Saxon.'"

It may also be observed that the title "Celt," as now used, has as little to recommend itself. And that had such titles ever been used by any British people, they would be quite inapplicable to any portion of the hybrid Modern-British nation.

† Which occurs in an article on "Old English Clans," contributed by Mr. Grant Allen to the "Cornhill Magazine" of September 1881.

one practises tattooing and the other does not, it may reasonably be argued that the former is in the least primitive condition : since tattooing not only shows a taste for artistic
decoration but also gives expression to many distinctions of
social, of family, or of religious nature. But "civilization"
is altogether relative. Customs that one society regards as
"barbarous" are held by others to be indispensable adjuncts
of "civilization." The mere custom of tattooing does not
really prove a want of "culture" among those early Saxons.

But the existence of those customs is what we have to
consider. And the practices of painting and tattooing show
us that those Saxon invaders were quite as much "Picts" as
were the "nimble blackamoors" who were their confederates.
While the fact that they, too, "scarified their faces" shows
that the self-styled "Hunes" of Britain followed at least
one fashion of the contemporary "Hunes" of the Continent.
And we have seen that each of these customs was practised
by British "tories" down to our own times.

This last is the most important point. When the
"gypsies" of Galloway—last century—painted their faces
with ruddle, they were following a custom that a Christianized
Goth (Jornandes, Bishop of Ravenna) ascribes to the Gothic
peoples. And in describing those "Galloways" as "Picts,"
it is no contradiction to assume that they were also "Goths"
and "Saxons." The Saxons were Picts ; and since their
era in Britain is the same, and their natures apparently
identical, it is likely enough that they were not very
different from each other—if at all. Such names as *Scot,
Attacott, Saxon,* and *Pict* do not necessarily imply *four*
different stocks. They may have been used to denote
tribes that were very closely allied to each other—if they
were not all so many different names for the one set of
people.

At any rate, the habits of those "Saxons" spoken of
above were the habits of our "gypsies." It is said of one of
the Border Faws that the hardest fight he ever had was
when capturing his bride from her relations. The antiquity
of this custom in North Britain is referred to by Scott,
when his fictitious "Richie Moniplies" states that he gained
his wife in "the auld Scottish fashion"—namely, by "his

bow and his spear." (And probably it yet survives, in a
modified form, in the rough treatment that is occasionally
given to bridegrooms, by people who are otherwise educated.)
If such a chief as Marshall of Galloway captured one of his
numerous wives by main force (as the neighbouring Faws
were recently accustomed to do), then that and his custom
of using war paint helped to connect him with those early
Saxons. Indeed, his district was largely overrun by Saxons ;
and, if there was any important difference between an early
" Saxon " and an early " Pict " (which is doubtful), this
Marshall may have been as much the descendant of the one
race as of the other.

It must be remembered that, to the early authors, the
" Saxons " were known as " Saracens."* If those early
Saxons were white Huns, then of course they were white
Saracens. Still, it is curious to notice that although the
traditional " Saracen " is sometimes represented as a white
man, yet the word is much more frequently used as a
synonym for " Moor." And it is certain that the early Saxons
were associated with the dark races—whatever their own
complexion may have been. We have seen that Theodosius
fought them at the same time as he fought the "nimble
blackamoors," and in like circumstances. Moreover, during
the attacks upon Menevia, in Wales,† during the tenth and
eleventh centuries, it does not seem that the "Saxons"
differed politically from the "black gentiles ;" in whose
company they made their forays. It is also worth noting
that such a title as *The Fair-haired* could not well have been
given (as a distinctive epithet) to a leader of fair-haired
people. When " *Godisric filius Harald cum nigris gentibus
vastavit Meneviam*," the leader—if white-skinned — was
apparently the only white " Saracen " in the pirate fleet.

But whether white or black, those Saracens whom history
knows as " Saxons " were, in manners, much like any other

---

* In a note to " The Minstrelsy of the Scottish Border " (p. 447 of the reprint
of 1869, A. Murray & Son, London), this statement is made :—" In the metrical
romance of ' Arthur ' and ' Merlin,' we have also an account of Wandlesbury
being occupied by the Saracens, *i.e.*, the Saxons ; for all pagans were Saracens
with the romancers. I presume the place to have been Wodnesbury, in Wilt-
shire. . . ."

† As chronicled in the *Annales Menevenses.*

of the Oriental invaders of the British Islands. And their latest distinct representatives have been rather our "gypsies" than the amalgamated mass of "Modern Britons;" who represent no race, era, or civilization so much as their own. The customs of stealing wives; beating them; buying and selling them; burning the dead; tattooing and painting the skin; "the great distinguishing feature" of robbery and oppression;—all these are customs common to British "tories" and to the various pagan invaders of our islands; who were, perhaps, the ancestors of all "Modern Britons."

Thus it seems that, although "gypsy" had once a special signification (which, even yet, it retains—in a measure), yet the word has more often been used as a synonym for "tory." And that the chief distinction between "gypsies" and British people, as understood by such writers as the Scotch gypsiologists, is that the former have adhered as much as possible to ancestral fashions and ideas, while the latter have gone over to the side of modernism and what at present we call "civilization."

APPENDIX.

THE likeness between Ancient Egypt and America has often been pointed out, and it is of too marked a nature to be the result of accident. Some of the resemblances which have been emphasized by Signor Gennarelli are of comparatively little weight; and indeed have not been everywhere admitted as deserving consideration. But the important points of resemblance can never be explained except by a belief in the common origin of the pyramid-builders of Central and Southern America and those of Ancient Egypt. Gennarelli does not only emphasize the pyramids; but he also draws attention to the fact that the title "Children of the Sun" was "borne both by the Incas and the Pharaohs"—that hieroglyphic languages are common to Egypt and America—that Ancient Egyptians and one or other of the American nations practised the embalming of the dead—and that the early races of America were connected in various other ways with the early races of Egypt. Not the least notable of these (although Signor Gennarelli does not seem to refer to it) is this— that the bricks employed by the older races of America are of precisely the same nature as those used by the Ancient Egyptians; being made of clay which has been rendered more compact by straw and hay intermingled with it—the blocks being afterwards dried in the sun. The very word by which these bricks are known in America (namely, *adobe* or *'dobie*) is the Egyptian word *adaub;* and it is pretty certain that on that memorable occasion on which the Egyptian overseers forced their Israelitish slaves to seek out the necessary straw and stubble for themselves—and when these slaves cried out against this extra labour—the word then employed, by taskmaster and servant, was the familiar American *adobe.* Of course, the *word* "adobe" may not have been used by the American nations prior to the Spanish Conquest;* but what is of much more importance is that the thing itself seems to be immemorially associated with the ante-Spanish races.

That mummies should (like pyramids) be common to America and to Egypt is a circumstance that would of itself suggest a remote kinship

* It is stated that the word *adaub* or *adobe* was brought into Spain from Egypt by the "Saracens," and then introduced into America at the Conquest. Still, if the Egyptian brick was manufactured in America many ages before the Spanish invasion, it is not unlikely that the Egyptian word was also used to denote it.

between the inhabitants of the countries in which they are found. In one instance, the resemblance between the American and the Egyptian mummy is singularly minute. A specimen of the Peruvian mummy, recently found in the vicinity of Iquique (and now preserved in the Museum at Arbroath) is thus described : " The features of the mummy . . . are strongly marked Indian, and the cheeks had apparently been painted a reddish colour." It has been pointed out that this reddish colour is given by the Ancient Egyptians to their own features, in their pictured representations ; and we have seen that it characterized the " Egyptians " of Galloway less than a century ago.* To refer to the modern " Egyptians " of this country is to lose sight, for a moment, of Ancient Egypt ; but it must be remembered that the Italian archæologist sees this Ancient-Egyptian identity in the peninsulas of Southern Europe as well as in Egypt and in Central America.

That some, at any rate, of the American " Red-Indian " nations may have entered America during the Christian era is by no means unlikely. It is notable that the tenth-century Northmen do not record the existence of *any* Red Indians in North America, at the period of their settlements. They found an Eskimo-Samoyed population in the New-England districts ; whom they styled Skraelings or Dwarfs ; and who are described as " black and ill-favoured, with large eyes and broad cheeks, and with coarse hair on their heads," while another version speaks of them as " sallow-coloured and ill-looking," with " ugly heads of hair, large eyes and broad cheeks." People of this kind are no doubt akin to certain modern American-Indian tribes ; but they are unquestionably far removed from the type that (with some reason) is held to stand for the American-Indian. The existing Eskimo races without doubt represent those tenth-century Skraelings more than any other variety of American humanity.

Inhabiting a large territory to the south of this Skraeling Land, at the time of the Norse explorations, there were people whom they styled " white men," and whose country they named " Great Ireland," and " The White Men's Land." These are pictured as " people who wore white dresses, and had poles borne before them on which were fastened lappets, and who shouted with a loud voice." It does not seem that their complexion is distinctly stated to have been white, but it is not likely that their white garments alone would have caused their country to be known as " The White Men's Land." There are other tokens of the early residence of white races in America. Mr. Désiré Charnay states that " Veytia describes the Toltec as a man of tall stature, *white*, and bearded ; " and he also remarks —" I have in my possession a bas-relief, found at Tula, coinciding very well with this description ; the man is full face, and has a large hooked nose, his beard being wide and fan-shaped."

* It ought to be observed that this particular Peruvian mummy is said to have been " mummified by the composition of the soil—nitrate of soda." If this means that the corpse had been *accidentally* preserved, this, of course, is not an illustration of the practice of embalming in America ; though interesting as showing the use of ruddle, or " keel," in painting the face. But the fact of the existence of mummies in America does not require an extra proof.

Again, in a "General Account of the Characters, Dispositions, and Numbers of the Indians in North America"—written last century—there is mention of "the white Panis," estimated at 2,000, and living "south of the Missouri," and also "the Blancs, Barbus, or white Indians with beards," said to number 1,500, but their residence not defined. (Besides the white Pawnees there are also 2,000 "freckled or pricked Panis," inhabiting the same or a contiguous district ; from which one may infer that their white confederates were *not* tattooed, and that the "pricked Panis" were not white.) In the present century, we are told :—" The eastern nations of Chili have but a slight tinge of the brown colour, and the Boroanes are still whiter. On the north-west coast, from latitude 43° to 60°, there are tribes who, though embrowned with soot and mud, were found, when their skins were washed, to have the brilliant white and red which is the characteristic of the Caucasian race : . . . within the tropics, the Malapoques in Brazil, the Guaranis in Paraguay, the Guiacas of Guiana, the Scheries of La Plata, have tolerably fair complexions, sometimes united with blue eyes and auburn hair; and in the hot country washed by the Orinoco, Humboldt found tribes of a dark, and others of a light hue, living almost in juxtaposition." In addition to these, the Guatosos of Costa Rica are believed to be fair-skinned, fair-haired, and blue-eyed ; but nothing definite seems to be known regarding them.*

All these people are described as living the life of "Indians," and as being "Indians" in every respect—except that their physical characteristics place them among the *Xanthochroi*. There have, no doubt, been many renegade Europeans who, at various periods, have joined Indian tribes, but the white tribes just referred to are regarded, as a matter of course, as "Indians." The 2,000 "white Pawnees," who inhabited a territory "south of the Missouri," sometime last century, are not only called "Indians" by the traveller who includes them in his "General Account ; " but more than one European of the same period has left on record† the existence of a nation of white-skinned Indians, whose country is sometimes described as "west of the Mississippi," and again as " seven hundred miles up the Red River" (both of these localizations pointing to a territory "South of the Missouri"). Such eighteenth-century " Indians " as these may reasonably be assumed as the progenitors of those who, in the present century, are said "to have the brilliant white

---

* The early Norse records may be consulted in "the ponderous volume called *Antiquitates Americanæ*; " which forms the basis of a more cheerful essay, contributed (by Mr. Thomas Wentworth Higginson) to "Harper's Magazine," September 1882. The information regarding the Toltecs is taken from Mr. Désiré Charnay's article on "The Ruins of Central America " (*North American Review*, October 1881) ; and the last-century "General Account " is quoted in the "New Annual Register" for the year 1784 (p. 87). The Costa Rican Guatosos are frequently referred to by Mr. Frederick Boyle, in his "Ride Across a Continent ; " at the date of which "ride" little or nothing was known as to the precise characteristics of those "Indians."

† See Vol. I. (pp. 66–75) of the "Popular History of the United States; " Sampson Low & Co., 1876.

and red" complexion which distinguishes the *Xanthochroic* type, although their proper hue is concealed by a covering of "soot and mud."

Of what lineage were those white Americans? Some of them—the Costa Rican Guatosos, for example—are supposed, by one set of theorists, to be the descendants of Drake's buccaneers, or of other European invaders of the sixteenth and seventeenth centuries. But it is by no means certain that those Europeans were mostly men of fair skins, with blue eyes and auburn hair. And there is evidence of white American races long before the sixteenth century. We have noticed that the tenth-century Norsemen called a large tract of North America "the White Men's Land;" and a skilled student of Central-American archæology has pronounced the Toltecs to have been white men—and *they* were "Americans" so far back as the seventh century. Those Toltecs are spoken of "as being wonderfully gifted, and as a typical race, cultivating land, erecting houses, working in stone and metal, weaving stuffs, using hieroglyphic characters, devising an ingenious astronomical instrument, and inventing a method of reckoning time." The Toltec builder "knew what a pier was, and not unfrequently introduced it into his edifices; he constructed columns, both free and attached, and even indulged in caryatides." He also understood the use of the arch, and "if we believe Veytia," he "had long known of the corbel vault." Add to this that the Toltec worshipped the sun and moon, besides other deities, built temples and pyramids, and amused himself by playing "a primitive kind of tennis," and it will be seen that those seventh-century Americans showed themselves to be connected in many ways with what is called the "Old World."

The assumption that the builders of the Yucatan pyramids were white-skinned men seems rather to conflict with Signor Gennarelli's "Redskin" theory. But then, if the Egyptian pyramids, though designed by an "Australioid" aristocracy, were actually reared by the hands of white-skinned slaves, then the latter were themselves pyramid-builders, in a sense. And the theory which assumes "that the lost Tribes of Israel wandered through Asia to the north-west coast [of America] and were the progenitors of the ancient Mexicans" is not all at variance with the statement that the Toltecs migrated into Mexico from California, and are held to be represented by a sculpture of a man (presumably white) with "a large hooked nose, his beard being wide and fan-shaped."

The necessity for considering those early races of white Americans is, that they seemed to have formed one of the most important of American races. The general name for them among ethnologists is that of "Nahua." "The name would appear to have been given to all the tribes, of the same race and tongue, who, during succeeding centuries from the seventh to the fourteenth, made their way into the high plateaus of Mexico, over Mexico itself, and into certain parts of Central America; their point of departure being generally regarded as lying anywhere between Aztlan (Lake Chapala), the country of the Aztecs, who were the last to arrive, and Huchuetlapalan, in California, the country of the

Toltecs, the first comers."* Now, at the period of their migrations between the seventh and fourteenth centuries of the Christian era, we have European testimony to the effect that a large country, supposed to be situated in North America, was known to the Northmen as "The White Men's Land." And it is believed that this "White Men's Land" is identical with the country reached by a European vessel in the eleventh century. "Gudleif Gudlaugson, brother of Thorfinn, . . . had made a trading voyage to Dublin ; but when he left that place again, with the intention of sailing round Ireland and returning to Iceland, he met with long continuing north-easterly winds, which drove him far to the south-west in the ocean, and at an advanced period of the summer he and his company arrived at last at an extensive country, but they knew not what country it was. On their landing, a crowd of the natives, several hundreds in number, came against them, and laid hands on them, and bound them."† And, among these, they found a brother-Northman, Biörn Asbrandson, who had left Iceland in the year 999, and had not been heard of since. Him they left there, and (being set free by his means) they "set sail again, and found their way back to Dublin."

The scene of this adventure, then, is believed to have been the "White Men's Land" of the Northern chroniclers. And the important consideration in all this is, that no mention whatever is made of a race of people who may have been the ancestors of the "Red Indians." Canada and New England were inhabited by Samoyeds and Esquimaux ; and south of these were the "White Men." But of "Red Indians" there is not a word.

Europe, however, has contained races that one may describe as "Red Indians"—although the characteristics which show this likeness have now, for the most part, faded away (partly through intermarriage and partly on account of altered fashions). That the early Scots formed one division of these races seems pretty certain. And it is curious to reflect that the two slaves, who, being "very swift of foot," were sent into the interior of Massachusetts on a scouting expedition, by the Norsemen of the year 1007—that these slaves, who were *Scots*, appear to have been the first *Red Indians* that history has recorded as inhabiting New England. And that they—being man and woman—may have been the "Adam and Eve" of one or many New-England "Indian" tribes. Another member of the expedition of 1007 was one "Thorhall," "a large man, and strong, black and like a giant, silent, and foul-mouthed in his speech," and characterized as "a bad Christian." Now, if this black man was one of the pagan Danes (which is probable), he was not unacquainted with the art of scalping ; and he, again, forms a suitable ancestor of the later "American Indians." These, of course, are only three individuals. But there is much reason for believing that the few instances on record of early intercourse between Europe and America do

---

* See Mr. Désiré Charnay's article on "The Ruins of Central America," in the *North American Review*, of October 1881.

† *Antiquitates Americanæ.*

not constitute the *only* links between the two " worlds "—of pre-Columbian date. Indeed, the idea that a West-Atlantic country was unknown to Europeans before the days of Columbus is profoundly heretical. Of such a country there are many traditions among British people (in addition to the incontrovertible statements of the Northmen). These traditions give various·names to such a territory. But one of the best known designations of what we now call " North America" was " Antilla," or "the Antillæ." " Before the discovery of America by Columbus, a tradition existed that far to the west of the Azores there lay a land called Antilla, whose position was vaguely indicated in the maps of the early cosmographers. Only eight months after Columbus's return, we find one Peter Martyr writing that the islands which the great navigator had touched upon must be the Antillæ."* And a reference made by a seventeenth-century author† leads one to believe that " the Antilles " signified the outlying parts of North America—as far north as Davis Straits—at no very remote date. It may be that the country, or archipelago, that originally formed " the Antilles," or "Antilla," has been submerged for many centuries ; and that "the banks of Newfoundland" represent one of its latest fragments. " There is no doubt that marked changes have taken place within the last few centuries along the outer coast of Cape Cod ; that an island called Nawset, and a cape called Point Gilbert . . . were known to Captain John Smith and Bartholomew Gosnold early in the seventeenth century,"‡ and have since disappeared. If similar disappearances had been taking place during the five, ten, or fifteen centuries that preceded the seventeenth, one can easily imagine an important archipelago, known as "the Antilles," where now there is nothing but the waves of the Atlantic.

Thus the voyages of the Norsemen, and those of the twelfth-century Madawg of Wales, may not have been so extended as our modern maps would lead us to believe. It is notable that, in either of these instances, a *continuous* intercourse is hinted at ; although only one special voyage may be chronicled. The Northmen of 999 must have had some *reason* for calling the trans-Atlantic country (or a part of it) " Great Ireland." And it is noteworthy that the speech of its people is said by them to have " resembled Irish." A parallel instance—though of far later date— is that of an Indian clan (the Doegs), who spoke "the British tongue," in the year 1660.§ The expressions " Irish" and "British" are, of course, very vague : and both may have applied to the speech of the Ancient Scots,—that is, to an " Egyptian " language.

The consideration of such statements as these, then, renders it by no means improbable that an important element in the North-American-Indian population was of European origin; though the intercourse

---

* *Chambers's Encyclopædia*, article " Antilles."

† Wallace, in a reference to "the natural and moral History of the *Antilles*," which he makes in his "Description of Orkney" (1693; reprinted at Edinburgh, 1883).

‡ Popular History of the United States; London, 1876; vol. I. p. 41.

§ *Ibid.* p. 70.

between the countries of the East Atlantic and those of the West was probably checked for several centuries prior to the time of Columbus.. Indeed, it would seem that the manners of certain North-American tribes represent very closely the real life of certain British tribes in early times. When Mr. Schoolcraft tells us * of Indians "who hold the relative rank of gamblers in Indian society," who are so fascinated by one particular game, that "they stake at it their ornaments, weapons, clothing, canoes, horses, everything in fact they possess," he is describing a caste that is almost identical with Spenser's Irish *carrows;* and when he further states that this class included "wanderers about the country, bragga-docios, or fops," who were also mountebanks and tale-tellers, he suggests the "bards, tale-tellers, and fancied fools or professed pleasants," whose idle, vagabond ways were suppressed in the British Islands. Moreover, on either side of the Atlantic, men of this caste used to paint their skins and shave their heads. And, in either case, the mistletoe was regarded as the most sacred of plants by the Magi, or Druids, or Medicine-men. And, just as (even in the present century) the horse of the British "tory" chief was killed at his funeral, or immediately after it, so is the same cere-monial still followed by the "tory" of North America. † The "Indians" of either country are alike in many ways; and not the least important resemblance consists in this—that each has a tradition of being preceded by earlier races, of like description, and actually known by a name that is almost, or quite, the same in "Indian" as in "English."

Resemblances such as these might be greatly enlarged upon, but this would be out of place here; and would require a thorough knowledge of the subject. But such likenesses can only be explained by a belief in the kinship—or, at least, the political union—of these long-separated com-munities. It is impossible to understand American archæology unless it is studied along with that of the "Old World."

* In one of the notes to "Hiawatha," these statements are quoted as from page 72 of Mr. Schoolcraft's *History, &c., of the Indian Tribes,* Part II.

† Mr. Edward King (*Southern States,* p. 194) refers to this as a custom of the "Kaws" of Kansas.

WOODFALL AND KINDER, PRINTERS, MILFORD LANE, STRAND, LONDON, W.C.